6x10/06 11/08

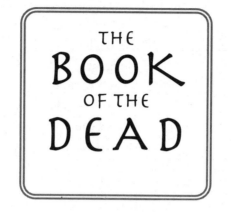

THE
BOOK
OF THE
DEAD

THE
BOOK
OF THE
DEAD

DOUGLAS PRESTON
& LINCOLN CHILD

WARNER BOOKS

NEW YORK   BOSTON

Copyright © 2006 by Splendide Mendax, Inc., and Lincoln Child
All rights reserved.

Warner Books
Hachette Book Group USA
1271 Avenue of the Americas, New York, NY 10020

Warner Books is a trademark of Time Inc. Used under license.

Printed in the United States of America

First Edition: May 2006
10 9 8 7 6 5 4 3 2 1

Library of Congress Cataloging-in-Publication Data

Preston, Douglas J.
    The book of the dead / Douglas Preston and Lincoln Child.—1st ed.
        p. cm.
    ISBN-13: 978-0-446-57698-7
    ISBN-10: 0-446-57698-0
    I. Government investigators—Fiction. 2. New York (N.Y.)—Fiction. 3. Sibling rivalry—Fiction. 4. Brothers—Fiction. 5. Psychological fiction. I. Child, Lincoln. II. Title.
    PS3566.R3982B66 2006
    813'.54—dc22   2006003058

Book design by Giorgetta Bell McRee

Lincoln Child dedicates this book to
his mother, Nancy Child

Douglas Preston dedicates this book to
Anna Marguerite McCann Taggart

ACKNOWLEDGMENTS

We would like to thank the following people at Warner Books: Jaime Levine, Jamie Raab, Beth de Guzman, Jennifer Romanello, Maureen Egen, and Devi Pillai. Thanks also to Larry Kirshbaum for being a believer in us almost from day one. We want to thank our agents, Eric Simonoff of Janklow & Nesbit Associates and Matthew Snyder of the Creative Artists Agency. A bouquet of hothouse orchids to Eadie Klemm for keeping us all neat and dusted off. Count Niccolò Capponi of Florence, Italy, suggested (brilliantly) our use of the Carducci poem. And, as always, we want to thank our wives and children for their love and support.

THE
BOOK
OF THE
DEAD

1

Early-morning sunlight gilded the cobbled drive of the staff entrance at the New York Museum of Natural History, illuminating a glass pillbox just outside the granite archway. Within the pillbox, a figure sat slumped in his chair: an elderly man, familiar to all museum staff. He puffed contentedly on a calabash pipe and basked in the warmth of one of those false-spring days that occur in New York City in February, the kind that coaxes daffodils, crocuses, and fruit trees into premature bloom, only to freeze them dead later in the month.

"Morning, doctor," Curly said again and again to any and all passersby, whether mailroom clerk or dean of science. Curators might rise and fall, directors might ascend through the ranks, reign in glory, then plummet to ignominious ruin; man might till the field and then lie beneath; but it seemed Curly would never be shifted from his pillbox. He was as much a fixture in the museum as the ultrasaurus that greeted visitors in the museum's Great Rotunda.

"Here, pops!"

Frowning at this familiarity, Curly roused himself in time to see a messenger shove a package through the window of his pillbox. The package had sufficient momentum to land on the little shelf where the guard kept his tobacco and mittens.

"Excuse me!" Curly said, rousing himself and waving out the window. "Hey!" But the messenger was already speeding away on his fat-tire mountain bike, black rucksack bulging with packages.

"Goodness," Curly muttered, staring at the package. It was about twelve inches by eight by eight, wrapped in greasy brown paper, and tied up with an excessive amount of old-fashioned twine. It was so beaten-up Curly wondered if the messenger had been run over by a truck on the way over. The address was written in a childish hand: *For the rocks and minerals curator, The Museum of Natural History.*

Curly broke up the dottle in the bottom of his pipe while gazing thoughtfully at the package. The museum received hundreds of packages every week from children, containing "donations" for the collection. Such donations included everything from squashed bugs and worthless rocks to arrowheads and mummified roadkill. He sighed, then rose painfully from the comfort of his chair and tucked the package under his arm. He put the pipe to one side, slid open the door of his pillbox, and stepped into the sunlight, blinking twice. Then he turned in the direction of the mailroom receiving dock, which was only a few hundred feet across the service drive.

"What have you got there, Mr. Tuttle?" came a voice.

Curly glanced toward the voice. It was Digby Greenlaw, the new assistant director for administration, who was just exiting the tunnel from the staff parking lot.

Curly did not answer immediately. He didn't like Greenlaw and his condescending *Mr. Tuttle.* A few weeks earlier, Greenlaw had taken exception to the way Curly checked IDs, complaining that he "wasn't really *looking* at them." Heck, Curly didn't have to look at them—he knew every employee of the museum on sight.

"Package," he grunted in reply.

Greenlaw's voice took on an officious tone. "Packages are supposed to be delivered directly to the mailroom. And you're not supposed to leave your station."

Curly kept walking. He had reached an age where he found the best way to deal with unpleasantness was to pretend it didn't exist.

He could hear the footsteps of the administrator quicken behind him, the voice rising a few notches on the assumption he was hard of hearing. "Mr. Tuttle? I said you should not leave your station unattended."

Curly stopped, turned. "Thank you for offering, doctor." He held out the package.

Greenlaw stared it at, squinting. "I didn't say *I* would deliver it."

Curly remained in place, proffering the package.

"Oh, for heaven's sake." Greenlaw reached irritably for the package, but his hand faltered midway. "It's a funny-looking thing. What is it?"

"Dunno, doctor. Came by messenger."

"It seems to have been mishandled."

Curly shrugged.

But Greenlaw still didn't take the package. He leaned toward it, squinting. "It's torn. There's a hole . . . Look, there's something coming out."

Curly looked down. The corner of the package did indeed have a hole, and a thin stream of brown powder was trickling out.

"What in the world?" Curly said.

Greenlaw took a step back. "It's leaking some kind of powder." His voice rode up a notch. "Oh my Lord. What is it?"

Curly stood rooted to the spot.

"Good God, Curly, drop it! It's anthrax!"

Greenlaw stumbled backward, his face contorted in panic. "It's a terrorist attack—someone call the police! I've been exposed! Oh my God, I've been exposed!"

The administrator stumbled and fell backward on the cobblestones, clawing the ground and springing to his feet, and then he was off and running. Almost immediately, two guards came spilling out of the guard station across the way, one intercepting Greenlaw while the other made for Curly.

"What are you doing?" Greenlaw shrieked. "Keep back! Call 911!"

Curly remained where he was, package in hand. This was something so far outside his experience that his mind seemed to have stopped working.

The guards fell back, Greenlaw at their heels. For a moment, the small courtyard was strangely quiet. Then a shrill alarm went off, deafening in the enclosed space. In less than five minutes, the air was filled with the sound of approaching sirens, culminating in an uproar of activity: police cars, flashing lights, crackling radios, and uniformed men rushing this way and that stringing up yellow biohazard tape and erecting a cordon, megaphones shouting at the growing crowds to back off, while at the same time telling Curly to *drop the package and step away, drop the package and step away.*

But Curly didn't drop the package and step away. He remained frozen in utter confusion, staring at the thin brown stream that continued to trickle out of the tear in the package, forming a small pile on the cobbles at his feet.

And now two strange-looking men wearing puffy white suits and hoods with plastic visors were approaching, walking slowly, hands outstretched like something Curly had seen in an old science fiction movie. One gently took Curly by the shoulders while the other slipped the package from his fingers and—with infinite care—placed it in a blue plastic box. The first man led him to one side and began carefully vacuuming him up and down with a funny-looking device, and then they began dressing him, too, in one of the strange plastic suits, all the time telling him in low electronic voices that he was going to be all right, that they were taking him to the hospital for a few tests, that everything would be fine. As they placed the hood over his head, Curly began to feel his mind coming back to life, his body able to move again.

"Scuse me, doctor?" he said to one of the men as they led him off toward a van that had backed through the police cordon and was waiting for him, doors open.

"Yes?"

"My pipe." He nodded toward the pillbox. "Don't forget to bring my pipe."

2

D~r.~ Lauren Wildenstein watched as the "first response" team carried in the blue plastic hazmat container, placing it under the fume hood in her laboratory. The call had come in twenty minutes earlier, and both she and her assistant, Richie, were ready. At first it sounded like it might be the real deal for a change, something that actually fit the profile of a classic bioterror attack—a package sent to a high-profile New York City institution, dribbling brown powder. But on-site testing for anthrax had already come up negative, and Wildenstein knew that this one would almost certainly be another false alarm. In her two years leading the New York City DOHMS Sentinel laboratory, they had received over four hundred suspicious powders to analyze and, thank God, not one had turned out to be a bioterror agent. So far. She glanced at the running tally they kept tacked to the wall: sugar, salt, flour, baking soda, heroin, cocaine, pepper, and dirt, in that order of frequency. The list was a testament to paranoia and too damn many terror alerts.

The delivery team left and she spent a moment staring at the sealed container. Amazing, the consternation a package of powder could cause these days. It had arrived half an hour ago at the museum, and already a guard and a museum administrator had been quarantined, given antibiotics, and were now being treated by mental health services. It seemed the administrator was particularly hysterical.

She shook her head.

"Whaddya think?" came a voice from over her shoulder. "Terrorist cocktail du jour?"

Wildenstein ignored this. Richie's work was top-notch, even if his emotional development had been arrested somewhere between the third and the fourth grade.

"Let's run an X-ray."

"Rolling."

The false-color X-ray that popped up on the monitor screen showed the package was full of an amorphous substance, with no letter or any other objects visible.

"No detonator," Richie said. "Darn."

"I'm going to open the container." Wildenstein broke the hazmat seals and carefully lifted out the package. She noted the crude, childish scrawl, the lack of a return address, the multiple strands of badly tied twine. It seemed almost designed to arouse suspicion. One corner of the package had been abraded by mishandling, and a light brown substance not unlike sand dribbled from it. This was unlike any bioterror agent she had studied. Awkwardly, on account of her heavy gloves, she cut the twine and opened the package, lifting out a plastic bag.

"We've been sandbagged!" said Richie with a snort.

"We treat it as hazardous until proven otherwise," said Wildenstein, although her private opinion was the same as his. Naturally, it was better to err on the side of caution.

"Weight?"

"One point two kilo. For the record, I'm noting that all the biohazard and hazmat alarms under the hood are reading zero."

Using a scoop, she took a few dozen grains of the substance and distributed them into half a dozen test tubes, sealed and racked them, then removed them from beneath the hood, passing them on to Richie. Without needing to be told, he started the usual set of chemical reagents, testing for a suite.

"Nice having a shitload of sample to work with," he said with a chuckle. "We can burn it, bake it, dissolve it, and still have enough left over to make a sand castle."

Wildenstein waited while he deftly did the workups.

"All negative," he reported at last. "Man, what is this stuff?"

Wildenstein took a second rack of samples. "Do a heat test in an oxidizing atmosphere and vent the gas to the gas analyzer."

"Sure thing." Richie took another tube and, sealing it with a vented pipette which led to the gas analyzer, heated the tube slowly over a Bunsen burner. Wildenstein watched, and to her surprise the sample quickly ignited, glowing for a moment before disappearing, leaving no ash or residue.

"Burn, baby, burn."

"What do you have, Richie?"

He scrutinized the readout. "Just about pure carbon dioxide and monoxide, trace of water vapor."

"The sample must have been pure carbon."

"Gimme a break, boss. Since when does carbon come in the form of brown sand?"

Wildenstein peered at the grit in the bottom of one of the sample tubes. "I'm going to take a look at this stuff under the stereozoom."

She sprinkled a dozen grains onto a slide and placed it on the microscope stage, turned on the light, and looked through the oculars.

"What do you see?" Richie asked.

But Wildenstein did not answer. She kept looking, dazzled. Under a microscope, the individual grains were not brown at all, but tiny fragments of a glassy substance in myriad colors—blue, red, yellow, green, brown, black, purple, pink. Still looking through the oculars, she picked up a metal spoon, pressed it on one of the grains, and gave a little push. She could hear a faint *scritch* as the grain scratched the glass.

"What're you doing?" Richie asked.

Wildenstein rose. "Don't we have a refractometer around here somewhere?"

"Yeah, a really cheap job dating back to the Middle Ages." Richie rummaged around in a cabinet and drew out a dusty machine in a yellowed plastic cover. He set it up, plugged it in. "You know how to work this puppy?"

"I think so."

Using the stereozoom, she plucked a grain of the substance and let it sink into a drop of mineral oil she put on a slide. Then she slid the slide into the reading chamber of the refractometer. After a few false starts, she figured out how to turn the dial and obtain a reading.

She looked up, a smile on her face.

"Just what I suspected. We have an index of refraction of two point four."

"Yeah? So?"

"There we are. Nailed it."

"Nailed what, boss?"

She glanced at him. "Richie, what is made of pure carbon, has an index of refraction above two, and is hard enough to cut glass?"

"Diamond?"

"Bravo."

"You mean, what we've got here is a bag of industrial diamond grit?"

"That's what it would seem."

Richie removed his hazmat hood, wiped his brow. "That's a first for me." He turned, reached for a phone. "I think I'll put a call in to the hospital, let them know they can stand down from biological alert. From what I heard, that museum administrator actually soiled his drawers."

3

Frederick Watson Collopy, director of the New York Museum of Natural History, felt a prickling of irritation on the back of his neck as he exited the elevator into the museum's basement. It had been months since he'd been down in these subterranean depths, and he wondered why the devil Wilfred Sherman, chairman of the Mineralogy Department, was so insistent on his coming to the mineralogy lab instead of Sherman's coming to Collopy's office on the fifth floor.

He turned a corner at a brisk walk, his shoes scraping the gritty floor, and came to the mineralogy lab door—which was shut. He tried the handle—locked—and in a fresh surge of irritation knocked sharply.

The door was opened almost immediately by Sherman, who just as quickly closed and locked it behind them. The curator looked disheveled, sweaty—not to put too fine a term on it, a wreck. *As well he should*, thought Collopy. His eye swept the lab and quickly fixed on the offending package itself, soiled and wrinkled, sitting in a double-ziplocked bag on a specimen table next to a stereozoom microscope. Beside it lay a half-dozen white envelopes.

"Dr. Sherman," he intoned, "the careless way this material was delivered to the museum has caused us major embarrassment. This is nothing short of outrageous. I want the name of the supplier, I want to know why this wasn't handled through proper procurement channels, and I want to know why such valuable material was handled so carelessly and misdelivered in such a way as to cause a panic. As I understand it, industrial-grade diamond grit costs several thousand dollars a pound."

Sherman didn't answer. He just sweated.

"I can just see the headline in tomorrow's newspaper: *Bioterror Scare at the Natural History Museum*. I'm not looking forward to reading it. I've just gotten a call from some reporter at the *Times*—Harriman something or other—and I have to call him back in half an hour with an explanation."

Sherman swallowed, still saying nothing. A drop of sweat trickled down his brow and he quickly wiped it away with a handkerchief.

"Well? *Do* you have an explanation? And is there a reason why you insisted on my coming to your lab?"

"Yes," Sherman managed to say. He nodded toward the stereozoom. "I wanted you to take a . . . take a look."

Collopy got up, went over to the microscope, removed his glasses, and put his eyes over the oculars. A blurry mess leaped into view. "I can't see a bloody thing."

"The focus needs adjustment, there."

Collopy fumbled with the knob, sweeping the specimen in and out of focus as he tried to find the right spot. Finally, he found himself staring at a breathtakingly beautiful array of thousands of brilliantly colored bits and pieces of crystal, backlit like a stained-glass window.

"What is it?"

"A sample of the grit that came in the package."

Collopy pulled away. "Well? Did you or someone in your department order it?"

Sherman hesitated. "No, we didn't."

"Then tell me, Dr. Sherman, how did thousands of dollars' worth of diamond grit come to be addressed and delivered to your department?"

"I have an explanation—" Sherman stopped. With a shaking hand, he picked up one of the white envelopes. Collopy waited, but Sherman seemed to have frozen up.

"Dr. Sherman?"

Sherman did not respond. He extracted the handkerchief and dabbed his face a second time.

"Dr. Sherman, are you ill?"

Sherman swallowed. "I don't know how to tell you this."

Collopy said briskly, "We have a problem, and I've now got"—he checked his watch—"only twenty-five minutes to call this fellow Harriman back. So just go ahead and lay it out for me."

Sherman nodded dumbly, dabbed yet again at his face. Despite his annoyance, Collopy felt pity for the fellow. In many ways, he was basically a middle-aged kid who never outgrew his rock collection . . . Suddenly, Collopy realized it wasn't just sweat the man was wiping away—his eyes were leaking tears.

"It's not industrial diamond grit," Sherman said at last.

Collopy frowned. "Excuse me?"

The curator took a deep breath, seemed to brace himself. "Industrial diamond grit is made from black or brown diamonds of no aesthetic value. Under a microscope, it looks like what you'd expect: dark crystalline particles. But when you look at *these* under the microscope, you see color." His voice quavered.

"That's what I saw, yes."

Sherman nodded. "Tiny fragments and crystals of color, every color in the rainbow. I confirmed that they were indeed diamond, and I asked myself . . ." His voice faltered.

"Dr. Sherman?"

"I asked myself: how in the world did a sack of diamond grit come to be made up of millions of fragments of fancy color diamonds? Two and a half pounds' worth."

The lab fell into a profound silence. Collopy felt himself go cold. "I don't understand."

"This is not diamond grit," said Sherman all in a rush. "This is the museum's diamond collection."

"What the devil are you saying?"

"The man who stole our diamonds last month. He must have pulverized them. *All* of them." The tears were now flowing freely, but Sherman no longer bothered to wipe them away.

"Pulverized?" Collopy looked around wildly. "How can you pulverize a diamond?"

"With a sledgehammer."

"But they're supposed to be the hardest thing in the world."

"Hard, yes. That doesn't mean they aren't *brittle*."

"How can you be sure?"

"Many of our diamonds have a unique color. Take the Queen of Narnia, for example. No other diamond has quite that blue color, with hints of violet and green. I was able to identify each tiny fragment. That's what I've been doing—separating them out."

He took the white envelope in his hand and tipped it out on a sheet of paper lying on the specimen table. A pile of blue grit poured out. He pointed to it.

"The Queen of Narnia."

He took out another envelope, tipped it over into a purple pile. "The Heart of Eternity."

One after another he emptied the little envelopes. "The Indigo Ghost. Ultima Thule. The Fourth of July. The Zanzibar Green."

It was like a steady drumbeat, one pounding blow after another. Collopy stared in horror at the tiny piles of glittering sand.

"This is a sick joke," he finally said. "Those *can't* be the museum's diamonds."

"The exact hues of many of these famous diamonds are quantifiable," Sherman replied. "I have hard data on them. I tested the fragments. They're diamonds with exactly the right hue. There can be no mistake. *There's nothing else they could be.*"

"But surely not *all* of them," said Collopy. "He can't have destroyed them *all.*"

"That package contained 2.42 pounds of diamond grit. That's equivalent to about 5,500 carats. Adding in the amount that spilled, the original shipment would have contained roughly 6,000 carats. I added up the carat weights of the diamonds that were stolen . . ." His voice trailed off.

"Well?" Collopy asked at last, no longer able to contain himself.

"The total weight was 6,042 carats," Sherman said in a whisper.

A long silence filled the laboratory, the only sound the faint hum of the fluorescent lights. At last Collopy raised his head and looked Sherman in the eye.

"Dr. Sherman," he began, but his voice cracked and he was forced to start over. "Dr. Sherman. This information *must not* leave this room."

Sherman, already pale, went white as a ghost. But after a moment, he nodded silently.

4

William Smithback Jr. entered the dark and fragrant confines of the pub known as the Bones and scanned the noisy crowd. It was five o'clock and the place was packed with museum staff, all lubricating themselves after the long and dusty hours spent laboring in the granite pile across the street. Why in the world they all wanted to hang out in a place whose every square inch of wall space was covered with bones, after escaping just such an environment at work, was a mystery to him. These days he himself came to the Bones for one reason only: the forty-year-old single malt that the bartender kept hidden under the bar. At thirty-six dollars a shot, it wasn't exactly a bargain, but it sure beat having your insides corroded by three dollars' worth of Cutty Sark.

He spied the copper-colored hair of his new bride, Nora Kelly, at their usual table in the back. He waved, sauntered over, and struck a dramatic pose.

" 'But, soft! What light through yonder window breaks?' " he intoned. Then he kissed the back of her hand briefly, kissed her lips rather more attentively, and took a seat across the table. "How are things?"

"The museum continues to be an exciting place to work."

"You mean that bioterror scare this morning?"

She nodded. "Someone delivered a package for the Mineralogy Department, leaking some kind of powder. They thought it was anthrax or something."

"I heard about that. In fact, brother Bryce filed a story on that today." Bryce Harriman was Smithback's colleague and archrival at the *Times*, but Smithback had secured himself a little breathing room with some recent—and very dramatic—scoops.

The hangdog waiter came by and stood by the table, silently waiting to take their drink orders.

"I'll take two fingers of the Glen Grant," Smithback said. "The good stuff."

"A glass of white wine, please."

The waiter shuffled off.

"So it caused a stir?" Smithback asked.

Nora giggled. "You should have seen Greenlaw, the guy who found it. He was so sure he was dying they had to carry him out on a stretcher, protective suit and all."

"Greenlaw? I don't know him."

"He's the new V.P. for administration. Just hired from Con Ed."

"So what'd it turn out to be? The anthrax, I mean."

"Grinding powder."

Smithback chuckled as he accepted his drink. "Grinding powder. Oh, God, that's perfect." He swirled the amber liquid around in the balloon glass and took a sip. "How'd it happen?"

"It seems the package was damaged in transit, and the stuff was dribbling out. A messenger dropped it off with Curly, and Greenlaw just happened by."

"Curly? The old guy with the pipe?"

"That's the one."

"He's still at the museum?"

"He'll never leave."

"How did he take it?"

"In stride, like everything else. He was back in his pillbox a few hours later, like nothing had happened."

Smithback shook his head. "Why in the world would anyone send a sack of grit by messenger?"

"Beats me."

He took another sip. "You think it was deliberate?" he asked absently. "Someone trying to freak out the museum?"

"You've got a criminal mind."

"Do they know who sent it?"

"I heard the package didn't have a return address."

At this small detail, Smithback grew suddenly interested. He wished he'd called up Harriman's piece on the *Times* internal network and read it. "You know how much it costs to send something by messenger in New York City these days? Forty bucks."

"Maybe it was valuable grit."

"But then, why no return address? Who was it addressed to?"

"Just the Mineralogy Department, I heard."

Smithback took another thoughtful sip of the Glen Grant. There was something about this story that set off a journalistic alarm in his head. He wondered if Harriman had gotten to the bottom of it. Not bloody likely.

He extracted his cell. "Mind if I make a call?"

Nora frowned. "If you must."

Smithback dialed the museum, asked to be put through to mineralogy. He was in luck: someone was still there. He began speaking rapidly. "This is Mr. Humnhmn in the Grmhmhmn's office, and I had a quick question: what kind of grinding powder was it that caused the scare this morning?"

"I didn't catch—"

"Look, I'm in a hurry. The director's waiting for an answer."

"I don't know."

"Is there anyone there who does?"

"There's Dr. Sherman."

"Put him on."

A moment later, a breathless voice got on. "Dr. Collopy?"

"No, no," said Smithback easily. "This is William Smithback. I'm a reporter for the *New York Times*."

A silence. Then a very tense "Yes?"

"About that bioterror scare this morning—"

"I can't help you," came the immediate response. "I already told everything I know to your colleague, Mr. Harriman."

"Just a routine follow-up, Dr. Sherman. Mind?"

Silence.

"The package was addressed to you?"

"To the department," came the terse reply.

"No return address?"

"No."

"And it was full of grit?"

"That's right."

"What kind?"

A hesitation. "Corundum grit."

"How much is corundum grit worth?"

"I don't know offhand. Not much."

"I see. That's all, thanks."

He hung up to find Nora looking at him.

"It's rude to use your cell phone in a pub," she said.

"Hey, I'm a reporter. It's my job to be rude."

"Satisfied?"

"No."

"A package of grit came to the museum. It was leaking, it freaked someone out. End of story."

"I don't know." Smithback took another long sip of the Glen Grant. "That guy sounded awfully nervous just now."

"Dr. Sherman? He's high-strung."

"He sounded more than high-strung. He sounded frightened."

He opened his cell phone again, and Nora groaned. "If you start making calls, I'm heading home."

"Come on, Nora. One more call, then we'll head over to the Rattlesnake Café for dinner. I gotta make this call now. It's already after five and I want to catch people before they leave."

Quickly, he dialed information, got a number, punched it in. "Department of Health and Mental Services?"

After being bounced around a bit, he finally got the lab he wanted.

"Sentinel lab," came a voice.

"To whom am I speaking?"

"Richard. And to whom am *I* speaking?"

"Hi, Richard, this is Bill Smithback of the *Times*. You in charge?"

"I am now. The boss just went home."

"Lucky for you. Can I ask a few questions?"

"You said you're a reporter?"

"That's right."

"I suppose so."

"This is the lab that handled that package from the museum this morning?"

"Sure is."

"What was in it?"

Smithback heard a snort. "Diamond grit."

"Not corundum?"

"No. Diamond."

"Did you examine the grit yourself?"

"Yup."

"What'd it look like?"

"Under coarse examination, like a sack of brown sand."

Smithback thought for a moment. "How'd you figure out it was diamond grit?"

"By the index of refraction of the particles."

"I see. And it couldn't be confused with corundum?"

"No way."

"You also examined it under a microscope, I assume?"

"Yup."

"What'd it look like?"

"It was beautiful, like a bunch of little colored crystals."

Smithback felt a sudden tingling at the nape of his neck. "Colored? What do you mean?"

"Bits and fragments of every color of the rainbow. I had no idea diamond grit was so pretty."

"That didn't strike you as odd?"

"A lot of things that are ugly to the human eye look beautiful under the microscope. Like bread mold, for instance—or sand, for that matter."

"But you said the grit looked brown."

"Only when blended together."

"I see. What'd you do with the package?"

"We sent it back to the museum and chalked it up as a false alarm."

"Thanks."

Smithback slowly shut the phone. *Impossible. It couldn't be.*

He looked up to find Nora staring at him, annoyance clear on her face. He reached over and took her hand. "I'm really sorry, but I've got another call to make."

She crossed her arms. "And I thought we were going to have a nice evening together."

"One more call. Please. I'll let you listen in. Believe me, this is going to be good."

Nora's cheeks grew pink. Smithback knew that look: his wife was getting steamed.

Quickly, he dialed the museum again, put the phone on speaker. "Dr. Sherman?"

"Yes?"

"This is Smithback from the *Times* again."

"Mr. Smithback," came the shrill reply, "I've already told you everything I know. Now, if you don't mind, I have a train to catch."

"I know that what arrived at the museum this morning was not corundum grit."

Silence.

"I know what it *really* was."

More silence.

"The museum's diamond collection."

In the silence, Nora looked at him sharply.

"Dr. Sherman, I'm coming over to the museum to talk to you. If Dr. Collopy is still around, he would be wise to be there—or, at least, to make himself available by phone. I don't know what you told my colleague Harriman, but you're not going to fob the same stuff off onto me. It's bad enough that the museum allowed its diamond collection—the most valuable in the world—to be stolen. I'm certain the museum trustees wouldn't want a cover-up scandal to follow hard on the heels of the revelation that the same diamond collection had just been reduced to industrial-strength grinding powder. Are we clear on that, Dr. Sherman?"

It was a very weak and shaky voice that finally issued from the cell phone. "It wasn't a cover-up, I assure you. It was, ah, just a delay in the announcement."

"I'll be there in ten minutes. Don't go anywhere."

Smithback immediately made another call, to his editor at the *Times*. "Fenton? You know that piece on the anthrax scare at the museum that Bryce Harriman filed? Better kill that. I've got the real story, and it's a bombshell. Hold the front page for me."

He shut the phone and looked up. Nora was no longer mad. She was white.

"Diogenes Pendergast," she whispered. "He *destroyed* the diamonds?"

Smithback nodded.

"But why?"

"That's a very good question, Nora. But now, darling, with my infinite apologies, and an IOU for dinner at the Rattlesnake Café, I have to go. I've got a couple of interviews to conduct and a story to file before midnight if I'm going to make the national edition. I'm really, really sorry. Don't wait up for me."

He rose and gave her a kiss.

"You're amazing," she said in an awed voice.

Smithback hesitated, feeling an unaccustomed sensation. It took him a moment to realize he was blushing.

5

Dr. Frederick Watson Collopy stood behind the great nineteenth-century leather-topped desk of his corner office in the museum's southeast tower. The huge desk was bare, save for a copy of the morning's *New York Times*. The newspaper had not been opened. It did not need to be: already, Collopy could see everything he needed to see, on the front page, above the fold, in the largest type the staid *Times* dared use.

The cat was out of the bag, and it could not be put back in.

Collopy believed that he occupied the greatest position in American science: director of the New York Museum of Natural History. His mind drifted from the subject of the article to the names of his distinguished forebears: Ogilvy, Scott, Throckmorton. His goal, his one ambition, was to add his name to that august registry—and not fall into ignominy like his two immediate predecessors: the late and not-much-lamented Winston Wright or the inept Olivia Merriam.

And yet there, on the front page of the *Times*, was a headline that might just be his tombstone. He had weathered several bad patches recently, irruptions of scandal that would have felled a lesser man. But he had handled them coolly and decisively—and he would do the same here.

A soft knock came at the door.

"Come in."

The bearded figure of Hugo Menzies, chairman of the Anthropology Department, dressed elegantly and with less than the usual degree of academic rumpledness, entered the room. He silently took a chair as Josephine Rocco, the head of public relations, entered behind him, along with the museum's lawyer, the ironically named Beryl Darling of Wilfred, Spragg and Darling.

Collopy remained standing, watching the three as he stroked his chin thoughtfully. Finally he spoke.

"I've called you here in emergency session, for obvious reasons." He glanced down at the paper. "I assume you've seen the *Times*?"

His audience nodded in silent assent.

"We made a mistake in trying to cover this up, even briefly. When I took this position as director of the museum, I told myself I would run this place differently, that I wouldn't operate in the secretive and sometimes paranoid manner of the last few administrations. I believed the museum to be a great institution, one strong enough to survive the vicissitudes of scandal and controversy."

He paused.

"In trying to play down the destruction of our diamond collection, in seeking to cover it up, I made a mistake. I violated my own principles."

"An apology to us is all well and good," said Darling in her usual crisp voice, "but why didn't you consult me before you made that hasty and ill-considered decision? You must have realized you couldn't get away with it. This has done serious damage to the museum and made my job that much more difficult."

Collopy reminded himself this was precisely the reason the museum paid Darling four hundred dollars an hour: she always spoke the unvarnished truth.

He raised a hand. "Point taken. But this is a development I never in my worst nightmares anticipated—finding that our diamonds have been reduced to . . ." His voice cracked: he couldn't finish.

There was an uneasy shifting in the room.

Collopy swallowed, began again. "We must take action. We've got to respond, and respond now. That is why I've asked you to this meeting."

As he paused, Collopy could hear, coming faintly from Museum

Drive below, the shouts and calls of a growing crowd of protesters, along with police sirens and bullhorns.

Rocco spoke up. "The phones in my office are ringing off the hook. It's nine now, and I think we've probably got until ten, maybe eleven at the latest, to make some kind of official statement. In all my years in public relations, I've never encountered anything quite like this."

Menzies shifted in his chair, smoothed his silver hair. "May I?"

Collopy nodded. "Hugo."

Menzies cleared his throat, his intense blue eyes darting to the window and back to Collopy. "The first thing we have to realize, Frederick, is that this catastrophe is beyond 'spinning.' Listen to the crowd out there—the fact that we even *considered* covering up such a loss has the people up in arms. No: we've got to take the hit, honestly and squarely. Admit our wrong. No more dissembling." He glanced at Rocco. "That's my first point and I hope we're all in agreement on it."

Collopy nodded again. "And your second?"

He leaned forward slightly. "It's not enough to respond. We need to go on the *offensive*."

"What do you mean?"

"We need to do something glorious. We need to make a fabulous announcement, something that will remind New York City and the world that, despite all this, we're still a great museum. Mount a scientific expedition, perhaps, or embark on some extraordinary research project."

"Won't that look like a rather transparent diversion?" asked Rocco.

"Perhaps to some. But the criticism will last only a day or two, and then we'll be free to build interest and good publicity."

"What kind of project?" Collopy asked.

"I haven't gotten that far."

Rocco nodded slowly. "Perhaps it would work. This event could be combined with a gala party, strictly A-list, the social 'must' of the season. That will mute museum-bashing among the press and politicians, who will naturally want to be invited."

"This sounds promising," Collopy said.

After a moment, Darling spoke. "It's a fine theory. All we lack is the expedition, event, or whatever."

At that moment, Collopy's intercom buzzed. He stabbed at it with irritation. "Mrs. Surd, we're not to be disturbed."

"I know, Dr. Collopy, but . . . well, this is highly unusual."

"Not now."

"It requires an immediate response."

Collopy sighed. "Can't it wait ten minutes, for heaven's sake?"

"It's a bank wire transfer donation of ten million euros for—"

"A gift of ten million euros? Bring it in."

Mrs. Surd entered, efficient and plump, carrying a paper.

"Excuse me for a moment." Collopy snatched the paper. "Who's it from and where do I sign?"

"It's from a Comte Thierry de Cahors. He's giving the museum ten million euros to renovate and reopen the Tomb of Senef."

"The Tomb of Senef? What the devil is that?" Collopy tossed the paper on the desk. "I'll deal with this later."

"But it says here, sir, that the funds are waiting in transatlantic escrow and must be either refused or accepted within the hour."

Collopy resisted an impulse to wring his hands. "We're awash in bloody restricted funds like this! What we need are *general* funds to pay the bills. Fax this count whoever and see if you can't persuade him to make this an unrestricted donation. Use my name with the usual courtesies. We don't need the money for whatever windmill he's tilting at."

"Yes, Dr. Collopy."

She turned away and Collopy glanced at the group. "Now, I believe Beryl had the floor."

The lawyer opened her mouth to speak, but Menzies held out a suppressing hand. "Mrs. Surd? Please wait a few minutes before contacting the Count of Cahors."

Mrs. Surd hesitated, glancing at Collopy for confirmation. The director nodded his confirmation and she left, closing the door behind her.

"All right, Hugo, what's this about?" Collopy asked.

"I'm trying to remember the details. The Tomb of Senef—it rings a bell. And, now that I recall, so does the Count of Cahors."

"Can we move on here?" Collopy asked.

Menzies sat forward suddenly. "Frederick, this *is* moving on! Think back over your museum history. The Tomb of Senef was an Egyptian tomb on display in the museum from its original opening until, I believe, the Depression, when it was closed."

"And?"

"If memory serves, it was a tomb stolen and disassembled by the French during the Napoleonic invasion of Egypt and later seized by the British. It was purchased by one of the museum's benefactors and reassembled in the basement as one of the museum's original exhibits. It must still be there."

"And who is this Cahors?" Darling asked.

"Napoleon brought an army of naturalists and archaeologists with his army when he invaded Egypt. A Cahors led the archaeological contingent. I imagine this fellow is a descendant."

Collopy frowned. "What does this have to do with anything?"

"Don't you see? This is precisely what we're looking for!"

"A dusty old tomb?"

"Exactly! We make a big announcement of the count's gift, set an opening date with a gala party and all the trappings, and make a media event out of it." Menzies looked inquiringly at Rocco.

"Yes," Rocco said. "Yes, that could work. Egypt is always popular with the general public."

"*Could* work? It *will* work. The beauty of it is that the tomb's already installed. The Sacred Images exhibition has run its course, it's time for something new. We could do this in two months—or less."

"A lot depends on the condition of the tomb."

"Nevertheless, it's still in place and ready to go. It might only need to be swept out. Our storage rooms are full of Egyptian odds and ends that we could put in the tomb to round out the exhibition. The count is offering plenty of money for whatever restoration is necessary."

"I don't understand," Darling said. "How could an entire exhibition be forgotten for seventy years?"

"For one thing, it would have been bricked up—that's often what they did to old exhibits to preserve them. " Menzies smiled a little sadly. "This museum simply has too many artifacts, and not enough money or curators to tend them. That's why I've lobbied for years now to create a position for a museum historian. Who knows what other secrets sleep in the long-forgotten corners?"

A brief silence settled over the room, broken abruptly as Collopy brought his hand down on his desk. "Let's do it." He reached for the phone. "Mrs. Surd? Tell the count to release the money. We're accepting his terms."

6

Nora Kelly stood in her laboratory, gazing at a large specimen table covered with fragments of ancient Anasazi pottery. The potsherds were of an unusual type that glowed almost golden in the bright lights, a sheen caused by countless mica particles in the original clay. She had collected the sherds during a summertime expedition to the Four Corners area of the Southwest, and now she had arranged them on a huge contour map of the Four Corners, each sherd in the precise geographical location where it had been found.

She stared at the glittering array, once again trying to make sense of it. This was the core of her major research project at the museum: tracing the diffusion of this rare micaceous pottery from its source in southern Utah as it was traded and retraded across the Southwest and beyond. The pottery had been developed by a religious kachina cult that had come up from Aztec Mexico, and Nora believed that—by tracing the spread of the pottery across the Southwest—she could thereby trace the spread of the kachina cult.

But there were so many sherds, and so many C-14 dates, that making all the variables work together was a thorny problem, and she had not even begun to solve it. She stared hard: the answer was there. She just had to find it.

She sighed and took a sip of coffee, glad she had her basement lab as a refuge from the storm raging outside the museum above. Yesterday it had been the anthrax scare, but today was worse—thanks in large part to her husband, Bill, who had a singular knack for stirring up trouble. He had broken the story in the *Times* this morning that the powder was, in fact, the museum's stolen diamond collection, worth hundreds of millions of dollars, pulverized to dust by the thief. The news had caused an uproar worse than anything Nora could remember. The mayor, cornered by a bevy of television cameras outside his office, had already blasted the museum and called for the immediate removal of its director.

She forced her mind back to the problem of the potsherds. All the lines of diffusion led back to one place: the source of the rare clay at the base of the Kaiparowits plateau of Utah, where it had been mined and fired by the inhabitants of a large cliff dwelling hidden in the canyons. From there, it had been traded to places as far away as northern Mexico and western Texas. But how? And when? And by whom?

She got up and went to a cabinet, removing the last ziplock bag of potsherds. The lab was as quiet as a tomb, the only sound the faint hiss of the forced-air ducts. Beyond the laboratory itself lay large storage areas: ancient oak cabinets with rippled glass windows, filled with pots, arrowheads, axes, and other artifacts. A faint whiff of paradichlorobenzene wafted in from the Indian mummy storage room next door. She began laying the sherds out on the map, filling in its last blank corner, double-checking the accession number on each sherd as she placed it.

Suddenly she paused. She had heard the creaking-open of the laboratory door and the sound of a soft footfall on the dusty floor. Hadn't she locked it? It was a silly habit, locking the door: but the museum's vast and silent basement, with its dim corridors and its dark storage rooms filled with strange and dreadful artifacts, had always given her the creeps. And she could not forget what had happened to her friend Margo Green just a few weeks earlier in a darkened exhibition hall, two floors above where she stood now.

"Is someone there?" she called out.

A figure materialized from the dimness, first the outlines of a face, then a closely trimmed beard with silvery-white hair—and Nora relaxed. It was only Hugo Menzies, chairman of the Anthropology Department and her immediate boss. He was still a little pale from his recent bout with gallstones, his cheerful eyes rimmed in red.

"Hello, Nora," said the curator, giving her a kindly smile. "May I?"

"Of course."

Menzies perched himself on a stool. "It's so lovely and quiet down here. Are you alone?"

"Yes. How are things up top?"

"The crowd outside is still growing."

"I saw them when I came in."

"It's getting ugly. They're jeering and hectoring the arriving staff and blocking traffic on Museum Drive. And I fear this is just the beginning. It's one thing when the mayor and governor make pronouncements, but it appears the people of New York have also been aroused. God save us from the fury of the *vulgus mobile.*"

Nora shook her head. "I'm sorry that Bill was the cause—"

Menzies laid a gentle hand on her shoulder. "Bill was only the messenger. He did the museum a favor in exposing this ill-advised cover-up scheme before it could take hold. The truth would have come out eventually."

"I can't understand why someone would go to the trouble to steal the gems and then destroy them."

Menzies shrugged. "Who knows what goes on in the mind of a deranged individual? It evinces, at the very least, an implacable hatred of the museum."

"What had the museum ever done to him?"

"Only one person can answer that question. But I'm not here to speculate on the criminal's mind. I'm here for a specific reason, and it has to do with what's going on upstairs."

"I don't understand."

"I've just come from a meeting in Dr. Collopy's office. We made a decision, and it involves you."

Nora waited, feeling a creeping sense of alarm.

"Are you familiar with the Tomb of Senef?"

"I've never heard of it."

"Not surprising. Few museum employees have. It was one of the museum's original exhibits, an Egyptian tomb from the Valley of the Kings that was reassembled in these basements. It was closed down and sealed off in the thirties and never reopened."

"And?"

"What the museum needs right now is some positive news, something that will remind everyone that we're still doing good things. A distraction, as it were. That distraction is going to be the Tomb of Senef. We're going to reopen it, and I want you as point person for the project."

"Me? But I put off my research for months to help mount the Sacred Images show!"

An ironic smile played over Menzies's face. "That's right, and that's why I'm asking you to do this. I saw the work you did on Sacred Images. You're the only one in the department who can pull this off."

"In how long?"

"Collopy wants it fast-tracked. We've got six weeks."

"You've got to be kidding!"

"We face a real emergency. Finances have been in a sorry state for a long time. And with this new spate of bad publicity, anything could happen."

Nora fell silent.

"What set this in motion," Menzies continued gently, "is that we just received ten million euros—thirteen million dollars—to fund this project. Money is no object. We'll have the unanimous support of the museum, from the board of trustees to all the unions. The Tomb of Senef has remained sealed, so it should be in fairly good condition."

"Please don't ask me to do this. Give it to Ashton."

"Ashton's no good at controversy. I saw how you handled yourself with those protesters at the Sacred Images opening. Nora, the museum is in a fight for its life. I need you. The *museum* needs you."

There was a silence. Nora glanced back over her potsherds with a horribly sinking heart. "I don't know anything about Egyptology."

"We're bringing in a top Egyptologist as a temporary hire to work with you."

Nora realized there was no escape. She heaved a huge sigh. "All right. I'll do it."

"Brava! That's what I wanted to hear. Now then, we haven't gotten very far with the idea yet, but the tomb hasn't been on display in seventy years, so it will obviously need some sprucing up. It's not enough these days to mount a static exhibition; you need multimedia. And of course, there will be a gala opening, something every New Yorker with social aspirations will *have* to get a ticket for."

Nora shook her head. "All this in six weeks?"

"I was hoping you might have some ideas."

"When do you need them?"

"Right now, I'm afraid. Dr. Collopy has scheduled a press conference in half an hour to announce about the show."

"Oh, no." Nora slumped on her stool. "Are you sure special effects will be necessary? I hate computerized window dressing. It distracts from the objects."

"That *is* what being a museum means these days, unfortunately. Look at the new Abraham Lincoln library. Yes, on a certain level, it's a bit vulgar perhaps—but this is the twenty-first century and we're competing with television and video games. Please, Nora: I need ideas now. The director will be bombarded with questions and he wants to be able to talk about the exhibit."

Nora swallowed. On the one hand, it made her sick to think of putting off her research yet again, working seventy-hour weeks, never seeing her husband of only a few months. On the other hand, if she was going to do this—and it seemed she had no choice—she wanted to do it well.

"We don't want anything cheesy," she said. "No mummies popping up from their sarcophagi. And it's got to be educational."

"My feelings exactly."

Nora thought a moment. "The tomb was robbed, am I right?"

"It was robbed in antiquity, like most Egyptian tombs, probably by the very priests who buried Senef—who, by the way, was not a pharaoh, but vizier and regent to Thutmosis IV."

Nora digested this. It was, she supposed, a huge honor to be asked to coordinate a major new exhibition—and this one would have exceptionally high visibility. It was intriguing. She found herself being drawn into it, despite herself.

"If you're looking for something dramatic," she said, "why not recreate the moment of the robbery itself? We could dramatize the robbers at work—show their fear of being caught, what would happen to them if they *were* caught—with a voice-over explaining what was happening, who Senef was, that sort of thing."

Menzies nodded. "Excellent, Nora."

Nora felt a mounting excitement. "If done right, with computerized lighting and so forth, it would give visitors an experience they'd never forget. Make history come alive inside the tomb itself."

"Nora, someday you'll be director of this museum."

She blushed. The idea did not displease her.

"I'd been thinking of some sort of sound-and-light show myself. It's perfect." With uncharacteristic exuberance, Menzies seized Nora's hand. "This is going to save the museum. And it will make your career here. As I said, you'll have all the money and support you'll need. As for the computer effects, let me manage that side of things—you focus on the objects and displays. Six weeks will be just enough time to get the buzz going, get out the invitations, and work the press. They won't be able to trash the museum if they're angling to be invited."

He glanced at his watch. "I've got to prepare Dr. Collopy for the press conference. Thank you so much, Nora."

He bustled out, leaving Nora alone in the silent laboratory. She turned her eye regretfully to the table she had so carefully arranged with potsherds, and then she started picking them up, one at a time, and returning them to their storage bags.

7

Special Agent Spencer Coffey rounded the corner and approached the warden's office, his steel-capped heels making a satisfying tattoo against the polished cement floor. Short, bottle-mustached Agent Rabiner followed, deferentially riding his wake. Coffey paused before the institutional oak door, gave a tap, then opened it without waiting for an invitation.

The warden's secretary, a thin bleach-blonde with old acne scars on her face and a no-bullshit attitude, gave him the once-over. "Yes?"

"Agent Coffey, Federal Bureau of Investigation." He waved his badge. "We've got an appointment, and we're in a hurry."

"I'll tell the warden you're here," she said, her upstate hick accent grating on his nerves.

Coffey glanced at Rabiner and rolled his eyes. He'd already had a run-in with the woman over a dropped connection when he called earlier that day, and now, meeting her in person, he confirmed she was everything he despised, a low-class hayseed who'd clawed her way into a position of semirespectability.

"Agent Coffey and—?" She glanced at Rabiner.

"*Special* Agent Coffey and *Special* Agent Rabiner."

The woman picked up the intercom phone with insolent slowness. "Agents Coffey and Rabiner to see you, sir. They say they have an appointment."

She listened for a moment, and then hung up. She waited just long enough to let Coffey know she wasn't in nearly the hurry he was. "Mr. Imhof," she finally said, "will see you."

Coffey started to walk past her desk. Then he paused. "So. How are things down on the farm?"

"Seems to be ruttin' season for hogs," she responded without a pause, not even looking at him.

Coffey continued into the inner office, wondering just what the bitch meant and whether he'd been insulted or not.

As Coffey shut the door behind them, Warden Gordon Imhof rose from behind a large Formica desk. Coffey hadn't seen him in person before, and found the man far younger than he expected, small and neat, with a goatee and cool blue eyes. He was impeccably dressed and sported a helmet of blow-dried hair. Coffey couldn't quite pigeonhole him. In the old days, wardens came through the ranks; but this fellow looked like he'd gotten some Ph.D. somewhere in correctional facility management and had never felt the satisfying *thok!* of a nightstick striking human flesh. Still, there was a thinness to the lips that boded well.

Imhof extended his hand to Coffey and Rabiner. "Have a seat."

"Thank you."

"How did the interrogation go?"

"Our case is developing," Coffey said. "If this doesn't fit the federal death penalty statute to a T, I don't know what does. But it's no slam dunk. There are certain complications." He didn't mention that the interrogation had, in fact, gone badly—very badly.

Imhof's face was inscrutable.

"I want to make something clear," Coffey continued. "One of this killer's victims was a colleague and friend of mine, the third most decorated agent in the history of the FBI."

He let that sink in. What he didn't mention was that this victim, Special Agent in Charge Mike Decker, was responsible for a humiliating demotion Coffey had been hit with seven years before, in the wake of the museum killings, and that nothing in his life had satisfied Coffey more than hearing about his death—except the news of who'd done it.

That had been a special moment.

"So you've got a very special prisoner, Mr. Imhof. He's a sociopathic serial killer of the most dangerous kind—murdered at least three people, although our interest in him is restricted to the murder of the federal agent. We're letting the State of New York worry about the others, but we hope by the time they convict we'll already have the prisoner strapped to a gurney with a needle in his arm."

Imhof, listening, inclined his head.

"The prisoner is also an arrogant bastard. I worked with him on a case years ago. He thinks he's better than everyone else, thinks he's above the rules. He's got no respect for authority."

At the mention of respect, Imhof finally seemed to respond. "If there's one thing I demand as warden of this institution, it's respect. Good discipline begins and ends with respect."

"Exactly," said Coffey. He decided to follow up this line, see if he could get Imhof to bite. "Speaking of respect, during the interrogation the prisoner had some choice things to say about you."

Now he could see Imhof getting interested.

"But they don't bear repeating," Coffey went on. "Naturally, you and I have learned to rise above such pettiness."

Imhof leaned forward. "If a prisoner has shown a lack of respect—and I'm not talking about anything personal here, but a lack of respect for the institution in any way—I need to know about it."

"It was the usual bullshit and I'd hate to repeat it."

"Nevertheless, I'd like to know."

Of course, the prisoner had, in fact, said nothing. That had been the problem.

"He referred to you as a beer-swilling Nazi bastard, a Boche, a Kraut, that sort of thing."

Imhof's face tightened slightly, and Coffey knew immediately he'd scored a hit.

"Anything else?" the warden asked quietly.

"Very crude stuff, something about the size of your—ah, well, I don't even recall the details."

There was a frosty silence. Imhof's goatee quivered slightly.

"As I said, it was all bullshit. But it points out an important fact:

the prisoner hasn't seen the wisdom of cooperating. And you know why? Everything stays the same for him whether he answers our questions or not, whether he shows respect for you or the institution or not. That's got to change. He has to learn that his wrong choices have consequences. And another thing: he's got to be kept in total, utter isolation. He can't be allowed to pass any messages to the outside. There have been allegations that he might be in league with a brother, still on the lam. So no phone calls, no more meetings with his lawyer, total blackout of communication with the outside world. We wouldn't want any further, ah, collateral damage to occur due to lack of vigilance. Do you understand what I mean, Warden?"

"I certainly do."

"Good. He's got to be made to see the advantages of cooperation. I'd love to work him over with a rubber hose and a cattle prod—he deserves nothing less—but unfortunately that's not possible, and we sure as hell don't want to do anything that could come back to haunt us at the trial. He may be crazy, but he's not dumb. You can't give a guy like that an opening. He's got enough money to dig up Johnnie Cochran and hire him for the defense."

Coffey stopped talking. Because for the first time, Imhof had smiled. And something about the look in the man's blue eyes chilled Coffey.

"I understand your problem, Agent Coffey. The prisoner must be shown the value of respect. I'll see to it personally."

8

On the morning appointed for opening the sealed Tomb of Senef, Nora arrived in Menzies's capacious office to find him sitting in his usual wing chair, in conversation with a young man. They both rose as she came in.

"Nora," he said. "This is Dr. Adrian Wicherly, the Egyptologist I mentioned to you. Adrian, this is Dr. Nora Kelly."

Wicherly turned to her with a smile, a thatch of untidy brown hair the only eccentricity in his otherwise perfectly dressed and groomed person. At a glance, Nora took in the understated Savile Row suit, the fine wing tips, the club tie. Her sweep came to rest on an extraordinarily handsome face: dimpled cheeks, flashing blue eyes, and perfect white teeth. He was, she thought, no more than thirty.

"Delighted to meet you, Dr. Kelly," he said in an elegant Oxbridge accent. He clasped her hand gently, blessing her with another dazzling smile.

"A pleasure. And please call me Nora."

"Of course. Nora. Forgive my formality—my stuffy upbringing has left me rather hamstrung this side of the pond. I just want to say how smashing it is to be here, working on this project."

Smashing. Nora suppressed a smile—Adrian Wicherly was almost a caricature of the dashing young Brit, of a type she didn't think even existed outside P. G. Wodehouse novels.

"Adrian comes to us with some impressive credentials," Menzies said. "D.Phil. from Oxford, directed the excavation of the tomb KV 42 in the Valley of the Kings, university professor of Egyptology at Cambridge, author of the monograph *Pharaohs of the XX Dynasty*."

Nora looked at Wicherly with fresh respect. He was amazingly young for an archaeologist of such stature. "Very impressive."

Wicherly put on a self-deprecating face. "A lot of academic rubbish, really."

"It's hardly that." Menzies glanced at his watch. "We're meeting someone from the Maintenance Department at ten. As I understand it, nobody knows quite precisely where the Tomb of Senef is anymore. The one certainty is that it was bricked up and has been inaccessible ever since. We're going to have to break our way in."

"How intriguing," said Wicherly. "I feel rather like Howard Carter."

They descended in an old brass elevator, which creaked and groaned its way to the basement. They emerged in the Maintenance Section and threaded a complex path through the machine shop and carpentry, at last arriving at the open door of a small office. Inside, a small man sat at a desk, poring over a thick press of blueprints. He rose as Menzies rapped on the door frame.

"I'd like to introduce you both to Mr. Seamus McCorkle," said Menzies. "He probably knows more about the layout of the museum than anyone alive."

"Which still isn't saying much," said McCorkle. He was an elvish man in his early fifties with a fine Celtic face and a high, whistling voice. He pronounced the final word *mitch*.

After completing the introductions, Menzies turned back to McCorkle. "Have you found our tomb?"

"I believe so." McCorkle nodded at the slab of old blueprints. "It's not easy, finding things in this old pile."

"Why ever not?" Wicherly asked.

McCorkle began rolling up the top blueprint. "The museum consists of thirty-four interconnected buildings, with a footprint of more than six acres, over two million square feet of space, and eighteen miles of corridors—and that's not even counting the sub-basement tunnels, which no one's ever surveyed or diagrammed. I once tried to figure out how many rooms there were in this joint, gave up when I hit a thousand. It's been under constant construction and renovation for every single one of its hundred and forty years. That's the nature of a museum—collections get moved around, rooms get joined together, others get split apart and renamed. And a lot of these changes are made on the fly, without blueprints."

"But surely they couldn't lose an entire Egyptian tomb!" said Wicherly.

McCorkle laughed. "That would be difficult, even for this museum. It's finding the entrance that might be tricky. It was bricked up in 1935 when they built the connecting tunnel from the 81st Street subway station." He tucked the blueprints under his arm and picked up an old leather bag that lay on his desk. "Shall we?"

"Lead the way," said Menzies.

They set off along a puke-green corridor, past maintenance rooms and storage areas, through a heavily trafficked section of the basement. As they went along, McCorkle gave a running account. "This is the metal shop. This is the old physical plant, once home to the ancient boilers, now used to store the collection of whale skeletons. Jurassic dinosaur storage . . . Cretaceous . . . Oligocene mammals . . . Pleistocene mammals . . . dugongs and manatees . . ."

The storage areas gave way to laboratories, their shiny, stainless-steel doors in contrast to the dingy corridors, lit with caged lightbulbs and lined with rumbling steam pipes.

They passed through so many locked doors Nora lost count. Some were old and required keys, which McCorkle selected from a large ring. Other doors, part of the museum's new security system, he opened by swiping a magnetic card. As they moved deeper into the fabric of the building, the corridors became progressively empty and silent.

"I daresay this place is as vast as the British Museum," said Wicherly.

McCorkle snorted in contempt. "Bigger. *Much* bigger."

They came to an ancient set of riveted metal doors, which McCorkle opened with a large iron key. Darkness yawned beyond. He hit a switch and illuminated a long, once-elegant corridor lined with dingy frescoes. Nora squinted: they were paintings of a New Mexico landscape, with mountains, deserts, and a multistoried Indian ruin she recognized as Taos Pueblo.

"Fremont Ellis," said Menzies. "This was once the Hall of the Southwest. Shut down since the forties."

"These are extraordinary," said Nora.

"Indeed. And very valuable."

"They're rather in need of curation," said Wicherly. "That's a rather nasty stain, there."

"It's a question of money," Menzies said. "If our count hadn't stepped forward with the necessary grant, the Tomb of Senef would probably have been left to sleep for another seventy years."

McCorkle opened another door, revealing another dim hall turned into storage, full of shelves covered with beautifully painted pots. Old oaken cabinets stood against the walls, fronted with rippled glass, revealing a profusion of dim artifacts.

"The Southwest collections," McCorkle said.

"I had no idea," said Nora, amazed. "These should be available for study."

"As Adrian pointed out, they need to be curated first," Menzies said. "Once again, a question of money."

"It's not only money," McCorkle added, with a strange, pinched expression on his face.

Nora exchanged glances with Wicherly. "I'm sorry?" she asked.

Menzies cleared his throat. "I think what Seamus means is that the, ah, first Museum Beast killings happened in the vicinity of the Hall of the Southwest."

In the silence that followed, Nora made a mental note to have a look at these collections later—preferably, in the company of a large group. Maybe she could write a grant to see them moved to updated storage.

Another door gave way to a smaller room, lined floor-to-ceiling with black metal drawers. Half hidden behind the drawers were ancient posters and announcements from the twenties and thirties, with art deco lettering and images of Gibson Girls. In an earlier era, it must have been an antechamber of sorts. The room smelled of paradichlorobenzene and something bad—like old beef jerky, Nora decided.

At the far end, a great dim hall opened up. In the reflected light, she could see that its walls were covered with frescoes of the pyramids of Giza and the Sphinx as they had appeared when first built.

"Now we're approaching the old Egyptian galleries," McCorkle said.

They entered the vast hall. It had been turned into storage space: shelving was covered in transparent plastic sheets, which were in turn overlaid with dust.

McCorkle unrolled the blueprints, squinted at them in the dim light. "If my estimations are correct, the entrance to the tomb was in what is now the annex, at the far end."

Wicherly went to one shelf, lifted the plastic. Beneath, Nora could make out metal shelves crowded with pottery vessels, gilded chairs and beds, headrests, canopic jars, and smaller figurines in alabaster, faience, and ceramic.

"Good Lord, this is one of the finest collections of ushabtis I've ever seen." Wicherly turned excitedly to Nora. "Why, there's enough material here alone to fill up the tomb twice over." He picked up an ushabti and turned it over with reverence. "Old Kingdom, II Dynasty, reign of the pharaoh Hetepsekhemwy."

"Dr. Wicherly, the rules about handling objects . . . ," said McCorkle, a warning note in his voice.

"It's quite all right," said Menzies. "Dr. Wicherly is an Egyptologist. I'll take responsibility."

"Of course," said McCorkle, a little put out. Nora had the feeling that McCorkle took a kind of proprietary interest in these old collections. They were his, in a way, as he was one of the few people ever to see them.

Wicherly went from one shelf to the next, his mouth practically watering. "Why, they even have a Neolithic collection from the Upper Nile! Good Lord, take a look at this ceremonial *thatof*!" He held up a foot-long stone knife, flaked from gray flint.

McCorkle cast an annoyed glance at Wicherly. The archaeologist laid the knife back in its place with the utmost care, then reshrouded it in plastic.

They came to another iron-bound door, which McCorkle had some difficulty opening, trying several keys before finding the correct one. The door groaned open at last, the hinges shedding clouds of rust.

Beyond lay a small room filled with sarcophagi made of painted wood and cartonnage. Some were without lids, and inside, Nora could make out the individual mummies—some wrapped, some unwrapped.

"The mummy room," said McCorkle.

Wicherly rushed in ahead of the rest. "Good heavens, there must be a hundred in here!" He swept a plastic sheet aside, exposing a large wooden sarcophagus. "Look at this!"

Nora went over and peered at the mummy. The linen bandages had been ripped from its face and chest, the mouth was open, the black lips shriveled and drawn back as if crying out in protest at the violation. In its chest stood a gaping hole, the sternum and ribs torn out.

Wicherly turned toward Nora, eyes bright. "Do you see?" he said in an almost reverential whisper. "This mummy was robbed. They tore off the linen to get at precious amulets hidden in the wrappings. And there—where that hole is—was where a jade and gold scarab beetle had been placed on the chest. The symbol of rebirth. Gold was considered the flesh of the gods, because it never tarnished. They ripped it open to take it."

"This can be the mummy we put in the tomb," Menzies said. "The idea—Nora's idea—was that we show the tomb as it appeared while being robbed."

"How perfect," said Wicherly, turning a brilliant smile to Nora.

"I *believe*," McCorkle interrupted, "that the tomb entrance was against that wall." Dropping his bag on the floor, he pulled the plastic sheeting away from the shelves covering the far wall, exposing pots, bowls, and baskets, all filled with black shriveled objects.

"What's that inside?" Nora asked.

Wicherly went over to examine the objects. After a silence, he straightened up. "Preserved food. For the afterlife. Bread, antelope joints, fruits and vegetables, dates—preserved for the pharaoh's journey to the afterworld."

They heard a growing rumble coming through the walls, followed by a muffled squeal of metal, then silence.

"The Central Park West subway," McCorkle explained. "The 81st Street station is very close."

"We'll have to find some way to dampen that sound," Menzies said. "It destroys the mood."

McCorkle grunted. Then he removed an electronic device from the bag and aimed it at the newly exposed wall, turned, aimed again. Then he pulled out a piece of chalk, made a mark on the wall. Taking a second device from his shirt pocket, he laid it against the wall and slid it across slowly, taking readings as he went.

Then he stepped back. "Bingo. Help me move these shelves."

They began shifting the objects to shelves on the other walls. When the wall was at last bare, McCorkle pulled the shelf supports from the crumbling plaster with a set of pliers and put them to one side.

"Ready for the moment of truth?" McCorkle asked, a gleam in his eye, good humor returning.

"Absolutely," said Wicherly.

McCorkle removed a long spike and hammer from his bag, positioned the spike on the wall, gave it a sharp blow, then another. The sounds echoed in the confined space and plaster began falling in sheets, exposing courses of brick. He continued to drive the spike in, dust rising . . . and then suddenly the spike slid in to the hilt. McCorkle rotated it, giving it a few side blows with the hammer, loosening the brick. A few more deft blows knocked free a large chunk of brickwork, leaving a black rectangle. He stepped back.

As he did so, Wicherly darted forward. "Forgive me if I claim explorer's privilege." He turned back with his most charming smile. "Any objections?"

"Be our guest," said Menzies. McCorkle frowned but said nothing.

Wicherly took his flashlight and shined it into the hole, pressing his face to the gap. A long silence ensued, interrupted by the rumble of another subway train.

"What do you see?" asked Menzies at last.

"Strange animals, statues, and gold—everywhere the glint of gold."

"What in heck?" said McCorkle.

Wicherly glanced back at him. "I was being facetious—quoting what Howard Carter said when he first peered into King Tut's tomb."

McCorkle's lips tightened. "If you'll step aside, please, I'll have this open in a moment."

McCorkle stepped back up to the gap, and with a series of expertly aimed blows of the spike, loosened several rows of bricks. In less than ten minutes, he had opened a hole big enough to step through. He disappeared inside, came back out a moment later.

"The electricity isn't working, as I suspected. We'll have to use our flashlights. I'm required to lead the way," he said with a glance at Wicherly. "Museum regulations. Might be hazards in there."

"The mummy from the Black Lagoon, perhaps," said Wicherly with a laugh and a glance at Nora.

They stepped carefully inside, then stopped to reconnoiter. In the glow of their flashlight beams, a great stone threshold was visible, and beyond, a descending staircase carved out of rough limestone blocks.

McCorkle moved toward the first step, hesitated, then gave a slightly nervous chuckle. "Ready, ladies and gents?"

9

Captain of Homicide Laura Hayward stood silently in her office, looking at the untidy forest that seemed to sprout from her desk, from every chair, and to spill over to the floor—chaotic heaps of papers, photographs, tangles of colored string, CDs, yellowing telex sheets, labels, envelopes. The outward disarray, she mused, was a perfect mirror of her inner state of mind.

Her beautiful layout of evidence against Special Agent Pendergast, with all its accusatory paraphernalia of colored strings, photos, and labels, was no more. It had fit together so well. The evidence had been subtle but clean, convincing, utterly consistent. An out-of-the-way spot of blood, some microscopic fibers, a few strands of hair, a knot tied in a certain way, the chain of ownership of a murder weapon. The DNA tests didn't lie, the forensics didn't lie, the autopsies didn't lie. They all pointed to Pendergast. The case against him was that good.

Maybe *too* good. And that, in a nutshell, was the problem.

A tentative knock came at the door and she turned to see the figure of Glen Singleton, local precinct captain, hovering outside. He was in his late forties; tall, with the sleek, efficient movements of a swimmer, a long face, and an aquiline profile. He wore a charcoal suit that was far too expensive and well cut for an NYPD captain, and every other week he dropped $120 at the barbershop in the lobby of the Carlyle to have his salt-and-pepper hair trimmed to perfection. But these were signs of personal fastidiousness, not a cop on the take. And despite the sarto-rial affectations, he was a damned good cop, one of the most decorated on active duty in the force.

"Laura, may I?" He smiled, displaying an expensive row of perfect teeth.

"Sure, why not?"

"We missed you at the departmental dinner last night. Did you have a conflict?"

"A conflict? No, nothing like that."

"Really? Then I can't understand why you'd pass up a chance to eat, drink, and be merry."

"I don't know. I guess I wasn't really in the mood to be merry."

There was an awkward silence while Singleton looked around for an empty chair.

"Sorry about the mess. I was just doing . . ." Her voice trailed off.

"What?"

Hayward shrugged.

"That's what I was afraid of." Singleton hesitated briefly, seemed to come to some decision, then shut the door behind him and stepped forward.

"This isn't like you, Laura," he said in a low voice.

So it's going to be like that, thought Hayward.

"I'm your friend, and I'm not going to beat around the bush," he went on. "I have a pretty good idea what you were 'just doing,' and you're asking for trouble by doing it."

Hayward waited.

"You developed the case in textbook fashion. You handled it per-fectly. So why are you beating yourself up about it now?"

She gazed steadily at Singleton for a moment, trying to control the surge of anger that she knew was directed more at herself than him.

"Why? Because the wrong man's in jail. Agent Pendergast didn't murder Torrance Hamilton, he didn't murder Charles Duchamp, and he didn't murder Michael Decker. His brother, Diogenes, is the real mur-derer."

Singleton sighed. "Look. It's clear that Diogenes stole the museum's diamonds and kidnapped Viola Maskelene. There are statements from Lieutenant D'Agosta, that gemologist, Kaplan, and Maskelene herself to that effect. But that doesn't make him a murderer. You have absolutely no proof of that. On the other hand, you've done a great job proving Agent Pendergast *did* commit those murders. Let it go."

"I did the job I was supposed to do, and that's the problem. I was set up. Pendergast was framed."

Singleton frowned. "I've seen plenty of frame jobs in my career, but for this to work, it would have to have been impossibly sophisticated."

"D'Agosta told me all along that Diogenes Pendergast was framing his brother. Diogenes collected all the physical evidence he needed during Pendergast's convalescence in Italy—blood, hair, fibers, everything. D'Agosta *insisted* Diogenes was alive; that he was the kidnapper of Viola Maskelene; that he was behind the diamond theft. He was right about those things, and it makes me think he might be right about everything else."

"D'Agosta messed up big-time!" Singleton snapped. "He betrayed my trust, and yours. I've no doubt that the disciplinary trial will confirm his dismissal from the force. You really want to tie your wagon to that star?"

"I want to tie my wagon to the truth. I'm responsible for putting Pendergast on trial for his life, and I'm the only one who can undo it."

"The only way to do that is to prove somebody *else* is the murderer. Do you have a single shred of evidence against Diogenes?"

Hayward frowned. "Margo Green described her assailant as—"

"Margo Green was attacked in a darkened room. Her testimony would never hold up." Singleton hesitated. "Look, Laura," he said in a gentler voice. "Let's not bullshit each other here. I know what you're going through. Hooking up with someone on the force is never easy. Breaking up with them is even harder. And with Vincent D'Agosta in the middle of this case, I don't wonder you feel a touch of—"

"D'Agosta and I are ancient history," Laura interrupted. "I don't appreciate that insinuation. And for that matter, I don't appreciate this visit of yours."

Singleton picked up a pile of papers from the guest chair, placed them on the floor, and sat down. He bowed his head, propped his elbows on his knees, sighed, then looked up.

"Laura, " he said, "you're the youngest female homicide captain in the history of the NYPD. You're twice as good as any man at your level. Commissioner Rocker loves you. The mayor loves you. Your own people love you. You're going to be commissioner someday—you're *that* good. I didn't come here at anyone's behest, I came here on my own. To warn you that you've run out of time on this. The FBI is moving ahead with their case against Pendergast. They think he killed Decker, and they aren't interested in inconsistencies. What you've got is a hunch, nothing more . . . and it's not worth throwing away your career on a hunch. Because that's what will happen if you go up against the FBI on this—and lose."

She looked at him steadily, took a deep breath. "So be it."

10

The small group descended the dust-laden staircase of the Tomb of Senef, their shoes leaving prints as in a coating of fresh snow.

Wicherly paused, shining his light around. "Ah. This is what the Egyptians called the God's First Passage along the Sun's Path." He turned toward Nora and Menzies. "Are you interested, or will I be making a bore of myself?"

"By all means," said Menzies. "Let's have the tour."

Wicherly's teeth gleamed in the dim light. "The problem is, much of the meaning of these ancient tombs still eludes us. They're easy enough to date, though—this seems a fairly typical New Kingdom tomb, I'd say late XVIIIth Dynasty."

"Right on target," said Menzies. "Senef was the vizier and regent to Thutmosis IV."

"Thank you." Wicherly absorbed the compliment with evident satisfaction. "Most of these New Kingdom tombs had three parts—an outer, middle, and inner tomb, divided into a total of twelve chambers, which together represented the passage of the Sun God through the underworld during the twelve hours of night. The pharaoh was buried at sunset, and his soul accompanied the Sun God on his solar barque as he made the perilous journey through the underworld toward his glorious rebirth at dawn."

He shone his light ahead, illuminating a dim portal at the far end.

"This staircase would have been filled with rubble, ending in a sealed door."

They continued descending the staircase, at last reaching a massive doorway topped by a lintel carved with a huge Eye of Horus. Wicherly paused, shining his light on the Eye and the hieroglyphics surrounding it.

"Can you read these hieroglyphics?" asked Menzies.

Wicherly grinned. "I make a pretty good show of it. It's a curse." He winked slyly at Nora. "*To any who cross this threshold, may Ammut swallow his heart.*"

There was a short silence.

McCorkle issued a high-pitched chuckle. "That's all?"

"To the ancient tomb robber," said Wicherly, "that would be enough—that's a heck of a curse to an ancient Egyptian."

"Who is Ammut?" Nora asked.

"The Swallower of the Damned." Wicherly pointed his flashlight on a dim painting on the far wall, depicting a monster with a crocodilian head, the body of a leopard, and the grotesque hindquarters of a hippo, squatting on the sand, mouth open, about to devour a row of human hearts. "Evil words and deeds made the heart heavy, and after death Anubis weighed your heart on a balance scale against the Feather of Maat. If your heart weighed more than the feather, the baboon-headed god, Thoth, tossed it to the monster Ammut to eat. Ammut journeyed into the sands of the west to defecate, and that's where you'd end up if you didn't lead a good life—a shite, baking in the heat of the Western Desert."

"That's more than I needed to hear, thank you, Doctor," said McCorkle.

"Robbing a pharaoh's tomb must have been a terrifying experience for an ancient Egyptian. The curses put on any who entered the tomb were very real to them. To cancel the power of the dead pharaoh, they didn't just rob the tomb, they destroyed it, smashing everything. Only by destroying the objects could they disperse their malevolent power."

"Fodder for the exhibit, Nora," Menzies murmured.

After the briefest hesitation, McCorkle stepped across the threshold, and the rest followed.

"The God's Second Passage," Wicherly said, shining his light around at the inscriptions. "The walls are covered with inscriptions from the *Reunupertembru,* the Egyptian Book of the Dead."

"Ah! How interesting!" Menzies said. "Read us a sample, Adrian."

In a low voice, Wicherly began to intone:

The Regent Senef, whose word is truth, saith: Praise and thanksgiving be unto thee, Ra, O thou who rollest on like unto gold, thou Illuminer of the Two Lands on the day of thy birth. Thy mother brought thee forth on her hand, and thou didst light up with splendor the circle which is traveled over by the Disk. O Great Light who rollest across Nu, thou dost raise up the generations of men from the deep source of thy waters . . .

"It's an invocation to Ra, the Sun God, by the deceased, Senef. It's pretty typical of the Book of the Dead."

"I've heard about the Book of the Dead," Nora said, "but I don't know much about it."

"It was basically a group of magical invocations, spells, and incantations. It helped the dead make the dangerous journey through the underworld to the Field of Reeds—the ancient Egyptian idea of heaven. People waited in fear during that long night after the burial of the pharaoh, because if he buggered up somehow down in the underworld and wasn't reborn, the sun would never rise again. The dead king had to know the spells, the secret names of the serpents, and all kinds of other arcane knowledge to finish the journey. That's why it's all written on the walls of his tomb—the Book of the Dead was a set of crib notes to eternal life."

Wicherly chuckled, shining his beam over four registers of hieroglyphics painted in red and white. They stepped toward them, raising clouds of deepening gray dust. "There's the First Gate of the Dead," he went on. "It shows the pharaoh getting into the solar barque and journeying into the underworld, where he's greeted by a crowd of the dead . . . Here in Gate Four they've encountered the dreaded Desert of

Sokor, and the boat magically becomes a serpent to carry them across the burning sands . . . And this! This is very dramatic: at midnight, the soul of the Sun God Ra unites with his corpse, represented by the mummified figure—"

"Pardon my saying so, Doctor," McCorkle broke in, "but we've still got eight rooms to go."

"Right, of course. So sorry."

They proceeded to the far end of the chamber. Here, a dark hole revealed a steep staircase plunging into blackness. "This passage would also have been filled with rubble," Wicherly said. "To hinder robbers."

"Be careful," McCorkle muttered as he led the way.

Wicherly turned to Nora and held out a well-manicured hand. "May I?"

"I think I can handle it," she said, amused at the old-world courtesy. As she watched Wicherly descend with excessive caution, his beautifully polished shoes heavily coated with dust, she decided that he was far more likely to slip and break his neck than she was.

"Be careful!" Wicherly called out to McCorkle. "If this tomb follows the usual plan, up ahead is the well."

"The well?" McCorkle's voice floated back.

"A deep pit designed to send unwary tomb robbers to their death. But it was also a way to keep water from flooding the tomb, during those rare periods when the Valley of the Kings flash-flooded."

"Even if it remains intact, the well will surely be bridged over," Menzies said. "Recall that this was once an exhibit."

They moved forward cautiously, their beams finally revealing a rickety wooden bridge spanning a pit at least fifteen feet deep. McCorkle, gesturing for them to remain behind, examined the bridge carefully with his light, then advanced out onto it. A sudden *crack!* caused Nora to jump. McCorkle grabbed desperately for the railing. But it was merely the sound of settling wood, and the bridge held.

"It's still safe," said McCorkle. "Cross one at a time."

Nora walked gingerly across the narrow bridge. "I can't believe this was once part of an exhibit. How did they ever install a well like this in the sub-basement of the museum?"

"It must have been cut into the Manhattan bedrock," Menzies said from behind. "We'll have to bring this up to code."

On the far side of the bridge, they passed over another threshold. "Now we're in the middle tomb," said Wicherly. "There would have been another sealed door here. What marvelous frescoes! Here's an image of Senef meeting the gods. And more verses from the Book of the Dead."

"Any more curses?" Nora asked, glancing at another Eye of Horus painted prominently above the once-sealed door.

Wicherly shone his light toward it. "Hmmm. I've never seen an inscription like this before. *The place which is sealed. That which lieth down in the closed place is reborn by the Ba-soul which is in it; that which walketh in the closed space is dispossessed of the Ba-soul. By the Eye of Horus I am delivered or damned, O great god Osiris.*"

"Sure sounds like another curse to me," said McCorkle.

"I would guess it's merely an obscure quotation from the Book of the Dead. The bloody thing runs to two hundred chapters and nobody's figured all of it out."

The tomb now opened up onto a stupendous hall, with a vaulted roof and six great stone pillars, all densely covered with hieroglyphics and frescoes. It seemed incredible to Nora that this huge, ornate space had been asleep in the bowels of the museum for more than half a century, forgotten by almost all.

Wicherly turned, playing his light across the extensive paintings. "This is rather extraordinary. The Hall of the Chariots, which the ancients called the Hall of Repelling Enemies. This was where all the war stuff the pharaoh needed in the afterlife would have been stored—his chariot, bows and arrows, horses, swords, knives, war club and staves, helmet, leather armor."

His beam paused at a frieze depicting beheaded bodies laid out by the hundreds on the ground, their heads lying in rows nearby. The ground was splattered with blood, and the ancient artist had added such realistic details as lolling tongues.

They moved through a long series of passageways until they came to a room that was smaller than the others. A large fresco on one side showed the same scene of weighing the heart depicted earlier, only much larger. The hideous, slavering form of Ammut squatted nearby.

"The Hall of Truth," Wicherly said. "Even the pharaoh was judged, or in this case, Senef, who was almost as powerful as a pharaoh."

McCorkle grunted, then disappeared into the next chamber, and the rest followed. It was another spacious room with a vaulted ceiling, painted with a night sky full of stars, the walls dense with hieroglyphics. An enormous granite sarcophagus sat in the middle, empty. The walls on each side were interrupted by four black doors.

"This is an extraordinary tomb," said Wicherly, shining the light around. "I had no idea. When you called me, Dr. Menzies, I thought it would be something small but charming. This is stupendous. Where in the world did the museum get it?"

"An interesting story," Menzies replied. "When Napoleon conquered Egypt in 1798, one of his prizes was this tomb, which he had disassembled, block by block, to take back to France. But when Nelson defeated the French in the Battle of the Nile, a Scottish naval captain finagled the tomb for himself and reassembled it at his castle in the Highlands. In the nineteenth century, his last descendant, the 7th Baron of Rattray, finding himself strapped for cash, sold it to one of the museum's early benefactors, who had it shipped across the Atlantic and installed while they were building the museum."

"The baron let go of one of England's national treasures, I should say."

Menzies smiled. "He received a thousand pounds for it."

"Worse and worse! May Ammut swallow the greedy baron's heart for selling the ruddy thing!" Wicherly laughed, casting his flashing blue eyes on Nora, who smiled politely. His attentiveness was becoming obvious, and he seemed not at all discouraged by the wedding band on her finger.

McCorkle began to tap his foot impatiently.

"This is the burial chamber," Wicherly began, "which the ancients called the House of Gold. Those antechambers would be the Ushabti Room; the Canopic Room, where all the pharaoh's preserved organs were stored in jars; the Treasury of the End; and the Resting Place of the Gods. Remarkable, isn't it, Nora? What fun we'll have!"

Nora didn't answer immediately. She was thinking about just how massive the tomb was, and how dusty, and how much work lay ahead of them.

Menzies must have been thinking the same thing, because he turned to her with a smile that was half eager, half rueful.

"Well, Nora," he said. "It should prove an interesting six weeks."

11

Gerry Fecteau slammed the door to solitary 44 hard, causing a deafening boom throughout the third floor of Herkmoor Correctional Facility 3. He smirked and winked at his companion as they paused outside the door, listening while the sound echoed through the vast cement spaces before dying slowly away.

The prisoner in 44 was a big mystery. All the guards were talking about him. He was important, that much was clear: FBI agents had come to visit him several times and the warden had taken a personal interest. But what most impressed Fecteau was the tight lid on information. For most new prisoners, it didn't take long for the rumor mill to grind out the accusation, the crime, the gory details. But in this case, nobody even knew the prisoner's name, let alone his crime. He was referred to simply by a single letter: A.

On top of that, the man was scary. True, he wasn't physically imposing: tall and slender with skin so pale it looked like he might have been born in solitary. He rarely spoke, and when he did, you had to lean forward to hear him. No, it wasn't that. It was the eyes. In his twenty-five years in corrections, Fecteau had never before seen eyes that were so utterly cold, like two glittering silvery chips of dry ice, so far below zero they just about smoked.

Christ, it gave Fecteau a chill just thinking about them.

There was no doubt in Fecteau's mind this prisoner had committed a truly heinous crime. Or series of crimes, a Jeffrey Dahmer type, a cold-blooded serial killer. He looked that scary. That's why it gave Fecteau such satisfaction when the order came down that the prisoner was to be moved to solitary 44. Nothing more needed to be said. It was where they sent the hard cases, the ones who needed softening up. Not that solitary 44 was any worse than the other cells in Herkmoor 3 Solitary—all the cells were identical: metal cot, toilet with no seat, sink with only cold running water. What made solitary 44 special, so useful in breaking a prisoner, was the presence of the inmate in solitary 45. The drummer.

Fecteau and his partner, Benjy Doyle, stood on either side of the cell door, making no noise, waiting for the drummer to start up again. He'd paused, as he always did for a few minutes when a new prisoner was installed. But the pause never lasted long.

Then, as if on schedule, Fecteau heard a faint soft-shoe shuffle start up again inside solitary 45. This was followed by the popping sound of lips, and then a low tattoo of fingers drumming against the metal rail of the bed. A little more soft-shoe, some snatches of humming . . . and then, the drumming. It started slowly, and quickly accelerated, a rapid roll breaking off into syncopated riffs, punctuated with a pop or a shuffle, a never-ending sonic flood of inexhaustible hyperactivity.

A smile spread across Fecteau's face and his eyes met those of Doyle.

The drummer was a perfect inmate. He never shouted, screamed, or threw his food. He never swore, threatened the guards, or trashed his cell. He was neat and tidy, keeping his hair groomed and his body washed. But he had two peculiar characteristics that kept him in solitary: he almost never slept, and he spent his waking hours—*all* his waking hours—drumming. Never loudly, never in-your-face. The drummer was utterly oblivious to the outside world and the many curses and threats directed at him. He did not even seem to be aware that there *was* an outside world, and he continued on, never varying, never ruffled or disturbed, totally focused. Curiously, the very softness of the drummer's sounds were the most unendurable aspect of them: Chinese water torture of the ear.

In transferring the prisoner known as A to solitary, Fecteau and Doyle had had orders to deprive the man of all his possessions, including—*especially* including, the warden had made clear—writing instruments. They had taken everything: books, sketches, photographs, journals, notebooks, pens and inks. The prisoner was left with nothing—and with nothing to do but listen:

Ba-da-ba-da-ditty-ditty-bop-hup-hup-huppa-huppa-be-bop-be-bop-ditty-ditty-ditty-boom! Ditty-*boom!* Ditty-*boom!* Ditty-*bada-boom-bada-boom-ba-ba-ba-boom!* Ba-da-ba-da-pop! Ba-pop! Ba-*pop!* Ditty-ditty-datty-shuffle-shuffle-ditty-da-da-da-dit! Ditty-shuffle-tap-shuffle-tap-da-da-dadadada-pop! Dit-ditty-dit-ditty-dap! Dit-ditty . . .

Fecteau had heard enough. It was already getting under his skin. He gestured toward the exit with his chin, and he and Doyle headed hurriedly back down the hall, the sounds of the drummer dying away.

"I give him a week," said Fecteau.

"A week?" Doyle replied with a snort. "The poor bastard won't last twenty-four hours."

12

Lieutenant Vincent D'Agosta lay on his belly, in a freezing drizzle, on a barren hill above the Herkmoor Federal Correctional and Holding Facility in Herkmoor, New York. Next to him crouched the dark form of the man named Proctor. The time was midnight. The great prison spread out in a flat valley below them, brilliantly illuminated by the yellow glare of overhead lights, as surreal an industrial confection as a giant oil refinery.

D'Agosta raised a pair of powerful digital binoculars and once again examined the general layout of the facility. It covered at least twenty acres, consisting of three low, enormous concrete building blocks, set in a U shape, surrounded by asphalt yards, lookout towers, fenced service areas, and guardhouses. D'Agosta knew the first building was the Federal Maximum Security Unit, filled with the very worst violent offenders contemporary America could produce—and that, D'Agosta thought grimly, was saying quite a bit. The second, much smaller area bore the official title of Federal Capital Sentence Holding and Transfer Facility. While New York State had no death penalty, there was a federal death penalty, and this is where those few who had been sentenced to death by the federal courts were held.

The third unit also had a name that could only have been invented by a prison bureaucrat: the Federal High-Risk Violent Offender Pretrial Detention Facility. It contained those awaiting trial for a small list of heinous federal crimes: men who had been denied bail and who were considered at especially high risk of escape or flight. This facility held drug kingpins, domestic terrorists, serial killers who had exercised their trade across state boundaries, and those accused of killing federal agents. In the lingo of Herkmoor, this was the Black Hole.

It was this unit that currently housed Special Agent A. X. L. Pendergast.

While some of the storied state prisons, such as Sing Sing and Alcatraz, were famed for never having had an escape, Herkmoor was the only federal facility that could boast a similar record.

D'Agosta's binoculars continued to roam the facility, taking in even the minute details he had already spent three weeks studying on paper. Slowly, he worked his way from the central buildings to the outbuildings and, finally, to the perimeter.

At first glance, the perimeter of Herkmoor looked unremarkable. Security consisted of the standard triple barrier. The first was a twenty-four-foot chain-link fence, topped by concertina wire, illuminated by the multimillion-candlepower brilliance of xenon stadium lights. A series of twenty-yard spaces spread with gravel led to the second barrier: a forty-foot cinder-block wall topped with spikes and wire. Along this wall, every hundred yards, was a tower kiosk with an armed guard; D'Agosta could see them moving about, wakeful and alert. A hundred-foot gap roamed by Dobermans led to the final perimeter, a chain-link fence identical to the first. From there, a three-hundred-yard expanse of lawn extended to the edge of the woods.

What made Herkmoor unique was what you couldn't see: a state-of-the-art electronic surveillance and security system, said to be the finest in the country. D'Agosta had seen the specs to this system—he had, in fact, been poring over them for days—but he still barely understood it. He did not see that as a problem: Eli Glinn, his strange and silent partner—holed up in a high-tech surveillance van a mile down the road—understood it, and that's what counted.

It was more than a security system: it was a state of mind. Although Herkmoor had suffered many escape attempts, some extraordinarily clever, none had succeeded—and every guard at Herkmoor, every employee, was acutely aware of that fact and proud of it. There would be no bureaucratic turpitude or self-satisfaction here, no sleeping guards or malfunctioning security cameras.

That troubled D'Agosta most of all.

He finished his scrutiny and glanced over at Proctor. The chauffeur was lying prone on the ground beside him, taking pictures with a digital Nikon equipped with a miniature tripod, a 2600mm lens, and specially made CCD chips, so sensitive to light they were able to record the arrival of single photons.

D'Agosta ran over the list of questions Glinn wanted answered. Some were obviously important: how many dogs there were, how many guards occupied each tower, how many guards manned the gates. Glinn had also requested a description of the arrival and departure of all vehicles, with as much information as possible on them. He wanted detailed pictures of the clusters of antennas, dishes, and microwave horns on the building roofs. But other requests were not so clear. Glinn wanted to know, for example, if the area between the wall and the outer fence was dirt, grass, or gravel. He had asked for a downstream sample from the brook running past the facility. Strangest of all, he had asked D'Agosta to collect all the trash he could find in a certain stretch of the brook. He had asked them to observe the prison through a full twenty-four-hour period, keeping a log of every activity they could note: prisoner exercise times, the movements of guards, the comings and goings of suppliers, contractors, and delivery people. He wanted to know the times when the lights went on and off. And he wanted it all recorded to the nearest second.

D'Agosta paused to murmur some observations into the digital recorder Glinn had given him. He heard the faint whirring of Proctor's camera, the patter of rain on leaves.

He stretched. "Jesus, it really kills me to think of Pendergast in there."

"It must be very hard on him, sir," said Proctor in his usual impenetrable way. The man was no mere chauffeur—D'Agosta had figured that out as soon as he saw him break down and stow away a CAR-15/XM-177 Commando in less than sixty seconds—but he could never seem to penetrate Proctor's Jeeves-like opacity. The soft click and whir of the camera continued.

The radio on his belt squawked. "Vehicle," came Glinn's voice.

A moment later, a pair of headlights flashed through the bare branches of the trees, approaching on the single road leading to Herkmoor, which ran up the hill from the town two miles away. Proctor quickly swung the lens of his camera around. D'Agosta clapped the binoculars to his eyes, the gain automatically adjusting to compensate for the changing contrasts of dark and light.

The truck came out of the woods and into the glow of lights surrounding the prison. It looked like a food-service truck of some kind, and as it turned, D'Agosta could read the logo on the side, *Helmer's Meats and By-Products.* It stopped at the guardhouse, presented a sheaf of documents, and was waved through. The three sets of gates opened automatically, one after the other, the gate ahead not opening until the one behind had closed. The soft clicking of the camera's shutter continued. D'Agosta checked his stopwatch, murmured into the recorder. He turned to Proctor.

"Here comes tomorrow's meat loaf," he said, making a feeble joke.

"Yes, sir."

D'Agosta thought of Pendergast, the supreme gourmet, eating whatever it was that truck was bringing. He wondered how the agent was handling it.

The truck entered the inner service drive, did a two-point turn, and backed up into a covered loading dock, where it was obscured from view. D'Agosta made another entry on the digital recorder, then settled down to wait. Sixteen minutes later, the vehicle drove back out.

He glanced at his watch. Almost one o'clock. "I'm heading down to get that water and air sample, and do the magnetic drag."

"Be careful."

D'Agosta shouldered his small knapsack and retreated to the back side of the hill, making his way down through bare trees, scrub, and mountain laurel. Everything was sopping wet, and water dripped from the trees. Here and there, small patches of damp snow glistened beneath the branches. He didn't need a light once he'd rounded the hill—

there was enough glow from Herkmoor to light up most of the mountain.

D'Agosta was glad of the activity. During the wait on top, he'd had too much time to think. And thinking was the last thing he wanted to do: thinking about his upcoming disciplinary trial, which might very well end in his dismissal from the NYPD. It seemed incredible what had happened in the last few months: his sudden promotion to the NYPD; his blossoming relationship with Laura Hayward; his reconnection with Agent Pendergast. And then it had all come crashing down. His career as a cop was in deep shit; he was estranged from Hayward; and his friend Pendergast was rotting in that damp hell below, shortly to go on trial for his life.

D'Agosta staggered, righted himself. He tilted his bleary face upward, letting the drops of icy rain lash a modicum of alertness into him.

He wiped his face and pushed on. Getting the water sample was going to be tricky, since the stream flowed along the edge of an open field outside the prison walls, completely exposed to the guards in the towers. But this was nothing compared to the magnetic drag he was charged with performing. Glinn wanted him to crawl as close to the outer perimeter fence as he could get, carrying a miniature magnetometer in his pocket, to see if there were any buried sensors or hidden electromagnetic fields . . . and then plant the damn thing in the ground. Of course, if there were any sensors, he might well set them off—and then things would get exciting.

He crept slowly downhill, the ground gradually leveling out. Despite his slicker and gloves, he could feel the icy water creeping down his legs and in through the poor sealing of his boots. A hundred yards farther on, he could make out the edge of the woods and hear the gurgle of the stream. He kept low in the laurel bushes as he moved forward. The last few yards he got down on his hands and knees and crawled.

A moment later, he was at the edge of the brook. It was dark and smelled of damp leaves, and along one bank a scalloped edge of old, rotten ice stubbornly remained.

He paused, looking at the prison. The guard towers loomed above now, only two hundred yards distant, the bright lights like multiple suns. He fumbled in his pocket and was about to remove the vial Glinn had given him when he froze. His assumption that the guards would be looking inward, toward the prison, had been wrong: he could clearly see one of them looking out, scanning the edge of the woods nearby with high-powered binoculars.

An important detail.

He froze, flattening himself in the laurel. He had already entered the forbidden perimeter, and he felt horribly exposed to view.

The guard's attention seemed to have swept past him. With exaggerated care, he edged forward and dipped the vial into the icy water, filled it, then screwed the top back on. Then he crept downstream, fishing out trash—old Styrofoam coffee cups, a few beer cans, gum wrappers—and putting it in the knapsack. Glinn had been quite insistent that D'Agosta collect everything. It was a highly unpleasant job, wading in the icy water, sometimes having to root about the cobbled stream bottom up to his shoulder in water. One jam-up of branches across the stream acted like a sieve and he hit the jackpot, collecting a good ten pounds of sodden garbage.

When he was done, he found himself at the point downstream where Glinn wanted the magnetometer placed. He waited until the guard's attention was at the farthest point; then he half waded, half crawled across the stream. The meadow that surrounded the prison was unkempt, grasses dead and flattened by the winter snows. But there were just enough skeletal weeds to provide at least the semblance of cover.

D'Agosta crawled forward, freezing in place every time the guard swept the binoculars his way.

The minutes crawled by. He felt the icy drizzle trickling down his neck and back. The fence grew closer only by excruciating degrees of slowness. But he had to keep going, and as fast as he dared: the longer he lingered, the higher the probability that one of the guards would spot him.

At last he reached the groomed part of the lawn. He removed the device from his pocket, pushed one hand out through the tall weeds, sank the magnetometer down to the level of the grass, then began an awkward retreat.

Crawling back was much more difficult. Now he was facing the wrong direction and unable to monitor the guard towers. He kept on, slowly but steadily, with frequent long pauses. Forty-five minutes after setting out, he once again crossed the stream and reentered the dripping woods, pushing up through the laurel bushes toward their spy nest on top of the hill, feeling half frozen, his back aching from lugging the knapsack of wet trash.

"Mission accomplished?" Proctor asked as he returned.

"Yeah, assuming I don't lose my frigging toes to frostbite."

Proctor adjusted a small unit. "Signal's coming in nicely. It appears you got within fifty feet of the fence. Nice work, Lieutenant."

D'Agosta turned wearily toward him. "Call me Vinnie," he said.

"Yes, sir."

"I'd call you by your first name, but I don't know what it is."

"Proctor is fine."

D'Agosta nodded. Pendergast had surrounded himself with people almost as enigmatic as himself. Proctor, Wren . . . and in the case of Constance Greene, maybe even *more* enigmatic. He checked his watch again: almost two.

Fourteen hours to go.

13

Rain hammered against the crumbling brick-and-marble facade of the Beaux Arts mansion at 891 Riverside Drive. Far above the mansard roof and its widow's walk, lightning tore at the night sky. The first-floor windows had been boarded up and covered with tin, and the windows of the upper three stories were securely shuttered—no light pierced through to betray life within. The fenced front yard was over-grown with sumac and ailanthus bushes, and stray bits of wind-whipped trash lay in the carriage drive and beneath the porte cochere. In every way, the mansion appeared abandoned and deserted, like many others along that bleak stretch of Riverside Drive.

For a great many years—a truly remarkable number of years, in fact—this house had been the shelter, redoubt, laboratory, library, museum, and repository for a certain Dr. Enoch Leng. But after Leng's death, the house had passed through obscure and secret channels—along with the charge of Leng's ward, Constance Greene—to his descendant, Special Agent Aloysius Pendergast.

But now, Agent Pendergast was in solitary confinement in the maximum security wing of Herkmoor Correctional Facility, awaiting trial for murder. Proctor and Lieutenant D'Agosta were away on a reconnaissance of the prison. The queer excitable man known as Wren, who was Constance Greene's nominal guardian while Pendergast was gone, was at his night job at the New York Public Library.

Constance Greene was alone.

She sat before a dying fire in the library, where neither the sounds of rain nor those of traffic penetrated. She had before her *My Life* by Giacomo Casavecchio, and she was intently studying the Renaissance spy's account of his celebrated escape from the Leads, the dreaded prison in the Venetian Ducal Palace from which no one had ever escaped before— or would escape again. A stack of similar volumes covered a nearby table: accounts of prison escapes from all over the world, but especially focusing on the federal correctional system in the United States. She read in silence, every so often pausing to make a notation in a leather-bound notebook.

As she finished one of these notations, the fire settled in the grate with a loud crack. Constance looked up abruptly, eyes widening at the sudden noise. Her eyes were large and violet, and strangely wise for a face that appeared to be no older than twenty-one. Slowly, she relaxed again.

It was not that she felt nervous, exactly. After all, the mansion was hardened against intruders; she knew its secret ways better than anyone; and she could vanish into one of a dozen hidden passages at a moment's notice. No—it was that she had lived here so long, knew the old dark house so well, that she could almost sense its moods. And she had the distinct impression something was not right; that the house was trying to tell her something, warn her about something.

A pot of chamomile tea sat on a side table beside the chair. She put the documents aside, poured herself a fresh cup, then rose. Smoothing down the front of her bone-colored pinafore, she turned and walked to the bookshelves set into the far wall of the library. The stone floor was covered in rich Persian rugs, and as she moved, Constance made no noise.

Reaching the bookshelves, she leaned close, squinting at the gilt bindings. The only light came from the fire and a lone Tiffany lamp beside her chair, and this far corner of the library was dim. At last she found what she was looking for—a Depression-era prison management treatise—and returned to her chair. Seating herself once again, she opened the book, leafed ahead to the contents page. Finding the desired chapter, she reached for her tea, took a sip, then moved to replace the cup.

As she did so, she glanced up.

In the wing chair next to the side table, a man was now seated: tall, aristocratic, with an aquiline nose and a high forehead, pale skin, dressed in a severe black suit. He had ginger-colored hair and a small, neatly trimmed beard. As he looked back at her, the firelight illuminated his eyes. One was a rich hazel green; the other, a milky, dead blue.

The man smiled.

Constance had never seen this man before, and yet she knew immediately who he was. She rose with a cry, the cup dropping from her fingers.

As fast as a striking snake, the man's arm shot out and deftly caught the cup just before it hit the ground. He replaced it on its silver salver, sat back again. Not a drop had spilled. It had happened so fast that Constance was hardly sure it had happened at all. She remained standing, unable to move. Despite her profound shock, one thing was clear: the man was seated between her and the room's only exit.

The man spoke softly, as if sensing her thoughts. "There is no need for alarm, Constance. I mean you no harm."

She remained where she was, standing motionless before the chair. Her eyes flickered about the room and returned to the seated man.

"You know who I am, don't you, child?" he asked. Even the buttery New Orleans tones were familiar.

"Yes. I know who you are." She choked on the uncanny resemblance to the man she knew so well, all except his hair—and his eyes.

The man nodded. "I am gratified."

"How did you get in here?"

"*How* I got in is unimportant. *Why* I am here is the true question, don't you think?"

Constance seemed to consider this for a moment. "Yes. Perhaps you are right." She took a step forward, letting the fingers of one hand drift from her wing chair and slide along the side table. "Very well, then: *why* are you here?"

"Because it's time we spoke, you and I. It's the least courtesy you could pay me, after all."

Constance took another step, her fingers trailing along the polished wood. Then she paused. "Courtesy?"

"Yes. After all, I—"

With a sudden motion, Constance snatched a letter opener from the side table and leaped at the man. The attack was remarkable not only for its swiftness, but for its silence. She had done nothing, said nothing, to warn the man of her strike.

To no avail. The man twitched aside at the last instant and the letter opener sank to its hilt in the worn leather of the wing chair. Constance jerked it free and—still without uttering a sound—whirled to face the man, raising the weapon above her head.

As she lunged, the man coolly dodged the stroke and with a flick of his arm seized her wrist; she thrashed and struggled, and they fell to the floor, the man pinning her body under his, the letter opener skidding across the rug.

The man's lips moved to within an inch of her ear. "Constance," he said in a quiet voice. "*Du calme. Du calme.*"

"Courtesy!" she cried once again. "How *dare* you speak of courtesy! You murder my guardian's friends, disgrace him, tear him from his house!" She stopped abruptly and struggled. A soft groan rose in her throat: a groan of frustration, mingled with another, more complex emotion.

The man continued to speak in a smooth undertone. "Please understand, Constance, I'm not here to hurt you. I'm restraining you simply to prevent harm to myself."

She struggled again. "Hateful man!"

"Constance, please. I have something to say to you."

"I'll *never* listen to you!" she gasped.

But he continued to pin her to the floor, gently yet firmly. Slowly her struggling ceased. She lay there, heart racing painfully. She became aware of the beating of his own heart—much slower—against her breasts. He was still whispering calming, soothing words into her ear that she tried to ignore.

He pulled away slightly. "If I release you, will you promise not to attack me again? To stay and hear me out?"

Constance did not reply.

"Even a condemned man has the right to be heard. And you may learn that everything is not as it seems."

Still, Constance said nothing. After a long moment, the man raised himself from the floor, then—slowly—released his grip on her wrists.

She stood at once. Breathing heavily, she smoothed down her pinafore. Her eyes darted around the library again. The man was still positioned strategically between her and the door. He raised a hand toward her wing chair.

"Please, Constance," he said. "Sit down."

Warily, she seated herself.

"May we speak now, like civilized people, without further outbursts?"

"You dare speak of yourself as civilized? You? A serial killer and thief." She laughed scornfully.

The man nodded slowly, as if ingesting this. "Naturally, my brother has taken a certain line with you. After all, it's worked so well for him in the past. He's an extraordinarily persuasive and charismatic individual."

"You can't presume to imagine I'd believe anything you say. You're insane—or worse, you do these things as a *sane* man." She again glanced past him, toward the library exit and the reception hall beyond.

The man gazed back at her. "No, Constance. I am not insane—on the contrary, like you, I greatly fear insanity. You see, the sad fact is, we have a great deal in common—and not just that which we fear."

"We haven't the slightest in common."

"No doubt this is what my brother would like you to believe."

It seemed to Constance that the man's expression had become one of infinite sadness. "It's true that I am far from perfect and cannot yet expect your trust," he went on. "But I hope you understand that I intend you no hurt."

"What you intend means nothing. You're like a child who befriends a butterfly one day to pull off its wings the next."

"What do you know of children, Constance? Your eyes are so wise and so old. Even from here, I can see the vast experience written there. What strange and terrible things they must have seen! How very penetrating your gaze! It fills me with sadness. No, Constance: I sense—I *know*—that childhood was a luxury you were denied. Just as I myself was denied it."

Constance went rigid.

"Earlier, I said I was here because it's time we spoke. It is time that you learned the truth. The *real* truth."

His voice had sunk so low that the words were only just audible. Against her will, she asked, "The truth?"

"About the relationship between me and my brother."

In the soft light of the dying fire, Diogenes Pendergast's peculiar eyes looked vulnerable, almost lost. Gazing back at her, they brightened slightly.

"Ah! Constance, it must sound impossibly strange to you. But gazing on you like this, I feel I would do anything in my power to lift from you that burden of pain and fear and carry it myself. And do you know why? Because when I look at you, I see *myself*."

Constance did not reply. She merely sat, motionless.

"I see a person who longs to fit in, to be merely human, and yet who is destined always to remain apart. I see a person who feels the world more deeply, more intensely, than she is willing to admit . . . even to her-self."

Listening, Constance began to tremble.

"I sense both pain and anger in you. Pain at being abandoned—not once, but several times. And anger at the sheer capriciousness of the gods. Why me? Why again? For it's true: you've been abandoned once again. Though not, perhaps, in exactly the way you imagined it. Here, too, we are the same. I was abandoned when my parents were burned to death by an ignorant mob. I escaped the flames. They did not. I've always felt that I should have died, not them; that it was my fault. You feel the same way about the death of your own sister, Mary—that it was you, instead of she, who should have died. Later, I was abandoned by my brother. Ah: I see the disbelief in your face. But then again, you know so little about my brother. All I ask is that you hear me with an open mind."

He rose. Constance took in a sharp breath, half rising herself.

"No," Diogenes said, and once again Constance stopped. There was nothing in his tone but weariness now. "There's no need to run. I'll take my leave of you. In the future, we'll speak again, and I'll tell you more about the childhood I was denied. About the older brother who took the love I offered and flung back scorn and hatred. Who took pleasure in destroying everything I created—my journals of childish poetry, my translations of Virgil and Tacitus. Who tortured and killed my favorite pet in a way that, even today, I can barely bring myself to think about. Who made it his mission in life to turn everyone against me, with lies and insinuations, to paint me as his evil twin. And when in the end none of this could break my spirit, he did something so awful . . . so, so *awful* . . ." But at this, his voice threatened to break. "Look at my dead eye, Constance: that was the *least* of what he did . . ."

There was a brief silence, broken only by the sound of labored breathing as Diogenes struggled to master himself, his opaque eye staring not quite at her, but not quite away from her, either.

He passed one hand across his brow. "I'll be going now. But you'll find I've left you with something. A gift of kinship, a recognition of the pain we share. I hope you'll accept it in the spirit in which it is offered."

"I want nothing from you," Constance said, but the hatred and conviction in her voice had ebbed into confusion.

He held her gaze a moment longer. Then—slowly, very slowly—he turned and walked away, toward the library exit. "Good-bye, Constance," he said quietly over his shoulder. "Take care. I'll see myself out."

Constance sat rooted in place as she listened to his departing footsteps. Only when silence had returned did she rise from her chair.

As she did so, something moved in the handkerchief pocket of her crinoline.

She started. The movement came again. And then a tiny pink nose appeared, bewhiskered and twitching, followed by two beady black eyes and two soft little ears. In wonder, she put her hand in her pocket and cupped it. The little creature climbed up on it and sat upright, his little paws curled as if begging, whiskers trembling, his bright eyes looking pleadingly up into her own. It was a white mouse: sleek, tiny, and perfectly tame—and Constance's heart melted with a suddenness so unexpected that the breath fled from her and tears sprang into her eyes.

14

Dust motes drifted in the still air of the Central Archives reading room, and it smelled not unpleasantly of old cardboard, dust, buckram, and leather. Polished oak paneling rose to an elaborately carved and gilded rococo ceiling, dominated by a pair of heavy chandeliers of gilt copper and crystal. Against the far wall stood a bricked-up fireplace of pink marble at least eight feet high and as many wide, and the center of the room was dominated by three massive oaken tables with claw feet, tops laid over with a heavy covering of baize. It was one of the most impressive rooms in the museum—and one of the least known.

It had been over a year since Nora was last in this room, and despite its grandeur, the memories it evoked were not good. Unfortunately, it was the only place where she could peruse the museum's most important historic files.

A faint tap came at the door and the stocky form of Oscar Gibbs entered, his muscular arms piled with ancient documents tied up with twine.

"There's quite a lot on this Tomb of Senef," he said, staggering a little as he laid out the documents on the baize table. "Funny that I never heard of it until yesterday."

"Very few have."

"It's become the talk of the museum overnight." He shook his head, which was shaved as bald as a billiard ball. "Only in a joint like this could you hide an Egyptian tomb."

He paused, catching his breath. "You remember the drill, right, Dr. Kelly? I have to lock you in. Just call extension 4240 when you're done. No pencils or paper; you have to use the ones in those leather boxes." He glanced at her laptop. "And wear linen gloves at all times."

"Got it, Oscar."

"I'll be in the archives if you need me. Remember, extension 4240."

The huge bronze door closed and Nora heard the well-oiled click of the lock. She turned to the table. The neat bundles of documents emanated a heavy odor of decay. She looked them over one by one, getting a general sense of what there was and how much of it she actually needed to read. There was no way she could read them all: it would be a question of triage.

She had asked for accession files to the Tomb of Senef and all related documents in the archives, from its discovery in Thebes to its final 1935 closing as an exhibition. It looked like Oscar had done a thorough job. The oldest documents were in French and Arabic, but they switched to English as the tomb's chain of ownership went from Napoleon's army to the British. There were letters, diagrams of the tomb, drawings, shipping manifests, insurance papers, excerpts from journals, old photographs, and scientific monographs. Once the tomb arrived at the museum, the number of documents exploded. A series of fat folders contained construction diagrams, plats, blueprints, conservators' reports, various pieces of correspondence, and innumerable invoices from the period of the tomb's construction and opening; and beyond that, letters from visitors and scholars, internal museum reports, more conservators' evaluations. The material ended with a flurry of documents relating to the new subway station and the museum's request to the City of New York for a pedestrian tunnel connecting the 81st Street subway station with a new basement entrance to the museum. The final document was a terse report from a long-forgotten curator indicating that the bricking-up of the exhibition had been completed. It was dated January 14, 1935.

Nora sighed, looking at the spread of bundled documents. Menzies wanted a summary report of them by the following morning so they could begin planning the "script" for the exhibition, drawing up label text and introductory panels. She glanced at her watch: 1:00 P.M.

What had she gotten herself into?

She plugged in her laptop and booted it up. At the insistence of her husband, Bill, she had recently switched from a PC to a Mac, and now the boot-up process took a tenth the time—zero to sixty in 8.9 seconds instead of two and a half plodding minutes. It had been like trading up from a Ford Fiesta to a Mercedes SL. As she watched the Apple logo appear, she thought that at least one thing in her life was going right.

She slipped on a pair of crisp linen gloves and began untying the twine that held the first bundle of papers together, but before she could get the century-old knot undone, the twine parted with a puff of dust.

With infinite care, she opened the first folder and slipped out a yellowed document, written in a spidery French script, and began the laborious process of working her way through it, taking notes on the PowerBook. Despite her difficulties with the script and the French language, she found herself becoming absorbed in the story Menzies had briefly touched on in the tomb the day before.

During the Napoleonic Wars, Napoleon had conceived a quixotic plan to follow Alexander the Great's route of conquest across the Middle East. In 1798, he mounted a huge invasion of Egypt, involving four hundred ships and 55,000 soldiers. In an idea radically modern for the time, Napoleon also brought with him more than 150 civilian scientists, scholars, and engineers, to make a complete scientific study of Egypt and its mysterious ruins. One of these scholars was an energetic young archaeologist named Bertrand Magny de Cahors.

Cahors was one of the first to examine the greatest Egyptological discovery of all time: the Rosetta stone, which Napoleon's soldiers had unearthed while digging a fort along the shore. The stone inflamed him with the possibilities that lay ahead. He followed the Napoleonic army as it pushed southward up the Nile, where they came across the great temples of Luxor and, across the river, the ancient desert canyon that became the most famous graveyard in the world: the Valley of the Kings.

Most of the tombs in the Valley of the Kings were cut out of the living rock and could not be moved. But there were a few tombs of lesser pharaohs, regents, and viziers, built higher up in the valley out of blocks of cut limestone. And it was one of these—the Tomb of Senef, vizier and regent to Thutmosis IV—that Cahors decided to disassemble and take back to France. It was an audacious and even dangerous engineering feat, since the blocks weighed several tons each and had to be individually lowered down a two-hundred-foot cliff in order to be carted to the Nile and floated downstream.

The project was plagued with disaster from the beginning. The locals refused to work on the tomb, believing it to be cursed, and so Cahors dragooned a group of French soldiers to undertake the job. The first calamity struck when the inner tomb—which had been resealed in antiquity after the tomb was robbed—was broached. Nine men died almost immediately. Later, it was hypothesized that carbon dioxide gas from acid groundwater moving through limestone far below had filled the tomb, causing the asphyxiation of the three soldiers who first entered, along with the half-dozen others sent in to rescue them.

But Cahors was singularly determined, and the tomb was eventually taken apart, block by numbered block, and barged down the Nile to the Bay of Aboukir, where it was laid out on the desert sands in a vast array, awaiting transport to France.

The famous Battle of the Nile ended those plans. After Admiral Horatio Nelson met Napoleon's grand flotilla—and soundly defeated it—in the most decisive naval battle in history, Napoleon fled in a small ship, leaving his armies cut off. Those armies soon capitulated, and in the terms of surrender, the British appropriated their fabulous collections of Egyptian antiquities, including the Rosetta stone—and the Tomb of Senef. A day after the signing of the terms of capitulation, Cahors stabbed himself in the heart with his sword while kneeling amid the stacks of blocks on the sands of Aboukir. And yet his fame as the first Egyptologist lived on, and it was a descendant of this same Cahors who was bankrolling the museum's reopening of the tomb, *à la distance*.

Nora put the first sheaf of documents aside and picked up the second. A Scottish officer with the Royal Navy, Captain Alisdair William

Arthur Cumyn, later Baron of Rattray, managed to acquire the Tomb of Senef in a murky transaction that appeared to involve a card game and two prostitutes. Baron Rattray had the tomb transported and reassembled on his ancestral estate in the Highlands of Scotland, went bankrupt doing so, and was forced to sell off most of his ancestral lands. The Barons of Rattray limped along until the mid–nineteenth century, when the last of the line, in a desperate bid to save what was left of the estate, sold the tomb to the American railroad magnate William C. Spragg. One of the museum's early benefactors, Spragg shipped the tomb across the Atlantic and had it reassembled in the museum, which was under construction at that time. It was his pet project and he spent months haunting the site, hounding the workers, and otherwise making a nuisance of himself. In a tragic irony, he was crushed under the wheels of a horse-drawn ambulance just two days before the grand opening in 1872.

Nora took a break from her perusal of the documents. It was not quite three o'clock, and she was making better progress than she'd expected. If she could get this done by eight, she might have time to share a quick bite with Bill at the Bones. He would love this dark, dusty history. And it might make a good piece for the *Times*'s cultural or metropolitan section when the tomb's opening neared.

She moved along to the next bundle, all museum documents and in much better condition. The first set of papers dealt with the opening of the tomb. In it were some copies of the engraved invitation:

The President of the United States of America
the Honorable General Ulysses S. Grant
The Governor of the State of New York the Honorable John T. Hoffman
The President of the New York Museum of Natural History
Dr. James K. Moreton
The Trustees and the Director of the Museum
Cordially invite you to a Dinner and Ball in honor of the opening of the

GRAND TOMB OF SENEF

Regent and Vizier to the Pharaoh Thutmosis IV,
Ruler of Ancient Egypt
1419–1386 B.C.

The Diva Eleonora de Graff Bolkonsky will perform Arias
from the New and Celebrated Opera Aïda
by Giuseppe Verdi

Egyptian Costume

Nora held the crumbling invitation in her hand. It amazed her that the museum commanded such a presence in those days that the president himself signed the invitation. She shuffled further and discovered a second document—a menu for the dinner.

Hors d'oeuvres Variés
Consommé Olga

Kebab Egyptien
Filet Mignon Lili
Vegetable Marrow Farcie

Roast Squab & Cress
Pâté de Foie Gras en Croûte
Baba Ghanouj

Waldorf Pudding
Peaches in Chartreuse Jelly

There were a dozen blank invitations in the file. She set one aside, along with the menu, in a "to be photocopied" folder. This was something Menzies should see. In fact, she thought, it would be marvelous if they could duplicate the original opening—without the costume ball, per-haps—and offer the same menu.

She began reading the press notices of the evening. It had been one of those great social events of late-nineteenth-century New York, the likes of which would never be seen again. The guest list read like a roll call at the dawn of the Gilded Age: the Astors and Vanderbilts, William Butler Duncan, Walter Langdon, Ward McAllister, Royal Phelps. There were engravings from *Harper's Weekly* showing the ball, with everyone dressed in the most outlandish interpretations of Egyptian costume . . .

But she was wasting time. She pushed the clippings aside and opened the next folder. It also contained a newspaper clipping, this time from the *New York Sun,* one of the scandal sheets of the time. It had an illustration of a dark-haired man in a fez, with liquid eyes, dressed in flowing robes. Quickly she scanned the article.

Sun Exclusive

Tomb in New York Museum Is Accursed!

Egyptian Bey Issues Warning

The Malediction of the Eye of Horus

New York—On a recent visit to New York by His Eminence Abdul El-Mizar, Bey of Bolbassa in Upper Egypt, the gentleman from the land of the pharaohs was shocked to find on display at the New York Museum the Tomb of SENEF.

The Egyptian and his entourage, who were being given a tour of the museum, turned away from the tomb in horror and consternation, warning other visitors that to enter the tomb was to consign oneself to certain and terrible death. "This tomb carries a curse well known in my own country," El-Mizar later told the *Sun.*

Nora smiled. The article went on in the same vein, mingling a stew of dire threats with wildly inaccurate historical pronouncements, ending, naturally, with a "demand" by the alleged "Bey of Bolbassa" that the tomb be returned forthwith to Egypt. At the conclusion, almost as an afterthought, a museum official was quoted as saying that several thousand visitors entered the tomb every day and that there had never been an "untoward incident."

This article was followed by a flurry of letters from various people, many of them clearly cranks, describing "sensations" and "presences" they had experienced while in the tomb. Several complained of sickness after visiting: shortness of breath, sweats, palpitations, nervous disorders. One, which merited a file all its own, told of a child who fell into the well and broke both his legs, one of which had to be amputated. An exchange of letters from lawyers resulted in a quiet settlement with the family for a sum of two hundred dollars.

She moved to the next file, which was very slender, and opened it, surprised to find inside a single yellowed piece of cardboard with a label pasted on it:

Contents moved to Secure Storage
March 22, 1938
Signed: Lucien P. Strawbridge
Curator of Egyptology

Nora turned this card over in surprise. Secure Storage? That must be what was now known as the Secure Area, where the museum kept its most valuable artifacts. What inside this file could have merited being locked away?

She replaced the piece of cardboard and put the file aside, making a mental note to follow up on this later. There was just one final bundle to go. Unsealing it, Nora found it to be full of correspondence and notes on the building of the pedestrian tunnel connecting the IND line subway station to the museum.

The correspondence was voluminous. As Nora read through it, she began to realize that the story the museum told—that the tomb had been sealed off because of the construction of the tunnel—was not exactly true. The truth, in fact, was just the opposite: the city wanted to route the pedestrian walkway from the front of the station well past the entrance of the tomb—a quicker and cheaper alternative. But for some reason, the museum wished to situate the tunnel toward the far end of the station. Then they argued that the new route would cut off the tomb's entrance and force its closure. It seemed as if the museum *wanted* to force the closure of the tomb.

She read on. Toward the end of the file, she found a handwritten note, from the same Lucien P. Strawbridge who'd placed the earlier file in Secure Storage, scribbled on a memo from a New York City official asking why the museum wanted the pedestrian walkway in that particular location, given the extra costs involved.

The marginalia read:

> *Tell him anything. I want that tomb closed. Let us not miss our last, best chance to rid ourselves of this damnable problem.*
> *L. P. Strawbridge*

Damnable problem? Nora wondered just what kind of problem Strawbridge was referring to. She flipped through the file again, but there didn't seem to be a problem connected with the tomb, beyond the annoyance of the Bey of Bolbassa's comments and the crank letters they had generated.

The problem, she decided, must be in the file in Secure Storage. In the end, it didn't seem relevant, and she had run out of time. When she had time, she might look into it. As it was, if she didn't get started on her report, she'd never make dinner with Bill.

She pulled her laptop toward her, opened a new file, and began typing.

15

The following day, Captain of Homicide Laura Hayward showed her ID and was deferentially ushered into the office of Jack Manetti, head of security for the New York Museum of Natural History. Hayward liked the fact that, in a museum where the administration seemed overly concerned with status, the head of security had chosen for himself a small, windowless office in the back of the security pool, and had furnished it with utterly functional metal desks and chairs. It said something positive about Manetti—at least she hoped it did.

Manetti was clearly not happy to see her, but he made an attempt at courtesy, offering her a chair and a cup of coffee, which she declined.

"I'm here on the Green assault," she said. "I wonder if you'd be willing to accompany me to the Sacred Images show so we can run through a few additional questions I have about ingress and egress, access, security."

"But we've been all over that, weeks ago. I thought the investigation was complete."

"*My* investigation isn't complete yet, Mr. Manetti."

Manetti licked his lips. "Did you go through the office of the director? We're supposed to coordinate all law enforcement—"

She cut him off and stood up, growing irritated. "I don't have the time, and neither do you. Let's go."

She followed the security director through a labyrinth of corridors and dusty halls, arriving at last at the exhibit entrance. The museum was still open and the security doors hooked back, but the exhibit itself was almost deserted.

"Let's begin here," said Hayward. "I've been going over the setup again and again, and there are a few things I just don't get. The perp had to enter the hall through this door, am I correct?"

"Yes."

"The door at the far end could be opened only from the inside, not from the outside. Right?"

"That's right."

"And the security system was supposed to automatically keep a log of all who came and went, because each magnetic card key is coded with the name of the owner."

Manetti nodded.

"But the system registered no entry other than Margo Green. The perp then stole her card and used it to leave by the rear exit."

"That's the assumption."

"Green could have entered and left this door hooked open."

"No. First, that would have been against the rules. Second, the system registered that she didn't do that. A few seconds after she entered, the door reengaged. We had an electronic log to that effect."

"So the perp must have been waiting in the hall, hiding, from the time it closed to visitors—five o'clock—until the time of the assault, two A.M."

Manetti nodded.

"Or else the perp managed to get around the security system."

"We think that's highly improbable."

"But *I* think it's almost certain. I've been through this hall a dozen times since the assault. There's no place for the perp to have hidden."

"It was under construction. Stuff was all over the place."

"It was two days from opening. It was almost finished."

"The security system is foolproof."

"Like the Diamond Hall. Right?"

She watched Manetti's lips tighten and felt a pang. This wasn't her style. She was becoming a bitch, and she didn't like it.

"Thank you, Mr. Manetti," she said. "I'd like to make another pass through the hall, if you don't mind."

"Be our guest."

"I'll be in touch."

Manetti disappeared and Hayward took a thoughtful turn around the room where Green had been attacked, picturing, yet again, each step of the assault in a kind of mental stop-motion. She tried to shut out the little voice in her head that said this was a wild-goose chase; that she wasn't likely to find anything of value here weeks after the attack, after a hundred thousand people had walked through; that she was doing this for all the wrong reasons; that she should just get on with her life and career while she still could.

She took another turn around the room, the little voice disappearing under the rap of her heels against the floor. As she came to the side of the case where the spot of blood had been found, she saw a crouched, dark-suited figure moving toward her from behind the case, ready to spring out.

She pulled out her weapon, drew down on the figure. "You! Freeze! NYPD!"

The person leaped up with a gargled shout, arms windmilling, an unruly cowlick of hair bobbing. Hayward recognized him as William Smithback, the *Times* city desk reporter.

"Don't shoot!" the journalist cried. "I was just, you know, looking around! Jesus, you're scaring the hell out of me with that thing!"

Hayward holstered her weapon, feeling sheepish. "Sorry. I'm a bit on edge."

Smithback squinted. "You're Captain Hayward, isn't that right?"

She nodded.

"I'm covering the Pendergast case for the *Times*."

"I'm aware of that."

"Good. In fact, I've been meaning to talk to you."

She glanced at her watch. "I'm very busy. Make an appointment through my office."

"I already tried that. You don't speak to the press."

"That's right." She gave him a stern look and took a step forward, but he didn't step aside to let her pass.

"Do you mind?"

"Listen," he said, talking fast. "I think we can help each other. You know, exchange information, that kind of thing."

"If you have any information of an evidentiary nature, you better divulge it now or get slapped with an obstruction charge," she said sharply.

"No, nothing like that! It's just that . . . well, I think I know why you're here. You're not satisfied. You think maybe Pendergast isn't the one who assaulted Margo. Am I right?"

"What makes you say that?"

"A busy homicide captain doesn't waste her valuable time visiting the scene of the crime when the case is wrapped up. You must have your doubts."

Hayward said nothing, concealing her surprise.

"You wonder if the killer might have been Diogenes Pendergast, the agent's brother. That's why you're here."

Still, Hayward said nothing, her surprise mounting.

"And that happens to be why *I'm* here, too." He paused and peered at her curiously, as if to gauge the effect of his words.

"What makes you think it wasn't Agent Pendergast?" asked Hayward cautiously.

"Because I *know* Agent Pendergast. I've been covering him—in a manner of speaking—since the museum murders seven years ago. And I know Margo Green. She phoned me from her hospital bed. She swears it wasn't Pendergast. She says her attacker had eyes of two different colors, one green, the other milky blue."

"Pendergast is known to be a master of disguises."

"Yeah, but that description fits his brother. Why would he disguise himself as his brother? And we already *know* his brother pulled the diamond heist and kidnapped that woman, Lady Maskelene. The only logical answer is that Diogenes also assaulted Margo and framed his brother. QED."

Once again, Hayward had to control her surprise, his thinking so closely paralleling her own. Finally she allowed a smile. "Well, Mr. Smithback, you seem to be quite the investigative reporter."

"That I am," he hastened to confirm, smoothing down his cowlick, which popped up again, unrepentant.

She paused a moment, considering. "All right, then. Maybe we can help each other. My involvement, naturally, will be strictly off the record. Background only."

"Absolutely."

"And I expect you to bring anything you find to me first. *Before* you bring it to your paper. That's the only way I'll consent to work with you."

Smithback nodded vigorously. "Of course."

"Very well. It seems Diogenes Pendergast has vanished. Completely. The trail stops dead at his hideout on Long Island, the place where he held Lady Maskelene prisoner. Such an utter disappearance just doesn't happen these days, except for one possible circumstance: he slipped into an alter ego. A *long-established* alter ego."

"Any ideas who?"

"We've drawn a blank. But if you were to publish a story about it . . . well, it just might shake something loose. A tip, a nosy neighbor's observation: you understand? Naturally, my name couldn't appear."

"I certainly do understand. And—and what do I get in return?"

Hayward's smile returned, broader this time. "You've got it backward. I just did *you* the favor. The question now is, what do you do for me in return? I know you're covering the diamond heist. I want to know all about it. Everything, big or small. Because you're right: I think Diogenes is behind the Green assault and the Duchamp murder. I need all the evidence I can get, and because I am in Homicide, it's difficult for me to access information at the precinct level."

She didn't say that Singleton, the precinct captain handling the diamond theft, was unlikely to share information with her.

"No problem. We have a deal."

She turned away, but Smithback called after her. "Wait!"

She glanced back at him, raising an eyebrow.

"When do we meet again? And where?"

"We don't. Just call me if—when—something important turns up."

"Okay."

And she left him in the semidarkness of the exhibition hall, jotting notes hurriedly onto the back of a scrap of paper.

16

Jay Lipper, computer effects consultant, paused in the empty burial chamber, peering about in the dim light. Four weeks had passed since the museum made the big announcement about the new opening of the Tomb of Senef; and Lipper himself had been on the job three weeks. Today was the big meeting, and he had arrived ten minutes early, to walk through the tomb and visualize the setup he'd diagrammed out: where to lay the fiber-optic cables, where to put the LEDs, where to mount the speakers, where to float the spots, where to put the holographic screens. It was two weeks before the grand opening, and an incredible amount still had to be done.

He could hear a medley of voices echoing down the multi-chambered tomb from somewhere near the entrance, distorted, mingled with the sound of hammering and the whine of Skilsaws. The teams of workmen were going flat out, and no expense was being spared. Especially *his* expense: he was charging $120 an hour, working eighty hours a week, making a fortune. On the other hand, he was earning every penny of it. Especially given the clown the museum had assigned him as cable-puller, duct-taper, and all-around electronic gofer. A real knuckle-dragger: if the guy was typical of the museum's tech staff, they were in trouble. The man was so buffed and toned he looked like a brick of meat, with a bullet head that contained about as much gray matter as a spaniel. The man probably spent his weekends in the gym instead of boning up on the technology he was supposed to understand.

As if on cue, the clown's voice rang down the corridor. "Dark as a tomb in here, hey, Jayce?" Teddy DeMeo came lumbering around the corner, arms full of an untidy bundle of rolled electronic diagrams.

Lipper tightened his lips and reminded himself once again of that $120 an hour. The worst of it was that, before he'd gotten to know what DeMeo was like, Lipper had unwisely mentioned to him the massively multiplayer online RPG he was involved in: *Land of Darkmord*. And DeMeo had immediately gone online and subscribed. Lipper's character, a devious half-elf sorcerer with a +5 onyx cape and a full book of offensive spells, had spent weeks organizing a military expedition to a distant castle stronghold. He'd been recruiting warriors—and suddenly, there was DeMeo, in the character of a slope-faced orc carrying a club, volunteering for military service, acting like his best friend, full of asinine questions and stupid off-color jokes and embarrassing him in front of all the other players.

DeMeo came to a halt beside him, breathing hard, the sweat pouring off his brow, smelling like a damp sock.

"All right, let's see . . ." He unrolled one of the plats. Naturally, DeMeo was holding it upside down, and it took him several seconds to right it.

"Give it to me," said Lipper, snatching it from him and smoothing it out. He glanced at his watch. Still five minutes before the curatorial committee was due to arrive. No problem—at two dollars a minute, Lipper would wait for Godot.

He sniffed, looked around. "Someone's going to have to do something about this humidity. I can't have my electronics sitting in a sweatshop."

"Yeah," said DeMeo, looking around. "And will you look at this weird shit? I mean, what the hell's *that*? Gives me the creeps."

Lipper glanced over at the fresco in question, depicting a human being with the black head of an insect, wearing pharaonic dress. The burial chamber *was* creepy: walls black with hieroglyphics, ceiling covered with a representation of the night sky, strange yellow stars and a moon against a field of deep indigo. But the truth was, Lipper liked being creeped out. It was like being inside the world of Darkmord for real.

"That's the god Khepri," he said. "A man with the head of a scarab beetle. He helps roll the sun across the sky." Working on the project had fascinated Lipper, and he'd delved deeply into Egyptian mythology over the last several weeks, looking for background and visual cues.

"*The Mummy* meets *The Fly*," said DeMeo with a laugh.

Their conversation was cut short by a rising hubbub of voices as a group entered the burial chamber: the man in charge, Menzies, followed by his curators.

"Gentlemen! I'm glad you're already here. We don't have much time." Menzies came forward, shook their hands. "You all know each other, of course."

They all nodded. How could they not, having practically been living together these past few weeks? There was Dr. Nora Kelly, someone Lipper could at least work with; the smug Brit named Wicherly; and Mr. Personality himself, the anthropology curator, George Ashton. The committee.

As the new arrivals talked briefly among themselves, Lipper felt a painful dig in his ribs. He looked over to see DeMeo, mouth open, winking and leering. "Man, oh man," he whispered, nodding at Dr. Kelly. "I'd climb all over that in a heartbeat."

Lipper glanced away, rolling his eyes.

"Well!" Menzies turned to address them again. "Shall we do the walk-through?"

"Sure thing, Dr. Menzies!" said DeMeo.

Lipper gave him a look he hoped would shut the moron up. This was his plan, his brainwork, his artistry: DeMeo's job was rack-mounting the equipment, pulling cable, and making sure juice got to all parts of the system.

"We should start at the beginning," Lipper said, leading them back to the entrance with another warning side glance at DeMeo.

They threaded their way back through the half-built exhibits and the construction teams. As they approached the entrance to the tomb,

Lipper felt his annoyance at DeMeo displaced by a growing excitement. The "script" for the sound-and-light show had been written by Wicherly, with various additions by Kelly and Menzies, and the end result was good. Very good. In turning it into reality, he'd made it even better. This was going to be one kick-ass exhibition.

Reaching the God's First Passage, Lipper turned to face the others. "The sound-and-light show will be triggered automatically. It's important that people be let into the tomb as a group and move through it together. As they proceed, they'll trip hidden sensors that in turn start each sequence of the show. When the sequence ends, they will move to the next part of the tomb and see the next sequence. After the show ends, the group will have fifteen minutes to look around the tomb before being escorted out and the next group brought in."

He pointed to the ceiling. "The first sensor will be up there, in the corner. As the visitors pass this point, the sensor will register, wait thirty seconds for stragglers to catch up, and start the first sequence, which I call act I."

"How are you hiding the cable?" asked Menzies.

"No problem," broke in DeMeo. "We're running it through black one-inch conduit. They'll never see it."

"Nothing can be affixed to the painted surface," said Wicherly.

"No, no. The conduit is steel, self-supporting, only needs to be anchored in the corners. It floats two millimeters above the surface of the paint, won't even touch it."

Wicherly nodded.

Lipper breathed out, thankful that DeMeo hadn't come across as an idiot—at least not yet.

Lipper led the party into the next chamber. "When the visitors reach the center of the God's Second Passage—where we're standing now—the lights will suddenly dim. There will be the sound of digging, furtive chatter, pickaxes striking stone—at first just sounds in the dark, no visuals. A voice-over will explain that this is the tomb of Senef and that it is about to be robbed by the very priests who buried him two months before. The sounds of digging will get louder as the robbers reach the first sealed door. They'll attack it with pickaxes—and then, suddenly, one will break through. That's when the visuals start."

"The point where they break through the sealed door is critical," Menzies said. "What's needed is a resounding blow from the pickax, a tumble of stones inward, and a piercing shaft of light like a bolt of lightning. This is a key moment and it needs to be dramatic."

"It *will* be dramatic." Lipper felt a faint irritation. Menzies, while charming enough, had been intrusive and meddlesome about certain technical details, and Lipper was worried he might micromanage the installation as well.

Lipper continued. "Then the lights come up and the voice-over directs the audience to the well." He led them through the long passageway and a broad staircase. Ahead, a new bridge had been built over the pit, broad enough to hold a large group.

"As they approach the well," Lipper went on, "a sensor in that corner will pick up their passage and begin act 2."

"Right," DeMeo interrupted. "Each act will be independently controlled by a pair of dual-processor PowerMac G5s, slaved to a third G5 that will act as backup and master controller."

Lipper rolled his eyes. DeMeo had just quoted, word for word, from Lipper's own spec sheet.

"Where will these computers be located?" asked Menzies.

"We're going to cable through the wall—"

"Look here," said Wicherly. "No one's going to drill any holes in the walls of this tomb."

DeMeo turned to him. "It just so happens that a long time ago somebody *already* drilled through the wall—in five places! The holes were cemented up, but I found them and cleared them out." DeMeo crossed his muscled arms in triumph, as if he'd just kicked sand in the face of a ninety-eight-pound weakling at the beach.

"What's on the far side?" Menzies asked.

"A storeroom," said DeMeo, "currently empty. We're converting it to a control room."

Lipper cleared his throat, forestalling any more interruptions by DeMeo. "In act 2, visitors will see the digitized images of the robbers bridging the well so they can break the second sealed door. A screen will lower on the far side of the well—unseen to the visitors, of course. Then a holographic projector in the far corner will project images of the robbers in the passageway ahead, carrying burning torches, breaking the seals of the inner door, smashing it down, and heading for the burial chamber. The idea here is to make the visitors feel like they're actually part of the gang of robbers. They'll follow the robbers into the inner tomb—where act 3 begins."

"Lara Croft, watch out!" DeMeo said, looking around and laughing at his witticism.

The group entered the burial chamber, where Lipper paused again. "The visitors will hear things before they see anything—breakage, shouting. As they enter this end of the burial chamber, they'll be stopped by a gate, here. And then the main event begins. First, it's dark, with frightened, excited voices. Then more smashing and breaking. A sudden flare, and another, and the torches are lit up. We see the sweaty, terrified, avaricious faces of the priests. And gold! Everywhere, the gleam of gold." He turned to Wicherly. "Just as you wrote in the script."

"Excellent!"

"As the torches are lit, the computer-controlled lighting will come up, dimly illuminating parts of the burial chamber. The thieves will shove off and smash the stone lid of the sarcophagus. Then they'll hoist up the top of the inner sarcophagus—the one in solid gold—and one of them will leap in and begin ripping off the linen wrappings. Then, with a shout of triumph, they'll hold up the scarab and smash it, thus breaking its power."

"That's the climax," said Menzies, breaking in excitedly. "That's where I want the peal of thunder, the strobes simulating flashes of lightning."

"And you'll have it," DeMeo said. "We got a complete Dolby Surround and Pro Logic II sound system and four Chauvet Mega II 750-watt strobes, along with a bunch of spots. All controlled by a twenty-four-channel DMX lighting console, fully automated."

He looked around proudly, as if he knew what the hell he was talking about instead of, once again, quoting verbatim from Lipper's carefully designed specs. God, Lipper couldn't stand him. He waited a moment before resuming.

"After the light and thunder, the holographic projectors will switch back on, and we'll see Senef himself rise from the sarcophagus. The priests will fall back, terrified. This is all meant to be in their minds, what they imagine, as was written in the script."

"But it will be realistic?" Nora asked, frowning. "Not hokey?"

"It'll all be 3-D, and the holographic images are a bit like ghosts—you can see through them, but only when there's strong light behind. We'll manipulate the light levels very carefully to exploit that illusion. Some of it's video-based, some of it C.G. Anyway, Senef rises, violated, and points a finger. To more flashes of lightning and thunder, he speaks of his life, what he has done, what a great regent and vizier he was to Thutmosis, and of course, this is where you slip in the educational stuff."

"Meanwhile," said DeMeo, "we've got a 500-watt Jem Glaciator hidden in the sarcophagus, pumping out an awesome ground fog. Two thousand cubic feet a minute."

"My script doesn't call for artificial smoke," said Wicherly. "This could damage the paintings."

"The Jem system uses only environmentally friendly fluids," Lipper said. "Guaranteed not to chemically alter anything."

Nora Kelly was frowning again. "Forgive me for raising this question, but is this level of theatricality really necessary?"

Menzies turned to her. "Why, Nora! This was your idea to begin with."

"I was imagining something lower-key, not strobe lights and fog machines."

Menzies chuckled. "As long as we're going this route, Nora, we should do it right. Trust me, we're creating an unforgettable educational experience. It's a marvelous way to slip a little learning to the *vulgus mobile* without them ever realizing it."

Nora continued to look doubtful, but said nothing further.

Lipper resumed. "As Senef speaks, the robbers fall to the floor in terror. Then Senef melts back into his sarcophagus, the robbers vanish, the holographic screens retract, the lights come up—and suddenly the tomb is as it was, before the robbery. A museum exhibit once again. The gate slides back and the visitors are free to tour the burial chamber as if nothing had happened."

Menzies raised a finger. "But they will do so having gained an appreciation of Senef and been entertained in the process. Now for the million-dollar question: can you finish by deadline?"

"We've already outsourced as much of the programming as possible," Lipper said. "The electrical staff are working flat out. I'd say we can have it installed and ready for alpha testing in four days."

"That's excellent."

"And then comes the debugging."

Menzies cocked his head questioningly. "Debugging?"

"That's the killer. A rule of thumb says the debugging takes twice as long as the original programming."

"Eight days?"

Lipper nodded, uneasy from the sudden darkening of Menzies's face.

"Four plus eight is twelve—two days before the gala opening. Can you finish the debugging in five?"

Something in Menzies's tone led Lipper to think it was more an order than a question. He swallowed: the schedule already verged on the insane. "We'll certainly try."

"Good. Now, let's talk for a minute about the opening. Dr. Kelly suggested we duplicate the original opening in 1872, and I wholeheartedly concurred. We are planning a cocktail reception, a bit of opera, and then the guests will be escorted into the tomb for the sound-and-light show. Dinner will follow."

"How many are we talking about?" Lipper asked.

"Six hundred."

"Obviously we're not going to fit six hundred people into the tomb at one time," Lipper said. "I've been estimating two hundred at a go for the sound-and-light show, which lasts about twenty minutes, but we could up that to, say, three hundred for the opening."

"Fine," said Menzies. "We'll divide them into two groups. The first in, of course, will be the A-list: the mayor, governor, senators and congressmen, the museum's top brass, the biggest patrons, movie stars. With two showings, we'll get guests through the exhibit within an hour. Finish off the entire crowd." He looked from Lipper to DeMeo. "You two are crucial. There can't be any mistakes. Everything's riding on you finishing that sound-and-light show on time. Four days plus five: that's nine days."

"I've got no problem," said DeMeo, all smiles and self-confidence: gofer and cable-puller extraordinaire.

Those disquieting blue eyes now turned back to Lipper. "And you, Mr. Lipper?"

"It'll happen."

"Delighted to hear it. I trust you'll keep me up-to-date with progress reports?"

They nodded.

Menzies glanced at his watch. "Nora, if you'll excuse me, I have to catch a train. I'll check in with you later."

Menzies and the curators were gone, leaving Lipper alone with DeMeo once again. He glanced at his watch. "We'd better get going, DeMeo, because I'd like to get to sleep tonight before four A.M. for a change."

"What about Darkmord?" DeMeo asked. "You promised to have the band of warriors ready for the attack by midnight."

Lipper groaned. *Shit.* They would just have to launch the attack on Castle Gloaming without him.

17

When Margo Green awoke, a bright afternoon sun was slanting in through the windows of the Feversham Clinic. Outside, puffy cumulus clouds drifted across a lazy blue sky. The distant call of waterbirds came from the direction of the Hudson River.

She yawned, stretched, then sat up in bed. Glancing at the clock, she noticed it was quarter to four. The nurse should be in soon with her afternoon cup of peppermint tea.

The hospital table beside her bed was crowded: back issues of *Natural History*, a Tolstoy novel, a portable music player, a laptop, and a copy of the *New York Times*. She reached for the newspaper, flipped through the C section. Maybe she could finish the crossword before Phyllis brought her tea.

Now that her condition was no longer critical, recovery at the clinic had settled into a kind of routine. She found that she looked forward to the afternoon chats with Phyllis. She hardly had any visitors—no visitors at all, actually, save her mother and Captain Laura Hayward—and the thing she missed most, other than her career, was companionship.

Picking up a pencil, she applied herself to the crossword. But it was one of those late-in-the-week puzzles, full of coy clues and obscure references, and mental exercise still tired her. After a few minutes, she put it aside. She found her thoughts straying back to Hayward's recent visit and the unpleasant memories it had reawakened.

It disturbed her that her memory of the attack remained shadowy. There were bits and pieces, disconnected, as if from a nightmare—but nothing coherent. She'd been inside the Sacred Images exhibition, checking the arrangement of some Native American masks. While there, she'd become aware of a presence: somebody else in the exhibition, lurking in the shadows. Following her. Stalking her. *Cornering* her. She dimly remembered making a stand, fighting with a box cutter. Had she wounded her pursuer? The actual attack itself was the most fragmentary: little more than a searing pain in her back. And that had been all—until she woke up in this room.

She folded up the newspaper, put it back on the table. The most disturbing thing was that, even though she knew her attacker had spoken to her, she couldn't remember anything he had said. His words were gone, fallen into the darkness. Curiously, she did remember, seared into her mind, the man's strange eyes and his hideous, dry chuckle.

She turned restlessly in her bed, wondering where Phyllis was, still thinking of Hayward's visit. The captain had asked a lot of questions about Agent Pendergast and his brother, a man with the peculiar name of Diogenes. It all seemed strange: Margo hadn't seen Pendergast in years, and she had never even known the FBI agent had a brother.

Now at last the door to her room opened and Phyllis walked in. But she wasn't carrying a tray of tea things, and her friendly face bore an official expression.

"Margo, you have a visitor," she said.

Margo barely had time to react to this announcement before a familiar figure appeared in the doorway: the chairman of her department at the museum, Dr. Hugo Menzies. He was dressed as usual in rumpled elegance, his thick white hair combed back from his forehead, his lively blue eyes darting briefly around the room before settling on her.

"Margo!" he cried, coming forward, patrician features breaking into a smile. "How wonderful to see you."

"Same here, Dr. Menzies," she replied. Her surprise at having a visitor was quickly replaced by embarrassment: she wasn't exactly dressed to receive her boss.

But Menzies, as if sensing her discomfort, was quick to put her at ease. He thanked Phyllis, waited until the nurse had left the room, then took a seat beside the bed.

"What a beautiful room!" he exclaimed. "And with an exquisite view of the Hudson River Valley. The quality of the light here is second only to Venice, I think; perhaps that's why it has drawn so many painters."

"They've been very good to me here."

"As well they should. You know, my dear, I've been terribly worried about you. The entire Anthropology Department has. We can't wait for your return."

"Neither can I."

"Your location has been almost a state secret. Until yesterday, I never even knew this place existed. As it was, I had to charm my way past half the staff." He smiled.

Margo smiled back. If anyone could charm his way in, Menzies could. She'd been lucky to get him as her supervisor: many museum curators lorded it over their minions, behaving like conceited philosopher-kings. Menzies was the exception: affable, receptive to the ideas of others, supportive of his staff. It was true—she couldn't wait to get out of here and back to work. *Museology*, the periodical she edited, was rudderless in her absence. If only she didn't grow tired so easily . . .

She realized her mind was drifting. She roused herself, glanced at Menzies. He was looking back at her, concern on his face.

"Sorry," she said. "I'm still a little out of it."

"Of course you are," he said. "Perhaps that's why this is still necessary?" And he nodded at the saline drip hanging beside the bed.

"The doctor said that's just a precautionary measure. I'm getting plenty of fluids now."

"Good, very good. The loss of blood must have been a severe shock. *So* much blood, Margo. There's a reason they call it the living liquid, don't you agree?"

A strange current, almost like a physical shock, passed through Margo. The weakness, the feeling of torpor, receded. She suddenly felt wide awake. "What did you say?"

"I said, have they given you any indication of when you can leave?"

Margo relaxed. "The doctors are very pleased with my progress. Another two weeks or so."

"And then bed rest at home, I assume?"

"Yes. Dr. Winokur—that's my primary physician here—said I would need another month's recuperation before returning to work."

"He would know best."

Menzies's voice was low and soothing, and Margo felt torpidity returning. Almost without realizing it, she yawned.

"Oh!" she said, embarrassed anew. "I'm sorry."

"Think nothing of it. I don't want to overstay my welcome, I'll leave shortly. Are you tired, Margo?"

She smiled faintly. "A little bit."

"Sleeping all right?"

"Yes."

"Good. I was worried you might have been having nightmares." Menzies glanced over his shoulder, toward the open door and the corridor beyond.

"No, not really."

"That's my girl! What spunk!"

There: that strange electric tingle again. Menzies's voice had changed—something about it was both foreign and disquietingly familiar. "Dr. Menzies," she began, sitting up once more.

"Now, now, you just sit back and rest." And with a gentle but firm pressure on her shoulder, he guided her back down onto the pillow. "I'm so glad to hear you're sleeping well. Not everybody could put such a traumatic event behind them."

"It's not exactly behind me," she said. "I just don't seem to remember what happened very well, that's all."

Menzies laid a comforting hand on hers. "That's just as well," he said, slipping his other hand inside his jacket.

Margo felt an inexplicable sense of alarm. She was tired—that's all it was. Much as she liked Menzies, much as she appreciated this break in the monotony, she needed to rest.

"After all, nobody would want such memories. The noises in the empty exhibition hall. Being followed. The invisible footfalls, the falling of boards. The sudden darkness."

Margo felt an unfocused panic well up within her. She stared at

Menzies, unable to wrap her mind around what he was saying. The anthropologist kept on talking in his low, soothing voice.

"Laughter in the blackness. And then, the plunge of the knife . . . No, Margo. Nobody would want those memories."

And then Menzies *himself* laughed. But it wasn't his voice. No: it was another voice, another voice entirely: a hideous, dry chuckle.

A sudden dreadful shock burned through the gathering lethargy. *No. Oh, no. It couldn't be . . .*

Menzies sat in the chair, looking at her intently, as if gauging the effect of his words.

Then he winked.

Margo tried to pull away, opened her mouth to scream. But even as she did so, the feeling of lassitude intensified, flooding her limbs, leaving her unable to speak or move. She had a desperate realization that the lethargy wasn't normal, that something was happening to her . . .

Menzies let his hand fall away from hers, and as he did so, she saw—with a thrill of horror—that his other hand had been concealed beneath. It held a tiny syringe, which was injecting a colorless liquid into the IV tube at her wrist. Even as she watched, he withdrew the syringe, palmed it, then replaced it in his suit jacket.

"My dear Margo," he said, sitting back, his voice so very different now. "Did you really think you'd seen the last of me?"

Panic, and a desperate desire to survive, surged within her—yet she felt utterly powerless against the drug that was spreading through her veins, silencing her voice and paralyzing her limbs. Menzies swept to his feet, placed a finger against his lips, and whispered, "Time to sleep, Margo . . ."

The hated darkness surged in, blotting out sight and thought. Panic, shock, and disbelief fell aside as the mere act of drawing breath became a struggle. As she lay paralyzed, Margo saw Menzies turn and hasten from the room, heard his faint yelling for a nurse. But then his voice, too, was subsumed into the hollow roar that filled her head, and darkness gathered in her eyes until the roar dwindled into blackness and eternal night, and she knew no more.

18

Four days after their meeting with Menzies, the sound-and-light show was finally installed and ready for debugging, and that night they were pulling the final cables, hooking everything up. Jay Lipper crouched by the dusty hole near the floor of the Hall of the Chariots, listening to various sounds emerging from the hole: grunts, heavy breathing, muttered curses. It was the third night in a row they'd worked on the install into the wee hours of the morning, and he was dog-tired. He couldn't take much more of this. The exhibition had basically taken over his life. All his guildmates in *Land of Darkmord* had given up on him and continued with the online game. By now, they'd leveled up once, maybe twice, and he was hopelessly behind.

"Got it?" came DeMeo's muffled voice from the hole. Lipper looked down to see the end of a fiber-optic cable poking out of the blackness.

Lipper seized the end. "Got it."

He pulled it through, then waited for DeMeo to come around from the other side. Soon DeMeo's blocky figure, backlit and faint in the dim light of the tomb, came huffing down the passageway, cables coiled about his massive shoulders. Lipper handed him the cable end and DeMeo plugged it into the back of a PowerBook sitting on a nearby worktable. Later, when the artifacts were all in place, the laptop would be artfully hidden behind a gilded and painted chest. But for now, it was out in the open, where they could access it.

DeMeo slapped the dust off his thighs with a grin, then held up his hand. "High five, bro. We did it."

Lipper ignored the hand, unable to disguise his irritation. He had had just about enough of DeMeo. The museum's two electricians had insisted on going home at midnight, and as a result he'd found himself on his hands and knees, acting as DeMeo's damn assistant.

"We've got a long way to go," he said in a sulky voice.

DeMeo's hand dropped. "Yeah, but at least, the cabling's been pulled, the software's loaded, and we're on schedule. You can't ask for better than that, right, Jayce?"

Lipper reached over and turned on the computer, initiating the boot sequence. He hoped to hell the computer would see the network and the remote devices, but he knew it wouldn't. It was never that easy— and besides, DeMeo was the one who set up the frigging network. Anything could happen.

The computer finished booting and, with a sinking heart, Lipper began sending pings over the network, checking to see how many of the two dozen remote devices were missing and would require time-consuming troubleshooting to locate. He'd be lucky if the computer saw half of the peripherals on first boot-up: it was the nature of the business.

But as he moused his way from one network address to another, a sense of disbelief stole over him. Everything seemed to be there.

He ran over his checklist. It was impossible, but true: the entire network was there, visible and operational. All the remote devices, the sound-and-light apparatus, were responding and seemed to be perfectly synchronized. It was as if someone had already worked out the kinks.

Lipper rechecked his list, but with the same result. Disbelief gave way to a kind of guarded jubilation: he could not recall a single job where such a complicated network was up and running on the first try. And it wasn't just the network: the entire project had been like that, everything coming together like a charm. It had taken days of seemingly endless work, but in the real world it would have taken even longer. Probably a lot longer. He fetched a deep breath.

"How's it look?" DeMeo asked, crowding up behind him to peer at the small screen. Lipper could smell his oniony breath.

"Looks good." Lipper edged away.

"Sweet!" DeMeo gave a whoop that echoed through the tomb, just about blowing out Lipper's eardrum. "I am the *man!* I'm a freaking network *monster!*" He danced around the room, doing an ungainly buck-and-wing, pumping his fist into the air. Then he glanced over at Lipper. "Let's do a test run."

"I have a better idea. Why don't you go out and get us a couple of pizzas?"

DeMeo looked at him in surprise. "What—now? You don't want to do an alpha?"

Lipper certainly did want to do a test run. But not with DeMeo breathing down his neck, whooping in his ear, and acting like an ass. Lipper wanted to admire his handiwork quietly, in a focused way. He needed a break from DeMeo, and he needed one bad.

"We'll do a run *after* the pizzas. On me."

He watched as DeMeo considered this.

"All right," DeMeo said. "What do you want?"

"The Neapolitan. With a large iced tea."

"I'm going for the Hawaiian double pineapple with honey-glazed ham, extra garlic, and two Dr Peppers."

It was typical of DeMeo to assume Lipper gave a shit what kind of pizza he wanted. Lipper pulled out two twenties, passed them over.

"Thanks, bro."

He watched DeMeo's form labor up the stone staircase and vanish in the gloom. The footsteps echoed slowly away.

Lipper breathed in the blessed silence. Maybe DeMeo would be run over by a bus on the way back.

With that pleasant thought in mind, he turned his attention back to the computer's control panel. He moused over each peripheral device in turn, checking to see that it was alive and functional, surprised again that each one responded perfectly, on cue, as if somebody had already debugged the network for them. DeMeo, for all his wisecracks and shenanigans, had actually done his job—and done it perfectly.

Suddenly he paused, frowning. A software icon was jumping frantically in the dock. Somehow the main routines for the sound-and-light show had loaded automatically, when, in fact, he had specifically programmed them to load manually, at least during the alpha testing, so he could step through the code and check each module.

So there *was* a glitch, after all. He'd need to fix it, of course: but not right now. The software was loaded, the controllers were online and ready, the screens in place, the fog machine filled.

He might as well run it.

He drew in another breath, savoring the peace and quiet, his finger over the return key, ready to execute the program. Then he paused. A sound had drifted toward him from the deeper part of the tomb: the Hall of Truth, or maybe even the burial chamber itself. Couldn't be DeMeo, since he'd be coming from the opposite direction. And the pizzas would take at least half an hour; if he were lucky, maybe even forty minutes.

Perhaps it was a guard or something.

The sound came again: a strange, dry, scurrying sound. No guard made a noise like that.

Mice, maybe?

He rose indecisively. It was probably nothing. Christ, he was letting himself get spooked by all this curse crap the guards had started to whisper about. It was probably just a mouse. After all, there'd been plenty of mice in the old Egyptian galleries, enough so the Maintenance Department had needed to place glue traps. Still, if some had gotten into the tomb itself—maybe through one of the cable holes DeMeo had opened up—all it would take was a pair of rodent teeth sunk into one cable to crash the whole system and cause a delay of hours, maybe even days, while they examined each cable. Inch by frigging inch.

Another scurry, like wind rustling dead leaves. Leaving the lights dimmed, he picked up DeMeo's coat—ready to throw it over a mouse if he found one—then rose and made his way stealthily into the deepest recesses of the tomb.

*   *   *

Teddy DeMeo fumbled for his key card, swiping it through the newly installed lock to the Egyptian gallery while trying not to drop the pizzas at the same time. The damn pies were cold—the guards at the security entrance had taken their sweet time clearing him through, when the same idiots had checked him out just twenty-five minutes earlier. Security? More like moronity.

The door to the Egyptian gallery whispered shut and he strode down the length of the hall, turned into the annex—and was surprised to find the doors to the tomb shut before him.

A suspicion took root in his mind: had Lipper gone and done the first run without him? But he quickly dismissed it. Lipper, though a fussy artiste type and cranky as hell, was basically a cool guy.

He fumbled out his key card and swiped it, hearing the locks disengage. Still balancing the pizzas and drinks, he got an elbow into the door and shoved it open, then slipped through, the door clicking shut behind him.

The lights had dimmed to level I—the level they would be at after a run—and once again, DeMeo felt a stab of suspicion.

"Hey, Jayce!" he called out. "Pizza delivery!"

His voice echoed and died away.

"Jayce!"

He descended the staircase, walked down the corridor, and went as far as the bridge over the well before pausing again.

"Jayce! Pizza time!"

He listened while the echoes died away. Lipper wouldn't have done an initial test run without him: not after all the time they'd put in on the project together. He wasn't that much of an asshole. He probably had his earphones on, checking the sound track or something. Or maybe he was listening to his iPod—sometimes he did that while working. DeMeo ventured across the bridge and entered their main work area in the Hall of the Chariots.

As he did so, he heard a distant footstep. At least he thought it was a footstep. But it had made an odd thumping sound. It came from deeper within the tomb, probably the burial chamber.

"That you, Jayce?" For the first time, DeMeo felt a creeping sense of alarm. He put the pizzas down on the worktable and took a few steps toward the Hall of Truth and the burial chamber beyond. He could see that it was quite dark—still at level I lighting, like the rest of the tomb. He couldn't see a damn thing, to tell the truth.

He went back to the worktable, looked at the computer. It was fully booted, the software loaded and waiting in standby mode. He moused over to the lighting icon, trying to remember how to raise the light levels. Lipper had done it a hundred times, but he'd never paid much attention. There were some software sliders visible in an open window and he clicked the one labeled Hall of the Chariots.

Christ! The lights *dimmed*, sending the disquieting Egyptian carvings and stone statuary even further into gloom. He quickly moused the slider in the other direction, and the lights intensified. Then he began brightening the lights in the rest of the tomb.

He heard a thump and turned with a jerk. "Jayce?"

It had definitely come from the burial chamber.

DeMeo laughed. "Hey, Jayce, c'mere. I got the pizzas."

There was that strange noise again: Draaaag-*thump*. Draaaag-*thump*. As if somebody, or some thing, was dragging one limb.

"It sounds just like *The Mummy's Curse*. Ha, ha, Jayce—good one!"

No answer.

DeMeo, still chuckling, turned from the computer and strode through the Hall of Truth. He turned his eyes away from the squatting form of Ammut—something about the Egyptian god, the eater of hearts with a crocodile head and lion's mane, creeped him out even worse than the rest of the tomb.

He paused beyond the door to the burial chamber. "You're a funny guy, Jayce."

He waited for Lipper's laugh, for the sight of his skinny form emerging from behind a pilaster. But there was nothing. The silence was absolute. With a nervous swallow, he ducked inside, peered about the tomb.

Nothing. The other doors leading away from the burial chamber were dark—they weren't part of the computer lighting scheme. Lipper must be hiding in one of those rooms, preparing to jump out and scare him half to death.

"Hey, Jayce, come on. The pizzas are cold and getting colder."

The lights suddenly went out.

"Hey!"

DeMeo spun around, but the tomb doglegged at the Hall of Truth and he could not see back into the Hall of the Chariots—nor could he see the comforting blue glow of the LCD screen.

He spun again, hearing the strange, dragging footfalls behind him, moving closer now.

"This isn't funny, Jay."

He felt for his flashlight—but of course he wasn't carrying it; it was back in the chariots hall, on the table. Why couldn't he see the indirect glow of the LCD? Had the power been cut as well? The darkness was total.

"Look, Jay, cut the crap. I'm serious."

He shuffled backward in the dark, came up against one of the pillars, began feeling his way around it. The steps drew still closer.

Draaaag-*thump.* Draaaag-*thump.*

"Jay, come on. Cut the bullshit."

Suddenly, from closer than he ever expected, he heard the raspy sound of air escaping from a dry throat. A rattle that was almost a hiss, full of something like hatred.

"Jesus!" DeMeo took a step forward and swiped his heavy fist through the air, striking something that shuffled back with another snakelike hiss.

"Stop it! Stop it!"

He both heard and felt the thing rush at him with a high keening sound. He tried to twist aside but felt, with astonishment, a terrible blow. Searing heat knifed through his chest. With a shriek, he fell backward, clawing at the darkness, and as he hit the ground, he felt something heavy and cold stamp on his throat and bear down with shocking weight. He lashed about with his hands as he heard the bones crackling in his neck and a sudden, dazzling explosion of urine-colored light flashed in his eyes—and then nothing.

19

The large, elegant library in Agent Pendergast's mansion on Riverside Drive was the last room one would expect to call crowded. And yet—D'Agosta reflected moodily—there was no other word for it this evening. Tables, chairs, and much of the floor were covered with plats and diagrams. Half a dozen easels and whiteboards had been erected, showing schematics, maps, routes of ingress and egress. The low-tech reconnaissance they had conducted of Herkmoor a few nights earlier had now been enhanced by high-tech remote surveillance, including false-color satellite images in radar and infrared wavelengths. Boxes lay shoved against one wall, overflowing with printouts, data dumps from computer probes of the Herkmoor network, and aerial photographs of the prison complex.

In the middle of the controlled chaos sat Glinn, nearly motionless in his wheelchair, speaking quietly in his usual monotone. He had begun the meeting with a crushingly detailed analysis of Herkmoor's physical plant and security measures. D'Agosta needed no convincing there: if any prison was escape-proof, it was Herkmoor. The old-fashioned defenses like redundant guard posts and triple fencing had been bolstered by cutting-edge instrumentation, including laser-beam "lattices" at every exit, hundreds of digital videocams, and a network of passive listening devices set into the walls and ground, ready to pick up anything from digging to stealthy footsteps. Every prisoner was required to wear an ankle bracelet with an embedded GPS device, which broadcast the prisoner's location to a central command unit. If the bracelet were cut, an alarm would immediately sound and an automatic lockdown sequence would begin.

As far as D'Agosta was concerned, Herkmoor was invincible.

From there, Glinn had segued to the next step in the escape plan. And this was where D'Agosta's simmering unease had boiled over. Not only did the idea seem simplistic and inept, but, even worse, it turned out that he, D'Agosta—and he alone—was the man assigned to carry it out.

He glanced around the library, waiting impatiently for Glinn to finish. Wren had arrived earlier that evening with a set of architectural plans of the prison, "borrowed" from the private records section of the New York Public Library, and now he hovered around Constance Greene. With his luminous eyes and almost translucent skin, the man looked like a cave creature, paler even than Pendergast . . . if that were possible.

Next, D'Agosta's gaze fell on Constance. She sat at a side table opposite Wren, a stack of books before her, listening to Glinn and taking notes. She was wearing a severe black dress with a row of tiny pearl buttons in the back, running from the base of her spine up to the nape of her neck. D'Agosta found himself wondering who had buttoned them up for her. More than once, he had caught her privately stroking one hand over the other, or gazing into the fire that crackled on the huge grate, lost in thought.

She's probably as skeptical about all this as I am, he thought. Because as he looked around at their little foursome—Proctor, the chauffeur, was unaccountably absent—he couldn't imagine a group less suited for such a daunting task. He had never really liked Glinn and his smooth arrogance, and he wondered if the man had finally met his match with the Herkmoor penitentiary.

There came a pause in Glinn's drone, and he turned toward D'Agosta.

"Do you have any questions or comments so far, Lieutenant?"

"Yeah. A comment: the scheme is crazy."

"Perhaps I should have phrased the question differently. Do you have any comments *of substance* to make?"

"You think I can just waltz in, make a spectacle of myself, and get out scot-free? This is Herkmoor we're talking about. I'll be lucky not to end up in the cell next to Pendergast."

Glinn's expression did not change. "As long as you stick to the script, there will be no problems and you will get off 'scot-free.' Everything has been planned down to the last eventuality. We know exactly how the guards and prison personnel will react to your every move." Glinn suddenly smiled, his thin lips stretching mirthlessly. "That, you see, is Herkmoor's fatal weakness. That and those GPS bracelets, which show the position of every inmate in the entire prison at the touch of a key . . . a most foolish innovation."

"If I go in there and make a scene, won't it put them on alert?"

"Not if you follow the script. There is some critical information which only you can get. And some prep work that only you can do."

"Prep work?"

"I'll get to that shortly."

D'Agosta felt his frustration rise. "Pardon my saying so, but all your planning isn't going to mean jack once I'm inside those walls. This is the real world, and people are unpredictable. You can't *know* what they're going to do."

Glinn looked at him without moving. "You'll forgive me for contradicting you, Lieutenant, but human beings are disgustingly predictable. Especially in an environment like Herkmoor, where the rules of behavior are mapped out in excruciating detail. The scheme may seem simple, even inane, to you. But that's its power."

"It's just going to get me into deeper shit than I am already."

After dropping this epithet, he glanced at Constance. But the young woman was staring into the fire with her strange eyes, not even seeming to have heard.

"We never fail," Glinn said, remaining unnervingly calm and neutral. "That's our guarantee. All you need to do, Lieutenant, is follow instructions."

"I'll tell you what we really need: a pair of eyes on the inside. You can't tell me none of those guards can be turned—blackmailed, whatever. Christ, prison guards are one step away from being criminals themselves, at least in my experience."

"Not these guards. Any attempt to turn one would be foolhardy." Glinn wheeled himself over to a desk. "If I told you we had somebody on the inside, however, would it reassure you?"

"Hell, yes."

"Would it secure your cooperation? Silence all these doubts?"

"If the source was reliable, yeah."

"I believe you will find our source to be above reproach." And with that, Glinn picked up a single piece of paper and handed it to D'Agosta.

D'Agosta glanced over the sheet. It contained a long column of numbers, with two corresponding times linked to each number.

"What's this?" he asked.

"A schedule of guard patrols in the solitary unit during lockdown, from ten P.M. to six A.M. And this is just one of the many useful pieces of information that have come our way."

D'Agosta stared in disbelief. "How the hell did you get it?"

Glinn allowed himself a smile—at least D'Agosta thought the faint thinning of the lips was a smile. "Our inside source."

"And who might that be, if you don't mind my asking?"

"You know him well."

Now D'Agosta was even more surprised. "Not—?"

"Special Agent Pendergast."

D'Agosta slumped in his chair. "How did he get this to you?"

This time a true smile broke over Glinn's features. "Why, Lieutenant, don't you remember? *You* brought it out."

"Me?"

Glinn reached behind the desk, pulled out a plastic box. Looking inside, D'Agosta was surprised to see some of the trash he'd collected in his recon of the prison perimeter—gum wrappers and scraps of linen—now carefully dried, pressed, and mounted between sheets of archival plastic. When he looked closely at the linen scraps, he could just make out faint markings.

"There's an old drain in Pendergast's cell—as in most of the older cells at Herkmoor—which was never hooked into the modern sewage treatment system. It drains into a catchment basin outside the prison walls, which in turn empties into Herkmoor Creek. Pendergast writes us a message on a scrap of trash, sticks it into the drain, and washes it down with water from the sink, which ends up in the creek. Simple. We discovered it because the DEP had recently cited Herkmoor for the water-quality violation."

"What about ink? Writing equipment? Those are the first things they'd have taken away."

"Frankly, I don't know how he's doing it."

There was a short silence.

"But you knew he'd communicate with us," D'Agosta said at last in a quiet voice.

"Naturally."

Despite himself, D'Agosta was impressed. "Now, if there was only some way to get information *to* Pendergast."

Wry amusement flickered briefly in Glinn's eyes. "As soon as we knew what cell he was in, that was simplicity itself."

Before D'Agosta could respond, a sudden noise rose in the library: a faint, urgent squeaking, coming from the direction of Constance. D'Agosta looked over in time to see her picking up a small white mouse from the carpet, which had apparently fallen from her pocket. She calmed it with soft words, petting it softly, before returning the mouse to its hiding place. Sensing the silence in the room and the eyes upon her, she looked up, coloring suddenly.

"What a delightful little pet," Wren said after a moment. "I didn't know you were fond of mice."

Constance smiled nervously.

"Wherever did you get it, my dear?" Wren went on, his voice high and tense.

"I . . . found it in the basement."

"Really?"

"Yes. Among the collections. The place is overrun."

"It seems awfully tame. And one doesn't usually find white mice running around loose."

"Perhaps it was somebody's pet that escaped," she said with some irritation, and rose. "I'm tired. I hope you'll excuse me. Good night."

After she had left, there was a moment of silence, and then Glinn spoke again, his voice low. "There was another message from Pendergast in those papers—urgent—not relating to the matter at hand."

"What was it about?"

"Her. He asked that you, Mr. Wren, keep a careful watch over her during the daytime—when you are not sleeping, of course. And that when you leave for your nighttime job at the library, you make sure the house is secure, and she in it."

Wren seemed pleased. "Of course, of course! Glad to, very glad indeed."

Glinn's eye turned to D'Agosta. "Even though you're living in the house, he asked if you could make it a point to drop in and check on her from time to time during working hours as well."

"He seems worried."

"Very." Glinn paused, then opened a drawer and began to remove items and place them on the desk: a hip flask of whiskey, a computer flash drive, a roll of duct tape, a rolled-up sheet of mirrored Mylar plastic, a capsule of brown liquid, a hypodermic needle, a small pair of wire cutters, a pen, and a credit card.

"And now, Lieutenant, let us go over the prep work you will be expected to accomplish once you are inside Herkmoor . . ."

Later on—once all the maps and boxes and charts had been packed away, and as D'Agosta was seeing Glinn and Wren out at the mansion's front door—the old librarian lingered behind.

"Listen a moment, if you would," he said, plucking at D'Agosta's sleeve.

"Sure," D'Agosta said.

Wren leaned in close, as if to impart a secret. "Lieutenant, you are not familiar with the—the *circumstances* of Constance's past existence. Let me just say that they are . . . unusual."

D'Agosta hesitated, surprised by the look of agitation in the strange man's eyes. "Okay," he said.

"I know Constance well: I was the person who found her in this house, where she'd been hiding. She has always been scrupulously honest—sometimes painfully so. But tonight, for the first time, she lied."

"The white mouse?"

Wren nodded. "I have no idea what it means, except that I'm convinced she's in some kind of trouble. Lieutenant, she's an emotional house of cards, just waiting for a puff of wind. We both need to keep a close eye on her."

"Thank you for the information, Mr. Wren. I'll check in as frequently as I can."

Wren held his gaze for a moment, staring at him with remarkable urgency. Then he nodded, grasped D'Agosta's hand briefly in his own bony claw, and vanished into the chill darkness.

20

The prisoner known only as A sat on the bunk in solitary 44, deep within the Federal High-Risk Violent Offender Pretrial Detention Facility—the Black Hole—of Herkmoor. It was a cell of monastic spareness, eight feet by ten, with freshly whitewashed walls, a cement floor with a central drain, a toilet in one corner, a sink, a radiator, and a narrow metal bed. A fluorescent bulb, recessed into the ceiling and protected by a wire cage, provided the cell's sole light. There was no switch: the bulb went on at 6 A.M. and went off at 10 P.M. High up on the far wall was the room's only window, deep and barred, two inches wide and fifteen inches high.

The prisoner, dressed in a neatly pressed gray jumpsuit, had been sitting on the mattress for many hours in utter stillness. His slender face was pale and without expression, the silvery eyes half hooded, white-blond hair combed back. Nothing moved, not even his eyes, as he listened to the soft, rapid sounds filtering from the cell next door: solitary 45.

They were the sounds of drumming: a tattoo of extraordinary rhythmic complexity that rose and fell, sped up and slowed down, moving from metal bed rail to mattress to the walls, toilet, sink, bars, and back again. At present, the prisoner was drumming on the iron bedstead rail with an occasional slap or turn played out on the mattress, while making rapid popping and clucking sounds with his lips and tongue. The endless rhythms rose and fell like the wind, working into a machine gun–like frenzy and then dying back into a lazy syncopation. At times, it almost—but not quite—seemed to come to a stop: except that a single ostinato *tap . . . tap . . . tap* indicated that the beat went on.

An aficionado of rhythm might have recognized the extraordinary diversity of rhythmical patterns and styles coming from solitary 45: a kassagbe Congo beat segueing into a down-tempo funk-out and then into a pop-and-lock, moving sequentially through a shakeout, a worm-hole, a glam, then into a long pseudo-electroclash riff; then a quick eurostomp ending in a nasty, followed by a hip-hop twist-stick and a tom club. A moment's silence . . . and then a slow Chicago blues fill began, evolving into innumerable other beats both named and name-less, twining and intertwining in an eternal braid of sound.

The prisoner known as A, however, was not an aficionado of rhythm. He was a man who knew many things—but drumming was not one of them.

And yet he listened.

Finally, half an hour before lights-out, the prisoner known as A shifted on his cot. He turned toward the headrail, gave it a cautious tap with his left index finger, then another. He began tapping out a simple 4/4 beat. As the minutes went on, he tried the beat on the mattress, then the wall and the sink—as if testing them for timbre, tone, and amplitude—before moving back to the bed rail. As he continued to beat out a 4/4 time with his left finger, he began beating a second rhythm with his right. As he played this simple rhythmic accompani-ment, he listened intently to the outpouring of virtuosity next door.

Lights-out arrived, and all went black. An hour went by, and an-other. The prisoner's approach subtly changed. Carefully following the drummer's lead, A picked up an unusual syncopation here, a three-against-two beat there, adding them to his simple repertoire. He meshed his own drumming ever more closely into the web of sounds coming from next door, taking cues from his neighbor, picking up the tempo or lowering it according to the drummer's lead.

Midnight, and the drummer in cell 45 continued—and so did the prisoner named A. A found that drumming—which he had always dismissed as a crude, primitive activity—was curiously pleasing to the mind. It opened a door from the tight, ugly reality of his cell into an expansive, abstract space of mathematical precision and complexity. He drummed on, still following the lead of the prisoner in 45, all the while increasing the complexity of his own rhythmical patterns.

The night wore on. The few other prisoners in solitary—there were not many, and they were far down the hall—were long asleep. Yet still the prisoners in 44 and 45 drummed on together. As the prisoner named A explored more deeply this strange new world of external and internal rhythm, he began to understand something about the man next door and his mental illness—as had been his intent. It was not something that could be put into words; it was not accessible to language; it was not reachable by psychological theorizing, psychotherapy, or even medication.

Yet nevertheless—through careful emulation of the complex drumming—the prisoner in 44 began to reach that place, to enter the drummer's special world. On a basic neurological level, he began to understand the drummer: what motivated him, why he did what he did.

Slowly, carefully, A took a measured foray into altering the rhythm along certain experimental pathways, to see if he could take the lead, induce the drummer to follow him for a moment. When this experiment proved successful, he very subtly began to alter the tempo, morph the rhythm. There was nothing sudden in his approach: every new beat, every altered rhythm, was carefully controlled and calculated to lead to a desired result.

Over the space of another hour, the dynamic between the two prisoners began to change. Without realizing it, the drummer became no longer the leader, but the follower.

Prisoner A continued to alter his own drumming, slowing it down and speeding it up by infinite degrees, until he was certain *he* was now setting the rhythm; that the Drummer in the cell next door was unconsciously following *his* tempo and lead. With infinite care, he then began to slow his own drumming: not in a steady way, but through speedups and slowdowns, through riffs and changeovers he had picked up from his neighbor, each time ending at a slightly slower tempo—until he was beating out a down-tempo as slow and sleepy as molasses.

And then he stopped.

The man in solitary 45, after a few tentative, lost beats, halted as well.

There was a long silence.

And then a breathy, hoarse voice came from cell 45. "Who . . . who are you?"

"I am Aloysius Pendergast," came the reply. "And I am pleased to make your acquaintance."

An hour later, blessed silence reigned. Pendergast lay on his bunk, eyes closed but still awake. At a certain moment, he opened his eyes and scrutinized the faintly glowing dial of his watch—the one item prisoners were allowed, by law, to keep. Two minutes to four in the morning. He waited, now with his eyes open, and at exactly four o'clock a brilliant pinpoint of green light appeared on the far wall, dancing and jittering before gradually settling down. He recognized it as the output of a 532nm green DPSS laser—nothing more than the beam from an expensive laser pen, aimed through his window from some concealed spot far beyond the prison walls.

When the light had stopped trembling, it began blinking, repeating a short introduction in a simple monophonic cipher, compressed to keep transmission short. The introduction was repeated four times, to make sure Pendergast recognized the code. Then, after a pause, the actual message began.

TRANSMISSION RECEIVED
STILL ANALYZING OPTIMAL ROUTES FOR EGRESS
CHANGE OF VENUE MAY BE REQUIRED ON YOUR END
WILL ADVISE ASAP
QUESTIONS FOLLOW—COMMUNICATE VIA PRIOR PROCEDURE
DESCRIBE YARD PRIVILEGES AND SCHEDULE
OBTAIN MATERIAL SAMPLES OF GUARD UNIFORM, SLACKS AND
    SHIRT

The requests and questions went on, some strange, some straight-forward. Pendergast made no move to take notes, committing everything to memory.

At the last question, however, he started slightly.

ARE YOU WILLING TO KILL?

With that, the laser light vanished. Pendergast rose to a sitting po-sition. Feeling under the mattress, he extracted a hard, frayed piece of canvas and a slice of lemon from a recent meal. Removing one shoe, he carried it to the sink, ran the water, placed a few drops into the soap depression, and dipped the shoe into it. Next, he squeezed the juice of the lemon slice into the water. With the piece of canvas, he proceeded to strip the shoe of some of its polish. Soon, a small amount of dark liquid stood in the enamel depression. He paused a moment in the gloom to make sure his movements were undetected. Then he unmade the corner of his bed, tore a long strip of sheet from beneath the tuck, laid it out on the rim of the sink. He removed one shoelace, dipped its previously sharpened and split metal edge into the liquid, and began to write in a fanatically small, neat hand, leaving a pale script on the strip of cotton.

By quarter to five, he had finished answering the questions. He laid the sheet on the radiator until it was baking hot, which darkened and fixed the writing; then he began to roll it up. But as he did so, he paused, and then added one more small line at the bottom: "Continue to keep a close eye on Constance. And be of good cheer, my dear Vincent."

He baked on this last part of the message, rolled it tight, and in-serted it into the drain in his cell. Then he filled his slop bucket at the sink and poured it down the drain, repeating the process a dozen times.

One hour to wake-up. He lay down on the bed, folded his hands across his chest, and went instantly to sleep.

21

Mary Johnson swung open the oversize door to the Egyptian gallery and stepped inside, feeling around on the cold marble wall for the light switches. Although she knew the technicians had been working late hours on the tomb recently, by six in the morning they were always gone. It was her job to unlock the area for the subcontractors, turn on the lights, and make sure all was well.

She found the bank of switches and brushed them on with a plump forefinger. Rows of old glass and bronze light fixtures blazed, casting a mellow incandescent glow over the partly refurbished hall. She paused for a moment in the doorway, fists parked on bulging hips, looking around to make sure all was in order. Then she began moving down the hall, her giant butt swaying as she hummed old disco tunes to herself, twirling a ring of keys in her hand. The jangling keys, clicking heels, and off-key voice echoed through the large chamber, creating a reassuring cocoon of noise that had seen her through thirty years of nighttime employment at the New York Museum of Natural History.

She reached the annex, smacked on the bank of lights there, then crossed the echoing space and swiped her card in the new security doors leading to the Tomb of Senef. The locks disengaged and the automatic doors opened with a humming sound, revealing the tomb beyond. She stopped, frowning. Normally, the tomb should be in blackness. But despite the hour, it was brilliantly lit.

Damn techies left the lights on.

She stood in the doorway, pausing. Then she tossed her head and sniffed disdainfully at her own uncertainty. Some of the guards who'd had family working here in the thirties had begun whispering about the tomb being cursed; how it had been boarded up for good reason; how it was a big mistake reopening it. But since when was an Egyptian tomb *not* cursed? And Mary Johnson prided herself on her brisk, matter-of-fact approach to her job. *Just tell me what to do and I'll do it. No bullshit, no whining, no excuses.*

Curse, hell.

With a cluck, she descended the broad stone stairs into the tomb, humming and singing, her voice echoing about the close space.

Stayin' alive, stayin' alive . . .

She walked across the well, her immense weight swinging the bridge, and passed into the chamber beyond. Here, the computer geeks had set up tables of equipment, and Johnson was careful not to trip on the cables snaking across the floor. She glanced disapprovingly at the greasy pizza boxes carelessly stacked on one table, at the Coke cans and candy bar wrappers lying about. Maintenance wouldn't be through until seven. Well, it wasn't her problem.

In her three decades at the museum, Mary Johnson had seen it all. She'd seen them come and go, she'd been through the museum murders and the subway murders, the disappearance of Dr. Frock, the killing of old Mr. Puck, and the attempted murder of Margo Green. It was the biggest museum in the world and it had proved to be a challenging place to work, in more ways than one. Still, the benefits were excellent and the leave was decent. Not to mention the prestige.

She moved on, passing into the Hall of the Chariots, stopping for a cursory visual check, and then stuck her head into the burial chamber. All seemed in order. She was on the verge of turning back when she caught the whiff of something sour. Her nose wrinkled instinctively as she searched for its source. There, on one of the nearby pillars, was a splatter of something wet and chunky.

She raised her radio. "M. Johnson calling Central. Do you read?"

"This is Central. Ten-four, Mary."

"We need a cleanup crew down here in the Tomb of Senef. Burial chamber."

"What's the problem?"

"Vomit."

"Christ. Not the night guards again?"

"Who knows? Maybe the techies, having themselves a big old time."

"We'll get maintenance on it."

Johnson snapped the radio off and did a brisk turn around the perimeter of the burial chamber. In her experience, piles of vomit seldom dropped alone: better to find out the rest of the bad news right away. Despite her size, she was a very fast walker, and she had completed more than half the circuit when her left shoe skidded on the slick floor and her momentum carried her sideways and down, landing her hard on the polished stone.

"Crap!"

She sat there, shaken but unhurt. She'd slipped in a puddle of something dark and coppery-smelling, and she'd broken the fall with both hands. When she held her hands up, she immediately recognized the substance as blood.

"Lord almighty."

She rose with care, looked around automatically for something to wipe her hands on, found nothing, and decided to go ahead and wipe them on her pants, since they were already ruined. She unhooked her radio.

"Johnson calling Central, do you read?"

"Roger that."

"Got a pool of blood here, too."

"What's that you say? *Blood?* How much?"

"Enough."

A silence. From the large pool of blood she'd slipped in, a dribbling trail of splatters led toward the huge, open granite sarcophagus that stood in the center of the room. The flank of the sarcophagus, engraved in hieroglyphics, had a prominent smear of gore along its side, as if something had been hoisted over and dropped inside.

Suddenly, the very last thing in the world Johnson wanted to do was look inside that sarcophagus. But something—perhaps her strong sense of duty—made her walk slowly forward. Her radio, held unheeded in one hand, squawked.

"Enough?" Central squawked again in a high voice. "What's that supposed to mean, *enough?*"

She reached the lip of the sarcophagus and looked inside. A body lay on its back. The body was human—that much she knew—but beyond that, she could tell nothing. The face was gashed and scored beyond recognition. The breastbone was split and the ribs yanked open like a set of double doors. Where the lungs and other organs should be was nothing but a red cavity. But what would really stick with her, and haunt her nightmares for years to come, was the pair of electric-blue Bermuda shorts the victim wore.

"Mary?" came the squawking radio.

Johnson swallowed, unable to answer. Now she noticed a smaller trail of blood and gore, dribbling its way into one of the small rooms that branched off from the burial chamber. The mouth of the room was dark and she couldn't see inside.

"*Mary? Do you read?*"

She slowly lifted the radio to her lips, swallowed again, found her voice. "I read you."

"What's going on?"

But Mary Johnson was slowly backing away from the sarcophagus, eyes on the little dark doorway in the far corner. No need to go in there. She'd seen enough. She continued backing up, then carefully turned her bulk around. And then, as she approached the exit to the burial chamber, something seemed to go wrong with her legs.

"Mary! We're sending security down right away! *Mary!*"

Johnson took another step, wobbled, then felt herself sink to the ground, as if borne down by an irresistible force. She rolled into a sitting position, then toppled backward almost in slow motion, coming to rest against the door lintel.

That was how they found her, eight minutes later, wide awake and staring at the ceiling, tears rolling out of her eyes.

22

Captain of Homicide Laura Hayward arrived after most of the crime scene investigation work had already been completed. She preferred it that way. She had come up through the homicide ranks and knew the scene-of-crime investigators didn't need a captain breathing down their necks to do good work.

At the entrance to the Egyptian gallery, where the crime scene perimeter had been erected, she passed through a knot of police and museum security personnel, talking in hushed, funereal voices. She spotted the museum's security director, Jack Manetti, and nodded at him to accompany her. She stepped up to the tomb's threshold, then paused, breathing in the close and dusty air, taking stock.

"Who was here last night, Mr. Manetti?" she asked.

"I have a list of all authorized employees and subcontractors. There are quite a few, but it seems all of them checked out of the museum through security except two technicians: the victim, and the one who's still missing. Jay Lipper."

Hayward nodded and began walking through the tomb, making a mental note of the progression of the rooms, stairs, passageways, building a three-dimensional image in her head. In a few minutes, she arrived at a large, pillared room. She quickly took it all in: the tables laden with computer equipment, the pizza boxes, the cables and wires running in all directions. Everything was festooned with evidence tags.

A sergeant came to greet her, a man older than her by a decade. She thought his name was Eddie Visconti. He looked competent, had a bright, clear eye, dressed neatly, deferential but only to a point. She knew it was tough for some of the rank and file to report to a woman younger than they were and twice as educated. Visconti looked as if he could handle it.

"You're the first responding officer, Sergeant?"

"Yes, ma'am. Me and my partner."

"All right. Let's have a quick summary."

"Two computer technicians worked late: Jay Lipper and Theodore DeMeo. They'd been working late every night this week—lot of pressure to open the exhibit by deadline."

She turned to Manetti. "And when's that?"

"Eight days from today."

"Proceed."

"DeMeo went out for pizza at around two, leaving Lipper behind. We checked with the pizzeria—"

"Don't tell me how you know what you know, Sergeant. Stick to the re-construction, please."

"Yes, Captain. DeMeo returned with pizza and drinks. We don't know if Lipper had already left or if he was attacked in the interim, but we do know they didn't have time to consume the food."

Hayward nodded.

"DeMeo put down the pizzas and drinks on that table and went into the burial chamber. It appears the killer was already there, and surprised him." He walked toward the burial chamber, Hayward following.

"Weapon?" Hayward asked.

"Unknown at this point. Whatever it was, it wasn't sharp. The cuts and lacerations are very ragged."

They entered the burial chamber. Hayward took in the extravagant pud-dle of blood, the smear on the stone coffin, the trail of gore into a side room, the bright yellow tags everywhere like fallen autumn leaves. She glanced around, locating each fleck of blood in turn, noting the shape and size of the droplets.

"A splatter analysis indicates the killer came at the victim from the left side with weapon raised, and brought it down in a way that partially cut through the victim's neck and severed the jugular vein. The victim fell but the perp continued to slash and cut, far more than necessary to kill. There were more than a hundred cuts to the victim's neck, head, shoulders, abdomen, legs, and buttocks."

"Any sign of a sexual motive?"

"No semen or other bodily fluids. Sex organs untouched, anal swab clean."

"Keep going."

"It appears the perp half chopped, half punched through the victim's breastbone with the weapon. Then he pulled out some of the internal organs and carried them into the Canopic Room and dumped them into a couple of very large jars."

"Did you say *pulled* out?"

"The viscera were torn away, not cut."

Hayward walked over to the small side chamber and looked in. A technician was on his hands and knees, photographing spots on the floor with a macro lens. A row of wet-evidence boxes stood against one wall, waiting to be carried away.

She looked around, trying to visualize the attack. She already knew that they were dealing with a disorganized killer, a disturbed individual, most likely a sociopath.

"After cutting out the organs," Sergeant Visconti continued, "the perp returned to the body, dragged it to the sarcophagus, and heaved it inside. Then he left by the main tomb door."

"He must've been covered with blood."

"Yes. And in fact, using a bloodhound, we've followed the trail as far as the fifth floor."

Hayward looked up sharply. This was a detail she hadn't heard before. "Not out of the museum?"

"No."

"Are you sure?"

"We can't be sure. But we found something else on the fifth floor. A shoe belonging to the missing technician, Lipper."

"Is that so? You think the killer's holding him hostage?"

Visconti grimaced. "Possible."

"Carrying his dead body?"

"Lipper was a small guy, five seven, about 135. That's also possible."

Hayward hesitated, wondering briefly what ordeal Lipper was going through now—or perhaps had already gone through. Then she turned toward Manetti.

"I want this museum sealed," she said.

The security director was sweating. "It's ten minutes to opening. We're talking two million square feet of exhibition space, two thousand staff—you can't be serious."

Hayward spoke softly. "If that's a problem, I can call Commissioner Rocker. He'll call the mayor, and the decision can come down through official channels—along with the usual shitstorm."

"That won't be necessary, Captain. I'll order the museum sealed. Temporarily."

She looked around. "Let's order up a forensic psychological profile."

"Already done," said the sergeant.

Hayward gave him an appraising glance. "We haven't worked together before, have we?"

"No, ma'am."

"It's a pleasure."

"Thank you."

She turned and walked briskly out of the room and the tomb, the others following. She crossed the length of the Egyptian gallery and approached the knot of people on the far side of the crime scene tape, gestured to Sergeant Visconti. "Are those bloodhounds still on the premises?"

"Yes."

"I want everyone here who's available, police and guards alike, to participate in searching this museum from attic to basement. Priority one: find Lipper. Assume he's alive and a hostage. Priority two: I want the killer. I want them both before the end of the day. Clear?"

"Yes, Captain."

She paused, as if remembering something. "Who's in charge of the tomb exhibit?"

"A curator named Nora Kelly," Manetti replied.

"Get her on the horn, please."

Hayward's attention was drawn to a sudden disturbance in the knot of guards and police, a voice raised in anguished pleading. A thin, slope-shouldered man in a bus driver's uniform wrenched free of two policemen and made a beeline for Hayward, his face distorted by grief.

"You!" he cried. "Help me! Find my son!"

"And you are?"

"Larry Lipper. I'm Larry Lipper. My son is Jay Lipper. He's missing, and a killer's on the loose, and I want you to find him!" The man burst into sobs. "*Find him!*"

The very intensity of his grief halted the two policemen pursuing him.

Hayward took his hand. "That's just what we're going to do, Mr. Lipper."

"*Find him! Find him!*"

Hayward looked around, spotted an officer she recognized. "Sergeant Casimirovic?"

The woman stepped forward.

Hayward gestured with her chin at Lipper's father and mouthed, "Help me out here."

The officer stepped over and, putting her arm around Larry Lipper, eased him away from Hayward. "You come with me, sir, and we'll find someplace quiet to sit down and wait." And Sergeant Casimirovic led him, crying loudly but unresisting, back through the crowd.

Manetti was at her side again, radio in hand. "I've got Kelly."

She took the radio, nodding her thanks. "Dr. Kelly? Captain Hayward, NYPD."

"How can I help?" came the voice.

"The Canopic Room in the Tomb of Senef. What's that for?"

"That's where the pharaoh's mummified organs were stored."

"Elaborate, please."

"Part of the mummification process is the removal of the pharaoh's internal organs for separate mummification and storage in canopic jars."

"The internal organs, you say?"

"That's right."

"Thank you." Hayward slowly passed the radio back to Manetti, a thoughtful look on her face.

23

ilson Bulke peered down the corridor that ran beneath the roofline of building 12. Dirty brown light struggled to penetrate the wire-mesh glass skylights, which were coated with at least a century of New York City soot. Air ducts and pipes ran in thick bundles on either side, where the rooflines almost touched the floor. Both sides of the long, low space were crammed with old collections—jars of animals floating in preservative, untidy stacks of yellowing journals, plaster models of animals—leaving a narrow passage down the center. It was a crazy, crooked space, with rooflines, pitches, and floor levels that changed half a dozen times just within eyesight. It was like a fun house at the fair, only there was nothing fun about it.

"My legs are killing me," Bulke said. "Let's take five." He eased himself down on an old wooden crate, the excess adipose tissue in his thighs stretching the material with an audible creak.

His partner, Morris, sat down lightly beside him.

"This is bullshit," said Bulke. "Day's almost over, and we're still at it. There's nobody up here."

Morris, who never saw the point in disagreeing with anybody, nodded.

"Lemme have another shot of that Jim Beam."

Morris slipped the hip flask from his pocket and passed it over. Bulke took a slug, wiped his mouth with the back of his hand, passed it back. Morris took a delicate sip himself and slid it back in.

"We shouldn't be working at all today," said Bulke. "This is supposed to be our day off. We're entitled to a little refreshment."

"That's the way I look at it, too," said Morris.

"You were smart to bring that along."

"Never go anywhere without it."

Bulke glanced at his watch. Four-forty. The light filtering in through the skylights was slowly dying, the shadows deepening in the corners. Night would be coming soon. And with this section of the attics undergoing repairs and currently without electricity, that meant switching to flashlights, making their search all the more annoying.

Bulke felt the creeping warmth of the whiskey in his gut. He sighed heavily, leaned his elbows on his knees, looked around. "Look at that shit, will you?" He gestured at a series of low metal shelves beneath the eaves, filled with countless glass jars containing jellyfish. "You think they actually *study* this crap?"

Morris shrugged.

Bulke reached out, fished a jar off the shelf, took a closer look. A whitish blob floated in the amber liquid, amidst drifting tentacles. He gave the jar a quick shake; when the turbulence settled, the jellyfish had been reduced to swirling shreds.

"Broke into a million pieces." He showed the jar to Morris. "Hope it wasn't *important*." He issued a guffaw and, with a roll of his eyes, shoved the jar back onto the shelf.

"In China, they eat 'em," said Morris. He was a third-generation museum guard and considered he knew a great deal more about the museum than the other guards.

"Eat what? Jellyfish?"

Morris nodded sagely.

"Frigging Chinese'll eat anything."

"They say they're crunchy." Morris sniffed, wiped his nose.

"Gross." Bulke looked around. "This is bullshit," he repeated. "There's nothing up here."

"The thing I don't get," Morris said, "is why they're reopening that tomb, anyway. I told you how my granddad used to talk about something that happened in there back in the thirties."

"Yeah, you've been telling everybody and his brother about that."

"Something real bad."

"Tell me some other time." Bulke glanced at his watch again. If they *really* thought there was something up there, they would have sent cops—not two unarmed guards.

"You don't think the killer dragged the body up here?" Morris asked.

"No way. Why the hell would he do that?"

"But the dogs—"

"How could those bloodhounds smell anything up here? The place reeks. They lost the trail down on the fifth floor, anyway—not up here."

"I suppose you're right."

"I *am* right. As far as I'm concerned, we're done up here." Bulke rose, slapped the dust off his butt.

"What about the rest of the attics?"

"We did 'em all, don't you remember?" Bulke winked.

"Right. Oh, right. Yeah."

"There's no exit up ahead, but there's a stairwell back a ways. We'll go down there."

Bulke turned, began shuffling in the direction from which they'd come. The attic corridor wandered up and down, so tight in places that he had to turn sideways to get through. The museum consisted of dozens of separate buildings joined together, and where they met the floor levels sometimes differed so greatly they had to be linked by metal staircases. They passed through a space filled with leering wooden idols, labeled *Nootka Graveposts*; another space filled with plaster casts of arms and legs; then yet another filled with casts of faces.

Bulke paused to catch his breath. A twilight gloom had descended. The face casts hung everywhere on the walls, white faces with their eyes closed, each one with a name attached. They all seemed to be Indians: *Antelope Killer, Little Finger Nail, Two Clouds, Frost on Grass . . .*

"Think all these are death masks?" asked Morris.

"Death masks? What do you mean, death masks?"

"You know. When you're dead, they take a cast of your face."

"I wouldn't know. Say, how about another shot of Mr. Beam?"

Morris obligingly removed the flask. Bulke took a swig, passed it back.

"What's that?" Morris asked, gesturing with the flask.

Bulke peered in the indicated direction. A wallet lay tossed in the corner, spread open, credit cards spilling out. He went over, picked it up.

"Shit, there must be two hundred bucks in here. What do we do?"

"Check out who it belongs to."

"What does that matter? Probably one of the curators." Bulke searched through, pulled out the driver's license.

"Jay Mark Lipper," he read, then looked at Morris. "Oh, shit. That's the missing guy."

Feeling a strange stickiness, he looked down at his hand. It was smeared with blood.

Bulke dropped the wallet with a jerk, then kicked it back into the corner with his foot. He felt abruptly nauseous. "Man," he said in a high, strained voice. "Oh, man . . ."

"You think the killer dropped it?" Morris asked.

Bulke felt his heart thumping in his chest. He looked around at all the shadowy spaces, the shelves covered with the leering faces of the dead.

"We gotta call Manetti," said Morris.

"Gimme a moment . . . Just gimme a moment here." Bulke tried to think through a fog of surprise and rising fear. "Why didn't we see this on the way in?"

"Maybe it wasn't there."

"So the killer's up ahead."

Morris hesitated. "I hadn't thought of that."

Bulke felt blood pounding in his temples. "If he's in front of us, we're trapped. There's no other way out."

Morris said nothing. His face looked yellow in the dim light. He pulled out his radio.

"Morris calling Central, Morris calling Central. Do you read?"

A steady hiss of static.

Bulke tried his radio, but the result was the same. "Jesus, this frigging museum is full of dead spots. You'd think with all the money they've spent on security, they'd put in a few more repeaters."

"Let's start moving. Maybe we'll get reception in another room." And Morris started forward.

"Not that way!" Bulke said. "He's ahead of us, remember?"

"We don't know that. Maybe we missed the wallet on the way in."

Bulke looked down at his bloody hand, the nausea growing in his gut.

"We can't just *stay* here," Morris said.

Bulke nodded. "All right. But move slowly."

It was now twilight in the attics, and Bulke slipped his flashlight out of its holster and flicked it on. They moved through the doorway to the next attic, Bulke flashing the light around. This space was crammed with elongated heads carved from black volcanic stone, packed so tightly that the two could just squeeze down the center.

"Try your radio," Bulke said in a low voice.

Again, nothing.

The attic corridor took a ninety-degree angle into a tight warren of cubicle-like rooms: rusted metal shelves stacked with cardboard cartons, each carton overflowing with tiny glass boxes. Bulke shone his light over them. Each contained a huge black beetle.

As they reached the end of the third cubicle, a crash came from the darkness ahead of them, dying away in a rattle of falling glass.

Bulke jumped. "Crap! What was that?"

"I don't know," said Morris. His voice was trembling and strained.

"He's ahead of us."

As they waited, another crash came.

"Jesus, sounds like someone's trashing the place."

More shattering glass, followed by a bestial, inarticulate scream.

Bulke backed up, groping for his own radio. "Bulke calling Central! Do you read?"

"This is Central Security, ten-four."

Crash! Another gargled scream.

"Jesus, we got a maniac up here! We're trapped!"

"Your location, Bulke?" came the calm voice.

"The attics, building 12! Section 5, maybe 6. Someone's up here, tearing up the place! We found the missing victim's wallet, too. Lipper's. What do we do?"

A hiss of static, the reply breaking up.

"I can't read you!"

"... retreat ... do not engage ... back ..."

"Retreat where? We're trapped, didn't you hear me?"

"... do not approach ..."

Another deafening crash, closer this time. The stench of alcohol and dead specimens wafted back through the darkness. Bulke backed up, screaming into the radio. "Send up the cops! Get a SWAT team up here! *We're trapped!*"

More static.

"Morris, try yours!"

When Morris didn't answer, Bulke turned. The radio lay on the floor, and Morris was running like hell down the crooked passageway, away from the noise, disappearing into the gloom.

"Morris! Wait!" Bulke tried to ship the radio, dropped it instead, and heaved along after Morris, putting one huge slow thigh after the other, desperately trying to overcome the inertia of his enormous body. He could hear the tearing, smashing, screaming thing coming up behind him, fast.

"Wait! *Morris!*"

A shelf covered with specimen jars went over with a massive crash behind him, and there was the sudden ripping stench of alcohol and rotting fish.

"No!"

Bulke lumbered forward as awkwardly as a walrus, groaning with both fear and effort, his fleshy arms and chest jiggling with each footfall.

Another scream, feral and chillingly inhuman, tore the darkness just behind him. He turned but could see nothing in the darkness except the flash of metal, the dim blur of movement.

"Noooo!"

He tripped and fell, the flashlight hitting the floor and rolling away, the beam wobbling crazily off the rows of jars before spotlighting a gape-mouthed fish floating upside down in a jar. He struggled, clawing the floor, trying to rise, but the screaming thing fell upon him as swiftly as a bat. He rolled, swatting feebly at it, hearing the tearing of cloth and then feeling the sudden biting sting of his flesh being slashed.

"*Noooooooo——!*"

24

Nora sat at a small baize-covered table in an open vault of the Secure Area, waiting. She was surprised at how easy it had been to gain access—Menzies had been instrumental in helping her with the paperwork. The fact was that very few curators, even the top ones, were allowed access without jumping through all sorts of bureaucratic hoops. The Secure Area wasn't just used for storing the most valuable and controversial collections—it was also where some of the museum's most sensitive papers were kept. It was a mark of how important the Tomb of Senef was to the museum that she had gotten access so quickly—and after five o'clock, at that, even while the museum was in a state of high alert.

The archivist appeared from the gloomy file room carrying a yellowing folder, placed it in front of her. "Got it."

"Great."

"Sign here."

"I'm expecting my colleague, Dr. Wicherly," she said, signing the form and handing it back to the archivist.

"I have the paperwork for him all ready to go."

"Thank you."

The woman nodded. "I'll lock you in now."

The archivist shut the vault door, leaving Nora in silence. She stared at the slender file, feeling a prickle of curiosity. It was marked simply *Tomb of Senef: correspondence, documents, 1933–35.*

She opened it. The first item was a typewritten letter, on elaborate stationery with a gold and red embossing. It was written by the Bey of Bolbassa, and it must have been the one described in the newspaper articles Nora had seen, full of assertions that the tomb was cursed—an obvious ploy to get the tomb back for Egypt.

She turned to the next documents: lengthy police reports from one Detective Sergeant Gerald O'Bannion, handwritten in the beautiful script once standard in America. She scanned the reports with interest, then reviewed the mass of papers beyond: memos and letters to city officials and the police in what appeared to have been a successful effort to squelch the real story described in the police reports and keep it from the press. She paged through the documents, fascinated by the tale they told, finally understanding why the museum had been so anxious to shut down the tomb.

She jumped when a faint tone announced that the vault door was opening. Turning, she saw the sleek, dapper form of Adrian Wicherly, leaning against the metal jamb, smiling.

"Hello, Nora."

"Hi."

He straightened up, giving his suit a little tug, adjusting his already perfect Windsor knot. "What's a nice girl like you doing in a dusty old place like this?"

"Have you signed in?"

"*Je suis en règle,*" he said with a little laugh, coming forward and leaning over her shoulder. She could smell expensive aftershave and mouthwashed breath. "What have we here?"

The archivist looked in. "Ready to be locked in?"

"Do. Lock us in." And Wicherly winked at Nora.

"Why don't you take a seat, Adrian?" she said coolly.

"Don't mind if I do." He pulled an old wooden chair up to the table, dusted the seat with a swipe of a silk handkerchief, and eased himself down.

"Any skeletons in the closet?" he asked Nora, leaning in.

"Definitely."

Wicherly was a bit too close and Nora edged away as subtly as she could. Although Wicherly had initially come across as the acme of good breeding, lately his smarmy winks and fingertip caresses had led her to believe he was operating more on the glandular level than she had initially thought. Still, things had remained on a professional level and she hoped they would continue that way.

"Do tell," Wicherly said.

"I've just skimmed the documents, so I don't have the full story, but here it is in brief. On the morning of March 3, 1933, the guards arriving to open the tomb realized it had been broken into. A lot of objects were vandalized. The mummy was missing, later found in an adjacent room, badly mutilated. When they looked in the sarcophagus, they found a different body in it. A freshly murdered body, as it happened."

"Amazing! Just like that fellow, what's-his-name. DeMeo."

"Sort of, except the resemblance stops there. The body belonged to Julia Cavendish, a wealthy New York socialite. She just happened to be the granddaughter of William C. Spragg."

"Spragg?"

"He was the man who bought the tomb from the last Baron Rattray and had it shipped to the museum."

"I see."

"Cavendish was a patroness of the museum. She appears to have had a rather notorious reputation as—well, for want of a better term, a female rake."

"How so?"

"She went to bars and picked up young working-class men—longshoremen, stevedores, and the like."

"And did what with them?" Wicherly asked with a leer.

"Use your imagination, Adrian," she said dryly. "Anyway, her body had been mutilated, but the papers don't offer details."

"Strong stuff for the thirties, I should say."

"Yes. The family and the museum were desperate to cover it up—

for different reasons, of course—and it seems they managed quite nicely."

"I imagine the press was a bit more cooperative in those days. Not the muckraking chaps we have today."

Nora wondered if Wicherly knew her husband was a reporter. "Anyway, the investigation into Cavendish's murder was still ongoing when it happened again. This time the mutilated body belonged to Mongomery Bolt, apparently a collateral descendant of John Jacob Astor, a remittance man and a sort of black sheep in the family. The tomb was now being guarded at night, but the murderer sapped the guard before dumping Bolt's body in the sarcophagus. A note was found on the body. There's a copy of it in this file."

She pulled out a yellowed sheet. On it was an Eye of Horus and several other hieroglyphs. Wicherly looked at it in bemusement.

"'The Curse of Ammut Strikes All Who Enter,'" he intoned. "Whoever wrote this was ignorant. The chap barely knew his hieroglyphs. They aren't even drawn properly. A crude fake."

"Yes. They realized that right away." She turned over some more papers. "Here's the police report on that crime."

"The plot thickens." Wicherly winked, edged his seat closer.

"The police took notice of the link to John Jacob Astor. He'd helped finance the installation of the Tomb of Senef. The police began to wonder if someone wasn't taking revenge on those responsible for bringing the tomb to the museum. Naturally, their suspicions fell on the Bey of Bolbassa."

"The fellow who claimed the tomb was cursed."

"Right. He'd gotten the newspapers all stirred up against the museum. Turns out he wasn't even a real bey—whatever that is. There's a report here on his background."

Wicherly picked it up, sniffed. "Former carpet merchant, made a lot of money."

"Again, the museum, along with the Astor family, was able to successfully quash any publicity—except it was impossible to stop the rumors circulating inside the museum itself. In time, the authorities established that the Bey of Bolbassa had returned to Egypt just before the killings, but they suspected he had hired operatives in New York. If he did, though, they were too clever to get caught. And when the third killing occurred—"

"Another?"

"This time it was an elderly lady who lived in the neighborhood. It took them a while to figure out the connection—turns out she was distantly descended from Cahors, the man who originally found the tomb. By now, the museum was boiling with rumors, and they were spreading to the general populace. Every crank spiritualist, medium, and tarot-card reader was converging on the museum, and New Yorkers were only too eager to believe the tomb was really cursed."

"Credulous fools."

"Perhaps. In any case, it just about emptied the museum. The police investigation wasn't going anywhere, and so the museum decided to take preemptive action. Using the pretext of the construction of the 81st Street station pedestrian tunnel, they closed the tomb and sealed it up. The killings stopped, the rumors gradually died down, and the Tomb of Senef was mostly forgotten."

"And the murder cases?"

"Never solved. Although they were convinced the bey was behind them, they couldn't get proof."

Wicherly rose from his chair. "That's quite a story, Nora."

"It certainly is."

"What are you going to do with it?"

"On the one hand, it might make an interesting sidebar to the history of the tomb. But I have a sense the museum wouldn't be too keen on publicizing it, and I'm not sure I'd like to, either. I'd rather focus on the archaeology, on teaching people about ancient Egypt."

"I agree with you, Nora."

"There's another reason, maybe even more important. This new murder in the museum—it has some resemblances to the old ones. People will talk, rumors will start."

"Rumors have already started."

"Well, yes. I've been hearing quite a few myself. At any rate, we don't want anything derailing this opening."

"Very true."

"Good. I'll write Menzies a report, with our recommendation that none of this is relevant and that it shouldn't be publicized." She closed the folder. "That settles it, then."

There was a silence. Wicherly had risen from his seat and was once again standing behind her, glancing down at the scattered papers of the file. He reached over and picked one up, perused it, put it back down. She felt his hand on her shoulder and stiffened.

A moment later, she felt his lips on the nape of her neck, barely touching her skin, caressing her as lightly as a butterfly.

She rose abruptly and turned. He stood close to her, blue eyes flashing. "I'm sorry if I startled you." He smiled, displaying his porcelain rack. "I couldn't help myself. I find you devastatingly attractive, Nora."

He continued smiling at her, radiating self-confidence and charm, elegant and more handsome than any man deserved to be.

"In case you hadn't noticed, I'm married," she said.

"We'll have a grand time and nobody need ever know."

"*I* will know."

He smiled, put a caressing hand on her shoulder. "I want to make love to you, Nora."

She took a deep breath. "Adrian, you're a charming and intelligent man. I'm sure that many women would like to make love to you, too."

She could see his smile broadening.

"But I'm not one of them."

"But, my lovely Nora—"

"Wasn't that plain enough for you? I haven't the slightest interest in making love to you, Adrian—even if I weren't married."

Wicherly stood there, dumbfounded, his face struggling to comprehend the sudden reversal of his expectations.

"I don't mean to be insulting, just unambiguous, since my earlier efforts to telegraph my lack of interest don't seem to have penetrated. Please don't make me be any more hurtful than necessary."

She saw the blood drain from his face. His easy self-possession vanished for a moment, exposing what Nora had begun to suspect: a spoiled child blessed with good looks and brilliance, who had developed the firm belief that whatever he wanted, he should get.

He began to stammer something that might have been intended as an apology, and Nora let her voice soften. "Look, Adrian, let's just forget it, okay? This never happened. We'll never mention it again."

"Quite right, yes. Very decent of you, thank you, Nora."

His face was now flaming with embarrassment, and he looked crushed. She couldn't help but feel sorry for him. She wondered if she was perhaps the first woman ever to turn him down.

"I've got a report to write for Menzies," she said as gently and lightly as possible. "And I believe you need a bit of fresh air. Why not take a brisk turn around the museum?"

"Yes, good suggestion, thank you."

"I'll see you in a bit."

"Yes."

And, moving as stiffly as a machine, Wicherly went to the intercom and pressed the button to be released. When the vault door opened, he vanished without another word, and Nora was once again left in peace to take notes and make her report.

25

D'Agosta turned the wheel of the meat van and slowed, guiding it out of the woods. Herkmoor rose ahead of him, a brilliant cluster of sodium lights bathing the maze of walls, towers, and cellblocks in an unreal topaz light. As he approached the first set of gates, he continued to slow, passing a cluster of warning signs telling drivers to have their paperwork in order and to expect a search, followed by a list of forbidden items so long it took two billboards to name them all: everything from fireworks to heroin.

D'Agosta took a deep breath, tried to calm his unsettled nerves. He'd been in prisons before, of course, but always on official business. Driving in like this, bent on some extremely *un*official business, was asking for trouble. Real trouble.

He stopped at the first chain-link gate. A guard came out of a pillbox and sauntered over, carrying a clipboard.

"You're early tonight," he said.

D'Agosta shrugged. "It's my first time up here. Left early, in case I got lost."

The guard grunted, shoved the clipboard in the window. D'Agosta attached his paperwork and handed it back. The guard flipped through it with the tip of a pencil, nodding.

"Know the drill?"

"Not really," D'Agosta answered truthfully.

"You'll get this back on your way out. Show your ID at the next checkpoint."

"Gotcha."

The chain-link gate withdrew on wheels, making a rattling noise.

D'Agosta eased forward, feeling his heart hammering in his chest. Glinn claimed to have planned everything down to the last iota—and had, with remarkable ease, secured his employment under an assumed name with the meatpacking company and arranged for him to get this route. But the fact was, you could never predict what people might do. That was where he and Glinn parted opinion. This little adventure could turn to shit in a heartbeat.

He drove the truck up to the second gate and, once again, a guard came out.

"ID?"

D'Agosta handed him the false driver's license and permit. The man looked them over. "New man?"

"Yeah."

"You familiar with the layout?"

"It wouldn't hurt to hear it again."

"Go straight through, then bear to the right. When you see the loading dock, back up to the first bay."

"Got it."

"You can exit the vehicle to supervise the unloading. You may not handle any of the merchandise or assist prison personnel. Stay with the vehicle at all times. As soon as you're unloaded, you leave. Understood?"

"Sure."

The guard spoke briefly into a radio and the final chain-link gate rolled up.

As D'Agosta eased the van through and made the right turn, he slipped his hand into his jacket pocket and removed a pint of Rebel Yell bourbon. He unscrewed the cap and took a slug, swishing it carefully around in his mouth before swallowing. He could feel the fiery bolus burn down his gullet into his stomach. He shook a few drops on his coat for good measure and slipped the bottle back into his jacket pocket.

In a moment, he had backed up to the loading dock. Two men in coveralls were already waiting, and as soon as he unlocked the back, they began off-loading the boxes and sides of frozen meat.

D'Agosta watched, hands in his pockets, whistling tunelessly. He glanced surreptitiously at his watch, then turned to a worker. "Say, you got a restroom around here?"

"Sorry. Not allowed."

"But I've gotta go."

"It's against the rules." The worker hefted two boxes of meats to his shoulders and disappeared into the back.

D'Agosta buttonholed the next man. "Look, I've *really* gotta go."

"You heard him. It's against the rules."

"Man, please don't tell me that."

The man put down his box and stared at D'Agosta with a long, tired look. "When you get out of here, you can piss in the woods. Okay?" He lifted the box.

"It ain't pissing I got to do."

"That's not my problem." He hoisted up the box and carried it off.

As the first man approached again, D'Agosta stepped in front of him, blocking his access and breathing heavily into the man's face. "This is no joke. I need to pinch one off, and I mean *now.*"

The man wrinkled up his nose and stepped back. He glanced at his fellow worker. "He's been drinking."

"What's that?" D'Agosta said belligerently. "What did you say?"

The man returned the look coolly. "I said, you've been drinking."

"Bullshit."

"I can smell it." He turned to his co-worker. "Get the super."

"What the hell for? You gonna give me a Breathalyzer?"

The other worker disappeared and a moment later he came back with a tall, grim-looking man incongruously dressed in a black blazer, with a belly that hung over his belt like a sack of grain.

"What seems to be the problem?" the supervisor asked.

"I think he's been drinking, sir," said the first worker.

The man hooked up his belt and stepped toward D'Agosta. "That right?"

"No, it isn't right!" D'Agosta said, getting in his face and breathing hard with indignation.

The man backed off, unshipped his radio.

"Look, I'm leaving," D'Agosta said, trying to make himself sound suddenly accommodating. "I've got a long drive to get back to the warehouse. This place is in the middle of frigging nowhere and it's six o'clock at night."

"You're not going anywhere, pal." The supervisor spoke briefly into the radio, then turned to one of the workers. "Take him into staff dining and have him wait there."

"Come this way, sir."

"This is bullshit. I'm not going anywhere."

"Come this way, *sir.*"

Grudgingly, D'Agosta followed the guard through the loading dock and into a large pantry, empty, dark, and smelling strongly of Clorox. They passed through a door in the far wall into a smaller room where, it seemed, the kitchen staff took their own meals when they were not on shift.

"Have a seat."

D'Agosta sat down at one of the stainless-steel tables. The man took a seat at the next table, folded his arms, looked away. A few minutes passed and the supervisor returned, an armed guard at his side.

"Stand up," the super said.

D'Agosta complied.

The super turned toward the guard. "Search him."

"You can't do that! I know my rights, and—"

"And this is a federal prison. It's all spelled out on the signs in front, if you bothered to read them. We have the right to search anyone at will."

"Don't you frigging touch me."

"Sir, at the moment, you've got a medium-sized problem. If you don't cooperate, you're going to have a *big* problem."

"Yeah? What kind of a problem?"

"How does resisting a federal law enforcement officer sound? Now, last time: raise your arms."

After a moment's hesitation, D'Agosta did as he was ordered. A pat-down quickly brought to light the pint bottle of Rebel Yell.

The guard pulled out the bottle, shaking his head sadly. He turned to the supervisor. "What now?" he asked.

"Call the local police department. Have them pick him up. A drunk driver is their problem, not ours."

"But I just took one sip!"

The supervisor turned back. "Sit down and shut up."

D'Agosta sat down again a little unsteadily, muttering to himself.

"And the truck?" the guard asked.

"Call his company. Have them send someone to pick it up."

"It's after six, there won't be any management there, and—"

"Call them in the morning, then. The truck isn't going anywhere."

"Yes, sir."

The supervisor glanced at the guard. "Stay here with him until the police arrive."

"Yes, sir."

The supervisor left. The guard sat down at the farthest table, eyeing D'Agosta balefully.

"I gotta go to the head," said D'Agosta.

The guard sighed heavily but said nothing.

"Well?"

The guard rose, scowling. "I'll take you."

"You gonna hold my hand while I take a dump, or can I do it by myself?"

The scowl deepened. "It's just down the hall, second door on the right. Hurry it up."

D'Agosta rose with a flabby sigh and walked slowly to the lunch-room door, opened it, and staggered through, holding on to the door-knob for support. As soon as the door closed, he turned left and ran silently down a long, empty corridor past a series of fortified lunch-rooms, barred doors all standing open. He ducked into the last one and yanked off the white driver's uniform, revealing a light tan shirt, which, with the dark brown pants he was wearing, gave him an uncanny resemblance to a typical Herkmoor guard. He stuffed the old shirt into a trash can at the door. Continuing down the hall, he passed a lit station. He nodded to the two officers as he walked by.

Beyond the station, he slipped a specially modified pen from his pocket, pulled off the cap, and began walking down the corridor, holding it in his hand, videotaping. He walked easily, nonchalantly, like a guard on his rounds, moving the pen this way and that, giving special attention to the placement of the security cameras and other high-tech sensing devices.

At last he ducked into a men's room, headed to the second-to-last stall, and closed the door. Digging into the crotch of his pants, he pulled out a small, sealed plastic bag and a small roll of duct tape. He stood on the toilet, lifted a ceiling tile, and used the duct tape to affix the bag to the upper side of the tile. Then he lowered the tile back in place. *Score one to Eli Glinn.* The man had insisted the pat-down would stop as soon as the bottle of booze was discovered—and he had been right.

Exiting the bathroom, D'Agosta continued down the hall. Moments later, he heard an alarm go off—not a loud one, just a high-pitched beeping. He walked to the end of the empty corridor, where he was confronted by a set of double doors with a magnetic security lock. Here, he removed his wallet, took out a certain credit card, and swiped it through the door.

A light turned green and he heard the whir and click of the lock disengaging.

Score another to Glinn. He quickly ducked through.

He was now in a small exercise yard, empty at this late hour, with high cinder-block walls on three sides and a chain-link fence on the other. He looked around, verifying that there was no security camera watching him: as Glinn had pointed out, even a prison as high-tech as Herkmoor had to limit its cameras to the most vital areas.

D'Agosta strolled around the yard quickly, videotaping all the while. Then, returning the pen to his pocket, he stepped toward one wall, loosened his belt and unzipped his pants, and removed a rolled sheet of Mylar, which had been strapped to the inside of his leg. He glanced over his shoulder, then stuffed the Mylar tube into a drainpipe in the corner of the yard, hooking it in place with a bent bobby pin.

This accomplished, he moved to the chain-link fence, put a hand on it, pulled at it gingerly. This was the part he really, really wasn't looking forward to.

Pulling a small pair of wire cutters from his socks, he snipped a three-foot vertical row of the chain links, directly behind one of the metal fence posts. He made sure the cut ends rejoined, the fence looking fully intact, and then he lobbed the wire cutters onto the nearest roof, where it would be a long time before they were found. He walked along the fence for half a dozen yards, taking a steadying breath, then another. Looking through the chain link, he could see the vague forms of the guard towers in the darkness beyond. He swallowed, rubbed his hands together. And then he hoisted himself up the chain link and began to climb.

Halfway up, he saw a colored wire strip woven through the chain link. As he passed it, a shrill alarm went off in the yard. Half a dozen sodium vapor lights snapped on around him. There was an immediate response from the guard towers along the perimeter: lights swiveled around, and in a moment they located him on the fence. He continued to climb to the top, and then, steadying himself, and concealing the movement with his arm, he pulled the pen from his pocket, aimed it through the link, and began videotaping the no-man's-land beyond and below him, now starkly illuminated by the lights focused on him.

"You are under surveillance!" came a bullhorned voice from the nearest tower. "Stop immediately!"

From over his shoulder, D'Agosta saw six guards burst into the yard and run like hell toward him. He replaced the pen in his pocket and glanced along the top edge of the fence. Two wires ran through the chain link here, one white, the other red. He grasped the red one, yanked as hard as he could.

Another alarm went off.

"Halt!"

The guards had reached the bottom of the fence and were climbing up after him. He felt first one, then two, then half a dozen hands grasping at his feet and legs. After a brief show of struggle, he let himself be dragged back down into the yard.

Guns drawn, they surrounded him in a circle. "Who the hell is this?" one barked. "Who are you?"

D'Agosta sat up. "I'm the truck driver," he said, slurring his words.

"The what?" another guard said.

"I just heard about this one. He did the meat delivery, got pulled off because he was drunk."

D'Agosta groaned and cradled his arm. "You hurt me."

"Jesus, you're right. He's drunk as a lord."

"I just took one sip."

"On your feet."

D'Agosta tried to rise, staggered. One of them caught his forearm and helped him up. There was a snicker. "He thought he was going to escape."

"Come on, pal."

The guards escorted him back to the kitchen, where his guard was standing, red-faced, along with the supervisor.

The super rounded on him. "What the hell do you think you're doing?"

D'Agosta slurred his words. "Got lost on the way to the john. Decided to blow the joint." He gave a drunken laugh.

More snickers.

The supervisor was not amused. "How did you get out into the yard?"

"What yard?"

"Outside."

"I dunno. Door was unlocked, I guess."

"That's impossible."

D'Agosta shrugged, slumped down in the chair, and promptly nodded off.

"Go check the yard 4 access," the supervisor snapped at one of the guards. Then he turned back to the first guard. "You *stay* here with him.

Do you understand? Don't let him go anywhere. Let him shit his pants if necessary."

"Yes, sir."

"Thank Christ he didn't make it over the fence and into no-man's-land. Do you know what a paperwork headache that would have caused?"

"Yes, sir. I'm sorry, sir."

D'Agosta noticed, to his great relief, that in the confusion and commotion, nobody noticed his shirt was a different color than before. *Score three to Glinn.*

At that moment, two local cops came in, looking bewildered. "This the guy?"

"Yeah." The guard prodded D'Agosta with his riot stick. "Wake up, asshole."

D'Agosta roused himself, stood up.

The policemen seemed at a loss. "So what do we do? We gotta sign something?"

The supervisor wiped his brow. "What do you do? Lock him up for drunk driving."

One of the policemen removed a notebook. "Break any laws on the premises? You filing any charges?"

A short silence followed, the guards glancing at each other.

"No," said the supervisor. "Just get him the hell out of here. After that, he's your headache. I don't want to see him around here, ever again."

He shut the notebook. "All right, we'll take him downtown, give him a Breathalyzer. Come on, pal."

"I'll pass! I only took one sip!"

"If that's the case, you don't have much to worry about, now, do you?" said the cop wearily as he led D'Agosta out the door.

26

Captain of Homicide Laura Hayward arrived on the scene a minute or two after the paramedics. She could hear the shrieks of the victim ringing down through the attic rooms, and they warmed her heart: nobody who was going to be dead any time soon could squall that lustily.

She ducked through a series of low doors until she arrived at the crime scene tape. With relief, she saw it was Sergeant Visconti and his partner, an officer named Martin.

"Brief me," she said as she approached.

"We were the closest team to the attack," Visconti replied. "We scared off the perp. He was bent over the victim, working him over. When he saw us approaching, he fled back into the attics."

"Get a look at him?"

"Just a shadow."

"Weapon?"

"Unknown."

She nodded.

"We also found Lipper's wallet." Visconti gestured with his chin toward a plastic evidence box, lined up with several others just outside the tape.

Hayward leaned over, opened the box. "I want a full battery on the wallet and everything inside—DNA, latents, trace fibers, the works.

And freeze a dozen swabs of blood and a dozen of organics for future workups."

"Yes, Captain."

"Is the other guard around, what's-his-name—Morris? I'd like to talk to him."

Visconti spoke into his radio, and a moment later a cop appeared at the far edge of the scene, leading the other guard. The man's comb-over was in disarray, hanging like a flap down the side of his head, and his clothes were disheveled. He stank of alcohol preservative.

"You okay?" she asked. "Able to talk?"

"I think so." His voice was high and breathy.

"Did you see the attack?"

"No. I was . . . too far away, and my back was turned."

"But you must have seen or heard something in the moments before it occurred."

Morris struggled to concentrate. "Well, there was this . . . scream-ing. Like an animal. And breaking glass. Then something came rushing out from the darkness . . ." His voice trailed off.

"Some*thing*? It wasn't a person?"

Morris's eyes slid from side to side. "It was just, like, a screaming, rushing shape."

Hayward turned to another of the officers. "Take Mr. Morris downstairs and have Detective Sergeant Whittier question him further."

"Yes, Captain."

Two EMTs came into view from behind a mountain of stacked boxes, pushing a stretcher with an enormous, groaning mound on top.

"What's his state?" she asked.

"Lacerated with what looks like a crude knife, or maybe a claw."

"Claw?"

The technician shrugged. "Some of the cuts are pretty ragged. Luckily, none of them reached vital organs—one advantage to being fat. Some blood loss, shock . . . He'll recover."

"Can he talk?"

"You're welcome to give it a shot," said an EMT. "He's been se-dated."

Hayward leaned over. The guard's damp, bulging face stared at the ceiling. The smell of liquor, formaldehyde, and dead fish assaulted her nostrils.

She spoke gently. "Wilson Bulke?"

His eyes flickered toward her, away again.

"I'd like to ask you a few questions."

No clear response.

"Mr. Bulke, did you see your attacker?"

The eyes gyrated in their sockets, and his wet mouth opened. "The . . . *face.*"

"What face? What did it look like?"

"Twisted . . . Oh, *God* . . ."

He groaned, mumbled something unintelligible.

"Can you be more specific, sir? Male or female?"

A whimper, a brief shake of the head.

"One, or more than one?"

"One," came the croaked reply.

Hayward looked at the EMT. He shrugged.

She turned, gestured to a detective waiting nearby. "Stay with him on the way to the hospital. If he becomes more coherent, get a complete description of his attacker. I want to know what we're up against."

"Yes, Captain."

She straightened up, looked around at the small group of police. "Whoever or whatever this is, we've got it cornered. I want us to go in. Now."

"Shouldn't we call for a SWAT team?" said Visconti.

"It would take hours before a SWAT team could gear up and get over here. And their rules of engagement are so ponderous they'd slow everything down. There was fresh blood on that wallet—there's a chance Lipper might still be alive and a hostage." She looked around. "I want you three to come with me: Sergeant Visconti, Officer Martin, and Detective Sergeant O'Connor."

There was a silence. The three officers exchanged glances.

"Is there a problem? It's four against one."

More hesitant looks.

She sighed. "Don't tell me you boys have bought into the rumors the museum guards are spreading? What, you think we're going to get jammed up by a mummy?"

Visconti colored, and by way of answer removed his weapon and gave it a quick check. The others followed suit.

"Turn off your radios, cell phones, pagers, everything. I don't want to be creeping up on the perp and suddenly hear Beethoven's Fifth coming from your BlackBerry."

They nodded.

Hayward took out a photocopy she'd requested of the attic layout of the museum and pressed it flat on a box. "Okay. This section of the attic is divided into sixteen narrow rooms—here—divided into two long lines under parallel roofs, with a connecting passage at the far end. Think of it as a U. Besides the stairway down, there's only one possible escape route: a rooftop accessible through this row of windows, here. I've already had it covered. The skylights are supposed to be barred. Which means the only way for the killer to escape is through us . . . He's cornered."

She paused, looked at them each in turn. "We advance in pairs: quick observation of each room and retreat, then move and cover. I'll partner with O'Connor. Martin, you and Visconti stay a half-room behind. Don't overcommit. And remember: we've got to proceed under the assumption—the hope—that Lipper's still alive and being held hostage. We can't risk killing him. Only if you have verification that Lipper's already wasted can you use deadly force—and then only if absolutely necessary. Are we clear on this?"

They all nodded.

"I'll lead."

When none of the three protested or made the usual faux-gallant comments about its being a job for a man, Hayward took it as a sign that women were finally being accepted in the force. Or maybe the three were just scared silent.

They stepped carefully through the crime scene, Hayward leading, O'Connor at her heels. The floor was smeared with blood, and a shelf of specimen jars lay where it had fallen, shards of glass and the broken,

putrid remains of eels scattered in puddles of foul-smelling preservative. They moved past the guard at the far end of the crime scene and
into the next room of the attic. The temporary lights set up around the
crime scene were fainter here, cloaking the room in near-darkness.

Hayward and O'Connor moved to either side of the doorway. She
gave a quick peek inside, ducked back, nodded to O'Connor, then proceeded.

Empty. More shelves had been thrown over, the glass littering the
floor, filling the room with the choking stench of preservative. These
jars seemed to have been filled with small rodents. A pile of papers had
been dashed about and numerous stored objects flung helter-skelter. It
reminded her, in a way, of the preliminary autopsy report on DeMeo:
the killer had rooted about haphazardly among his internal organs, ripping and pulling stuff out with a kind of crazy, disorganized violence.
A sick kind of vandalism.

She crept up to the next door, waited until the others were in position, ducked around for a visual. Another room, like the previous, completely trashed. One of the dingy skylights had been broken, but the
bars above it were still intact. No escape that way.

She froze, suddenly listening. A faint sound was echoing back from
the dark attics beyond.

"Hush!" she whispered. "Hear that?"

It was a strange kind of stumbling, limping gait: a dragging sound,
followed by an unsettling thump: Draaag-*thump*. Draaag-*thump*.

Hayward moved into the next room, almost pitch-dark now. Pulling
out her flashlight, she used it to illuminate the dark corners. The room
contained thousands of plaster faces—death masks—staring at them
from every square foot of wall surface. Some of the masks showed
signs of recent damage: someone, apparently the killer, had slashed at
the masks, gouging out their eyes, leaving smears of blood everywhere.

The lights were off in the next room. Crouching beside the door
frame of the next room, Hayward gestured for the men behind to stay
put.

She leaned forward, listening intently. The strange sound had ceased: the killer was waiting, listening. She sensed, rather than knew, that he was near: very near.

She could feel the level of tension within their little group rising. Better to keep going: the less thinking the better.

Hayward ducked forward, swept the room with her flashlight, then ducked back again as quickly as she could. Something was crouching in the middle of the next room—naked, bestial, bloody . . . but definitely human, and surprisingly small and thin.

She gestured to the others, held one finger upward, then rotated it slowly toward the doorway: one perp, in the room beyond.

There was a tense moment as they gathered themselves. And then Hayward spoke in a firm, clear voice: "Police officers. Do not move. We're armed and we've got you covered. Walk to the doorway with your hands up."

She heard a scrambling noise, a thumping and banging like a beast shambling on all fours.

"He's running!"

Gun drawn, Hayward ducked around the corner just in time to see a dark figure scuttle into the darkness of the room beyond. This was followed by a tremendous crash.

"Let's go!"

She ran across the room to the far doorway, paused, gave a quick look into the next with the flashlight. There was no sign of the figure, but there were plenty of nooks and crannies where the killer could hide.

"Again!" They charged into the next room, immediately spreading out and taking cover.

This was the largest attic room yet, filled with gray metal shelves tightly packed with jars. In each jar resided a single staring eye, the size of a cantaloupe, roots dangling like tentacles. One shelf of jars had been thrown to the ground, and the eyeballs lay ruptured, oozing jelly amid the glass and preservative.

A quick search disclosed the room was empty. Hayward gathered the team.

"Slowly but surely," she said, "we're driving him into a corner. Remember that people, like animals, get progressively more dangerous as they become cornered."

Nods all around.

She glanced around. "The whale eyeball collection, it seems."

A few nervous, steadying laughs.

"Okay. We'll take it one room at a time. No hurry."

Hayward moved to the edge of the next door, listened, then ducked her head around, flashed the light. Nothing.

As they moved into the room, Hayward heard a sudden, rending scream from beyond the far doorway, followed by the tremendous crash of glass and the sound of running liquid. The men jumped as if they'd been shot. A strong odor of ethyl alcohol drifted back.

"That stuff is flammable," Hayward said. "If he's got a match, get ready to run."

She moved forward, raking the next room beyond with her flashlight.

"I see it!" O'Connor cried.

Draaag-*thump!* A shriek like a banshee, and then a dark figure, scuttling sideways but with horrifying single-mindedness, came rushing at them, gray flint knife raised in a fisted hand; Hayward jumped back as it crossed the threshold, knife slashing the air.

"Police!" she called out. "Drop your weapon!"

But the figure paid no heed, shambling crablike at them, knife still slashing the air.

"Don't shoot!" Hayward cried. "Mace him!"

She dodged the figure, drawing it around, while the other three cops flanked it on both sides, holstering their guns and pulling out their riot sticks and Mace. Visconti jumped forward and Maced the attacker and he howled like a demon, spinning and whipping the stone knife around blindly; Hayward deftly stepped in and gave a sharp, plunging kick to the inside of one leg, sending him sprawling. A second kick sent the knife skittering across the floor.

"Cuff him!"

But Visconti had already sprung into action, slapping the cuffs on one wrist and then, with the help of O'Connor, wrestling the other flailing arm down and cuffing it as well.

He screamed and bucked maniacally.

"Do his ankles!" Hayward ordered.

A minute later, the perp lay on his stomach, still pinned, writhing and shrieking in a voice so high it cut the air like a scalpel.

"Get the EMTs in here," Hayward said. "We need a sedative."

Most suspects, when cuffed hand and foot and pinned to the floor, settled down. Not this one. He continued to writhe and scream, twisting, rolling, thrashing about, and, small as he was, it was all that Hayward and the cops could do to hold him down.

"Must be on angel dust," said one of the cops.

"I've never seen angel dust do this."

A minute later, an EMT arrived and plunged a needle into the shrieking man's buttock. A few moments later, he began to quiet down. Hayward got up and dusted herself off.

"Jesus," said O'Connor. "Looks like he's taken a shower in gore."

"Yeah, and it's gone off in this heat. He *stinks*."

"Fucker's naked, too."

Hayward stepped back. The perp was still lying on his stomach, face pressed to the floor by Visconti, whimpering and quivering in an unsuccessful attempt to fight off the sedative.

She bent down. "Where's Lipper?" she asked him. "What did you do to him?"

More whimpering.

"Turn him over, I want to see his face."

Visconti complied. The man's face and hair were caked with dried blood and offal. He was grimacing strangely, his face seized by tics.

"Clean him up."

The EMT broke out a pack of sterile gauze wipes and cleaned up his face.

"Oh, Christ," Visconti said involuntarily.

Hayward merely stared. She could barely believe her eyes.

The killer was Jay Lipper.

27

Spencer Coffey settled himself in a chair in Warden Imhof's office, impatiently flicking his trouser crease. Imhof sat behind his desk, looking much as he had during the first meeting: cool and neat, with the same blow-dried helmet of light brown hair on his head. Nevertheless, Coffey could see the uneasy, perhaps even defensive look in his eye. Special Agent Rabiner remained standing, arms crossed, leaning against the wall.

Coffey let a strained silence build in the office before speaking.

"Mr. Imhof," he began, "you promised you would take care of this personally."

"As I have," said Imhof in a coldly neutral voice.

Coffey leaned back. "S.A. Rabiner and I have just come from an interview with the prisoner. I'm sorry to say there's been no progress— none—in teaching him the value of respect. Now, I told you earlier I wasn't really interested in *how* you accomplished the task we set for you, that I was only interested in *results*. Whatever you're doing, it isn't working. The prisoner's the same cocky, arrogant bastard who first walked in here. Refused to answer questions. Insolent as well. When I asked him how he was enjoying solitary confinement, he said, 'I rather prefer it.'"

"Prefer it to what?"

"Being mixed in with 'former clients' is how he put it, the sarcastic bastard. Really emphasizing the point that he didn't want to be mixed with the general prison population. He's as unrepentant and combative as ever."

"Agent Coffey, sometimes these things take time."

"Which is exactly what we don't have, Mr. Imhof. We've got a second bail hearing coming up, and Pendergast's going to have a day in court. We can keep him from his lawyer only so long. I need him broken by then; I need a confession." What he didn't add were the growing problems they were having nailing down some of the evidence. That would make the bail hearing very tricky—whereas a confession would make it all so nice and clean.

"As I said, it takes time."

Coffey took a breath, remembering Imhof's particular buttons. A little carrot, a little stick.

"Meanwhile, our man is down there bad-mouthing you and Herkmoor to all who will listen: guards, staff, everyone. And he's an eloquent bastard, Imhof."

The warden remained silent, but Coffey noticed—with satisfaction—a slight twitching at one corner of his mouth. And yet the man made no move to suggest stronger measures. Maybe there *weren't* any stronger measures . . .

And that's when the idea came to him—the masterstroke. It was the "former clients" phrase that did it. So Pendergast was afraid of being mixed up with "former clients"?

"Mr. Imhof," he said—but quietly, as if to disguise the freshness of his brainstorm—"is that computer on your desk linked to the Department of Justice database?"

"Naturally."

"Well, then. Let's check up on some of these 'former clients.' "

"I don't understand."

"Access Pendergast's arrest records. Run them against your current prison population, see if you can find any matches."

"You mean, see if any of the perps Pendergast arrested are currently in Herkmoor?"

"That's the idea, yes."

Coffey glanced over his shoulder at Rabiner. The agent had a wolfish smirk on his face.

"Boss, I like the way you think," he said.

Imhof pulled the keyboard toward him and began typing. Then he stared at the screen for a long moment while Coffey waited in growing impatience.

"Strange," Imhof said. "Pendergast's collars seem to have suffered a rather high mortality rate. Most never made it to trial."

"Surely, there have to be some live ones who made it through the legal system and ended up in prison."

More typing. Then Imhof leaned back from the monitor. "There are two currently residing in Herkmoor."

Coffey looked at him sharply. "Tell me about them."

"One is named Albert Chichester."

"Go on."

"He's a serial killer."

Coffey rubbed his hands together, glanced again at Rabiner.

"Poisoned twelve people in the nursing home where he was employed," Imhof went on. "Male nurse. Seventy-three years old."

As quickly as it had come, Coffey's exhilaration fell away. "Oh," he said.

There was a brief silence.

"What about the other one?" S.A. Rabiner asked.

"A serious felon named Carlos Lacarra. They call him El Pocho."

"Lacarra," Coffey repeated.

Imhof nodded. "Former drug kingpin. Real hard case. Worked his way up through East L.A. street gangs and then came east. Took over much of the Hudson County and Newark enforcement action."

"Yeah?"

"Tortured a whole family to death, including three kids. Revenge for a deal gone bad. Says here Pendergast was the S.A. in charge on that one—funny, I didn't remember that."

"What's Lacarra's record here?"

"Leads a gang in here known as the Broken Teeth. A major pain in the rear for our guards."

"The Broken Teeth," Coffey murmured. The exhilaration was quickly returning. "Now, tell me, Mr. Imhof. Where does this Pocho Lacarra currently enjoy his exercise privileges?"

"Yard 4."

"And what would happen if you transferred Agent Pendergast to, ah, yard 4 for his daily exercise period?"

Imhof frowned. "If Lacarra recognized him, it would be ugly. Or even if he didn't."

"How so?"

"Lacarra . . . Well, there isn't a delicate way of putting it: he likes a white boy for his bitch."

Coffey thought for a moment. "I see. Please give the order at once."

Imhof's frown deepened. "Agent Coffey, that's a rather extreme step—"

"I'm afraid our man has left us with no choice. I've seen hard cases in my time, I've seen sullen impudence before, but nothing like this. The way he disrespects the legal process, this prison—and you, in particular—is shocking. It really is."

Imhof drew in a breath. Coffey noticed, with satisfaction, that the man's nostrils flared briefly.

"Stick him in there, Imhof," Coffey said quietly. "Stick him in there, but keep an eye on the situation. Extract him if things get out of hand. But don't extract him too soon, if you get my meaning."

"If something does happen, there could be fallout. I'll need you to back me up."

"You can count on me, Imhof. I'm behind you, in all the way." And with that, Coffey turned, nodded to the still-grinning Rabiner, and left the office.

28

Captain of Homicide Laura Hayward sat at her desk, gazing at the storm of paperwork in front of her. She hated disorder; she hated mess; she hated unsquared papers and shabby piles. And yet it seemed no matter how much she sorted and squared and organized, it ended up this way: the desk a physical manifestation of the disorder and frustration within her own mind. By rights, she should be typing up a report on the murder of DeMeo. Yet she felt paralyzed. It was damned hard to work on open cases when you felt you'd royally screwed up on a previous one; that maybe an innocent—or mostly innocent—man was in prison, unjustly charged with a crime that carried a potential death sentence . . .

She made another enormous effort to impose order on her mind. She had always organized her thoughts in lists: she was forever making lists nested within lists within lists. And she was finding it difficult to move forward with her other cases while the Pendergast case remained unresolved in her mind.

She sighed, focused, and began again.

One: a possibly innocent man was in prison, charged with a capital crime.

Two: his brother, long thought dead, had resurfaced, kidnapped a woman with apparently no connection to anything, stolen the world's most valuable diamond collection . . . and then destroyed it. Why?

Three—

A knock on the door interrupted her.

Hayward had asked her secretary to make sure she was not disturbed, and she struggled with a momentary anger that shocked her with its intensity. She brought herself back under control and said coldly, "Come in."

The door opened slowly, tentatively—and there stood Vincent D'Agosta.

There was a brief moment of frozen stasis.

"Laura," D'Agosta began. Then he fell silent.

She maintained an utter coolness even as she felt the color mounting in her face. For a moment, she could think of nothing to say except "Please sit down."

She watched him enter the office and take a seat, crushing with ruthless efficiency the emotions that welled up inside her. He was surprisingly trim and reasonably well dressed in a suit and a twenty-dollar sidewalk tie, his thinning hair combed back.

The moment of awkward silence lengthened.

"So . . . How's everything?" D'Agosta asked.

"Fine. You?"

"My disciplinary trial is scheduled for early April."

"Good."

"Good? If they find me guilty, there goes my career, pension, benefits—everything."

"I meant, it will be good to have it over with," she said tersely. Is that what he'd come here to do—complain? She waited for him to get to the point.

"Look, Laura: first, I just want to tell you something."

"Which is?"

She could see him struggling. "I'm sorry," he said. "I'm *really* sorry. I know I hurt you, I know you think I treated you like dirt . . . I wish I knew how to make it up."

Hayward waited.

"At the time, I thought, I really thought, I was doing the right thing. Trying to protect you, keep you safe from Diogenes. I thought that by moving out I could keep the heat off you. I just didn't figure on how it would look to you . . . I was winging it. Things were happening fast and I didn't have time to work everything out. But I've had plenty of time to think about it since. I know that I looked like a cold bastard, walking out on you with no explanation. It must have seemed like I didn't trust you. But that wasn't it at all."

He hesitated, chewing his lip as if working up to something. "Listen," he began again. "I really want us to get back together. I still care about you. I know we can work this out . . ."

His voice trailed off miserably. Hayward waited him out.

"Anyway, I just wanted to say I'm sorry."

"Consider it said."

Another excruciating silence.

"Is there anything else?" Hayward asked.

D'Agosta shifted uncomfortably. Slats of sunlight came in through the blinds, striping his suit.

"Well, I heard . . ."

"What did you hear?"

"That you were still looking into the Pendergast case."

"Really?" she said coolly.

"Yeah. From a guy I know, works for Singleton." He shifted again. "When I heard that, it gave me hope. Hope that maybe I could still help you. There are things that I didn't tell you before, things that I felt sure you wouldn't believe. But if you're really still on the case, after all that's happened . . . well, I thought maybe you should hear some of these things. To, you know, give you as much ammunition as possible."

Hayward kept her face neutral, not willing to give him anything but a thunderous silence. He was looking older, a little drawn, but his clothes were new and his shirt was well ironed. She wondered, briefly and searingly, who was taking care of him. Finally she said, "The case is settled."

"Officially, yeah. But this friend said that you were—"

"I don't know what you heard, and I don't give a damn. You should know better than to listen to departmental gossip from so-called friends."

"But, Laura—"

"Refer to me as Captain Hayward, please."

Another silence.

"Look, this whole thing—the killings, the diamond theft, the kidnapping—was all orchestrated by Diogenes. All of it. It was his master plan. He played everyone like a violin. He murdered those people, then framed Pendergast for it. He stole the diamonds, kidnapped Viola Maskelene—"

"You've told me all this before."

"Yes, but here's something you don't know, something I never told you—"

Hayward felt a rush of anger that almost overwhelmed her icy control. "Lieutenant D'Agosta, I don't appreciate hearing that you've continued to withhold information from me."

"I didn't mean it that—"

"I know exactly what you meant."

"Listen, damn it. The reason Viola Maskelene was kidnapped is that she and Pendergast—well, they're in love."

"Oh, *please.*"

"I was there when they met on the island of Capraia last year. He interviewed her as part of the investigation into Bullard and the lost Stradivarius. When they met, I could see this connection between them. Diogenes somehow learned of it."

"They've been seeing each other?"

"Not exactly. But Diogenes lured her here using Pendergast's name."

"Funny she never mentioned that during her debriefing."

"She was trying to protect Pendergast and herself. If it got out that they had a thing for each other—"

"From one brief meeting on an island."

D'Agosta nodded. "That's right."

"Agent Pendergast and Lady Maskelene. In love."

"I can't speak one hundred percent about the strength of Pendergast's feelings. But as for Maskelene—yeah, I'm convinced."

"And how did Diogenes discover this touching bit of sentiment?"

"There's only one possibility: while Diogenes was nursing Pendergast back to health in Italy, after rescuing him from Count Fosco's castle. Pendergast was delirious, he probably said something. So, you see? Diogenes kidnapped Viola to ensure that Pendergast was maximally distracted at *precisely* the moment he undertook the diamond heist."

D'Agosta fell silent. Hayward took the time for a long breath and another effort at control.

"This," she said quietly, "is a story straight out of a romance novel. This isn't the way things happen in real life."

"What happened with us wasn't all that different."

"What happened with us was a mistake I'm trying to forget."

"Listen, please, Laura—"

"Call me Laura again and I'll have you escorted out of the building."

D'Agosta winced. "There's something else you ought to know. Have you heard of the forensic profiling firm of Effective Engineering Solutions, down on Little West 12th Street, run by an Eli Glinn? I've been spending most of my time down there recently, moonlighting."

"Never heard of it. And I know all the legitimate forensic profilers."

"Well, they're more of an engineering firm, and they're pretty secretive, but they recently did a forensic profile of Diogenes. It backs up everything I've told you about him."

"A forensic profile? At whose request?"

"Agent Pendergast's."

"That inspires confidence," she said sarcastically.

"The profile indicated that Diogenes *isn't through*."

"Isn't through?"

"All of what he's done so far—the killings, the kidnapping, the diamond theft—has been leading up to something else. Something bigger, maybe *much* bigger."

"Such as?"

"We don't know."

Hayward picked up some files and squared them on the desk with a crack. "That's quite a story."

D'Agosta began to get angry. "It's not a story. Look, this is Vinnie you're talking to, Laura. It's *me*."

"That's it." Hayward pressed an intercom button. "Fred? Please come to my office and escort Lieutenant D'Agosta off the premises."

"Don't do this, Laura . . ."

She turned to him, finally losing it. "Yes, I *will* do it. You lied to me. Played me for a fool. I was willing to offer you anything. Everything. And you—"

"And I am so very sorry. God, if only I could turn back the clock, do things differently. I tried my best, tried to balance my loyalty to Pendergast with my . . . loyalty to you. I know I screwed up a wonderful thing—and I believe that what we had is worth saving. I want your forgiveness."

The door was opened by a police sergeant. "Lieutenant?" he said.

D'Agosta rose, turned, and exited without even a look back. The sergeant shut the door, leaving Hayward behind her heaped-up desk, silent and trembling, looking at the mess but seeing nothing, nothing at all.

29

A dark, chill night had fallen over the restless streets of Upper Manhattan, but even on the brightest noon no sunlight ever penetrated the library of 891 Riverside Drive. Metal shutters were closed and fastened over mullioned windows, and drapes of rich brocade hid the shutters in their turn. The room was lit only by fire: the glow of candelabra, the flicker of embers dying on the wide grate.

Constance sat in a wing chair of burnished leather. She was very erect, as if at attention, or perhaps poised for flight. She was looking tensely at the other occupant of the room: Diogenes Pendergast, who sat on the couch across from her, a book of Russian poetry in his hands. He spoke softly, his voice as liquid as honey, the warm cadence of the Deep South strangely appropriate to the flow of the Russian.

"Память о солнце в сердце слабеет. Желтей трава," he finished, then laid the book down and looked over at Constance. "'Heart's memory of sun grows fainter, sallow is the grass.'" He laughed quietly. "Akhmatova. No one else ever wrote about sorrow with the kind of astringent elegance she did."

There was a short silence.

"I don't read Russian," Constance replied at last.

"A beautiful, poetic language, Constance. It's a shame, because I sense hearing Akhmatova speak of her sorrow in her own tongue would help you bear your own."

She frowned. "I bear no sorrow."

Diogenes raised his eyebrows and laid the book aside. "Please, child," he said quietly. "This is Diogenes. With others, you may put up a brave front. But with me, there's no reason to hide anything. I know you. We are so very alike."

"Alike?" Constance laughed bitterly. "You're a criminal. And me— you know *nothing* about me."

"I know a great deal, Constance," he said, voice still quiet. "You are unique. Like me. We are alone. I know you've been blessed and cursed with a strange and terrible burden. How many would wish for such a gift as you were given by my great-uncle Antoine—and yet how few could understand just what it would be like. Not liberation, not at all. So many, many years of childhood . . . and yet, to be deprived of *being* a child . . ."

He looked at her, the fire illuminating his strange, bicolored eyes. "I have told you. I, too, was denied a childhood—thanks to my brother and his obsessive hatred of me."

Immediately, a protest rose to Constance's lips. But this time she suppressed it. She could feel the white mouse shifting in her pocket, contentedly curling himself up for a nap. Unconsciously she moved a hand over the pocket, stroking it with slender fingers.

"But I've already spoken to you about those years. About my treatment at his hands." A glass of pastis sat at his right hand—he had helped himself from the sideboard earlier—and now he took a slow, thoughtful sip.

"Has my brother communicated with you?" he asked.

"How can he? You know where he is: you put him there."

"Others in similar situations find ways to get word to those they care about."

"Perhaps he doesn't want to cause me further discomfort." Her voice fell as she spoke. Her eyes dropped to her fingers, still absently stroking the sleeping mouse, then rose again to look at Diogenes's calm, handsome face.

"As I was saying," he went on after a pause, "there is much else we share."

Constance said nothing, stroking the mouse.

"And much that I can teach you."

Once again, she summoned a tart retort; once again, it remained unvoiced. "What could you possibly teach me?" she replied instead.

Diogenes broke into a gentle smile. "Your life—not to put too fine a term to it—is dull. Even stultifying. You're trapped in this dark house, a prisoner. Why? Aren't you a living woman? Shouldn't you be allowed to make your own decisions, to come and go as you please? Yet you've been forced to live in the past. And now, you live for others who only take care of you through guilt or shame. Wren, Proctor—that busybody policeman D'Agosta. They're your jailers. They don't love you."

"Aloysius does."

A sad smile creased Diogenes's face. "You think my brother is capable of love? Tell me: has he ever told you he loved you?"

"He doesn't have to."

"What evidence do you have that he loves you?"

Constance wanted to answer, but she felt herself coloring in confusion. Diogenes waved a hand as if to imply his point was made.

"And yet you don't have to live this way. There's a huge, exciting world out there. I could show you how to turn your amazing erudition, your formidable talents, toward fulfilling, toward pleasing, *yourself*."

Hearing this, Constance felt her heart accelerate despite her best intentions. The hand stroking the mouse paused.

"You must live not only for the mind, but for the senses. You have a body as well as a spirit. Don't let that odious Wren jail you with his daily babysitting. Don't crush yourself any longer. Live. Travel. Love. Speak the languages you've learned. Experience the world directly, and not through the musty pages of a book. Live in color, not black and white."

Constance listened intently, feeling her confusion mount. The fact was, she felt she knew so little of the world—nothing, in fact. Her entire life had been a prelude . . . to what?

"Speaking of color, note the ceiling of this room. What color is it?"

Constance glanced up at the library ceiling. "Wedgwood blue."

"Was it always that color?"

"No. Aloysius had it repainted during—during the repairs."

"How long do you suppose it took him to pick that color?"

"Not long, I imagine. Interior decorating is not his forte."

Diogenes smiled. "Precisely. No doubt he made the decision with all the passion of an accountant selecting an itemization. Such an important decision, made so flippantly. But this is the room you spend most of your time in, isn't it? Very revealing of his attitude toward you, don't you think?"

"I don't understand."

Diogenes leaned forward. "Perhaps you will understand if I tell you how *I* choose color. In my house—my *real* house, the one that is important to me—I have a library like this. At first I thought of draping it in blue. And yet after some consideration and experimentation, I realized blue takes on an almost greenish tint in candlelight—which is the only light in that room after the sun has set. Further examination revealed that a dark blue, such as indigo or cobalt, appears black in such light. If pale blue, it fades to gray; if rich, like turquoise, it becomes heavy and cold. Clearly blue, though my first preference, would not work. The various pearl grays, my second choice, were also unacceptable: they lose their bluish gloss and are transformed into a dead, dusky white. Dark greens react like dark blues and turn almost black. So at length I settled on a light summery green: in shimmering candlelight, it gives the dreamy, languorous effect of being underwater." He hesitated. "I live near the sea. I can sit in that room, all lights and candles extinguished, listening to the roar of the surf, and I become a pearl diver, within, and as one with, the lime-green waters of the Sargasso Sea. It is the most beautiful library in the world, Constance."

He fell silent for a moment, as if in contemplation. Then he leaned forward and smiled. "And do you know what?"

"What?" she managed to say.

"You would *love* that library."

Constance swallowed, unable to formulate a response.

He glanced at her. "The presents I brought you last time. The books, the other items . . . have you opened them?"

Constance nodded.

"Good. They will show you there are other universes out there—perfumed universes, full of wonder and delight, ready to be enjoyed. Monte Carlo. Venice. Paris. Vienna. Or, if you prefer: Katmandu, Cairo, Machu Picchu." Diogenes waved his hand around the walls of leather-bound books. "Look at the volumes you're surrounded by. Bunyan. Milton. Bacon. Virgil. Sobersided moralists all. Can an orchid flower if you water it with quinine?" He stroked the copy of Akhmatova. "*That* is why I've been reading you poetry this evening: to help you see that these shadows you surround yourself with need not be merely monochrome."

He picked up another slender volume from the pile beside him. "Have you ever read Theodore Roethke?"

Constance shook her head.

"Ah! Then you are about to experience a most delicious, undiscovered pleasure." He opened the book, selected a page, and began.

I think the dead are tender. Shall we kiss?—

Listening, Constance suddenly felt a strange feeling blossom deep within her: something faintly grasped at in fleeting dreams and yet still unknown, something rich and forbidden.

We sing together; we sing mouth to mouth . . .

She rose abruptly from the chair. The mouse in her frock pocket righted itself in surprise.

"It's later than I realized," she said in a trembling voice. "I think you had better leave."

Diogenes glanced at her mildly. Then he closed the book with perfect ease and rose.

"Yes, that would be best," he said. "The scolding Wren will be in shortly. It would not do for him to find me here—or your other jailers, D'Agosta and Proctor."

Constance felt herself flush, and immediately hated herself for it.

Diogenes nodded toward the couch. "I'll leave these other volumes for you, as well," he said. "Good night, dear Constance."

Then he stepped forward and—before she could react—inclined his head, took her hand, and raised it to his lips.

The gesture was executed with perfect formality and the best of breeding. Yet there was something in the way his lips lingered just out of contact with her fingers—something in the warm breath on her skin—that made Constance curl inwardly with unease . . .

And then he was gone, suddenly, wordlessly, leaving the library empty and silent, save for the low crackle of the fire.

For a moment, she remained motionless, aware of her own quickened breathing. He had left nothing of himself behind, no trace of his scent, nothing—save for the small stack of books on the couch.

She came forward and picked up the top volume. It was exquisitely bound in silk, with gilt edging and hand-marbled endpapers. She turned it over in her hands, feeling the delicious suppleness of the material.

Then, quite suddenly, she placed it back on the pile, picked up the half-finished glass of pastis, and exited the library. Making her way into the back parts of the house, she entered the service kitchen, where she rinsed and dried the glass. Then she returned to the central stairway.

The old mansion was silent: Proctor was out, as he had been so frequently on recent nights, assisting Eli Glinn in his plans; D'Agosta had looked in earlier, but only to make sure the house was secure, and had left again almost immediately. And "scolding Wren" was, as always at this hour, at the New York Public Library. His tiresome self-imposed babysitting duties were, thankfully, confined to the daylight hours. There was no point in checking to see whether the front door was still locked—she knew it would be.

Now, slowly, she ascended the stairs to her suite of rooms on the third floor. Gently removing the white mouse from her pocket, she placed him in his cage. She slipped out of her frock and undergarments and folded them neatly. Normally, she would have gone through her evening ablutions next, donned a nightgown, and read in the chair beside her bed for an hour or so before retiring—at present, she was working her way through Johnson's *Rambler* essays.

But not tonight. Tonight, she drifted into her bathroom and filled the oversize marble bath with hot water. Then she turned to a beautifully papered gift box, resting on a brass server nearby. Inside the box were a dozen small glass bottles from a Parisian manufacturer of bath oils: a gift from Diogenes on his last visit. Selecting one, she poured the contents into the water. The heady scent of lavender and patchouli perfumed the air.

Constance walked over to the full-length mirror and regarded her nude form for a long moment, sliding her hands over her sides, along her smooth belly. Then, turning away, she slipped into the bath.

This had been Diogenes's fourth visit. Before, he had often spoken of his brother and made several allusions to a particular Event—Diogenes seemed to speak the word with a special emphasis—an Event of such horror that he could not bring himself to talk of it, except to say it had left him blind in one eye. He had also described how his brother had gone out of his way to poison others against him—herself in particular—by telling lies and insinuations, making him out to be evil incarnate. At first she had objected vehemently to that kind of talk. It was a perversion of the truth, she'd protested—teased out now for some twisted end of his own. But he had been so calm in the face of her anger, so reasonable and persuasive in his rebuttals, that despite herself, she had grown confused. It was true that Pendergast was remote and aloof at times, but that was just his way . . . wasn't it? And wasn't it true the reason he'd never contacted her from prison was to simply spare her additional anxiety? She loved him, silently, from afar—a love he never seemed to return or acknowledge.

It would have meant so much to have heard from him.

Could there be some truth to Diogenes's stories? Her head told her he was untrustworthy, a thief, perhaps a sadistic killer . . . but her heart told her differently. He seemed so understanding, so vulnerable. So *kind*. He had even shown her evidence—documents, old photographs—that seemed to undercut many of the things Aloysius had told her about him. But he hadn't denied everything; he had also accepted a share of blame, admitted to being a less-than-perfect brother—a deeply flawed human being.

Everything was so confused.

Constance had always trusted her head, her intellect—even though, in many ways, she knew her mind was fragile and capable of betraying her. And yet now it was her heart that spoke the loudest. She wondered if Diogenes was telling the truth when he said he understood her—because, at some deep level she had yet to plumb, she believed him: she felt a connection. Most important, she was beginning to understand him as well.

At last she rose from the bath, dried herself, and completed her preparations for bed. She chose to wear not one of her cotton nightgowns, but rather one of finely milled silk that lay, unworn and half forgotten, at the bottom of a drawer. Then she slipped into bed, propped up her down pillows, and opened the collection of *Rambler* essays.

The words all ran together without meaning, and she grew restless. She flipped ahead to the next essay, scanned its stentorian opening, then closed the book. Getting out of bed again, she walked over to a heavy Duncan Phyfe armoire and opened it. Inside was a velvet-lined box containing a small collection of octavo books Diogenes had brought on his last visit. She carried the box back to bed and sorted through its contents. They were books she had heard about but never read, books that had never been a part of Enoch Leng's extensive library. The *Satyricon* of Petronius; Huysmans's *Àu rebours*; Oscar Wilde's letters to Lord Alfred Douglas; the love poetry of Sappho; Boccaccio's *Decameron*. Decadence, opulence, and passionate love clung to these pages like musk. Constance dipped into one and then another—at first gingerly, then curiously, then with something like hunger, reading late into the restless night.

30

Gerry Fecteau found a sunny spot on the walkway overlooking yard 4 and snugged up the zipper of his guard's jacket. A late-winter light filtered down from a whiskey sky, not strong enough to melt the patches of dirty snow that still edged the yards and building corners. From where he stood, he had a good view of the yard. He glanced over at his partner, Doyle, placed strategically at the other corner.

The nature of their assignment had not been explained to them, not even hinted at. In fact, they had been given only one order: watch the yard from above. But Fecteau had been around long enough to read between the lines. The mystery prisoner, still in solitary, had been given yard privileges for good behavior—in yard 4. *Obligatory* yard privileges. With Pocho and his gang. Fecteau knew very well what was going to happen to the prisoner—who was about as white as a white man could get—when he was turned out in yard 4 with Lacarra and his thugs. And watching the yard from the walkway above, like he was doing, it would take a couple of minutes at least to get down to the yard if any trouble erupted.

There was only one reason for an order like that. The drummer hadn't worked—for some inexplicable reason, he'd actually grown *quiet*—and now they were on to something new.

He licked his lips and scanned the empty yard: the basketball hoop with no net, the parallel bars, the quarter acre of asphalt. Five minutes until the exercise hour. Fecteau wasn't exactly thrilled with the assignment. If anybody got killed, it would be his ass. And he sure didn't relish the thought of pulling Lacarra off someone. On the other hand, another part of him relished the thought of violence. His heart rate accelerated with anticipation and apprehension.

At the appointed time, to the second, he heard the bolts shoot back, and the double doors to the yard opened. Two guards stepped into the weak sunlight, hooked the doors open, and stood on either side while Pocho ambled out—always first—his eyes squinting around the cement yard, stroking the tuft of hair under his lip. He was wearing the standard prison jumpsuit, no coat despite the winter temperature. He turned as he walked, twisting the tuft of hair, muscles rippling under his sleeves. His shaved head gleamed dully in the weak light and across his face, making his old acne scars look like lunar craters.

Lacarra sauntered into the center of the yard as the six other inmates filed out after him, heading off in different directions, striking casual poses as they looked around, chewing gum, walking aimlessly across the tarmac. One guard tossed out a basketball, which bounced toward one of the men; he flipped it up with his foot, caught it, then began bouncing it idly.

A moment later, the new prisoner stepped out, tall and straight. He paused just beyond the threshold, looking around, with a degree of casualness that made Fecteau tingle. The poor guy hadn't a clue.

Pocho and his boys didn't even seem to notice the newcomer—except that they all stopped chewing. But only for an instant. The ball continued its steady bounce, like the slow beating of a drum, *bom . . . bom . . . bom.* It was as if nothing out of the ordinary had happened.

The mystery prisoner began to walk along the cinder-block wall of the yard. As he walked, he looked about, face neutral, his moves easy and smooth. The others followed him with their eyes.

The yard was enclosed on three sides by the cement walls of Herkmoor, with chain link topped by concertina wire forming the fourth barrier at the far end. The prisoner walked alongside the wall until he came to the chain link, then turned to follow the line of the fence, staring out through it as he walked. Prisoners, Fecteau had noticed, always looked out or up—never back in toward the grim building. A guard tower dominated the middle distance; and beyond that, the tops of the trees rose above the prison's outer wall.

One of the delivery guards looked up, caught Fecteau's eye, and shrugged as if to say, "What's going on?" Fecteau shrugged back and signaled them to leave, that the transfer of prisoners to the yard was good. The two disappeared back into the building, shutting the doors behind them.

Fecteau raised the radio to his lips and spoke in a low tone. "You reading me, Doyle?"

"I read you."

"You thinking what I'm thinking?"

"Yup."

"We better be ready to run down there and break things up."

"Ten-four."

They waited. The sound of the bouncing ball continued steadily. Nobody moved except the mystery prisoner, who continued his slow perambulation along the fence.

Bom . . . bom . . . bom, went the ball.

Doyle's voice crackled over the radio again. "Hey, Gerry, this remind you of anything?"

"Like what?"

"You remember the opening scene of *The Good, the Bad, and the Ugly?*"

"Yeah."

"This is it."

"Maybe. Except one thing."

"What's that?"

"The outcome."

Doyle snickered over the radio. "Don't worry. Pocho wants his meat alive, only tenderized."

Now Lacarra removed his hands from his pockets, straightened up, and pimp-rolled over to a point on the fence thirty feet ahead of the prisoner. He hooked a hand on the chain link and watched the prisoner come toward him. Instead of varying his route to avoid Lacarra, the prisoner continued his leisurely stroll, not pausing for an instant, until he had come right up to Lacarra. And then he spoke to him. Fecteau strained to hear.

"Good afternoon," said the prisoner.

Lacarra looked away. "Got a cigarette?"

"I'm sorry, I don't smoke."

Lacarra nodded, still looking off into the distance, his eyes half closed, like two black slits. He began stroking the tuft of hair, pulling his lip down with each stroke, exposing a row of yellow, broken teeth.

"You don't smoke," Lacarra said quietly. "Isn't that *healthy*."

"I used to enjoy the occasional cigar, but I quit when a friend of mine developed cancer. They had to cut off most of his lower jaw, poor fellow."

At this, Lacarra's head swiveled toward him, as if in slow motion. "He must've been one ugly motherfucker after that."

"It's amazing what they can do with plastic surgery these days."

Lacarra turned. "Hey, you hear that, Rafe? This boy's got a friend with no mouth."

As if on cue, Lacarra's gang started to move again—all except the one with the ball. They began drifting in, like wolves.

"I think I'll continue my walk now," said the prisoner, moving to one side.

With a casual step, Lacarra moved to block the prisoner's path.

The prisoner paused, and fixed a pair of silvery eyes on Lacarra. He said something in a low voice that Fecteau didn't catch.

Lacarra didn't move, didn't look at the prisoner. After a moment he replied, "And what's that?"

The prisoner spoke more clearly now. "I hope you're not going to make the second worst mistake of your life."

"What the fuck you talking about, second mistake? What's the first mistake?"

"Murdering those three innocent children."

There was an electric silence. Fecteau shifted, stunned by what he had heard. The prisoner had broken one of the most sacred rules of prison life—and what was more, had done it with Pocho Lacarra. And how in hell did he even know Lacarra? The man had been in solitary

retreated, temporarily at her had de
y a blow to the chin.
ed and ran down the walk ng into h or
ay was he going to break th just Do
oice rose up. "You gonna le kick yo
moved in and around. One t and the er
was a feint so another could while a thir ck
ut—getting him good this tim w they all wed
ng, and the prisoner began to st heath the blow
burst through the upper doors er able to see he
own the stairs, unlocked another dashed along he
Doyle was just arriving, along with er backup guards
rom the station, riot sticks drawn. locked the dou-
to the yard and they jumped throu
! Cut the shit!" Fecteau screamed as t cross the cement
small knot of Lacarra's men, hunch invisible figure
ground, kicking the crap out of it. Tw now lay on the
nearby, while Lacarra himself seemed disappeared.
nough!" Fecteau waded in with Doyle a thers, grabbing
llar of one thug and jerking him back, w another across
ar with his stick.
Cut it! Enough!"
Doyle charged in beside him, Taser in hand, e other guards
ed in as well. In less than thirty seconds, the s had been re-
ained. The special prisoner lay on his back, un ous, the blood
vering his face a striking contrast to his skin, his nearly torn off
the waistband, his shirt split down the side.
One of the other prisoners was screaming hyster somewhere in
he background. "You seen what that crazy fucker do? een that, man?"
"What's happening, Fecteau?" came the warden oice over the
radio. "What's this about a fight?"
As if he didn't know. "The new prisoner got nailed, s
"What happened to him?"
"We need EMTs!" one of the other guards was calling in the background. "We got at least three prisoners hurt bad! EMTs!"

since
to hap
La
yellow
ejecte   egr
with   "W
"   rst, th
are.   ldn't   en-year
h   f yurs   o?"
Fectea   ly believe
sure. Lacarr emed equal
waiting for l of signal.
Pocho laugh: a slow, u
Rafe," he ca his shoulder. "I
me, know an?"
Rafe sa   ver. "Oh, yeah?"
The pri   nothing. Now the o
a pack of ecteau felt his heart po
"You h elings, man," Pocho said
"Indeed the reply. "And what feel
Pocho s back and Rafe came in, all
then—fast ring-loaded trap—he swung
The pri moved like a blur, one leg flash
Rafe was d l up, on the ground. Then, wi
sound, he ved.
"Knock !" Fecteau screamed down at them,
call Doyle.
The oth moved in fast while Pocho took anoth
ting the oth   o the dirty work. Watching, Fecteau wa
founded, to   the prisoner move in a way he never tho
faster than h ought possible, some kind of martial art
miliar with—ut of course, he was up against six gang m
had spe   t th   entire lives street-fighting and nobody could
that. As   f   r the gang itself, they were so surprised by the

mov es they had
Rafe, stunned
Fecteau tur
backup. No w
Lacarra's
The rest
spun, but it
him in the
in, fists flyi
Fecteau
yard, ran d
corridor.
running f
ble door
"He
toward
on the
ground
"E
the c
the e

wa
str
c
a

"Fecteau, are you there?" came Imhof's strident voice.

"Yeah, the new prisoner's hurt, don't know how bad, though."

"Find out!"

"Yes, sir."

"Another thing: I want the EMTs on the new prisoner first. You understand?"

"Copy, sir."

Fecteau looked around. Where the hell was Pocho?

Then he saw the form of Pocho huddled in a frozen corner of the yard, motionless.

"Oh, God," he said. "Where are those EMTs? Get them here *now!*"

"Motherfucker!" came the hysterical voice. "You *seen* what he done?"

"Secure the others," Fecteau cried. "Hear me? Cuff them and get them the hell out of here into lockdown!"

It was an unnecessary order. The gang members who could still stand were already being marched to the yard door. The shouting faded, leaving behind the high-pitched whimpering of one of the injured inmates. Lacarra lay in grotesque imitation of a supplicant, knees and face in the snow, head twisted in an unnatural angle. His motionlessness creeped out Fecteau most of all.

The EMTs arrived, two of them, followed by two more wheeling stretchers.

Fecteau pointed to the special prisoner. "Warden wants him taken care of first."

"What about that one?" The EMTs had fixed their horrified eyes on Lacarra.

"Take care of the new prisoner first."

Even as they worked on the new prisoner, Fecteau couldn't take his eyes off Lacarra. And then, as if in slow motion, Lacarra's body began to move, began to topple on its side, where it lay, again unmoving, the grinning face and wide-open eyes now turned to the sky.

Fecteau raised the radio to his lips, wondering just what to tell the warden. One thing was clear: Pocho Lacarra wasn't likely to be making anybody his bitch, ever again.

31

On a cold March day, eastern Long Island did not much look like the playground of the rich and famous it was supposed to be. At least, that was Smithback's impression as he cruised past yet another muddy, stubble-strewn potato field, a bedraggled flock of crows wheeling about overhead.

Since his meeting with Hayward, Smithback had tried everything in his journalistic bag of tricks to find out more about Diogenes. He'd written suggestive articles, hinting at imminent breakthroughs and soliciting tips. He'd poked around the museum, asking questions and sifting rumors. Nothing. Pendergast remained in prison on charges of murder. Just as bad, Diogenes remained utterly vanished, free. The image of Pendergast's brother at large and no doubt hatching some fresh outrage both angered and frightened Smithback.

He wasn't sure, exactly, when the idea had come to him. But come it had . . . and now he was driving eastward on the island, heading for a house that he hoped—rather fervently hoped—was unoccupied.

Chances were, he'd find nothing. After all, what could he find that the police hadn't? But it was the only thing still left for him to do.

"In five hundred feet, turn right on Springs Road," spoke a mellifluous female voice from the dashboard.

"Thanks, Lavinia darling," Smithback said with a jauntiness he didn't feel.

"Turn right on Springs Road."

Smithback complied, swinging onto a cracked macadam road sandwiched between more potato fields, shuttered beach houses, and barelimbed trees. Beyond lay a marsh of dead cattails and sawgrass. He passed a faded wooden sign in a picturesque state of dilapidation. *Welcome to the Springs,* it told him. This was an unpretentious corner of eastern Long Island, only faintly perfumed with the odor of quiet money.

"The town, my dear Lavinia, is small and unremarkable, but not wholly without atmosphere," said Smithback. "Wish you could see it."

"In five hundred feet, turn right on Glover's Box Road."

"Very well."

"Turn right on Glover's Box Road," came the smooth response.

"With a voice like that, you could make a fortune in the phone sex business, you know that?" Smithback was glad Lavinia was only a voice in his dashboard. The GPS navigation system couldn't know just how nervous he felt.

He now found himself on a broad sandy spit of land, beach houses on either side among scraggly pines, cattail marshes, and scrub. A gray sheet of water lay to his left: Gardiners Bay. On his right was a bedraggled harbor, shut up for the winter, the yachts gone into tender.

"In three hundred feet, you will arrive at your destination."

Smithback slowed. Ahead, he could see a sandy driveway leading through a sparse scattering of oaks to end at a gray, shingled house. Police sawhorses had been placed across the driveway, but there was no sign of a police presence. The house was shut up and dark.

The road curved past a few more houses, then ended in a loop where the spit came to an end. A sign to one side announced a public beach. Smithback pulled the car onto the side of the loop—he was the only one there—and stepped out, inhaling the fresh cold air. He zipped his jacket against the damp wind, shrugged his arms into a backpack, picked up a rock from the ground, placed it in his pocket, and strolled out onto the beach. The small waves slopped and hissed up the strand in a regular cadence. Strolling along, he picked up a few shells, tossed them back again, scuffed his sneakers along the sand, all the time making his way down the beach.

The houses stood just beyond the beginning of the sawgrass and dunes: gray shingles and white trim, silent and boarded up for the winter. The house he wanted was easy to identify: pieces of yellow crime scene tape still fluttered from stakes driven into the unkempt yard. It was a large house from the twenties, weather-beaten, with pitched roofs, a deep sea-facing porch, and two gables. Smithback continued past the house, but still there was no sign of any official presence. Still kicking sand nonchalantly, he strolled up through the dunes and sawgrass, hopped over a split rail fence, ducked under the police tape, and scooted across the yard into the lee of the house.

He pressed himself against the wall, hidden from sight behind a half-dead yew, and slipped on a pair of leather gloves. The house would be locked, of course. He edged around until he came to a side door, then peered inside. He made out a tidy, old-fashioned kitchen, devoid of the usual utensils.

Smithback removed the rock from his pocket, along with a handkerchief. He wrapped the handkerchief around the rock, gave the window a smart rap.

Nothing happened. He struck harder, this time making a fairly audible thump, but still it did not break.

He took a closer look at the glass and noticed something unusual: it was thick and blue-green in color, and the light dividers were of painted metal, not wood.

Bulletproof glass?

Somehow, Smithback wasn't surprised. Diogenes would have retrofitted the house to be impregnable from the outside as well as escape-proof from the inside.

He paused, hoping he hadn't just wasted a three-hour drive. Certainly Diogenes would have thought of everything—how could he have forgotten that? There was no point in probing for weaknesses: there would be none.

On the other hand, the police might have left a door open.

Keeping hidden in the shrubbery, he crept around to the front porch. The door had crime scene tape stretched across it. He hopped onto the porch, glanced up and down the road, then turned to examine the door. This was how the cops had broken in—the door frame had been bent by crowbars and the door itself was bowed, the lock shattered. It appeared as if a remarkable amount of force had been necessary. Having destroyed the door lock, the police had affixed a padlock of their own, and this Smithback examined carefully. It was of case-hardened steel, too thick to cut with bolt cutters; but the fasteners had been screwed into fresh holes drilled in the metal door.

Smithback dipped into the leather backpack and pulled out a Phillips-head screwdriver. In five minutes, he had unscrewed one side. He pulled the fastener back and eased open the badly warped metal door. In a moment, he was inside, the door shut behind him.

He paused for a moment, rubbing his hands together. It was warm in the house—the heat was still on. He was standing in a typical beach-house living room, with comfortable wicker furniture, braided and hooked rugs scattered about the floor, a gaming table set for chess, a grand piano in one corner, and a huge fireplace built from beach stones in the far wall. The light in the house was a curious green from the thick-glassed windows.

What was he looking for? He wasn't sure. Some clue to where Diogenes might be, perhaps, or under what other identity or identities he might be hiding. He had a moment's feeling of dismay, wondering how he could possibly find something that the police had missed or that—even more improbably—Diogenes himself had overlooked. Of course, the man had left in a hurry, leaving behind a slew of equipment and material, enough for the police to positively identify him as the museum diamond thief. Even so, he had proved himself to be not only exceptionally intelligent but also exceptionally careful. Diogenes wasn't the type to make mistakes.

Walking noiselessly, Smithback moved through an archway into a dining room beautifully paneled in oak, with a heavy table and Chippendale chairs. Paintings and prints hung on the dark red walls. A door in the far wall led to the tiny kitchen, also spotless. The police would not have cleaned the house: he figured this was the way Diogenes habitually kept it.

Back in the living room, Smithback wandered to the piano, hit a few keys. It was beautifully in tune, the hammers working smoothly.

Okay, that was one thing: Diogenes played the piano.

He looked at the music open on the stand: Schubert's Impromptus, opus 90. Under that, sheet music for Debussy's "Clair de Lune," a book of Chopin's nocturnes. A relatively accomplished pianist at that, but probably not at the concert level.

Next to the piano was another archway, leading into the library. This room was unaccountably disordered. Books lay on the floor, some open, with gaps on the shelves. The rug was rumpled and turned up at one end, and a table lamp lay broken on the floor. A large table dominated the middle of the space, covered with black velvet; above stood a row of bright spotlights.

In one corner, Smithback saw something that sent a shiver down his spine: a large, finely machined, stainless-steel anvil. Next to it lay some rumpled rags and a strange kind of hammer made out of a gray, gleaming metal—titanium, perhaps?

Smithback backed out of the library, turned, and ascended the wooden stairs. At the top was a landing with a long hall, paintings of seascapes on both walls. A small, stuffed capuchin monkey crouched on a table, next to a glass dome under which stood a fake tree festooned with butterflies.

The doors to the rooms were all open.

Walking into the room directly at the top of the stairs, Smithback realized it must have been the one where Viola Maskelene was held prisoner. The bed was in disarray, there was a broken glass on the floor, and someone had scraped off the wallpaper on one wall, revealing metal underneath.

Metal. Smithback went over and carefully peeled off some more wallpaper. The walls were made of solid steel.

He shivered again, feeling a creeping sensation of alarm. The window was of the same thick blue-green glass as downstairs, and was barred. The door, which he examined next, was extremely heavy, also of steel, and it moved noiselessly on oversize hinges. He peered at the lock—superheavy machined brass and stainless steel.

Smithback's feeling of nervousness increased. What if Diogenes came back? But of course he wouldn't come back—that would be crazy. Unless there was something in the house he had forgotten . . .

He made a quick tour of the other bedrooms. On a hunch, he took his screwdriver and poked the wall of another room. It, too, was steel.

Did Diogenes plan to imprison more than one person? Or was the whole house fortified like this as a matter of course?

He skipped downstairs, heart pounding in his chest. The whole place was giving him the creeps. The day had proved a total waste: he'd come out there without a real plan, without looking for anything specific. He wondered if he should take notes—but of what? Maybe he should just forget it and go visit Margo Green. He was already out of the city. But that would be an equally useless journey—she had taken an abrupt turn for the worse, he understood, and was now comatose and unresponsive . . .

Suddenly he froze. Soft footsteps were moving across the porch.

With a sudden feeling of terror, he ducked into the coat closet at the bottom of the stairs. He pushed his way toward the back, nestling himself behind the row of cashmere, camel's-hair, and tweed coats. He could hear the rattle of the door, and then the groan as it slowly opened.

Diogenes?

The closet was thick with the smell of wool. He could hardly breathe from fear.

Footsteps moved quietly across the carpeted entry and into the living room, then stopped. Silence.

Smithback waited.

Next, the footsteps moved into the dining room, then faded away into the kitchen.

Should he run for it?

But even before he could consider, the steps returned: slow, soft, deliberate steps. Now they moved toward the library, back out, and up the stairs.

Now. Smithback flitted out of the closet, scurried across the living room, and dashed out the open door. As he rounded the corner of the porch, he saw that a cop car was standing in the driveway, engine running, door open.

He skipped through the backyard of the house next door and ran down onto the beach, almost laughing with relief. What he had assumed was Diogenes was only a cop, coming to check on the place.

He got back in his car and spent a moment recovering his breath. A wasted day. But at least he'd exited the house in one piece.

He started the car, turned on the navigator.

"Where would you like to go?" came the smooth, sexy voice. "Please enter the address."

Smithback punched up the menu and chose the "Office" option. He knew his way back, but he liked listening to Lavinia.

"We are going to the location called Office," came the voice. "Proceed north on Glover's Box Road."

"Righty-o, darling."

He drove slowly and nonchalantly past the house. The cop was now outside, standing next to his cruiser with a mike in his hand. He watched Smithback drive by but made no move to stop him.

"In five hundred feet, turn left on Springs Road."

Smithback nodded. He raised a hand to brush away a wisp of tweed wool from his face. As he did so, he stiffened with an almost electric shock.

"That's it, Lavinia!" he cried. "The coats in the closet!"

"Turn left on Springs Road."

"There were *two kinds* of coats! Super-expensive cashmere and mohair, and then a bunch of heavy, hairy, itchy tweed coats. Do you know of anyone who wears both? Hell, no!"

"Proceed for one mile on Springs Road."

"Diogenes is the cashmere-and-mohair type, for sure. That means his alter ego wears tweeds. He's disguised as a professorial type. It's perfect, Lavinia, it feels right. He's a professor. No, wait! *Not* a professor, not exactly. After all, he knows the museum so well . . . The police are saying the diamond heist had to have had inside help—but can you imagine Diogenes enlisting help? Hell, it's staring us right in the face. Holy shit, Lavinia: we nailed it! *I* nailed it!"

"In five hundred feet, take a left on the Old Stone Highway," came the placid response.

32

What repelled Hayward most about the Bellevue psych ward wasn't the dingy, tiled corridors, or the locked steel doors, or the mingled smell of disinfectant, vomit, and excrement. It was the sounds. They came from everywhere—a cacophony of mutterings, shrill outbursts, monotonic repetitions, glottal explosions, whining, soft high-speed babblings: a symphony of misery, now and then punctuated by a cry so hideous, so full of despair, that it wrenched her heart.

Meanwhile, Dr. Goshar Singh walked beside her, speaking in a calm, rational voice as if he heard nothing—and maybe, she thought, he didn't. If he did, he would no longer be sane himself. It was that simple.

Hayward tried to focus on the doctor's words. "In all my years of clinical psychiatry," he was saying, "I've never seen anything quite like it. We're trying to get a handle on it. We've made some progress, although not yet as much as I'd like."

"It seems to have happened so suddenly."

"The sudden onset is a puzzling feature, indeed. Ah, yes, Captain Hayward: here we are."

Singh unlocked a door and held it open, ushering Hayward into an almost bare room, divided in half by a long counter, a thick plate-glass window above separating it from the other half—exactly like a visitors' room at a prison. An intercom was set into the glass.

"Dr. Singh," said Hayward, "I requested a face-to-face meeting."

"I'm afraid that won't be possible," Singh replied almost sadly.

"I'm afraid it *will* be possible. I can't question a suspect under these conditions."

Again, Singh shook his head sadly, his plump cheeks wagging. "No, no, we're in charge here, Captain. And I think when you see the patient, you'll realize that it wouldn't make a difference, no difference at all."

Captain Hayward said nothing. Now was not the time to fight with the doctors. She would evaluate the situation and, if necessary, return under her own conditions.

"If you would care to have a seat?" Singh asked solicitously.

Hayward seated herself at the counter and the doctor settled into the seat beside her. He glanced at his watch.

"The patient will be out in five minutes."

"What kind of preliminary results do you have?"

"As I say, it is a most puzzling case. Most puzzling indeed."

"Can you elaborate?"

"The preliminary EEG showed significant focal temporal abnormalities, and an MRI revealed a series of small lesions to the frontal cortex. It is these lesions that seem to have triggered severe cognitive defects and psychopathology."

"Can you translate that into English?"

"The patient seems to have suffered severe damage to the part of the brain that controls behavior, emotions, and planning. The damage is most pronounced in an area of the brain we psychiatrists sometimes call the Higginbottom region."

"Higginbottom?"

Singh smiled at what was evidently an inside psychiatric joke. "Eugenie Higginbottom worked on an assembly line in a ball-bearing factory in Linden, New Jersey. One day in 1913, there was a boiler explosion in the factory. Blew apart the stamper. It was as if a huge shotgun shell had gone off: ball bearings flew everywhere. Six people were killed. Eugenie Higginbottom miraculously survived: but with some two dozen ball bearings embedded in the frontal cortex of her brain."

"Go on."

"Well, the poor woman suffered a complete personality change. She was instantly transformed from a kind, gentle person to a foulmouthed slattern, given to outbursts of profanity and violence, a drunkard, and, ah, sexually promiscuous. Her friends were astounded. It underscored the medical theory that personality is hardwired in the brain and that damage can literally transform one person into another. The ball bearings, you see, destroyed Higginbottom's ventromedial frontal cortex—the same area that is affected in our patient."

"But there are no ball bearings in this man's brain," Hayward said. "What could have caused it?"

"This is the crux of the matter. Initially, I hypothesized a drug overdose, but no drug residues were found in his system."

"A blow to the head? A fall?"

"No. No evidence of coup/contrecoup, no edema or bruising. We've also ruled out a stroke: the damage was simultaneous in several widely separated areas. The only possible explanation I can come up with is an electrical shock administered directly to the brain. If only we had a dead body—an autopsy would show *so* much more."

"Wouldn't a shock leave burn marks?"

"Not a low-voltage, high-amperage shock—such as one generated by electronic or computer equipment. But there's no damage anywhere but to the brain. It's hard to see how such a shock might have occurred, unless our patient was performing some kind of bizarre experiment on himself."

"The man was a computer technician installing an exhibit at the museum."

"So I've heard."

An intercom chimed, and a voice sounded softly. "Dr. Singh? The patient is arriving."

Beyond the glass window, a door opened, and a moment later Jay Lipper was wheeled in. He sat in a wheelchair, restrained. He was making slow circles with his head, and his lips were moving, but no sound came out.

His face was shocking. It was as if it had caved in, the skin gray and slack and hanging in leathery folds, the eyes jittery and unfocused, the tongue hanging out, as long and pink and wet as that of an overheated retriever.

"Oh my God . . . ," Hayward said involuntarily.

"He's heavily sedated, for his own safety. We're still trying to adjust the meds, find the right combination."

"Right." Hayward looked at her notes. Then she leaned forward, pressed the talk switch on the intercom. "Jay Lipper?"

The head continued its slow orbit.

"Jay? Can you hear me?"

Was there a hesitation there? Hayward leaned forward, speaking softly into the intercom.

"Jay? My name is Laura Hayward. I'm here to help you. I'm your friend."

More slow rolling.

"Can you tell me what happened at the museum, Jay?"

The rolling continued. A long gobbet of saliva, which had gathered on the tip of his tongue, dripped to the floor in a foamy thread.

Hayward leaned back and looked toward the doctor. "Have his parents been in?"

Singh bowed. "Yes, they were here. And a very painful scene it was."

"Did he respond?"

"That was the only time he's responded, and then only briefly. He emerged from his inner world for less than two seconds."

"What did he say?"

" 'This isn't me.' "

" 'This isn't me?' Any idea what he meant by that?"

"Well . . . I imagine he retains some faint recollection of who he was, along with a vague realization of what he's become."

"And then?"

Singh seemed embarrassed. "He became suddenly violent. He said he was going to kill them both and . . . rip out their guts. He had to be further sedated."

Hayward glanced at him a moment longer. Then, thoughtfully, she turned back toward Lipper, still rolling his head, his glassy eyes a million miles away.

33

He got into a fight with Carlos Lacarra," Imhof told Special Agent Coffey as they strode down the long, echoing corridors of Herkmoor. "Lacarra's friends weighed in, and by the time the guards broke it up, a certain amount of damage had been done."

Coffey listened to the public recitation of events with Rabiner at his side. Two prison guards walking behind completed the entourage. They rounded a corner and continued down another long corridor.

"What kind of damage?"

"Lacarra's dead," said the warden. "Broken neck. Don't know what happened, exactly—not yet. None of the prisoners are talking."

Coffey nodded.

"Your prisoner got pretty banged up—mild concussion, contusions, bruised kidney, a couple of cracked ribs, and a shallow puncture wound."

"Puncture wound?"

"Seems somebody shanked him. That was the only weapon recovered at the scene of the fight. All in all, he's lucky to be alive." Imhof coughed delicately and added, "He certainly didn't *look* like a fighter."

"And my man is back in his cell, as per my orders?"

"Yes. The doctor wasn't happy."

They cleared a security gate, and Imhof keyed an elevator for them. "At any rate," he said, "I expect he'll be a lot more amenable to questioning now."

"You didn't sedate him, did you?" Coffey asked as the elevator chimed open.

"We don't habitually dispense sedatives here at Herkmoor—potential for abuse and all that."

"Good. We don't want to waste our time with a nodding vegetable."

The elevator rose to the third floor, opening onto a pair of steel doors. Imhof swiped a card and punched in a code and they slid back, revealing a cinder-block corridor, painted stark white, with white doors on either side. Each door had a tiny square window and a foot slot.

"Herkmoor Solitary," Imhof said. "He's in cell 44. Normally, I'd escort him to a visiting room, but in this case he's not exactly mobile."

"I'd rather speak to him in his cell, anyway. With the guards on hand . . . in case he should become aggressive."

"Not much chance of that." Imhof leaned forward and lowered his voice. "I don't want to tell you how to do your job, Agent Coffey, but I would imagine that any suggestion that he might be put back in yard 4 for exercise would get him talking a mile a minute."

Coffey nodded.

They approached the cell door and one of the guards gave it several whacks with his riot stick. "Make yourself pretty, you got a visitor!"

Whang, whang! went the nightstick against the door. The guard removed his weapon and stood aside while the other unlocked the door and glanced in. "All clear," he said.

The first guard holstered his weapon and stepped inside.

"How much time do you need?" Imhof asked.

"An hour should do it. I'll have the guard call you when we're done."

Coffey waited until Imhof was gone, then he stepped into the small immaculate cell, followed by Rabiner. The second guard closed the door from the outside and locked it, preparing to stand watch.

The prisoner lay on the narrow bed, propped up on a thin pillow, dressed in a fresh jumpsuit so orange it almost glowed. Coffey was shocked by his appearance—head bandaged, one eye swollen shut and the other dark, the entire face a palette of black, blue, and green. Behind the puffy slit in the prisoner's good eye, Coffey could see the glitter of silver.

"Agent Coffey?" the guard asked. "Do you want a chair?"

"No, I'll stand." He turned to Rabiner. "Ready?"

Rabiner had removed a microcassette recorder. "Yes, sir."

Coffey folded his arms and looked down at the battered and bandaged prisoner. He grinned. "What happened to you? Try to kiss the wrong guy?"

No answer, but then, Coffey expected none.

"Let's get down to business." He took out a sheet of paper with his notations. "Roll the tape. This is Special Agent Spencer Coffey, in prison cell number C3-44 at Herkmoor Federal Correctional and Holding Facility, interviewing the prisoner identified as A. X. L. Pendergast. The date is March 20."

A silence.

"Can you talk?"

To Coffey's surprise, the man said, "Yes." His voice was barely a whisper and a little thick on account of his puffy lips.

Coffey smiled. This was a promising beginning. "I'd like to get this over with as soon as possible."

"Likewise."

It seemed the softening up had worked even better than he had anticipated.

"All right, then. I'm going to return to my previous line of questioning. This time I expect a response. As I've already explained, the evidence puts you in Decker's house at the time of the killing. It provides means, motive, and opportunity, and a direct link between you and the murder weapon."

The prisoner said nothing, so Coffey continued.

"Point one: the forensic team recovered half a dozen long black fibers at the crime scene, which we found came from a highly unusual cashmere/merino blended Italian fabric made in the 1950s. An analysis of the suits in your wardrobe indicate that all of them were made from the same fabric, even the very same bolt of cloth.

"Point two: at the scene of the crime, we found three hairs, one with root. A PCR analysis proved it matched your DNA to a probability of error of one in sixteen billion.

"Point three: a witness, a neighbor of Decker's, observed a pale-complected individual in a black suit entering Decker's house ninety minutes before the murder. In no less than three photo lineups, he positively and categorically identified you as that person. As a member of the U.S. House of Representatives, he is about as unimpeachable a witness as you could find."

If the prisoner sneered momentarily, it happened so fast that Coffey wasn't sure he had seen it at all. He took a moment to read the man's face, but it was impossible to discern any kind of emotion in a face so swollen and bandage-covered. All he could really see of the man was the silver glitter behind the slitted eye. It made him uneasy.

"You're an FBI agent. You know the ropes." He shook the piece of paper at Pendergast. "You're going to be convicted. If you want to avoid the needle, you'd better start cooperating, and cooperating now."

He stood there, breathing hard, staring at the bandaged prisoner.

The prisoner gazed back. After a moment, he spoke.

"I congratulate you," he said. His slurred voice sounded submissive, even obsequious.

"May I make a suggestion, Pendergast? Confess and throw yourself at the mercy of the court. It's your only option—and you know it. Confess, and save us the shame of seeing one of our own dragged through a public trial. Confess, and we'll get you transferred out of yard 4."

Another brief silence.

"Would you consider a plea bargain?" Pendergast asked.

Coffey grinned, feeling a flush of triumph. "With evidence like this? Not a chance. Your only hope, Pendergast—and I repeat—is to store up a bit of goodwill with a nice, round confession. It's now or never."

Pendergast seemed to consider this for a moment. Then he stirred on the cot. "Very well," he said.

Coffey broke into a smile.

"Spencer Coffey," Pendergast went on, honeyed voice dripping with obsequiousness, "I have watched your progress in the Bureau for almost ten years, and I *confess* I've been amazed by it."

He paused to breathe in.

"I knew from the beginning you were a special, even unique individual. You—what is the term?—*nailed* me."

Coffey felt his smile broaden. This was good; this was the moment of humiliation against a hated rival that most people only dreamed about.

"Remarkable work, Spencer. May I call you Spencer? Peerless, I might even say."

Coffey waited for the confession he was now certain was coming. The poor bastard thought flattering him would gain some sympathy. That's what they all did: *Oh, you're so clever to have caught me.* He gestured behind his back for Rabiner to move closer with the recorder, not to miss a word. The beauty of it was, Pendergast was only digging his own grave deeper. There would be no mercy, even with a confession: not for the man responsible for murdering a top FBI agent. A confession would shave ten years off his death-penalty appeals—that was all.

"I've been lucky enough to witness some of your work in person. For example, your performance during that harrowing night of the museum massacre many years ago, manning the mobile command station. That was truly unforgettable."

Coffey felt a stirring of unease. He didn't remember much from that awful night—to be truthful, it hadn't been his best moment. But then, maybe he was just being too hard on himself, as usual.

"I remember that night vividly," Pendergast went on. "You were in the thick of it, nerves of steel, barking orders."

Coffey shifted. He wished the man would get on with the confession. This was getting a bit maudlin. Pathetic how quickly the man had been reduced to groveling.

"I felt bad about what happened afterward. You didn't deserve that reassignment to Waco. It wasn't fair. And then, when you mistook that teenager carrying home a prize catfish for a Branch Davidian terrorist with an RPG—well, that could have happened to anybody. Luckily, your first shot missed and your partner was able to tackle you before you squeezed off a second—although perhaps the teenager was in little danger, since I understand you came in dead last in your Firearms Training Unit at the Academy."

The segue had happened so smoothly, Pendergast's tone of voice never varying from its whining submissiveness, that it took Coffey a moment to realize the effusive praise had morphed into something else. The stifled snicker of the guard stung him to the quick.

"I happened upon a Bureau study of the Waco field office while it was under your benevolent leadership. It seems your office enjoyed being at the top of several lists. For example, the smallest number of cases successfully closed for three years running. The largest number of agents requesting transfers. The most internal investigations for incompetence or ethics violations. One could argue that your being transferred back to New York could not have come at a more convenient time. So nice to have an ex–U.S. senator for a father-in-law, Spencer, is it not?"

Coffey turned to Rabiner and said, as calmly as possible, "Turn it off."

"Yes, sir."

Pendergast didn't pause, although his voice changed in tone to cool sarcasm. "How's the PTSD treatment coming, by the way? I understand they've got a new approach that works wonders."

Coffey gestured to the guard and said, with an effort at detachment, "I can see that further questioning of the prisoner is pointless. Open the door, please."

Even as the guard outside fumbled with the door, Pendergast continued speaking.

"On another note, knowing your love of great literature, I recommend to you Shakespeare's marvelous comedy *Much Ado About Nothing*. Particularly the character of Constable Dogberry. You could learn much from him, Spencer. Much."

The cell door opened. Coffey glanced at the two guards, their expressions studiously neutral. Then, straightening his back, he proceeded down the corridor toward the solitary confinement security doors, Rabiner and the guards following in silence.

* · * *

It took almost ten minutes of walking through endless corridors to reach Imhof's office, located in a sunny corner of the administrative building. By that time, some of the color had returned to Coffey's face.

"Wait outside," he told Rabiner, then marched stiffly past the obnoxious secretary, entered Imhof's office, and shut the door.

"How did it—?" Imhof began, but fell silent when he saw Coffey's face.

"Put him back in yard 4," Coffey said. "Tomorrow."

Surprise blossomed on the warden's face. "Agent Coffey, when I mentioned that earlier, it was suggested merely as a threat. If you put him back there, they'll kill him."

"Social conflicts among prisoners are *their* business, not ours. You assigned this prisoner to exercise in yard 4, and yard 4 is where he will stay. To move him now would be to let him win."

Imhof began to speak, but Coffey cut him off with a sharp gesture. "Listen to me well, Imhof. I'm giving you a direct, official demand. The prisoner stays in yard 4. The FBI will take full responsibility."

There was a silence.

"I'll need that in writing," said Imhof at last.

Coffey nodded. "Just tell me where to sign."

34

Dr. Adrian Wicherly walked through the deserted Egyptian gallery, feeling a certain smug satisfaction at the special assignment Menzies had charged him with—him, and not Nora Kelly. He flushed at the thought of the way she had led him on and then humiliated him; he had heard that American women liked to burst one's bollocks, and now he'd had a taste of it, good and proper. The woman was as common as muck.

Well, he would be back in London soon enough, his C.V. nicely buffed up from this plum little assignment. His thoughts strayed to all the young, eager docents who volunteered at the British Museum—they had already proved to be delightfully flexible in their thinking. A pox on American women and their hypocritical puritanical moralism.

On top of that, Nora Kelly was bossy. Although he was the Egyptologist, she had never relinquished the riding crop; she had always remained firmly in charge. Although he had been hired to write the script for the sound-and-light extravaganza, she had insisted on proofreading it, making changes, and in general making a bloody nuisance of herself. What was she doing working in a big museum, anyway, when she really should be tucked away in some semidetached house in the suburbs with a pack of squalling brats? Who was this husband she was allegedly so loyal to? Maybe the problem was she was rogering someone on the side *already*. Yes, that was probably it . . .

Wicherly arrived at the annex and paused. It was very late—Menzies had been quite insistent on the time—and the museum was almost unnaturally silent. He listened to that silence. There were some sounds—but what, exactly, he couldn't say. A faint sighing somewhere of . . . what? Forced-air ducts? And then a slow, methodical ticking: *tick . . . tick . . . tick . . .* every two or three seconds, like a moribund clock. There were also faint thumps and groans, which could be ducts or something to do with the museum's mechanical systems.

Wicherly smoothed down his thatch of hair, glancing around nervously. They had caught the killer the day before and there was nothing to worry about. Nothing. Strange, though, what had happened to Lipper . . . typical smart-arsed New Yorker, one wouldn't have thought he would snap like that. Well, they were all a little tense. These Americans worked themselves half to death—he couldn't believe the hours they worked. Back at the British Museum, such demands would be looked on as downright uncivilized, if not illegal. Look at him now, for example: three o'clock in the bloody morning. Of course, given the nature of Menzies's assignment, it was understandable.

Wicherly swiped his card through the reader attached to the wall, punched in his code, and the gleaming new stainless-steel doors to the Tomb of Senef opened with a whisper of well-machined metal. The tomb exhaled the scent of dry stone, epoxy glue, dust, and warm electronics. The lights came up automatically. Nothing had been left to chance; everything was now fully programmed. A backup tech to succeed poor Lipper had already reported for duty, but so far had proved superfluous. The grand opening was only five days away, and although the tomb's collections were only partially installed, the lighting, electronics, and the sound-and-light show were ready to go.

Still, Wicherly hesitated. His eye strayed down the long, sloping staircase to the corridor beyond. He felt a small tingle of apprehension. Trying to shake it off, he stepped inside and walked down the stairs, his oxfords making a *chuff-chuff* sound on the worn stones.

At the first door, he paused, almost against his will, glance arrested by the great Eye of Horus and the hieroglyphs below. *To any who cross this threshold, may Ammut swallow his heart.* It was a standard enough curse; he had entered a hundred tombs under a similar threat, and never once had it put the wind up him. But the image of Ammut on the far wall was unusually hideous. And then, there was the strange, dark history of the tomb, not to mention the business with Lipper . . .

The ancient Egyptians believed in the magical powers of the incantations and images written on tomb walls, especially in the Book of the Dead. These were not mere decoration: they had a power against which the living were helpless. In studying Egypt for so long, in learning to read hieroglyphics fluently, in immersing himself in their ancient beliefs, Wicherly had come to half believe them himself. Of course, they were all rubbish, but at one level he understood them so thoroughly they almost seemed real.

And never had they seemed more real than at that moment: especially the squatting, grotesque form of Ammut, its slavering crocodile jaws open and glistening, the scaly head morphing into a leopard's spotted body, which in turn segued into the hindquarters of a hippo. Those hindquarters were the most vile of all: a bloated, slimy, misshapen fundament spreading over the ground. All three animals, Wicherly knew, were common killers of people during the time of the pharaohs, and greatly feared. A monstrous amalgamation of all three was the worst creature the ancient Egyptians could imagine.

Shaking his head and forcing a rueful chuckle, Wicherly walked on. He was letting himself get spooked by his own erudition, by all the ridiculous talk and silly rumors circulating through the museum. After all, this was not some tomb lost in the wastes of the Upper Nile: one of the biggest, most modern cities in the world was sitting right on top of him. Even as he stood there, he heard the distant, muffled rumble of a late-night subway. It annoyed him: despite all their efforts, they had been unable to block out totally the sound of the Central Park West subway.

He crossed the well and glanced up at the dense script from the Book of the Dead, his eye arrested by the odd inscription that he had so cavalierly dismissed during his first visit:

The place which is sealed. That which lieth down in the closed place is reborn by the Ba-soul which is in it; that which walketh in the closed space is dispossessed of the Ba-soul. By the Eye of Horus I am delivered or damned, O great god Osiris.

Like many inscriptions from the Book of the Dead, it was well-nigh opaque. But as he read it a second time, a glimmer of understanding came to him. The ancients believed people had five distinct souls. The Ba-soul was the ineffable power and personality each person possessed: this soul flew back and forth between the tomb and the underworld, and it was the means by which the deceased kept in touch with the underworld. But the Ba-soul had to reunite with the mummified corpse every night, or the deceased would die again: this time permanently.

The passage, it seemed to Wicherly, implied that those who invaded the place which was sealed—the tomb—would be deprived of their Ba-soul and thus damned by the Eye of Horus. In ancient Egypt, the insane were considered to be people who had somehow lost their Ba-soul. In other words, those who defiled the tomb would be driven insane.

Wicherly shivered. Isn't that just what had happened to that poor bugger Lipper?

Suddenly he found himself laughing out loud, his voice echoing unpleasantly in the close confines of the tomb. What was the matter with him? He was becoming as superstitious as a bloody Irishman. He gave his head another, more vigorous shake and proceeded into the inner tomb. He had work to do. He had a special errand to run for Dr. Menzies.

35

Nora unlocked her office door, laid her laptop and mail on the desk, then shrugged out of her coat and hung it up. It was a cold, sunny late-March morning, and yellow light streamed in the window, making an almost horizontal bar of gold light, raking the spines of the books crowding the shelves along the opposite wall.

Four more days until the opening, she thought with satisfaction, and then she could get back to her potsherds—and her husband, Bill. Because of her long hours at the museum, their lovemaking had been so scarce of late he'd even stopped bothering to complain. *Four more days.* It had been a long, stressful haul—and bizarre even by museum standards—but it was almost over. And who knew? The opening might actually be fun. She'd be taking Bill, and she knew how much he liked a good gorge—and the museum, for all its shortcomings, knew how to throw a party.

She settled at her desk and had just begun slitting open the letters when a knock sounded at the door.

"Come in," she said, wondering who else would be in so early—it was barely eight o'clock.

The avuncular form of Menzies appeared in the doorway, his blue eyes worried, his brow furrowed with concern.

"May I?" he asked, gesturing at the guest chair.

"Please."

He came in and sat down, folding one leg over the other and tugging at the crease in his herringbone slacks. "You haven't seen Adrian, have you?"

"No. But it's very early, he probably isn't in yet."

"That's just the thing. He did come in: at three this morning. Checked in through security and accessed the tomb, according to the electronic security logs. Then he left the tomb at three-thirty, locked it up tight. Strange thing is, he didn't leave the museum—he hasn't checked out. Security shows him as still on the premises, but he's not in his office or lab. In fact, I can't find him anywhere. I thought perhaps he might have said something to you."

"No, nothing. Do you know why he came in at three?"

"He might have wanted to get a head start on the day: as you know, we have to start moving in the final artifacts at nine. I've got the carpenters, the Exhibition Department, and the conservation staff all mobilized. But no Adrian. I can't believe he would just vanish like this."

"He'll show up. He's always been reliable."

"I should hope so."

"I should hope so, too," came another voice.

Nora glanced up, startled. Wicherly stood in the doorway, looking at her.

Menzies seemed startled himself and then smiled with relief. "There you are! I was starting to get worried."

"No need to worry about me."

Menzies rose. "Well then, much ado about nothing. Adrian, I'd like to have a chat with you in my office about the artifact placements. We have a big day ahead of us."

"Mind if I have a word with Nora first? I'll see you in a few minutes."

"Fine." Menzies left and shut the door behind him.

Wicherly sat himself down, uninvited, in the wing chair Menzies had just vacated. Nora felt a twitch of annoyance. She hoped he wasn't going to repeat his asinine behavior of the previous week.

When he spoke again, his voice was laced with sarcasm. "Worrying that I might try to slip something unwelcome into your knickers?"

"Adrian, I don't have time for this. I've got a busy day ahead of me, and so do you. Give it a rest."

"Not after your abominable behavior."

"*My* behavior?" Nora took a breath: this was not the time to get into it. "The door is over there. Please use it."

"Not until we settle this thing."

Nora looked at Wicherly more closely, feeling a twinge of alarm. She was suddenly struck by how tired he looked—wiped out, even. His face was white; gray pouches had formed under his blue eyes; and his hair was damp and disordered. Most surprising of all, his suit and tie, always immaculate, looked untidy, even disheveled. Beads of sweat stood on his brow.

"Are you all right?"

"I'm *fine!*" But as he spoke, one side of his face suddenly contracted in a grotesque twitch.

"Adrian, I honestly think you need a break. You've been working too hard." She kept her voice calm and cool. As soon as he left, she would call Menzies and suggest he order Wicherly home for the day. Much as they needed his expertise—and despite his obnoxious behavior, he'd proved invaluable—they couldn't afford a crack-up just before the opening.

His face twitched again, a horrible muscular contraction that screwed his handsome features into a brief grimace before allowing them to spring back into normalcy.

"Why did you ask me that, Nora? Don't I seem all right?"

His voice had risen in volume. She noticed his hands were gripping the arm of the chair so hard that the fingernails were digging into the fabric.

Nora rose from her seat. "You know, with all your hard work, I really think you've earned a day off." She decided she wouldn't even check with Menzies: she was the curator of the show, and she was going to send him home. Wicherly was in no condition to be supervising the moving of millions of dollars' worth of artifacts.

Another hideous twitch. "You still haven't answered my question."

"You're exhausted, that's all. I'm giving you the day off. This is not optional, Adrian. I want you to go home and get some rest."

"Not optional? And since when have you been my boss?"

"Since the day you arrived here. Now, please go home or I'll be forced to call security."

"Security? They're a ruddy joke!"

"Please remove yourself from my office." And Nora reached for the phone.

But suddenly Wicherly—rising—lunged forward and swept it from the desk to the floor, stomped on the cradle, yanked the wire out the back, and tossed it aside.

Nora froze. Something terrible was happening to Wicherly, something utterly beyond her experience.

"Look, Adrian," she said calmly. "Let's just cool down here." She stood up, then began edging along the desk.

"You bloody *tart*," he said in a low, menacing tone.

Nora could see his fingers twitching now, contracting a little more with each twitch until they formed a spastically clutching fist. She could almost smell the air of violence gathering around him. She came around the desk, not fast, but with slow determination.

"I'm leaving," she said as firmly as she could. At the same time, she braced for a fight. If he came at her, she'd go straight for his eyes.

"The *fuck* you are." Wicherly stepped across her path while at the same time reaching behind his back and turning the lock in the door.

"Get away from me *now!*"

He stood his ground, eyes bloodshot, pupils like tiny black bullets. She struggled against a rising panic. What would work: calm persuasion or stern command? She could smell his sweat, almost as strong as urine. His face had screwed itself up again in a series of spastic jerks, his right fist clenching and unclenching. He looked exactly as if he'd been possessed by demonic forces.

"Adrian, everything's okay," she said, working a soothing note into her trembling voice. "You just need help. Let me call for a doctor."

More twitching, his neck muscles knotting and bulging.

"I think you might be having a seizure of some kind," she said. "Do you understand, Adrian? You need a doctor immediately. Please let me help you."

He tried to say something but instead he spluttered, spittle drooling down his chin.

"Adrian, I'm going to step outside now and call you a doctor—"

His right hand jerked up like a shot, striking her hard across the face, but she had been tensing for just such an attack and she managed to sidestep the main force of the blow. She fell backward. "Somebody help me! *Guards! Call the guards!*"

"Shut up, *bitch!*" He shuffled forward, dragging one leg, and struck at her again, wildly. She stumbled against the side of her desk, off balance, and he leaped on top of her immediately, slamming her down and sending her laptop crashing to the floor.

"*Help! I'm being attacked!*"

She stabbed at his eyes with the rigid fingers of her hand, but he swatted her arm away and dealt her a blow across the side of her head, while his other hand grabbed the top of her blouse and ripped downward, scattering buttons.

She screamed again and tried to twist away from his grip, but his free hand came around and wrapped around her neck with shocking force, cutting off the sound. She scrabbled with her legs, trying to find a purchase, but he scissored them in his own.

"So, you think you're the boss?" He raised his other hand and together they began squeezing her neck harder. She flailed, tore at his hair, pounded his back, but he seemed not even to notice, so fixated was he on the grip of his hands, his sweaty, stinking, twitching face shoved into hers.

"I'll show you who's boss around here."

Nora punched and clawed helplessly, her diaphragm heaving to suck in air that wouldn't come. Her larynx felt nearly crushed under the awful pressure. He'd blocked the blood flow to her brain and she felt the strength draining away like water from a burst hose; her eyes were suddenly flecked with a million exploding stars, and a spreading stain of darkness began clouding the edges of her vision like ink poured into water.

"How does it feel, *bitch?*"

She heard sounds in the background, as if from far away; a violent hammering and splintering of wood; and then, from the furthest edge of consciousness, she felt the iron grip of his hands loosen and fall away. She was still swimming in a sea of dimness when she was jolted by a burst of shouting and an incredibly loud bang.

She rolled over, coughing violently and holding her bruised neck . . . and suddenly Menzies was there, cradling her in his arms and calling for a doctor. She felt utter confusion. There seemed to be a terrific commotion beyond the desk, a knot of museum guards, shouting . . . and then she saw a river of blood spreading out across the floor. What had happened?

"I had to do it, he came at me with a knife!" came a desperate voice, edging into her returning consciousness.

". . . just a letter opener, you idiot!"

". . . a doctor! *Now!*"

". . . tried to strangle her . . ."

The cacophony of loud, panicky voices continued, the shattered phrases sounding in her head as it all began to come back . . . She coughed, trying to block it all out, trying not to think, while Menzies eased her down into the wing chair, whispering all the time: "You're all right, my dear, everything's fine, the doctor's on his way. No, don't look over there . . . Close your eyes and all will be fine . . . Don't look, don't look . . ."

36

Captain Hayward looked down at the huge puddle of blood on the linoleum floor of the office, all smeared about by the frantic and useless efforts of the EMTs trying to restart a heart that had been obliterated by a point-blank 9mm round fired from a Browning Hi. The scene was now being carefully examined, sorted, tagged, and bottled by the forensic teams and a variety of specialized crime scene investigators.

She backed out of the office, leaving it to the experts to make sense of what was clearly a senseless, tragic act. She had another assignment: to speak with the victim before she was taken to the hospital.

She found Nora Kelly waiting in the staff lounge, with her husband, Bill Smithback; the chairman of the Anthropology Department, Hugo Menzies; and several EMTs, police officers, and museum guards. The EMTs were arguing with Kelly about whether she would go to the hospital for a checkup and treatment.

"I want the guards and museum staff out," said Hayward. "Except Drs. Kelly and Menzies."

"I'm not going," said Smithback. "I'm not leaving my wife."

"You can stay, then," said Hayward.

One of the EMTs, who had obviously been arguing with Nora for a while, leaned in for one last try. "Listen here, miss, your neck is bruised and you might have a concussion. The effects can be delayed. We've got to take you in for tests."

"Don't 'miss' me. I'm a Ph.D."

"The paramedic's right," Smithback added. "You need to go for at least a quick exam."

"Quick? I'll be in the emergency room all day. You know what St. Luke's is like!"

"Nora, we can get along quite well without you today," Menzies said. "You've had a terrible shock—"

"With all due respect, Hugo, you know as well as I do that with Dr. Wicherly . . . Oh, God, this is *terrible!*" She choked up for a moment, and Hayward used the opportunity to speak.

"I know this is a bad time, Dr. Kelly, but can I ask you a few questions?"

Nora wiped her eyes. "Go ahead."

"Can you tell me what happened leading up to the attack?"

Nora took a deep, steadying breath. Then she proceeded to relate the events that had occurred in her office just ten minutes before, as well as the pass Wicherly had made at her a few days before. Hayward listened without interrupting, as did her husband, Smithback, his face darkening with anger.

"Bastard," he muttered.

Nora waved an impatient hand at him. "Something happened to him today. He wasn't the same person. It was like he had . . . a *seizure* of some kind."

"Why were you in the museum so early?" Hayward asked.

"I had—*have*—a busy day ahead of me."

"And Wicherly?"

"I understand he came in at three A.M."

Hayward was surprised. "What for?"

"I've no idea."

"Did he go into the tomb?"

It was Menzies who answered. "Yes, he did. The security log shows he entered the tomb just after three, spent half an hour in there, then left. Where he was between then and the attack, we don't know. I looked all over for him."

"I assume you checked his background before you hired him. Did he have a criminal record, a history of aggression?"

Menzies shook his head. "Absolutely nothing like that."

Hayward looked around and saw to her relief that Visconti had been assigned to the museum that day. She motioned him over.

"I want you to take statements from Dr. Menzies and the guard who shot Wicherly," she said. "We can get Dr. Kelly's when she returns from the hospital."

"No way," Nora said. "I'm ready to give a statement now."

Hayward ignored her. "Where's the M.E.?"

"Went to the hospital with the body."

"Get him on the radio."

A moment later, Visconti handed her a radio. Then he led Menzies off to take a statement.

"Doctor?" Hayward spoke into the radio. "I want an autopsy performed as soon as possible. I want you to look for lesions to the temporal lobe of the brain, particularly to the ventromedial frontal cortex . . . No, I'm not a neurosurgeon. I'll explain later."

She handed the radio back to Visconti, then cast a firm eye on Nora. "You're going to the hospital. Now." She gestured to the EMTs. "Help her to her feet and get moving."

Then she turned to Smithback. "I want to talk to you privately, in the hall."

"But I want to go with my wife—"

"We'll have a police car take you after we speak, sirens, the works. You'll get there at the same time as the ambulance."

She exchanged a brief word with Nora, gave her a reassuring pat on her shoulder, and then nodded Smithback into the hall. They found a quiet corner and Hayward faced the journalist.

"We haven't spoken in a while," she said. "I was hoping you might have something to share with me."

At the question, Smithback looked a little uncomfortable. "I published that story we talked about. Two, even. They didn't shake free any leads—at least none that I heard about."

Hayward nodded, waiting. Smithback glanced at her, then glanced away. "Every trail I tried turned cold. That's when I . . . paid a visit to the house."

"House?"

"You know. *His* house. The one where he held Viola Maskelene."

"You snuck in? I didn't know they'd finished the investigation. When did the crime scene tape come down?"

Now Smithback looked even more uncomfortable. "It wasn't down."

"What?" Hayward raised her voice. "You trespassed on an active crime scene?"

"It wasn't all *that* active!" Smithback said quickly. "I only saw one cop the whole time I was there!"

"Look, Mr. Smithback, I don't want to hear any more. I can't and won't have you operating extralegally—"

"But it was in the house that I found it."

Hayward stopped and looked at him.

"Well, it's nothing I can prove. It's just a theory, really. At first I really thought it was something, but later on . . . Anyway, that's why I didn't call you about it earlier."

"Out with it."

"In a coat closet, I found a bunch of Diogenes's coats."

Hayward crossed her arms, waiting.

"Three were very expensive cashmere or camel's-hair, elegant, Italian-designed. Then there were a couple of big, bulky, itchy tweed jackets, also expensive but of a totally different style—you know, stodgy English professor."

"And?"

"I know this sounds strange, but something about those tweeds—well, they almost seemed like a disguise. Almost as if Diogenes—"

"Has an alter ego," Hayward said. She realized where this was going, and she was suddenly very interested.

"Right. And what kind of alter ego would wear tweeds? A professor."

"Or a curator," Hayward said.

"*Exactly*. And then it dawned on me he's probably a curator in the museum. I mean, they're all saying the diamond heist had to have been an inside job. He didn't have a partner—maybe he himself was the inside man. I know it sounds a little crazy . . ." His voice trailed off, uncertain.

Hayward looked at him intently. "Actually, I think it's far from crazy."

Smithback stopped to glance at her in surprise. "You do?"

"Absolutely. It fits the facts better than any other theory I've heard. Diogenes is a curator in this museum."

"But it just doesn't make sense. Why would Diogenes steal the diamonds . . . and then pound them into dust and mail them back here?"

"Maybe he has some personal grudge against the museum. We won't know for sure until we catch him. Good job, Mr. Smithback. There's just one more thing."

Smithback's gaze narrowed. "Let me guess."

"That's right. This conversation never took place. And until I say otherwise, these speculations are to go no further. Not even to your wife. And certainly not to the *New York Times*. Are we clear?"

Smithback sighed, nodded.

"Good. Now I need to track down Manetti. But first, let me get that squad car to take you to the hospital." She smiled. "You've earned it."

37

In the great paneled office of Frederick Watson Collopy, director of the New York Museum of Natural History, a silence reigned. Everyone had arrived: Beryl Darling, the museum's general counsel; Josephine Rocco, head of PR; Hugo Menzies. The short list of Collopy's most trusted staff. They were all seated and looking in his direction, waiting for him to begin.

At last Collopy laid a hand on his leather-topped desk and looked around. "Never in its long history," he began, "has the museum faced a crisis of these proportions. Never."

He let that sink in. The silence, the immobility, of his audience held.

"In short order, we have been dealt several blows, any one of which could cripple an institution such as ours. The theft and destruction of the diamond collection. The murder of Theodore DeMeo. The inexplicable attack on Dr. Kelly, and the subsequent killing of the assailant— the very distinguished Dr. Adrian Wicherly of the British Museum—by a trigger-happy guard."

A pause.

"And in four days, one of the biggest openings in the museum's history is scheduled. The very opening that was to put the diamond theft behind us. The question I pose to you now is this: how do we respond? Do we postpone the opening? Do we hold a press conference? I've gotten calls from twenty trustees so far this morning, and every single one has a different idea. And in ten minutes, I have to face a homicide captain named Hayward who—I have no doubt—will demand that we postpone the opening. It's up to us four, at this moment, to set a course and stick with it."

He folded his hands on the desk. "Beryl? Your thoughts?"

Collopy knew that Beryl Darling, the museum's general counsel, would speak with brutal clarity.

Darling leaned forward, pencil poised in her hand. "The first thing I'd do, Frederick, is disarm every museum guard in the building."

"Already done."

Darling nodded with satisfaction. "Next, instead of a press conference—which can spin out of control—I would immediately issue a statement."

"Saying?"

"It will be an unvarnished recitation of the facts, followed by a mea culpa and an expression of profound sympathy to the families of the victims—DeMeo, Lipper, and Wicherly—"

"Excuse me. Lipper and Wicherly? Victims?"

"The expression of regret will be strictly neutral. The museum doesn't want to get in the business of throwing stones. Let the police sort out the facts."

A frosty silence.

"And the opening?" Collopy asked.

"Cancel it. Shut the museum down for two days. And make sure nobody—and I mean *nobody*—at the museum talks to the press."

Collopy waited a moment, then turned to Josephine Rocco, head of public relations.

"Your comments?"

"I'm in agreement with Ms. Darling. We've got to show the public that it's not business as usual."

"Thank you." Collopy turned to Menzies. "Do you have anything to add, Dr. Menzies?" He was amazed at how cool, collected, and composed Menzies looked. He wished he had the same sangfroid.

Menzies nodded toward Darling and Rocco. "I would like to commend Ms. Darling and Ms. Rocco for their well-considered comments, which under almost any other circumstances would be excellent advice."

"But you differ?"

"I do. Most decidedly." Menzies's blue eyes, so full of calm self-assurance, impressed Collopy.

"Let's hear it, then."

"I hesitate to contradict my colleagues, whose wisdom and experience in these matters exceeds my own." Menzies glanced around humbly.

"I've asked for your unvarnished opinion."

"Well, then. Six weeks ago, the diamond collection was stolen and destroyed. Now an outside contractor—not a museum employee—kills a co-worker. Then a museum consultant—a temporary hire, not an employee—assaults one of our top curators and is killed by a guard in the ensuing melee. Now, I ask you: what do these events have in common?" Menzies looked around inquiringly.

No one answered.

"Ms. Darling?" Menzies persisted.

"Well, nothing."

"*Exactly.* During the same six-week period, New York City had sixty-one homicides, fifteen hundred assaults, and countless felonies and misdemeanors. Did the mayor shut down the city? No. What did he do instead? He announced the good news: the crime rate is down four percent from the previous year!"

"So," drawled Darling, "what 'good news' would you announce, Dr. Menzies?"

"That despite recent events, the grand opening of the Tomb of Senef is still on schedule and will go off exactly as planned."

"And just ignore the rest?"

"Of course not. By all means, issue a statement. But be sure to point out that this *is* New York City and that the museum is a vast place covering twenty-eight acres of Manhattan with two thousand employees and five million visitors a year, and that under these circumstances it's surprising that *more* random crimes don't happen. Be sure to emphasize the latter point: the crimes are not connected, they're random, and they've all been solved. The perpetrators have been caught. A run of bad luck, that's all."

He paused. "And there's one final point to consider."

"What's that?" Collopy asked.

"The mayor is coming and plans to give an important speech. It's possible he might just use the auspicious occasion to announce his bid for re-election."

Menzies smiled and fell silent, his bright blue eyes surveying the room, challenging them all to respond.

The first to stir was Beryl Darling. She uncrossed her legs, tapped the pencil on the table. "I must say, Dr. Menzies, that's a rather interesting take on things."

"I don't like it," said Rocco. "We can't just dismiss all this, sweep it under the rug. We'll be crucified."

"Who suggested sweeping anything under the rug?" said Menzies. "On the contrary, we'll release all the facts. We'll hide nothing. We'll beat our breasts and take full responsibility. The facts work in our favor because they clearly demonstrate the random nature of the crimes. And the perpetrators are either dead or behind bars. Case closed."

"What about the rumors?" asked Rocco.

Menzies turned a pair of surprised blue eyes on her. "Rumors?"

"All the talk about the tomb being cursed."

Menzies chuckled. "The mummy's curse? It's marvelous. Now everyone will want to come."

Rocco's bright red lips tightened, cracking her heavy lipstick.

"And let's not forget the original purpose of the Tomb of Senef— to remind the city that we are still the greatest natural history museum in the world. We need this distraction more than ever."

A long silence settled on the group. Collopy finally stirred. "That's damned persuasive, Hugo."

"I find myself in the curious position of changing my mind," said Darling. "I believe I concur with Dr. Menzies."

Collopy looked at the PR head. "Josephine?"

"I still have my doubts," she replied slowly. "But it's worth a try."

"Then that's settled," said Collopy.

As if on cue the door opened, with no knock, no announcement. A policewoman stood there, dressed in a smart gray suit, brass on her collar. Collopy glanced at his watch—she was on time to the second.

He rose. "May I introduce Captain of Homicide Laura Hayward. This is—"

"We're all acquainted," she said crisply. She turned a pair of violet eyes on him. She was disconcertingly young and attractive. Collopy wondered if she was some kind of affirmative-action type, advanced beyond her competence. Somehow, looking at those eyes, he doubted it.

"I'd like to speak with you privately, Dr. Collopy," she said.

"Of course."

The door closed after Menzies—the last to leave—had said his good-byes. Collopy turned his attention on Hayward. "Would you like to take a seat, Captain?"

After the briefest of hesitations, she nodded. "I think I will." She sank down in a wing chair and Collopy noted that her skin was pale and she looked exhausted. And yet her violet eyes were anything but dull.

"What can I do for you, Captain?" he asked.

She withdrew a sheaf of folded papers from her pocket. "I've got here the results of the autopsy on Wicherly."

Collopy raised his eyebrows. "Autopsy? Is there some mystery about how he died?"

By way of answer, she withdrew another piece of paper. "And here's a diagnostic report on Lipper. The bottom line is they both suffered identical, sudden brain damage to the ventromedial cortex of the brain."

"Indeed?"

"Yes. In other words, they both went insane in *exactly the same way*. The damage produced a sudden, violent psychosis in each of them."

Collopy felt a cold sensation along the base of his spine. This was exactly what they had dismissed—that the incidents were somehow connected. This could ruin everything.

"The evidence suggests there's some kind of environmental cause, and that it may be in or around the Tomb of Senef."

"The tomb? Why do you say that?"

"Because that's where both of them were immediately prior to the onset of symptoms."

Collopy swallowed painfully, pulled at his collar. "This is astonishing news."

"The M.E. thinks the cause could be anything: electrical shock to the head, poison, fumes or perhaps a malfunction in the ventilation system, an unknown virus or bacterium . . . We don't know. This is, by the way, confidential information."

"I'm glad of that." Collopy felt the sensation of cold begin to spread. If this got out, it could put the lie to their statement and destroy all they had worked so hard for.

"Since I received this information two hours ago, I've put a special toxicological forensic team into the tomb. They've been at it for an hour and so far haven't found anything. Of course, it's early in their search."

"This is very disturbing, Captain," Collopy replied. "Is there any way the museum could be of assistance?"

"That's exactly why I'm here. I want you to postpone the opening until we can locate the source."

This was precisely what Collopy had been afraid of. He let a beat pass. "Captain, forgive me for saying so, but it seems you've jumped to two huge conclusions here: first, that the brain damage was caused by a toxin, and second, that this toxin is present in the tomb. It could have been anything—and happened anywhere."

"Perhaps."

"And you forget that others—many others—have spent significantly more time in the Tomb of Senef than Lipper and Wicherly. They've manifested no symptoms."

"I didn't forget that, Dr. Collopy."

"In any case, the opening isn't for four days. Surely, that's enough time to check out the tomb."

"I'm not taking any chances."

Collopy took a long, deep breath. "I understand what you're saying, Captain, but the fact is, we simply can't delay the opening. We've invested millions. I've got a new Egyptologist arriving in less than an hour, flown in all the way from Italy. The invitations have been mailed and acceptances returned, the catering paid for, the musicians hired—everything's done. To back out now would cost a fortune. And it would send the wrong message to the city: that we're frightened, that we're stymied, that the museum is a dangerous place to visit. I can't allow that."

"There's something else. It's my belief that Diogenes Pendergast, the person who attacked Margo Green—and who stole the diamond collection—has a second identity as a museum employee. Most likely a curator."

Collopy looked at her, shocked. "What?"

"I also believe this person is somehow connected with what's happened to Lipper and Wicherly."

"These are very serious accusations. Who's your suspect?"

Hayward hesitated. "I don't have one. I asked Mr. Manetti to comb the personnel records—without telling him what I was looking for, of course—but no criminal histories or any other red flags came to light."

"Naturally not. Our employees all have spotless records, especially the curatorial staff. I find this whole line of speculation to be personally offensive. And it certainly doesn't change my position about the opening. A postponement would be fatal to the museum. Absolutely fatal."

Hayward looked at him a long time, her violet eyes weary yet alert. They seemed almost sad, as if she had already known the conclusion was foregone. "By not postponing, you risk putting many lives in danger," she said quietly. "I must insist on it."

"Then we are at an impasse," said Collopy simply.

Hayward rose. "This isn't over."

"Correct, Captain. A higher power than us will have to make the decision."

She nodded and left the office without further comment. Collopy watched the door close behind her. He knew, and she knew, that it would boil down to a decision by the mayor himself. And in that case, Collopy knew exactly how the chips would fall.

The mayor wasn't one to miss the opportunity for a good party and speech.

38

Mrs. Doris Green paused at the open doorway to the intensive-care room. The afternoon light filtered through the partly screened windows, throwing peaceful stripes of light and shadow across her daughter's bed. Her eye moved across the bank of medical equipment, which sighed and beeped softly in a regular cadence, and came to rest on her daughter's face itself. It was pale and thin, a stray lock of hair running over the forehead and cheek. Mrs. Green took a few steps inside and gently moved the lock to its proper place.

"Hello, Margo," she said softly.

The machines continued to beep and sigh.

She eased herself down on the side of the bed and took her daughter's hand. It was cool and light as a feather. She gave it a gentle squeeze.

"It's a beautiful day outside. The sun's shining, and the cold weather seems to have broken. The crocuses are already coming up in my garden, just poking their little green shoots out of the ground. Do you remember when you were a little girl, just five years old—you couldn't resist picking them? You brought me a fistful of half-crushed flowers one day, cleaned out the whole garden. I was so upset at the time . . ."

Her voice faltered and she fell into silence. A moment later, the nurse entered, her cheerful, rustling presence adding a sudden efficiency to the gauzy atmosphere of bittersweet memory.

"How are you, Mrs. Green?" she asked, straightening up some flowers in a vase.

"All right, thank you, Jonetta."

The nurse checked the machines, jotting quick notes on a clipboard. She adjusted the IV, examined the breathing tube, then bustled about, plumping up more flowers and adjusting some of the get-well cards that covered the table and shelves.

"The doctor should be in at any moment, Mrs. Green," she said, smiling and heading for the door.

"Thank you."

Peace descended once more. Doris Green stroked her daughter's hand ever so lightly. The memories came back, crowding in with no discernible order: diving with her daughter off the dock at the lake; opening the envelope containing her SAT scores; roasting Thanksgiving turkey; standing hand in hand beside her husband's grave . . .

She swallowed, continued to stroke Margo's hand. And then she felt a presence behind her.

"Good afternoon, Mrs. Green."

She turned. Dr. Winokur was standing there, a dark, handsome man in crisp white, exuding self-confidence and sympathy. Doris Green knew it wasn't just his bedside manner: this doctor really cared.

"Would you care to talk in the waiting room?" he asked.

"I'd prefer to stay here. If Margo could hear—and who knows, maybe she can—she'd want to know everything."

"Very well." He paused, seated himself in the visitor's chair, rested his hands on his knees. "The bottom line is this: we simply don't have a diagnosis. We've performed every test we can think of and then some; we've consulted with the country's top coma and neurology specialists, at Doctors' Hospital in New York and Mount Auburn Hospital in Boston—and we just don't have a handle on it yet. Margo is in a deep coma, and we don't know why. The good news is that there's no evidence of permanent brain damage. On the other hand, her vital signs are not improving, and some important ones are slowly declining. She simply isn't responding to the normal treatments and therapies. I could load you down with a dozen theories we've had, a dozen treatments we've tried, but they all add up to one fact: she's not responding. We could move her to Southern Westchester. But to tell you the truth, there isn't anything down there that we don't have here, and the move might not be good for her."

"I'd prefer she stay here."

Winokur nodded. "I have to say, Mrs. Green, you've been a wonderful patient's mother. I know this is extremely hard on you."

She shook her head slowly. "I thought I had lost her. I thought I'd buried her. After that, nothing could be worse. I know she's going to recover—I *know* it."

Dr. Winokur gave a small smile. "You could be right. Medicine doesn't have all the answers, especially in a case like this. Doctors are more fallible—and illness a great deal more complex—than most people realize. Margo is not alone. There are thousands like her all over the country, very ill and without a diagnosis. I'm not telling you this to comfort you so much as to give you all the information I have. I sense that is how you'd prefer it."

"It is." She glanced from the doctor to Margo and back again. "Funny, I'm not much of a religious person, but I find myself praying for her every day."

"The longer I'm a doctor, the more I believe in the healing power of prayer." He paused. "Do you have any questions? Is there anything I can do?"

She hesitated. "There is one thing. I got a call from Hugo Menzies. Do you know him?"

"Yes, of course—her employer at the museum. He was with her when she had her seizure?"

"That's right. He called me to tell me what had happened, what he'd seen—he knew I'd want to know."

"Of course."

"Have you spoken to him?"

"Yes, certainly. He's been very good—he's dropped in to check on Margo's condition more than once since her relapse. He seems most concerned."

Mrs. Green smiled faintly. "Having such a caring employer is a blessing."

"It most certainly is." The doctor rose.

"I'll just stay here a little while with her, Doctor, if you don't mind," Doris Green said.

39

Thirty hours before the grand opening, the Tomb of Senef was boiling like a nest of angry hornets. And the swarm was no longer comprised of simply curators, electricians, carpenters, and technicians: a new element had been added to the mix. As Nora walked down the God's Second Passage toward the Hall of the Chariots, she was met with the glare of television lights and a knot of men setting up cameras and mikes at the far end of the hall.

"Over there, dear boy, over *there!*"

A slender man with clenched buttocks, wearing a camel's-hair sport jacket and yellow pinpoint bow tie, stood to one side. He was gesturing furiously with slender hands toward a burly soundman. Nora realized he must be the director Randall Loftus, whom Menzies had recently spoken to her about. He had won huge acclaim for his documentary series *The Last Cowboy on Earth*, and since then had produced a string of award-winning documentaries for public television.

As she approached, the babel of overlapping voices grew more shrill. "Testing. Testing . . ."

"Ugh! We've got the acoustics of a barn in here!"

Loftus and his crew were setting up to broadcast the premiere of the sound-and-light show on the night of the opening. The local PBS station planned to cover the opening live, and they had energetically syndicated the show to ensure it would not only go out to most PBS affiliates across the nation, but also be carried by the BBC and the CBC. It was a public relations coup that Menzies himself had worked hard to arrange. The resulting international attention, Nora knew, could go a long way toward saving the museum's bacon. But at the moment, they were causing utter chaos—and at the worst possible time. Their cables lay all over the ground, tripping up assistants carrying priceless Egyptian antiquities. The brilliant lights only added to the heat generated by hot electronics and the dozens of frantic people rushing about in a kind of controlled panic: the air-conditioning system ducts were roaring in a futile effort to lower the exhibit's temperature.

"I want two six-inch, one-kilowatt Mole Babies in the corner, there," Loftus was saying. "Will somebody move that jar?"

Nora quickly stepped up. "Mr. Loftus?"

He turned to her, squinting over the tops of his John Mitchell glasses. "Yes?"

She gamely stuck out her hand. "I'm Dr. Nora Kelly, curator of the exhibition."

"Oh! Of course. Randall Loftus. Delighted." He began to turn away.

"Excuse me, Mr. Loftus? You mentioned something about moving a jar. I'm sure you'll understand that nothing can be moved—or even touched—except by museum staff."

"Nothing moved! How am I supposed to set up?"

"You'll just have to work around things, I'm afraid."

"Work *around* things! I've never been asked to perform in such conditions. This tomb is like a straitjacket. I can't get any good angles or distance. It's impossible!"

She gave him a brilliant smile. "I'm sure, with your talent, you'll find a way to make it work."

The smile had no effect, but at the word *talent* Loftus seemed to pause.

"I've admired your work," Nora continued, sensing her opening. "I'm personally thrilled that you agreed to direct the show. And I know that, if anyone can make it work, you can."

Loftus touched his bow tie. "Thank you indeed. Flattery will get you everywhere."

"I wanted to introduce myself, see if there's anything I can do to help."

Loftus spun abruptly, shouted to someone in a dim corner teetering on a ladder, "Not that one, the *other* light, the LTM Pepper spot! I want it mounted on that ceiling rack on a three-sixty."

He turned back to her. "You're a dear, but we simply *must* move that jar."

"I'm sorry," said Nora. "There's no time to move anything even if we wanted to. That jar is three thousand years old and invaluable—you can't just pick it up and move it. It takes special equipment, specially trained conservators . . . As I said, you'll just have to work with what's here. I'll help you any way I can, but that's one thing I can't do. I'm sorry."

Loftus drew in a long breath. "I can't work around that jar. It's so fat and horrible."

When Nora didn't reply, the director waved his hand. "I'll talk to Menzies about it. Really, this is impossible."

"I'm sure you're as busy as I am, so I'll leave you," she replied. "As I said, if you need anything, let me know."

He turned away instantly, zeroing in on another hapless production assistant laboring in the shadows. "The low crankovator goes where the tape is. On the floor. You're *standing* on it! Look down, it's between your *legs*, for heaven's sake!"

Nora moved out of the Hall of the Chariots toward the burial chamber, leaving the gesticulating Loftus behind. The conservators had finished placing all the objects in the chamber—the last to be done—and Nora wanted to check the label copy against her master design. A knot of technicians was working on the fog machines inside the great stone sarcophagus. Earlier in the day, they'd run through a dress rehearsal of the entire sound-and-light show, and Nora had to admit that it was more than good. Wicherly may have been an ass, and possibly deranged, but he was also a brilliant Egyptologist and—what was more—an excellent writer. The script was an amazing tour de force; and the finale, when Senef came suddenly to life, rising out of a bubbling pool of mist, hadn't seemed hokey at all. Wicherly had managed to slip quite a lot of good, solid information into the show. People would leave not just entertained, but educated.

She paused. It was strange how such a competent archaeologist could crack up so quickly. Unconsciously, she rubbed her throat, still raw and bruised. She still felt uncomfortable going back into her lab after what had happened. It was bizarre, tragic, inexplicable . . . But once again, she tried to push the attack from her mind. She would digest it all after the opening.

She felt a light tap on her shoulder.

"Dr. Kelly, I presume?" The voice was a dusky, cultured English contralto.

She turned to find herself face-to-face with a tall woman with long, glossy black hair, dressed in old canvas pants, sneakers, and a dusty work shirt. One of the workers, evidently, but one she hadn't seen before: she would have remembered someone with such striking looks. And yet, as she looked at this stranger, she sensed she *had* seen her before.

"That's me," Nora said. "And you are—?"

"Viola Maskelene. I'm an Egyptologist and the new visiting curator for the show." She stuck out her hand, seized Nora's, and gave it a very vigorous shake. The grip was strong, the hand a little callused. This was someone who spent a lot of time outdoors—judging from her tan and her lean, one might even say weather-beaten, look.

"Very glad to meet you," Nora said. "I hadn't expected you so soon."

"I'm very pleased to meet you," Maskelene said. "Dr. Menzies has spoken so highly of you, and everyone just *adores* you! Dr. Menzies is tied up at present, but I wanted to come down and meet you right away . . . and see this marvelous exhibit!"

"As you can see, we're down to the wire."

"I'm sure you've got everything under control." Maskelene looked around with relish. "I was so surprised to receive the museum's invitation, and I can't tell you how delighted I am to be here. XIX Dynasty tombs are my specialty. And, incredibly, the Tomb of Senef has never been studied or published, although it apparently contains one of the most complete texts to the Book of the Dead ever found. Very few scholars even knew it existed! I'd always thought it was mere rumor, an urban myth like the alligators in your sewers. This is an incredible opportunity."

Nora smiled and nodded, studying the woman intently. The speed with which Wicherly had been replaced—he'd been dead only a few days—surprised her. But then, she reflected, the opening was looming and the museum absolutely had to have an Egyptologist in residence for the run of the show.

Viola, oblivious to the sound and chaos beyond, was looking around at the tomb with wonder. "What a treasure!"

Nora found herself liking the woman's high-spirited attitude. Her open, frank enthusiasm was infinitely preferable to the pontifications of some dusty old professor.

"I've just been checking the placement of the artifacts and doing a final run-through on the label copy," she said. "Care to come along? You might catch some errors."

"I'd adore it," she said, practically beaming. "Although with Adrian having done the work, I'm sure it's solid."

Nora turned. "You knew him?"

Viola's face clouded. "We Egyptologists are a rather small club. Dr. Menzies told me what happened. I can't understand it. How terribly frightening for you."

Nora simply nodded.

"I knew Adrian professionally," Viola said, her voice more quiet now. "He was a brilliant Egyptologist, although he rather fancied himself God's gift to women. Still, I never would have thought that . . . What a terrible shock." She broke off.

For a moment, an awkward silence settled over them. Then Nora roused herself.

"He left a fine legacy behind him," she said. "In his work for the exhibition. And I know it sounds crass, but the show must go on."

"I suppose so," Viola replied. Then she brightened a little. "I hear the sound-and-light show is quite spectacular."

"It has just about everything, even a talking mummy."

Viola laughed. "That sounds delicious!"

They walked on, Nora checking her clipboard. She took the opportunity to examine Viola Maskelene more closely out of the corner of her eye as the Egyptologist looked over the cases full of antiquities.

They paused at one spectacular canopic jar. "I'm afraid this is XVIII Dynasty," Viola said. "It's a bit anachronistic, compared to the other objects."

Nora smiled. "I know. We didn't quite have all the XIX Dynasty objects we needed, so we expanded—fudged—the time period a bit. Adrian explained that antiques, even at the time of the pharaohs, were often put in burials."

"Quite true! Sorry for bringing it up—I'm a bit of a stickler for details."

"Being a stickler for details is exactly what we need."

They circled the burial chamber, Nora checking items off her list, Viola parsing the label copy and examining the objects.

"Can you read hieroglyphics?" Nora asked.

Viola nodded.

"What do you make of the curse above the door, the one with the Eye of Horus?"

A laugh. "One of the nastiest I've ever seen."

"Really? I thought they were all nasty."

"On the contrary. Many Egyptian tombs aren't even protected with curses. They didn't need to be—everyone knew that to rob a pharaoh's tomb was to steal from the gods themselves."

"So why put a curse in this tomb?"

"I imagine it was because, unlike a pharaoh, Senef wasn't a god. He may have felt that the additional protection of the curse might be warranted. That painting of Ammut . . . whew!" Viola shuddered. "Goya couldn't do better."

Nora glanced at the painting, nodding grimly.

"I understand word of this curse has gotten around," Viola said.

"The guards started it. Now the whole museum is abuzz. A few of the maintenance staff flat-out refuse to go into the tomb after hours."

They came around a pilaster, only to find a woman in a gray suit kneeling on the stone floor, scraping dust out of a crack and putting it in a test tube. Nearby, a man in a white lab coat was organizing what looked like samples in a portable chemical laboratory.

"What in the world is she doing?" Viola whispered.

Nora had never seen the woman before. She certainly didn't look much like a museum employee. In fact, she looked like a cop.

"Let's find out." Nora walked over. "Hello. I'm Nora Kelly, curator of the exhibition."

The woman rose. "I'm Susan Lombardi, with the Occupational Safety and Health Administration."

"May I ask what you're doing?"

"We're testing for any environmental hazards—toxins, microbes, that sort of thing."

"Really? And why is that necessary?"

She shrugged. "All I know is, the request came from the NYPD. A rush job."

"I see. Thank you."

Nora turned away and the woman went back to work.

"That's odd," said Viola. "Are they worried about some kind of infectious disease, perhaps, endemic to the tomb itself? Some Egyptian tombs have been known to harbor ancient viruses and fungus spores."

"I suppose so. Strange that no one told me."

But Viola had turned away. "Oh, look—what a fabulous unguent container! It's better than *anything* in the British Museum!" And she rushed over to a large glass case containing an artifact carved in white alabaster and decorated with paint, a lion crouching on the lid. "Why, it has the cartouche of Thutmosis himself on it!" She knelt, examining it with rapt attention.

There was something refreshingly spontaneous, even rebellious, about Viola Maskelene. Nora took in the woman's beaten-up canvas pants, lack of makeup, and dusty work shirt, wondering if this was going to be her standard museum uniform. She looked just the opposite of a stuffy British archaeologist.

Viola . . . Viola Maskelene. It was a strange name, and it rang a bell . . . Had Menzies mentioned her before? No, not Menzies . . . somebody else . . .

And then, quite suddenly, she remembered.

"You were the one kidnapped by the jewel thief!" It came out in a rush, before she'd had time to think, and Nora immediately colored.

Viola rose quietly from the case and brushed off her knees. "Yes. That was me."

"I'm sorry. I didn't mean to fling it out like that."

"Actually, I'm glad you mentioned it. Better to get it out in the open and get past it."

Nora felt her cheeks flaming.

"It's fine, Nora—really. Actually, all that was just another reason I was glad to take this job and return to New York."

"Really?"

"To me, it's sort of like falling off a horse—you've got to get right back on if you ever hope to ride again."

"That's a good way to look at it." Nora paused. "So you're Agent Pendergast's friend."

Now it was time for Viola Maskelene to color. "You might say that."

"My husband, Bill Smithback, and I are well acquainted with Special Agent Pendergast."

Viola looked at her with fresh interest. "Really? How did you meet?"

"I helped with a case of his a few years ago. I feel terrible about what's happened to him." She didn't mention her husband's activities, which he had insisted on keeping confidential.

"Agent Pendergast is the other reason I returned," Viola said in a low voice. Then she fell into silence.

After they had finished up in the burial chamber, they followed with a quick check of the side chambers. Then Nora glanced at her watch. "One o'clock. You want some lunch? We're going to be here until after midnight, and you don't want to be caught running on empty. Come on—the shrimp bisque in the staff cafeteria is actually worth making a trip for."

At this, Viola Maskelene brightened. "Lead the way, Nora."

40

In the close darkness of cell 44, high within the isolation cellblock of Herkmoor Federal Correctional Facility, Special Agent Aloysius Pendergast lay at rest, his eyes open and staring at the ceiling. The dark was not absolute: an unchanging bar of light from the lone window streaked across the ceiling, formed by the harsh glare of the illuminated yards and grounds outside. From the next cell, the soft sounds of the drummer continued, muted and thoughtful now, a mournful adagio which Pendergast found curiously conducive to concentration.

Other sounds reached his sensitive ears: the clang of steel against steel; a distant gargled cry of anger; the endless repetition of a cough, coming in groups of three; footsteps of a guard on his rounds. The great prison of Herkmoor was resting but not sleeping—a world unto its own, with its own rules, food chain, rituals, and customs.

As Pendergast lay there, a trembling green dot appeared on the opposite wall: the beam of a laser, shot in through the window from a great distance. It quickly steadied itself. Then, after a moment, the dot began to blink off and on. Pendergast watched as it spelled out its coded message. The only sign of his comprehension was a slight quickening of breath toward the end of the message.

And then, as abruptly as it had come, the dot vanished. The faintly murmured word "Excellent" could be heard in the darkened cell.

Pendergast closed his eyes. Tomorrow at two o'clock he would once again have to face Lacarra's gang, the Broken Teeth, in yard 4. And then—assuming he survived the encounter—an even greater task would follow.

Right now, he required sleep.

Employing a specialized and secretive form of meditation known as Chongg Ran, Pendergast identified and isolated the pain in his broken ribs; then he turned the pain off, one rib at a time. His consciousness moved to the torn rotator cuff in his shoulder, the puncture wound in his side, the dull ache of his cut and bruised face. One by one, with cold mental discipline, he isolated and extinguished the pain in each part.

Such discipline was necessary. A most challenging day lay ahead.

41

The ancient Beaux Arts mansion at 891 Riverside Drive boasted many spacious halls, but none were grander than the broad gallery that ran across the entire front portion of the second floor. The wall facing the street was composed of a series of floor-to-ceiling windows, sealed and shuttered. At each end of the hall, arched doorways led back to other parts of the mansion. Between the two doors, along the inside wall, stretched an unbroken succession of life-sized oil portraits. The gallery was lit by dim electric candelabra, which threw lambent light over the heavy gilt frames. Piano music sounded from hidden speakers: dense, lush, and demonically complex.

Constance Greene and Diogenes Pendergast walked slowly down the gallery, pausing at each portrait while Diogenes murmured the history of its subject. Constance wore a pale blue dress, set off by a black lace front whose buttons ran up to the low neckline that surrounded her throat. Diogenes wore dark trousers and a silver-gray cashmere jacket. Both held tulip-shaped cocktail glasses.

"And this," Diogenes said as he stopped before a portrait of a splendidly dressed nobleman whose air of dignity was strangely offset by a rakish mustache, "is le Duc Gaspard de Mousqueton de Prendregast, the largest landholder in Dijon during the late sixteenth century. He was the last respectable member of the noble line which began with Sieur de Monts Prendregast, who won his title fighting in England with

William the Conqueror. Gaspard was something of a tyrant: he was forced to flee Dijon when the peasants and villeins working his lands revolted. He took his family to the royal court, but a scandal ensued and they were forced to leave France. Exactly what next happened to the family remains something of a mystery, but there was a dreadful split. One branch moved to Venice, while the other—those left without favor, title, or money—fled to America."

He moved to the next portrait, of a young man with flaxen hair, gray eyes, and a weak chin, whose full and sensual lips seemed almost the mirror of Diogenes's own. "This is the scion of the Venice branch of the family, the duke's son, Comte Lunéville—the title was by this point, alas, already honorary. He sank into idleness and dissipation, and for several generations his descendants followed suit. For a time, in fact, the lineage was sadly reduced. It did not regain its full flower for another hundred years, when the two family lines were reunited by marriage in America . . . but even that, of course, proved a fleeting glory."

"Why fleeting?" Constance asked.

Diogenes looked at her a moment. "The Pendergast family has been in a long, slow decline. My brother and I are the last. Although my brother married, his charming wife . . . met an *untimely* end before she could reproduce. I have neither wife nor child. If we die without issue, the Pendergast line will vanish from the earth."

They proceeded to the next painting.

"The American branch of the family ended up in New Orleans," he continued. "They moved comfortably in the wealthy circles of antebellum society. There, the last of the Venetian branch of the family, il Marquese Orazio Paladin Prendergast, married Eloise de Braquilanges in a wedding so lavish and brilliant it was talked about for generations. Their only child, however, became fascinated with the peoples, and the *practices*, of the surrounding bayous. He took the family in a wholly unexpected direction." He gestured at the portrait, displaying a tall, goateed man in a brilliant white suit with a blue ascot. "Augustus Robespierre St. Cyr Pendergast. He was the first fruit of the reunited family lines, a doctor and a philosopher, who dropped an *r* from the last name to make it more American. He was the cream of old New

Orleans society—until he married a ravishingly beautiful woman from the deep bayou who spoke no English and was given to strange nocturnal practices." Diogenes paused a moment, as if reflecting on something. Then he chuckled.

"It's remarkable," Constance breathed, fascinated despite herself. "All these years I've stared at these faces, trying to put names and histories to them. A few of the most recent ones I could guess at, but the rest . . ." She shook her head.

"Great-Uncle Antoine never told you of his ancestry?"

"No. He never spoke of it."

"I'm not surprised, really—he left the family on bad terms. As, in fact, did I." Diogenes hesitated. "And it's clear my brother never spoke much of the family to you, either."

Constance took a sip from her glass in lieu of reply.

"I know a great deal about my family, Constance. I have taken pains to learn their secret histories." He glanced at her again. "I can't tell you how happy it makes me to be able to share this with you. I feel I can talk to you . . . like no other."

She met his eyes only briefly before returning them to the portrait.

"You deserve to know it," he continued. "Because after all, you're a member of the family, too—in a way."

Constance shook her head. "I'm only a ward," she said.

"To me, you are more than that—much more."

They had hesitated before the portrait of Augustus. Now, to break a silence that threatened to grow awkward, Diogenes said, "How do you like the cocktail?"

"Interesting. It has an initial bitterness that blossoms on the tongue into . . . well, something else entirely. I've never tasted anything like it."

She looked at Diogenes for approval and he smiled. "Go on."

She took another small sip. "I detect licorice and aniseed, eucalyptus, fennel perhaps—and notes of something else I can't identify." She lowered the glass. "What is it?"

Diogenes smiled, sipped from his own glass. "Absinthe. Hand-macerated and distilled, the finest available. I have it flown in from Paris for my personal consumption. Diluted slightly with sugar and water, as is the classic preparation. The flavor you can't identify is thujone."

Constance stared at the glass in surprise. "Absinthe? Made from wormwood? I thought it was illegal."

"We should not be concerned with such trifles. It is powerful, mind-expanding: which is why great artists from Van Gogh to Monet to Hemingway made it their drink of choice."

Constance took another, cautious sip.

"Look into it, Constance. Have you ever seen a drink of such a pure and unadulterated color? Hold it up to the light. It's like gazing at the moon through a flawless emerald."

For a moment, she remained motionless, as if searching for answers in the green depths of the liqueur. Then she took another, slightly less tentative sip.

"How does it make you feel?"

"Warm. Light."

They continued slowly down the gallery.

"I find it remarkable," she said after a moment, "that Antoine fitted up this interior into a perfect replica of the family mansion in New Orleans. Down to the last detail—including these paintings."

"He had them re-created by a famous artist of the day. He worked with the artist for five years, reconstructing the faces from memory and a few faded engravings and drawings."

"And the rest of the house?"

"Almost identical to the original, save for his choice of volumes in the library. The use he devoted all the sub-basement chambers to, however, was . . . *unique*, to say the least. The New Orleans mansion was effectively below sea level and so had its basements lined with sheets of lead: that wasn't necessary here." He sipped his drink. "After my brother took over this house, a great many changes were made. It is no longer the place Uncle Antoine called home. But then, you know that all too well."

Constance did not reply.

They reached the end of the gallery, where a long, backless settee awaited, cushioned in plush velvet. Nearby lay an elegant English game bag by John Chapman in which Diogenes had brought the bottle of absinthe. Now he lowered himself gracefully onto the settee and motioned for Constance to do the same.

She sat down beside him, placing the glass of absinthe on a nearby salver. "And the music?" she asked, nodding as if to indicate the shimmering piano scales that freighted the air.

"Ah, yes. That is Alkan, the forgotten musical genius of the nineteenth century. You will never hear a more luxuriant, cerebral, technically challenging artist—never. When his pieces were first played—a rare event, by the way, since few pianists are up to the challenge—people thought them to be diabolically inspired. Even now Alkan's music inspires strange behavior in listeners. Some think they smell smoke while listening; others find themselves trembling or growing faint. This piece is the Grande Sonate, 'Les Quatre Âges.' The Hamelin recording, of course: I've never heard more assured virtuosity or more commanding finger technique." He paused, listening intently a moment. "This fugal passage, for instance: if you count the octave doublings, it has more parts than a pianist has fingers! I know you must appreciate it, Constance, as few do."

"Antoine was never a great appreciator of music. I learned the violin entirely on my own."

"So you can appreciate the intellectual and sensual heft of the music. Just listen to it! And thank God the greatest musical philosopher was a romantic, a decadent—not some smug Mozart with his puerile false cadences and predictable harmonies."

Constance listened a moment in silence. "You seem to have worked rather hard to make this moment agreeable."

Diogenes laughed lightly. "And why not? I can think of few pastimes more rewarding than to make you happy."

"You seem to be the only one," she said after a pause, in a very low voice.

The smile left Diogenes's face. "Why do you say that?"

"Because of what I am."

"You are a beautiful and brilliant young woman."

"I'm a freak."

Very quickly—yet with exceptional tenderness—Diogenes took her hands. "No, Constance," he said softly and urgently. "Not at all. Not to me."

She looked away. "You know my history."

"Yes."

"Then surely you, of all people, would understand. Knowing how I've lived—the *way* in which I've lived, here in this house, all these years . . . don't you find it bizarre? Repugnant?" Suddenly she looked back at him, eyes blazing with strange fire. "I am an old woman, trapped in the body of a young woman. Who would ever want me?"

Diogenes drew closer. "You have acquired the gift of experience—without the awful cost of age. You are young and vibrant. It may feel a burden to you now, but it doesn't have to be. You can be free of it any-time you choose. You can begin to live whenever you want. *Now*, if you choose."

She looked away again.

"Constance, look at me. No one understands you—except me. You are a pearl beyond price. You have all the beauty and freshness of a woman of twenty-one, yet you have a mind refined by a lifetime . . . no, *lifetimes* . . . of intellectual hunger. But the intellect can take you only so far. You are like an unwatered seed. Lay your intellect aside and recog-nize your other hunger—your *sensual* hunger. The seed cries for water—and only then will it sprout, rise, and blossom."

Constance, refusing to look back, shook her head violently.

"You have been cloistered here—shut up like a nun. You've read thousands of books, thought deep thoughts. But you haven't *lived*. There is another world out there: a world of color and taste and touch. Constance, we will explore that world together. Can't you feel the deep connection between us? Let me bring that world here, to you. Open yourself to me, Constance: I am the one who can save you. Because I'm the only person who truly understands you. Just as I am the one per-son who shares your pain."

Now, abruptly, Constance tried to pull her hands away. They re-mained gently—but firmly—clasped in Diogenes's own. But in the brief struggle, her sleeve drew back from her wrist, exposing several slashing scars: scars that had healed imperfectly.

Seeing this secret revealed, Constance froze: unable to move, even to breathe.

Diogenes also seemed to go very still. And then he gently released one hand and held out his own arm, sliding up the cuff from his wrist. There lay a similar scar: older but unmistakable.

Staring at it, Constance drew in a sharp breath.

"You see now," he murmured, "how well we understand each other? It is true—we are alike, so *very* alike. I understand you. And you, Constance—you understand me."

Slowly, gently, he released her other hand. It fell limply to her side. Now, raising his hands to her shoulders, he turned her to face him. She did not resist. He raised a hand to her cheek, stroking it very lightly with the backs of his fingers. The fingers drifted softly over her lips, then down to her chin, which he grasped gently with his fingertips. Slowly, he brought her face closer to his. He kissed her once, ever so lightly, and then again, somewhat more urgently.

With a gasp that might have been relief or despair, Constance leaned into his embrace and allowed herself to be folded into his arms.

Adroitly Diogenes shifted his position on the settee and eased her down onto the velvet cushions. One of his pale hands strayed to the lacy front of her dress, undoing a row of pearl buttons below her throat, the slender fingers gliding down, gradually exposing the swelling curve of her breasts to the dim light. As he did so, he murmured some lines in Italian:

> *Ei s'immerge ne la notte,*
> *Ei s'aderge in vèr' le stelle . . .*

As his form moved over her, nimble as a ballet dancer, a second sigh escaped her lips and her eyes closed.

Diogenes's eyes did not close. They remained open and fixed upon her, wet with lust and triumph—

Two eyes: one hazel, one blue.

42

Gerry sheathed his radio and cast a disbelieving look in Benjy's direction. "You won't frigging believe this."

"What now?"

"They're still bringing that special prisoner into yard 4 for the two o'clock exercise shift."

Benjy stared. "Bringing him *back*? You're shittin' me."

Gerry shook his head.

"It's murder. And they're doing it on our watch."

"Tell me about it."

"On whose orders?"

"Straight from the horse's ass: Imhof."

A silence gathered in the long empty hall of Herkmoor's building C.

"Well, two o'clock is in fifteen minutes," Benjy said at last. "We'd better get our butts in gear."

He led the way as they exited the cellblock into the weak sunlight of yard 4. A smell of springlike decay and dampness drifted on the air. The sodden grass of the outer yards was still matted and brown, and a few bare branches could be seen rising beyond the perimeter walls. They took up positions, not on the catwalk above this time, but in the actual yard.

"I'm not going to see my corrections career get flushed down the toilet," said Gerry darkly. "I swear, if any of Pocho's gang makes a move toward the guy, I'll use the Taser. I wish to hell they gave us guns."

They took up positions on either side of the yard, waiting for the prisoners in isolation to be escorted out for their lone hour of exercise. Gerry checked his Taser, his pepper spray, adjusted his side-handle baton. He wouldn't wait to see what happened, like he'd done last time.

A few minutes later, the doors opened and the escort guards filed out with their prisoners, who sidled out into the yard, blinking in the bright light, looking as shit-stupid as they were.

The last prisoner to come out was the special one. He was as pale as a maggot and looked a mess: face bruised and bandaged, one eye nearly swollen shut. Despite being numbed by years of working in pens, Gerry felt a creeping sense of outrage that the man had been put back in the yard. Pocho was dead, true enough; but that had been an open-and-shut case of self-defense. This was different. This was cold-blooded murder. And if it didn't happen today, it would happen to-morrow or the next day, on their watch or someone else's. It was one thing to stick the guy in a cell next to the drummer, or put him in soli-tary, or take away his books, but this was out of line. *Way* out of line.

He braced himself. Pocho's boys were spreading out, doing their slow pimp-roll, hands in their pockets. The tall one, Rafael Borges, was bouncing the usual basketball, moving in a slow arc toward the hoop. Gerry glanced at Benjy and saw his partner was equally on edge. The es-cort guards made a gesture toward him and he gestured back, signifying the handoff was complete: they would take over the prisoners. The es-cort guards filed out, closing the double metal doors behind them.

Gerry kept his eye on the special prisoner. The man was strolling along the brick wall toward the chain-link fence, moving alertly but without undue alarm. Gerry wondered if he was all right in the head. If it were him out there, he'd have stained his shorts by now.

He watched as the special prisoner sidled over behind the basketball backboard and placed a casual hand on the chain-link fence, leaning against it. He looked up, then peered from side to side, almost as if waiting for something. The other prisoners slowly circled, none even looking in his direction, acting as if he didn't exist.

When a call came over his radio with a burst of static, Gerry jumped. "Fecteau here."

"This is Special Agent Spencer Coffey, FBI."

"Who?"

"Wake up, Fecteau, I don't have all day. As I understand it, you and the other one, Doyle, are in yard 4 on exercise duty."

"Yes, yes, sir," Gerry stammered. Why the hell was Agent Coffey talking directly to him? It must be true what they were whispering, that the special prisoner was a fed—although he sure didn't look like one.

"I want both of you up here in Main Security, on the double."

"Yes, sir, as soon as we hand over yard duty—"

"I said, on the double. That means *right now*."

"But, sir, there's just the two of us guarding the yard—"

"I gave you a *direct order*, Fecteau. If I don't see you in *ninety* seconds, I swear to God you'll be in North Dakota tomorrow, on the midnight shift at Black Rock."

"But you're not—"

His reply was drowned out by a short blast of static as the FBI agent signed off. He looked over at Benjy, who had, of course, heard everything over his own radio. Benjy walked over, shrugging his shoulders faintly.

"We don't report to that bastard," Gerry said. "Do you think we have to do what he says?"

"You want to take that kind of chance? Let's get going."

Gerry replaced the radio, feeling sick to his stomach. It was murder, pure and simple. But at least they wouldn't be there when it happened—and they couldn't be blamed for that, now, could they?

Ninety seconds . . . He moved swiftly across the yard and opened the metal doors. Then he turned and threw one last glance back at the special prisoner. The man was still leaning against the chain-link fence behind the backboard. Pocho's gang was already starting to close in, packlike.

"God help him," he murmured to Benjy as the doors swung shut behind them with a deep metallic boom.

43

J uggy" Ochoa sauntered across the asphalt of the yard, glancing at the sky, the fence, the basketball backboard, his brothers scattered about. His eye turned back to the metal doors that had just clanged shut. The two guards had split. Just like that. He could hardly believe they'd put "Albino" back in the yard—and left him there.

There the sucker was, leaning against the fence, coolly returning his gaze.

Ochoa glanced around again through slitted eyes. His prison instincts told him something was going on. It was some kind of setup. Ochoa knew the others felt the same way. They didn't need to talk; everyone knew already what everyone else was thinking. The guards hated Albino as much as they did. Somebody in high places *wanted* him dead.

Ochoa was only too eager to oblige.

He spit on the asphalt and scuffed it in with his shoe while he watched Borges pound the basketball on the ground with his fist, once, twice, as he made a slow round toward the hoop. Borges was going to reach Albino first, and Ochoa knew Borges could be relied on to be cool and sit tight. There would be plenty of time to take care of the problem, nice and quiet, in a way that nobody got singled out. Sure, it would mean a few months in solitary, loss of privileges—but they were all lifers, anyway. And this was *sanctioned*. Whatever the consequences, they'd be mild.

He glanced up at the distant tower. Nobody was looking their way: the tower guards mostly looked to the side and out, toward the perimeter fences. Their view of the interior of yard 4 was limited.

He turned his gaze back to Albino, disconcerted to see the man was still staring at him. Let him stare. In five minutes, he'd be dead, ready to be rinsed off and shipped out.

Juggy glanced around at the *hermanos*. They, too, were taking it slow. Albino was a fighter, a motherfucking dirty fighter, but this time they'd be more careful. And he was banged up; he'd be slower. They'd take him down as a pack.

They continued to slide in, tightening the ring.

Borges had reached the three-point line. With a smoothly practiced motion, he tossed the ball up and it swished through the hoop, dropping down—into the waiting hands of the Albino, who had stepped forward with a sudden deft movement to catch it.

They all stood and stared at him, hard. He held the ball, returning their looks, his stitched-up face utterly neutral. Juggy felt a surge of rage at the raw challenge in his look.

He glanced over his shoulder. Still no guards.

Borges stepped forward and the Albino said something to him, talking in a rapid undertone, so low Juggy couldn't hear what he said. As he approached, Juggy reached down and pulled the little shank out of the crotch seam of his underwear. The time was now: shank the bastard and have it done.

"Hold on, man," said Borges, gesturing with his palm out as Ochoa stepped forward. "I want to hear this."

"Hear what?"

"You know you're being set up," Albino was saying. "They *want* you to kill me. And you know it—every single one of you. Do you know why?"

He stared in turn at the group that now encircled him.

"Who the fuck cares?" said Juggy, taking a step forward and readying the shank.

"Why?" said Borges, holding his arm out toward Juggy again.

"Because *I know how to escape from here.*"

An electric silence.

"Bull*shit*," said Juggy, darting forward with the shank. But the Albino was ready and shot the ball at him, taking him by surprise, and in dodging it Juggy lost his stride. The ball bounced off and rolled away.

"Are you going to kill me and then spend the rest of your lives in here, never knowing if I was telling the truth?"

"He's full of shit," said Juggy. "He did Pocho, remember?" He lunged forward again, but the Albino skipped sideways and turned, like a matador. Borges grabbed Juggy's arm with a grip of steel.

"He fucking did Pocho!"

"Let the man talk."

"*Freedom*," Albino continued, his drawling accent making the word sound delicious. "Have you been caged up so long you've forgotten what the word means?"

"Borges, nobody gets out of here," Juggy said. "Let's finish this."

"Jug, don't fucking do *anything*."

Juggy looked around and saw that the others were staring at him. He felt incredulous: the Albino was sweet-talking his way out of a shank.

"Hear the man out," said another gang member, Roany. The others nodded.

"This is the guy that waxed Pocho," Juggy said again, feeling the conviction begin to drain out of his voice.

"So?" said Borges. "Maybe Pocho needed a little waxing."

The Albino continued, speaking in a low voice. "Borges is going out first," he said. "He believed me first. Jug, if you're ready, you're next."

"Going out? When?" Borges asked.

"Right now, while the guards are gone."

"The hell with this," Juggy snarled.

"Okay, instead of Jug, I'll take you." And the Albino pointed to Roany. "Are you ready?"

"You *know* I am."

"Wait a goddamn minute." Ochoa took another lunge with the

shank, but there was a sudden flashing movement that took him utterly by surprise, and when it was over, Albino held the shank.

Ochoa backed up. "You son of a bitch——"

"He's just wasting our time," said Albino. "Another word out of him and I'll cut out his tongue. Any objections?" He looked around the group.

Nobody responded.

Ochoa stood there, breathing hard, saying nothing. The bastard had killed Pocho and taken over, just like that. How could it have happened so fast?

"Anyone who doubts me, look at this." Albino reached over to the fence and grasped the links at a welded seam at a post, giving a sharp tug. The links parted effortlessly. He drew them back a bit more, stretching out an opening just large enough to admit a human being.

They stared in disbelief.

"Follow my instructions and you'll all get out of here—even you, Mr. Jug. To prove my sincerity, I'll go last. I've worked it out to the final detail. On the far side of the fence, you will scatter, each going out by a different route. Here's the plan . . ."

44

Pendergast waited until the last one, Jug, had climbed through the slit in the fence and disappeared, all of them tumbling through the gap so quickly they hardly cared whether he followed or not—which was precisely what Pendergast had hoped. They would each be following separate escape routes, exquisitely choreographed by Eli Glinn to create a maximal uproar and response.

After Jug had disappeared, Pendergast grasped the cut fence, which had sprung back into place, and pulled it as wide as he could, stretching and bending the metal to leave the gap obvious for the guards who would soon be coming. He stepped back and examined the digital watch on his wrist, which in Pendergast's case had far more sophisticated guts inside than its cheap plastic casing suggested. Those guts included a receiver unit that downloaded ACTS satellite time signals, which would be of the utmost importance for the impending operation. He waited until the precise appointed time, then pressed a button on the watch, activating a timer. The display began counting down from 900 seconds.

Pendergast stepped back and waited.

At 846 seconds, the sudden howl of emergency sirens filled the air. Pendergast turned and walked swiftly across the yard into the angle of the building closest to the door, where two shabby cement walls came together at a right angle. There, he reached down into a drainpipe and retrieved a long, thin tube: the same tube D'Agosta had placed inside it a few days earlier. He released the catches at both ends, unrolled it like a flag, and gave it a sharp shake. Immediately, it popped out into its intended shape: two equal squares of fabric about three feet per side, joined along one edge by plastic stays to create a V shape. The squares were coated in very thin sheets of brilliantly reflective Mylar. The entire construction, in fact, had been modified by Glinn from a standard portable light reflector such as those used in outdoor advertising shoots.

Now Pendergast moved into the corner, putting his back against the bricks and crouching low to the ground. He positioned the device in front, snugging it up close to him and making sure the outer two edges of the V-shaped reflector were tight against the walls on each side, forming a ninety-degree angle.

It was a simple but highly refined application of one of the oldest stage illusions of magic: using carefully angled mirrors to make someone vanish. It had been used as early as the 1860s, when Professor John Pepper's "Proteus Cabinet" and Colonel Stodare's "Sphinx" act—in which a woman was placed in a box that was subsequently shown to be empty—were the rage of Broadway. Pressed into the corner of the prison yard, the reflector accomplished the same effect: creating in essence a mirrored box that Pendergast could hide behind. Its mirrored surfaces reflected the cement walls on either side, creating the illusion of a vacant corner where the two walls came together. Only someone actually walking over to examine the corner would discover the deception—and the current panic was calculated to prevent that.

At 821, Pendergast heard the electronic bolts disengage; the doors were flung open, and four "first responder" guards from nearby guard station 7 charged into yard 4, Tasers at the ready.

"Fence is cut!" one cried, pointing to the gaping hole at the far end.

As the four sprinted across the asphalt toward the gap, Pendergast stood, snapped the two sides of the Mylar reflector together, rolled it back into a compact tube, and returned it to the drainpipe. Then he slipped through the doors into the prison, sprinting around a corner and into the nearby bathroom. Quickly, he entered the second-to-last stall, stood on the toilet, and lifted the acoustic ceiling tile overhead. There, taped to the upper side, he found a plastic bag containing a slim four-gigabyte flash-memory chip, a credit card, a small hypodermic needle and syringe, some duct tape, and a tiny capsule of brown liquid. Pocketing the items, he exited the bathroom and darted down the hall to guard station 7. Just as Glinn had predicted: of the five guards on duty, four had responded to the escape call, leaving the lone commanding guard at the console, surrounded by a wall of live video feeds. The man was shouting orders into a microphone and punching up feed after feed, frantically searching for the loose inmates. An overwhelming response had been mobilized to deal with the mass escape attempt. Based on the guard's excited chatter, already one of the inmates had been run down and recaptured.

As Glinn had anticipated, the door to guard station 7 had been left unlocked in the hasty departure of the first responders.

Pendergast slipped inside, then threw an arm around the guard's neck and injected him. The guard slumped without a word and Pendergast laid him out on the floor, then half covered the guard's comm mike with his hand and yelled hoarsely into it, "I see one of them! I'm going after him!"

He quickly undressed the unconscious guard while a burst of shouted countermands came over the speaker, ordering him to remain at his station. In less than a minute, Pendergast was dressed in the guard's uniform, equipped with badge, Mace, Taser, stick, radio, and emergency call unit. He was more slender than the unconscious guard, but a few minor adjustments rendered the disguise quite acceptable.

Next, he reached behind the large rack of servers until he had located the correct port. Then, taking the flash drive from the plastic bag, he inserted it into the port. He then turned his attention back to the guard, taping his mouth shut, his hands behind his back, and his knees together. He dragged the drugged guard back to the nearby men's room, seated him on a toilet, taped his torso to the toilet tank to keep him from falling over, locked the stall, and crawled out beneath the door.

Moving to a mirror, Pendergast pulled the bandages from his face and stuffed them into the waste can. He broke the glass capsule over a sink and massaged the dye into his hair, turning it from white blond to an unremarkable dark brown. Exiting the men's room, he walked down the hall, made a right turn, and—just before coming to the first video camera—he paused to glance at his watch: 660 seconds.

He waited until the display read 640, then continued on, moving at an easy pace, all the while keeping one eye fixed on his watch. He knew that many eyes would be watching the video feeds. Even though he was dressed in a guard's uniform, he was walking in the wrong direction— away from the breakout—and his face was still battered and bruised. They knew him well in building C. Anyone catching a glimpse of him would recognize him.

But he also knew that for ten seconds—from 640 to 630—this particular video feed would be controlled by the flash drive he had plugged into the security computer. The drive would temporarily store the previous ten seconds of feed from that camera and play it back again. It would then leapfrog to the next video camera in the chain and repeat the process. The loop would run only once for each camera: Pendergast had a ten-second window, no more, to pass through each field of view. The timing had to be perfect.

He walked past the camera without incident and continued down the long, vacant corridors of building C—the guards had been drawn off to other areas by the escapees. Sometimes he quickened his step, sometimes he slowed it, passing each camera at the precise moment in which its video signal would be replayed. Frequently his radio blared. Once, he was passed by a knot of running guards, and he quickly dropped to tie a shoe, turning his swollen, bruised face away from them. They tore by without a glance, their interest otherwise engaged.

He passed the dining hall and kitchen of building C, the smell of disinfectant strong in the air. He took another turn, then another, at last reaching the final stretch of corridor before the checkpoint and security door between Herkmoor Building C/Federal and Herkmoor Building B/State.

Pendergast's face was well known in building C. He was not known at all in building B.

He approached the security door, swiped the credit card, placed his hand on the fingermatrix screen, and waited.

His heart was beating at rather more than its customary rate. This was the moment of truth.

At exactly 290 seconds, the security light glowed green and the metal locks disengaged.

Pendergast stepped through into building B. He walked around the first bend in the corridor, then paused in the dark corner made by the dogleg of the hallway. He reached up to the deepest cut on his cheek and, with a vicious tug, pulled out the row of stitches. When the warm blood began to run, he smeared it over his face, neck, and hands. Then he pulled up his shirt, examining the stitched wound in his side where the shank had penetrated. He took a deep breath. Then he yanked that wound open as well.

They had to look as fresh as possible.

At 110 seconds, he heard running footsteps, and, as previously planned, one of the escapees ran by—Jug—who had dutifully followed the escape plan laid out for him by Glinn. Of course, it would not be successful—he would be apprehended at the exit to building B if not before—but this, too, was part of the plan. Pocho's gang was a smoke screen—that was all. None would actually escape.

As soon as Jug passed him, Pendergast screamed and threw himself down onto the floor of the corridor, while at the same time pressing the emergency button on his comm unit:

"Officer down! Immediate response! Officer down!"

45

Staff Nurse Ralph Kidder kneeled over the supine form of the guard—who was sobbing like a baby, babbling about being attacked, being afraid of dying—and tried to focus on the problem at hand. He checked the man's heart with a stethoscope—strong and fast—examined the neck and limbs for any broken bones, took the blood pressure—excellent—examined the cut on the face: nasty but superficial.

"Where are you hurt?" he asked again, exasperated. "Where are your injuries? Talk to me!"

"My face, he cut my face!" the man shrieked, finally gaining a measure of coherence.

"I see that. Where else?"

"He stabbed me! Oh, my chest, it hurts!"

The nurse gently felt the ribs, noting the swelling and faint gravelly feel of a couple of broken ones, not displaced. There was indeed a stab wound, bleeding copiously, but a quick check indicated a rib had deflected the blade and prevented it from piercing the pleura.

"It's nothing that a convalescence won't fix," Kidder said sharply, turning to the two responding EMTs. "Load him and take him down to infirmary B. We'll do a blood workup, an X-ray series, stitch up a few of those cuts. Tetanus booster and a course of amoxicillin. I don't see anything so far that'll require a transfer to an outside hospital."

One of the EMTs snorted. "Nothing's going in or out until the escapees are apprehended and all prisoners accounted for, anyway. They've had a morgue-mobile idling outside the gate for half an hour already."

"The morgue-mobile's never in a rush," said Kidder dryly. He wrote down the guard's name and badge number on his clipboard. He didn't recognize the man—but then, he was from building C and his face was cut up pretty bad.

As they were loading the patient onto the stretcher, Kidder heard a sudden uproar of shouting from down the corridor as another prisoner was apprehended. Kidder had been working at Herkmoor for almost twenty years and this was the biggest escape attempt yet. Of course it had no chance of succeeding. He just hoped the guards weren't beating hell out of too many would-be escapees.

The EMTs raised the stretcher and trundled the whimpering guard off to the infirmary, Kidder following. These guards acted so tough when everything was under control, he thought, but knock them around a bit and they fell apart like so much overcooked meat.

The infirmary in building B, like the other infirmaries in Herk-moor, was divided into two completely separate, walled-off areas: the free area for staff and guards, and the incarceration area for prisoners. They wheeled the guard to the free area and covered him with a blanket. Kidder worked up the man's chart, ordered some X-rays. He was starting to prep the guard for stitching when his radio beeped. He lifted it to his ear, listened, spoke briefly. Then he turned to the patient. "I've got to leave you for a while."

"Alone?" the injured guard cried in a panic.

"I'll be back in about half an hour, maybe forty-five minutes, with the radiologist. We have some injured inmates—"

"Taking care of inmates before me?" the man whined.

"They're in need of rather more urgent care." Kidder didn't tell him about the call he'd just received. It was as he feared: the guards had beat the crap out of several of the escapees.

"How long will I have to wait?"

Kidder sighed irritably. "Like I said, maybe forty-five minutes." He readied a needle with a mild sedative and painkiller.

"Don't stick me with that!" the man cried. "I've an awful fear of needles!"

Kidder made an effort to control his annoyance. "This'll ease the pain."

"It's not *that* bad! Turn on the TV for me. That'll distract me."

Kidder shrugged. "Have it your way." He put away the syringe and handed the patient the remote. The man immediately turned it to an asinine game show and cranked up the volume. Kidder left, shaking his head, his already low opinion of prison guards having sunk even lower.

Fifty minutes later, Kidder returned to the infirmary in a ferociously bad mood. Some of the guards had jumped at the chance to settle scores with a particularly unsavory group of inmates, breaking half a dozen bones in the process.

He checked his watch, wondering about the guard he'd left behind. Fact was, in any of the big New York emergency rooms the man would have had to wait at least twice as long. He pulled back the curtain and gazed at the guard, all bundled up and turned toward the wall, sleeping heavily despite the excessively loud game show playing on the television.

Are you sure, Joy, that door number 2 is your choice? All right, then, let's open it up! Behind door number 2 is . . . (huge groan from the audience) . . .

"Time for your X-rays, Mr.—" Kidder glanced at the clipboard. "Mr. Sidesky."

No response.

. . . a cow! Now, isn't that the most beautiful Holstein cow you've ever seen, ladies and gentlemen? Fresh milk every morning, Joy, think of it!

"Mr. Sidesky?" Kidder said, raising his voice. He reached for the remote, turned off the TV. A sudden, blessed silence.

"X-ray time!"

No response.

Kidder reached over and gave the man's shoulder a gentle push—then jerked back with a muffled cry. Even through the covers, the body felt *cold*.

It wasn't possible. The man had been brought in an hour ago, alive and healthy.

"Hey, Sidesky! Wake up!" With a trembling hand, he reached out again, pressed on the shoulder—and once again felt that hideous muffled cold.

With a feeling of dread, he grasped the corner of the covers and drew them back, exposing a naked corpse, purple and grotesquely bloated. The stench of death and disinfectants rose up, enveloping him like a miasma.

He staggered, hand over his mouth, choking, mind reeling in confusion and disbelief. The man had not only died, he had started to decay. How was it possible? He looked around wildly but there was no other patient in the ward. There had been some terrible mistake, some crazy mix-up . . .

Kidder took a steadying breath. Then he grasped the figure by the shoulder and pulled him over onto his back. The head flopped around, eyes staring, tongue lolling like a dog, face horribly blue and bloated, mouth draining some kind of yellow matter.

"God!" he moaned, backing up. It wasn't the injured guard at all. It was the dead prisoner he had worked on just the day before, helping the radiologist produce a series of forensic X-rays.

Trying to keep his voice normal, he paged the Herkmoor chief physician. A moment later the man's irritated voice came over the intercom.

"I'm busy, what is it?"

For a moment, Kidder didn't quite know what to say. "You know that dead prisoner in the morgue—"

"Lacarra? They carted him away fifteen minutes ago."

"No. No, they didn't."

"Of *course* they did. I signed the transfer myself, I saw them load the body bag into the morgue-mobile. It was waiting outside the gate for the all-clear so it could come in for the corpse."

Kidder swallowed. "I don't think so."

"You don't think what? What the hell are you talking about, Kidder?"

"Pocho Lacarra . . ." He swallowed, licked dry lips: ". . . is still here."

Twenty miles to the south, the mortuary vehicle was on the Taconic State Parkway, heading toward New York City through light traffic. Within minutes, it pulled over at a rest area and cruised to a stop.

Vincent D'Agosta tore off his white morgue uniform, climbed into the rear, and unzipped the body bag. Inside was the long, white, nude form of Special Agent Pendergast. The agent sat up, blinking.

"Pendergast! Damn, we did it! We frigging did it!"

The agent held up a hand. "My dear Vincent, please—no effusive demonstrations of affection until I am showered and dressed."

46

At 6:30 that evening, William Smithback Jr. stood on the sidewalk of Museum Drive, looking up at the brilliantly lit facade of the New York Museum of Natural History. A broad velvet carpet had been unrolled down the great granite steps. A seething crowd of rubberneckers and journalists was held back by velvet ropes and phalanxes of museum guards, while one limousine after another rolled up, disgorging movie stars, city officials, kings and queens of high finance, society matrons, gaunt vacant-eyed fashion models du jour, managing partners, university presidents, and senators—a stupendous parade of money, power, and influence.

The great and powerful ascended the museum steps in a measured flow of black, white, and glitter, looking neither left nor right, heading through the pillared facade and vast bronze doors into a great blaze of light—while the rabble, held back by velvet and brass, gaped, squealed, and photographed. Above, a four-story banner draped over the museum's neoclassical facade billowed in a light breeze. It depicted a gigantic Eye of Horus with words in faux Egyptian script written underneath:

GRAND OPENING
THE GREAT TOMB OF SENEF

Smithback adjusted the silk tie of his tuxedo and smoothed his lapels. Having arrived in a cab instead of a limo, he had been forced to get out a block shy of the museum and had pushed his way through the crowd until he'd arrived at the ropes. He showed his invitation to a suspicious guard, who called over another, and after several minutes of confabulation they grudgingly allowed him through—right in the perfumed wake of Wanda Meursault, the actress who had made such a fuss at the Sacred Images opening. Smithback considered how distressing it must have been when she lost out in her bid for Best Actress at the recent Academy Awards. With a thrill of pleasure, he marched in the parade of power and passed through the shining gates.

This was going to be the mother of all openings.

The velvet carpet led across the Great Rotunda, with its brace of mounted dinosaurs, through the magnificent African Hall, and from there wound its way through half a dozen musty halls and half-forgotten corridors to arrive at a set of elevators, where the crowd had backed up. It was quite a distance from the entrance, Smithback thought as he waited in line for the next elevator—but the Tomb of Senef was located in the very bowels of the museum, about as far from the front entrance as you could get. He adjusted the knot of his tie. *The hike might just pump a little blood through some of these dried-out old husks,* he thought. *Do them good.*

A chime announced the arrival of the next car and he filed in with the rest of them, packed in like black and white sardines, waiting for the elevator to make the crawl to the basement. The doors opened again at last and they were greeted with another blaze of light, the swirling sounds of an orchestra, and beyond, the great Egyptian Hall itself, its nineteenth-century murals beautifully restored. Along the walls, gold, jewels, and faience glittered from every case, while exquisitely laid tea tables and dining tables, flickering with thousands of candles, covered the marble floors. Most important, Smithback thought as his eye roved about, were the long tables along the walls groaning with smoked sturgeon and salmon, crusty homemade breads, huge platters of hand-cut San Daniele prosciutto, silver tubs of pearly-gray sevruga and beluga caviar. Massive silver cauldrons heaped with shaved ice stood at either end, bristling with bottles of Veuve Clicquot like so many batteries of artillery, waiting to be fired and poured.

And these, Smithback thought, were merely the hors d'oeuvres—the dinner was yet to come. He rubbed his hands together, savoring the splendid sight and looking about for his wife, Nora, whom he had hardly seen in the past week, and shivering slightly at the thought of other, more intimate pleasures to be enjoyed later, once this party—and this whole hectic and dreadful week—had finally come to a close.

He was contemplating which of the food tables to assault first when he felt an arm slip through his from behind.

"Nora!" He turned to embrace her. She was dressed in a sleek black gown, tastefully embroidered with silver thread. "You look ravishing!"

"You don't look so bad yourself." Nora reached up and smoothed his unrepentant cowlick, which promptly sprang up again, defying gravity. "My handsome overgrown boy."

"My Egyptian queen. How's your neck feeling, by the way?"

"It's fine, and please stop asking."

"This is amazing. Oh, God, what a spread." Smithback looked around. "And to think—you're the curator. This is your show."

"I had nothing to do with the party." She glanced over at the entrance to the Tomb of Senef, closed and draped with a red ribbon, waiting to be cut. "My show's in there."

A slim waiter came sweeping by, bearing a silver tray loaded with flutes of champagne, and Smithback snagged two as the man passed, handing one to Nora.

"To the Tomb of Senef," he said.

They clinked glasses and drank.

"Let's get some food before the crush," said Nora. "I've only got a few minutes. At seven, I've got to say a few words, and then there'll be other speeches, dinner, and the show. You won't see much of me, Bill. I'm sorry."

"Later, I'll see more."

As they approached the tables, Smithback noticed a tall, striking, mahogany-haired woman standing nearby, dressed incongruously in black slacks and a gray silk shirt, open at the neck, set off by a simple string of pearls. It was down-dressing in the extreme, and yet somehow she managed to pull it off, make it look classy, even elegant.

"This is the museum's new Egyptologist," said Nora, turning to the woman. "Viola Maskelene. This is my husband, Bill Smithback."

Smithback was taken aback. "Viola Maskelene? The one who . . . ?" He quickly recovered, extending his hand. "Very pleased to meet you."

"Hullo," the woman said in a cultured, faintly amused accent. "I've enjoyed working with Nora these past few days. What a museum!"

"Yes," said Smithback. "Quite the noble pile. Viola, tell me . . ." Smithback could hardly restrain his curiosity. "How, er, did you happen to end up here in the museum?"

"It was a last-minute thing. With Adrian's tragic death, the museum needed an Egyptologist right away, someone with expertise on the New Kingdom and the tombs in the Valley of the Kings. Hugo Menzies knew of my work, it seems, and suggested my name. I was delighted to take the job."

Smithback was about to open his mouth to ask another question when he caught Nora casting him a warning look: now was not the time to start pumping her for information about the kidnapping. Still, he reflected, it was mighty strange that Maskelene was so suddenly back in New York—and at the museum, no less. All Smithback's journalism bells were ringing: this was far too much a coincidence. It bore looking into . . . tomorrow.

"Quite a spread," Viola said, turning to the food tables. "I'm starving. Shall we?"

"We shall," said Smithback.

They elbowed up to the teeming tables, and Smithback, gently easing aside a meek curator, reached out and loaded up a plate with a good two ounces of caviar, a tall stack of blinis, and a dollop of crème fraîche. Out of the corner of his eye, he saw, with surprise, that Viola was heaping her plate with an even more unseemly amount of food, apparently as dismissive of decorum as he was.

She caught his eye, colored slightly, then winked. "Haven't eaten since last night," she said. "They've had me working nonstop."

"Go right ahead!" Smithback said, scooping up a second mound of caviar, delighted to have a partner in crime.

A sudden burst of music came from the small orchestra at the end of the hall, and there was a smattering of applause as Hugo Menzies, magnificent in white tie and tails, mounted a podium next to the orchestra. A hush fell on the hall as his glittering blue eyes surveyed the crowd.

"Ladies and gentlemen!" he said. "I won't inflict a long speech on you tonight, because we have far more interesting entertainment planned. Let me just read you an e-mail I received from the Count of Cahors, who made this all possible with his extraordinarily generous donation:

> My dear Ladies and Gentlemen,
>
> I am desolate not to join you in these festivities celebrating the re-opening of the Tomb of Senef. I am an old man and can no longer travel. But I shall raise a glass to you and wish you a spectacular evening.
>
> With kindest regards,
>
> Le Comte Thierry de Cahors

A thunder of applause greeted this short missive from the reclusive count. When it died down, Menzies resumed.

"And now," he said, "I have the pleasure of introducing to you the great soprano Antonella da Rimini as Aïda, joined by tenor Gilles de Montparnasse as Radamès, who will sing for you arias from the final scene of *Aïda*, 'La fatal pietra sovra me si chiuse,' which will be sung in English, for the benefit of those of you who do not speak Italian."

More applause. An enormously fat woman, heavily painted and eye-lined, and squeezed to bursting into a faux Egyptian costume, stepped onto the stage, followed by an equally large man in similar garb.

"Viola and I have to go," Nora whispered to Smithback. "We're on next." She gave his hand a squeeze, then left with Viola Maskelene in tow, disappearing into the crowd.

Another round of applause shook the hall as the conductor mounted the stage. Smithback marveled at the enthusiasm of the guests—they had hardly had time to get lubricated. Glancing around while munching a blini, he was surprised at the number of notable faces: senators, captains of industry, movie stars, pillars of society, foreign dignitaries, and of course, the full spread of museum trustees and assorted bigwigs. If somebody nuked the joint, he reflected ghoulishly, the repercussions wouldn't be just national—they'd be global.

The lights dimmed and the conductor raised his baton, the audience falling into silence. Then the orchestra began a dolorous motif as Radamès sang:

> *The fatal stone above has sealed my doom,*
> *Here is my tomb! The light of day*
> *I shall never see again . . . Nor shall I see Aïda.*
> *Aïda, my love, where are you? May you live happily,*
> *My hideous fate forever unknown!*
> *But what is that sound? A slithering serpent? A ghoulish vision?*
> *No! A dim human form I see.*
> *By the gods! Aïda!*

And now the diva sang out:

> *Yes, it is I.*

Smithback, a confirmed opera-hater, made an effort to shut out the shrieking voice while he returned his attention to the loaded tables. Shouldering his way through the crowd, he took advantage of the temporary lull in the feeding frenzy to scoop up half a dozen oysters; on top of this, he laid two thick slabs cut from an ancient, moldy round of French cheese, added a stack of paper-thin slices of prosciutto and two slices of tongue. Balancing the tottery stack, he moved to the next table and snagged a second flute of champagne, asking the bartender to top it off for efficiency's sake so he wouldn't have to return as quickly for a refill. Then he made his way to one of the candlelit tables to enjoy his booty.

A free feed like this came only rarely, and Smithback was determined to make the most of it.

47

Eli Glinn was waiting for the morgue vehicle at the anonymous door to the EES building. Sending someone to deal with the vehicle, he whisked Pendergast off for a shower and change of clothes and assigned D'Agosta to a robotically silent, white-coated technician. The technician had D'Agosta wait while he made a few brief phone calls; then he led the way through the cavernous, echoing space that comprised the heart of the Effective Engineering Solutions building. The large room was quiet, as one would expect at half past seven on a week-night: even so, several scientists could be seen scribbling on whiteboards or peering at computer monitors, amidst an air of studious efficiency. As he walked past the lab tables, the scientific equipment, and the models, he wondered just how many of the employees knew that their building currently harbored one of the fed's top fugitives.

D'Agosta followed the technician into a waiting elevator in the rear wall. The man inserted a key into a control panel and pressed the down button. The car descended for a surprisingly long interval before the doors opened onto a pale blue corridor. Motioning D'Agosta to follow, the technician strode down it, stopping at last before a door. He smiled, nodded, then turned and walked back in the direction of the elevator.

D'Agosta stared at the retreating form. Then he glanced back at the unmarked door. After a moment, he gave a tentative knock.

It was immediately opened by a short, cheerful-looking man with a florid face and a closely cropped beard. He ushered D'Agosta in and closed the door behind him.

"You are Lieutenant D'Agosta, yes?" he asked in an accent D'Agosta assumed to be German. "Please have a seat. I am Dr. Rolf Krasner."

The office had the spare, clinical air of a doctor's consultation room, with gray carpets, white walls, and anonymous furnishings. A rosewood table stood in the middle, brilliantly polished. In its center sat what looked like a technical manual—thick as the Manhattan telephone book and bound in black plastic. Eli Glinn had already wheeled himself into position at the far side of the table. He nodded silently to D'Agosta and gestured toward an empty chair.

As D'Agosta seated himself, a door in the back of the room opened and Pendergast appeared. His wounds had been freshly dressed and his hair, still damp from being washed, had been combed back. He was dressed, most incongruously, in a white turtleneck and gray wool pants, which—different as they were from his habitual black suit—almost had the effect of a disguise.

D'Agosta rose instinctively.

Pendergast's eyes met his, and after a moment he smiled. "I fear I neglected to express my gratitude to you for freeing me from prison."

"You know you don't have to do that," said D'Agosta, coloring.

"But I will. Thank you very much, my dear Vincent." He spoke softly, taking D'Agosta's hand in his own and giving it a curt shake. D'Agosta felt strangely moved by this man who sometimes found even the simplest human courtesies awkward.

"Please sit down," said Glinn in the same neutral voice—devoid of any human feeling—that had so annoyed D'Agosta on their first meeting.

He complied. Pendergast slipped into a seat opposite—a little stiffly, D'Agosta thought, yet with his usual feline grace. "And I owe an enormous debt of gratitude to you as well, Mr. Glinn," Pendergast went on. "A most successful operation."

Glinn nodded curtly.

"Although I deeply regret having to kill Mr. Lacarra to do so."

"As you know," Glinn replied, "there was no other way. You had to kill an inmate in order to escape in his body bag, and that inmate, furthermore, had to take his exercise in yard 4, the ideal spot for an abortive escape. We were *fortunate*—if I may be permitted that expression—to identify a yard 4 inmate who was so thoroughly evil that some might say he deserved to die: a man who tortured three children to death in front of their mother. It was then a simple matter to hack into the Justice Department database and change Lacarra's arrest records to identify him as one of your 'collars'—thus baiting the trap for Coffey. Finally, I might point out that you were forced to kill him: it was self-defense."

"No amount of sophistry will change the fact it was a premeditated killing."

"Strictly speaking, you are correct. But as you know yourself, his death was necessary to save more lives—perhaps *many* more lives. And our model indicated his death sentence appeals would have been denied, anyway."

Pendergast silently inclined his head.

"Now, Mr. Pendergast, let us lay trivial ethical dilemmas aside. We have urgent business to take care of, relating to your brother. I assume no news from the outside world reached you while in solitary confinement?"

"None whatsoever."

"Then it would be a surprise to learn that your brother destroyed all the diamonds he stole from the museum."

D'Agosta saw Pendergast stiffen visibly.

"That's right. Diogenes pulverized the diamonds and returned them to the museum as a sack of powder."

After a silence, Pendergast said, "Once again, his actions were beyond my ability to predict or comprehend."

"If it's any consolation to you, they surprised us as well. It meant our assumptions about him were wrong. We believed that after being cheated of Lucifer's Heart—the one diamond he most desired—your brother would go to ground for a period, lick his wounds, plot his next move. Clearly, that was not the case."

Krasner broke in, his cheerful voice in stark contrast to Glinn's monotone. "By destroying the very diamonds he had spent many years planning to steal, diamonds that he both desired and needed, Diogenes was destroying a part of himself. It was a suicide of sorts. He was abandoning himself to his demons."

"When we learned what happened to the diamonds," Glinn went on, "we realized our preliminary psychological profile was woefully insufficient. And so we went back to the drawing board, reanalyzed existing data, gathered additional information. *That* is the result." He nodded to the thick volume. "I'll spare you the details. It boils down to one thing."

"And that is?"

"The 'perfect crime' which Diogenes spoke of was *not* the theft of the diamonds. Nor was it the outrage he perpetrated on you: killing your friends and then framing you for the crimes. Whatever his original intent was we are in no position to speculate. But the fact remains that his ultimate crime *has yet to be committed*."

"But the date in his letter?"

"Another lie, or at least diversion. The theft of the diamonds *was* part of his plan, but their destruction was apparently a more spontaneous act. That doesn't change the fact that his series of crimes was carefully planned to keep you occupied, to mislead you, to stay one step ahead of you. I must say, the depth and complexity of your brother's plan is quite breathtaking."

"So the crime is yet to come," Pendergast said in a dry, quiet voice. "Do you know what it is, or when it will take place?"

"No—except that all indications are that this crime is imminent. Perhaps tomorrow. Perhaps tonight. Hence the need for your immediate liberation from Herkmoor."

Pendergast was silent a moment. "I fail to see how I can be of any help," he said, his voice tinged with bitterness. "As you see, I've been wrong at every turn."

"Agent Pendergast, you are the one person—the *only* person—who can help. And you know how."

When Pendergast did not immediately respond, Glinn went on. "We had hoped our forensic profile would have predictive power—that it would provide a sense of what Diogenes's future action would be. And it has . . . to a point. We know he's motivated by a powerful feeling of victimization, the sense that a terrible wrong was done to him. We believe his 'perfect crime' will attempt to perpetrate a similar wrong on a large number of people."

"That is correct," Krasner broke in. "Your brother wants to *generalize* this wrong, to make it public, to force others to share his pain."

Glinn leaned over the table and stared at Pendergast. "And we know something else. *You* are the person who inflicted this pain on your brother—at least, that's how he perceives it."

"That is absurd," said Pendergast.

"Something happened between you and your brother at an early age: something so dreadful it twisted his already warped mind and set in motion the events he's playing out now. Our analysis is missing a vital piece of information: what happened between you and Diogenes. And the memory of that event is locked up *there*." Glinn pointed at Pendergast's head.

"We've been through this before," Pendergast replied stiffly. "I've already told you everything of importance that has passed between my brother and myself. I even submitted to a rather curious interview with the good Dr. Krasner here—without result. There is no hidden atrocity. I would remember: I have a photographic memory."

"Forgive my disagreeing with you, but this event happened. It must have. There's no other explanation."

"I'm sorry, then. Because even if you're right, I have no recollection of any such event—and there's clearly no way for me to recall it. You've already tried and failed."

Glinn tented his hands, looked down at them. For a moment, the room went still.

"I think there is a way," he said without looking up.

When there was no response, Glinn raised his head again. "You're schooled in a certain ancient discipline, a secret mystical philosophy practiced by a tiny order of monks in Bhutan and Tibet. One facet of this discipline is spiritual. Another is physical: a complex series of ritualized movements not unlike the *kata* of Shotokan karate. And still another is intellectual: a form of meditation, of concentration, that allows the practitioner to unleash the full potential of the human mind. I refer to the secret rituals of the Dzogchen and its even more rarefied practice, the Chongg Ran."

"How did you come by this information?" Pendergast asked in a voice so cold D'Agosta felt his blood freeze.

"Agent Pendergast, please. The acquisition of knowledge is our primary stock-in-trade. In trying to learn more about you—for purposes of better understanding your brother—we have spoken to a great many people. One of them was Cornelia Delamere Pendergast, your great-aunt. Current residence: the Mount Mercy Hospital for the Criminally Insane. Then there was a certain associate of yours, Miss Corrie Swanson, enrolled as a senior at Phillips Exeter Academy. She was a rather more difficult subject, but we ultimately learned what we needed to."

Glinn regarded Pendergast with his Sphinx-like gaze. Pendergast returned the look, his pale cat's eyes hardly blinking. The tension in the conference room increased rapidly; D'Agosta felt the hairs on his arms standing on end.

At last Pendergast spoke. "This prying into my private life goes far beyond the bounds of your employ."

Glinn did not reply.

"I use the memory crossing in a strictly impersonal way—as a forensic tool, to re-create the scene of a crime or a historical event. That is all. It would have no value with such a . . . personal matter."

"No value?" A dry tone of skepticism crept into Glinn's voice.

"On top of that, it is a very difficult technique. Attempting to apply it here would be a waste of time. Just like the little game that Dr. Krasner tried to play with me."

Glinn leaned forward again in his wheelchair, still staring at Pendergast. When he spoke, his voice carried a sudden urgency.

"Mr. Pendergast, isn't it possible that the same event which has marred your brother so terribly—which turned him into a monster—scarred you as well? Isn't it possible you have walled up its memory so completely that you no longer have any conscious recollection of it?"

"Mr. Glinn—"

"Tell me," Glinn said, his voice growing louder. "Isn't it possible?"

Pendergast looked at him, gray eyes glinting. "I suppose it is remotely possible."

"If it *is* possible, and if this memory does exist, and if this memory will help us find that last missing piece, and if by doing so we can save lives and defeat your brother . . . isn't it at least worth *trying*?"

The two men held each other's gaze for less than a minute, but to D'Agosta it seemed to last forever. Then Pendergast looked down. His shoulders slumped visibly. Wordlessly he nodded.

"Then we must proceed," Glinn went on. "What do you require?"

Pendergast did not reply for a moment. Then he seemed to rouse himself. "Privacy," he said.

"Will the Berggasse studio suffice?"

"Yes."

Pendergast placed both hands on the arms of the chair and pushed himself upright. Without a glance at the others in the room, he turned and made his way back toward the room from which he'd emerged.

"Agent Pendergast . . . ?" Glinn said.

Hand on the doorknob, Pendergast half turned.

"I know how difficult this ordeal will be. But this is not the time for half measures. There can be no holding back. Whatever it is, it must be faced—and confronted—in its totality. Agreed?"

Pendergast nodded.

"Then good luck."

A wintry smile passed briefly over the agent's face. Then, without another word, he opened the door to the study and slipped out of sight.

48

Captain of Homicide Laura Hayward stood to the left of the Egyptian Hall entrance, gazing dubiously over the crowd. She had dressed in a dark suit, the better to blend in with the crowd, the only sign of her authority the tiny gold captain's bars pinned to her lapel. Her weapon, a basic Smith & Wesson .38, was in its holster under her suit jacket.

The scene that greeted her eyes was one of textbook security. Her people, plainclothed and uniformed, were all at their appointed stations. They were the best she had—truly New York's finest. The museum guard presence was there as well, deliberately obtrusive, adding at least a psychological sense of security. Manetti had so far been fully cooperative. The rest of the museum had been painstakingly secured. Hayward had run dozens of disaster scenarios through her head, drawing up plans to deal with every contingency, even the most unlikely: suicide bomber, fire, security system malfunction, power failure, computer failure.

The only weakness was the tomb itself—it had only one exit. But it was a large exit, and at the insistence of the NYC fire marshals, the tomb and all its contents had been specially fireproofed. She herself had made sure the tomb's security doors could be opened or closed from the inside or outside, manually or electronically, even in the case of a total power failure. She had stood in the control room, occupying the empty room next to the tomb, and had operated the software that opened and closed the doors.

The toxicological teams had made not one sweep, not two, but three—the results uniformly negative. And now she stood, surveying the crowd, asking herself, *What could possibly go wrong?*

Her intellect answered loud and clear: *Nothing.*

But her gut sensed otherwise. She felt almost physically sick with unease. It was irrational; it made no sense.

Once more, she delved deep into her cop instincts, trying to discover the source of the feeling. As usual, her thoughts formed almost automatically into a list. And this time the list was all about Diogenes Pendergast.

> Diogenes was alive.
> He had kidnapped Viola Maskelene.
> He had attacked Margo.
> He had stolen the diamond collection—and then
>   destroyed it.
> He had probably been responsible for at least some of
>   the killings ascribed to Pendergast.
> He spent a great deal of time in the museum in some
>   unknown capacity, most likely posing as a curator.

Both perps—Lipper and Wicherly—had been involved with the Tomb of Senef, and both had suddenly gone mad after being in the tomb. And yet a meticulous examination of the tomb and the hall had produced no evidence whatsoever of any kind of environmental or electrical problem—certainly nothing that could trigger psychotic breaks or brain damage. Was Diogenes somehow to blame? What on earth was he planning?

Against her will, her mind returned to the conversation she'd had with D'Agosta in her office days before. *All of what he's done so far—the killings, the kidnapping, the diamond theft—has been leading up to something else.* Those had been his words. *Something bigger, maybe much bigger.*

She shivered. Her conjectures, her questions about Diogenes—it *was* all linked, it had to be. It *was* part of a plan.

But what was the plan?

Hayward hadn't the slightest idea. And yet her gut told her it would happen tonight. It couldn't be coincidence. This was the "something else" D'Agosta had talked about.

Her eyes traveled around the room, making contact with her people, one by one. As she did so, she picked out the many famous faces in the hall: the mayor, the speaker pro tem of the House, the governor, at least one of the state's two senators. And there were many others: CEOs of Fortune 500 companies, Hollywood producers, a smattering of actors and television personalities. Then there were the museum staff she knew: Collopy, Menzies, Nora Kelly . . .

Her eyes moved to the PBS television crew, which had set up at one end of the hall and was filming the gala live. A second crew had set up inside the as-yet-unopened tomb, ready to film the first VIP tour of the exhibition and the sound-and-light show that would be part of it.

Yes—that would be part of the plan. Whatever was going to happen would happen live, with millions watching. And if Diogenes's alter ego was a curator, or somebody else highly placed in the museum, he would have the power and the access necessary to engineer almost anything. But who could he be? Manetti's careful probing of the museum's personnel files turned up nothing. If only they had a picture of Diogenes that was less than twenty-five years old, a fingerprint, a bit of DNA . . .

What was the plan?

Her eye ended up at the closed door to the tomb, the steel now covered with a faux stone finish, a huge red ribbon stretched across its front.

Her feeling of sickness increased. And along with it came a desperate feeling of isolation. She had done everything in her power to stop, or at least postpone, this opening. But she had convinced nobody. Even Police Commissioner Rocker, her ally in the past, had demurred.

Was it all in her mind? Had the pressure finally gotten to her? If only she had someone who saw things her way, who understood the background, the true nature of Diogenes. Someone like D'Agosta.

D'Agosta. He had been ahead of her at every step of the investigation. He knew what was going to happen before it happened. Long before anyone else, he'd known the kind of criminal they were up against. He had insisted Diogenes was alive even when she and everyone else had "proved" he was dead.

And he knew the museum—knew it cold. He'd been involved in cases connected to the museum going back half a dozen years or more. He knew the players. God, if only he were here now . . . Not D'Agosta the man—that was over—but D'Agosta the *cop.*

She controlled her breathing. No point wishing for the impossible. She had done all she could. There was nothing left now but to wait, watch, and be ready to act.

Once again her eye roved the crowd, gauged the flow, examined each face for unnatural tension, excitement, anxiety.

Suddenly she froze. There, standing by the group of dignitaries near the podium, stood the tall figure of a woman: a woman she recognized.

All her alarm bells went off. Making an effort to control her voice, she raised her radio. "Manetti, Hayward here, do you read?"

"Copy."

"Is that Viola Maskelene I'm looking at? Over by the podium."

A pause. "That's her."

Hayward swallowed. "What's *she* doing here?"

"She was hired to replace that Egyptologist, Wicherly."

"When?"

"I don't know. A day or two ago."

"Who hired her?"

"Anthropology, I think."

"Why wasn't her name on the guest list?"

A hesitation. "I'm not sure. Probably because she was such a recent hire."

Hayward wanted to say more. She wanted to curse into the radio. She wanted to demand to know why she hadn't been told. But it was too late for all that. Instead, she merely said, "Over and out."

The profile indicated that Diogenes isn't through.

The whole gala opening looked like a meticulous setup—but for what?

D'Agosta's words rang in her ears like a Klaxon. *Something bigger, maybe much bigger.*

Jesus, she needed D'Agosta—she needed him right now. He had the answers she didn't.

She pulled out her personal phone, tried his cellular. No response.

She glanced at her watch: 7:15. The evening was still young. If she could find him, get him back here . . . Where the hell could he be? Once again, his words echoed in her mind:

There's something else you ought to know. Have you heard of the forensic profiling firm of Effective Engineering Solutions, down on Little West 12th Street, run by an Eli Glinn? I've been spending most of my time down there recently, moonlighting . . .

It was just a chance—but it was better than nothing. It sure beat waiting here, twiddling her thumbs. With luck, she could be there and back in less than forty minutes.

She lifted her radio again. "Lieutenant Gault?"

"Copy."

"I'm heading out briefly. You're in charge."

"May I ask—?"

"There's somebody I need to speak with. If anything—*anything*—out of the ordinary happens, you have my authority to shut this down. Totally. You understand?"

"Yes, Captain."

She pocketed the radio and walked briskly out of the hall.

49

Pendergast stood in the small study, back pressed against the door, motionless. His eyes took in the rich furnishings: the couch covered with Persian rugs, the African masks, the side table, bookshelves, curious objets d'art.

He took a steadying breath. With a great effort of will, he made his way to the couch, lay down upon it slowly, folded his hands over his chest, crossed his ankles, and closed his eyes.

Over his professional career, Pendergast had found himself in many difficult and dangerous circumstances. And yet none of these equaled what he now faced in this little room.

He began with a series of simple physical exercises. He slowed his breathing and decelerated his heartbeat. He blocked out all external sensation: the rustle of the forced-air heating system, the faint smell of furniture polish, the pressure of the couch beneath him, his own corporeal awareness.

At last—when his respiration was barely discernible and his pulse hovered close to forty beats per minute—he allowed a chessboard to materialize before his mind's eye. His hands drifted over the well-worn pieces. A white pawn was moved forward on the board. A black pawn responded. The game continued, moving to stalemate. Another game began, ending the same way. Then another game, and another . . .

. . . but without the expected result. Pendergast's memory palace—

the storehouse of knowledge and information in which he kept his most personal secrets, and from which he carried out his most profound meditation and introspection—did not materialize before him.

Mentally, Pendergast switched games, moving from chess to bridge. Now, instead of setting two players against each other, he posited four, playing as partners, with the infinity of strategy, signals both missed and made, and plays of the hand that could result. Quickly he played through a rubber, then another.

The memory palace refused to appear. It remained out of reach, shifting, insubstantial.

Pendergast waited, reducing his heartbeat and respiration still further. Such a failure had never occurred before.

Now, delving into one of the most difficult of the Chongg Ran exercises, he mentally detached his consciousness from his body, then rose above it, floating incorporeal in space. Without opening his eyes, he recreated a virtual construct of the room in which he lay, imagining every object in its place, until the entire room had materialized in his mind, complete to the last detail. He lingered over it for several moments. And then, piece by piece, he proceeded to remove the furnishings, the carpeting, the wallpaper, until at last everything was gone once again.

But he did not stop there. Next, he proceeded to remove all the bustling city that surrounded the room: initially, structure by structure, then block by block, and then neighborhood by neighborhood, the act of intellectual oblivion gaining speed as it raced outward in all directions. Counties next; then states; nations, the world, the universe, all fell away into blackness.

Within minutes, everything was gone. Only Pendergast himself remained, floating in an infinite void. He then willed his own body to disappear, consumed by darkness. The universe was now entirely empty, stripped clean of all thought, all pain and memory, all tangible existence. He had reached the state known as Sunyata: for a moment—or was it an eternity?—time itself ceased to exist.

And then at last, the ancient mansion on Dauphine Street began to materialize in his mind: the Maison de la Rochenoire, the house in which he and Diogenes had grown up. Pendergast stood on the old cobbled street before it, gazing through the high wrought-iron fence to the mansion's mansard roofs, oriel windows, widow's walk, battlements, and stone pinnacles. High brick walls on one side hid lush, interior parterre gardens.

In his mind, Pendergast opened the huge iron gates and walked up the front drive, pausing on the portico. The whitewashed double doors lay open before him, giving onto the grand foyer.

After a moment of uncharacteristic indecision, he stepped through the doors and onto the marble floor of the hall. A huge crystal chandelier sparkled brilliantly overhead, hovering beneath the trompe l'oeil ceiling. Ahead, a double curved staircase with elaborately beaded newels swept up toward the second-floor gallery. On the left, closed doors led into the long, low-ceilinged exhibition hall; on the right lay the open doorway into a dim, wood-paneled library.

Although the real family mansion had been burned to the ground by a New Orleans mob many years before, Pendergast had retained this virtual mansion within his memory ever since: an intellectual artifact, perfect down to the last detail; a storehouse in which he kept not only his own experiences and observations, but innumerable family secrets as well. Normally, entering into this palace of memory was a tranquilizing, calming experience: each drawer of each cabinet of each room held some past event, or some personal reflection on history or science, to be perused at leisure. Today, however, Pendergast felt a profound unease, and it was only with the greatest mental effort he was able to keep the mansion cohesive in his mind.

He crossed the foyer and mounted the stairs to the wide second-floor hallway. Hesitating only briefly at the landing, he moved down the tapestried corridor, the broad sweep of the rose-colored walls broken at intervals by marble niches or ancient gilt frames containing portraits in oils. The smell of the mansion now swept over him: a combination of old fabric and leather, furniture polish, his mother's perfume, his father's Latakia tobacco.

Near the center of this hallway lay the heavy oak door to his own room. But he did not proceed that far. Instead, he stopped at the door just before it: a door that, strangely, had been sealed in lead and covered with a sheet of hammered brass, its edges nailed into the surrounding door frame.

This was the room of his brother, Diogenes. Pendergast himself had mentally sealed this door years before, locking the room forever inside the memory palace. It was the one room into which he had promised himself never again to enter.

And yet—if Eli Glinn was right—he must enter it. There was no choice.

As Pendergast paused outside the door, hesitating, he became aware that his pulse and respiration were increasing at an alarming rate. The walls of the mansion around him flickered and glowed, growing brighter, then fading, like the filament of a lightbulb failing under too much current. He was losing his elaborate mental construct. He made a supreme effort to concentrate, to calm his mind, and managed to steady the image around him.

He had to move quickly: the memory crossing could shatter at any moment under the force of his own emotions. He could not maintain the necessary concentration indefinitely.

He willed a pry bar, chisel, and mallet to appear in his hands. He wedged the pry bar under the brass sheet, pulling it away from the door frame, moving around the four sides until he had pried it off. Dropping the bar, he took up the chisel and mallet and began hammering loose the soft lead that had been packed in the cracks between the door and the frame, digging and carving it out in chunks. He worked rapidly, trying to lose himself in the task, thinking of nothing but the job at hand.

Within minutes, curls of lead lay over the carpeting. Now the only impediment to what lay on the far side of the door was its heavy lock.

Pendergast stepped forward, tried the handle. Normally, he would have picked it with the set of tools he always carried with him. But there was no time even for this: any pause, however brief, might be fatal. He stepped back, raised his foot, aimed at a point just below the lock, and gave the door a savage kick. It flew back, slamming against the interior wall with a crash. Pendergast stood in the doorway, breathing heavily. The room of Diogenes, his brother, lay beyond.

And yet there was nothing visible. The mellow light of the hallway did not penetrate the infinite gloom. The doorway was a rectangle of blackness.

Pendergast tossed aside the chisel and mallet. A moment's thought brought a powerful flashlight into his hand. He snapped on the light and pointed the beam into the gloom, which seemed to suck the very light out of the air.

Pendergast tried to take a step forward but found he could not will his limbs to move. He stood there, on the threshold, for what seemed like an eternity. The house began to wobble, the walls evaporating as if made of air, and he realized he was once again losing the memory palace. He knew if he lost it now, he'd never return. Ever.

It was only by a final act of supreme will—the most focused, draining, and difficult moment he had ever faced—that Pendergast forced himself over the threshold.

He stopped again just beyond, prematurely exhausted, playing the flashlight around, forcing the beam to lick ever farther into the darkness. It was not the room he expected to find. Instead, he was at the top of a narrow stairway of undressed stone, winding down into the living rock, twisting deeply into the earth.

At this sight, something dark stirred within Pendergast's mind: a rough beast that had slumbered, undisturbed, for over thirty years. For a moment, he felt himself falter and his will fail. The walls trembled like a candle flame in the wind.

He recovered. He had no choice now but to go forward. Taking a fresh grip on the flashlight, he began to descend the worn, slippery steps of stone: deeper, ever deeper, into a maw of shame, regret—and infinite horror.

50

Pendergast descended the staircase, the smell of the sub-basement coming up to him: a cloying odor of damp, mold, iron rust, and death. The staircase ended in a dark tunnel. The mansion had one of the few belowground basements in New Orleans—created at great expense and labor by the monks who originally built the structure, and who had lined the walls with sheets of hammered lead and carefully fitted stone to make cellars for aging their wines and brandies.

The Pendergast family had converted it to another use entirely.

In his mind, Pendergast made his way down the tunnel, which opened onto a broad, low open space, the irregular floor part earth, part stone, with a groined ceiling. The walls were encrusted with niter, and dim marble crypts, elaborately carved in Victorian and Edwardian style, filled the expanse, separated from one another by narrow walkways of brick.

Suddenly he became aware of a presence in the room: a small shadow. Then he heard the shadow speak with a seven-year-old voice: "Are you sure you want to keep going?"

With another shock, Pendergast realized there was a second figure in the dim space: taller, more slender, with white-blond hair. He felt chilled to the bone—it was himself, nine years old. He heard his own smooth, childish voice speak: "You're not afraid?"

"No. Of course not," came the small, defiant return—the voice of his brother, Diogenes.

"Well, then."

Pendergast watched as the two dim figures made their way through the necropolis, candles in hand, the taller one leading the way.

He felt a rising dread. He didn't remember this at all—and yet he knew something fearful was about to happen.

The fair-haired figure began examining the carved fronts of the tombs, reading the Latin inscriptions in a high, clear voice. They had both taken to Latin with great enthusiasm. Diogenes, Pendergast remembered, had always been the better Latin student; his teacher thought him a genius.

"Here's an odd one," said the older boy. "Take a look, Diogenes."

The smaller figure crept up and read:

ERASMUS LONGCHAMPS PENDERGAST
1840 – 1932
De mortiis aut bene aut nihil

"Do you recognize the line?"

"Horace?" said the younger figure. " 'Of the dead' . . . hmmm . . . 'speak well or say nothing.' "

After a silence, the older boy said, with a touch of condescension, "Bravo, little brother."

"I wonder," asked Diogenes, "what it was about his life he didn't want talked about?"

Pendergast remembered his youthful rivalry with his brother over Latin . . . one in which he was eventually left far behind.

They moved on to an elaborate double crypt, a sarcophagus in the Roman style topped with a man and woman in marble, both laid out in death with hands crossed on their breasts.

"Louisa de Nemours Prendergast. Henri Prendergast. *Nemo nisi mors,*" read the older boy. "Let's see . . . That must be 'Till death do us part.' "

The smaller boy had already moved to another tombstone. Crouching, he read, "*Multa ferunt anni venientes commoda secum, Multa recedentes adimiunt.*" He looked up. "Well, Aloysius, what do you make of that?"

A silence followed, and then the response came, bravely but a little uncertain. " 'Many years come to make us comfortable, many receding years diminish us.' "

The translation was greeted with a sarcastic snicker. "That doesn't make any sense."

"Of course it does."

"No, it doesn't. 'Many receding years diminish us'? That's nonsense. *I* think it means something like 'The years, as they come, bring many comforts. As they recede, they . . .' " He paused. "*Adimiunt?*"

"Just what I said: diminish," said the older boy.

" 'As they recede, they diminish us,' " finished Diogenes. "In other words, when you're young, the years bring good. But as you grow old, the years take it all away again."

"That makes no more sense than mine," said Aloysius, annoyance in his voice. He moved on toward the back of the necropolis, down another narrow row of crypts, reading more names and inscriptions. At the end of the cul-de-sac, he paused at a marble door set into the back wall, a rusted metal grate over it.

"Look at this tomb," he said.

Diogenes came up close, peered at it with his candle. "Where's the inscription?"

"There isn't one. But it's a crypt. It's got to be a door." Aloysius reached up, gave the grate a pull. Nothing. He pushed at it, pulled it, and then picked up a stray fragment of marble and began tapping around its edges. "Maybe it's empty."

"Maybe it's meant for *us*," the younger boy said, a ghoulish gleam appearing in his eyes.

"It's hollow back there." Aloysius redoubled his tapping and gave the grate another tug—and then suddenly, with a grinding sound, it opened. The two stood there, frightened.

"Oh, the *stink!*" said Diogenes, backing up and holding his nose.

And now Pendergast, deep within his mental construct, smelled it, too—an indescribable odor, foul, like a rotten, fungus-covered liver. He swallowed as the walls of the memory palace wavered, then came back into solidity.

Aloysius shone his candle into the freshly exposed space. It wasn't a crypt at all, but rather a large storage room, set into the rear of the sub-basement. The flickering light played off an array of strange contraptions made of brass, wood, and glass.

"What's in there?" Diogenes said, creeping back up behind his brother.

"See for yourself."

Diogenes peered in. "What are they?"

"Machines," the older brother said positively, as if he knew.

"Are you going in?"

"Naturally." Aloysius stepped through the doorway and turned. "Aren't you coming?"

"I guess so."

Pendergast, from the shadows, watched them go in.

The two boys stood in the room. The lead walls were streaked with whitish oxides. The space was packed floor-to-ceiling with contraptions: boxes painted with grimacing faces; old hats, ropes, and moth-eaten scarves; rusted chains and brass rings; cabinets, mirrors, capes, and wands. Cobwebs and thick layers of dust draped everything. At one end, propped up sideways, stood a sign, painted in garish colors and embellished with curlicues, a pair of pointing hands, and other nine-teenth-century American carnival flourishes.

Late from the Great Halls of Europe
The Illustrious and Celebrated Mesmerist
☛ PROFESSOR COMSTOCK PENDERGAST ☚
Presents
THE GRAND THEATRE AND ILLUMINATED PHANTASMAGORIA
Of
Magick, Illusion, and Prestidigitation

Pendergast stood in the shadows of his own memory, filled with the helpless foreboding of nightmare, watching the scene unfold. At first the two boys explored cautiously, their candlelight throwing elongated shadows among the boxes and piles of bizarre devices.

"Do you know what all this is?" whispered Aloysius.

"What?"

"We've found all the stuff from Great-Grand-Uncle Comstock's magic show."

"Who's Great-Grand-Uncle Comstock?"

"Only the most famous magician in the history of the world. He trained Houdini himself."

Aloysius touched a cabinet, ran his hand down to a knob, and cautiously pulled out a drawer: it contained a pair of manacles. He opened another drawer, which seemed to stick, and then it gave with a sudden *pop!* A pair of mice shot out of the drawer and scurried off.

Aloysius moved on to the next item, his younger brother following close behind. It was a coffin-like box standing upright, with a screaming man painted on the lid, numerous bloody holes piercing his body. He opened it with a groan of rusty hinges to reveal an interior studded with wrought-iron spikes.

"That looks more like torture than magic," said Diogenes.

"There's dried blood on those spikes."

Diogenes peered closely, fear temporarily overcome by a strange eagerness. Then he stepped back again. "That's just paint."

"Are you sure?"

"I know dried blood when I see it."

Aloysius moved on. "Look at that." He pointed to an object in the far corner. It was a huge box, much larger than the others, rising from floor to ceiling, the size of a small room itself. It was garishly painted in red and gold with a grinning demon's face on the front. Flanking the demon were odd things—a hand, a bloodshot eye, a finger—floating against the crimson background almost like severed body parts loosed in a tide of blood. Arched over a door cut into the side was a legend painted in gold and black:

The Doorway to Hell

"If it were my show," said Aloysius, "I would have given it a much grander name, something more like 'The Gates of the Inferno.' 'The Doorway to Hell' sounds boring." He turned to Diogenes. "Your turn to go first."

"How do you figure that?"

"I went first last time."

"Then you can go first again."

"No," said Aloysius. "I don't care to." He put his hand on the door and gave Diogenes a nudge with his elbow.

"Don't open it. Something might happen."

Aloysius opened it to reveal a dim, stifling interior, lined with what looked like black velvet. A brass ladder stood just inside, disappearing up through a hatch in a low false ceiling set into the box.

"I could dare you to go in there," Aloysius went on, "but I'm not going to. I don't believe in childish games. If you want to go in, go in."

"Why don't *you* go in?"

"I freely admit it to you: I'm nervous."

With a creeping feeling of shame, Pendergast could see his knack for psychological persuasion, already developed as a boy, coming into play. He wanted to see what was in there—but he wanted Diogenes to go in first.

"You're scared?" Diogenes asked.

"That's right. So the only way we're ever going to know what's in there is if *you* go in first. I'll be right behind you, I promise."

"I don't want to."

"Scared?"

"No." The quaver in his high-pitched voice said otherwise.

Pendergast reflected bitterly that Diogenes, who was only seven, hadn't yet learned that truth is the safest lie.

"Then what's stopping you?"

"I . . . I don't feel like it."

Aloysius snickered dryly. "I admitted I was scared. If you're scared, say so, and we'll go back upstairs and forget all about it."

"I'm *not* scared. It's just some stupid fun house."

Pendergast watched, horrified, as his childish doppelganger reached over and grasped Diogenes by the shoulders. "Go ahead, then."

"Don't *touch* me!"

Firmly and gently, Aloysius urged him through the little doorway of the box and crowded in behind him, blocking his retreat. "As you said, it's just some stupid fun house."

"I don't *want* to stay in here."

They were both inside the first compartment in the box, jammed up against each other. Clearly, the fun house was meant to admit one adult at a time, not two half-grown children.

"Get going, brave Diogenes. I'll be right behind."

Wordlessly, Diogenes began to climb the little brass ladder, and Aloysius followed.

Pendergast watched them disappear as the hinged box door closed automatically behind them. His heart was beating so hard in his chest he thought it might explode at any moment. The walls of his memory construct flickered and shook. It was almost unbearable.

But he could not stop now. Something terrible was about to happen, but what exactly he still hadn't the slightest idea. He had not yet excavated that deeply into old, repressed memories. He had to keep going.

In his mind, he opened the box door and climbed the brass ladder himself, passing into a crawl space above, which turned horizontally and gave onto a low chamber above the false ceiling but below the top of the box. The two boys were there ahead of him, Diogenes in the lead. He was crawling toward a circular porthole in the far wall of the crawl space. Diogenes hesitated at the entrance to the porthole.

"Go on!" Aloysius urged.

The little boy glanced back once at his brother, a strange expression in his eyes. Then he crawled through the porthole and disappeared.

Moving toward the porthole himself, Aloysius paused, peering round with the candle, apparently noticing for the first time that the walls seemed to be covered with photographs shellacked to the wood.

"Aren't you coming?" came a small, scared, angry voice from the darkness beyond. "You *promised* you would stay right behind me."

Pendergast, watching, felt himself begin to shake uncontrollably.

"Yes, yes. I'm coming."

The young Aloysius crept up to the round, dark portal, looked inside—but went no farther.

"Hey! Where are you?" came the muffled cry from the darkness beyond. Then suddenly: "What's happening? What's *this*?" A shrill boyish scream cut through the little chamber like a scalpel. Ahead, through the porthole, Pendergast saw a light appear; saw the floor tip; saw Diogenes slide to the far end of a small room and tumble into a lighted pit below. There was a sudden low sound, like the rumble of an animal— and dreadful, unspeakable images appeared within the pit—and then with a swift *thunk!* the porthole snapped shut, blocking his view.

"No!" screamed Diogenes from deep within. "*Nooooooo!*"

And then quite suddenly, Pendergast remembered all. It came rushing back in perfect, exquisite detail, every hideous second, every moment of the most terrifying experience in his life.

He remembered the Event.

As the memory crashed over him like a tidal wave, he felt his brain overload, his neurons shut down—and he lost control of the memory crossing. The mansion trembled, shivered, and exploded in his mind, the walls igniting and flying apart, a huge roar filling his head, the great palace of memory blazing off into the darkness of infinite space, dissolving into glittering shards of light like meteors streaking into the void. For a brief moment, the anguished cries of Diogenes continued from out of the limitless gulf—then they, too, fell away and all was quiet once again.

51

Warden Gordon Imhof glanced around the table of the spartan conference room deep within Herkmoor's Command Block, microphone clipped to his lapel. All things considered, he felt good. The response to the breakout had been immediate and overwhelming. Everything had worked like clockwork, by the book: as soon as the Code Red was given, the entire complex had been electronically locked down, all ingress and egress halted. The escapees had run around for a time like headless chickens—theirs had been a totally senseless escape plan—and within forty minutes they had all been rounded up and put back either in their cells or in the infirmary. The obligatory anklet sensor check, which ran automatically every time a Code Red was suspended, confirmed that all prisoners in the complex were accounted for.

In the corrections business, Imhof mused, the way to get noticed was through a crisis. A crisis created visibility. Depending on how the crisis was handled, it created an advancement opportunity or a ruined career. This particular one had been handled flawlessly: a single guard hurt (and not badly at that), no hostages taken, nobody killed or seriously injured. Under his leadership, Herkmoor had retained its flawless no-escape record.

Imhof glanced at the clock, waited for the second hand to sweep around to exactly 7:30. Coffey hadn't shown up, but he wasn't going to wait. The truth was, the smug FBI agent and his lackey had really begun to get on his nerves.

"Gentlemen," he began, "let me start this meeting by saying to all of you: well done."

A murmuring and a vague shifting greeted this opening.

"Today, Herkmoor faced an extraordinary challenge—a mass escape attempt. At two-eleven P.M., nine inmates cut the fence in one of the building C exercise yards and fanned out through the inner perimeter fields. One got as far as the security station at the south end of building B. The cause of the breakout is still under investigation. Suffice to say, it appears that the prisoners in yard 4 were not under direct guard supervision at the time of the escape, for reasons that remain unclear."

He paused, giving the group around the table a stern look. "We will be addressing that failure in the course of this debriefing."

Then he relaxed his features. "Overall, the response to the escape attempt was immediate and by the book. First responders were at the scene at two-fourteen and a Code Red was immediately sounded. More than fifty guards were mobilized for the response. In well under an hour, every single escapee had been recaptured and all prisoners had been accounted for. By three-oh-one, the Code Red had ended. Herkmoor returned to business as usual."

He paused for a moment. "Once again, I offer my congratulations to all involved. Everyone can relax, this is merely a pro forma meeting—as you know, a formal debriefing is required by regulation to occur within twelve hours of any Code Red. I apologize for keeping you here past your normal workday: let's see if we can't tie up any loose ends quickly so we can all get home to dinner. I urge any of you with questions to ask them as we proceed. Do not stand on ceremony."

He looked around the room. "I call first on building C security manager James Rollo. Jim, could you talk about the role of Officer Sidesky? There seems to be some confusion about that."

A man with a pour-over belly arose with the sound of jingling keys, adjusted his belt with more jingling. His face had assumed a stolid look of high seriousness.

"Thank you, sir. As you mentioned, the Code Red was sounded at two-fourteen. The first responders came from guard station 7. Four responded, leaving Officer Sidesky to man the guard station. It appears one of the escapees overpowered Officer Sidesky, drugged him, tied him up, and left him in the nearby men's room. He's still disoriented, but as soon as he is lucid we'll get a statement."

"Very well."

At this point, a restless-looking man in a nurse's uniform rose. "I'm Staff Nurse Kidder, sir, in charge of the building B infirmary."

Imhof looked at him. "Yes?"

"There seems to have been some kind of mix-up. Early in the escape attempt, the EMTs brought down an injured guard claiming to be Sidesky, in uniform with his badge and ID. He then disappeared."

"That's easily explained," said Rollo. "We found Sidesky without his uniform and badge. He must have left the infirmary. And then, evidently, one of the prisoners must have stripped Sidesky after knocking him out."

"That sounds logical to me," said Imhof. He hesitated. "Only thing is, all the escapees were apprehended in their prison garb. None were wearing uniforms."

Rollo rubbed his wattle. "The prisoner who stripped Sidesky probably didn't have time to put on the uniform."

"That must be it," said Imhof. "Mr. Rollo, please record those items as missing: uniform, badge, and ID belonging to Sidesky. I expect they'll be found in the trash or in a dark corner somewhere. Can't have them falling into prisoner hands."

"Yes, sir."

"Mystery solved. Continue, Mr. Rollo."

"Forgive me for interrupting," said Kidder, "but I'm not sure the mystery *is* solved. This man claiming to be Sidesky was left in the infirmary awaiting the radiologist while I attended to some of the escapees. He had several broken ribs, contusions, a facial laceration, a—"

"We don't need the complete diagnosis, Kidder."

"Right, sir. Anyway, he was in no condition to go anywhere. And when I returned, Sidesky—I mean, the guy claiming to be Sidesky—had disappeared, and in his bed was the corpse of the prisoner, Carlos Lacarra."

"Lacarra?" Imhof frowned. He hadn't heard this part before.

"That's right. Someone had moved his cadaver and stuck him in Sidesky's bed."

"Somebody's idea of a joke?"

"I don't know, sir. I was wondering if . . . well, if it could be involved with the escape attempt somehow."

There was a silence.

"If so," Imhof finally said, "then we're dealing with a more sophisticated plan than we initially assumed. But the bottom line is this: every single escapee was recaptured and is accounted for. We'll be interrogating them in the days ahead to unravel exactly what happened."

"One other thing troubles me," Kidder went on. "During the escape, a morgue-mobile arrived to take Lacarra's body away. It was kept waiting outside the gates until the Code Red came down."

"And?"

"When the code was called off, the ambulance came in and loaded the body. The chief physician witnessed the loading and signed the papers."

"I don't see the problem."

"The problem, sir, is that it wasn't until fifteen minutes *later* that I found Lacarra's body in Sidesky's bed."

Imhof raised his eyebrows. "So the wrong stiff got picked up in the confusion. That's understandable. Don't be too hard on yourself, Kidder. Just call the hospital and sort it out."

"I did that, sir. And when I called the hospital, they said our call to pick up the body this morning was canceled right after it came in. They swear they never even *sent* a morgue-mobile."

Imhof snorted. "That damn hospital is always screwing up, a dozen layers of administrators who don't know their ass from a hole in the ground. Call them back in the morning, tell them we sent them the wrong stiff and they should go look for it." He shook his head in disgust.

"But that's just the problem, sir. We didn't *have* any other corpse at Herkmoor. I can't figure out what cadaver went to the hospital."

"You say the chief physician signed the papers?"

"Yes. He went home at the end of his shift."

"We'll get a statement from him tomorrow. No doubt we'll straighten out this confusion in the morning. Anyway, it's tangential to the escape attempt. Let's get on with the debriefing."

Kidder fell silent, his face troubled.

"All right. The next question is why the yard seemed to have no supervision at the time of the breakout. My time sheets show Fecteau and Doyle were on yard 4 duty at the time of the escape. Fecteau, could you please explain your absence?"

A very nervous guard at the far end of the table cleared his voice. "Yes, sir. Officer Doyle and I had yard duty that day—"

"The nine prisoners were escorted to the yard on schedule?"

"Yes, sir. They arrived at two P.M. sharp."

"Where were you?"

"At our yard posts, just as required."

"So what happened?"

"Well, about five minutes later, we got the call from Special Agent Coffey."

"Coffey called you?" Imhof was truly astonished. This was way out of line. He glanced around: Coffey still hadn't shown up.

"Tell us about the call, Fecteau."

"He said he needed us right away. We explained we were on yard duty, but he insisted."

Imhof felt his anger rising. Coffey had told him nothing about this. "Tell us Agent Coffey's exact words, please."

Fecteau hesitated, colored. "Well, sir, he said something like 'If you're not here in ninety seconds, I'll have you transferred to North Dakota.' Something like that, sir. I tried to explain that we were the only two on yard duty, but he cut me off."

"He threatened you?"

"Basically, yes."

"And so you left the yard unattended, without checking with either the chief of security or me?"

"I'm sorry, sir. I thought he must have authorized it with you."

"Why in hell, Fecteau, would I *authorize* the removal of the only two guards on yard duty, leaving a gang of prisoners to their own devices?"

"I'm sorry, sir. I assumed it was . . . because of the special prisoner."

"The special prisoner? What are you talking about?"

"Well . . ." Fecteau had begun to stumble over his words. "The special prisoner who had exercise privileges in yard 4."

"Yes, but he never made it to yard 4. He remained in his cell."

"Um, no, sir. We saw him in yard 4."

Imhof took a deep breath. Things were more screwed up than he had thought. "Fecteau, you're getting confused. The prisoner remained in his cell all day and was never escorted to yard 4. I checked on it personally during the code—I have the electronic logs right here. The anklet scans show he never left solitary."

"Well, sir, my best recollection is that the special prisoner was there." He cast an inquiring glance toward the other guard, Doyle, who looked equally flummoxed.

"Doyle?" Imhof asked sharply.

"Yes, sir?"

"Don't 'yes, sir' me, I want to know: did you see the special prisoner in yard 4 today?"

"Yes, sir. I mean, that's my recollection, sir."

A long silence. Imhof screwed his eye around to Rollo, but the man was already murmuring into his radio. It took only moments for the security manager to put it aside and look up again. "According to the electronic monitor, the special prisoner's still in his cell. Never left it."

"Better send someone to do a cell check, just to make sure." Imhof boiled with fury at Coffey. Where the hell was he? This was all his fault.

As if on cue, the door flew open and there was Special Agent Coffey, trailed by Rabiner.

"It's about time," said Imhof darkly.

"It certainly *is* about time," said Coffey, striding into the room, face red. "I left *specific* orders for the special prisoner to be put into yard 4, and now I find out it was never done. Imhof, when I give an order, I expect it to be—"

Imhof rose. He'd had it with this asshole, and he wasn't going to let him bully him, especially in front of his staff. "Agent Coffey," he said in an icy voice, "we had a serious escape attempt today, as you surely know."

"That's no concern of—"

"We are conducting a debriefing related to said escape. You are interrupting. If you will sit down and await your turn to speak, we will continue."

Coffey remained standing, looking at him, face turning red. "I don't appreciate being addressed in that tone of voice."

"Agent Coffey, I am asking you one more time to sit down and allow this debriefing to continue. If you continue to speak out of turn, I will have you removed from the premises."

A thunderstruck silence ensued. Coffey's face contorted with fury and he turned to Rabiner. "You know what? I think our presence at this meeting is no longer required." He swiveled back to Imhof. "You'll be hearing from me."

"Your presence certainly *is* required. I have two guards here who say you gave them orders and threatened them with termination if they didn't obey—despite the fact that you have absolutely no authority here. As a result, prisoners were left unattended and attempted escape. *You*, sir, are responsible for the escape attempt. I make this statement for the record."

Another electric silence. Coffey looked around, the imperious look on his face softening as he began to absorb the seriousness of the accusation. His eyes locked on the tape recorder in the middle of the table, the microphones in front of each seat.

Stiffly Coffey sat down, swallowed. "I'm sure we can straighten out this, ah, misunderstanding, Mr. Imhof. There's no need to make rash accusations."

In the ensuing silence, Rollo's radio chimed—he was receiving the callback about the cell check for the special prisoner. As Imhof watched, the security manager lifted the radio to his ear and listened, his face gradually turning a slack, dead white.

52

Glinn glanced down at Special Agent Pendergast. He lay unmoving on the couch of burgundy-colored leather, arms over his chest, ankles crossed. He had been like that for almost twenty minutes. With his unnaturally pale complexion and gaunt features, the man looked remarkably like a corpse. The only signs of life were the beads of sweat that had sprung out across Pendergast's forehead and a faint trembling in his hands.

His body jerked once, suddenly, then fell still. The eyes slowly opened—remarkably bloodshot, the pupils like pinpricks in the silvery irises.

Glinn wheeled forward, leaned close. Something had happened. The memory crossing was over.

"You stay. Alone," Pendergast said in a husky whisper. "Send Lieutenant D'Agosta and Dr. Krasner away."

Glinn closed the door quietly behind him, turned the lock. "Done."

"What is to come . . . must take the form of an interrogatory. You will ask questions. I will answer them. There is no other way. I . . ." And here the whisper stopped for a long moment. "I am unable to speak about what I have just witnessed—voluntarily."

"Understood."

Pendergast lay silent. After a moment, Glinn spoke again. "You have something to tell me."

"Yes."

"About your brother, Diogenes."

"Yes."

"The Event."

A pause. "Yes."

Glinn glanced at the ceiling, where a tiny camera and high-gain microphone were concealed. Reaching into his pocket, he pressed a small remote control, deactivating them. Some inner sense told him that whatever was to come should remain solely the province of their collective memory.

He inched his wheelchair forward. "You were there."

"Yes."

"You and your brother. No others."

"No others."

"What was the date?"

Another pause. "The date is not important."

"Let me decide that."

"It was spring. The bougainvillea was in bloom outside. Beyond that, I don't know."

"How old were you?"

"Nine."

"And your brother must have been seven, correct?"

"Yes."

"Location?"

"Maison de la Rochenoire, our ancestral home on Dauphine Street, New Orleans."

"And what were you doing?"

"Exploring."

"Go on."

Pendergast was silent. Glinn remembered his words: *You will ask questions. I will answer them.*

He cleared his throat quietly. "Did you frequently explore the house?"

"It was a large mansion. It had many secrets."

"How long had it been in the family?"

"It had originally been a monastery, but an ancestor purchased it in the 1750s."

"And which ancestor was that?"

"Augustus Robespierre Pendergast. He spent decades refashioning it."

Glinn knew most of this, of course. But it had seemed better to keep Pendergast talking for a bit—and answering the easy questions—before venturing deeper. Now he would penetrate.

"And where were you exploring on this particular day?" he asked.

"The sub-basements."

"Were they one of the secrets?"

"My parents didn't know we had found our way into them."

"But you had discovered a way."

"Diogenes did."

"And he shared it with you."

"No. I—followed him once."

"That's when he told you."

A pause. "I made him tell me."

The sweat was thicker on Pendergast's brow now, and Glinn did not press this point. "Describe the sub-basements to me."

"They were reached through a false wall in the basement."

"And beyond, a staircase leading down?"

"Yes."

"What was at the bottom of the staircase?"

Another pause. "A necropolis."

Glinn paused a moment to master his surprise. "And you were exploring this necropolis?"

"Yes. We were reading inscriptions on the family tombs. That is how . . . how it started."

"You found something?"

"The entrance to a secret chamber."

"And what was inside?"

"The magical equipment of my ancestor, Comstock Pendergast."

Glinn paused again. "Comstock Pendergast, the magician?"

"Yes."

"So he stored his stage equipment in the sub-basement?"

"No. My family hid it there."

"Why did they do that?"

"Because much of the equipment was dangerous."

"But while you were exploring the room, you didn't know that."

"No. Not at first."

"At first?"

"Some of the devices looked strange. Cruel. We were young, we didn't fully understand . . ." Pendergast hesitated.

"What happened next?" Glinn asked gently.

"In the back, we found a large box."

"Describe it."

"Very large—almost the size of a small room itself—but portable. It was garish. Red and gold. The face of a demon was painted on its side. There were words above the face."

"What did the words say?"

" 'The Doorway to Hell.' "

Pendergast was trembling slightly now, and Glinn let some more time pass before speaking again. "Did the box have an entrance?"

"Yes."

"And you went inside."

"Yes. No."

"You mean, Diogenes went first?"

"Yes."

"Willingly?"

Another long pause. "No."

"You goaded him," Glinn said.

"That, and . . ." Pendergast stopped once more.

"You used force?"

"Yes."

Glinn now kept utterly still. He did not allow even the slightest squeak of the wheelchair to break the tense atmosphere.

"Why?"

"He had been sarcastic, as usual. I was angry with him. If there was something a little frightening . . . I wanted him to go first."

"So Diogenes crawled inside. And you followed him."

"Yes."

"What did you find?"

Pendergast's mouth worked, but it was some time before the words emerged. "A ladder. Leading up to a crawl space above."

"Describe it."

"Dark. Stifling. Photographs on the walls."

"Go on."

"There was a porthole in the rear wall, leading into another room. Diogenes went first."

Watching Pendergast, Glinn hesitated, then said, "You made him go first?"

"Yes."

"And you followed."

"I . . . I was about to."

"What stopped you?"

Pendergast gave a sudden, spasmodic twitch, but did not answer.

"What stopped you?" Glinn pressed suddenly.

"The show began. Inside the box. *Inside*, where Diogenes was."

"A show of Comstock's devising?"

"Yes."

"What was its purpose?"

Another twitch. "To frighten someone to death."

Glinn leaned back slowly in his wheelchair. He had, as part of his research, studied Pendergast's ancestry, and among his many colorful antecedents Comstock stood out. He had been the agent's great-grand-uncle, in his youth a famed magician, mesmerist, and creator of illusions. As he grew old, however, he became increasingly bitter and misanthropic. Like so many of his relatives, he ended his days in an asylum.

So this was where Comstock's madness had led.

"Tell me how it began," he said.

"I don't know. The floor tilted or collapsed beneath Diogenes. He fell into a lower chamber."

"Deeper into the box?"

"Yes, back down to the first level. That was where the . . . *show* took place."

"Describe it," Glinn said.

Suddenly Pendergast moaned—a moan of such anguish, such long-repressed suffering, that Glinn was for a moment left speechless.

"Describe it," he urged again as soon as he could speak.

"I only had a glimpse, I didn't really see it. And then . . . *they* closed around me."

"They?"

"Mechanisms. Driven by secret springs. One behind me, shutting off escape. Another that locked Diogenes inside the inner chamber."

Pendergast fell silent again. The pillow beneath his head was now soaked in perspiration.

"But for a moment . . . you saw what Diogenes saw."

Pendergast lay still. Then—very slowly—he inclined his head. "Only for a moment. But I *heard* it all. All of it."

"What was it?"

"A magic-lantern show," Pendergast whispered. "A phantasmagoria. Operated by voltaic cell. It was . . . Comstock's specialty."

Glinn nodded. He knew something of this. Magic-lanterns were devices that passed light through sheets of glass onto which images had been etched. Projected onto a slowly rotating wall with uneven surfaces to reinforce the illusion, and supplemented by sinister music and repetitious voices, it was the nineteenth-century equivalent of the horror movie.

"Well then, what did you see?"

Abruptly the agent leaped from the couch, suddenly full of feverish action. He paced the room, hands clenching and unclenching. Then he turned toward Glinn. "I beg you, *do not ask me that*."

He mastered himself with a supreme effort, still pacing the room like a caged beast.

"Go on, please," said Glinn tonelessly.

"Diogenes shrieked and screamed from within the inner chamber. Again and again . . . and again. I heard a terrible scrabbling as he tried to claw his way out—I could hear his nails breaking. Then there was a long silence . . . And then—I don't know how much later—I heard the shot."

"Gunshot?"

"Comstock Pendergast had furnished his . . . house of pain with a single-shot derringer. He gave his victim a choice. You could go mad; you could die of fright—or you could take your life."

"And Diogenes chose the last."

"Yes. But the bullet didn't . . . didn't kill him. It only damaged him."

"How did your parents react?"

"At first they said nothing. Then they pretended Diogenes was sick, scarlet fever. They kept it secret. They were afraid of the scandal. They told me the fever had altered his vision, his sense of taste and smell. That it deadened one eye. But now I know it must have been the bullet."

Glinn felt a chill horror settle over him, and he felt an illogical need to wash his hands. The thought of something so awful, so utterly terrifying, that a *seven-year-old* could possibly be induced to . . . He forced the thought away.

"And the small chamber you were imprisoned in," he said. "These photographs you mention—what were they of?"

"Official crime scene photographs and police sketches of the world's most terrible murders. Perhaps a way to prepare for the . . . the horror beyond."

An awful silence settled over the small room.

"And how long was it before you were rescued?" Glinn asked at last.

"I don't know. Hours, a day perhaps."

"And you awakened from this living nightmare under the impression Diogenes had become sick. And that accounted for his long absence."

"Yes."

"You had no idea of the truth."

"No, none."

"And yet *Diogenes* never realized that you had repressed the memory." Abruptly Pendergast stopped in his pacing. "No. I suppose he didn't."

"As a result, you never apologized to your brother, tried to make it up to him. You never even mentioned it, because you had utterly blocked out all memory of the Event."

Pendergast looked away.

"But to Diogenes, your silence meant something else entirely. A stubborn refusal to admit your mistake, to ask forgiveness. And that would explain . . ."

Glinn fell silent. Slowly he pushed his wheelchair back. He did not know everything—that would await the computer analysis—but he knew enough to see it now, clearly, in its broadest brushstrokes. Almost from birth, Diogenes had been a strange, dark, and brilliant creature, as had many Pendergasts before him. He might have swung either way, if the Event had not occurred. But the person who emerged from the Doorway to Hell—ravaged emotionally as well as physically—had turned into something else entirely. Yes, it all made sense: the gruesome images of crime, of murder, that Pendergast had endured . . . Diogenes's hatred of the brother who refused to speak of the ordeal he had caused . . . Pendergast's own unnatural attraction to pathological crimes . . . Both brothers now made sense. And Glinn now knew why Pendergast had repressed the memory so utterly. It was not simply because it was so awful. No—it was *because the guilt was so overwhelming it threatened his very sanity.*

Remotely, Glinn became aware that Pendergast was looking at him. The agent was standing as stiff as a statue, his skin like gray marble.

"Mr. Glinn," he said.

Glinn raised his eyebrows in silent query.

"There is nothing more I can or will say."

"Understood."

"I will now require five minutes alone, please. Without interruptions of any kind. And then we can . . . proceed."

After a moment, Glinn nodded. Then he turned the wheelchair around, opened the door, and exited the studio without another word.

53

With sirens shrieking, Hayward was able to get down to Greenwich Village in twenty minutes. On the way, she had tried the few other contact numbers she had for D'Agosta—none connected. She had tried to find a listing for Effective Engineering Solutions or Eli Glinn, without success. Even the NYPD telephone and Manhattan business databases didn't have a number, although EES was registered as a legitimate business, as required by law.

She knew the company existed, and she knew its address on Little West 12th Street. Beyond that, nothing.

Sirens still blaring, she pulled off the West Side Highway onto West Street, and from there turned into a narrow lane, crowded on both sides by dingy brick buildings. She shut off her sirens and crawled along, glancing at the building numbers. Little West 12th, once the center of the meatpacking district, was a single block in length. The EES building had no number, but she deduced it must be the correct one by the numbers on either side. It was not exactly what she imagined: perhaps a dozen stories tall, with the faded name of some long-defunct meatpacking company on the side—except it betrayed itself by tiers of expensive new windows on the upper floors and a pair of metal doors at the loading dock that looked suspiciously high-tech. She double-parked in front, blocking the narrow street, and went up to the entrance.

A smaller door sat beside the loading dock, an intercom with a buzzer its only adornment. She pressed the intercom and waited, her heart racing with frustration and impatience.

Almost immediately a female voice answered. "Yes?"

She flashed her badge, not sure where the camera was but certain there was one. "Captain Laura Hayward, NYPD Homicide. I demand immediate access to these premises."

"Do you have a warrant?" came the pleasant answer.

"No. I'm here to see Lieutenant Vincent D'Agosta. I've got to see him immediately—it's a matter of life and death."

"We don't have a Vincent D'Agosta on staff here," came the female voice, still maintaining a tone of bureaucratic pleasantness.

Hayward took a breath. "I want you to carry a message to Eli Glinn. If this door isn't opened within thirty seconds, here's what'll happen: the NYPD will stake out the entrance, we'll photograph everyone coming in or out, and we'll get a search warrant looking for a meth lab and bust a lot of glass. You understand me? The countdown just began."

It took only fifteen seconds. There came a faint click and the doors sprang open noiselessly.

She stepped into a dimly lit corridor that ended in doors of polished stainless steel. They opened simultaneously, revealing a heavily muscled man in a warm-up suit emblazoned with the logo of Harvey Mudd College. "This way," he said, and turned unceremoniously.

She followed him through a cavernous room to an industrial elevator, which led via a short ascent to a maze of white corridors, finally ending up at a pair of polished cherry doors. They opened onto a small, elegant conference room.

Standing at the far end was Vincent D'Agosta.

"Hi, Laura," he managed after a moment.

Hayward suddenly found herself at a loss for words. She'd been so intent on getting to see him that she hadn't thought ahead to what she would say if she succeeded. D'Agosta, too, was silent. It seemed that beyond a greeting, he was also unable to speak.

Hayward swallowed, found her voice. "Vincent, I need your help."

Another long silence. "My help?"

"At our last meeting, you spoke about Diogenes planning something bigger. You said, 'He's got a plan which he's put in motion.'"

Silence. Hayward found herself coloring; this was a lot harder than she'd thought. "That plan is tonight," she went on. "At the museum. At the opening."

"How do you know?"

"Let's call it a gut feeling—a pretty damn strong gut feeling."

D'Agosta nodded.

"I think Diogenes *works* at the museum, in some kind of alter ego. All the evidence shows the diamond theft had inside help, right? Well, *he* was the inside help."

"That isn't what you and Coffey and all the others concluded—"

She waved her hand impatiently. "You said Viola Maskelene and Pendergast were romantically involved. That's why Diogenes kidnapped her. Right?"

"Right."

"Guess who's at the opening."

Another silence—this one not awkward, but surprised.

"That's right. Maskelene. Hired at the last minute to be Egyptologist for the show. To replace Wicherly, who died in the museum under very strange circumstances."

"Oh, Jesus." D'Agosta glanced at his watch. "It's seven-thirty."

"The opening's going on as we speak. We need to go *right now*."

"I—" D'Agosta hesitated again.

"Come on, Vinnie, there's no time to waste. You know the place better than I do. The brass isn't going to do anything—I have to do it myself. That's why I need you there."

"You need more than me," he said, his voice now quiet.

"Who else did you have in mind?"

"You need Pendergast."

Hayward laughed mirthlessly. "Brilliant. Let's send a chopper up to Herkmoor and see if we can't borrow him for the evening."

Another silence. "He isn't at Herkmoor. He's here."

Hayward stared at him, uncomprehending.

"Here?" she repeated at last.

D'Agosta nodded.

"You busted him out of Herkmoor?"

Another nod.

"My God, Vinnie. Are you frigging crazy? You're already hip-deep in shit . . . and now this?" Without thinking, she sank into one of the chairs at the conference table, then sprang immediately back to her feet. "I can't believe it."

"What are you going to do about it?" D'Agosta asked.

Hayward stood there, staring at him. Slowly the enormity of the choice she had to make became clear to her. It was a choice between playing it by the book—taking Pendergast into custody, calling in backup and transferring custody, then getting back to the museum— or . . .

Or what? There was no other option. That was what she should do—what she *had* to do. Everything she had learned as a cop, every fiber of her cop's soul, told her so.

She took out her radio.

"Calling for backup?" D'Agosta asked in a low voice.

She nodded.

"Think about what you're about to do, Laura. Please."

But fifteen years of training had already thought for her. She raised the radio to her lips. "This is Captain Hayward calling Homicide One, come in."

She felt D'Agosta's hand gently touch her shoulder. "You *need* him."

"Homicide One? This is a Code 16. I've got a fugitive and need backup . . ." Her voice trailed off.

In the silence, she could hear the dispatcher's inevitable question. "Your location, Captain?"

Hayward said nothing. Her eyes met D'Agosta's.

"Captain? I need your location."

There was a silence broken only by the crackle of the radio.

"I read you, over," Hayward said.

"Your location?"

Another silence. Then she said, "Cancel that Code 16. Situation re-solved. This is Captain Hayward, over and out."

54

Hayward tore away from the curb, made a U-turn, and drove the wrong way down Little West 12th, peeled right onto West Street, and rocketed uptown, cars braking and pulling off to the left and right as she flashed past, sirens screaming. If all went well, they would be at the museum no later than 8:20 P.M. D'Agosta sat in the passenger's seat next to her, saying nothing. She glanced at Pendergast in the rearview mirror—face badly bruised, a freshly dressed cut along one cheek. He wore a ghostly expression, one she had never seen on his face before— or anybody else's, for that matter. He had the look of somebody who had just peered into his own personal hell.

Hayward returned her gaze to the street ahead. She knew, in some profound way, that she had just crossed the Rubicon. She had done something that went against all her training, everything she knew about what it meant to be a good cop.

Funny how, at the moment, she didn't seem to care.

A strange, uncomfortable silence hung over the three. She would have expected Pendergast to be peppering her with questions, or at least thanking her for not turning him in. Instead, he sat there wordlessly, the same awful expression on his bruised features.

"Okay," she said. "Here it is. Tonight's the big opening of the new exhibition at the museum. Everyone's there: top museum brass, mayor, governor, celebrities, tycoons. *Everyone.* I tried to stop it, postpone it, but I got vetoed. Problem is, I didn't—still don't—have any really hard information. All I know is this: something's coming down. And your brother, Diogenes, is behind it."

She glanced at Pendergast again. But he did not respond, did not return the glance. He just sat there, withdrawn, detached. He might have been a million miles away.

The wheels squealed a little as she negotiated a city bus, then accelerated onto the West Side Highway.

"After the diamond heist," she went on, "Diogenes vanished. I figure he already had an alter ego prepared and just stepped into it. I've done some sniffing around, and so has that journalist Smithback. We're both convinced Diogenes's alter ego is a staff member of the museum, probably a curator. Think about it: the diamond heist had to be an inside job, but he's not the kind of guy to take in partners. That's also how he managed to penetrate the security of the Sacred Images exhibition and attack Margo Green. Vinnie, you'd told me from the start Diogenes was working up to something big. You were right all along. And it's going to happen tonight, at the opening."

"You'd better bring Pendergast up to speed on the new exhibition," D'Agosta said.

"After the fiasco with the diamonds, the museum announced it was going to reopen an old Egyptian tomb in its basement—the Tomb of Senef. Some French count gave them a ton of money to do it. It was obviously a way to distract public attention from the destruction of the diamond collection. Tonight's the opening gala."

"Name?" Pendergast asked. His voice was barely audible, as if emerging from deep within a sepulcher.

It was the first word Hayward had heard him utter. "I'm sorry?" she replied.

"The name of the count?"

"Thierry de Cahors."

"Did anyone actually meet this count?"

"I wouldn't know."

When Pendergast lapsed back into silence, she continued. "Over the past six weeks, there've been two deaths associated with the reopening of the tomb, supposedly unconnected with each other. The first was a computer technician working inside the tomb, killed by his partner. The guy went crazy, murdered his pal, stuffed his organs into nearby ceremonial jars, and fled to the museum attics. Attacked a guard when they tried to flush him out. The second death was a curator named Wicherly, a Brit brought in specially to curate the show. He went nuts, tried to strangle Nora Kelly—you know her, Vinnie, right?"

"She all right?"

"She's fine—in fact, she's handling the opening tonight. Wicherly, on the other hand, was shot and killed by a panicked museum guard during the attack on Kelly. Now here's the kicker: autopsies showed both aggressors suffered the exact same kind of brain damage."

D'Agosta looked over at her. *"What?"*

"Both were working in the tomb just before they went psycho. But we went over everything with a fine-tooth comb, found nothing—no environmental or other cause. As I said, the official line is that the two deaths are unconnected. But I'm not buying the coincidence. Diogenes is planning something—I've felt it all evening. And when I saw *her* at the opening, I knew I was right."

"Who?" Pendergast murmured.

"Viola Maskelene."

Hayward sensed a sudden stillness behind her.

"Did you inquire as to how she happened to be there?" came the very cool voice from the backseat.

Hayward swerved around a lumbering garbage truck. "She was hired by the museum at the last minute to replace Wicherly."

"Hired by whom?"

"The head of the Anthropology Department. Menzies. Hugo Menzies."

Another pause, much briefer, before Pendergast spoke again. "Tell me, Captain, what's the program for this evening?"

Pendergast seemed, in a way, to be waking up.

"Hors d'oeuvres and cocktails, seven to eight. The ribbon cutting and opening of the tomb, eight to nine. Dinner at nine-thirty."

"Opening of the tomb—I assume that includes a tour?"

"A tour with a sound-and-light show. Nationally televised."

"A *sound-and-light* show?"

"Yes."

Pendergast's voice—which had been so hollow and remote—was now laced with urgency. "For God's sake, Captain, *hurry!*"

Hayward shot between two cabs that were stubbornly refusing to let her pass, clipping one bumper in the process. Glancing in the rearview mirror, she saw it fly upward, bouncing and flipping in a shower of sparks.

"What am I missing here?" D'Agosta asked.

"Captain Hayward is right," Pendergast said. "This is it—the 'perfect crime' Diogenes boasted about."

"Are you sure?"

"Listen carefully," Pendergast said. He hesitated briefly. "I will only speak of this once. A wrong was done to my brother, many years ago. He was exposed—inadvertently, but exposed nevertheless—to a sadistic device. It was a 'house of pain,' its sole purpose to drive its victim insane or kill him from sheer fright. And now Diogenes—in the person of Menzies, whom he is no doubt posing as—will, through some hidden means of his own, *re-create* this at the opening tonight. Eli Glinn said it: Diogenes is motivated by a feeling of victimization. My brother wants to perpetrate the wrong done to him, but on a large scale. And, with a live television broadcast, the scale could be large indeed. *This* is what he has been building up to. All the rest was merely sideshow."

He sank back in the rear seat and fell silent once again.

The car careened off the West Side Highway at the 79th Street exit ramp, then accelerated eastward toward the rear of the museum. In the distance ahead, all seemed calm—there were no flashing police lights, no hovering helicopters.

Maybe it hasn't happened yet.

She tore right on Columbus, made the dogleg around 77th Street with a screeching of rubber, and flew onto Museum Drive, jamming on her brakes before a crush of idling limousines, taxis, and spectators. The squad car slewed sideways before the crowd and she leaped out, waving her badge, D'Agosta already in the lead, a one-man flying wedge.

"Captain Hayward, NYPD Homicide!" she cried. "Make way!"

The crowds parted in confusion, the slower ones scattered by D'Agosta, and in a moment they were at the velvet ropes. Without even pausing, D'Agosta knocked down a guard who had stepped in front of them. Hayward flashed her shield at the astonished police officers on duty and they sprinted up the carpeted steps toward the huge bronze doors of the museum.

55

Nora Kelly stepped down from the podium into a sea of applause, enormously relieved that her short speech had gone well. She had been the last speaker, directly following George Ashton, the mayor, and Viola Maskelene, and now the main event was about to begin: the cutting of the ribbon and the opening of the Tomb of Senef.

Viola joined up with her. "Brilliant speech," she said. "You were actually interesting."

"As were you."

She saw Hugo Menzies gesturing for them to come over. She pushed through the crowd, Viola following. Menzies's face was florid, his blue eyes sparkling, his white tie and tails giving him the air of an impresario. His arm was linked with that of the mayor of New York, Simon Schuyler, a balding, owlish man with spectacles, whose appearance belied an interior of slick and utterly lethal political genius. He was scheduled to give a short speech at dinner, and he looked the part. He was standing next to a brunet who was so well put together she could only have been a politician's wife.

"Nora, my dear, you know Mayor Schuyler, of course," Menzies said. "And this is Mrs. Schuyler. Simon, this is Dr. Nora Kelly, head curator of the Tomb of Senef and one of our most brilliant and interesting young scientists. And this is Dr. Viola Maskelene, the formidable British Egyptologist."

"I'm delighted to meet you," said Schuyler, eyeing Viola with interest through his thick lenses, then transferring that interest to Nora and back again, highly approving. "Marvelous talk you gave, Ms. Maskelene, especially that part about weighing the heart after death. I'm dreadfully afraid my heart has gotten rather heavy these last few years, thanks to New York City politics." He laughed merrily and Nora and Viola dutifully laughed along with him, joined by Menzies. Schuyler was known for his huge appreciation of his own wit, an appreciation not shared by many of his acquaintances. Tonight he seemed in high good humor. Funny how, just six weeks ago, he'd been calling for Collopy's resignation. So it was in big-city politics.

"Nora," said Menzies, "the mayor and his wife would love to have you and Dr. Maskelene accompany them in the tomb."

"Delighted," said Viola, smiling.

Nora nodded. "It would be our pleasure." It was standard museum practice, she knew, for VIP guests at openings to get museum staff as private tour guides. And while Mayor Schuyler was not the highest-ranking politician at the opening, he was the most important, holder of the museum's purse strings, who had been loudest in decrying the destruction of the diamonds.

"Yes, how lovely," said his wife, who seemed less than enthusiastic about being escorted by two such attractive guides.

Menzies bustled off. Nora watched as he paired up the governor with the museum's associate director, a New York senator with George Ashton, and various VIPs with other staff to ensure that everyone felt special.

"That fellow's a regular matchmaker," said the mayor, following him with his eyes, chuckling. "I could use him on my staff." The hall's warm overhead lighting shone off his bald pate, illuminating it like a billiard ball.

"Ladies and gentlemen, may I have your attention!" came the rich, aristocratic voice of Frederick Watson Collopy, the museum's director, who had positioned himself in front of the tomb doors, wielding the same tiresome pair of gigantic scissors that were trotted out at every opening. With a little help from an assistant, he got them positioned and ready to cut.

The tympanist in the small orchestra let fly a tolerable drumroll.

"I hereby officially reopen, after more than half a century of darkness, the Grand Tomb of Senef!"

With a mighty heave, Collopy shut the scissors, and the two ends of the cut ribbon fluttered to the floor. With a rumble, the faux stone doors slid open. The orchestra immediately sounded the famous theme of *Aïda* once again and those in the crowd with passes to the first of the two shows surged toward the dimly lit rectangle of darkness.

The mayor's wife shivered. "I don't like tombs. Is it really three thousand years old?"

"Three thousand three hundred and eighty," said Viola.

"My goodness, you know so much!" said Mrs. Schuyler, turning to her.

"We Egyptologists are veritable founts of useless knowledge."

The mayor chuckled at this.

"Is it true what they say, that it's cursed?" Mrs. Schuyler went on.

"In a manner of speaking," said Viola. "Many Egyptian tombs had inscriptions that threatened harm to those who disturbed them. This one has a stronger curse than most—but that's probably because Senef wasn't a pharaoh."

"Oh, dear, I hope nothing happens to *us*. Who was this Senef?"

"They don't really know—probably the uncle of Thutmosis IV. Thutmosis became pharaoh at age six, and Senef acted as regent while Thutmosis grew up."

"Thutmosis? You mean King Tut?"

"Oh, no," said Viola. "Tut was Tutankhamen, another pharaoh—far less important than Thutmosis."

"I get so *confused*," said the wife.

They passed through the doors, into the sloping corridor.

"Watch your step, dear," said the mayor.

"This is the God's First Passage," said Viola, and launched into a brief description of the tomb's layout. As she listened, Nora recalled the enthusiastic tour Wicherly had given only a few weeks before. Despite the warmth, she shivered.

They moved forward slowly toward the first stop on the sound-and-light show, hemmed in on all sides by the crowd. In a few minutes, the three hundred guests were all inside and she heard the rumble as the tomb doors closed, ending with a hollow clang. A sudden silence fell on the crowd and the lights dimmed even further.

Out of the darkness came the faint sound of a shovel digging in sand. Then another—and then a chorus of picks, all striking the soil. Then came the furtive voices of the tomb robbers, speaking in tense, muffled tones. Nora glanced over and saw, in the far corner, the PBS camera crew filming.

The sound-and-light show had begun, and millions were watching.

56

Hayward arrived in the hall just behind D'Agosta, stepping into a blaze of light and color. To her dismay, she saw that the doors to the Tomb of Senef were closed, the decorative red ribbon lying cut on the floor. The most important guests were already inside, while the others were scattered about the hall, seated at cocktail tables or clustered in knots by the food and liquor.

"We've got to get those doors open—now," said Pendergast, coming up beside her.

"The computer control room is this way."

They ran across the hall—receiving startled glances from some of the guests—and burst through a door at the far end.

The computer control room for the Tomb of Senef was small. At one end was a long table on which stood several computer monitors and keyboards. On either side rose up racks of equipment: hard drives, controllers, synthesizers, video equipment. A muted television was tuned to the local PBS affiliate, currently simulcasting the opening. Two technicians sat at the table, observing a brace of monitors displaying video feeds from inside the tomb, as well as a third monitor, on which scrolled a long series of numbers. They turned, surprised at the sudden entry.

"What's the status of the sound-and-light show?" Hayward asked.

"Going like clockwork," said one of the technicians. "Why?"

"Shut it down," Hayward said. "Open the tomb doors."

The technician removed a pair of earphones. "I can't do that without authorization."

Hayward stuck her badge in his face. "Captain Hayward, NYPD Homicide. How's that?"

The technician hesitated, staring at the badge. Then he shrugged and turned to the other. "Larry, initiate the door release sequence, please."

Hayward glanced at the second technician and noted it was Larry Enderby, a staff member she had questioned about the attempted murder of Margo Green, and again about the diamond theft. He seemed to be in the wrong place at the wrong time a lot these days.

"If you say so," Enderby said a little dubiously.

He had just begun to type when Manetti charged in, his face red, followed by two guards.

"What's going on?" he said.

"We've got a problem," said Hayward. "We're stopping the show."

"You aren't stopping *anything* without a damn good reason."

"No time to explain."

Enderby had paused in his typing, his fingers hovering over the keyboard, looking from Hayward to Manetti and back.

"I've been as accommodating as I can, Captain Hayward," Manetti said. "But now you've gone too far. This opening is critical to the museum. Everyone who counts is here and we've got a live audience of millions. No *way* am I going to allow anything or anybody to disrupt that."

"Stand down, Manetti," Hayward said in a clipped voice. "I'll take full responsibility. Something is about to go terribly wrong."

"No go, Captain," Manetti said brusquely. He gestured at the television. "See for yourself. Everything's fine." He reached over and turned up the sound:

In the fifth year of the reign of the pharaoh Thutmosis IV . . .

Hayward turned back to Enderby. "Open those doors *now*."

"Hold off on that order, Enderby," Manetti said.

The technician's hands, still poised above the keyboard, began to tremble.

Manetti glanced past Hayward and abruptly caught sight of Pendergast. "What the *hell*? Aren't you supposed to be in prison?"

"I said, *open the goddamn doors*," Hayward barked.

"Something's not right." Manetti began to fumble for his radio.

Pendergast moved smoothly forward. He turned his bruised face to Manetti and said in a courteous voice, "My sincerest apologies."

"What for?"

The blow came so fast that it was little more than a blur, and with a muffled *oof!* Manetti doubled over. With a smooth, swift gesture, Pendergast whisked Manetti's sidearm out of its holster and pointed it at the two guards.

"Weapons, batons, pepper spray, radios, on the floor," he said.

The two guards obeyed.

Pendergast plucked one of their guns from its holster and handed it to D'Agosta. "Watch them."

"Right."

Pendergast took the second guard's gun and tucked it in his waistband as a spare. Then he turned back to Manetti, who was on his knees, one hand cradling his midriff, trying to suck in air.

"I am truly sorry. There's a conspiracy under way to destroy everybody in the tomb. We're going to try to stop it, whether you like it or not. Now: where is Hugo Menzies?"

"You're in big trouble, pal," Manetti gasped. "Even bigger than you were before." And he began to rise.

D'Agosta raised the gun threateningly, and Manetti froze. "Menzies is in the tomb with the rest," he said after a moment.

Pendergast turned to the technicians and spoke, his voice icy and laced with menace. "Mr. Enderby? You heard the order: open the doors."

The technician, thoroughly frightened, nodded and began to type on the keyboard. "No problem, sir, I'll have them open in a jiffy."

A momentary silence.

Another staccato bunch of keystrokes, then another pause. Enderby frowned.

"Seems we got a glitch here . . ."

57

In the fifth year of the reign of the pharaoh Thutmosis IV, Senef—the grand vizier and former regent to the young pharaoh—died of unknown causes. He was buried in a grand tomb in the Valley of the Kings that had been under construction for twelve years. Although Senef had never been a pharaoh himself, he was buried in the Valley of the Kings as befitted one who acted as regent to a pharaoh and who probably retained pharaonic-like power after the assumption to the throne of his former ward. The Great Tomb of Senef was filled with all the riches ancient Egypt could provide: grave goods in gold and silver, lapis, carnelian, alabaster, onyx, granite, and adamant, as well as furniture, foodstuffs, statues, chariots, games, and weapons. No expense was spared.

In the tenth year of his reign, Thutmosis fell ill. His son, Amenhotep III, was declared pharaoh by a faction of the army, opposed by the priesthood. There was a rebellion in Upper Egypt, and the Land of the Two Kingdoms fell into strife and chaos.

It was a good time to rob a tomb.

And so, one morning at dawn, the high priests assigned to guard the Great Tomb of Senef began to dig . . .

The voice-over paused. Nora stood in the darkened corridor of the God's Second Passage, shoulder-to-shoulder with the mayor and his wife. Viola Maskelene stood just beyond them. The sounds of digging grew louder, the *chuff-chuff* of the shovels rising in crescendo with the excited voices of the tomb robbers. A muffled cheer, the scraping of shovel on stone, and then the sharp crack of plaster seals being struck off with a pick, one by one. All around her, the audience—three hundred hand-picked VIPs, the movers and shakers of New York—watched, enthralled.

As the show continued, there was a rumble and grinding of stone: the robbers were dragging aside the outer tomb door. A crack of light appeared, throwing a brilliant beam into the dim space. A moment later, the digitized faces of the tomb robbers appeared, eagerly scurry-ing in and lighting torches. They were dressed in the garb of ancient Egyptians. Although Nora had seen this all before, she was still amazed at how realistic the holographic robbers looked.

A new set of projectors took over seamlessly, throwing images onto artfully placed screens, and the tomb robbers appeared to creep fear-fully along the passageway ahead of the visitors. With gestures and hisses, the ghostly robbers turned and urged the audience to follow along behind them—including them as accomplices. This helped as-sure that the crowd would now move on to the next stage of the sound-and-light show—which took place in the Hall of the Chariots.

As she moved with the crowd, Nora felt a shiver of pride. It was an excellent script—Wicherly had done a masterful job. For all his per-sonal failings, he had been abundantly talented. She was also proud of her own creative contribution. Hugo Menzies had guided the overall project with a subtle and sure hand, while proving equally clever with the nuts and bolts of bringing the show together. The technicians and A/V crew had done a splendid job with the visuals. Judging from the mesmerized audience, so far it was going very well.

As the crowd walked down the corridor toward the well, following the video images of the tomb robbers, lights placed behind hidden panels flickered, simulating the effect of torchlight on the walls. The crowd flow was working perfectly, the audience automatically moving at the pace of the robbers.

At the well, the robbers paused, their voices raised in discussion of how to bridge the dangerous pit. Several of them carried thin tree trunks over their shoulders, which they proceeded to lash together.

Using a crude pulley and winch system, they lowered the logs and swung them across the well to make a bridge. The projected images then inched across the swaying, creaking bridge as if on a tightrope. A cry rang out as one of the figures slipped from the bridge, plunging with a hideous scream into the darkness of the pit—cut off suddenly in a sickening smack of meat hitting stone. The audience gasped.

"Goodness," said the mayor's wife. "That was rather . . . *realistic*."

Nora glanced around. Initially, she had been against that little piece of drama, but she had to admit that—judging by the excited murmurs and gasps of the audience—it had been effective. Even the mayor's wife, despite her faint objection, seemed enthralled.

More invisible holographic screens now descended as others rose, and the computer-controlled video projectors seamlessly transferred the images of the robbers from one screen to the next, giving them the illusion of three-dimensional motion. The effect was extraordinarily real. And yet—the moment the last visitor left the tomb—the screens would all retract and the images of death and destruction would be cut off, leaving the hall in its original pristine shape and ready for the next performance.

The guests followed the holographic figures into the Hall of the Chariots. Here, the robbers fanned out, awestruck at the incredible wealth spread out before them—heaped-up gold and silver, lapis, and gemstones, all gleaming dully by torchlight. The audience itself was halted by a lowered barrier at the far end of the hall, and the second section of the show began with another voice-over:

The Tomb of Senef, like many ancient Egyptian tombs, contained an inscription that cursed those who would despoil it. But an even greater deterrent than a curse was the robbers' own terror of the power of the pharaoh. For these high priests, although greedy and corrupt, were also believers. They believed in the divinity of the pharaoh and in his everlasting life. They believed in the magical properties which had been invested in the objects buried in the tomb with him. The magic in these objects was extremely dangerous and would do the robbers great harm if it were not canceled.

For this reason, the first thing the robbers did was destroy all the grave goods in the tomb, as a way to expunge their magical powers.

The robbers, having recovered from their initial awe, began to pick up objects and hurl them about—tentatively at first, then working up to an orgy of destruction, smashing furniture, vases, armor, and statues, hurling them against the walls, dashing them onto the stone floors, or swinging them into square pillars, sending ghostly projections of gemstones, gold, and fragments of alabaster skittering and rattling everywhere. They screamed and cursed as they worked. Other robbers scrambled about on their hands and knees, sorting through the destruction for things of value and stuffing them into sacks.

Once again, the illusion was remarkable.

Everything would be destroyed. The only things of value taken from the tomb would be taken in pieces and further reduced as soon as possible. Metals would be melted down into bullion; jewels, inlaid lapis, turquoise, and jasper would be pried from their settings and recut. All this treasure would then be quickly exported from Egypt, where any residual power of the godlike pharaoh still residing in the objects would be lost.

That would be the fate of all the beautiful and precious objects in the tomb—total annihilation. The work of thousands of craftsmen over years, reduced in a single day to broken shards.

The frenzy of cursing, screaming, and destruction grew. Nora glanced at the mayor and his wife; both were staring at the scene, mouths open, astonished and utterly captivated. It was the same for the rest of the crowd. Even the police officers and the camera crew looked spellbound. Viola Maskelene caught her eye. The Egyptologist nodded and gave her a thumbs-up.

Nora shivered once again. The Tomb of Senef was going to be a success—a huge success. And—she couldn't help but think—she was the chief curator of the tomb. This was to her credit. Menzies had been right: this would make her career.

The voice-over resumed:

And now, having destroyed the Hall of the Chariots and gleaned all treasure of value, the robbers moved into the deepest section of the tomb: the so-called House of Gold, the burial chamber itself. This was the richest—and most dangerous—part of the tomb. Because here is where the pharaoh himself rested, his body—it was believed—mummified but not dead.

Still clutching their torches, sweaty and frenzied from their spree of destruction, the holographic figures moved through the far archway and into the burial chamber. The retaining gates opened and the crowd followed them across the Hall of the Chariots and into the burial chamber, gathering behind another barrier that descended from the ceiling. The voice-over continued as the show began to move toward its climax:

> The burial chamber was the resting place of the mummified body of the pharaoh, which contained the pharaoh's Ba-soul, one of the five souls of the dead.
>
> The robbery was planned for broad daylight. That was deliberate: according to Egyptian belief, the pharaoh's Ba-soul was absent from the tomb during the day, journeying with the sun across the sky. At sunset, the Ba-soul would reunite with the pharaoh's mummy. Woe to the robber caught in the tomb after dark, when the mummy came back to life!
>
> But these robbers have not been careful. Clocks did not yet exist, and in the darkness of the tomb a sundial was useless. They have no way of keeping track of time. And little do they know that, outside the tomb, the sun is already setting . . .

Once again, the robbers flung themselves into an orgy of violence, smashing the canopic jars, scattering Senef's mummified organs, breaking open baskets of grains and breads, tossing about mummified foodstuffs and pets, decapitating statues. Then they set to work on the great stone sarcophagus itself, jamming cedar poles under one side, slowly dislodging the one-ton lid and wedging it back, millimeter by millimeter, until it toppled from the sarcophagus and broke in two on the floor. Through the magic of holographic projection, the effect was again remarkably real.

Nora felt somebody touch her elbow, and she glanced down to see the mayor smiling at her. "This is utterly fantastic," he whispered with a wink. "It looks like the curse of Senef has finally been lifted."

Looking at his bald pate and round, shiny face, Nora had to smile to herself. He was eating it up, just like an overgrown kid. They *all* were.

There was no longer any doubt in her mind: the show was a huge— a monster—success.

58

D'Agosta watched in sick disbelief as the technicians, both of them now working frantically, continued to type commands on their keyboards.

"What's wrong?" Hayward demanded.

Enderby wiped his forehead nervously. "I don't know. The terminal isn't accepting my commands."

"Manual override?" Hayward asked.

"Tried that already."

Hayward turned to Manetti. "Notify the guards in the tomb. Tell them we're shutting down the show." She pulled out her radio, preparing to talk to her own officers on the inside. Then she paused, staring at Manetti, who had gone pale. "What is it?"

"That's just it. I'm trying to contact my men in the tomb. There's no communication. None."

"How can that be? They're less than fifty yards away!"

"The tomb has been shielded against radio frequencies," said Pendergast quietly.

Hayward put down her radio. "Use the P.A. system. It's hardwired, right?"

More furious typing from Enderby. "That's down, too."

Hayward stared at him. "Cut power to the doors. In the event of a total power failure, they can be levered open by hand."

Enderby typed some more, then raised his hands in a gesture of futility.

Suddenly, Pendergast pointed at one of the monitors displaying a live feed of the hall. "Did you see that? Rewind it, please."

One of the technicians digitally rewound the image.

"*There.*" And Pendergast indicated the blurry outline of a figure, off to one side in the shadows.

"Can you sharpen the image?" he asked urgently. "Magnify it?"

D'Agosta stared as the feed jumped into clearer focus. They all watched as the man slipped a hand inside his dinner jacket, casually extracted a black eye-mask, and put it on. A pair of earplugs followed.

"Menzies," Hayward murmured.

"Diogenes," Pendergast said, almost to himself, his voice as cold as ice.

"We need to call for backup," said Manetti. "Get a SWAT team in here, and—"

"No!" Pendergast broke in. "We don't have time. That will delay everything—they'll want to set up a mobile command unit, there will be rules of engagement to follow. We've got ten minutes—at the outside."

"I can't believe these doors won't open!" Enderby said, banging at the keyboard. "We programmed two completely independent backups. This doesn't make sense. Nothing's responding—"

"And nothing *will* respond," said Pendergast. "Those doors aren't going to open no matter what you do. Menzies—Diogenes—has no doubt hijacked the systems controlling both the show and the hall." Pendergast turned back to Enderby. "Can you get a list of all running processes?"

"Yes." Enderby typed a series of commands. D'Agosta glanced over: a small window had opened on the screen, filled with a list of mysterious lowercase words like *asmcomp, rutil, syslog, kcron.*

"Examine all the process names," Pendergast said. "Especially the system processes. See anything unusual?"

"No." Enderby peered at the screen. "Yes. This one called *kernel_con_fund_o.*"

"Any idea what it's for?"

Enderby blinked. "Judging by the name, it's some kind of console file that accesses the system kernel. That zero at the end also implies it's a beta version."

"Reverse-engineer the code if you can, get a sense of what it does." Pendergast turned toward Hayward and D'Agosta. "Although I'm afraid I already know the answer."

"What's that?" Hayward asked.

"That's not a zero at the end—it's the letter *o. Confundo* in Latin means to trouble, distress, throw into confusion. It's no doubt a system routine added by Diogenes to hijack the show." He gestured at the room full of equipment. "I would guess all this equipment—everything—is now under Diogenes's control."

Meanwhile, Enderby was peering at his screen. "There seems to be another server actually running the show, and it's inside the tomb itself. All the systems in the control room, here, are slaved to it."

Pendergast leaned over the technician's shoulder. "Can you attack it, disable it?"

More furious typing. "No. Now it isn't even accepting my input anymore."

"Cut all power to the tomb," Pendergast said.

"It'll just switch to backup—"

"Cut that, too."

"That'll leave them in darkness."

"Do it."

More typing, followed by a frustrated curse. "Nothing."

Pendergast looked around. "In that case, the breaker box." He strode over, flung open the box, and threw the main circuit breaker.

Although the little room was immediately plunged into darkness, the computers remained online. Within seconds, there was a sharp click as the backup power system kicked in, rows of emergency fluorescent tubes flicking on.

Enderby stared at the monitors in disbelief. "Incredible. There's still full power in the tomb. The show's going on like nothing's happened. There must be an internal generator somewhere inside. But that wasn't on any of the plans I—"

"Where's the backup power source for this room?" Pendergast interrupted.

Manetti nodded toward a large gray metal cabinet in the corner. "That contains the relays connecting the tomb's main power cables to the museum's auxiliary generator."

Pendergast stepped back and pointed Manetti's weapon at the cabinet. He emptied a full clip into it—the gunshots incredibly loud in the soundproofed space—walking the rounds from one side of the cabinet to the other, each round punching a large dark hole in the metal and sending chips of gray paint flying. There was a sound of crackling electricity, a massive blue arc, and the lights flickered and went out—leaving only the glow of the computer screens and the stench of cordite and melted insulation.

"These computers are still on," said Pendergast. "Why?"

"They've got their own local battery backup."

"Force a hard reboot, then. Pull the power cords and plug them back in."

Enderby crawled under the table and began yanking out cords, throwing the room into utter darkness and silence. There was a snap, then a sudden glow of light as Hayward switched on her flashlight.

The door was abruptly flung open and a tall man with a red ascot and round black glasses advanced. "What is going *on* here?" he asked in a shrill voice. "I'm directing a *live simulcast* to *millions* of people, and you can't even keep the power on? Listen, my backup power won't last more than fifteen minutes."

D'Agosta recognized Randall Loftus, the famous director, his face mottled with anger.

Pendergast turned to D'Agosta, leaned in close. "You know what has to be done, Vincent?"

"Yes," D'Agosta said. Then he turned toward the director. "Let me help you."

"I should *hope* so." And Loftus turned and walked stiffly out of the room, D'Agosta following.

In the hall beyond, guests were milling around in a darkness relieved only by the glow from hundreds of tea candles set on the tables, excited but not yet alarmed, apparently treating it as an adventure. Museum guards were circulating, reassuring people that the power would be restored at any moment. D'Agosta followed the director to the far end of the hall, where his crew was set up. They were all working quickly and efficiently, murmuring into mikes or observing small camera-mounted monitors.

"We've lost touch with the crew inside," said one. "But it seems their power is still on. They're still broadcasting, and the feed to the uplink is good. In fact, I don't even think they know we've lost power out here."

"Thank God for that," said Loftus. "I'd rather *die* than deliver dead airtime."

"This feed you mention," D'Agosta asked. "Where is it?"

Loftus nodded toward a thick cable that snaked its way out of the hall, covered with a strip of rubber and secured by gaffer tape.

"I see," said D'Agosta. "And if that cable got cut?"

"God *forbid*," said Loftus. "We'd lose our simulcast. But it won't be cut, believe me. It would take more than an accidental kick to damage that cable."

"You don't have a backup cable?"

"No need. That cable's got a rubber-and-epoxy-clad sheath, with woven steel—it's indestructible. Well, Officer . . . ?"

"Lieutenant D'Agosta."

"It appears we don't need you, after all." Loftus turned his back and pointed to another crew member. "You ninny, *never* leave an open monitor unattended like that!"

D'Agosta looked around. At the far end of the hall, near the entrance, was the obligatory fire station case, containing a coiled hose and a massive Pulaski axe behind a sheet of breakable glass. He strode over, gave the glass a sharp kick, and extracted the Pulaski. Then he walked over to where the taped-down cable turned the corner, braced himself, and raised the axe above his head.

"Hey!" called one of the crew members. "What the *hell*!"

D'Agosta brought the axe down smartly, neatly chopping the cable in half with a shower of sparks.

An inarticulate howl of rage went up from Randall Loftus.

A moment later, D'Agosta was back in the control room. Pendergast and the technicians were still laboring over the newly rebooted computer system, which was still refusing to accept commands.

Pendergast turned toward him. "Loftus?"

"Beside himself with anger at the moment."

Pendergast nodded, his lips twitching in a brief semblance of a smile.

Suddenly a barrage of flashing lights on one of the live monitors attracted D'Agosta's notice.

"What's that?" Pendergast asked sharply.

"The strobes are firing up," said Enderby, hunched over the keyboard.

"There are *strobe lights* in the show?"

"In the later part, yeah. You know, for special effects."

Pendergast turned his attention to the monitor, the blue glow reflecting his intense gray eyes. More strobe lights flashed on, followed by a strange rumble.

Enderby suddenly sat up. "Wait. That's not how it's supposed to go."

The audio feed from the tomb continued over the monitor, carrying a rising murmur from the audience along with it. Pendergast turned to Hayward. "Captain, during your security review, you consulted a set of plans to the tomb and adjacent areas, I assume?"

"I did."

"If you had to, what would the best point be to force an entry into the tomb from outside?"

Hayward thought for a moment. "There's a corridor that connects the 81st Street subway station to the museum's subway entrance. It goes behind the back of the tomb, and there's a point where the masonry's only twenty-four inches thick between the walkway and the burial chamber."

"Twenty-four inches of what?"

"Concrete and rebar. It's a load-bearing wall."

"Twenty-four inches of concrete," D'Agosta murmured. "Might as well be a hundred feet. We can't shoot through that, and we can't chop through it. Not in time."

A dreadful hush fell over the little room, punctuated only by the strange booming from inside the hall, and the accompanying murmur of the crowd. As D'Agosta watched, Pendergast's shoulders sank visibly. *It's happening,* he thought with a thrill of horror. *Diogenes is winning. He's thought of everything and there's not a damn thing we can do about it.*

But then, as he watched, he saw Pendergast start visibly. The agent's eyes grew bright, and he breathed in sharply. Then he turned toward one of the guards.

"You—your name?"

"Rivera, sir."

"You know where the Taxidermy Department is?"

"Yes, sir."

"Go down there and find me a bottle of glycerol."

"Glycerol?"

"It's a chemical used for softening animal skins—there's certain to be some down there." Next, Pendergast turned to Manetti. "Send a couple of your guards down to the chemistry lab. I need bottles of sulfuric acid and nitric acid. They'll find them where the hazardous chemicals are stored."

"May I ask—?"

"No time to explain. I'm also going to need a separation funnel with a stopcock on the bottom, as well as distilled water. And a thermometer, if they can find one." Pendergast looked around, found a sheet of paper and a pencil, scribbled some quick notes, and handed the paper to Manetti. "Have them ask a lab technician if they have any problems."

Manetti nodded.

"In the meantime, clear the hall, please. I want everyone out except NYPD and museum guards."

"Done." Manetti motioned to the two guards and they exited the control room.

Pendergast turned to the technicians. "There's nothing more you can do here. Evacuate with the others."

They both jumped up, only too eager to get out.

Now Pendergast turned to D'Agosta. "Vincent? I have a job for you and Captain Hayward. Go to the subway station. Help her identify that weak point in the wall."

D'Agosta exchanged glances with Hayward. "Right."

"And Vincent? That cable you just cut?" Pendergast gestured toward one of the screens. "Diogenes must have arranged a hidden backup: the simulcast is continuing. Please take care of it."

"We're on it." And D'Agosta left the room, Hayward at his side.

59

T his is just *marvelous!*" said the mayor, whispering loudly in Nora's ear. The holographic tomb robbers, having trashed the burial chamber, were now approaching the open sarcophagus itself. They trembled, hesitated—until one finally dared look in.

"Gold!" the man's recorded voice gasped. "Solid gold!"

The voice-over intoned:

And now comes the moment of truth. The robbers are gazing inside the sarcophagus at the solid gold coffin of Senef. To the ancient Egyptians, gold was more than a precious metal. They worshiped it as sacred. It was the only substance they knew that didn't tarnish, fade, or corrode. They considered it to be immortal, the substance making up the very skin of the gods themselves. The coffin represented the immortal pharaoh, resurrected in his skin of gold: the same skin that Ra, the Sun God, wore on his journey across the sky, showering his golden light over the earth.

Everything else they have stolen is merely a prelude to this: the heart of the tomb.

The show continued as the robbers threw up a makeshift tripod of wooden timbers over the sarcophagus, rigged with a block and tackle, to lift off the top of the heavy gold coffin. Two of them climbed into the sarcophagus and began affixing ropes to the coffin inside—and then, with a shout of triumph, the others began to heave and the huge gold coffin lid rose into the light, glittering and magnificent. The audience gasped.

The narrator's recorded voice began again:

Unbeknownst to the robbers, the sun has now set. The Ba-soul of Senef will be returning to inhabit his mummy for the night, where it will reanimate his dry bones during the hours of darkness.

Here it was: the unleashing of the Ba-soul, the culmination of the curse of Senef. Nora, knowing what was about to come, braced herself.

There was a noise from inside the coffin—a muffled groan. The robbers paused in their work, the gold coffin lid swinging from the ropes. And then the fog machines kicked in and a whitish mist began bubbling up out of the sarcophagus and sliding down its sides. A gasp went up from the audience. Nora smiled to herself. A trifle hokey, perhaps, but effective.

Now a roll of thunder sounded, and through the rising fog the strobes in the corners of the ceiling began to flash, to the accompaniment of ominous rumblings. The strobes began to speed up . . . and then all four went out of sync, flashing at different rates.

Damn, a glitch. Nora looked around for a technician before realizing they were, of course, all in the control room, monitoring the show by remote. No doubt they would fix it in a moment.

As the strobes continued to accelerate and decelerate at opposing rates, a second rumble sounded—an incredibly low and deep vibration, just at the threshold of human hearing. Now it seemed the sound system was malfunctioning, too. The deep sound was joined by another, and then another: more like physical vibrations in the gut than actual sound.

Oh, no, she thought. *The computers are royally messing up. And it was all going so well . . .*

She glanced around again, but the crowd hadn't noticed the glitch—they assumed it was just part of the show. If the technicians could fix it soon, maybe nobody would know. She hoped they were on the ball.

Now the strobes were speeding up even further, except for one—

particularly bright—that kept flashing, not quite in time . . . the lights blended to form a kind of visual Doppler effect that almost made Nora dizzy.

With a deep groaning sound, the mummy abruptly rose from the sarcophagus. The holographic robbers fell back with shrieks of terror—at least that part of the show was still working—some dropping their torches in fright, the light flickering off their staring faces as they cringed in fear.

Senef!

But somehow the mummy didn't look right to Nora—it was bigger, darker, somehow more menacing. Then a bony arm broke free of its bandages—something not even in the script—and, clawing and twitching, reached up to its own swathed face. The arm was distorted, as elongated as an ape's. The bony fingers sank into the linen wrappings and ripped them away, revealing a visage of such horror that Nora gasped, backing up instinctively. This was over-the-top—*way* over-the-top. Was this some joke of Wicherly's? Obviously, something this dreadful, this effective, had to be carefully programmed—it wasn't a mere glitch.

There were audible gasps from the audience. "Oh, my goodness!" the mayor's wife said.

Nora looked around. The crowd continued to stare at the still-rising mummy as if mesmerized, swaying, uncomfortable now. She could feel their fear rising like a miasma, their voices tight and hushed. Viola caught her eye, gave her a questioning frown. Beyond, Nora could make out the face of Collopy, the museum director. He looked pale.

The malfunctioning strobe lights kept flashing, flashing, *flashing* in her peripheral vision, so very brightly, and Nora felt a real twinge of dizziness. Another gut-twisting low note sounded, and she closed her eyes momentarily against the combined assault of the brilliant lights and the deep sounds. She heard more gasps around her, then a scream, choked off almost before it started. What the hell was this? Those sounds—she had never heard anything like them. They were like the sounding of the last trump, full of dread and horror, so loud it seemed to violate her very being.

The mummy now began to open its jaw, the dry lips cracking and flaking off as they drew back from a rack of brown, rotting teeth. The mouth became a sinkhole of black slime, which began to seethe and wriggle. Then, as she watched in horror, it morphed into a swarm of greasy black cockroaches, which began rustling and crawling their way out of the ruined orifice. Another horrible groaning, and then there was a second explosion of strobe flashes of such incredible intensity that, when she closed her eyes, she could still see them flashing through her eyelids . . .

. . . but a hideous buzzing sound forced her to open her eyes again. It now looked as if the mummy were vomiting blackness—the swarm of insects had taken flight, the cockroaches morphing into fat lubricious wasps, their mandibles clicking like knitting needles as they flew toward the audience with a horrible believability.

She felt a sudden wave of vertigo, and she swayed, instinctively grabbing the person next to her—the mayor—who was himself stumbling and unsteady.

"Oh my God—!"

She heard someone vomiting, a cry for help—and then a flurry of short screams as the crowd surged back, trying to escape the insects. Although Nora knew they had to be holographically generated, like everything else, they looked amazingly real as they came straight at her, each with a vicious stinger extruded from its abdomen, gleaming with venom. She stumbled backward instinctively, felt herself falling, with no bottom, falling like the robber in the well, to a chorus of wails around her like the shrieks of the damned being sucked into hell itself.

60

Constance was awakened by a discreet rapping on her bedroom door. Without opening her eyes, she turned over with a sigh, nuzzling gently at the down pillow.

The knock came again, a little louder now. "Constance? Constance, is everything all right?" It was the voice of Wren—shrill, worried.

Constance stretched languorously—deliciously—then sat up in bed. "I'm fine," she said with a twinge of irritation.

"Is anything the matter?"

"Nothing's the matter, thank you."

"You're not ill?"

"Certainly not. I'm fine."

"You'll forgive my intrusion. It's just that I've never known you to sleep all day like this. It's eight-thirty, past time for supper, and you're still abed."

"Yes," was all Constance said in return.

"Would you care for your usual breakfast, then? Green tea and a piece of buttered toast?"

"Not the usual breakfast, thank you, Wren. If you could manage it, I'd like poached eggs, cranberry juice, kippers, half a dozen rashers of bacon, a grapefruit half, and a scone with a pot of jam, please."

"I—very well." She heard Wren fussing his way back down the hall toward the stairs.

Constance settled back into the pillows, closing her eyes again. Her sleep had been long and deep and completely dreamless—most unusual for her. She recalled the bottomless emerald green of the absinthe, the strange feeling of lightness it gave her—as if she were watching herself from a distance. A private smile flitted across her face, vanished, then returned again, as if prompted by some recollection. She settled deeper into the pillows, letting her limbs relax beneath the soft sheets.

Gradually, very gradually, she became aware of something. There was a scent in the room, an unusual scent.

She sat up in bed again. It was not the scent of—of *him*; it was something she didn't think she'd ever smelled before. It was not unpleasant, really . . . just different.

She looked around for a moment, trying to trace the source. She checked the bedside table without success.

It was only as an afterthought that she slipped a hand beneath the pillows.

There she found something: an envelope, and a long box, wrapped in an antique paper and tied with a black ribbon. These were the source of the scent: a musky smell redolent of the deep woods. Quickly, she pulled them out.

The envelope was of cream-laid linen paper, and the box was just large enough to hold a diamond choker, or perhaps a bracelet. Constance smiled, then flushed deeply.

She opened the envelope eagerly. Out fell three pages of dense, elegant handwriting. She began to read.

I hope you slept well, my dearest Constance: the sweet sleep of the innocent.

There is a good chance it will be your last such sleep for some time. Then again—if you take the advice in this letter—sleep may come again, and very soon.

As I've whiled away these pleasant hours with you, I must admit to having wondered something. What has it been like, all these many years, to live under the same roof as Uncle Antoine, the man you called Enoch Leng: the man who brutally murdered your sister, Mary Greene?

Did you know this, Constance? That Antoine killed and vivisected your sister? Surely you must have. Perhaps at first it was just a supposition, a strange twinge of dark fancy. No doubt you ascribed it to your own perverse cast of mind. But over time—and you two had so very *much* time—it must have come to seem, first a possibility, then a certainty. Yet no doubt this was all subconscious, buried so deep as to be almost undiscoverable. And yet *you knew it:* of course you did.

What a deliciously ironic situation. This man, Antoine Pendergast, killed your very own sister—for the furthering of his own mortal life . . . and ultimately yours as well! This is the man to whom you owe everything! Do you know how many children had to die so that he could develop his elixir, so that you could enjoy your abnormally extended childhood? You were born normal, Constance; but thanks to Uncle Antoine, you became a freak of nature. That was your word, wasn't it? *Freak.*

And now, my dear, duped Constance, you can no longer shove this idea aside. You can no more dismiss it as a flight of imagination, or a dark irrational fear on those nights when the thunder rumbles and you cannot sleep. Because the worst is, in fact, true: this is precisely what happened. Your sister was murdered to prolong your life. I know, because before he died, *Uncle Antoine told me so himself.*

Oh, yes: I had several chats with the old gentleman. How could I not seek out a dear relative with such a colorful history, with a worldview so similar to my own? The very possibility that he might still be alive after all those decades added excitement to my search, and I did not rest until I at length tracked him down. He quickly sensed my own true nature, and naturally became most anxious that your path should never cross mine—but in return for my promise never to meet you, he seemed happy enough to discuss his, shall we say, *unique* solution for a broken world. And he confirmed everything: the existence of his concoction for the prolongation of life—although he withheld from me the manner of its preparation. Dear Uncle Antoine, I was sorry to see him go; the world was a most interesting place with him in it. But at the time of his murder, I was too closely involved in my own plans to help him escape his fate.

So I ask one more time: what was it like for you to live in this house for so many, many years as helpmate to your sister's killer? I can't even begin to imagine it. No wonder your psyche is so frail—no wonder my brother fears for the soundness of your mind. Together, alone, in this house: was it possible that you even grew to become, shall we say, on *intimate terms* with Antoine? But no, not that: I am the first man to become master of that shrine, dearest Constance: the physical evidence was incontrovertible. But you loved him—no doubt *you loved him.*

And so what now is left for you, my poor pitiable Constance? My precious fallen angel? Handmaiden to fratricide, consort to your sister's murderer? The very air you breathe you owe to her, and to Antoine's other victims. Do you deserve to continue this perverse existence? And who will mourn your passing? My brother, surely not: you would be a guilty burden to him no more. Wren? Proctor? How risible. *I* shall not mourn you: you were a toy; a mystery easily solved; a dull box forced and found empty; an animal spasm. So let me give you a piece of advice, and please believe this to be the one honest, altruistic thing I have ever told you.

Do the noble thing. End your unnatural life.

Ever your

Diogenes

P.S. I was surprised to see how juvenile your earlier attempt at suicide was. Surely, you now know not to slash willy-nilly *across* your wrists; the knife is arrested by the tendons. For a more satisfactory result, cut lengthwise, between the tendons: just one cut: slow, forceful, and above all, *deep*. As for my own scar: isn't it remarkable what one can do with a bit of greasepaint and wax?

A long, unfathomable moment passed.

Then, Constance turned her attention to the small present. She picked it up and unwrapped it, slowly, gingerly, as one might a bomb. Inside was a hinged box of beautifully polished rosewood.

Just as slowly, she opened the box. Within, nestled on purple velvet, rested an antique scalpel. The handle was of yellowed ivory; the blade itself was polished to great brilliance. Extending an index finger, she stroked the handle of the scalpel. It was cool and smooth. Carefully she drew the scalpel out of the box, balancing it in the palm of her hand, turning it in the light, staring at the mirrored blade that flashed like a diamond in the firelight.

61

When the lights went out, Smithback paused, a raw oyster halfway to his mouth. There was a millisecond of utter darkness before a deep clunk sounded somewhere and the emergency lights came on, rows of fluorescent tubes in the ceiling, bathing everything in a hideous greenish-white light.

He looked around. Most of the VIPs in the crowd had gone into the tomb, but the second shift remained, with plenty of serious drinkers and eaters, standing around or sitting at tables. They remained calm, taking the power failure in stride.

Shrugging, he tipped the oyster shell into his mouth and sucked in the briny, still-living slithery bolus, smacked his lips in enjoyment, and plucked a second oyster from the plate, readying it for the same operation.

And then he heard the shots: six muffled reports from the darkness beyond the far end of the hall: a heavy-caliber handgun firing in a measured cadence, one shot after another. With a dying crackle, the emergency lights went out—and Smithback knew immediately that something big was going down, that there was a story happening. The only light in the hall now came from the hundreds of tea candles spread out on the dinner tables. There were murmurings from the remaining crowd, a rising sense of alarm.

Smithback looked in the direction of the gunshots. He recalled seeing various technicians and staff going in and out of a door in the rear of the hall as the evening progressed, and he figured it must lead to the control room for the Tomb of Senef. As he watched, somebody he recognized—Vincent D'Agosta—came through that door. Not in uniform at the moment, but still looking every inch the cop. With him was somebody else Smithback recognized: Randall Loftus, the well-known director. He watched them make their way toward the small knot of television cameras.

A stab of uneasiness struck Smithback as he realized his wife, Nora, was inside the tomb. Probably stuck in utter darkness. But the tomb had a full complement of guards and cops, so she was certainly safe. Something was happening here, and it was his job as a reporter to find out just what it was. He watched D'Agosta cross the hall, break the glass in an emergency fire station, and remove an axe.

He pulled out his notebook and pencil, noted the time, and jotted down what he was seeing. D'Agosta walked over to a cable, positioned the axe, and brought it down with a clunk, eliciting a roar of protest from Loftus and the PBS technicians. Ignoring them, D'Agosta walked calmly back, axe in hand, to the small door in the rear of the hall, which he then closed behind him.

The tension in the hall increased by an order of magnitude.

Whatever was happening, it was big.

Smithback swiftly followed in D'Agosta's wake. Reaching the door to the control room, he put his hand on the knob. Then he paused. If he barged in there, he was likely to be ejected. Better to hang back, mingle with the crowd, and wait for the other shoe to drop.

It didn't take long. Within minutes, D'Agosta, still carrying the axe, and Captain Hayward burst out the door, jogged down the hall, and disappeared out the main exit. A moment later, Manetti, the director of security, came out, climbed onto the darkened podium, and addressed the remaining partygoers.

Again, Smithback noted the time and began to take notes.

"Ladies and gentlemen!" he cried out, his voice barely penetrating the vast murky interior.

A hush fell.

"We're experiencing some power problems, some technical problems. Nothing to be alarmed about, but we're going to have to clear the hall. The guards will escort you out the way you came in and up to the rotunda. Please follow their instructions."

A murmur of disappointment rose up. Someone shouted out, "What about the people in the tomb?"

"The people in the tomb will be escorted out as soon as we open the doors. There's nothing to be concerned about."

"Are the doors stuck?" Smithback yelled.

"Momentarily, yes."

More restlessness. It was clear people did not want to go, leaving their friends or loved ones behind in the tomb.

"Please move toward the exit!" Manetti shouted. "The guards will escort everyone out. There is nothing to be alarmed about." There were some murmurs of protest from guests clearly unused to being told what to do.

Bullshit, thought Smithback. If there was nothing to be alarmed about, why was there a quaver in Manetti's voice? There was no way in hell he was going to allow himself to be "escorted" out of the building just as the story was breaking—and especially with Nora still stuck in the tomb.

He looked around, then ducked outside the hall. The velvet ropes ran down the basement corridor, lit only by the battery-operated exit signs. Another corridor sat at right angles to the main hallway, roped off, running into darkness. Guards with flashlights were already herding groups of protesting people toward the exit.

Smithback sprinted on ahead to where the corridor branched off, vaulted the velvet rope, ran through the darkness, and ducked into an entryway marked *Alcoholic Storage, Genus Rattus.*

He flattened himself against the shallow door frame and waited.

62

Vincent D'Agosta and Laura Hayward sprinted between the velvet ropes, down the front steps of the museum, and along Museum Drive. The entrance to the subway stood at the corner of 81st Street, a dingy metal kiosk with a copper roof, perched on the corner. Parked near it, just beyond the seething crowd of rubberneckers, D'Agosta spotted the PBS television van, cables snaking from it across the lawn and through a window into the museum. A white satellite dish was set atop the van.

"Over here!" D'Agosta began to push his way through the crowd toward the van, gripping the axe. Hayward was at his side, hand up displaying her shield.

"NYPD!" she cried. "Make way, please!"

When the crowd seemed reluctant to part, D'Agosta raised the axe over his head with both hands and began to pump it up and down. The crowd parted before them, exposing a thin path to the van.

They ran around to the rear of the vehicle. Hayward held back the crowd while D'Agosta stepped up onto the bumper. Grasping the rack on top of the van, he pulled himself onto the roof.

A man leaped out of the van. "What the hell are you doing?" he cried. "We've got a live broadcast in session!"

"NYPD Homicide," said Hayward, positioning herself between him and the bumper.

D'Agosta steadied himself on top of the van, legs apart. Then he raised the axe above his head again.

"Hey! You can't do that!"

"Watch me." With one tremendous swing, D'Agosta struck through the metal posts supporting the satellite dish, popping the bolts and sending them flying. Then he swung the flat end of the axe against the dish: once, twice. With a creaking groan of metal, it toppled over the edge of the roof and crashed to the street below.

"Are you *crazy*—?" the technician began.

Ignoring him, D'Agosta leaped off, tossed the axe aside, and he and Hayward shoved their way through the fringes of the crowd, heading for the subway entrance.

Dimly, D'Agosta was aware it was Laura Hayward at his side: his own Laura, who'd had him escorted out of her office just days before. He thought he had lost her irretrievably—and yet, she had sought him out.

She had sought him out. It was a delicious thought. He reminded himself to return to it if he survived the rest of the night.

Reaching the entrance to the subway, they ran down the stairs and sprinted over to the ticket booth. Hayward flashed her shield at the woman inside.

"Captain Hayward, NYPD Homicide. There's a situation in the museum and we need to clear this station. Call Transit Authority HQ and have them flag the station as a skip until further notice. I don't want any trains stopping. Understand?"

"Yes, ma'am."

They jumped the turnstiles, ran down the corridor, and entered the station proper. It was still early—not yet nine—and there were several dozen people waiting for the train. Hayward trotted along the platform, and D'Agosta followed. At the far end, a corridor branched off, with a large tiled sign above:

New York Museum of Natural History
Walkway to Entrance
Open During Museum Hours Only

An accordion grille of dingy, rusted metal sealed off the corridor, secured with a massive padlock.

"Better talk to those people," murmured Hayward, pulling out her gun and pointing it at the lock.

D'Agosta nodded. He walked back along the platform, waving his shield. "NYPD! Clear the station! Everybody out!"

People looked over at him disinterestedly.

"Out! Police action, clear the station!"

The sound of two gunshots thundered down the platform, waking everyone up. They began to move back toward the exits, suddenly alarmed, and amidst the confused hubbub of the increasingly rapid retreat D'Agosta heard the words *terrorist* and *bomb* drifting toward him.

"I want everyone to leave in a calm and orderly fashion!" he called after them.

A third ripping gunshot cleared the station completely. D'Agosta ran back to find Hayward wrestling with the grille. He helped push it back and together they ducked through.

Ahead of them, the corridor stretched for a hundred yards before taking a sharp turn toward the museum's subway entrance. Tilework along the walls showed images of mammal and dinosaur skeletons, and there were framed posters announcing upcoming museum exhibitions, including several for the Grand Tomb of Senef. Hayward pulled a small set of plans from her pocket and unrolled them on the cement floor. The plans were covered with scribbled notations—it looked to D'Agosta as if she had gone over them many times.

"That's the tomb," said Hayward, pointing at the map. "And there's the subway tunnel. And look—right over here, there's only about two feet of concrete between the corner of the tomb and this tunnel."

D'Agosta squatted, examined the plat. "I don't see any exact measurements on the subway side."

"There aren't any. They only surveyed the tomb, estimating the rest."

D'Agosta frowned. "The scale is ten feet to the inch. That doesn't give us much precision."

"No."

She consulted the map a moment longer, then, gathering it up, she paced off about a hundred feet down the corridor before stopping again. "My best guess is that this is the thin spot, right here."

The rumble of a subway car began to fill the air, followed by a roar as it passed the station without stopping, the noise quickly fading.

"You've been in the tomb?" said D'Agosta.

"Vinnie, I've practically been *living* in the tomb."

"And you can hear the subway in there?"

"All the time. They couldn't get rid of it."

D'Agosta pressed his ear to the tiled wall. "If they can hear out, we should be able to hear in."

"They'd have to be making a lot of noise in there."

He straightened up, looked at Hayward. "They are."

Then he pressed his ear to the wall again.

63

From his hiding place in the dim doorway, Smithback watched the murmuring, complaining crowds being ushered out of the hall toward the elevators. He lingered a few minutes after the last had passed by, then crept forward, ducked under the velvet rope, and inched along the wall to the corner, where he could peer into the Egyptian Hall. It wasn't difficult to stay hidden: the only light came from the hundreds of candles still flickering in the hall, leaving much of the antechamber in darkness.

Pressed into the shadows beside the entrance, he watched a small knot of people emerge from the side door leading to the control room. He recognized Manetti, in his usual ugly brown suit, sporting an impressive comb-over. The rest were museum guards except for one man who, in particular, attracted his attention. He was tall and brown-haired, wearing a white turtleneck and slacks. Although his face was turned away, a large bandage was clearly visible on one cheek. What attracted Smithback's attention wasn't so much the man's appearance as the way he moved: so smoothly and gracefully it seemed almost feline. It reminded him of someone . . .

He watched as the man strode to a huge silver cauldron of crushed ice. Dozens of champagne bottles had been pressed into the ice, their snouts pointing upward.

"Help me get rid of these bottles," Smithback heard the man say to Manetti—and the instant he spoke, Smithback recognized that honeyed voice.

Special Agent Pendergast. Out of prison? What's he doing here? He felt a sudden thrill of excitement and surprise: here was the man whose name he'd been working to clear, walking around as casually as if he owned the place. But along with the excitement came a sudden sinking feeling—in his experience, Pendergast appeared only when the shit was really hitting the fan.

Two of the guards jogged up to the tomb entrance, and Smithback watched as they made an attempt to lever open the doors with a wrecking bar and a sledgehammer, without success.

Smithback felt the sinking feeling increase. People were trapped inside the tomb—he knew that—but why this sudden desperate effort to get them out? Was something going wrong inside?

His blood ran cold with speculation. Fact was, the tomb presented a perfect opportunity to launch a terrorist attack. An incredible concentration of money, power, and influence was inside: dozens of political bigwigs, along with an elite slice of the country's corporate, legal, and scientific leadership—not to mention everybody of importance at the museum itself.

He returned his attention to Pendergast, who was pulling the bottles of champagne out of the ice and hurling them into a trash can. In another moment, he'd emptied the cauldron, leaving only a heap of crushed and melting ice. Now he stepped to an adjoining food table and, with a great sweep of his hand, cleared it of its contents, sending platters of oysters, mounds of caviar, cheeses, prosciutto, and breads crashing to the floor. Aghast, Smithback watched a massive Brie roll like a white wheel all the way across the hall before coming to a gluey rest in a dark corner.

Next, Pendergast went from table to table, collecting dozens of tea candles and arranging them in a circle around the cleared area to provide illumination.

What the hell is he doing?

A man came into the hall at a dead run, carrying a bottle of something, which Pendergast immediately snatched up, checked, then shoved into the mound of crushed ice. Two more men arrived, one pushing a cart crammed with bottles and laboratory equipment—beakers and flasks—which were also shoved into the ice.

Pendergast straightened and, his back to Smithback's hiding place, began rolling up his sleeves. "I need a volunteer," he said.

"What exactly are you doing?" asked Manetti.

"Making nitroglycerin."

There was a silence.

Manetti cleared his throat. "This is crazy. Surely there's a better way to get into the tomb than blowing your way in."

"No volunteers?"

"I'm calling for a SWAT team," said Manetti. "We need professionals to break in there. We can't just blow it up willy-nilly."

"Well, then," said Pendergast, "how about you, Mr. Smithback?"

Smithback froze in the blackness, hesitated, looked around. "Who, me?" he said in a small voice.

"You're the only Smithback here."

Smithback emerged from the shadows of the doorway and stepped into the hall, and only now did Pendergast turn and look him in the eye.

"Well, sure," Smithback stammered. "Always happy to help a—Wait. Did you say *nitro*?"

"I did."

"Will it be dangerous?"

"Given my inexperience at the synthesis, and the impurity of the formulation that will inevitably result, I'd estimate our chances are slightly better than fifty percent."

"Chances at what?"

"Enduring a premature detonation."

Smithback swallowed. "You must . . . be worried about what's happening in the tomb."

"I am, in fact, terrified, Mr. Smithback."

"My wife's in there."

"Then you have a special incentive to help."

Smithback stiffened. "Just tell me what to do."

"Thank you." Pendergast turned to Manetti. "See to it that everyone leaves the hall and takes cover."

"I'm calling for a SWAT team, and I strongly suggest—"

But the look on Pendergast's face silenced the security director. The guards hastened out of the hall, Manetti following, his radio crackling.

Pendergast glanced back at Smithback. "Now, if you will kindly follow my instructions *to the letter*, we will have a fair chance of pulling this off."

He went back to setting up the equipment: rotating the bottles in the ice to chill them more quickly; taking a flask, shoving it deep into the ice, setting a glass thermometer within it. "The problem, Mr. Smithback, is that we have no time to do this properly. We need to mix the chemicals quickly. And that sometimes provokes an undesirable result."

"Look, what's happening in the tomb?"

"Let us concentrate on the problem at hand, please."

Smithback swallowed again, trying to get a grip on himself. All thought of a big story had vanished. *Nora is in there, Nora is in there*—the phrase pounded in his head like a drumbeat.

"Hand me the bottle of sulfuric acid, but wipe it off first."

Smithback located the bottle, pulled it out of the ice, wiped it down, and handed it to Pendergast, who poured it carefully into the chilled flask. A nasty, acrid smell arose. When the agent was satisfied he had poured in the requisite amount, he stepped back and capped the bottle. "Check the temperature."

Smithback peered down at the glass thermometer, pulled it from the flask, held it close enough to a candle to read.

"Needless to say," said Pendergast dryly, "you will take exquisite care with that candle flame. I should also mention these acids will dissolve human flesh in a matter of seconds."

Smithback's hand jerked away.

"Give me the nitric acid. Same procedure, please."

Smithback wiped off the bottle and handed it to Pendergast. The agent unscrewed the top and held it up, examining the label.

"As I pour this in, I want you to stir the solution with the thermometer, reading off the temperature at thirty-second intervals."

"Right."

Pendergast measured the acid into a graduated cylinder, then began pouring it, a tiny amount at a time, into the chilled flask while Smith-back stirred.

"Ten degrees," said Smithback.

More exquisitely slow pouring.

"Eighteen . . . twenty-five . . . Going up fast . . . Thirty . . ."

The mixture began to foam and Smithback could feel the heat of it on his face, along with a hideous stench. The ice began melting around the beaker.

"Don't breathe those fumes," said Pendergast, pausing in his pour-ing. "And keep stirring."

"Thirty-five . . . thirty-six . . . thirty-four . . . thirty-one . . ."

"It's stabilizing," said Pendergast, relief audible in his voice. He resumed pouring in the nitric acid, a tiny bit at a time.

In the silence, Smithback thought he could hear something. He lis-tened intently: it was the sound of distant screaming, muffled to a faint whisper. And then a thud sounded from the direction of the tomb, and then another, which rapidly became a dull pounding.

He straightened suddenly. "Jesus, they're pounding on the tomb door!"

"*Mr. Smithback!* Continue reading the temperatures."

"Right. Thirty . . . twenty-eight . . . twenty-six . . ."

The muffled pounding continued. Pendergast was pouring so slowly Smithback thought he would be driven mad.

"Twenty." Smithback tried to concentrate. "Eighteen. Please, *hurry.*" He found his hand shaking, and as he removed the thermometer to read it, he fumbled and splashed some drops of the sulfuric-nitric acid mix on the back of his hand.

"Oh, shit!"

"Keep *stirring,* Mr. Smithback."

It felt like his hand had been splattered with molten lead, and he could see smoke rising from the black spots where the acid had fallen on his skin.

Pendergast finished pouring. "I'll take over. Put your hand in the ice."

Smithback plunged his hand into the ice while Pendergast grabbed a small box of baking soda, ripped off the top. "Give me your hand."

He extracted it from the ice. Pendergast shook baking powder over the burn marks with one hand while stirring with the other. "The acids are neutralized now. It'll be a nasty scar—no more. Please resume stirring while I prepare for the next addition."

"Right." Smithback's hand felt like it was on fire, but the thought of Nora trapped in the tomb reduced the pain to insignificance.

Pendergast removed another bottle from the ice, wiped it off, and measured some of the contents carefully into a small beaker.

The pounding, the screaming, seemed to be getting even more frantic.

"While I pour, you slowly rotate the flask in its ice bath like a cement mixer, keeping it tilted, and read off the temperature every fifteen seconds. *Do not stir*—don't even knock the thermometer against the glass. Understand?"

"Yes."

With excruciating slowness, Pendergast poured while Smithback kept rotating.

"The temperature, Mr. Smithback?"

"Ten . . . twenty . . . It's shooting up . . . Thirty-five . . ." The sweat appearing now on Pendergast's forehead frightened Smithback almost more than anything else. "Thirty-five still . . . Hurry, please, for God's sake!"

"Keep rotating," the agent said, his calm voice in sharp contrast to his damp brow.

"Twenty-five . . ." The distant pounding continued unabated. "Twenty . . . twelve . . . ten . . ."

Pendergast poured another small amount in, and once again, the temperature shot up. They waited for what seemed an eternity.

"Look, can't you just mix it all up now?"

"If we blow ourselves up, there's no hope for them, Mr. Smithback."

Smithback forced down his impatience, reading off the temperature and rotating the flask, while Pendergast continued pouring bit by bit, pausing between pours. At last he tipped up the beaker.

"First stage complete. Now grab that separatory funnel and pour in some distilled water from that jug, there."

Smithback picked up the funnel, which looked like a drawn-out glass bulb, a long glass tube with a stopcock angling away from its bottom. Taking the glass plug from its top, he filled the funnel with water from a jug sitting in the ice.

"Shove it upright into the ice, if you please."

Smithback pushed the funnel into the ice.

Pendergast picked up the flask and, with infinite care, poured the contents into the separatory funnel. As Smithback looked on apprehensively, the agent performed the last several steps. Now a white paste lay in the beaker. Pendergast held up the beaker, examined it briefly, then turned to Smithback. "Let's go."

"That's it? We're done?" Smithback could still hear the pounding: rising to a crescendo now, backed up by ever-more-hysterical screaming.

"Yes."

"Well, let's hurry up and blow the door!"

"No—that door's too heavy. Even if we could, we'd kill people: they're all assembled just on the other side, by the sound of it. I've got a better entry point."

"Where?"

"Follow me." Pendergast had already turned and was heading out the door, breaking into a catlike run, cradling the beaker protectively. "It's outside, in the subway station. To get there, we'll have to leave the museum and run the gauntlet of bystanders outside. Your job, Mr. Smithback, is to *get me through that crowd*."

64

With a superhuman effort, Nora steadied herself, tried to focus her mind. She realized she was not falling into the well: that the sensation of falling was, in fact, an illusion. The holographic insects had scattered the crowd, inducing a growing panic. The dreadful low throbbing sounds were getting louder, like an infernal drumbeat, and the strobe lights were brighter and more painful than any she had ever experienced. These were not the strobes she had seen in the equipment tests: these flashed so violently that they seemed to be penetrating into her very brain.

She swallowed, looked around. The holographic image of the mummy had vanished, but the fog machines had accelerated and mist was boiling out of the sarcophagus, filling the burial chamber like rising water. The strobes were flashing into the rising fog with extreme rapidity, and each flash blossomed horribly in the mist.

Beside her, Nora felt Viola stumble, and she reached out and grasped the Egyptologist's hand. "Are you all right?" she asked.

"No, I'm not. What in bloody hell is going on, Nora?"

"I . . . I don't know. Some kind of terrible malfunction."

"Those insects were no malfunction. Those had to be programmed. And these *lights* . . ." Viola winced, averting her eyes.

The fog had reached their waists and was still rising. Staring into it, Nora felt an indescribable panic welling up in her. Soon it would fill the room, engulfing them all . . . It felt as if they were about to drown in the mist and the welter of flashing lights. There were shouts, scattered screams, as the crowd panicked.

"We've got to get this crowd out," she gasped.

"Yes, we must. But, Nora, I can hardly think straight . . ."

Not far away, Nora saw a man gesticulating madly. In one hand, he held a shield that flashed brilliantly in the winking strobes. "If everybody would please stay calm!" he cried. "I'm a New York City police officer. We're going to get you out of here. But please, everybody, *stay calm!*"

Nobody paid the slightest attention.

Closer at hand, Nora heard a familiar voice cry out for help. Turning, she saw the mayor a few feet away, bent over, groping downward into the fog. "My wife—she fell! Elizabeth, where are you?"

The crowd suddenly surged backward in a violent crush, accompanied by a ripple of screams, and Nora felt herself borne along against her will. She saw the undercover cop go down beneath the press of bodies.

"Help!" cried the mayor.

Nora struggled to reach him, but the enormous press of the crowd carried her farther away, and a fresh rumble from the sound system drowned out the mayor's frantic calls.

I've got to do something.

"Listen!" she cried at the top of her lungs. "Listen to me! *Everyone listen!*"

A lessening of the cries close around her proved that at least some people had heard.

"We have to work together if we're going to get out. Understand? *Everyone join hands and move toward the exit!* Do not run or push! Follow me!"

To her amazement and relief, her little speech seemed to have a calming effect. The cries lessened further, and she felt Viola grasp her hand.

The fog was now up to her chest, its surface roiled and tendril-strewn. In a moment, they would be covered, blinded.

"Pass the word along! Keep holding hands! Follow me!"

Nora and Viola moved forward, guiding the crowd. Another enormous boom that was more a sensation than sound—and the crowd surged again in utter panic, abandoning any pretense to order.

"Hold hands!" she cried.

But it was too late: the crowd had lost its mind. Nora felt herself borne along, crushed in the press, the air literally squeezed from her lungs.

"Stop pushing!" she cried, but no one was listening any longer. She heard Viola beside her, also calling for calm, but her voice was swallowed up in the panic of the crowd and the deep booming sounds that filled the tomb. The strobes kept flashing, each flash causing a brief, brilliant explosion of light in the fog. And with each flash, she seemed to feel stranger, heavy . . . almost drugged. This wasn't just fear she was feeling: it was something else. What was happening to her head?

The crowd surged toward the Hall of the Chariots, possessed by a mindless, animal panic. Nora clung to Viola's hand with all her might. Suddenly a new sound cut in over the deep booming—a high keening at the threshold of audibility, rising and falling like a banshee. The razor-sharp shriek seemed to riddle her consciousness like a shotgun blast, increasing the strange sensation of alienness. Another surge in the crowd caused her to lose her grip on Viola's hand.

"Viola!"

If there was an answering cry, it was lost in the tumult.

All of a sudden, the pressure around her relented, as if a cork had been released. She gasped, sucking air into her lungs, shaking her head in an attempt to clear it. The fog without seemed mirrored by another fog, growing within her mind.

A pilaster loomed into view through the gloom ahead. She clung to it, recognized a bas-relief: and suddenly knew where she was. The door to the Hall of the Chariots was just up ahead. If they could just get through it and away from the infernal fog . . .

She flattened herself against the wall, then felt her way along it, keeping out of the panicked crowd, until she could make out the door ahead. People were squeezing through, fighting and clawing, ripping at one another's clothes, forming a bloody bottleneck of insanity and panic. More grotesque, deep groaning from the hidden speakers, along with an intensification of the bansheelike wail. Under this assault of noise, Nora felt a sudden vertigo, as if she were sinking; the kind of awful swoon she sometimes experienced in the throes of a fever. She staggered, fought to keep her feet: to fall now might mean the end.

She heard a cry and saw, through the swirling mist, a woman nearby, lying on one side, being trampled by the crowd. Instinctively, she bent forward, grabbed an upraised hand, and hauled her to her feet. The woman's face was bloody, one leg crooked and obviously broken—but she was still alive.

"My leg," the woman groaned.

"Put your arm around my shoulder!" Nora yelled.

She forced herself into the stream of people and the two were borne along through the doorway into the Hall of the Chariots. A dreadful, growing pressure . . . and then suddenly there was space, people milling about, disoriented, their clothes torn and bloody, weeping, shrieking for help. The woman sagged on her shoulder like a dead weight, whimpering. At least here they would be rid of the murderous barrage . . .

And yet, strangely, they were not. She had not escaped the sound, or the fog, or the strobe lights. Nora looked around, disbelieving. The fog was still rising fast, and more lights flashed from the ceiling—relentless, blinding bursts that each seemed to cloud her brain a little further.

Viola's right, she thought in a vague, confused way. This was no malfunction. The script didn't call for strobes or fog in the Hall of the Chariots; only in the burial chamber itself.

This was something planned—deliberate.

She clutched her throbbing head with one hand, urging the woman along, plodding slowly forward toward the God's Second Passage and the tomb exit that lay beyond. But once again, a seething mass blocked the narrow door at the far end.

"One at a time!" Nora screamed.

Directly ahead of her, a man was trying to beat his way through the crowd. With her free arm, she seized him by his tuxedo collar, yanking him off balance. He looked around wildly, took a swing at her.

"Bitch!" he yelled. "I'll kill you!"

Nora backed off in horror and the man turned back, grabbing and tearing at the people before him. But it wasn't just him: all around, people were screaming, boiling with rage, eyes rolling in their sockets—utter bedlam, a Boschean vision of hell.

She felt it even within herself: overwhelming agitation; a muddy, unfocused fury; an impending sense of doom. Yet nothing had actually *happened*. There was no fire, no mass murder—nothing to justify this kind of mass insanity . . .

Nora spotted the museum's director, Frederick Watson Collopy. His face looked shattered and he was staggering forward toward the doorway, one dead-looking leg trailing behind him: Draaaag-*thump!* Draaaag-*thump!*

He spied her and his ravaged face grew bright and hungry. He staggered toward her through the crush. "Nora! Help me!"

He seized the injured woman. Nora was about to thank him for his help, when he tossed her roughly to the ground.

Nora looked at him in horror. "What the hell are you doing?" She stepped forward to help the woman but Collopy seized her with incredible force, his hands clawing and grasping at her like a drowning man. She tried to twist free, but his desperate strength was shocking. In his frenzy, he twisted one arm around her neck.

"Help me!" he screamed again. *"I can't walk!"*

Nora jabbed him in the solar plexus with her elbow and he staggered, but still clung to her.

There was a sudden flash by her side and Nora saw Viola, kicking Collopy fiercely in the shins. With a shriek, Collopy released his grip and collapsed to the floor, writhing and spitting curses.

Nora grabbed Viola and together they backed away from the writhing crowd, staggered toward the rear wall of the Hall of the Chariots. There was a crash and the sound of shattering glass as a display case toppled over.

"My head, my head!" Viola groaned, pressing her hands to her eyes. "I can't think straight."

"It's like everyone's gone crazy."

"I feel like *I'm* going crazy."

"I think it's the strobe lights," Nora said, coughing. "And the sounds . . . or maybe some chemical in the fog."

"What do you mean?"

And then a swirling image appeared above them—a huge three-dimensional spinning spiral. With a thudding groan of sound, it twisted slowly . . . and then a piercing tone sounded, and another a quarter tone away, and another, throbbing and beating in dissonance, as the spiral began to rotate faster. Nora stared at it, instantly mesmerized. It was a holographic projection, it had to be. And yet it was *real* . . . it was like nothing she had ever seen before. It drew her forward, sucking her in, pulling her down into a maelstrom of insanity.

With a huge effort, she tore her eyes away. "Don't look at it, Viola!"

Viola trembled all over, her eyes still fixated on the swirling image.

"Stop it!" Nora slapped her across the face with her free hand.

Viola just shook her head to clear the blow, her eyes wild, still staring.

"The show!" Nora said, shaking her. "It's doing something to our minds!"

"What . . . ?" Viola's voice sounded drugged. And when she looked at Nora, her eyes were bloodshot—just like Wicherly's had been.

"The show. It's affecting our minds. Don't look at it, don't listen!"

"I don't . . . understand." Viola's eyes rolled backward in her head.

"Down on the floor! Cover your eyes and your ears!"

Nora tore a strip off her gown and blindfolded Viola. Just as she was about to blindfold herself, she caught a glimpse of a man standing in an alcove in the far corner, dressed in white tie and tails, utterly calm, an eye-mask over his face, head tilted up, hands clasped in front, standing stock-still, as if waiting. Menzies.

Another illusion?

"Fingers in your ears!" Nora cried, hunching down next to Viola.

They huddled in the corner, eyes squeezed shut, ears stopped, trying to shut out the hideous, grotesque show of death.

65

Smithback followed Pendergast at a dead run through the emptied museum halls, the beam from the agent's flashlight licking its way along the velvet ropes. Within minutes, they had reached the rotunda, their footsteps clattering on the white marble, and seconds later, they emerged onto the grand, red-carpeted staircase before the museum. Police cars were arriving in force along Museum Drive now, sirens wailing and brakes screeching. Smithback could hear the thudding of helicopters overhead.

Many of the police were engaged in crowd control, trying to clear Museum Drive of the panicked guests, onlookers, and press. Numerous other police officers were clustered together at the foot of the great steps, where they were setting up a mobile command center. There was pushing and shoving, and a hubbub of shouting filled the air. The flashes of photographers exploded like a fireworks display.

Pendergast hesitated at the top of the stairs, then turned to Smithback. "That's the subway entrance we need," he said, pointing to the far end of Museum Drive. Their route was blocked by a seething mass of guests and onlookers.

"It's going to take twenty minutes to force our way through that crowd," Smithback said. "And for sure somebody's going to knock that beaker out of your hands along the way."

"That would be unacceptable."

A hell of an understatement, Smithback thought. "What do you plan to do about it, then?"

"We shall simply have to part the crowds."

"How?" But even as he asked the question, Smithback saw a gun appear in Pendergast's hand. "Jesus, don't tell me you're going to use that."

"*I'm* not going to use it. *You* are. I wouldn't dare fire a gun while carrying this—the proximity of the discharge could set it off."

"But I'm not going to—"

Smithback felt the gun placed in his hand. "Fire into the air, *high* up into the air. Aim out over Central Park."

"But I've never used this model—"

"All you need to do is pull the trigger. It's a Colt .45 Model 1911, kicks like a mule, so wrap both hands on the grip and keep your elbows slightly bent."

"Look, *I'll* carry the nitro."

"I'm afraid not, Mr. Smithback. Now, get moving, if you please."

Reluctantly, Smithback advanced toward the crowd. "FBI!" he said unconvincingly. "Make way!"

The crowds didn't even notice him.

"Make way, damn it!"

Now some of the crowd stared back at him like a herd of cows, placid, unmoving.

"The sooner you fire, the sooner you will have their attention," Pendergast said.

"Make way!" Smithback raised the gun. "Emergency!"

A few at the front perceived what was coming, and there was a flurry of action, but the mass of the crowd between them and the subway entrance just stood there dumbly.

Bracing himself, Smithback squeezed the trigger. Nothing. He squeezed harder—and the gun went off with a terrific boom, jolting him.

A chorus of screams erupted and the crowd parted like the Red Sea.

"What the hell you think you're doing?" Two cops started running toward them from where they'd been pushing back the crowd nearby, their own guns drawn.

"FBI!" Pendergast shouted as they rushed forward into the breach. "This is an emergency federal action. Do not interfere!"

"Let's see your shield, sir!"

The back of the crowd was already coalescing and Smithback realized his mission was not yet accomplished. *"Make way!"* he yelled, firing the gun again while walking forward, to dramatic effect.

A series of screams, and a fresh pathway appeared almost miraculously before them.

"You crazy bastard!" somebody shouted. "Firing a gun like that!"

Smithback broke into a run, Pendergast following as quickly as he dared behind him. The cops attempted to give chase, but the crowd had already drawn together behind them. Smithback could hear the cops cursing as they tried to fight their way through.

A minute later, they'd reached the entrance to the subway, and here Pendergast went ahead, taking the stairs quickly yet with remarkable smoothness, still cradling the small flask. They trotted along the deserted platform, ducked around a corner at the far end, into the museum's subway entrance. Halfway down it, Smithback could see two figures: D'Agosta and Hayward.

"Where's our entry point?" Pendergast called out as he arrived.

"Between those lines," said Hayward, indicating two lines that had been marked on the tiles with lipstick.

Pendergast knelt and placed the flask carefully against the wall, positioning it between the lines. Then he stood and turned to face the little group. "If you would all please withdraw around the corner? My sidearm, Mr. Smithback?"

As Smithback handed the gun to the agent, he heard the sound of feet charging down the stairwell into the station. He followed Pendergast back around the corner onto the platform proper, where they crouched against the wall.

"NYPD!" came a shouted command from the far end of the station. *"Drop your weapons and freeze!"*

"Stay back!" Hayward shouted, waving her badge. "Police action in progress!"

"Identify yourself!"

"Captain Laura Hayward, Homicide!"

That seemed to flummox them.

Smithback saw Pendergast taking careful aim. He shrank closer to the wall.

"Stand *down*, Captain!" one of the policemen yelled.

"Take cover *now!*" came Hayward's reply.

"Ready?" Pendergast asked quietly. "On the count of three. One . . ."

"I repeat, Captain, *stand down!*"

"Two . . ."

"And I repeat, you idiots: take cover!"

"Three."

There was another gunshot, followed immediately by a terrific, earthshaking roar, and then a concussive blast that smacked Smithback hard against the chest and knocked him to the cement floor. Instantly the entire station filled with cement dust. Smithback lay on his back, dazed, the wind temporarily knocked from him. Chips of cement pattered down around him like rain.

"Holy shit!" It was D'Agosta's voice, but the man himself was invisible in the sudden gloom.

Vaguely, Smithback could hear confused shouting from the other end of the station. He pulled himself to a sitting position, choking and spluttering, ears ringing, and felt a reassuring hand on his shoulder. Then Pendergast's voice was in his ear.

"Mr. Smithback? We're going in now, and I'll need your help. Stop the show—rip out wires, rip down screens, smash lights, but *stop the show.* We must do that before we do anything else—even before we help the people. Do you understand?"

"Call for backup!" came the choking cry from somewhere at the far end of the platform.

"Do you understand?" Pendergast asked urgently.

Smithback coughed, nodded. The agent pulled him to his feet.

"Now!" Pendergast whispered.

They bolted around the corner, D'Agosta and Hayward at their heels. The dust had cleared just enough to show a gaping hole in the wall. From it gushed billows of fog, brilliantly illuminated by the maniacal flashing of strobe lights.

Smithback held his breath, readied himself. Then he ducked inside.

66

Just inside the breach, they paused. The heavy mist was pouring out of the gap like water from a broken dam, filling the tunnel and the subway station beyond; within the tomb itself, it was already subsiding below eye level, allowing them to see the upper portions of the tomb. Smithback immediately recognized it, from Nora's descriptions, as the burial chamber. Strobe lights of extraordinary, even painful intensity were flashing from every corner, and an unholy rumble filled the tomb, overlaid by a throbbing, nerve-shredding, high-pitched shriek.

"What the hell is going on?" D'Agosta asked behind him.

Pendergast moved forward without answering, waving away the swirling tendrils of fog. As they approached the huge stone sarcophagus in the center of the chamber, the agent paused, looked around at the ceiling, took aim, and fired: a fixture in the corner exploded in a flash of sparks and streamers of glass. He rotated his stance, fired again, and then again, until all the strobes were dead—although flashing could still be seen coming through the doorway to the next room of the tomb, and the hideous sounds continued.

They moved forward again. Smithback felt a sudden lurch in his gut: as the fog cleared, he could see bodies on the ground, moving feebly. The floor was slick with blood.

"Oh, no." Smithback looked around wildly. "Nora!"

But it was impossible to hear anything over the maddening wall of noise that seemed to penetrate his very bones. He took a few more steps, frantically waving away the mist. Another explosion from Pendergast's gun, followed by the hollow screech of feedback and an electric arc as an audio speaker crashed to the floor. Still, the sound throbbed on, unabated. Smithback grabbed some loose wires, yanked.

A plainclothes policeman approached them, staggering as if half drunk. His face was scratched and bleeding, and his shirt was torn and hanging in strips. His shield flapped on his belt as he moved, and his service piece dangled from one hand like a forgotten appendage.

Hayward frowned in surprise. "Rogerson?" she asked.

The cop's eyes swiveled toward her briefly, then swiveled away. After a second, he turned his back on them and began staggering off. Hayward reached over and plucked the gun from the man's unresisting hand.

"What the hell happened here?" D'Agosta cried, looking around at the scattering of torn clothes, shoes, blood, and injured guests.

"There's no time to explain," Pendergast said. "Captain Hayward, you and Lieutenant D'Agosta head up to the front of the tomb. You will find most of the guests up there, clustered at the entrance. Lead them back here and out through the gap in the wall. But be careful: many of them have undoubtedly become unhinged as a result of this sound-and-light show. They may be violent. Take care not to cause a stampede." He turned to Smithback. "We must find that generator."

"The hell with that. I'm finding Nora."

"You won't be able to find anyone until we stop this infernal show."

Smithback stopped. "But—"

"Trust me, I *know* what I'm doing."

Smithback hesitated, then nodded reluctantly.

Pendergast slipped a second flashlight out of his pocket and handed it to him, and they moved forward into the fog, side by side. It was a horrifying scene of carnage—wounded were sprawled across the marble floor, groaning, and more than one body lay motionless in a grotesque, unnatural position . . . apparently trampled to death. The floor was littered with shards of pottery. Smithback swallowed and tried to control his wildly beating heart.

Pendergast shone his light across the ceiling, the beam finally coming to rest on a long stone molding. He aimed his gun, fired, and blew off a corner of the molding, exposing a power cable that smoked and sparked.

"They would not have been allowed to bury the cables in the walls of the tomb," he explained. "We need to search for more false moldings."

Slowly, he traced his light along the molding, which had been plastered, textured, and painted to look like stone. It ran to a corner, where it was joined by a second molding, and from there a larger molding headed through the doorway to the adjoining room.

They picked their way over several bodies piled before the door and entered the next chamber of the tomb. Smithback winced at the blinding strobes, which Pendergast dispatched with four well-placed shots.

As the last shot reverberated through the gloom, a figure emerged from the dissipating fog, shambling, picking up and dropping its feet as if shackled with heavy weights. The mouth moved as if in violent speech, but Smithback could hear nothing over the thundering sound.

"Look out!" Smithback cried as the man abruptly lunged at Pendergast. The agent stepped aside deftly, tripping the stumbling figure and pushing him to one side. The man fell heavily to the ground and rolled, unable to get up.

They moved into a third room, Pendergast following the lines of molding with his flashlight. They appeared to all converge at a fake half-pilaster set into the far wall. Beneath stood a large XX Dynasty chest, gilded and intricately carved. It was set within a glass display case, unbroken despite the carnage.

"There!" Pendergast walked over, picked up a broken chariot wheel, and swung it into the case, shattering the glass. He stepped back and, raising his gun again, shot the ancient bronze lock off the chest. After holstering his weapon, he swept away the lock and the broken glass and lifted the lid from the heavy chest. Inside, a large generator hummed and vibrated. Pendergast slipped a knife out of his pocket, reached in, and cut a wire; the generator coughed, choked, and died—plunging the tomb into utter darkness and silence.

And yet the silence was not complete. Smithback could now hear a cacophony of cries and shrieks from the front section of the tomb: a moblike hysteria. He stood up, probing the darkness with his own flashlight.

"Nora!" he cried out. *"Nora!"*

Suddenly the beam of his light was arrested by a figure standing, half hidden, in a far alcove. Smithback stared in surprise. Although the man was dressed in impeccable white tie and tails, he wore a black mask over his face, and a set of headphones covered his ears. A small device that looked like a remote control was in his hand. He was standing so still Smithback wondered if perhaps he was just another holographic projection, but then, as if on cue, he reached up and pulled off the mask.

Pendergast had been staring at the man, and the effect of his unmasking was remarkable. He stiffened and jerked, like a man who has received an electric shock. His face, normally so pale, flushed crimson.

It seemed to Smithback that the tuxedoed figure's reaction was even stronger. He went into a sudden, instinctive crouch, like a man poised to spring. Then he gathered himself together and slowly rose to his full height.

"You!" he said. For a moment, he went still again. And then—with a long, spidery hand—he removed the headphones and earplugs, and slowly and deliberately dropped them to the floor.

Fresh surprise blossomed over Smithback. He recognized this man: it was Nora's boss, Hugo Menzies. And yet he looked so different. His eyes were flaming red, his limbs quivered. His face was flushed as deeply as Pendergast's was—he was filled with rage.

Pendergast's hand went for his gun. Then he stopped, weapon half drawn, as if paralyzed.

"Diogenes . . . ," he said in a strangled voice.

At the same time, Smithback heard his own name being called from a far corner. He looked over to see Nora staggering to her feet, supported by Viola Maskelene. Pendergast glanced over, noticing them as well.

In that moment, Menzies darted to one side with incredible speed and vanished into the darkness. Pendergast turned, tensed for pursuit—and then he turned back again toward Viola, face contorted with indecision.

Smithback dashed over to the two women and helped them to their feet. A moment later, Pendergast was beside him, taking Viola into his arms.

"Oh my God," she said, gasping and half weeping. "Oh my God, Aloysius . . ."

But Smithback barely heard. His arms were around Nora, one hand caressing her smudged and bloodied face. "Are you all right?" he asked.

She winced. "A headache. A few scratches. It was so *horrible.*"

"We'll get you out." Smithback turned back to Pendergast. The agent was still holding Viola in his embrace, his hands resting on her shoulders, but again, his gaze had darted toward the darkness into which Hugo Menzies had vanished.

Behind, from the burial chamber, Smithback heard the muffled blaring of police radios. Flashlight beams lanced through the murk, and the police were there, a dozen or more uniformed officers looking confused, moving into the Hall of the Chariots, guns drawn.

"What the hell's going on?" said the commander, a lieutenant. "What is this place?"

"You're in the Tomb of Senef," said Pendergast.

"What about the explosion?"

"Necessary to gain entry, Lieutenant," said Captain Hayward, walking toward them and showing her shield. "Now, listen carefully. We have injured in here, and a lot more up ahead. We're going to need EMTs, mobile first-aid stations, ambulances. Do you understand? Lieutenant D'Agosta is in the front of the tomb, about to escort the trapped victims back here to the exit. He needs help."

"Understood, Captain." The lieutenant turned to his officers and began barking orders. Several of them holstered their weapons and began moving deeper into the tomb, flashlight beams bobbing. Beyond them, Smithback could hear the approach of the crowd, the sounds of moaning, sobbing, and coughing, punctuated now and again by angry, incoherent cries. It sounded like an insane asylum on the move.

Pendergast was already helping Viola toward the exit. Smithback put his arm around Nora, and they fell in behind, headed for the gap blown in the corner of the burial chamber. Moments later, they were out of the mephitic tomb and inside the brightly lit subway station. A group of EMTs came running down the platform toward them, some carrying collapsible stretchers.

"We'll take them, gentlemen," one of the medical technicians said as they came up, while the rest rushed through the gap into the tomb.

In moments, Viola and Nora were strapped into stretchers and being carried up the stairs. Pendergast led the way. The flush had gone from his face, leaving it ashen and unreadable. Smithback walked beside Nora.

She smiled and reached up to grasp his hand. "I knew you'd come," she said.

67

"We serve breakfast beginning at six, sir," the porter said to the handsome, impeccably dressed gentleman in the private compartment.

"I would prefer to be served in my bedroom. Thank you in advance for obliging me."

The porter glanced down at the twenty-dollar bill being pressed into his hand. "No problem, sir, not a problem at all. Is there anything else I can do for you?"

"Yes. You could bring me a chilled glass, some crushed ice, a bottle of cold spring water, and a tin of sugar cubes."

"Very good, sir. I'll be back in a jiffy." The man stepped out of the compartment, smiling and bowing, and shut the door with almost reverential caution.

Diogenes Pendergast watched the dwarfish man disappear down the corridor and out of sight. He heard the footsteps patter away, heard the clunk of the heavy door at the end of the railroad car. He heard the myriad sounds of Penn Station, commingled and yet disparate in his mind: the ebb and flow of conversation outside the train, the sonorous droning of the stationmaster's announcements.

He shifted his gaze to the window, looked idly out at the platform. A landscape in shades of gray greeted him. A portly conductor stood there, patiently giving directions to a young woman, baby in her arms. A commuter trotted by, briefcase in hand, hurrying to catch the last

Midtown Express to Dover on the adjoining track. An elderly woman tottered slowly by, frail and thin. She stopped to stare at the train, then at her ticket, before continuing on her precarious way.

Diogenes saw them all, yet he paid them little heed. They were simply visual ephemera, a distraction for his mind . . . to keep it from drifting toward other, more maddening thoughts.

After the first few minutes—moments of anguish, disbelief, and white-hot rage—he had more or less managed to keep the thought of his failure at arm's length. The fact was, under the circumstances he had managed quite well: he always had multiple exit plans in place, and this evening he'd followed the most appropriate one to the letter. Barely half an hour had passed since he'd fled the museum. And yet already he was safely aboard the Lake Champlain, the overnight Amtrak train to Montreal. It was an ideal train for his purposes: it stopped at Cold Spring, on the Hudson, to change from electric to diesel, and all passengers were given thirty minutes to stretch their legs.

Diogenes would use the time to pay a final visit to his old friend Margo Green.

The hypo was already filled and lovingly nestled in its gift box, beautifully wrapped and beribboned. It was tucked safely away in his valise along with his most precious items—his scrapbooks, his personal pharmacopoeia of hallucinogens and opioids, his ghastly little trinkets and playthings of which nobody who'd ever caught sight had been permitted to live—all stowed in the overhead compartment. Enough clothing and disguises to get him safely home were hanging in the garment bag inside the small closet by the door. And safely tucked into his pocket were his documents and passports.

Now all that remained was to think as little as possible about what had happened. He did this by turning again, contemplatively, to Margo Green.

In his exhaustive, disciplined preparations for the sound-and-light show, *she* was the one indulgence he allowed himself. *She* was the only carryover from the earlier stage of his plan. Unlike the others, she was a sitting duck, to be played with and dispatched with little risk, time, or effort.

What about her, in particular, had drawn him back—more than, say, William Smithback, Nora Kelly, Vincent D'Agosta, or Laura Hayward? He wasn't sure, but he guessed it was her long connection to the museum—to the pontificating, pedestrian, whoreson, didactic, beggarly, jejune, ossified, shit-encrusted minds amongst whom he had been *buried*—as Hugo Menzies—for more years than he cared to count. It had been an insufferably extended torture. The whole lot of them would have been dispatched by the sound-and-light show—except for her. He had failed with the others, but he would not fail with her.

It had pleased him to pay her frequent sympathetic visits in her comatose state—which he had been at pains to extend, keeping her on the brink of expiration, teasing out her widowed mother's pain to the greatest possible extent. It was a brew of suffering from which he drank deep, and whose astringent taste renewed his own thirst for the living death that was his life.

There was a knock on the door.

"Come in," Diogenes said.

The porter entered rolling a portable bar, which he set up on an adjoining table. "Anything else, sir?"

"Not at the moment. You may make up my bed in an hour."

"Very good, sir. I'll get your breakfast order then." The man retreated with another deferential bow.

Diogenes sat for a moment, once again glancing out at the platform. Then, slowly, he drew a silver flask from his breast pocket. Opening it, he poured several ounces of a brilliant green liquid—which to him looked pale gray—into the glass on the portable bar. Then he retrieved a spoon from his leather valise: a silver spoon with the Pendergast family crest stamped on its handle, somewhat melted at one corner. He handled it as one might handle one's newborn child. Carefully, lovingly, he laid the spoon across the top of the glass and placed a sugar cube inside it. Then, taking the chilled water, he poured it onto the cube, drop by drop. Spilling over the edges of the spoon like a sugary fountain, the sweetened water fell into the liqueur below, turning it first a milky green, then a beautiful opalescent jade—if his eyes could only see in color.

All of this was done without the slightest trace of hurry.

Diogenes put the spoon carefully aside and lifted the glass to his lips, savoring the faintly bitter taste. He screwed the cap back on the flask and returned it to his pocket. It was the only modern absinthe he had found that had the same high proportion of essences of wormwood as the old nineteenth-century brands. As such, it deserved to be drunk in the traditional manner.

He took another sip, settling back comfortably into the chair. What was it Oscar Wilde had said of drinking absinthe? "The first stage is like ordinary drinking, the second when you begin to see monstrous and cruel things, but if you can persevere you will enter in upon the third stage, where you see things that you *want* to see, wonderful curious things."

Strange how, no matter how much he drank, Diogenes never seemed to get past the second stage—nor did he particularly care to.

A small speaker set high up in the wall came to life.

> *Ladies and gentlemen, this is the conductor speaking. Welcome aboard the Lake Champlain, making stops at Yonkers, Cold Spring, Poughkeepsie, Albany, Saratoga Springs, Plattsburg, St.-Lambert, and Montreal. This is your final boarding call. All visitors, please exit the train at this time . . .*

Listening, Diogenes smiled faintly. The Lake Champlain was one of only two luxury passenger trains still operated by Amtrak. By taking two adjoining first-class bedrooms and having the partition between them unlocked, Diogenes had secured himself a passably comfortable suite. It was a criminal disgrace the way politicians had allowed America's passenger train system, once the envy of the world, to fall into insolvency and disrepair. But this, too, was but a passing inconvenience: he would soon be back in Europe, where people understood how to travel in dignity and comfort.

Outside the window, a heavyset woman wobbled quickly by, a porter burdened down with suitcases trotting in her wake. Diogenes held up his glass, stirring the pearly liquid gently. The train would depart within moments. And now for the first time—cautiously, like a man approaching a dangerous animal—he allowed himself a brief moment of reflection.

It was almost too dreadful to contemplate. Fifteen years of planning, careful disguise, artful intrigue, ingenious contrivance . . . all for naught. The thought of all the work and time he had put into Menzies *alone*— fashioning his backstory, learning his trade, obtaining employment, working for years and years, attending vapid meetings and listening to the asinine mutterings of desiccated curators—was almost enough to send him spiraling into a pit of madness. And then there was the final extravaganza, in all its intricate and fearsome glory: the meticulous medical research into how one could contrive to transform ordinary people into murderous sociopaths using nothing more than sound and light— the ablation of the inhibitory cerebral pathway by laser light, traumatizing the entorhinal cortex and amygdala and allowing for disinhibition of rudimentary function . . . And then, there had been the painstaking implementation of his own special sound-and-light show hidden *within* the multimedia presentation everybody else had slaved over—and the testing of it on the technician and that ass, Wicherly . . .

It had all been so perfect. Even the tomb's curse, which he'd exploited so beautifully, added an exquisite touch: softening people up, preparing them psychologically for the terror of his sound-and-light show. It would have worked. In fact, it *did* work—except for the one element he could never have predicted: his brother escaping from Herkmoor. How had he managed that? And then he had appeared on the scene just in time to once again ruin everything.

How very like Aloysius. Aloysius, who—as the less gifted brother— had always taken grim pleasure in tearing down those things he himself lovingly constructed. Aloysius who, realizing he would always be bested intellectually, had taken the ultimate step of subjecting him to an Event that would ensure . . .

But here the hand holding the glass began to shake, and Diogenes immediately shut down this line of thought. Never mind: he would leave his brother one more gift for the delectation of his conscience: the gruesome death of Margo Green.

☼   ☼   ☼

There was a hiss of brakes; another announcement from the conductor; and then, with a squealing of metal wheels, the train began to creep forward along the platform. He was on his way: Cold Spring, Canada, Europe, and home.

Home. Just the thought of being back in his library, among his treasured possessions, within the embrace of a structure lovingly designed to spoil his every whim, helped restore his equanimity. It was from home that, over many years, he'd planned his perfect crime. From there he could do it again. He was still relatively young. He had many years left, more than enough to develop a plan—a *better* plan.

He took a deeper sip of absinthe. In his rage and shock, he was forgetting something. He *had* succeeded, at least in part. He had hurt his brother terribly. Aloysius had been publicly humiliated, charged with the murders of his own friends, sent to prison. He might be free, temporarily, but he was still a wanted man: the prison break would only deepen the hole he was in. He could never rest, never take an easy breath. He would be hunted endlessly. For somebody so private, the prison ordeal must have been mortifying.

Yes, he had accomplished much. He had struck his brother in a most vital, most sensitive spot. While Aloysius had been languishing in prison, he had seduced his brother's ward. What an abominable, delicious pleasure it had been. Remarkable: a hundred years of childhood . . . and yet still so fresh, so innocent and naive. Every web he had spun, every cynical lie he had told, had been a joy: especially his long and windy disquisitions on color. She would be dead by now, lying in a pool of her own blood. Yes, murder was one thing: but suicide, genuine *suicide*, struck the hardest blow of all.

He took another slow sip and watched the platform glide by over the rim of the glass. He was approaching Oscar Wilde's second stage of absinthe drinking, the contemplation of monstrous and cruel things— and he wanted to hold in his mind, like a soothing balm, one particular image: his brother standing over the dead body of Constance, reading the letter. This was the image that would comfort, nourish, and sustain him until he reached home . . .

The door to his stateroom rolled back with a clatter. Diogenes sat up, smoothing his shirtfront and slipping a hand into his jacket pocket for the ticket. But it was not the conductor who stood in the corridor beyond: it was the frail old woman he had seen walk past on the platform a few minutes earlier.

He frowned. "This is a private room," he said in a clipped tone.

The woman did not answer. Instead, she took a step forward into the compartment.

Instantly, Diogenes grew alarmed. It was nothing he could immediately put his finger on, but some sixth sense abruptly screamed danger. And then, as the woman reached into her handbag, he realized what it was: these were no longer the slow, hesitant movements of an old lady. They were lithe and quick—and they seemed to have a dreadful purpose. But before he could move, the hand came out of the bag holding a gun.

Diogenes froze. The gun was ancient, practically a relic: dirty, webbed with rust. Almost against his will, Diogenes found his eyes traveling up the woman's form until they reached her face—and he recognized the bottomless, expressionless eyes that looked back at him from beneath the wig. Recognized them well.

The barrel rose toward him.

Diogenes leaped to his feet, absinthe sloshing over his shirt and spattering the front of his pants, and flung himself backward as she squeezed the trigger.

Nothing.

Diogenes straightened, heart beating madly. It dawned on him that she had never fired a weapon before—she did not know how to aim, she had not yet turned off the safety. He sprang at her, but even as he did so, he heard the click of a safety being released, and a shattering explosion filled the compartment. A bullet punched a hole in the skin of the train car above his head as he twisted and fell sideways.

He scrambled to his feet as the woman took a step forward, wraithlike in the billows of cordite and dust. Once again—with perfect, terrible composure—she leveled the gun, took aim.

Diogenes threw himself at the door to the adjoining compartment, only to find that the porter had not yet unlocked it.

Another deafening explosion, and splinters flew from the molding mere inches from his ear.

He turned around to face her, his back against the window. Perhaps he could rush her, knock her from the door . . . But once again, with a deliberation so slow it was unspeakably awful, she leveled the old pistol, took aim.

He jerked to one side as a third bullet shattered the window where just a moment before he had been standing. As the echoes of the shot died away, the clank of the train wheels drifted in. There were shouts and screams in the corridor of the train now. Outside, the end of the platform was in sight. Even if he overcame her, wrestled away the gun—it would be all over. He would be caught, exposed.

Instantly, without conscious thought, Diogenes whirled around and dived out through the shattered window, landing heavily on the concrete platform and rolling once, twice, a confused welter of dust amidst bits of safety glass. He picked himself up, half dazed, heart beating madly, just in time to see the last car of the train disappear beyond the platform and into the dark mouth of the tunnel.

He stood there, stunned. And yet, through his daze, through his shock and pain and fear, an image persisted: the terrible calm with which she—Constance—had corrected her aim. There had been a lack of emotion, expression, *anything*, in those strange eyes . . .

Except utter conviction.

68

Anyone observing the gentleman going through security at terminal E in Boston's Logan Airport would have noticed a dapper man in his mid-sixties, with brown hair graying at the temples, a neatly trimmed salt-and-pepper beard, wearing a blue blazer with a white shirt open at the collar and a red silk handkerchief poking from his breast pocket. His eyes were a sparkling blue, his cheekbones broad, and his face open, ruddy, and cheerful. A black cashmere overcoat was slung over his arm, and he laid it on the security belt along with his shoes and watch.

Past security, the gentleman strode vigorously down the terminal corridor, pausing only at a Borders near gate 7. He ducked inside, perused the shelves of thrillers, and was delighted to find that a new James Rollins had been published. He took up the book, plucked a *Times* from the rack, and brought them to the cashier, greeting her with a cheery "Good day," betraying in accent and diction his Australian origins.

The gentleman then chose a seat near the gate, seated himself, and unfolded the paper with a snap. He took in the world and national news, turning the pages with a crisp, practiced motion. In the New York Report, his notice fell on a small item: *Mysterious Shooting on Amtrak Train.*

A sweep of his eyes took in the salient details: a man had been shot at on the Lake Champlain out of Penn Station; witnesses described the shooter as an elderly woman; the would-be target threw himself off the train and disappeared in the tunnels underneath Penn Station; a thorough search failed to identify the assailant or recover the weapon. The police were still investigating.

He turned the page and scanned the editorials, a slight frown gathering over some point he apparently disagreed with, soon clearing up.

A meticulous observer—and, in fact, there was one—would have seen nothing more remarkable than a wealthy Australian reading the *Times* while waiting for his flight. But the pleasant, somewhat vacant expression on his face was no more than skin-deep. Inside, his head was a boiling stew of fury, disbelief, and savage self-reproach. His world was upended, his careful planning destroyed. Nothing had succeeded. The Doorway to Hell: ruined. Margo Green: still alive. His brother: free. And most unacceptable of all: Constance Greene, undead.

Smiling, he turned to the sports section.

Constance, unsuicided. With her, he had miscalculated disastrously. Everything he knew of human nature indicated that she would take her own life. She was a freak, mentally unstable—hadn't she been stumbling blindfolded along the cliff's edge of sanity for decades? He had given her a push—a hard shove. Why hadn't she fallen? He had destroyed every pillar in her life, every support she had—undermined her every belief. He had drowned her existence with nihilism.

> *With rude haste the bloomy girl deflow'r'd,*
> *Tender, defenceless, and with ease o'erpower'd.*

In her long, sheltered, uneventful life, Constance had always drifted hesitantly, uncertain what she was intended for, confused about the meaning of her life. With bitter clarity, Diogenes now saw that he had cleared up her confusion and given her the one thing no one else could have: something to live for. She had found a new, shining purpose in life.

To kill *him*.

Normally, this would not be a problem. Those who interfered with him—there had been several—hadn't survived long enough to make a second attempt. He had washed away his sins in their blood. But already he could see that she was not like the others. He could not understand how she had identified him on the train—unless she had somehow physically followed him from the museum. And he was still unnerved from the utter self-possession of mind with which she had shot at him. She had forced him to leap out a window, flee in undignified panic, abandoning his valise with its treasured contents.

Fortunately, he had retained his various passports, wallet, credit cards, and identifications. The police would trace the valise and luggage back to Menzies; but they could not identify his traveling alter ego from them: Mr. Gerald Boscomb of South Penrith, Sydney, NSW. Now it was time to put aside all extraneous thoughts, all the little voluntary and involuntary mental tics and flourishes and whispered voices that made up his internal landscape—and identify a plan of action.

Closing the sports section, he turned to business.

> *No thought of right and wrong—only her fury*
> *With all her being speeded toward revenge.*

Constance Greene alone could identify him. She was an unacceptable danger. As long as she pursued him, he could not retreat to his bolt-hole and regroup. And yet all was not lost. He had failed this time, at least in part, but he had many years of life left to establish and execute a new plan, and he would not fail a second time.

But as long as *she* lived, he would never be safe.

Constance Greene had to die.

Mr. Gerald Boscomb picked up the novel he'd purchased, cracked it, and began reading.

Killing her would require a finely tuned plan. His thoughts turned to the Cape buffalo—the most dangerous animal hunted by man. The Cape buffalo employed a peculiar strategy when hunted: alone among animals, it knew how to turn the hunter into the hunted.

As he read, a plan formed in his mind. He thought it over, considered various locations for its execution, and discarded each in turn, before arriving—at chapter 6—at the perfect setting. The plan *would* work. He would turn Constance's very hatred for him against her.

He placed a bookmark in the novel, shut it, and tucked it under his arm. The first part of the plan was to show himself to her, to be in-tentionally seen—if she had managed to follow him here. But he could take no more chances, make no more assumptions.

He rose, slung his coat over his arm, and strolled down the termi-nal, glancing casually left and right, observing the masses of humanity as they ebbed and flowed on their futile business, a tidal flow of grays and more grays: layers of gray, an infinitude of gray. As he passed the Borders once again, his eye paused fleetingly on a dowdy woman buy-ing a copy of *Vogue;* she was dressed in a brown woolen skirt of African design with a white shirt, a cheap scarf wrapped around her neck. Her brown, unwashed hair fell limply to her shoulders. She carried a small black leather backpack.

Diogenes passed slowly by the bookstore and went into the Star-bucks next door, shocked that Constance had made such a poor effort to disguise herself. Shocked, also, that she had managed to follow him.

Or had she?

She must have. To find him any other way would take a mind reader.

He purchased a small organic green tea and croissant and made his way back to his seat, taking care not to look at the woman again. He could kill her here—it would be easy—but he would not be able to es-cape the layers of airport security. Would she make an attempt on his life in this exposed place? Did she care enough about her own life to take greater care—or was her sole aim to end his?

He had no answer.

Mr. Gerald Boscomb finished his tea and croissant, brushed the crumbs off the tips of his fingers, dusted his coat, and resumed read-ing his newly acquired thriller. A moment later, the first-class cabin of his flight was called to board. As he proffered his boarding pass to the gate attendant, his eye swept the terminal aisle again, but the woman had disappeared.

"G'day," he said cheerily, as he took the ticket stub and entered the jetway.

69

Vincent D'Agosta entered the library of 891 Riverside Drive, pausing in the doorway. A fire blazed on the hearth, the lights were up, and the room was a hive of concentrated activity. The chairs had been pushed back against the bookcases, and a large table covered with papers dominated the center of the room. Proctor was at one side, murmuring into a cordless phone, while Wren, his hair even wilder than usual, pored over a stack of books at a desk in the corner. The little man looked pinched and ancient.

"Vincent. Please come in." Pendergast called D'Agosta over with a curt gesture.

D'Agosta complied, shocked at the agent's uncharacteristically haggard appearance. It was the only time he remembered ever seeing Pendergast unshaven. And, for once, the man's suit jacket was unbuttoned.

"I got the details you wanted," D'Agosta said, holding up a manila folder. "Thanks to Captain Hayward." He dropped it on the table, flipped it open.

"Proceed."

"Witnesses say the shooter was an old woman. She got on the train with a first-class ticket to Yonkers, paid in cash. Gave the name Jane Smith." He snorted. "Just as the train was pulling out of Penn Station, while it was still underground, she entered the first-class berth of a passenger named . . . Eugene Hofstader. Pulled a gun and fired four shots.

Forensics recovered two .44-40 rounds embedded in the walls and another on the tracks outside. Get this: they were antique rounds—probably shot from a nineteenth-century revolver, a Colt perhaps."

Pendergast turned to Wren. "Check to see if we're missing a Colt Peacemaker or similar revolver from the collection, along with any .44-40 rounds, please."

Wordlessly, Wren stood up and left the room. Pendergast glanced back at D'Agosta. "Go on."

"The old woman vanished, although no one saw her get off the train, which was sealed almost immediately following the shooting. If she was wearing a disguise and discarded it, it was never found."

"Did the man leave anything behind?"

"You bet: a valise and a garment bag full of clothes. No papers or documents, or even a clue to his true identity. All labels had been carefully razored off the clothing. But the valise . . ."

"Yes?"

"They brought it into the evidence room, and when the warrant came down, they opened it up. Apparently, the evidence officer took one look and, well, whatever happened next he had to be sedated. A hazmat team was called in, and the stuff is now under lock and key—nobody seems to know where."

"I see."

"I guess we're talking about Diogenes here," said D'Agosta, slightly annoyed that he'd been sent out on the assignment with less-than-complete information.

"That is correct."

"So who's this old lady who shot at him?"

The agent gestured toward the table at the center of the room. "When Proctor returned here last night, he found Constance missing, along with a few articles of clothing. In her room, he found her pet mouse, its neck broken. Along with that note and the rosewood box."

D'Agosta walked over, picked up the indicated note, read it quickly. "Jesus. Oh, Jesus, what a sick fuck . . ."

"Open the box."

He opened the small antique box a little gingerly. It was empty, a long dimple left in the purple velvet interior by some object, now gone. A faded label on the inside cover read *Sweitzer Surgical Instrument Company*.

"A scalpel?" he asked.

"Yes. For Constance to cut her wrists with. She seems to have taken it for another purpose."

D'Agosta nodded. "I think I'm getting the picture. The old woman was Constance."

"Yes."

"I hope she succeeds."

"The thought of their meeting again is too terrible to contemplate," Pendergast replied, his face grim. "I must catch up with her—and stop her. Diogenes has been preparing for this escape for years, and we have no hope of tracing him . . . unless, of course, he *wishes* to be traced. Constance, on the other hand, will not be trying to conceal her tracks. I must follow her . . . and there is always a chance that, in finding her, I will find him as well."

He turned to an iBook sitting open on the table, began typing. A few minutes later, he looked over. "Constance boarded a flight to Florence, Italy, at five o'clock this afternoon, out of Logan Airport in Boston." He turned. "Proctor? Pack my things and book a ticket to Florence, if you please."

"I'm coming with you," said D'Agosta.

Pendergast looked back at him, his face gray. "You may accompany me to the airport. But as for going with me—no, Vincent, you will not. You have a disciplinary hearing to prepare for. Besides, this is a . . . *family* matter."

"I can help you," said D'Agosta. "You need me."

"Everything you say is true. And yet I must, and I *will*, do this alone."

His tone was so cold and final that D'Agosta realized any reply was useless.

70

Diogenes Pendergast, a.k.a. Mr. Gerald Boscomb, passed the Palazzo Antinori and turned into the Via Tornabuoni, breathing in the damp winter air of Florence with a certain bitter nostalgia. So much had happened since he was last here, mere months ago, when he had been filled with plans. Now he had nothing—not even his clothes, which he had abandoned on the train.

Not even his treasured valise.

He strolled pass Max Mara, remembering with regret when it was once the fine old Libreria Seeber. He stopped in at Pineider, bought some stationery, purchased luggage at Beltrami, and picked up a raincoat and umbrella at Allegri—all of which he had sent over to his hotel, keeping only the raincoat and umbrella, for which he had paid cash. He stopped at Procacci, settled himself at a tiny table in the crowded shop, and ordered a truffle sandwich with a glass of vernaccia. He sipped his drink thoughtfully, watching passersby through the window.

> *Fourmillante cité, cité pleine de rêves*
> *Où le spectre en plein jour raccroche le passant*

The sky was threatening rain, the city dark and narrow. Perhaps that was why he had always liked Florence in winter—it was monochromatic, the buildings pale, the surrounding hills gray humps spiked with cypress trees, the river a sluggish ripple of dull iron, its bridges almost black.

He dropped a bill on the table and left the café, continuing his stroll down the street. He paused to examine the display window at Valentino, using the reflection of the glass to observe the other side of the street. He went inside and purchased two suits, one in silk and the other a black double-breasted *completo* with a broad pinstripe, which he favored because of its faint thirties gangsterish flavor—and had them, as well, sent to his hotel.

Back on the street, he turned his footsteps toward the grim medieval facade of the Palazzo Ferroni, an imposing castle of dressed stone with towers and crenellated battlements, now the world headquarters of Ferragamo. He crossed the small piazza in front of the castle, past the Roman column of gray marble. Just before he entered the castle proper, a swift, sidelong glance identified the dowdy woman with brown hair—*her*—just at that moment entering the church of Santa Trinità.

Satisfied, he entered Ferragamo and spent a good deal of time looking over shoes, buying two pairs, and then completing his wardrobe with purchases of underwear, socks, nightshirt, undershirts, and bathing suit. As before, he sent his purchases over to his hotel and exited the store, encumbered with nothing more than the furled umbrella and the raincoat.

He walked toward the river and paused along the *lungarno*, contemplating the perfect curve of the arches of the Ponte Santa Trinità, designed by Ammanati: curves that had confounded the mathematicians. His yellowed eye examined the statues of the four seasons that crowned both ends.

None of it gave him pleasure anymore. It was all useless, futile.

The Arno below, swollen by winter rains, shuddered along like the back of a snake, and he could hear the roar of water going over the *pescaia* a few hundred yards downriver. He felt a faint raindrop on his cheek, then another. Black umbrellas immediately began appearing among the bustling crowds, and they bobbed over the bridge like so many black lanterns . . .

e dietro le venìa sì lunga tratta
di gente, ch'i' non averei creduto
che morte tanta n'avesse disfatta.

He put on his own raincoat, belted it tightly, unfurled the umbrella, and experienced a certain nihilistic frisson as he joined the crowds crossing the bridge. On the far side, he paused at the embankment, looking back over the river. He could hear the *tick-tick* of raindrops on the fabric of the umbrella. He could not see *her,* but he knew she was there, somewhere under that moving sea of umbrellas, following him.

He turned and strolled across the small piazza at the far end of the bridge, then took a right on Via Santo Spirito and an immediate left onto Borgo Tegolaio. There he paused to look in the rear display window of one of the fine antique shops that fronted on Via Maggio, stuffed with gilt candlesticks, old silver saltcellars, and dark still lifes.

He waited until he was sure that she had observed him—he caught just a glimpse of her through a double reflection in the shop window. She was carrying a Max Mara bag, and for all the world looked like one of the swinish American tourists who visited Florence in mindless shopping herds.

Constance Greene, just where he wanted her.

The rain slackened. He furled his umbrella but remained at the shop window, examining the objects with apparent interest. He watched her distant, almost unreadable reflection, waiting for her to move forward into the sea of umbrellas and thus lose sight of him for a moment.

As soon as she did so, he burst into a run, sprinting silently up Borgo Tegolaio, his raincoat flying behind him. He ducked across the street and darted into a narrow alley, Sdrucciolo de' Pitti; tore along its length; then took another left, racing down Via Toscanella. Then he ran across a small piazza and continued down Via dello Sprone until he had made a complete circuit and come back around to Via Santo Spirito, some fifty yards *below* the antique shop where he had dallied moments earlier.

He paused just short of the intersection with Via Santo Spirito, catching his breath.

Rat's coat, crowskin, crossed staves
In a field

He forced his mind back to business, angry at the whispered voice that never gave him peace. When she saw he was no longer on the street, she would assume—she would *have* to assume—that he had taken a right turn down the tiny alley just beyond the antique shop: Via dei Coverelli. She would think him *ahead* of her, walking in the opposite direction toward her. But, like the Cape buffalo, he was now behind her, their positions reversed.

Diogenes knew Via dei Coverelli well. It was one of the darkest, narrowest streets in Florence. The medieval buildings on both sides had been built out over the street on arches of stone, which blocked the sky and made the alley, even on a sunny day, as dim as a cave. The alley made a peculiar dogleg as it wormed past the back of the Santo Spirito church, two ninety-degree turns, before joining Via Santo Spirito.

Diogenes trusted in Constance's intelligence and her uncanny research abilities. He knew she would have studied a map of Florence and considered deeply the *momento giusto* in which to launch her attack on him. He felt sure that she would see the Coverelli alleyway as an ideal point of ambush. If he had turned down Coverelli, as she must believe, then this would be her chance. All she had to do was backtrack, enter Coverelli from the other end, and then wait in the crook of the dogleg for Diogenes to arrive. A person lurking in that dark angle could not be seen from either opening of the alleyway.

All this Diogenes had already thought out, the day before, on the plane ride to Italy.

She did not know that he had already anticipated her every action. She did not know that his flanking dash in the other direction would turn the tables. He would now be approaching her from behind, instead of from the front.

The hunter is now the hunted.

71

The Rolls tore across the upper deck of the Triborough Bridge, the skyline of Manhattan rising to the south, slumbering in the predawn. Proctor drove effortlessly through the traffic—heavy even at 4:00 A.M.—leaving drivers in his wake, their angry horns Doppler-shifting downward as he passed.

Pendergast sat in the back, in disguise as an investment banker on a business trip to Florence, equipped with the appropriate documents supplied by Glinn. Next to him sat D'Agosta, silent and grim.

"I don't get it," D'Agosta said at last. "I just don't understand how Diogenes could call this a perfect crime."

"I *do* understand—and rather too late," Pendergast replied bitterly. "It's as I explained on the ride to the museum last night. Diogenes wanted to inflict on the world the pain that had been inflicted on him. He wanted to re-create the . . . the terrible Event that ruined his life. You recall I mentioned he had been victimized by a sadistic device, a 'house of pain'? The Tomb of Senef was nothing less than a re-creation of that house of pain. On a grand and terrible scale."

The Rolls slowed for the tollbooth, then accelerated again.

"So what was going on in the tomb, then? What happened to all those people?"

"I'm not yet sure precisely. But did you notice that some of the victims were walking with a peculiar, shuffling gait? It put me in mind of the neurological effect known as drop foot, which sometimes afflicts people suffering from brain inflammation. Their ability to walk is impaired in a very specific manner, making it difficult to lower their feet smoothly to the ground. And if you ask Captain Hayward to inspect the tomb, I feel certain she will find powerful lasers hidden among the strobe lights. Not to mention a superfluity of fog machines and subwoofers far beyond anything the original design called for. It seems Diogenes engineered a combination of strobe light, laser, and sound to induce lesions in a very particular part of the brain. The flashing lasers and sound overwhelmed the ventromedial cortex of the brain, which inhibits violent and atavistic behavior. Victims would lose all inhibition, all sense of restraint, prey to every passing impulse. The id unleashed."

"It's hard to believe that light and sound could actually cause brain damage."

"Any neurologist will tell you that extreme fear, pain, stress, or anger can *damage* the human brain, kill brain cells. Post-traumatic stress disorder in its extreme form does, in fact, cause brain damage. Diogenes simply brought that to its ultimate conclusion."

"It was a setup from the very beginning."

"Yes. There was no Count of Cahors. Diogenes fronted the money for the restoration of the tomb. And the ancient curse itself provided just the kind of flourish that Diogenes delights in. Clearly, he secretly installed his own version of the show, a hidden version unknown to the technicians and programmers. He tested it first on Jay Lipper, then on the Egyptologist, Wicherly. And recall, Vincent, his ultimate aim was not just the people in the tomb: a live feed was going out over public television. Millions could have been affected."

"Unbelievable."

Pendergast bowed his head. "No. Utterly logical. His aim was to recreate the terrible, unforgivable Event . . . for which I was responsible."

"Don't start blaming yourself."

Pendergast looked up again, the silvery eyes suddenly dark in his bruised face. He spoke in a low voice, almost as if he were talking to himself. "I *am* my brother's creator. And all this time, I never knew it——

I never apologized or atoned for what I did. That is something I'll have to live with for the rest of my life."

"Forgive me for saying it, but that's a load of crap. I don't know much about it, but I do know what happened to Diogenes was an accident."

Pendergast went on, voice even lower, almost as if he hadn't heard. "Diogenes's entire reason for existence is I. And, perhaps, *my* reason for existence is *him*."

The Rolls entered JFK Airport and drove along the circulation ramp toward terminal 8. As it pulled up to the curb, Pendergast leaped out and D'Agosta followed.

Pendergast hefted his suitcase, grasped D'Agosta's hand. "Good luck on the hearing, Vincent. If I don't return, Proctor will handle my affairs."

D'Agosta swallowed. "Speaking of returning, there's something I've been meaning to ask you."

"Yes?"

"It's . . . a difficult question."

Pendergast paused. "What is it?"

"You realize there's only one way to take care of Diogenes."

Pendergast's silvery eyes hardened.

"You know what I'm talking about, right?"

Still, Pendergast said nothing, but the look in his eyes was so cold that D'Agosta almost had to look away.

"When the moment comes, if you hesitate . . . he won't. So I need to know if you'll be able to . . ." D'Agosta couldn't finish the sentence.

"And your question, Vincent?" came the icy reply.

D'Agosta looked back at him, saying nothing. After a beat, Pendergast turned abruptly and disappeared into the terminal.

72

Diogenes Pendergast strolled around the corner of the Via dello Sprone and back into Via Santo Spirito. Constance Greene was gone, having ducked into the Via dei Coverelli as he'd anticipated. And now she would be waiting for him, in ambush, to round the corner.

To confirm this, he walked briskly down Via Santo Spirito and paused just before the entrance to Coverelli, flattening himself against the ancient *sgraffito* facade of some long-forgotten palace. With enormous caution, he peered around the corner.

Excellent. She was still not to be seen—she had already turned the first angle of the dogleg and was no doubt waiting for him to come from the opposite direction.

His hand slipped into his pocket and removed a leather case, from which he took an ivory-handled scalpel identical to the one he had left beneath her pillow. The cool weight of it comforted him. Counting out the seconds, he opened his umbrella and made the turn. Then he began walking boldly down Via dei Coverelli, his shoes echoing on the cobblestones in the confined alleyway, his upper body hidden beneath the black umbrella. Disguise was unnecessary: she would not look back around the corner to see who was coming from the *other* direction. She would not expect his approach from that side.

He strode on boldly, inhaling the scent of urine and dog feces, of vomit and wet stone—the ancient alleyway retained even the smell of medieval Florence. Keeping the scalpel poised in his gloved hand, he approached the first corner of the dogleg. As he did so, he previsualized his strike. She would have her back to him; he would come up from the side, grab her neck with his left arm while aiming the scalpel for that sweet spot just below the right clavicle; the length of the scalpel blade would be sufficient to sever the brachiocephalic artery at the point where it divided into the carotid and subclavian arteries. She would not even have time to cry out. He would then hold her while she died; he would cradle her; he would allow her blood to flow over him as it had done once before . . . under very different circumstances . . .

. . . and then he would leave both her and his raincoat in the alley.

He approached the corner. Fifteen feet, ten, eight, *now* . . .

He turned the corner and paused, tense and then astonished. There was no one there. The dogleg was empty.

He quickly looked around, forward and back: no one. And now *he* was in the dogleg, blind, unable to see who was coming from either direction.

He felt a twinge of panic. Somewhere he had miscalculated. Where had she gone? Had she tricked him in some way? It didn't seem possible.

He paused, realizing that he was now stuck in the blind spot. If he walked around the corner ahead of him, out into Borgo Tegolaio, a much broader and more visible street, and she was there, she would see him—and all his advantage would be lost. On the other hand, if she was behind him, and he went back, that would also destroy his advantage.

He stood motionless, thinking furiously. The sky continued to darken, and now he realized that it wasn't merely the rain, but the evening was falling like a dead hand over the city. He couldn't stay there forever: he would have to move, to turn either one corner or the other.

Despite the chill, he felt himself growing warm under the raincoat. He had to abandon his plan, turn around, and walk back the way he had come—to unwind, so to speak, his flanking maneuver as if it had never happened. That would be best. Something had happened. She had taken another turn somewhere and he had lost her—that was it. He would then have to think of another attack. Perhaps he should go to Rome and allow her to follow him into the Catacombs of St. Callixtus. That popular tourist site, with its anonymous dead ends and doubling-backs, would be an excellent place to kill her.

He turned and walked back along Via dei Coverelli, cautiously rounding the first dogleg. The alleyway was empty. He strode down it—and then suddenly, out of the corner of his eye, he saw a flash of movement from one of the archways above; he instinctively threw himself sideways even as a shadow dropped upon him and he felt the resistless swipe of a scalpel cutting through the layers of his raincoat and suit, followed by the searing burn of cut flesh.

With a cry, he twisted around and—even as he fell—drove his own scalpel in a glittering arc toward her, aiming for the neck. His greater experience with the blade, combined with superior speed, paid off as his scalpel met flesh in a mist of blood; but as he continued to fall, he realized she had twisted her head at the last moment and his blade, instead of cutting her throat, had merely slashed the side of her head.

He fell hard onto the cobblestones, his mind swept clean by astonishment, rolled over, and leaped up, scalpel in hand—but she was already gone, vanished.

In that moment, he understood *her* plan. Her poor disguise had been no accident. She had been showing herself to him, just as he had been revealing himself to her. She had allowed him to lead her to a point of ambush, and she had then used it against him. She had countered his countermove.

The simple brilliance of it astounded him.

He stood there, looking up at the crowded stone arches above him. He made out the crumbling ledge of *pietra serena* from which she had no doubt launched her attack. Far above he could see the tiniest sliver of steel-gray sky, out of which were spinning raindrops.

He took a step, staggered.

ὤμοι, πέπληγμαι καιρίαν πληγὴν ἔσω!

He felt a wave of faintness as the burning sensation in his side increased. He dared not open his coat and inspect; he could not afford to get blood on the outside of his clothing—it would draw attention. He belted his raincoat as tightly as possible, trying to bind the wound.

Blood would draw attention.

As the feeling of faintness receded and his brain emerged from the shock of the attack, he realized that an opening had presented itself to him. He had cut her head, and no doubt it was bleeding copiously, as all such cuts did. She could not hide such a cut and the blood, not even with a scarf. She could not pursue him around Florence with blood pouring down her face. She would have to retreat somewhere, clean herself up. And that gave him the window of opportunity he needed to escape from her, to shake her off—forever.

Now was the moment. If he could escape from her cleanly, he could assume another identity, and from there proceed to his final destination. She would never find him there—never.

He strolled as casually as possible through the streets toward the taxi stand at the end of Borgo San Jacopo. As he walked, he could feel the blood soaking through his clothes, trickling down his leg. The pain was minor, and he was sure the cut had merely sliced along his rib cage without penetrating his vitals.

He had to do something about the blood, however—and fast.

He turned into a little café at the corner of Tegolaio and Santo Spirito, went up to the bar, and ordered an espresso and a *spremuta*. He downed both, one after the other, dropped a five-euro bill on the zinc, and went into the bathroom. He locked the door and opened his raincoat. The amount of blood was shocking. He quickly probed the wound, confirming that it hadn't pierced his peritoneum. Using paper towels, he mopped up as much blood as he could; and then, tearing away the lower half of his blood-soaked shirt, he tied the strips around his torso, closing the wound and stanching the flow of blood. Then he washed his hands and face, put on his raincoat, combed his hair, and left.

He felt the blood pooling now into his shoe, and he looked down to see that his heel was leaving a bloody quarter-moon on the sidewalk. But it was not fresh blood, and he could sense that the bleeding had slowed. A few more steps and he arrived at the taxi stand, slid into the backseat of a Fiat.

"Speak English, mate?" he asked, smiling.

"Yes," came the gruff reply.

"Good man! The railroad station, please."

The cab shot forward and he lay back in the seat, feeling the blood sticky in his groin, his mind suddenly loosening itself in a tumult of thoughts, a shower of broken memories, a cacophony of voices:

> *Between the idea*
> *And the reality*
> *Between the motion*
> *And the act*
> *Falls the Shadow*

73

In the convent of the Suore di San Giovanni Battista in Gavinana, Florence, twelve nuns presided over a parochial school, a chapel, and a villa with a *pensione* for religious-minded visitors. As night gathered over the city, the *suora* behind the front desk noted with unease the return of the young visitor who had arrived that morning. She had come back from her tour of the city cold and wet, her face bundled up in a woolen scarf, body hunched against the weather.

"Will the signora be having dinner?" she began, but the woman silenced her with a gesture so brusque the *suora* closed her mouth and sat back.

In her small, simply furnished room, Constance Greene furiously flung off her coat on her way to the bathroom. She bent over the sink, turning on the hot water tap. As the sink filled, she stood before the mirror and unwound the woolen scarf from her face. Beneath it was a silk scarf, stiff with blood, which she gingerly unwrapped.

She peered closely at the wound. She could not see much; her ear and the side of her head were crusted with clotted blood. She dipped a washcloth in the warm water, wrung it out, and gently placed it over her skin. After a moment, she removed, rinsed, and reapplied it. Within minutes, the blood had softened enough for her to cleanse the cut and examine it more clearly.

It wasn't as bad as it had looked at first. The scalpel had scored deeply across her ear but had only nicked her face. She gently probed with her fingers, noting that the cut was exceedingly sharp and clean. It was nothing, although it had bled like a stuck pig—it would heal with hardly a scar.

Scar. She almost laughed out loud as she threw the bloody washcloth into the sink.

She leaned over and examined her face in the mirror. It was thin and haggard, her eyes hollow, lips cracked.

The novels she had read made pursuit sound easy. Characters followed other characters halfway around the world, all the while remaining well rested, fed, refreshed, and groomed. In reality, it was an exhausting, brutal business. She had hardly slept since she first picked up his trail at the museum; she had barely eaten; she looked like a derelict.

On top of that, the world had proved to be a nightmare beyond all imagining: noisome, ugly, chaotic, and brutally anonymous. It was not at all like the comfortable, predictable, moral world of literature. The great welter of human beings she had encountered were hideous, venal, and stupid—indeed, mere words failed to describe their true loathsomeness. And chasing Diogenes had proved expensive: through inexperience, being cheated, and rash expenditure, she had run through almost six thousand euros in the past forty hours. She had only two thousand left—and no way of getting more.

For forty hours, she had followed him relentlessly. But now he had escaped her. His wound would not slow him down: it was undoubtedly a trifle, like hers. She was certain she had lost his trail for good—he would see to that. He was gone, on to a new identity, and no doubt heading for the safe place he had prepared for just such a flight, years ago.

She had come so close to killing him—twice. If she had a better handgun . . . if she had known how to shoot . . . if she had been a millisecond quicker with the blade . . . he would be dead.

But now he had escaped her. She had lost her chance.

She gripped the sink, staring into her bloodshot eyes. She knew with a certainty the trail would end here. He would flee by taxi, train, or plane, cross a dozen borders, crisscross Europe, before ending up in a place and in a persona he had carefully cultivated. It would be somewhere in Europe, she was sure of that—but the certainty was of little help. It might take a lifetime to find him—or even more.

Nevertheless, a lifetime was what she had. And when she found him, she would know him. His disguises had been good—but no disguise would deceive her. She *knew* him. He could alter everything possible about his appearance: his face, clothes, eyes, voice, body language. But there were two things he could not alter. His stature was the first. The second, the more important, was something she was sure Diogenes had not thought of: and that was his peculiar scent. That scent she remembered so well, strange and heady, like a mixture of licorice underscored by the keen, dark smell of iron.

A lifetime . . . She felt a wave of despair so overwhelming that she swayed over the sink.

Could he have left some clue behind in his hasty departure? But that would mean returning to New York, and by the time she did so, the trail would have grown too cold.

Perhaps he had dropped some unconscious reference, then, in her presence? It seemed most unlikely—he had been so careful. But perhaps, because he had expected her to die, he might have been less than vigilant.

She walked out of the bathroom, sat down on the edge of the bed. She paused a moment to clear her mind as best she could. Then she thought back to their earliest conversations in the library of 891 Riverside. It was a mortifying exercise, excruciatingly painful, like peeling back a raw bandage of memory: and yet she forced herself to continue, summoning up their first exchanges, his whispered words.

Nothing.

She then went over their later meetings, the books he had given her, his decadent disquisitions on sensual living. But there was still nothing, not even the hint of a geographical location.

In my house—my real *house, the one that is important to me—I have a library* . . . That was what he had told her once. Was it, like everything else, just a cynical lie? Or was there perhaps a glimmer of truth?

I live near the sea. I can sit in that room, all lights and candles extinguished, listening to the roar of the surf, and I become a pearl diver . . .

A library, in a house by the sea. That wasn't much help. She ran over the words again and again. But he had been so careful to hide any personal details, except for those lies he had so carefully crafted, such as the suicide scars.

The suicide scars. She realized that, in her recollections, she had been unconsciously avoiding the one event that held out the greatest chance of revealing something. And yet she could not bear to think of it again. Reliving those final hours together—the hours in which she gave herself to him—would be almost as painful as first reading the letter . . .

But once again a coldness descended over her. Slowly she lay back on the bed and stared upward into the darkness, remembering every exquisite and painful detail.

He had murmured lines of poetry in her ear as his passion mounted. They had been in Italian:

> *Ei s'immerge ne la notte,*
> *Ei s'aderge in vèr' le stelle.*

> He plunges into the night,
> He reaches for the stars.

She knew that the poem was by Carducci, but she had never made a careful study of it. Perhaps it was time that she did.

She sat up too quickly and winced from a sudden throbbing in her ear. She went back into the bathroom and went to work on the injury, cleaning it thoroughly, covering it with antibiotic ointment, and then bandaging it as unobtrusively as possible. When she was done, she undressed, took a quick bath, washed her hair, put on fresh clothes. Next, she stuffed the washcloth, towel, and bloody clothes into a garbage bag she found stored in the back of the room's armoire. She gathered up her toiletries and returned them to her suitcase. Pulling out a fresh scarf, she wrapped it carefully around her face.

She closed the suitcase, buckled and strapped it. Then she took the garbage bag and descended to the greeting room of the convent. The sister was still there, and she looked almost frightened by this sudden reappearance.

"Signora, is there something not to your liking?"

Constance opened her wallet. "*Quanto costa?* How much?"

"Signora, if there is a problem with your room, surely we can accommodate you."

She pulled out a rumpled hundred-euro bill, placed it on the counter.

"That is too much for not even one night . . ."

But Constance had already vanished into the cold, rainy dark.

74

Two days later, Diogenes Pendergast stood on the port rail of the *traghetto* as it plowed through the heaving blue waters of the southern Mediterranean. The boat was passing the rocky headland of Capo di Milazzo, crowned by a lighthouse and a ruined castle; behind him, sinking into the haze, stood the great hump of Sicily, the blue outline of Mount Etna thrusting into the sky, a plume of smoke trailing off. To his right lay the dark spine of the Calabrian coast. Ahead lay his destination, far, far out to sea.

The great eye of the setting sun had just dipped behind the cape, casting long shadows over the water, limning the ancient castle in gold. The boat was heading north, toward the Aeolian islands, the most remote of all the Mediterranean islands—the dwelling place, or so the ancients believed, of the Four Winds.

Soon he would be home.

Home. He rolled the bittersweet word around in his mind, wondering just what it meant. A refuge; a place of retreat, of peace. He removed a packet of cigarettes from his pocket, took shelter in the lee of the deck cabin, and lit one, inhaling deeply. He had not smoked in more than a year—not since he had last returned home—and the nicotine helped calm his agitated mind.

He thought back to the two days of hectic traveling he had just completed: Florence, Milan, Lucerne—where he'd had his wound stitched at a free clinic—Strasbourg, Luxembourg, Brussels, Amsterdam, Berlin, Warsaw, Vienna, Ljubljana, Venice, Pescara, Foggia, Naples, Reggio di Calabria, Messina, and finally Milazzo. A forty-eight-hour ordeal of train travel that had left him weak, sore, and exhausted.

But now, as he watched the sun dying in the west, he felt strength and presence of mind returning. He had shaken her in Florence; she had not, *could* not have, followed him. From there, he had changed identities several times, confused his trail to such an extent that neither she nor anyone else could hope to untangle it. The open borders of the EU, combined with the crossing into Switzerland and re-entry into the EU under a different identity, would confound even the most persistent and subtle pursuer.

She would not find him. Nor would his brother. Five years, ten years, twenty—he had all the time in the world to plan his next—his final—move.

He stood at the rail, inhaling the breath of the sea, feeling a modicum of peace steal over him. And for the first time in months, the interminable, dry, mocking voice in his head fell to a susurrus, almost inaudible amid the sound of the bow plowing the sea:

Goodnight Ladies: Goodnight sweet Ladies: Goodnight, goodnight.

75

Special Agent Aloysius Pendergast got off the bus at Viale Giannotti and walked through a small park of sycamore trees past a shabby merry-go-round. He was dressed as himself—now that he was safely out of the United States, there was no need for disguise. At Via di Ripoli, he took a left, pausing before the huge iron gates that led into the convent of the Sisters of San Giovanni Battista. A small sign identified it only as *Villa Merlo Bianco*. Beyond the gates, he could hear the mingled cries of schoolchildren at recess.

He pressed the buzzer and, after a moment, the gates opened automatically, leading into a graveled courtyard before a large ocher villa. The side door was open, and a small sign identified it as guest reception.

"Good morning," he said in Italian to the small, plump nun at the desk. "Are you the Suor Claudia I spoke to?"

"Yes, I am."

Pendergast shook her hand. "Pleased to know you. As I mentioned over the phone, the guest we spoke of—Miss Mary Ulciscor—is my niece. She has run away from home, and the family is extremely worried about her."

The plump nun was almost breathless. "Yes, signore, in fact I could see she was a very troubled young lady. When she arrived, she had the most haunted look in her face. And then she didn't even stay the night—arrived in the morning, then returned that evening and insisted on leaving—"

"By car?"

"No, she came and left on foot. She must have taken the bus, because taxis always come in through the gates."

"What time would that have been?"

"She returned about eight o'clock, signore. Soaking wet and cold. I think she might have been sick."

"Sick?" Pendergast asked sharply.

"I couldn't be sure, but she was hunched over a bit, and her face was covered."

"Covered? With what?"

"A dark blue woolen scarf. And then not two hours later, she came down with her luggage, paid too much money for a room she hadn't even slept in, and left."

"Dressed the same?"

"She'd changed her clothes, had on a red woolen scarf this time. I tried to stop her, I really did."

"You did all you could, Suora. Now, may I see the room? You needn't bother coming—I'll take the key myself."

"The room's been cleaned, and there's nothing to see."

"I would prefer to check it myself, if you don't mind. One never knows. Has anyone else stayed there?"

"Not yet, but tomorrow a German couple . . ."

"The key, if you would be so kind."

The nun handed him the key. Pendergast thanked her, then walked briskly through the piano nobile of the villa and mounted the stair.

He found the room at the end of a long hall. It was small and simple. He closed the door behind him, then immediately dropped to his knees. He examined the floor, searched under the bed, searched the bathroom. To his great disappointment, the room had been fanatically cleaned. He stood up, looked around thoughtfully for a minute. Then he opened the armoire. It was empty—but a careful look revealed a small, dark stain in the far corner. He dropped to his knees again, reached in, and touched it, scratching a bit up with his fingernail. Blood—dry now, but still relatively fresh.

Back in the reception room, the nun was still deeply concerned.

"She seemed troubled, and I can't imagine where she went at ten o'clock at night. I tried to talk to her, signore, but she—"

"I'm sure you did all you possibly could," Pendergast repeated. "Thank you again for your help."

He exited the villa onto Via di Ripoli, deep in thought. She had left at night, in the rain . . . but for where?

He entered a small café at the corner of Viale Giannotti, ordered an espresso at the bar, still pondering. She had encountered Diogenes in Florence, that much was certain. They had fought; she had been wounded. It seemed incredible that she was only hurt, for normally, those who came within Diogenes's orbit did not leave it alive. Clearly, Diogenes had underestimated Constance. Just as he himself had done. She was a woman of vast, unexpected depths.

He finished the coffee, bought an ATAF ticket at the bar, and stepped across the viale to wait for the bus into the city center. When it arrived, he made sure he was the last one on. He held up a fifty-euro note to the driver.

"You don't pay me, stamp your ticket at the machine," the driver said crossly, pulling roughly out of the bus stop, his hammy arms swinging the wheel around.

"I want information."

The driver continued to ignore the money. "What kind of information?"

"I'm looking for my niece. She got on this bus around ten o'clock two nights ago."

"I drive the day bus."

"Do you have the name of the night driver and his cell number?"

"If you weren't a foreigner, I'd say you were a *sbirro*, a cop."

"It's not a police matter. I'm just an uncle looking for his niece." Pendergast softened his voice. "Please help me, signore. The family is frantic."

The driver negotiated a turn, then said, his tone more sympathetic,

"His name is Paolo Bartoli, 333-662-0376. Put your money away—I don't want it."

Pendergast got off the bus at Piazza Ferrucci, pulled out the cell phone he had acquired on arrival, dialed the number. He found Bartoli at home.

"How could I forget her?" the bus driver said. "Her head was swaddled in a scarf, you couldn't see her face, her voice all muffled. She spoke an old-fashioned Italian, used the *voi* form with me—I haven't heard that since the days of the Fascists. She was like a ghost from the past. I thought maybe she was crazy."

"Do you remember where she got off?"

"She asked me to stop at the Biblioteca Nazionale."

It was a long walk from Ferrucci to the National Library, which stood across the Arno River, its brown baroque facade rising in sober elegance from a dirty piazza. In the cold, echoing reading room, Pendergast found a librarian who remembered her as well as the bus driver had.

"Yes, I was working the night shift," the librarian told him. "We have few visitors at that hour—and she looked so lost, so desolate, I couldn't keep my eyes off her. She stared at a particular book for over an hour. Never turning the pages, always on the same page, murmuring to herself like a crazy woman. It got on toward midnight and I was getting ready to ask her to leave so I could close. But then all of a sudden, she jumped up, consulted another book—"

"What other book?"

"An atlas. She pored over it for perhaps ten minutes—scribbling furiously in a small notebook as she did so—and then ran out of the library as if the hounds of hell were after her."

"Which atlas?"

"I didn't notice—it's one of those on the far reference shelf, she didn't have to fill out a slip to look at them. But let's see, I do still have the slip she filled out for the book she stared at for so long. Just a moment, I'll collect it for you."

A few minutes later, Pendergast was seated where Constance had sat, staring at the same book she had stared at: a slim volume of poems by Giosuè Carducci, the Italian poet who had won the Nobel Prize for Literature in 1906.

The volume sat in front of him, unopened. Now, with infinite care, he upended it and allowed it to fall open naturally; hoping, as books will sometimes do, that it would open to the last page that had been read. But it was an old, stiff book, and it merely fell open to the front endpapers.

Pendergast reached into the pocket of his suit jacket, drew out a magnifying glass and a clean toothpick, and began turning the pages of the book. For each page he turned, he gently dragged the toothpick along the gutter, then examined the dirt, hair, and fibers that had been exposed with his magnifying glass.

An hour later, on page 42, he found what he was looking for: three red fibers of wool, curled as if from a knitted scarf.

The poem that straddled both pages was called "La Leggenda di Teodorico," the Legend of Theodoric.

He began to read:

> *Su 'l castello di Verona*
> *Batte il sole a mezzogiorno,*
> *Da la Chiusa al pian rintrona*
> *Solitario un suon di corno . . .*

> Above the great castle of Verona,
> Beats the brutal midday sun,
> From the Mountains of Chiusa, across the plains,
> Resounds the dreaded horn of doom . . .

The poem recounted the strange death of the Visigothic king Theodoric. Pendergast read it once, and then again, failing to see what momentous importance Constance could have attached to it. He read it again slowly, recalling the obscure legend.

Theodoric was one of the earliest of the great barbarian rulers. He carved a kingdom for himself from the corpse of the Roman Empire, and among other brutal acts he executed the brilliant statesman and philosopher Boethius. Theodoric died in 526. Legend had it that a holy hermit, living alone on one of the Aeolian islands off the coast of Sicily, swore that in the very hour of Theodoric's death, he witnessed the king's shrieking soul being cast into the throat of the great volcano of Stromboli, believed by the early Christians to be the entrance of hell itself.

Stromboli. The Doorway to Hell. In a flash, Pendergast understood.

He rose, walked over to the shelf of atlases, and selected the one of Sicily. Returning to his seat, he carefully opened it to the page displaying the Aeolian islands. The outermost of these was the island of Stromboli, which was essentially the peak of a live volcano that rose abruptly from the sea. A lone village hugged its surf-pounded shore. The island was exceedingly remote and difficult to reach, and the volcano of Stromboli itself had the distinction of being the most active in Europe, in almost continual eruption for at least three thousand years.

He carefully wiped the page with a folded white linen handkerchief, then examined it with his magnifying glass. There, stuck to the linen weft, was another curled red wool fiber.

76

Diogenes Pendergast stood on the terrace of his villa. Below him, the tiny whitewashed village of Piscità crowded down to the broad, black-sand beaches of the island. A wind came in from the sea, bringing with it the scent of brine and flowering ginestra. A mile out to sea, the automatic lighthouse on the immense rock of Strombolicchio had begun winking in the gathering dusk.

He sipped a glass of sherry, listening to the distant sounds from the town below—a mother calling her children in to dinner, a dog barking, the buzz of a three-wheeled Ape, the only kind of passenger vehicle used on the island. The wind was rising, along with the surf—it was going to be another roaring night.

And behind him, he heard the thunderous rumble of the volcano.

Here, at the very edge of the world, he felt safe. *She* could not follow him here. This was his home. He had first come here twenty years before, and then almost every year since, always arriving and departing with the utmost care. The three hundred or so year-round residents of the island knew him as an eccentric and irascible British professor of classics who came periodically to work on his magnum opus—and who did not look with favor on being disturbed. He avoided the summer and the tourists, although this island, being sixty miles from the mainland and inaccessible for days at a time due to violent seas and the lack of a port, was far less visited than most.

Another rolling boom. The volcano was active tonight.

He turned, glancing up its steep, dark slopes. Angry clouds writhed and twisted across the volcanic crater, towering more than a half mile above his villa, and he could see the faint flashes of orange inside the jagged cone, like the flickering of a defective lamp.

The last gleam of sunlight died on Strombolicchio and the sea turned black. Great rollers creamed in long white lines up the black beach, one after another, accompanied by a monotonous low roar.

Over the past twenty-four hours, with enormous mental effort, Diogenes had expunged from his mind the raw memory of recent events. Someday—when he had acquired a little distance—he would sit down and dispassionately analyze what had gone wrong. But for now he needed to rest. After all, he was in his prime; he had all the time in the world to plan and execute his next attack.

> *But at my back I always hear*
> *Time's wingèd chariot hurrying near*

He gripped the delicate glass so tightly it snapped, and he dashed the stem to the ground and went into the kitchen, pouring himself another. It was part of a supply of amontillado he had laid down years before, and he hated to waste a drop.

He took a sip, calming himself, then strolled back onto the terrace. The town was settling down for the night: a few more faint calls, a wailing baby, the slamming of a door. And the buzz of the Ape, closer now, in one of the crooked streets that rose toward his villa.

He put the glass down on the parapet and lit a cigarette, drawing in the smoke, exhaling into the twilit air. He peered down into the streets below. The Ape was definitely coming up the hill, probably on Vicolo San Bartolo . . . The tinny whine drew still closer, and for the first time Diogenes felt a twinge of apprehension. The dinner hour was an unusual time for an Ape to be out and about, especially in the upper village—unless it was the island taxi taking someone somewhere. But it was early spring and there were no tourists: the ferry he had taken from Milazzo had carried no visitors, only produce and supplies; and besides, it had departed hours ago.

He chuckled at himself. He had grown too wary, almost paranoid. This demonic pursuit—coming hard on the heels of such a huge failure—had left him shaken, unnerved. What he really needed was a long period of reading, study, and intellectual rejuvenation. Indeed, now would be the perfect time to begin that translation of *Aureus Asinus* by Apuleius that he had always intended.

He drew in more smoke, exhaled easily, turned his eyes to the sea. The running lights of a ship were just rounding Punta Lena. He went inside, brought out his binoculars, and—looking to sea again—was able to make out the dim outline of an old wooden fishing boat, a real scow, heading away from the island toward Lipari. That puzzled him: it had not been out fishing, not in this weather at this time of day. It had probably been making a delivery.

The sound of the Ape approached and he realized it was now coming up the tiny lane leading to his villa—hidden by the high walls surrounding his grounds. He heard the engine slow as it came to a stop at the bottom of his wall. He put down the binoculars and strode to the side terrace, from where he had a view down the lane; but by the time he got there, the Ape was already turning around—and its passenger, had there been one, was nowhere to be seen.

He paused, his heart suddenly beating so hard he could hear the roar of blood in his ears. His was the only residence at the end of the lane. That old fishing scow hadn't brought cargo—it had brought a *passenger*. And that passenger had taken the Ape to the very gates of his villa.

He exploded into silent action, running inside, dashing from room to room, shuttering and barring the windows, turning off the lights, and locking the doors. The villa, like most on the island, was built almost like a fortress, with heavy wooden shutters and doors bolted with hand-wrought iron and heavy locks. The masonry walls themselves were almost a meter thick. And he had made several subtle improvements of his own. He would be safe in the house—or at least he could gain enough time to think, to consider his position.

In a few minutes, he had finished locking himself in. He stood in his dark library, breathing hard. Once again he had the feeling he had reacted out of sheer paranoia. Just because he'd seen a boat, heard the taxi . . . It was ridiculous. There was simply no way for her to have found him—certainly not this quickly. He had arrived on the island only the evening before. It was absurd, impossible.

He dabbed his brow with a pocket handkerchief and began to breathe easier. He was being utterly foolish. This business had unnerved him even more than he realized.

He was just feeling around for the light when the knock came: slow—mockingly slow—each boom on the great wooden door echoing through the villa.

He froze, his heart wild once again.

"*Chi c'è?*" he asked.

No answer.

With trembling fingers, he felt along the library drawers, found the one he was looking for, unlocked it, and removed his Beretta Px4 Storm. He ejected the magazine, checked that it was full, and eased it back into place. In the next drawer, he found a heavy torch.

How? *How?* He choked down the rage that threatened to overwhelm him. Could it really be her? If not, why hadn't there been an answer to his call?

He turned on the torch and shone it around. Which was the likeliest entry point? It would probably be the door on the side terrace, closest to the lane and easiest to get to. He crept over to it, unlocked it silently, then carefully balanced the metal key on top of the wrought-iron door handle. Then he retreated to the center of the dark room and knelt in firing stance, letting his eyes adjust to the dark, gun aimed at the door. Waiting.

It was silent within the thick walls of the house. The only sound that penetrated was the periodic deep-throated rumble of the volcano. He waited, listening intently.

Five minutes passed, then ten.

And then he heard it: the clink of the falling key. He instantly fired four shots through the door, covering it in a diamond-shaped pattern. The 9mm rounds would have no trouble penetrating even the thickest part of the door with plenty of velocity left to kill. He heard a gasp of pain; a thud; a scrabbling noise. Another gasp—and then silence. The door, now ajar, creaked open an inch in a gust of wind.

It sounded as if he had killed her. And yet he doubted it. She was too smart. She would have anticipated that.

Or *would* she? And on the other hand, was it even her? He might have just killed some hapless burglar or delivery boy.

Crouching low, he crept toward the door. As he drew close, he lay flat on the floor and crawled the final few feet. He stopped, his gaze on the narrow crack below the doorjamb. He needed to ease the door open another inch before he could see whether a body lay on the terrace beyond—or whether it was a trick.

He waited—and, when another gust of wind came, he used the opportunity to creak the door a little farther open to expose the terrace to view.

Instantly, two shots rang out, slamming through the door just inches above his head, showering him with splinters. He rolled quickly away, heart pounding. The door was now open a foot, and each gust of wind pushed it farther ajar. She had fired very low—expecting him to be crouching. If he hadn't been completely prone, he would have been hit.

He stared at the holes her rounds had torn in the woodwork. She had managed to get her hands on a mid-caliber semiautomatic, a Glock from the sound of it. And she had learned at least the basics of how to shoot.

Another, heavier gust of wind blew the door wide open, and it slammed against the wall, then swung to, creaking loudly. Slowly he maneuvered around to its far side, and then with one swift movement kicked the door shut, rolled to a sitting position, and shot the bolt. As he rolled away again, another shot blew a hole in the wood inches from his ear, prickling him with splinters.

As he lay on the floor, breathing hard, he realized now the disadvantage of shutting himself up in the house. He could not see out; he could not know from what direction she would come. Although the house had been somewhat hardened against entry, he had seen no need to arouse local suspicion by making it as secure as the Long Island structure: with a gun, she could shoot the locks or bolts off any door and window. No—it would be better to fight her outside, where his superior strength, his expert shooting ability, and his knowledge of the terrain would put him at a decided advantage.

Had the gunshots been heard? People in town might be calling the police, and that could be awkward. But *had* they heard? With the wind coming off the water and roaring up through the figs and olive groves—not to mention the periodic booms from the restless volcano—perhaps the sound of the gunshots would not be noted. And as for the police, the only law enforcement on the island during the winter was a *nucleo investigativo* headed by a lone *maresciallo* of the carabiniere—who spent his evenings playing *briscola* at the bar in Ficogrande.

He felt a rush of limb-trembling rage. She had invaded his home, his bolt-hole, his ultimate refuge. This was it: he had nowhere else to go, no other identity to assume. Flushed from here, he would be put to flight like a dog, pursued relentlessly. Even if he eventually escaped, it would take years to find a new safe haven, establish a secure identity.

No: he had to finish it here and now.

Three shots sounded in rapid succession, and he heard one of the shutters in the breakfast nook hurl open, slamming against the wall with a shuddering crash. He jumped up and, scuttling ahead at a crouch, took cover behind a half-wall of masonry separating the kitchen from the dining area. The wind howled through the open window, banging the shutter.

Had she gotten inside?

He scrambled around the half-wall, jumped up at a run, and swept the torch across the kitchen: nothing. Still running, he slid into the dining room, braced himself against a wall. The key was to keep moving . . .

Three more shots resounded, this time from the direction of the library, and he could hear another shutter begin to swing wildly in the wind.

That was her game, then: punch holes in his defenses, one by one, until the house was no protection at all. He wouldn't play that game. He had to seize the initiative. He, not she, would choose the terrain for the final confrontation.

He *had* to get outside—and not only outside, but up the mountain. He knew every switchback of the steep and dangerous trail. She was comparatively weak and would be weaker after her long and exhausting pursuit. On the mountain, every advantage would be his—including the use of a handgun in the dark. Nevertheless, he reminded himself that he had underestimated her at each turn. That could not be permitted to happen again. He was up against the most determined, and perhaps most deadly, adversary of his career.

His thoughts returned to the mountain. The ancient trail had been built almost three thousand years ago by Greek priests to offer sacrifices to the god Hephaestus. About halfway up, the trail branched. A newer trail ran to the summit along the Bastimento Ridge. The ancient Greek trail continued westward, where it had been cut centuries earlier by the Sciara del Fuoco, the legendary Slope of Fire. The Sciara was a continuous avalanche of red-hot lava blocks forced from the crater, which tumbled down a vast ravine a mile broad and three thousand feet deep, to ultimately crash into the sea in explosions of steam. The cliff edge of the Sciara was a hellish, dizzying place, like no other on earth, swept by raging winds of heated air coming off the lava flow.

The Sciara del Fuoco. A perfect solution to his problem. A body that fell in there would virtually disappear.

Exiting the house would be his point of greatest vulnerability. But she could not be everywhere at once. And even if she was waiting, expecting his exit, she had little chance of hitting him if he kept moving in the dark. It took years to develop handgun skills at that level.

Diogenes crept up to the side door, paused briefly. And then, in one explosive movement, he kicked it open and charged into the darkness. The shots came, as he knew they would, missing him by inches. He dived for cover and returned the shots, suppressing her fire. Then he jumped up, sprinted through the gate, and turned sharply right, racing up a series of ancient lava steps at the top of the lane, which would connect to the trail that wound up the side of the volcano of Stromboli toward the Slope of Fire.

77

Special Agent Pendergast leaped off the swaying fishing boat onto the quay at Ficogrande, the boat already backing its engines to get away from the heavy surf along the exposed shore. He stood for a moment on the cracked cement, looking up at the island. It rose abruptly from the water like a black pillar against the dim night sky, illuminated by a fitful quarter-moon. He saw the reddish play of lights in the clouds capping the mountain, heard the boom and roll of the volcano, mingling with the roar of surf at his back and the howling of wind from the sea.

Stromboli was a small, round island, two miles in diameter and conical in shape: barren and forbidding. Even the village—a scattering of white-washed houses stretched out along a mile of shoreline—looked battered, windswept, and austere.

Pendergast breathed in the moist, sea-laden air and drew his coat more closely around his neck. At the far end of the quay, across the narrow street that paralleled the beach, a row of crooked stuccoed buildings sat crowded together: one was evidently a bar, although the faded sign that rocked in the wind had lost its electric light.

He hurried up the quay, crossed the street, and entered.

A thick atmosphere of cigarette smoke greeted him. At a table sat a group of men—one in the uniform of the carabiniere—smoking and play-ing cards, each with a tumbler of wine in front of him.

He went to the bar, ordered an *espresso completo*. "The woman who arrived on the chartered fishing boat earlier this evening . . . ?" he said in Italian to the bartender, and then paused, waiting expectantly.

The man gave the zinc a swipe with a damp cloth, served the espresso, tipped in a measure of grappa. He didn't seem inclined to answer.

"Young, slender, her face swathed in a red scarf?" Pendergast added.

The bartender nodded.

"Where did she go?"

After a silence, he said, in Sicilian-accented Italian, "Up to the professor's."

"Ah! And where does the professor live?"

No answer. He sensed that the card game behind him had paused.

Pendergast knew that, in this part of the world, information was never given out freely: it was exchanged. "She's my niece, poor thing," he offered. "My sister's heart is just about broken, her daughter chasing after that worthless man, that so-called professor, who seduced her and now refuses to do the right thing."

This had the desired effect. These were Sicilians, after all—an ancient race with antique notions of honor. From behind him, Pendergast heard the scrape of a chair. He turned to see the carabiniere drawing himself up.

"I am the *maresciallo* of Stromboli," he said gravely. "I will take you up to the professor's house." He turned. "Stefano, bring up the Ape for this gentleman and follow me. I will take the *motorino*."

A dark, hairy man rose from the table and nodded at Pendergast, who followed him outside. The three-wheeled motorized cart stood at the curb and Pendergast got in. Ahead, he could see the carabiniere kick-starting his *moto*. In a moment, they were off, driving along the beach road, the surf roaring on their right, pounding up beaches that were as dark as the night.

After a short drive, they swung inland, winding through the impossibly narrow lanes of the town, rising steeply up the side of the mountain. The lanes grew even steeper, now running through dark vineyards and olive groves and kitchen gardens, enclosed by walls made of mortared lava cinders. A few sprawling villas appeared, dotting the upper slopes. The last one stood hard against the rising mountain, surrounded by a high lava-stone wall.

The windows were dark.

The carabiniere parked his motorbike at the gate and the Ape stopped behind it. Pendergast jumped out, looking up at the villa. It was large and austere, more like a fortress than a residence, graced with several terraces, the one facing the sea colonnaded with old marble columns. Beyond the lava wall stood a lush and extensive garden of tropical plants, birds of paradise, and giant exotic cacti. It was the very last house on the mountainside, and from Pendergast's vantage point below, it almost seemed as if the volcano were leaning above the house, its rumbling, flickering peak reflecting a menacing bloody orange against the lowering clouds.

Despite everything—despite the extremity of the moment—Pendergast continued to stare. *This is my brother's house*, he thought.

With an officious swagger, the carabiniere went to the iron gate—which stood open—and pressed the buzzer. And now, spell broken, Pendergast brushed past him, ducked through the gate, and ran at a crouch toward the side door on the terrace, which was banging in the wind.

"Wait, signore!"

Pendergast slipped out his Colt 1911 and pressed himself on the wall against the door, catching it in his hand as it swung to. It was riddled with bullet holes. He glanced around: a shutter outside the kitchen was also open, swinging in the wind.

The carabiniere came puffing up beside him. He eyed the door. *"Minchia!"* His own firearm came out immediately.

"What is it, Antonio?" said the Ape driver, coming up, the tip of his cigarette dancing in the roaring dark.

"Go back, Stefano. This does not look good."

Pendergast pulled out a flashlight, ducked into the house, shone it around. Splinters of wood lay scattered across the floor. The beam of the flashlight illumined a large living room in the Mediterranean style, with cool plastered surfaces, a tiled floor, and heavy antique furniture: spare and surprisingly austere. He had a glimpse, beyond an open door, of an extraordinary library, rising two stories, done up in a surreal pearl gray. He ducked inside, noting that a second shutter in the library had been shot open.

Still, no signs of a struggle.

He strode back to the side door, where the carabiniere was examining the bullet holes. The man straightened up.

"This is a crime scene, signore. I must ask you to leave."

Pendergast exited onto the terrace and squinted up the dim mountain. "Is that a trail?" he asked the Ape driver, who was still standing there, gaping.

"It goes up the mountain. But they would not have taken that trail—not at night."

The carabiniere appeared a moment later, radio in hand. He was calling the carabiniere *caserma* on the island of Lipari, thirty miles away.

Pendergast exited through the gate and walked up to the end of the lane. A ruined staircase in stone ran up the side of the hill, joining a larger, very ancient trail on the slope just above. Pendergast knelt, shone his light on the ground. After a moment, he rose and took a dozen steps up the trail, examining it with his light.

"Do not go up there, signore! It is extremely dangerous!"

He knelt again. In a thin layer of dust protected from the wind by an ancient stone step, he could make out the impression of a heel—a small heel. The impression was fresh.

And there, above it, another small, faint print, lying on top of a larger one. Diogenes, pursued by Constance.

Pendergast rose and gazed up the dizzying slope of the volcano. It was so black he could see nothing except the faint flicker of muffled orange light around its cloud-shrouded summit.

"This trail," he called back to the policeman. "Does it go to the top?"

"Yes, signore. But once again, it is very dangerous and is for expert climbers only. I can assure you, they did not go up there. I have called the carabinieri on Lipari, but they cannot come until tomorrow. And maybe not even then, with this weather. There is nothing more I can do, aside from searching the town . . . where surely your niece and the professor have gone."

"You won't find them in the town," Pendergast said, turning and walking up the trail.

"Signore! Do not take that trail! It leads to the Sciara del Fuoco!"

But the man's voice was carried away in the wind as Pendergast climbed with all the speed he could muster, his left hand gripping the flashlight, his right the handgun.

78

Diogenes Pendergast jogged along a windswept shoulder of lava 2,500 feet up the side of the mountain. The wind blew demonically, lashing the dense ginestra brush that crowded the trail. He paused to catch his breath. Looking down, he could just barely see the dim surface of the sea, flecked with bits of lighter gray that were whitecaps. The lighthouse of Strombolicchio sat alone on its rock, surrounded by a gray ring of surf, blinking its mindless, steady message out to an empty sea.

His eye followed the sea in toward land. From his vantage point, he could make out fully a third of the island, a great swerve of shoreline from Piscità to the crescent beach below Le Schiocciole, where the sea raged in a broad band of white surf. The dim illumination of the town lay sprinkled along the shore: dirty, wavering points of light, an uncertain strip of humanity clinging to an inhospitable land. Beyond and above, the volcano rose massively, like the ribbed trunk of a giant mangrove, in great parallel ridges, each with its own name: Serra Adorno, Roisa, Le Mandre, Rina Grande. He turned, looked up. Above him loomed the immense black fin of the Bastimento Ridge, behind which lay the Sciara del Fuoco—the Slope of Fire. That ridge ran up to the summit itself: still shrouded in fast-moving clouds, blooming with the lurid glow of each fresh eruption, the thunderous booms shaking the ground.

A few hundred meters up, Diogenes knew, the trail split. The left fork cut eastward and switchbacked to the summit crater up the broad cinder slopes of the Liscione. The right fork, the ancient Greek trail, continued westward, climbing the Bastimento and ending abruptly where it was cut by the Sciara del Fuoco.

She would be at least fifteen, twenty minutes behind him by now—he had been pushing himself to the utmost, climbing at maximum speed up the crumbling stone staircases and cobbled switchbacks. It was physically impossible for her to have kept up. That gave him time to think, to plan his next step—now that he had her where he wanted her.

He sat down on a crumbling wall. The obvious mode of attack would be an ambush from the almost impenetrable brush that crowded each side of the trail. It would be simple: he could hide himself in the ginestra at, say, one of the switchback turns, and shoot straight down the trail as she came up. But this plan had the great disadvantage of being the obvious one, a plan she would most certainly anticipate. And the brush was so thick he wondered if he could even push into it without leaving a ragged hole behind or, at the least, signs of damage visible to a keen eye—and she had a damnably keen eye.

On the other hand, she did not know the trail—*could* not know the trail. She had arrived at the island and come straight to his villa. No map could convey the steepness, the danger, the roughness of the trail. There was a spot ahead, just below the fork, where the trail ran close under a bluff of hardened lava, looped back around, and then topped the bluff. There were cliffs all around it—there was no way for her to get off the trail at that point. If he waited for her on the bluff above, she would have to pass almost directly underneath him. There was simply no other way for her to go. And because she did not know the trail, she could not anticipate that it doubled back over the bluff.

Yes. That would serve nicely.

He continued up the mountain and in another ten minutes had reached the final switchback and gained the top of the bluff. But as he looked around for a hiding place, he saw there was an even better position—indeed, it was nearly perfect. She would see the bluff as she approached and might anticipate a strike from it. But well before the bluff itself was another ambush point—in the deep shadows below it, half obscured by rocks—that looked to be far subtler; indeed, it was completely invisible from farther down the trail.

With an unutterable feeling of relief that it would soon be over, he carefully took up a position in the shadow of the switchback and prepared to wait. It was a perfect spot: the deep darkness of the night and the natural lines of the terrain making it appear there was no break at all in the rocks behind which he hid. Within fifteen minutes or so, she should appear. After he killed her, he would throw her body into the Sciara, where it would vanish forever. And he would once again be free.

The fifteen minutes that passed next were the longest of his life. As they ticked on into twenty, he became increasingly uneasy. Twenty-five minutes passed . . . thirty . . .

Diogenes found his mind racing with speculation. She could not possibly know that he was there. He was certain she could not have been alerted to his presence.

Something else might be wrong.

Was she too weak to have climbed this high up the mountain? He had assumed her hatred would carry her far past the point of normal exhaustion. But she was only human; she had to have a breaking point. She had been following him for days, hardly eating and sleeping. On top of that, she would have lost a fair amount of blood. To then climb almost three thousand vertical feet up an unknown and exceedingly dangerous trail at night . . . maybe she just couldn't make it. Or perhaps she'd been hurt. The decrepit cobbled path was strewn with loose stones and eroded blocks, and the steepest parts—where the ancients had built stone staircases—were slick with rubble and missing many steps, a veritable death trap.

A *death trap*. It was entirely possible—indeed, even probable—that she had slipped and hurt herself; fallen and twisted an ankle; perhaps even been killed. Did she have a flashlight? He didn't think so.

He checked his watch: thirty-five minutes had now passed. He wondered what to do. Of all the possibilities, the likeliest was that she had been hurt. He would go back down the trail and see for himself. If she was lying there with a broken ankle, or collapsed in exhaustion, killing her would be simple . . .

He paused. No, that would not do. That was, perhaps, *her* game plan: to make him believe she'd been hurt, to lure him back down—and then ambush him. A bitter smile passed across his face. That was it, wasn't it? She was waiting him out, waiting for him to descend. But he would not fall into that trap. He would wait *her* out. Eventually her hatred would force her up the mountain.

Ten more minutes passed, and once again he was beset by doubts. What if he waited for her all night? What if she had declined to bring the battle into the terrain of the mountain itself? What if she had gone back to town and was lying low, planning something new? What if she had alerted the police?

He couldn't bear the thought that this might continue. He could not go on in this manner. It must end *this very night*. If she would not come to him, he had to force the issue by coming to her.

But how?

He lay on the hard ground, peering down into the murk, his agitation increasing. He tried to think as she would, anticipate what she would do. He could not afford to underestimate her again.

I escape the house, run up the trail. She stands there, wondering if she should follow. What would she do? She knew he would be going up the mountain; she knew he would wait for her, that he intended to fight her on his own ground, on his own terms.

What would she do?

The answer came to him in a flash: find another route. A shorter route. And cut him off. But of course there wasn't another route—

With a sudden, dreadful prickling sensation along his neck, he recalled an old story he had heard told around the island. Back in the eighth century, the Saracens had attacked the island. They had landed at Pertuso, a cove on the far side, and made a bold and dangerous crossing, which required climbing up one side of the volcano and down the other. But they had not taken the Greek trail down—they had blazed their own route in order to fall upon the town from an unexpected direction.

Could *she* have taken the Saracen trail up?

His mind worked feverishly. He hadn't paid any attention to the old story, treating it as yet another colorful legend, like so many others attached to the island. Did anyone even know today where the Saracen trail went? Did it still exist? And how could Constance have known about it? There probably weren't more than half a dozen people in the world who would know the actual route.

He cursed savagely, racked his brains, trying to remember more of the story. Where did the Saracen trail go?

There was something in the legend about the Saracens losing men into the Filo del Fuoco, a narrow gorge that split off from the Sciara. If that were the case, the trail must have hugged the edge of the Sciara all the way down the Bastimento Ridge—or up it, as the case may be—

He rose abruptly. He knew—*he knew!*—this was what Constance had done. She was a consummate researcher; she had gotten hold of some old atlas of the island. She'd studied it, memorized it. She'd flushed him from his house, like a badger from a bolt-hole, driven him up the more familiar trail. Allowing him to think that it was his *own* plan all the time . . . And meanwhile, she would have cut to the west and taken the secret trail up, flanking him as he'd waited in ambush, wasting minute after precious minute. And now she was above. Waiting for him.

A cold sweat broke out on his brow. He could see the breathtaking subtlety of her plan. She had worked it all out ahead of time. She had *expected* him to flee his house, run up the trail. And she had *expected* him to pause somewhere along the trail and wait in interminable ambush, giving her—the weaker one—all the time she needed to get up the Saracen trail to the Bastimento Ridge—

He stood abruptly in horror, eyes focusing on the great black fin of the Bastimento above him. The clouds were tumbling across the peak, the mountain groaning and shaking with each explosion—and then they parted, exposing the ridge to the glare of the eruptions: and in that moment he spied, silhouetted against the horrid lambent glow, a figure in white, *dancing* . . . And despite the roar of the wind and the rumbling of the mountain, he was sure he could hear a shrill, manic laughter echoing down toward him . . .

In a convulsion of fury, he aimed his gun and fired again and again, the bright flashes blinding his own night vision. After a moment, he cursed and lowered the gun, his heart pounding. The ridge was bare, the figure gone.

It was now or never. The end was upon them. He tore up the trail, moving as fast as he could, knowing that she could never hit him in the dark. The fork in the trail loomed ahead, the newer trail running off to the left on a graded path. The right fork was blocked by a fence, rusty concertina wire rattling in the wind, marked by a weather-beaten sign in two languages:

Sciara del Fuoco!
Pericolosissimo!
Vietato a Passare!

Active Lava Flow Ahead!
Extreme Danger!
Do Not Pass!

He leaped over the fence and scrambled up the ancient trail toward the top of the Bastimento Ridge. There was only one possible outcome. One of them would walk back down the mountain; the other would be thrown into the Sciara.

It remained to be seen who, in the end, would prevail.

79

Aloysius Pendergast paused at the fork in the trail, listening intently. Not five minutes before, he had distinctly heard shots—ten of them in all—over the thundering of the volcano. He knelt and examined the ground with his light, quickly determining that Diogenes—and Diogenes alone—had taken the fork blocked by a fence.

There was much about this situation that he had not yet untangled, enigmas wrapped in mysteries. There had been very few footprints—only where dust or sand had blown into pockets of the rock—but even so, Constance's prints had ceased, almost at the beginning of the trail. And yet Diogenes had continued on. Why? Pendergast had been forced to make a choice: search for Constance's prints or follow Diogenes's. And this was no choice at all—Diogenes was the danger, he needed to be found first.

And then, there had been gunshots—but whose? And why so many? Only a person in the grip of panic would fire ten shots in a row like that.

Pendergast scaled the fence and continued up the ancient trail, which had fallen into dangerous ruin. The top of the ridge was perhaps a quarter mile distant, and beyond that he could see only the sky, stained by an angry orange glow. He had to move fast—but with care.

The trail came to a steep part of the ridge, carved into a staircase that ran up the rough lava itself. But the staircase was badly eroded, and

Pendergast was forced to holster his sidearm and use both hands to climb it. Just before cresting the top, he leaned into the slope, paused, and removed his gun again, listening. But it was hopeless: the roar and bellow of the volcano was even louder here, and the wind howled ever more fiercely.

He crawled to the top of the ridge, into the stinging wind, and paused once again to reconnoiter. The exposed trail ran along the crest before turning and disappearing around a spike of frozen lava. He jumped to his feet, ran across the exposed ground, and took cover behind the lava, peering ahead. He could see now that a great chasm must lie to his right—no doubt the Sciara del Fuoco. The reddish glow coming up from it provided an excellent backdrop against which to identify a figure.

He edged around the lava spike, and the Sciara suddenly appeared on his right: a sheer cliff falling away into a steeply pitched chasm, like a huge cleft in the side of the island: half a mile broad, plunging precipitously into a churning, boiling sea hundreds of feet below. Heated air came roaring up the chasm, screaming diagonally over the ridge, carrying with it stinging particles of ash and clouds of sulfurous fumes. And now, in addition to the roar from the mountain, Pendergast could hear a new sound: the crackling and rumbling of huge blocks of living lava, some glowing red-hot, that came bounding down from the crater above, leaping and tumbling into the sea below, where they blossomed into dim white flowers.

He staggered forward into the tearing wind, finding his balance while compensating for the hellish force pushing him back from the brink of the cliff. He examined the ground, but all possible tracks had been scoured away by the wind. He sprinted along the ragged trail, taking cover behind old blocks of lava whenever possible, keeping his center of gravity low. The trail continued, still climbing the ridgeline. Ahead stood an enormous pile of lava blocks, an arrested rockfall, which the trail skirted around, making a sharp right toward the cliff's edge.

He crouched in the shelter of the lava fall, gun at the ready. If there was anyone on this trail, they would be directly ahead of him, at the edge of the cliff.

He spun around the edge of the rock, gun in both hands—and saw a terrifying sight.

At the very edge of the chasm, he could see two figures, silhouetted against the dull glow of the volcano. They were locked in a curious, almost passionate embrace. And yet these were not lovers—these were enemies, joined in mortal struggle, heedless of the wind, or the roar of the volcano, or the extreme peril of the cliff edge on which they stood.

"Constance!" he cried, racing forward. But even as he ran, they began to tip off balance, each raking and clawing at the other, each pulling the other into the abyss—

And then, with a silence worse than any cry, they were gone.

Pendergast rushed up to the edge, almost blown onto his back by the force of the wind. He dropped to his knees, shielding his eyes, trying to peer into the abyss. A thousand feet below, hardened blocks of dull red lava the size of houses rolled and bounced like pebbles, shedding clouds of orange sparks, the wind screaming up from the volcano's flanks like the wail of the collective damned. He remained on his knees, the wind whipping salt tears from his eyes.

He could barely comprehend what he had seen. It was incredible to him, an impossibility, that Constance—sheltered, fragile, confused Constance—could have pursued his brother to the very ends of the earth, driven him up this volcano, and flung herself into it with him . . .

He swiped savagely at his eyes, made a second attempt to peer down into the hellish cleft, in the faint hope that something, *anything*, might be left—and there, not two feet below him, he saw a hand, completely covered with blood, clutching at a small projection of rock with almost superhuman strength.

Diogenes.

And now he heard D'Agosta's voice in his head: *You realize there's only one way to take care of Diogenes. When the moment comes . . .*

Without a second thought, Pendergast reached down to save his brother, grasped the wrist with one hand and clutched the forearm with the other, and with a mighty heave leaned back, pulling him up and away from the lip of the inferno. A ragged, wild face appeared over the crest of the rock—not that of his brother, but of Constance Greene.

Seconds later, he had pulled her away from the brink. She rolled onto her back, her chest heaving, arms spread, ragged white dress whipping in the wind.

Pendergast bent over her. "Diogenes . . . ?" he managed to ask.

"He's *gone!*" A laugh tore from her bloodied lips and was instantly whisked away by the wind.

80

The waiting area for hearing room B consisted of an impromptu collection of seventies-era Bauhaus benches lining an anonymous hallway on the twenty-first floor of One Police Plaza. D'Agosta sat on one of these benches, breathing in the stale air of the hallway: the mingled smells of bleach and ammonia from the nearby men's room; stale perfume; perspiration; and old cigarette smoke, which had permeated the walls too deeply to ever be completely eradicated. Underlying all was the acrid, omnipresent tang of fear.

Fear, however, was the last thing on his own mind. D'Agosta was about to undergo a formal disciplinary hearing that would decide if he could ever serve in law enforcement again—and all he felt was a weary emptiness. For months, this trial had been hanging over his head like the sword of Damocles—and now, for better or worse, it was almost over.

Beside him, Thomas Shoulders, his union-appointed lawyer, shifted on the bench. "Anything else you'd like to review one last time?" he asked in his thin, reedy voice. "Your statement, or their likely line of questioning?"

D'Agosta shook his head. "Nothing more, thanks."

"The department advocate will be presenting the case for the NYPD. We might have caught a break there. Kagelman's tough but fair. He's old-school. The best approach is to play it straight: no evasions, no bull. Answer the questions with a simple yes or no, don't elaborate unless asked. Present yourself along the lines we discussed—a good cop caught in a bad situation, doing the best he could to see that justice was served. If we can keep it at that level, I'm guardedly optimistic."

Guardedly optimistic. Whether spoken by an airplane pilot, a surgeon, or one's own lawyer, the words were not exactly encouraging.

He thought back to that fateful day in the fall, when he had run into Pendergast at the Grove estate, tossing bread to the ducks. It was only six months ago, but what a long strange journey it had been . . .

"Holding up?" Shoulders asked.

D'Agosta glanced at his watch. "I just want the damn thing to be over with. I'm tired of sitting here, waiting for the axe to drop."

"You shouldn't think about it that way, Lieutenant. A disciplinary hearing is just like a trial in any other American court. You're innocent until proven guilty."

D'Agosta sighed, shifted disconsolately. And in so doing, he caught a glimpse of Captain Laura Hayward, walking down the busy corridor.

She was coming toward them with that measured, purposeful stride of hers, wearing a gray cashmere sweater and a pleated skirt of navy wool. Suddenly the drab corridor seemed charged with life. And yet the last thing he wanted was for her to see him like this: parked on a bench like some truant awaiting a whipping. Maybe she'd walk on, just walk on, like she'd done that day back in the police substation beneath Madison Square Garden.

But she did not walk on. She stopped before the bench, nodded nonchalantly to him and Shoulders.

"Hi," D'Agosta managed. He felt himself blushing with embarrassment and shame and felt furious for doing so.

"Hey, Vinnie," she replied in her dusky contralto. "Have a minute?"

There was a moment of stasis.

"Sure." He turned to Shoulders. "Could you spare me for a sec?"

"Don't go far—we're up soon."

D'Agosta followed Hayward down to a quieter section of the hallway. She paused, looking at him, one hand unconsciously smoothing down her skirt. Glancing at her shapely legs, D'Agosta felt his heart accelerate further. He searched his mind for something to say, came up with nothing.

Hayward, too, seemed uncharacteristically at a loss for words. Her face looked clouded, conflicted. She opened her handbag, fumbled in it a moment, closed it, tucked it under her arm. They stood there another moment in silence as police officers, technicians, and court personnel passed by.

"Are you here to give a statement?" D'Agosta finally asked.

"No. I gave my deposition over a month ago."

"Nothing more to say, then?"

"No."

A peculiar thrill went through D'Agosta as he realized the implications of this. *So she's kept quiet about my role in the Herkmoor breakout,* he thought. *She hasn't told anybody.*

"I got a call from an acquaintance in the Justice Department," she said. "The word's just come down. As far as the feds are concerned, Special Agent Pendergast has been formally cleared of all charges. Homicide's officially reopened the case on our end, and it looks as though we're going to drop all charges against him, too. Based on evidence retrieved from Diogenes Pendergast's valise, fresh warrants have been issued for Diogenes. Thought you'd want to know."

D'Agosta slumped with relief. "Thank God. So he's completely cleared."

"Of criminal charges, yes. But it's safe to say he hasn't made any new friends in the Bureau."

"Popularity never was Pendergast's strong suit."

Hayward smiled faintly. "He's been given a six-month leave. Whether requested by him or demanded by the Bureau, I don't know."

D'Agosta shook his head.

"I thought you might also like to hear about Special Agent Spencer Coffey."

"Oh?"

"In addition to royally screwing up the Pendergast case, he got embroiled in some kind of scandal at Herkmoor. Seems he was busted down to GS-11 and had a notice of censure placed in his jacket. They've reassigned him to the North Dakota field office in Black Rock."

"He's gonna need a new pair of long underwear," D'Agosta said.

Hayward smiled, and an awkward silence settled over them again.

The deputy commissioner of trials approached them from the elevator bank, along with the department special prosecutor. They passed by D'Agosta and Hayward, nodding distantly, then turned and proceeded into the courtroom.

"With Pendergast cleared, you should be, too," Hayward said.

D'Agosta looked down at his hands. "It's a different bureaucracy."

"Yes, but when—"

Abruptly she stopped. D'Agosta looked up to see Glen Singleton walking down the hall, immaculately dressed as usual. Captain Singleton was officially still D'Agosta's boss and was there, no doubt, to testify. When he saw Hayward, he paused in surprise.

"Captain Hayward," he said stiffly. "What are you doing here?"

"I came to watch the proceedings," she replied.

Singleton frowned. "A disciplinary hearing is not a spectator sport."

"I'm aware of that."

"You've already been deposed. Your showing up here in person, without being called to provide fresh information, may imply . . ." Singleton hesitated.

D'Agosta flushed at the insinuation. He stole a glance at Hayward and was surprised by what he saw. The cloudiness had left her face, and she suddenly looked calm. It was as if, after struggling for a long time, she had reached some private decision.

"Yes?" she asked mildly.

"Might imply a lack of impartiality on your part."

"Why, Glen," Hayward said, "don't you wish the best for Vinnie, here?"

Now it was Singleton's turn to color. "Of course. Of course I do. In fact, that's why I'm here—to bring to the attention of the prosecutor certain new developments that have recently come to our attention. It's just that we wouldn't want any hint of any improper . . . well, *influence.*"

"Too late," she replied briskly. "I've already been influenced."

And then—very deliberately—she clasped D'Agosta's hand in her own.

Singleton stared at them for a moment. He opened his mouth, closed it again, at a loss for words. Finally he gave D'Agosta a sudden smile and laid a hand on his shoulder. "See you in court, Lieutenant," he said, giving the word *lieutenant* special emphasis. Then he turned and was gone.

"What was that supposed to mean?" D'Agosta asked.

"If I know Glen, I'd say you've got a friend in court."

D'Agosta felt his heart accelerate again. Despite the imminent ordeal, he suddenly felt absurdly happy. It was as if a great weight had just been lifted from him: a weight he hadn't even been fully conscious he was carrying.

He turned toward her in a rush. "Listen, Laura—"

"No. *You* listen." She wrapped her other hand around his, squeezed it tightly. "It doesn't matter what happens in that room. Do you understand me, Vinnie? Because whatever happens, happens to both of us. We're in this together."

He swallowed. "I love you, Laura Hayward."

At that moment, the door of the courtroom opened and the court clerk called his name. Thomas Shoulders rose from the bench, caught D'Agosta's gaze, nodded.

Hayward gave D'Agosta's hand a final squeeze. "Come on, big boy," she said, smiling. "It's showtime."

81

Afternoon sun bronzed the hills of the Hudson Valley and turned the wide, slow-moving river into an expanse of brilliant aquamarine. The forests that covered Sugarloaf Mountain and Breakneck Ridge were just leafing out in new bloom, and the entire Highlands wore a feathery mantle of spring.

Nora Kelly sat in a deck chair on the broad porch of the Feversham Clinic, looking down over Cold Spring, the Hudson River, and the red brick buildings of West Point beyond. Her husband prowled back and forth at the edge of the porch, now and then gazing out over the vista, other times darting glances up at the genteel lines of the private hospital.

"It makes me nervous, being back here," he muttered. "You know, Nora, I haven't been in this place since I was a patient here myself. Oh, God. I don't know if I've ever told you, but when the weather changes, I can sometimes still feel an ache in my back where the Surgeon—"

"You've told me, Bill," she said with mock weariness. "Many times."

The turning of a knob, the soft squeak of hinges, and a door opened onto the porch. A nurse in crisp whites stuck out her head. "You can come in now," she said. "She's waiting for you in the west parlor."

Nora and Smithback followed the nurse into the building and down a long corridor. "How is she?" Smithback asked the nurse.

"Much improved, thank goodness. We were all so worried for her—

such a dear thing. And she's getting better every day. Even so, she gets tired easily: you'll have to restrict your visit to fifteen minutes."

"The *dear thing*," Smithback whispered in Nora's ear. She poked him playfully in the ribs.

The west parlor was a large, semicircular room that reminded Nora of an Adirondack lodge: polished ceiling beams, pine wainscoting, paper-birch furniture. Oils of sylvan landscapes hung on the walls. A merry fire leaped and crackled in the massive stone fireplace.

And there—propped in a wheelchair in the center of it all—sat Margo Green.

"Margo," said Nora, and stopped, almost afraid to speak. Beside her, she heard Smithback draw in his breath sharply.

The Margo Green who sat before them was a mere shadow of the feisty woman who had been both academic rival and friend to her at the museum. She was frighteningly thin, and her white skin lay like tissue paper over her veins. Her movements were slow and considered, like someone long unfamiliar with the use of their limbs. And yet her brown hair was rich and glossy, and in her eye was the same spark of life Nora well recalled. Diogenes Pendergast had sent her to a dark and dangerous place—had almost ended her life—but she was on her way back now.

"Hello, you two," she said in a thin, sleepy voice. "What day is it?"

"It's Saturday," Nora said. "April 12."

"Oh, good. I hoped it was still Saturday." She smiled.

The nurse came in and bustled around Margo a moment, propping her up more comfortably in the wheelchair. Then she walked around the room, opening curtains and fluffing pillows before leaving them again. Shafts of radiant light streamed into the parlor, falling over Margo's head and shoulders and gilding her like an angel. Which in a way, Nora thought, she was: having been brought almost to the brink of death by an unusual cocktail of drugs administered to her by Diogenes.

"We brought you something, Margo," Smithback said, reaching into his coat and bringing out a manila envelope. "We thought you might get a kick out of it."

Margo took it, opened it slowly. "Why, it's a copy of my first issue of *Museology!*"

"Look inside, it's been signed by every curator of the Anthropology Department."

"Even Charlie Prine?" Margo's eyes twinkled.

Nora laughed. "Even Prine."

They pulled two seats up beside the wheelchair and sat down.

"The place is just plain *dull* without you, Margo," Nora said. "You have to hurry up and get well."

"That's right," said Smithback, smiling, his irrepressible good humor returning. "The old pile needs someone to shake it up from time to time, raise some fossil dust."

Margo laughed quietly. "From what I've been reading, the last thing the museum needs right now is more controversy. Is it true four people died in the crush at that Egyptian opening?"

"Yes," Nora said. "And another sixty were injured, a dozen of them severely."

She exchanged glances with Smithback. The story that had come out in the two weeks since the opening was that a glitch in the system software caused the sound-and-light show to go out of control, in turn triggering a panic. The truth—that it could have been much, much worse—was so far known only to a select few in the museum and in law enforcement circles.

"Is it true the director was among the injured?" Margo asked.

Nora nodded. "Collopy suffered a seizure of some kind. He's under psychiatric observation at New York Hospital, but he's expected to make a full recovery."

This was true—as far as it went—but of course it wasn't the full story. Collopy, among several others, had fallen victim to Diogenes's sound-and-light show, driven half psychotic by the laser pulsing and the low-frequency audio waves. The same might have happened to Nora had she not closed her eyes and covered her ears. As it was, she had suffered nightmares for a week. Pendergast and the others had stopped the show before it could run its full course and inflict permanent damage: and as a result, the prognosis was excellent for Collopy and the others—much better than for the unfortunate tech, Lipper.

Nora shifted in her chair. Someday she would tell Margo everything—but not today. The woman still had a lot of recovery ahead of her.

"What do you think it means for the museum?" Margo asked. "This tragedy at the opening, coming on the heels of the diamond theft?"

Nora shook her head. "At first everybody assumed it was the final straw, especially since the mayor's wife was among the injured. But it turns out that just the opposite has happened. Thanks to all the controversy, the Tomb of Senef is the hottest show in town. Requests for ticket reservations have been pouring in at an unbelievable rate. I even saw somebody hawking *I Survived the Curse* T-shirts on Broadway this morning."

"So they're going to reopen the tomb?" Margo asked.

Smithback nodded. "Fast-tracking it, too. Most of the artifacts were spared. They hope to have it up and running within the month."

"Our new Egyptologist is recasting the show," Nora said. "She's revising the original script, removing some of the cheesier special effects but keeping much of the sound-and-light show intact. She's a great person, wonderful to work with, funny, unpretentious—we're lucky to have her."

"The news reports mentioned some FBI agent as instrumental in the rescue," Margo said. "That wouldn't happen to be Agent Pendergast, by any chance?"

"How did you guess?" Nora asked.

"Because Pendergast always manages to get into the thick of things."

"You're telling me," Smithback said, smile fading. Nora noticed him unconsciously massaging the hand that had been burned by acid.

The nurse appeared in the doorway. "Margo, I'll need to take you back to your room in another five minutes."

"Okay." She turned back to them. "I suppose he's been haunting the museum ever since, asking questions, intimidating bureaucrats, and making a nuisance of himself."

"Actually, no," Nora said. "He disappeared right after the opening. Nobody has seen or heard from him since."

"Really? How strange."

"Yes, it is," Nora said. "It's very strange indeed."

82

In late May, on the island of Capraia, two people—a man and a woman—sat on a terrace attached to a neat whitewashed house overlooking the Mediterranean. The terrace stood near the edge of a bluff. Below the bluff, surf crawled around pillars of black volcanic rock, wreathed in circling gulls. Beyond lay a blue immensity, stretching as far as the eye could see.

On the terrace, a table of weather-beaten wood was spread with simple food: a round of coarse bread, a plate of small salamis, a bottle of olive oil and a dish of olives, glasses of white wine. The scent of flowering lemons lay heavy in the air, mingling with the perfume of wild rosemary and sea salt. Along the hillside above the terrace, rows of grapevines were shooting out of coiling tendrils of green. The only sound was the faint cry of gulls and the breeze that rustled through a trellis of purple bougainvillea.

The two sat, sipping wine and speaking in low voices. The clothes the woman wore—battered canvas pants and an old work shirt—stood in contrast to her finely cut features and the glossy mahogany hair that spilled down her back. The man's dress was as formal as the woman's was informal: black suit of Italian cut, crisp white shirt, understated tie.

Both were watching a third person—a beautiful young woman in a pale yellow dress—who was strolling aimlessly through an olive grove beside the vineyard. From time to time, the young woman stopped to pick a flower, then continued on, twisting the flower in her hands, plucking it to pieces in an absentminded way.

"I think I understand everything now," the woman on the terrace was saying, "except there's one thing you didn't explain: how in the world did you remove the GPS anklet without setting off the alarm?"

The man made a dismissive gesture. "Child's play. The plastic cuff had a wire inside it that completed a circuit. The idea was that, in removing the cuff, you'd need to cut the wire—thus breaking the circuit and triggering an alarm."

"So what did you do?"

"I scratched away the plastic in two places along the circuit to expose the wire. Then I attached a loop of wire to each spot, cut the bracelet in between—and took it off. Elementary, my dear Viola."

"Ah, *je vois!* But where did you get the loop of wire?"

"I made it with foil gum wrappers. I was, unfortunately, obligated to masticate the gum, since I needed it to affix the wire."

"And the gum? Where did you get that?"

"From my acquaintance in the cell next door, a most talented young man who opened a whole new world for me—that of rhythm and percussion. He gave me one of his precious packs of gum in return for a small favor I did him."

"What was that?"

"I listened."

The woman smiled. "What goes around comes around."

"Perhaps."

"Speaking of prison, I can't tell you how thrilled I was to get your wire. I was afraid you wouldn't be permitted to leave the country for ages."

"Diogenes left behind enough evidence in his valise to clear me of the murders. That left only three crimes of substance: stealing Lucifer's Heart; kidnapping the gemologist, Kaplan; and breaking out of prison. Neither the museum nor Kaplan cared to press charges. As for the prison, they would like nothing more than to forget their security was fallible. And so here I am."

He paused to sip his wine. "That leads me to a question of my own. How is it that you didn't recognize Menzies as my brother? You'd seen him in disguise before."

"I've wondered about that," Viola replied. "I saw him as two different people, but neither one was Menzies."

There was a silence. Viola let her gaze drift again toward the younger woman in the olive grove. "She's a most unusual girl."

"Yes," the man replied. "More unusual than you could even imagine."

They continued to watch the younger woman drift aimlessly through the twisted trees, like a restless ghost.

"How did she come to be your ward?"

"It's a long and rather complicated story, Viola. Someday I'll tell you— I promise."

The woman smiled, sipped her wine. For a moment, silence settled over them.

"How do you like the new vintage?" she asked. "I broke it out especially for the occasion."

"As delightful as the old one. It's from your grapes, I assume?"

"It is. I picked them myself, and I even stomped out the juice with my own two feet."

"I don't know whether to be honored or horrified." He picked up a small salami, examined it, quartered it with a paring knife. "Did you shoot the boar for these, as well?"

Viola smiled. "No. I had to draw the line somewhere." She looked at him, her gaze growing concerned. "You're making a valiant effort to be amusing, Aloysius."

"Is that all it appears to be—an effort? I am sorry."

"You're preoccupied. And you don't look especially good. Things aren't going well for you, are they?"

He hesitated a moment. Then, very slowly, he shook his head.

"I wish there was something I could do."

"Your company is tonic enough, Viola."

She smiled again, her gaze returning to the young woman. "Strange to think that murder—and there's really no other word for it, is there?—could have been such a cathartic experience for her."

"Yes. Even so, I fear she remains a damaged human being." He hesitated. "I realize now it was a mistake to keep her shut up in the house in New York. She needed to get out and see the world. Diogenes exploited that need. I made a mistake there, too—allowing her to be vulnerable to him. The guilt, and the shame, are with me always."

"Have you spoken of this to her? Your feelings, I mean. It might be good for both of you."

"I've tried. More than once, in fact. But she violently rejects any possibility of a discussion on that topic."

"Perhaps that will change with time." Viola shook out her hair. "Where do you plan to go next?"

"We've already toured France, Spain, and Italy—she seems interested in the ruins of ancient Rome. I've been doing everything I can to take her mind off what happened. Even so, she's preoccupied and distant—as you can see."

"I think what Constance needs most is direction."

"What sort of direction?"

"You know. The kind of direction a father would give a daughter."

Pendergast shifted in his chair, ill at ease. "I've never had a daughter."

"You've got one now. And you know what? I think this whole Grand Tour you've been taking her on isn't working."

"The same thought had occurred to me."

"You need healing—*both* of you. You need to get over this, together."

Pendergast was silent for a moment. "I've been thinking about retreating from the world for a time."

"Oh?"

"There's a monastery I once spent some time at. A very secluded one, in western Tibet, exceedingly remote. I thought we might go there."

"How long would you be gone?"

"As long as it takes." He took a sip of wine. "A few months, I'd imagine."

"That might be most beneficial. And it brings me to something else. What's next . . . for us?"

He slowly put down the glass. "Everything."

There was a brief silence. "How do you mean?" Her voice was low.

"Everything is open to us," said Pendergast slowly. "When I have settled Constance, then it will be our turn."

She reached out and touched his hand. "I can help you with Constance. Bring her to Egypt this winter. I'll be resuming work in the Valley of the Kings. She could assist me. It's a rugged, adventurous life, working as an archaeologist."

"Are you serious?"

"Of course."

Pendergast smiled. "Excellent. I think she would like that."

"And you?"

"I suppose . . . I would like that, too."

Constance had drifted closer, and they fell silent.

"What do you think of Capraia?" Viola called over as the girl stepped onto the terrazzo.

"Very nice." She walked to the balustrade, tossed over a mangled flower, and rested her arms on the warm stone, staring out to sea.

Viola smiled, nudged at Pendergast. "Tell her the plan," she whispered. "I'll be inside."

Pendergast stood and walked over to Constance. She remained at the railing, looking out to sea, the air stirring her long hair.

"Viola's offered to take you to Egypt this winter, to assist her with her excavations in the Valley of the Kings. You could not only learn about history, you could touch it with your own hands."

Constance shook her head, still staring out to sea. A long silence followed, filled by the distant cries of the seagulls, the muffled whisper of the surf below.

Pendergast drew closer. "You need to let go, Constance," he said. "You're safe now: Diogenes is dead."

"I know," she replied.

"Then you know there's nothing more to fear. All that's past. Finished."

Still she said nothing, her blue eyes reflecting the vast azure emptiness of the sea. Finally she turned toward him. "No, it isn't," she said.

Pendergast looked back at her, frowning. "What do you mean?"

For a moment, she did not answer.

"What do you mean?" he repeated.

At last Constance spoke. And when she did, her voice was so weary, so cold, that it chilled him despite the warm May sunshine.

"I'm pregnant."

THE PRESTON-CHILD NOVELS
A WORD FROM THE AUTHORS

We are frequently asked in what order, if any, our books should be read.

The question is most applicable to the novels that feature Special Agent Pendergast. Although most of our novels are written to be stand-alone stories, very few have turned out to be set in discrete worlds. Quite the opposite: it seems the more novels we write together, the more "bleed-through" occurs between the characters and events that comprise them all. Characters from one book might appear in a later one, for example, or events in one novel could spill into a subsequent one. In short, we have slowly been building up a universe in which all the characters in our novels, and the experiences they have, take place and overlap.

Reading the novels in a particular order, however, is rarely necessary. We have worked hard to make almost all of our books into stories that can be enjoyed without reading any of the others, with a few exceptions.

Here, then, is our own breakdown of our books.

THE PENDERGAST NOVELS

Relic was our first novel, and the first to feature Special Agent Pendergast, and as such has no antecedents.

Reliquary is the sequel to *Relic*.

The Cabinet of Curiosities is our third Pendergast novel, and it stands completely on its own.

Still Life with Crows is next. It is also a self-contained story (although people curious about Constance Greene will find a little information here as well as in *The Cabinet of Curiosities*).

Brimstone is next, and is the first novel in what we informally call the Pendergast trilogy. Although it is also self-contained, it does pick up some threads begun in *The Cabinet of Curiosities*.

Dance of Death is the middle novel of the Pendergast trilogy. While it can be read as a stand-alone book, readers may wish to read *Brimstone* before *Dance of Death*.

The Book of the Dead is the last, culminating novel in the Pendergast trilogy. For greatest enjoyment, the reader should read at least *Dance of Death* first.

THE NON-PENDERGAST NOVELS

We have also written a number of self-contained tales of adventure that do not feature Special Agent Pendergast. They are, by date of publication, *Mount Dragon*, *Riptide*, *Thunderhead*, and *The Ice Limit*.

Thunderhead introduces the archaeologist Nora Kelly, who appears in all the later Pendergast novels. *The Ice Limit* introduces Eli Glinn, who appears in *Dance of Death* and *The Book of the Dead*.

In closing, we want to assure our readers that this note is not intended as some kind of onerous syllabus, but rather as an answer to the question *In what order should I read your novels?* We feel extraordinarily fortunate that there are people like you who enjoy reading our novels as much as we enjoy writing them.

With our best wishes,

REFERENCES

Original Russian poetry on page 169 is from "Heart's Memory of Sun" by Anna Akhmatova, 1911. Translation by Stanley Kunitz © 1967–1973.

Original poetry on page 173 is from "She" by Theodore Roethke © 1958.

Original Italian poetry on pages 243, 406, and 414 is from "La Leggenda di Teodorico" (The Legend of Theodoric) by Giosuè Carducci, 1896. Translations on pages 406 and 414 by Douglas J. Preston © 2006.

Original lyrics on page 266 are from *Aida*. Opera written by Giuseppe Verdi from Italian libretto by Antonio Ghislanzoni; first performed 1871. Translation by Douglas J. Preston © 2006.

Original poetry on page 385 is from "Metamorphoses" by Ovid, 43 BC to circa AD 17. Translation under the direction of Sir Samuel Garth, 1717.

Original poetry on page 386 is from "Metamorphoses" by Ovid, 43 BC to circa AD 17. Translation by Horace Gregory © 1958.

Original French poetry on page 391 is from "Les Fleurs du Mal" by Charles Baudelaire, 1857.

Original Italian poetry on page 393 is from "Inferno" from *The Divine Comedy* by Dante Alighieri, 1308–1320.

Original poetry on page 394 and page 402 is from "The Hollow Men" by T.S. Eliot © 1925.

Original Greek quote on page 400 is from "Agamemnon," part one of *The Oresteia* by Aeschylus. First performed 458 BC.

Original quote on page 409 is from *Hamlet* by William Shakespeare, 1600–1602.

Original poetry on page 417 is from "To His Coy Mistress" by Andrew Marvell, 1649–1660.

A SPECIES OF REVENGE

Marjorie Eccles

HarperCollins*Publishers*

Collins Crime
An imprint of HarperCollins*Publishers*
77–85 Fulham Palace Road, London W6 8JB

First published in Great Britain
in 1996 by Collins Crime

1 3 5 7 9 10 8 6 4 2

© Marjorie Eccles 1996

The Author asserts the moral right to be
identified as the author of this work

A catalogue record for this book is
available from the British Library

ISBN 0 00 232616 7

Set in Meridien and Bodoni

Photoset by Rowland Phototypesetting Ltd
Bury St Edmunds, Suffolk
Printed and bound in Great Britain by
Caledonian International Book Manufacturing Ltd, Glasgow

PART I

The house had a bad feeling again.

It was an atmosphere hard to describe. It hung on the air in spider's webs, invisible until you felt it clinging to your face; or it waited for you behind closed doors, and as you entered a room it curled to the ceiling, thick as smoke. It was unclean, like a fog seeping in around the edges of the windowpanes . . .

But no, it didn't come from outside.

It came from the unspoken tensions of the occupants, from within, from emotions and resentments bottled up for years and about to erupt again like some evil genie. It was there in the silences and the covert glances, in the sum of what was known, and remembered.

Patti Ryman is whistling as she pushes her bike to the summit of the hill, ready to deliver her newspapers on Saturday morning.

'A whistling woman and a crowing hen, Will bring the devil from his den,' her granddad used to say. Patti grins. She isn't scared of the devil because she knows he doesn't exist. It isn't that which makes her hurry to get the deliveries to the two old houses over and done with. First, to Edwina Lodge, with its familiar 'For Sale' notice still in the garden but now with a red 'SOLD' sticker plastered across it, and the Guardian *ordered to start on Monday. Having delivered the other papers there, she leaves her bike against the wall near the shrubbery inside the gates, and goes on to the next house, Simla, with the* Independent *for Miss Kendrick and* The Times *for her brother, being careful not to tear these as they're pushed through the letter-box: Miss Kendrick teaches maths at Patti's school, she'll be her form tutor when the new school year starts in a few days' time, and Patti is more afraid of her than any old devil who may be hanging around. The brother, she's never seen, only heard of, so he doesn't bother her.*

No, it's something more than either Miss Kendrick or the devil which causes her to hurry through the dark shrubs and trees surrounding both houses, that makes her want to look back over her shoulder, as if something nasty is lurking in the undergrowth, that starts her heart jumping into her mouth.

She has every cause to be uneasy, though not just now.

She turns with relief into Ellington Close, the cul-de-sac of modern houses separating the two bigger ones, although, for a different reason, she never feels entirely comfortable there, either.

1

It could have been a surprise to nobody, thought Sarah Wilmot, a few hours later, gazing round the kitchen with disbelief, that the house had remained unsold for so long, and it was typical of her brother-in-law's state of mind that he should have been the sucker to buy it. Though 'sucker' wasn't a word that normally sprang to mind to describe Dermot.

Bought it he had, however. As if by taking a new job in a new place, by leaving the bright, modern new-town house and saddling himself with this Victorian monstrosity, by burying himself here in this backwater on the edge of the Black Country, he could make himself sufficiently miserable to forget what had happened. But it was barely three months since Lisa had died, and no one had yet got over the shock, least of all Dermot.

Except, to some extent, the children. Children were resilient. They couldn't sustain misery and grief forever – and who would want them to? Bereft and bewildered at first, they were gradually learning to come to terms with the situation. Playing outside now, oblivious of the sultry heat, discovering the new garden, two brown-haired little girls, Lucy leading as usual, red-cheeked in her excitement, Allie quieter, stopping occasionally to stand and stare, to take it all in. Lucy was all Dermot's daughter, in looks, charm and temperament, at nearly ten, an energetic and confident child. But Allie?

Younger than Lucy by eighteen months, she was a different matter altogether. She'd accepted news of the move meekly,

unlike Lucy, who'd kicked up a fuss about leaving her school-friends and Granny and Grandpa, but had soon changed her mind when the idea of a new school and new friends was presented to her, and had then hardly been able to wait until they moved in. With Allie, it was hard to tell.

Now, in some indefinable way, she already looked more at home in the garden than Lucy did, as if she belonged there, standing underneath the pear tree, with the hot breeze of a threatening thunderstorm blowing her cotton dress against her thin, tense body.

The garden was decidedly the nicest thing about Edwina Lodge. Secluded and large, running down into thick, long grass at its end, spiked with foxgloves and overhung with big trees from the small wood beyond. The trees were heavy-leafed and lax with the heat of late summer, the garden overgrown, apart from a small tended area adjacent to the house, but all of a piece: a pear tree simply asking for a swing to hang from it, a broken-down pergola burdened with a rampant rose, tile-edged, blue-brick paths, a vegetable garden. Large enough to grow their own vegetables, said Dermot, airily optimistic, he who'd never done more than push a reluctant lawn mower on Sunday mornings – when he was there – in Milton Keynes. Sarah visualized tidy rows of peas and beans. Courgettes, herbs, lettuces and salad onions. Maybe some rocket . . .

No chance! The arrangement was that she wouldn't be here any longer than it took to do her duty. Then back to her job in London, and concerts, exhibitions, theatres, shops, sophisticated dinners *à deux*. Simon. Dark-haired, guardsman-tall, immaculate, urbane. More than comfortably off. Everything a girl could want, in fact. She was very lucky, it went without saying.

She ran a hand through the short swing of thick, sun-streaked brown hair and went back with determination to her lists.

Ominously long, those lists, but it was a matter of principle that she should do as much as she could in the couple of weeks or so she was scheduled to stay: just until the girls

had settled into school, getting the house shipshape, and finding for Dermot a housekeeper who would be willing to face up to the horrors of the house and, more specifically, the kitchen. The Aga was the most up-to-date piece of equipment there and was unquestionably prewar, second if not first. Sarah made a face at it, refused to contemplate the geyser over the sink and the pipe-festooned corners, abandoned it and took herself to the drawing room, via the dark and echoing hall which, with its cold, Minton-tiled floor and depressing stained glass, was no better.

Given time, money, know-how – none of which Dermot had – something might be done with the drawing room. The *pièce de résistance* of 'this valuable part-investment property' as the house agents' blurb had it – the investment being that part of the house already split up into three self-contained flats and which was, theoretically, to finance the whole. Huge and high-ceilinged, with elaborate plasterwork and a heavy, ornate black marble fireplace, the drawing room was solid and handsome, needing little more than a lick of paint and new wallpaper – but Dermot would need to think seriously about new furniture. Lisa's light, pretty things would fit in here no better than Lisa herself would have done. Only too easily could Sarah imagine her sister's reactions to the very idea of living here at all: turning her eyes up comically at the notion of such a place as home, at its size, at the cavernous kitchen and the dark, narrow staircases, of which there were two, plus the ones to the attics and cellars. Death traps, all of them.

And yet, heavily pregnant, tripping over the loose belt of her dressing gown, Lisa had lost her footing on the upper treads of the wide, well-lit, open staircase in their modern house in Milton Keynes, fallen from top to bottom and broken her neck.

Another of those swift, futile moments of pain and anger at the unnecessary waste, the misery of it, touched Sarah with a cold finger. She hugged herself, despite the heat.

A clock somewhere chimed a distant, silvery four. Dermot had been gone three-quarters of an hour, inspecting the flats

with Mrs Burgoyne, receiving last-minute instructions. Dermot, a landlord!

'Don't be spiky, Sarah,' he'd said, not appreciative of opposition at any time, particularly not now. 'Mrs Burgoyne's convinced me the flats are a worthwhile proposition, and very little trouble.'

It had seemed to Sarah, and her parents too, that the whole enterprise was fraught with trouble, and this was one of the reasons why she'd volunteered to help Dermot over the settling-in period – although he might have cause to rethink his good luck, she thought, a quick bubble of laughter sending the shivers packing, given that housekeeping wasn't exactly one of her more conspicuous talents. But if she hadn't volunteered, her mother would certainly have felt compelled to do so, foregoing the cruise which Sarah's father had booked to mark his retirement, and to which they'd looked forward for years. A holiday which her mother so desperately needed, after the shock and heartbreak and subsequent upheaval of Lisa's death.

Sarah's whole warm, generous nature had rebelled at such needless sacrifice, and she'd said, impulsively, 'I'll go,' earning both Dermot's and her father's gratitude. And, unfortunately, Simon's disapproval.

'The whole scheme's preposterous – and what am I going to do without you? In the office, not to mention otherwise?'

Sarah told herself that this apparent self-interest hid his real concern, and the 'otherwise' pleased her, but she stuck to her guns, reminding him that Devora Vine had supposedly been trained to take over in an emergency – and had been breathlessly waiting for just such an opportunity to prove she could – though she thought this last better not said, unwise to put thoughts into his head about the crush the Divine Devora had on him.

Simon owned and ran a glossy art and antiques magazine, a rather chichi, expensive quarterly with a small but steady, even growing, circulation. Its success wasn't surprising; he worked hard and was extremely knowledgeable in the field,

having grown up with a silver spoon in his mouth, surrounded by the sort of things he wrote about.

She promised to stay no more than a few weeks, until the children were settled into school. They'd only be apart for two or three weekends, four at most.

'Or you could come up here and stay,' she'd suggested.

'I could.' His tone implied that the possibility was remote. As if Lavenstock were Alaska or Australia, and not barely an hour and a half from London by InterCity. 'Well, maybe,' he added after some consideration, and she'd chalked up a small victory, seeing the smile he allowed himself. 'You know I can deny you nothing, my lovely.'

An exaggeration, on both counts, that she let pass. She'd been his personal assistant on the magazine for four years, and the possibility of a directorship was in the air, though an association of a different kind was more what he had in mind. Sarah suspected he was using the one as a carrot for the other, to try and make her see the sense of becoming Mrs Simon Asshe. Well, it was time she settled down, everyone thought so, including Sarah. Thirty-five was on the horizon. So why the hesitation?

'I can see you're set on going,' Simon had finally admitted, seeing the predicament and reluctantly conceding the reasons for her offer, 'so it's no use my trying to dissuade you. You must do what you have to – only don't make it too long, out there in the sticks. I fear Dermot could only too easily become used to you as an unpaid housekeeper.'

Sarah might have feared this, too, had she not already been well-armed against Dermot's admitted tendency to make use of people, especially his womenfolk: first, of his pretty Irish mother who, being as adept as he was at withdrawing from an unsatisfactory situation and with no intention of being burdened with motherless grandchildren, had circumspectly taken herself off to live permanently in Marbella; and thereafter of Mrs Wilmot, his mother-in-law. He was on the surface easy-going and optimistic, full of good ideas, which other people unfortunately tended to get landed with – though he was generally thought well-meaning and was therefore

9

forgiven, until patience wore thin. He had reason to be grateful to a great many people, though in the end, underneath the lazy, blue-eyed, inherited Celtic charm, Dermot was quite capable of looking after his own affairs. The Voss side of his nature, from his German father, perhaps. When you thought about that, it wasn't really all that astonishing that he'd taken this unprecedented step, made the decision to do it off his own bat, and carried it through all of a rush, against all the opposition. And surely understandable that he should be so devastated by Lisa's untimely end that he could no longer bear to stay in the place where they'd been so happy together.

She could hear the children's voices, clear on the heavy air as they played, blissfully unaware of the changes that lay ahead of them. Nothing would ever be the same for them again. Life with a daddy whom they'd hitherto only infrequently seen, apart from flying visits home, one who wasn't going to find such a drastic change in his lifestyle easy, either. And, in between, being looked after by a strange housekeeper.

Dermot had been a TV cameraman, our man in whatever trouble spots of the world demanded his presence, alighting in England only long enough to spoil the girls outrageously before leaving on yet another assignment. It had been an unsatisfactory sort of family life, though Lisa, loyal and good, had never complained. Well, Dermot had now been thrust into the realities and responsibilities of parenthood with a vengeance and, to do him justice, he'd faced up squarely to what had to be done, wangled himself out of his contract with the BBC and found himself a job working with a corporate film and video company. But how long would this satisfy him, after the excitements and dangers of his previous job?

Footsteps at last sounded on the stairs, Dermot with Mrs Burgoyne. The erstwhile owner of the house, she was a tiny, white-haired old lady with a soft pink and white, powdery skin and eyes like an electric drill. 'No trouble at all, the tenants,' she was repeating her assurances as they came into

10

the drawing room with even Dermot, who was only just above middle height, appearing to tower over her. 'Because, of course, I've always made sure, as you must, I warn you, Mr Voss, to take only the *right* sort of person in to Edwina Lodge.' And she went on to detail, for Sarah's information, what Dermot already knew about his tenants.

The house was split more or less right down the middle, one half for the owners, one for the tenants. Upstairs, on the first floor, lived Mr Pitt, a librarian. Below him was the Baverstocks' flat – he was employed in the borough accounts department, and she ran a wholefood shop in Folgate Street. Unexceptionable, all of them.

And the attic-floor flat, inquired Sarah, the one where the huge window had been built out over the roof? The eyesore, she added to herself, the incongruity stuck like a blister to the side of the property, doing its bit to add to the ugliness of the house. There was a slight pause. Oh, that was Mr Fitzallan's furnished flat. The window had been added many years ago, by a previous owner of Edwina Lodge, simply for the view, which was magnificent. On a clear day you could see the Rotunda in Birmingham.

'And that reminds me, Mr Voss,' Mrs Burgoyne went on swiftly, 'did you pull that door smartly to, as I told you? I didn't hear you, come to think of it, and if you didn't, it won't have closed properly. Mr Fitzallan won't be pleased to come home and find his front door wide open, I can tell you. It's these little things that count.'

Dermot, restless, chafing under the weight of all this instruction, running his hand through his black curls, smiled disarmingly and admitted ruefully that he couldn't remember.

'I'll go up and check,' Sarah offered, looking at her watch. 'You'd better get off, hadn't you, if you want to get Mrs Burgoyne to the station to catch her train?'

Dermot flashed her a relieved smile. 'I'll be about half an hour, then I'll take you and the children straight to the hotel – we're staying at the Saracen's Head for a couple of nights,

Mrs Burgoyne. An early night for all of us seems indicated in view of what we've to face in the next few days.'

'Monday's when your furniture arrives, isn't it?' Mrs Burgoyne asked, eyeing Sarah, clearly not equating a short skirt and bare legs with someone capable of dealing with the removal, as though she would dearly have loved to superintend it personally to prevent anything going wrong. But finally, with a last sharp look round, though with what seemed to Sarah an ultimately unregretful eye, she departed with Dermot for the train which was to carry her to retirement in her south-coast bungalow.

Sarah checked that the children were still safely and happily occupied – Allie, for one, was dreamily accident prone, seeming destined to go through life permanently sticking-plastered somewhere about her person; a recently broken collar bone and a small chip off one of her permanent front teeth from a fall off her bicycle was present testimony to this.

She ran up the two flights of stairs to the attic flat, to find its front door was, after all, closed. But when she leaned her hand against it, it gave against her weight, and swung open. Before giving it the required slam, natural curiosity made her step forward a few paces and take a look round the room. Mrs Burgoyne certainly hadn't spread herself here with regard to the furniture. The few cheap and unmistakably second-hand, unrelated pieces added nothing to the room's character, nondescript with all-over, porridge-coloured paint and a curtainless window. This wasn't, however, the big, ugly protruding window at the side, with its vaunted view. Evidently, this room in which she was standing was the first of two rooms, and the window in question was in the second one, through the opposite door. She felt a sudden urge to see it for herself, curious to know whether you really could see as far as the Birmingham Bull Ring . . . She walked across and tried the door handle.

'It's locked.'

She whipped round. A man stood in the doorway. Mr Fitzallan, I presume. She had a feeling he'd been standing

12

there for some time, and she was distinctly put out to know that guilty colour had flown to her cheeks, to hear herself stumbling apologies like an adolescent schoolgirl. He had, after all, given his permission for the flat to be inspected. If not by her.

'I – didn't hear you coming up the stairs.'

He inclined his head, not deigning to reply to this fatuously obvious statement. Mrs Burgoyne's warning had conjured up an elderly fusspot, a cantankerous, intolerant person. Looking at him, she saw no reason to change her opinion, except in regard to age. In his mid-forties, maybe, over six foot, wide-shouldered with tousled dark hair, wearing a beautiful slate-blue silk shirt and an unstructured suit in cream linen, polished loafers. Casually cool and elegant in a loose-limbed way, making her aware of every crease and crumple collected on the hot, sweaty journey here.

Boardroom and top management, every inch of him – and living *here*?

Sarah looked into a face as dark as the thunderheads piling up outside, saw a square jaw, a strong nose, felt a sense of harsh purpose. Their eyes met and held, hers wide and brown, his a brilliant and unexpected grey under lowering brows. For an instant, she thought she saw a hint of trouble behind them, in the lines of pain drawn down towards the mouth, but quickly decided it was simply general disagreeableness.

'I'm sorry, I don't usually trespass without invitation,' she admitted, his lack of response to her warm smile transferring itself to her and making her unusually stilted. 'I was curious about that big window . . . Mrs Burgoyne says you can see the Rotunda from it. I saw it from the garden, the window, I mean.'

He stood aside for her to pass. 'It's hard to miss, Mrs Voss.' He didn't offer to show her the view.

'Good heavens, I'm not Mrs Voss! I'm just living with Dermot for the time being.' Realizing what she'd said, Sarah laughed and an explanation was on the tip of her tongue when the expression of either acute disinterest or dis-

approval, the one raised eyebrow, brought her to a halt. Her smiled died. No sense of humour, either. A spark of antagonism cracked across the space between them.

'I'm very sorry,' she repeated, and turned to go. There was nothing for it other than that, a dignified exit and as graceful an apology as she could muster. He made no attempt to detain her, and she escaped.

And hoped, as she fled down the stairs, that his elegant silk tie might choke him on a sweltering day like this, and thought the other tenants were certainly going to be interesting to meet, if this was Mrs Burgoyne's idea of 'the right sort of person'.

She'd just filled the kettle ready to make tea the moment Dermot got back – the girls would love a picnic out in the garden, sandwiches and Granny's jam tarts, never mind the wasps or the possibility of thunderstorms – when there was a knock on the back door. The woman who stood there was plump and pleasant, in her early forties, her hair done in a top-heavy mop of curls over her forehead, otherwise shorn into a short back and sides, like a man's. She introduced herself as Doreen Bailey.

'Oh, do come in and sit down; Mrs Burgoyne mentioned your name.' Not intending to make the same mistake twice, Sarah this time made it clear who she was.

Mrs Bailey smiled and settled her ample figure with the ease of familiarity on to the ugly fifties vinyl-covered banquette seat which someone had once mistakenly fitted in a half-hearted attempt to modernize the kitchen. Sarah rummaged in the picnic basket. 'I'm just about to make some tea, if I can sort some cups out. Hope you don't mind plastic.'

'Better than Mrs B's cast-offs, I'll bet. She said she'd leave one or two mugs and plates for you to use while your stuff was being unpacked, but I should use your own – anything *she* hasn't taken, it won't be worth much, I can tell you. She'd cut a currant in two, that one.' She laughed and got up to open a cupboard next to the sink, sniffing. 'As I thought! Chipped, *and* cracked, what cheek! Only fit for the dustbin.

14

She tell you I'd be willing to come and help out with the cleaning a couple of mornings a week?' she continued, without pause. 'I work afternoons at the checkout down at Safeway's, but I've come to Edwina Lodge twice a week, mornings, getting on for twelve years. I'd be willing to carry on, if that's all right with you.'

Sarah said, perhaps unwisely on such short acquaintance, but she'd taken one of her immediate likings to Mrs Bailey, 'I'm sure Dermot would be delighted if you could manage it.'

Mrs Bailey gave a satisfied nod and, having drawn breath, went on, 'I do for Miss Kendrick and her brother as well – they live at Simla, next house along. Makes a change from the supermarket – I feel like a battery hen there, sometimes, and the housework gives me a bit of exercise, besides helping with the mortgage. I was determined we should go for one of the houses in the Close when they went up, but it's a struggle, sometimes.'

Sarah assumed she was referring to the cul-de-sac of new-ish houses which lay between this house and the next one in Albert Road, the one she'd called Simla. 'Ellington Close, you mean? That's convenient.'

'That's right. They pulled a big old house down and built our houses on the site. Heath Mount, the house was called – the Kendricks had lived there all their lives, their great-grandfather or some such built it, but you know what it's like trying to keep places like that going. They sold it in the end and moved into Simla. Bit of a comedown for them, but I shouldn't waste your breath feeling sorry for them, they couldn't have done so bad out of the deal, my Bob says, and he's in the building trade, painter and decorator, so he should know. Two sugars, m'duck, I know I shouldn't but I use a lot of energy.'

'What are they like?' asked Sarah, grabbing the opportunity to speak as Mrs Bailey paused to take possession of her tea.

'The Kendricks? All right. Bit on the snooty side. Clever, highbrow, you know. College types – Cambridge, I think it

was. He writes books. And of course there's Mrs Loxley, the other sister.'

'What sort of books does he write?'

Mrs Bailey was vague. 'About art, and that sort of stuff. His study's full of pictures, not that I'm allowed in there, except to take him his coffee when his sister's not there. She teaches maths at the Princess Mary – the girls are all terrified of her, but they respect her, if you know what I mean. She's strict, but fair – got my niece through her maths GCSEs, and that's saying something! Patti's a lovely girl, and bright with it, but not when it comes to figures.'

Doreen Bailey's flow of chat was interrupted by the arrival of Dermot, Lucy hanging on his arm, Allie a step behind. 'Do I smell tea?' he demanded, smiling engagingly at the older woman who, in turn, was gazing admiringly at the handsome man with the tanned skin and the smiling blue eyes that exactly matched his open-necked shirt.

Damn, thought Sarah, who'd sensed a rich vein of information waiting to be tapped in Mrs Bailey, now I shall have to wait to find out more about the tenants – though the obnoxious Mr Fitzallan could go and jump in the lake for all the interest she had in him.

2

St Nicholas's church, Lavenstock, was tolling its single melancholy note for eight o'clock communion as Harry Nevitt arrived at his council-owned allotment the next morning. The thunderstorms of the previous day had cleared the air, and it was a little cooler, though there was promise of returning heat later on. Meanwhile, the morning sparkled. Everything appeared clean and new-washed. Ruby beetroot leaves gleamed, celery stood erect and waved its bright green fronds, cabbages were diamond-studded. The earth was warm and damp and Harry was anxious to get cracking with the hoe, put paid to the weeds that would have come out in full marching order.

He considered himself lucky that his allotment was in one of the prime positions, in a coveted spot which not only had the best of the sun but also allowed him to park his car nearby, since it ran alongside the narrow dirt road that cut through the middle of the site. He'd worked it for twenty-odd years, getting the soil into good heart and growing prize-winning onions and chrysanthemums, and now he was retired, and a widower, he happily spent most of his day here. He lacked nothing: tea-making facilities and a radio, his daily paper and a deck chair in the little green hut where he kept his tools and his garden supplies. Even a much-disparaged mobile phone which his daughter insisted on him carrying around. Today, he'd also brought writing materials; he was working on yet another petition to the council to do something about repairing the road behind his allotment.

The state of it after the heavy rain proved his point. He'd

17

had to park his car as near as he could get, which wasn't near enough. Swearing at the potholes in the surface, and because the half-hundredweight polythene bag of fertilizer he'd picked up at the allotment store – where they bought in bulk for economy – was slippery and awkward, and heavy for a seventy-four-year-old, he made his way clumsily towards the hut. He wasn't as nippy on his pins as he had been, and it was a wonder he didn't trip over the prone form and join it where it lay right across his path.

' 'Ere,' said Harry. 'What d'you think you're playing at?'

He wasn't an imaginative man, but it didn't take him long to realize this wasn't just a drunk still sleeping it off after a Saturday-night binge, nor was it a tramp, that the man was lying with his head in one of the rain-filled potholes and certainly wasn't going to stand up and apologize for getting in Harry's way. He looked pretty dead to Harry, and he'd seen a few corpses during his war service, but he put down his fertilizer sack and tentatively took hold of the outflung wrist. Then he picked up the bag again and carefully deposited it in his hut before getting out the despised phone and punching in 999.

The church bell stopped tolling just as the Town Hall clock began to strike eight.

'Dead for roughly twelve hours, probably less, that's as near as I can tell you at the moment. And *that*,' pronounced the pathologist, pointing to the shallow puddle of clay-coloured water, 'is almost certainly what killed him.'

The body had already been photographed *in situ*, and the video cameramen and the SOCO team were now busy on the surrounding area. The police surgeon, automatically summoned to what was an unexplained death and having done his duty of pronouncing an obviously dead body offici-ally dead, but seeing grounds for suspicion, had given his opinion that his eminent colleague, the Home Office pathol-ogist, Professor Timpson-Ludgate, who fortunately lived in the area, should be called in. He was now working on the body, speaking into a small tape recorder hung around his

neck as he worked, a photographer in attendance to take close-ups at his instructions.

Familiarly known throughout the police as T-L, the pathologist glanced up at the detective inspector from his kneeling position, his bulk obscuring the body. 'He's been roughed up more than a bit, but I can tell you he died from drowning, unless I'm very much mistaken.'

Abigail Moon nodded. She knew it was perfectly possible to drown in two inches of water. 'Drunk?'

'No smell of drink on him, no vomit. Tell you better when I've opened him up.' He lifted the recorder from round his neck. 'He's all yours, meanwhile, and the best of British. Not a pretty sight, I'm afraid.'

The professor was a big, jovial man of Falstaffian appearance, a bit of a throwback, Abigail thought him, quite aware that under the nod to equality he privately thought feminism had gone too far, still had quaint, old-fashioned notions that women should be at home having babies and looking after their menfolk, rather than doing hard, difficult and often distasteful jobs. He gave her a quizzical glance as he spoke but he should have known her well enough by now to know that she wasn't about to have the vapours at the sight of a dead body. Not even ones much more horrible than this was likely to be. It didn't mean she didn't mind. Only that she'd trained herself to look, without actually *looking*. She'd already seen this one, anyway, when she'd first arrived at the scene.

'He'd been fighting, you say?'

'Well, these aren't love bites he's got. There's bruising to the jaw and cheekbone, a cut lip and a black eye, consistent with the sort of injuries you might expect from fighting, though they're superficial, and if he hit back there's no bruising or broken skin on his knuckles to show it.'

The morning was warming up by the minute. Abigail pushed her heavy bronze hair behind her ears and frowned. 'If he didn't fall down drunk, how did he drown? Running away from a fight, fell, knocked himself unconscious? He must have been unconscious or he'd have rolled away.'

19

The pathologist peeled off his gloves and levered himself to his feet, not without difficulty. He was carrying more weight than he should and knew it, but like most doctors, he didn't always follow his own advice. 'But there's this, too, which is what interests me more than anything.' Saving the best for last, he turned the body slightly and indicated a nasty-looking wound on the back of the head. 'I'll reserve judgement until I can take a closer look at him, but off the record, there's not much doubt it would at least be the cause of him losing consciousness.'

'So some other person was definitely involved, then?'

'Since the wound's on the back of the head, yes. Unless, of course, he fell, then rolled over before he lost consciousness. Remote, but possible. And in the absence of anything obvious he could have fallen against . . .' He shrugged his big shoulders. 'No point in speculating. The PM will resolve which it was, fall or a blow. In the meantime, it looks as though we're into your department, Inspector. Find me a rock or something similar, that fits the injury, preferably one with blood and hairs on it.'

'Could the same fall – supposing he did fall – account for his other injuries?'

'Not a chance. Take it from me, he'd been in some sort of rough-house. I'll do the PM as soon as possible, since I know you're impatient for a result. Not today – maybe tomorrow.' He made it sound like a favour. 'No one would think it, but we are allowed to have social commitments,' he added, squinting with disfavour down at his ruined, light-coloured trousers.

You and who else? thought Abigail, seeing her own day disappearing, fast, down the drain.

'I'm snowed under with bodies just now,' the professor saw fit to add, explaining with a lugubrious smile, 'Why they all seem to come at once, I don't know, you tell me, but they're dying like flies at the moment. Must be something in the water.'

'I'll take care to stick to the bottled sort,' Abigail said as he finally departed, picking his way back between the puddles to

where he'd left his distinctive vintage Rover. Water might be all she'd get the chance of that day. She was officially off duty and had planned a grand slam on the domestic chores, the afternoon working in her garden, and a deliciously relaxed evening with Ben Appleyard, intending to astonish him with the virtuosity of her cooking and a bottle of wine. Alas! As a newspaperman, editor of the local newspaper, he understood and forgave these sort of emergencies better than most men would, but even his apparently inexhaustible patience must have its limits. This wasn't the place to examine what those limits were, however. She gave the SOCOs the nod that it was their turn with the body. Cameras began flashing again and ex-Sergeant Dexter came forward and began his task with his usual thoroughness and practicality. The Scenes-of-Crime department had recently been civilianized, but Dexter had liked his job so much he had quit the Force in order to carry on. She was glad he was the one to be assigned to this case; he was moody, sometimes, could be taciturn if he was that way inclined, but he was knowledgeable, unflappable and meticulous to a degree. If Dave Dexter didn't find evidence, it usually wasn't there.

While he was occupied with searching for anything foreign to the scene, collecting trace evidence – hairs, fibres and dust samples from the victim's clothing in addition to those already taken from the surrounding area – bottling water samples from the puddle, she used the time to talk to the elderly man who'd found the body. He was sitting on an upended bale of peat inside his hut, a tall, thin man, smoking, drinking a mug of tea and looking blankly out over the neat rows of vegetables, the serried ranks of dahlias and chrysanthemums for cutting. If he was shaken, he wasn't showing it. All the same, the sort of discovery he'd made was a facer for anyone and he wasn't young any more. She went carefully with him.

'We're going to need an official statement from you, Mr Nevitt. I've a car coming to take you down to the station, but to give me something to be going on with, perhaps you

could just tell me now how you found him – that is, if you feel up to it?'

He took another drag on his cigarette and assured her he was all right but there wasn't much more he could sa,, other than that he'd all but fallen over the body when he arrived at the allotment first thing. 'What I can tell you is, he wasn't there at half past eight last night. That were a heavy old thunderstorm we had around tea-time and I come down here, after, to see whether my chrysanths was still standing. What with one thing and another, I was here best part of an hour.'

'This road – is it used a lot? By people other than the allotment-holders, I mean?'

'It's a short cut through from Colley Street to the Lea-sowes.' He pronounced it 'Lezzers' in the time-honoured local way. 'That and the path at the back. We get a fair number of them joggers coming through, and kids on bikes and that, but the road's too bad for folks as don't have to, to risk their car suspensions. We've complained and complained to the council about it – what's the use of having a road if we can't use it? – but you might as well save your puff. They reckon there's no money for it, these days.'

Abigail nodded and looked around at the allotment holdings. It was a roughly triangular site, pointing down towards the river and the Riverside Community Centre on Stockwell Street. Along one side was Colley Street, a busy road that ran up through the town towards Holden Hill; along the other was the shorter street called the Leasowes, a much sought-after council-improved street of small, artisan-type houses. A narrow path ran along the base of the triangle at the back of the allotments, connecting the two streets, while running up from Stockwell Street and roughly bisecting the site was the unnamed, unmade-up road Harry Nevitt was complaining about.

'Hello, young Peter, thought you might be around somewhere,' the old man greeted D C Deeley, who'd arrived with the announcement that the car to take the old man down

22

to the police station was ready, if Mr Nevitt was. 'Your mum were telling me you was a detective now.'

'Her allus did say I were destined for better things than a uniform, Harry,' Deeley answered, with a wink at Abigail, employing his broadest dialect.

'Oh ar. Dow let it go to your head, then.'

Built like a steamroller, cheerful, unflappable, Pete Deeley grinned and walked with the old man to the car and drove off with him.

'Right, Inspector. You can have another look at him now if you want, before we get him bagged up and taken away,' Dexter said.

'Nothing to identify him?'

'No wallet or credit cards, just his car keys and a handful of loose change in his trouser pocket – though the label on his pants says they were made in Germany, if that's any use to you . . . not that it counts for a lot nowadays, last pair I bought was made in Sweden . . . and his shirt and underpants are St Michael. I'll tell you where his shoes came from when we've dried them off in the lab and scraped the mud off.'

'Probably Taiwan,' Abigail said, ducking under the tape. Conscientiously, but without noticeable enthusiasm, she took a better view of the body. He was a youngish man – not yet forty, the pathologist had estimated, slightly built and of middle height, dark-haired and seen to be clean-shaven. Froth ballooned from his nose and mouth. The front of his clothing was still caked with mud, but appeared to have been otherwise respectable.

'Not your usual yob that gets mixed up in a fight.'

The comment came from Sergeant Kite, who'd just arrived. The scene was now crowded with police, the allotments having been taped off and a uniformed P C detailed to keep away the disgruntled tenants as they arrived.

'T-L thinks he'd been in some sort of punch-up, Martin, for all that. If he was mugged, they've left him his ring and his watch.' She indicated the plain band on the wedding finger and the flat gold watch with the leather strap.

'In too much of a hurry, maybe. Just grabbed his wallet and scarpered.'

'I'm wondering if he had one with him. It was a muggy night, after the rain, too warm for a jacket. You men are at a disadvantage, no handbag, nowhere to put your wallet except your back pocket, but that's still buttoned up. And I can't see anybody stopping to do it up again if they'd just pinched a wallet from it. He'd loose change and car keys in his other pocket.'

Hitching her bag on to her shoulder, she thought about the keys, and the possibility that his car was somewhere near . . .

'We shan't get much from the immediate area around, I have to tell you,' Dexter was grumbling. 'Footprints or vehicle marks – forget it.'

The loose sharp stones, the potholes all over the place, would make this impossible, Abigail could see that. She repeated what the pathologist had said about the wound on the back of the victim's head possibly having been caused by a heavy stone.

'Keep an eye out for anything likely, Dave. And Martin,' she said to Kite. 'Get them knocking on doors.'

'We're not going to be popular.' Starting with Colley Street and the Leasowes, disturbing folks from their weekend lie-in this fine Sunday morning to find out whether anyone had heard a commotion last night. Would anyone have even remarked on it if they had, this end of Colley Street? Commotion was its normal condition, especially Friday and Saturday nights. 'We shall need more manpower – more uniforms from Reader,' he said.

Abigail pulled down her mouth. The chief inspector in charge of the uniformed branch wasn't exactly a pushover where his scarce resources were concerned. 'If he's awkward, shunt him over to me and I'll twist his arm. Meantime, all the pubs, not forgetting the Punch Bowl.'

'As if!'

'As if you could.' Saturday night without some sort of disturbance needing police intervention at the sleazy dive in

24

Colley Street would indeed be a night to remember. 'But if we can find anyone who came along here after Mr Nevitt left at half past eight, it'd help – maybe somebody took a short cut after closing time.'

'We'll be lucky! Anybody from the Punch, they wouldn't remember if they fell over an elephant.'

Abigail laughed. 'All the same . . . Right, I'll get back to the station now and report to the Super before he leaves.' Mayo would want a full briefing on what was happening before his departure for the Police Staff College, where he was leading a three-day seminar on the treatment of young offenders, and a start must be made on establishing the identity of the man, finding his car.

It was too early yet for anyone to have come forward to report him missing, but doubtless someone would, sooner or later. A thought enough to sober anyone: that on this bright and beautiful morning, among the dahlias and gladioli and all the fruitful produce of the earth, a young man, with all the expectancy of his life in front of him, should now lie mysteriously dead. While somewhere a wife, maybe children, waited for him.

3

There were sixteen houses in the Close that dipped down from the brow of the hill, sixteen where previously one had stood, that one having been Heath Mount, a Victorian edifice much bigger than Simla, or even Edwina Lodge. Most of the houses in Albert Road had been of that ilk, built at the time when the Industrial Revolution which had made Britain prosperous had been at its height and made its masters rich. Here on the edge of Lavenstock, their foundries, brickworks, claypits and glass kilns, chainworks and nail shops, had grown and spread out towards the great sprawl of Birmingham, and here they had built their splendid houses high on the ridge of Holden Hill, from whence they could look down on their creations and see that they were good. Imposing once, monuments to Victorian self-help, the houses had enjoyed their moment of glory but by now they'd had their day; most had been either split up into flats, taken over for business enterprises or pulled down and the land sold for development.

The houses that formed Ellington Close were mostly occupied by young families, childless couples and one or two retired people, though advertised as starter homes when they were built five years ago. It had begun to lose the raw look of a new housing development, to acquire some semblance of permanence, now that the flowering cherries were maturing and the rockeries flourishing . . . almost every garden had a rockery, a practical solution to gardens built on a slope. The houses were stepped down the hill in a rough crescent, away from Albert Road, in a pleasantly irregular pattern. The

builder, or the architect who designed the site, had, to do him credit, used his imagination and had staggered them so that most of them had a magnificent view across workaday Holden Hill, down to the flat band of the canal in the bottom and the silvery dance of the river running parallel with it, right across Lavenstock and then up to the blue, tree-crowned hills which rose on the far side and looked out over three counties.

Everyone knew everyone else in the Close, although several of the houses had changed hands since they were built. They were three-bedroomed and detached – if only just – and in order to pack that number of houses on to a site of this size, they were dolls' houses, their dimensions minute. For two young people, to whom proximity is more important than space, this had a certain advantage, but when children arrived, the picture changed. Number thirteen had been on the market for almost as long as Edwina Lodge. The number wasn't regarded as a significant cause of their not being able to sell. It was generally thought that the occupants, Gail and Trevor Lawley, were asking too much, but what could they do when they owed more on their mortgage than the house was worth? Negative equity acquires a sharper edge when you find yourselves locked into it.

Monday morning, and Stanley Loates was, as usual, stationed at the front bay window of number seven, where he lived with his horrible old mother, when Patti Ryman entered the Close and began delivering her newspapers. She loathed him, the way he never smiled or came to the door to take the paper from her, just watched in that creepy way, day after day. She didn't give him the friendly wave she used to, not on your nelly! Not now she'd twigged he was only hoping for a look of her knickers as she bent down to push the delivery through number eight's letter-box. She yanked the newspaper bag further on to her shoulder. It was heavy, and she was tiny, but that didn't bother her. She was tough despite her size, as tough as any of the male oiks of her own age. She could cope. The money she got for this paper

27

round was a joke, of course, but she hadn't yet been able to find a proper weekend job, and meanwhile it all helped, though her mum wasn't happy about it, you heard such stories. She'd have had a fit if she knew about Stanley Loates, but Patti hadn't mentioned the dirty old perv to her.

He was still standing there when she finished her round. It was all she could do not to knock on his door and tell him what she thought about him – but she didn't want to lose her job through his complaints. She decided it might be a very good idea to ask Mr Patel to put her on another round. Better still, tell her Aunt Doreen, who also lived in the Close, what was going on, and let her deal with Stanley Loates.

Patti grinned. That'd fix him, all right!

Hope Kendrick heard the papers slide through the letter-box and land on the floor, but she was on her way to her brother's study with a tray and left them where they were.

She was careful to knock lightly before she entered the study. They'd always been meticulous about respecting each other's privacy, and Francis didn't like to be interrupted without warning when he was working.

'Coffee,' she announced, moving aside a pile of art magazines to find room for the tray on the table under the window. It was a dark, untidy room, where books took preference over human comfort, spilling off the shelves into hazardous piles on the floor, and where pictures of all kinds rubbed egalitarian shoulders in what space there was left.

Francis grunted, hunched over the work spread out on the big desk, and didn't immediately look up. It was barely half past eight but he liked his coffee early. He invariably rose at six, either to start work immediately, breakfastless, or to take one of his solitary walks, covering miles with his long strides before returning home to his desk.

As Hope put down the tray, it struck her with a pang how pronounced the academic stoop of his shoulders was becoming. He needed glasses now for close work. His head was bowed over the coloured prints and his hair was ruffled where he'd run his hands through it. She could see the slight

thinning of his pate but resisted the temptation to smooth the floppy hair back over it. The back of his neck looked so vulnerable. It was difficult to remember, sometimes, that he was forty-six, no longer a little boy, though God knew he still needed looking after. Salutary to think that he was the same age as she was, her twin.

She poured two mugs of coffee. 'Want me to bring it over to you?' she asked, after a minute or two. The question was superfluous, more of a reminder to come and drink it before it grew cold, since he never drank or ate at his desk. Unnoticing and untidy about most other things, he was scrupulous where his work was concerned, and would never have risked spilling coffee over it.

He pushed his chair back, knocking over a leaning tower of books stacked on the floor beside it, and lounged over to sit by her at the chenille-covered table in front of the stone-mullioned window, open to a warm morning that promised another hot day. The roses that he loved and so carefully tended were in their second flush, and sent waves of perfume into the room. He leaned back and stuck out his long legs, clad in baggy cotton. He was thin and very tall, six foot three, and gangly. She was five foot ten herself, with the same sort of frame, although more tidily held together, and all her movements were, unlike his, quick and decisive. She had the same disregard for appearances; her hair, streaked with grey, was chopped off in an uncompromising bob, pushed back behind her ears, her face was innocent of make-up. She wore a faded cotton skirt and a man's shirt, though she'd omitted her usual big, enveloping sweater this morning in deference to the warm promise of the day. Her feet, in flat sandals, were almost as large as his. It was only her thick-lensed glasses that made any appreciable difference to their appearance.

He nodded towards a pile of manuscript on the table, fresh from the typist. 'Came this morning. That woman got a move on, for once.'

'Pleased with it?'

'As a first draft, it's not bad.'

29

In Francis-speak, this meant that he was. She picked the papers up, clipped together, neatly typed by Liz Fawcett, who was always quick and efficient, despite what Francis affected to believe, though they wouldn't remain in that state of perfection for long. The first of many drafts, it would be scribbled over and rewritten six or seven times before Francis was satisfied with the result. He was such a clear thinker, it always astonished Hope that he needed to work over his material to such an extent – but Francis was a complex character, never as straightforward as he seemed, slow to anger but formidable when roused. Suppressing this unprofitable line of thought, she peered through her spectacles in order to read the title on the cover sheet: 'The Cave and the Mountain: The importance of Symbolism in Mediaeval Iconography'. Francis was an authority on Byzantine art and had published several books on similar themes. Each one had made quiet ripples in the academic art world, but with this one she knew he was hoping to stir up more significant waves.

'They're moving into Edwina Lodge today,' she said, as she sipped her coffee. 'The new people.'

'Oh?'

He wasn't really interested. He cradled the coffee mug in his huge hands as he drank, in between each large gulp reaching out for a couple of his favourite jammy dodgers, scrunching them in his strong teeth, impatient to get back to work. His gaze strayed to the prints spread out on his desk. They were all of icons – madonnas, saints, the Christ. The reds and golds of the Greek icons glowed against the soft, pure colours of the Russian ones. *Our Lady of Vladimir* shone out in blue. There were two copies of the *Black Madonna of Czestochowa*. He went back to the desk and picked one up, studying it intently, back in his own world.

'A young couple,' Hope said.

And two little girls. She'd heard them calling out to each other as they played. Lucy and Allie (or some such) were their names, seemingly. She fervently wished there hadn't been children. Weren't they surrounded by too many of them already, in the Close? The summer holidays weren't

quite over and you couldn't get away from them. We should have moved further away than just next door when the old house was sold, Hope thought, not for the first time – to the cottage, perhaps. But Francis hadn't wanted to move permanently to Shropshire, it was too far from the reference library in Birmingham and the availability of trains to London for him; it would have meant her finding another job in another school . . .

'I wonder at them – taking on all that responsibility,' she mused, her mind turning again to the new people. 'All right for the Burger, she was used to it, but young people like that, they don't usually take to that sort of thing . . . Imogen says we should ask them over for drinks.'

'What?' She had his attention now. An almost panic-stricken look crossed his face, to be replaced by the sort of stubbornness only Francis was capable of showing. 'Count me out. If Imogen wants them over, let her do the entertaining.'

'Francis, we can't. They're going to be our new neighbours, after all. We have to be civil to them; it needn't amount to anything more than that.'

'They'll ask us back. If they're young, they'll have parties, there'll be no end to it.'

'Francis – '

'You and Imogen do the necessary. She enjoys that sort of thing. You don't need me.'

He swung his chair round, dismissively held up the two Black Madonna prints, holding them side by side. 'Which do you prefer?'

'Not that one,' she said. She privately thought it rather vulgar, the way the beautiful simplicity of the original was obscured, 'dressed' as the Mother and Child were in their richly jewelled frames of robes and crowns. Adorned with hundreds of votive offerings in the form of rubies and other precious stones and hundreds of gold wedding rings, said to have been offered by pious couples.

'Ah, the Robe of Faithfulness,' Francis murmured. 'Both, I think, should be included.'

Hope let the subject of the new neighbours drop for the

31

moment. She'd sowed the seeds, he'd have time to think about it before Imogen approached him, and though his agreement couldn't be guaranteed, Imogen was unlikely to meet with the outright refusal she'd have encountered if she'd had to mention it to him cold.

She would, of course, be expecting opposition. Hope knew very well that Imogen was always prepared for that when confronting either of them with suggestions, admittedly not without cause. They rarely thought the same way. Sometimes Hope wondered how the three of them could have sprung from the same stock, so unlike were they. But, although everything the older twins were not, Imogen was unquestionably their sibling. She was their mother incarnate, in looks and in spirit, from the tips of her pretty, impatient feet to the crown of her shining dark hair (nature helped along by art, but Imogen was the last to let Hope's disapproval bother her). She not only had their mother's surprisingly practical, common-sense approach to life, but also their father, Roland's, undeniable charm, gambler and reprobate though he'd been, he who'd gone with the speed of light through the proceeds of the family business.

The money had originally been made through fireclay, rich deposits of which Great-great-grandfather Kendrick had discovered lay all around Holden Hill, waiting to be dug to make firebricks and furnaces. He'd made his pile by the time he died, leaving behind a legacy of ugly and dangerous clay-pits for future generations to deal with, and a comfortable lifestyle for the Kendrick descendants – who were numerous, since he'd had nine children. Most of them, however, despised the business, sold their shares profitably and became doctors, teachers, lawyers. One became a bishop and one – Roland, the grandson of the only son to carry on the business – a good-for-nothing. When he died, the debts he left were staggering. Their solicitor had told his children bluntly that they had no option but to get rid of Heath Mount. An opportunity to sell it for building development had just arisen and they'd be well advised to grab it with their three pairs of hands. He pointed out the advantages of living in a smaller,

more manageable house, and sitting on a comfortable amount of money, having sold at the top of the market, instead of struggling with the upkeep of Heath Mount without the means to do so.

Sell Heath Mount? Pull it down? It was quite possible the elder Kendricks might never recover from the shock.

In the end, it had been Imogen who'd pushed them into the move. Left to themselves, the twins would have lived on in Heath Mount until it crumbled around their ears, shutting their eyes to the need for running repairs until it was too late. Francis with his head in the clouds over his Byzantine art and icons and Hope with her books and her senior maths syllabuses . . . did they exist on another planet, divorced from such humdrum things? Imogen demanded.

They tried to ignore her but she could be ruthless. She'd forced them to look at the situation fair and square, made them see that their only option was to do as Mr Crytch advised and move somewhere smaller. Francis had immediately assumed this to mean a custom-built bungalow or a luxury flat and had retreated into one of his haughty silences, refusing to discuss the matter. Hope had tried to be slightly more amenable but nevertheless managed to find some excuse to turn down every suggestion Imogen made. Imogen might never have succeeded in prising them out if Simla had not come on the market at about the same time, a face-saving solution, in that the vendor was almost as stubborn as they were, having inserted a proviso on the sale that the house should not be sold to a developer. It was smaller and better looked-after than Heath Mount, but of the same vintage, and it would mean they could live more or less in the same way they'd always been used to.

Well, that was Imo's version of the situation! Hope thought. Perhaps she wouldn't have been so keen on the idea herself if she'd known she'd be back living with them within five years, back from Brussels, her marriage to Tom Loxley, Euro MP, all but over. But five years ago she'd been comfortably off, and secure enough to claim only a modest sum out of the sale of Heath Mount, with the promise of a

couple of rooms at the new house whenever she might need them on her visits home.

With her usual efficiency, she'd overseen the move to Simla, insisting on having the plumbing at least updated and a new kitchen installed before they moved in. But Hope had scorned attempts to get them to abandon the old sagging armchairs, bookcases and sideboards like mausoleums, all of them familiar and less alarming than new things would have been. The old curtains had been made over somehow to fit the new windows, despite Imogen having actually sought the advice of an interior designer in the town. She might just as well have gone down to Lavenstock market and bought curtaining by the yard to machine up, for all the interest Hope could summon up. So that in the end, Simla, lacking only the Benares brass and elephant-foot coffee tables brought home from India by the general who'd first inhabited and named the house, looked much as Heath Mount had always done. And by now, even the new kitchen had acquired a decent lived-in air.

But still, Hope considered the price for freedom from financial worries was high: to be living in the middle of a housing development like the Close, with what seemed like more than its fair share of children, when they'd been used to space and privacy, was a lot to pay. Certainly, more than she'd bargained for.

'Mother would have sent round a note, asking them to tea,' Imogen remarked, not without irony, still thinking about the new people at Edwina Lodge when Hope returned with the coffee things. 'On the lawn, perhaps, with cucumber sandwiches. I shall have to go and knock on the door like the Avon lady, since I don't know their name or telephone number. Oh, but of course, they'll have the same number as the Burger, won't they?'

'I'll warn you, Francis is being difficult,' Hope said.

Imogen raised expressive eyebrows. 'What's new?' She added, despite her promises to herself, before she could bite it off, 'Do rinse those mugs out and empty the pot, don't just

34

leave them there,' which had patently been Hope's intention. Instead of saying, 'Wash them yourself, if you're so concerned,' as any other sister might have done, Hope washed and dried them with a meticulousness which, even if she hadn't meant it, was even more insulting. Imogen tried not to sigh.

They were just too damned exasperating for words, her brother and sister, too brainy and too superior to bother about mundane tasks until they assumed crisis proportions. She hadn't yet got over her fury, on her return from Brussels, at seeing the scruffy state of the kitchen she'd left newly refurbished. Hope had declared loftily that she'd got rid of Doreen Bailey, it was demeaning to both parties to pay someone to do menial work, which was all very well, but not if you then shut your own eyes to it. It was only Doreen's good nature that allowed her to return. She was independent enough not to share Hope's views on what was demeaning, and she'd worked for the Kendricks, as well as Mrs Burgoyne, even before their father had died and the old house had been sold, so she knew what she was letting herself in for.

By now, the house was at least liveable in, and Imogen felt better for having asserted herself, banished the memory of that terrible old house. As a child, she had felt extinguished in the presence of her older brother and sister, in the shadow of their intellectual superiority, and frequently afraid of them. It hadn't been until she'd married Tom, in fact, and found that she could hold her own in his sophisticated world that she began to gain self-confidence.

It had been a mistake to think of Tom.

She hurriedly began with the list of neighbours and friends she might ask to the proposed welcome party, concentrating fiercely and pressing so hard with the ballpoint that it nearly tore through the cheap paper of the kitchen pad. She tried to ignore the nasty, lurching pain in the pit of her stomach. When was she going to be able to go through a single day without thinking about him?

Tom. A humorous, tolerant man. Threads of grey in his hair, small lines etched at the corners of his kind eyes. The look of utter desolation when she told him she was leaving

him. The words had come out of her mouth, unintended until given voice. Nothing, he'd repeated, his face bleak, the girl had meant nothing to him. Propinquity, an overconvivial evening, an adjacent hotel room, nothing else.

Nothing to him, perhaps, but everything to her.

She should have tried to shrug it off. Lots of men had their bit on the side, it was irrelevant, in some circles it almost seemed mandatory – their wives forgave them, in public at any rate. But she couldn't. Theirs hadn't been a relationship like that, it had been based on mutual trust, on knowing the other person through and through. It was this that had shattered her, the realization that she hadn't, in fact, known him at all. Was he, then, like every other man, not special as she'd always believed? She'd only his word that it had been no more than a one-night stand, that there'd been nothing of the sort before, and never would be again, she'd told herself, trying to make herself doubt him.

Why? she'd asked herself repeatedly. Why did he have to do it? Is there something wrong with me?

She'd scrutinized herself in every available mirror and found nothing physically wrong, apart from the usual female dissatisfactions with a body less than perfect. Glossy dark hair, discreetly and expensively hennaed, trim figure, tall but not, like Hope, enough to intimidate shorter men. Beautiful clothes that she'd learned how to wear.

Me, myself then. It must be I who am lacking.

Her own subsequent behaviour had helped nothing.

She closed her eyes. What are you doing now, Tom?

She saw him in her mind's eye in the elegant Brussels apartment, unlikely as it was that he'd be there at that time of day, listening to the opera recordings he loved: a world of music contained within softly coloured walls, pale spreads of carpet, cushioned chairs and sofas in jewel-coloured fabrics. Lamps that lit the gilt-framed Georgian mirrors, the deeply glowing pictures, the oil paintings that were his other passion in life. Nothing spared in the way of expense and taste. Nothing lacking, except a wife.

4

Abigail Moon hurriedly splashed a watering can over the few tomato plants in growing bags outside the back door of her foursquare little house under the hill, briefly envying Harry Nevitt's spruce allotment as it had appeared on Sunday. Passionate as she'd become about gardening since acquiring her cottage, hers was necessarily of the low-maintenance variety – nothing so ambitious as growing vegetables, which needed more constant attention than she could give. The tomatoes were as far as she could go in that direction, and as for the rest, if it couldn't look after itself when necessary, it didn't get garden room here.

She loved her little plot to bits, though. Nonexistent when she'd taken it over, her knowledge of gardening at the same level, she'd learned as she went along, and though small, it had burgeoned into a restful place, lush with exuberant greenery that hid twisting little paths and unexpected viewpoints to give an illusion of glamour to the flat fields and woods beyond.

Thinking about the allotment brought the dead man vividly to mind again as she left the country lane that led to the cottage, having been allowed through by her nearest neighbours' huge black dog, who guarded the entrance to the lane like Cerberus at the gates of Hades. It was four days since the man had been found, and still no positive identification, with the initial inquiries seeming to have reached a plateau. All available manpower had been deployed on the investigation, and throughout Sunday and Monday every inch of the area surrounding the spot where

the unknown man had been found had been thoroughly searched. His car had been sought, without success. House-to-house inquiries had so far been fruitless. The media had been informed and brief announcements had appeared in the press and on local radio and television that the body of an unidentified man had been found behind the Colley Street allotments. As yet, this had brought forth no response from anyone who might have recognized him, though there was still time for this: there were bound to be some who'd missed tuning in or reading the papers.

But neither had there been any inquiries from relatives worried about loved ones, and that was more puzzling.

She arrived at Milford Road without getting snarled up in traffic, and parked in the station yard, noticing with a resigned grimace that the Super had, as usual, beaten her to it. His car was in its appointed place after his return from the staff college. After signing in, she checked with the night duty officer's occurrence book and found that nothing out of the ordinary had happened during the night, certainly nothing relevant to Sunday morning's body finding.

It was, however, only one of several investigations which needed her urgent attention. She was currently working on a spate of motor thefts which appeared to be more organized than the usual opportunist heists, there was a factory surveil-lance to be organized today with a depleted staff – Sergeant Carmody on leave on the Costa Brava and Kite due in court this morning. And she'd come in early to get her thoughts straightened out on a possible child-abuse case which had also landed on her desk, needing time alone to be able to think about the harrowing facts dispassionately – if anyone could be dispassionate about such a subject – before the busy day got under way and she was inundated with interruptions from all directions. With a cup of coffee at her elbow, she worked steadily on, regardless of people arriving in the CID room and the growing noise level outside her glass partition, and had collated enough material into a file to pass on to the Child Protection Unit by the time her telephone rang.

'Ready when you are, Abigail.'

Satisfied with what she'd achieved, she closed the file and went upstairs to Mayo's office. It was a daily routine that had developed, given time and opportunity, which was valuable to both of them. They'd worked closely together when Gil Mayo was a chief inspector, before he'd been made up to superintendent, and still maintained a brisk and friendly relationship which suited both of them. A big, forceful man who'd come up through the ranks, he didn't let it get under his skin that she was a graduate entrant who could well leave him behind within a few years.

She found him tinkering with the old clock he kept on the bookcase. Clocks were his hobby – the collecting, restoring, and timing thereof – and he preferred this unreliable old Victorian mantel clock with its comforting tick, needing daily tender loving care to keep it up to scratch, to the official one on the wall which kept perfect time and marked off its movements with an unnerving clunk.

The seminar had evidently gone well. He was cheerful and alert and got straight to the point. One thing you could always guarantee with Mayo, he didn't hang about. After a swift canter through the details of the rest of her cases, he said, 'Give me a rundown on what you've gathered on the Colley Street job so far. I don't like the way it appears to be shaping up – or not, as the case may be.'

'Not's the right word,' she said, taking the point that he'd already made himself familiar with what had been going on in that direction while he'd been away. But he listened attentively to what she had to tell him.

An active and practical man, he fitted into the chair of Super somewhat ambivalently, playing his new role to his own rules, more than he'd felt able to do in his previous job. Impatient of the amount of time needed for endless committees and policy meetings, he took every chance he could to play an active part whenever possible, to be in at the sharp end. It didn't worry Abigail, as long as he didn't interfere with her own responsibilities. He'd earned the reputation of being a good boss from those he outranked . . . if you toed the line. If not . . . well, it wasn't often he let fly.

He kept his powder dry until he needed it for his big guns, but when he did – take cover!

'Let's hear what you've got, all the same. Sit down and have some coffee. You look as though you could do with it.' He poured her a cup from the fresh pot which had just been brought in.

God, did she look that bad? Probably. She wondered if he remembered she'd had her day off cancelled on Sunday, with fat chance of being able to make it up, never mind take time off for an overdue hairstyling, which always made her feel a hag. She took a drink of coffee and vowed she'd make time to visit the hairdresser, somehow. She could take on board as much pressure as anybody, but she'd enough common sense to grab time off in lieu as soon as she could manage it. Which might, in the circumstances, unfortunately for her, be some time in coming, all things considered. Too bad. No use complaining. It went with the territory.

'We've had the PM report through,' she said. 'It's fairly conclusive.'

Asphyxial death due to drowning in water, was how Timpson-Ludgate had phrased it. The occipital fracture of the skull had resulted in loss of consciousness, whereby the victim, lying face downwards in the puddle, had subsequently drowned. Diatoms, or microscopic water algae, in the blood, proved conclusively that he was alive before the water entered his air passages. There were no *contre-coup* injuries to the brain to indicate that the fracture was due to his fall. Translated, this meant that he had been hit with, rather than fallen on to, some irregularly shaped, heavy object, possibly a stone. Had he fallen, the brain damage would have showed up on the opposite side to where the skull injury had been sustained, a seeming anomaly which occurred for some complex and not yet fully understood reason. A nice distinction, but important, since it proved conclusive evidence that his death was no accident.

'But the weapon hasn't turned up. We've combed the area, and found nothing. Plenty of stones, but none that obviously fit the bill. And nothing else that looks likely.'

'So we're talking murder. At the least manslaughter, a fight that got out of hand?'

'We've had no reports of any undue disturbances nearby, either in the Leasowes or Colley Street, apart from the usual Saturday-night rumpus at the Punch Bowl – bikers and some drunken louts celebrating United's win. Ending up with one youth in hospital, several others enjoying free lodging here for the night. We've ascertained it had nothing to do with our man.'

And in any case, she added, the Punch Bowl, or any other pub, was probably a nonstarter, since the medical evidence had revealed no traces of alcohol in the victim's system. 'The car keys are for a last year's BMW, but so far we haven't had any reports of one being abandoned. Kite's been on to the manufacturers . . . they've given him the model, and the retail outlets they were sent to – but it'll be a long job tracing it that way – could've changed hands several times since then. And of course, our man could have disturbed thieves or joyriders in the act and tackled them as they were taking it away.'

'Might be some connection with your motor thefts, is that what you're thinking? They've all been prestigious type cars so far.'

'I'm currently working on the theory, but I'm not optimistic, if it's part of the same scam. Respray, new numberplates and its chassis number ground off, you name it, and it'll be over the channel before you can blink.'

'On the other hand, the dead man's car may be tucked up tidily in his own garage. What about Missing Persons?'

'Not a hope. No one even remotely conforming to his description. And his prints aren't on the Index, either. He was wearing a wedding ring, which indicates the presence of a wife somewhere or other, but maybe she thinks she knows where he is.'

She hesitated. 'Among the loose change in his pocket were a couple of Belgian francs. Might have been left over from a recent holiday, of course, or it could just be that he actually is Belgian. We've put out the usual inquiries, on the

41

offchance, but no luck there either, yet. We might get some response from the fly-posters we're organizing. Heigh-ho.' She grinned suddenly. 'Well, we've had worse than this; it's early days, yet.'

'We've tried taxi drivers? Or bus conductors, if it comes to that, or if he came here by train from somewhere else? Just because he had his car keys in his pocket it doesn't necessarily mean he used his car on that occasion.'

'It's a reasonable assumption,' Abigail said.

'We seem to be running out of reasonable assumptions as far as he's concerned. Let's try the other kind, now.'

She'd learned to respect what some jaundiced people called Mayo's good luck, what some dared to call his intuition and he himself insisted was gut feeling. Whatever it was, he had an uncanny knack of being right.

She hoped he was wrong this time. What he was implying was the worst-case scenario. Unknown victim, unknown killer, with every chance of this remaining a case marked 'Closed'.

5

'*Why* can't I have my ears pierced?' nagged Lucy.

She'd been at her new school for only two days but, typically, had already acquired a best friend named Jodie, who not only had her ears pierced but also, if what she'd told Lucy was to be believed, had her hair highlighted and possessed a pair of black patent-leather ankle boots which were the immediate and passionate object of Lucy's envy.

'When you're older, perhaps,' Sarah temporized.

'Why not *now*?'

'Because you'd have to wear sleepers if you did and your daddy doesn't think that suitable at your age – do you, Dermot?'

'Not really,' Dermot answered unconvincingly, and added weakly, 'We'll see,' thus storing up further trouble for himself.

Sarah poured herself a strong cup of coffee. 'Get on with your cornflakes, Lucy, or you'll be late for school.'

'Angel doesn't have her ears pierced,' said Allie.

There was a pause. 'Oh God,' Dermot said.

So Angel was back.

Angel, who'd lived and slept and played with Allie for months, her imaginary friend who'd then simply disappeared one day about six months ago, without explanation from Allie, greatly to everyone else's relief. Nobody was sorry that this smugly self-righteous child, aptly named from Allie's favourite story-book character, no longer formed part of the family, or was the unseen guest at the table, that Allie was at last able to do things without a prolonged discussion with

her, something which irritated everyone else unbearably, especially her father. Sarah shot a warning glance at Dermot, who was showing every sign of his previous impatience with Allie over this. After a moment, with a shrug and a grunt, he subsided behind yesterday's newspaper.

Despite assurances that many children went through this stage, not to make too much of it, it would pass, Lisa had worried that the phantom child's presence was a sign of Allie's insecurity. Did her return signal some desperate need in Allie for comfort and reassurance? Sarah worried in her turn now. Was it a belated reaction to the loss of her mother? There'd been nightmares at first, sleepwalking, after Lisa had died, but she was sleeping peacefully through the nights now, just as Lucy had ceased to wail, 'I want my mummy, it's not *fair*!' every bedtime.

Sarah felt out of her depth, catapulted into family responsibilities she didn't feel fitted to cope with – and Dermot wasn't going to be much help over this, she could see. He was on edge and unapproachable, had been all week, ever since they'd moved in. His original enthusiasm for the whole project seemed to have evaporated. Reminding him that he'd brought it on himself – much as she'd have enjoyed doing so – would cut no ice with him; he'd pointed out only last night that the most stressful things which could happen to anyone were supposed to be divorce, bereavement and moving house – and he'd just suffered the last two.

But she knew it was mainly because this new venture was so far not coming up to his expectations, that this wasn't exactly the new life he'd envisaged when the idea of taking over Edwina Lodge had transferred itself from Mrs Burgoyne's mind to his own. The actuality, she suspected, had been enough to make him wonder if he hadn't been too easily seduced by her weasel words, by the brilliant idea of having his mortgage paid by the tenants' rents, plus a little over. Dermot-like, he hadn't actually thought it through, considered the responsibilities ensuing from living in a house that included three other units. Already, the tenant of the downstairs flat, Tina Baverstock, was becoming a major pain,

buttonholing him like the Ancient Mariner on some pretext or other every time she saw him. The venture had, like so many of Dermot's notions, seemed like a good idea at the time, a sort of bohemian, extended-family situation where he'd imagined there would be plenty of social interaction, plus someone on hand when he needed to park his children.

But still, Sarah wouldn't have expected disillusionment to have set in so quickly. The honeymoon was over before it had begun.

Allie seemed oblivious to the tension her announcement had created. She was going on with her cereal, carefully scraping the dish clean, spooning up every drop of milk. Lucy, munching toast, showed no sign of being bothered that Angel was amongst them again, either. For all her elder-sister superiority, she'd never either laughed at, or questioned the existence of, Angel.

At the moment, in fact, Angel seemed to have had the last word on the subject of pierced ears. Lucy finished her breakfast without further nagging, though this didn't by any means signify that they'd heard the end of it. Lucy was nothing if not relentless.

As Dermot folded the newspaper, he glanced out of the window and gave a sudden choked exclamation. 'That bloody Baverstock woman! She was complaining to me yesterday about the paper girl leaving her bike here – I suppose that must be the girl – what's she going on at her again for? I *told* the woman it was all right!'

Before Sarah could answer, he'd rushed out. He was gone several minutes and when he came back, he had the morning's paper with him and was looking rather white around the mouth.

The telephone rang.

'I'll get it!' Lucy cried, jumping down from her chair.

'No!' Sarah said firmly, preparing to answer it herself. 'You get your things ready for school, if you've finished your breakfast.'

Lucy looked smug. 'I put them in my school bag *before* breakfast.'

'Well, *check* – and then help Allie.' Allie was capable of dawdling indefinitely over collecting two exercise books and some coloured pencils, and then forgetting something essential, and panicking.

Sarah's heart skipped when she heard the voice. Simon, showing all the signs of being prepared for a lengthy conversation, full of how he was missing her, when was she coming back to London . . . ?

They spoke for several minutes and she looked anxiously at her watch as Simon began on what was evidently going to be a complicated saga, involving the Divine Devora. Well, of course, he would simply have no idea of what the morning scramble was like – the girls, in their new maroon blazers and little round grey hats, were now hopping on one foot, waiting for her to drive them to school.

'We'll be *late*,' Allie hissed, in a tizzy. To be late, the third day at their new school – ! Not to be borne.

'Simon, I'm sorry, I'll have to ring you back. I have to drive the girls to school.'

A slight pause. 'I've a full day ahead of me, Sarah, that's why I rang now.'

'Oh, Lord, I'm sorry! It's just that –'

'I'll try again tonight – if you're sure you won't be too busy reading nursery rhymes and making cocoa,' he said stiffly.

'Not if you ring after seven thirty, I won't,' Sarah replied, equally cool, a little nettled by the sarcasm, wondering how she was going to tell him that she hadn't yet found anyone to run the house and look after the children, that Dermot wasn't making any effort himself in that direction, that she'd have to stay on here at least another week.

Later that afternoon, James Fitzallan paced the floor of his comfortless attic flat, hands shoved deep in his pockets. It wasn't the place he called home, so the comfort or otherwise of it scarcely mattered. It served its purpose. Occasionally he stayed the night if circumstances warranted it, but its principal use to him was as a studio, and a place which had for

several years accommodated his need to get away and be alone, when things had become intolerable. His impatient strides brought him to the big, protuberant window where he came to a halt, looking out, trying to fill his mind and his eyes with the sight of the changing clouds, the pearlescent sky, willing himself into the right mood. Easel and paintbrushes stood ready. It was no use. He couldn't seem to get started.

Skyscapes were what he painted. Nothing but treetops and sky, the same trees, differently hued in their due seasons, and skies that changed with the dawn and the sunset, with storm and wind and rain, with moonlight and sun, through spring and summer, to autumn and into winter. The immensity of the sky, and the clouds with their infinite mutations, the possibilities were endless.

He was no expert, no Constable. Nor fooled into thinking himself any more than a talented amateur, but painting had always released something in him that might otherwise have soured and curdled irreparably. Until recently. It was doing nothing for him now.

Down below in the garden, on the bumpy, weed-infested patch of grass that was the back lawn, the children, Lucy and Allie, played mock tennis with a motheaten ball and a couple of old racquets they'd discovered in the garden shed. They had, it seemed, cajoled the woman he now knew was their aunt, Sarah, to show them how to serve, which she was doing with more enthusiasm than skill, impatient with the bumps in the lawn that bounced the ball in the wrong direction, though she was evidently enjoying herself, from the way she laughed. He'd seen them often since they'd arrived here, spoken to them several times: the two small girls, Lucy and Allie, and this warm and vibrant woman, with her quick laugh and shining brown hair, like pulled toffee. Amends would have to be made for that first meeting, which had started them off wrong-footed. He'd found himself thinking of her, a lot, in odd moments, since then. So far, she'd treated him with polite reserve whenever they happened to meet, though she didn't, despite her coolness

47

towards him, look the sort to hold on to a grudge. She'd caught him at a bad moment, the worst possible one, after a difficult out-of-hours meeting called for Saturday morning and an unexpected quarrel with his normally mild-tempered and long-suffering father. It had been his own fault, Fitzallan admitted it. His father didn't lose his temper without a great deal of provocation. It had ended with his own apologies, no bones broken, but not liking himself very much, realizing how damned difficult to live with he'd become over the last years.

He couldn't tear himself away from the window. He hadn't been able to bring himself so much as to look at a child since it had happened, but now he indulged himself, watching the three energetic bodies in the garden, the brown limbs flashing. From this distance Sarah could have been an older sister. She wasn't pretty until she smiled, then she was enchanting. Allie had the same quality.

He'd never before painted a living figure, but the desire to do so was suddenly overwhelming – a kind of catharsis? He doubted whether he'd even ask for permission, he'd look such a bloody fool if it should turn out badly, as it might well do.

Sarah called a halt, declaring it was too hot for more, and all three of them flopped down in a laughing heap on to the grass. Fitzallan found the beginnings of a smile in himself, too. It felt to have been a very long time since he'd last smiled, and stranger still that he welcomed it. In the last few years he'd gone through his own private hell, but now he was suddenly sick of himself and what he'd become. He wanted to rejoin the human race.

Rodney Shepherd returned home with his wife from his holiday in the Canaries with a fine deep tan, several bottles of cheaply acquired wine in his baggage and a few extra pounds around his waistline which he could have done without. Despite this last, he was well pleased with life. He remarked to his wife, as they picked the Rover up from the long-stay car park at the airport in Birmingham and drove

home, that their twenty-fifth wedding anniversary celebration holiday had been one to remember. They'd escaped both sunburn and travellers' trots, the hotel had been brilliant – two swimming pools – that foreign food hadn't been half bad, really, but it was great to be home and how about some good old fish and chips from Fryer Tuck's for supper –?

'What the hell does that fool think he's doing, parking there?' he demanded, braking hard after manoeuvring the car down the narrow entry and around the corner to the back of his premises.

Rodney was an electrical supplier, he and Moira lived in the flat above the shop in Colley Street, and the only parking space he had was in the tiny yard behind the shop. It was awkward enough to get into at the best of times, the access lane behind being so narrow, but now a dark-red car was carelessly parked just before the double gates, leaving several feet of its front end protruding across them.

'You'll not get the Rover in, Rod,' Moira said, unwisely.

'You see if I damn well won't,' answered Rodney, his bonhomie quickly evaporating, macho instincts taking its place.

'You'll scratch the paintwork.'

'Not mine, I won't. He gets an inch off his, tough! No way am I going knocking on doors halfway down to Lavenstock to find who it belongs to. Some buggers'll park anywhere for free.'

But it was the three gins he'd had on the aircraft talking. Rodney wouldn't have dreamed of damaging any car if he could help it, no matter whose it was, never mind a car like that. He'd more respect for a good paint job, and with some fancy manoeuvring, and a lot of swearing, he successfully squeezed his own car past, though he'd no space to turn into the yard, the access being to his premises only, and ending at the point where high chain-link fencing separated it from the supermarket car park next door.

'Professor Kendrick, Cambridge? Good Lord. Surprising world we live in!' declared Dermot that evening, once more having arrived home too late to see the girls before they

49

went to bed. He wasn't used to what he called 'office hours' and had evidently made up for it by spending the intervening time somewhere convivial. 'Professor Kendrick!' he repeated. His eyes were bright with malicious amusement.

'I don't know about professor,' Sarah said, 'but yes, I think he *was* at Cambridge.'

'Then it's sure to be the same one. He was a lecturer there – we went out to do a story on some scandal he was connected with, years ago – though I only remember vaguely what it was.'

But there'd been nothing vague about Dermot's reaction to the name. He hadn't needed to think, and Sarah was sure he hadn't forgotten the circumstances, either. Dermot rarely forgot anything to do with his work. She wondered what his reasons were for keeping it to himself, but she didn't press him in view of what she might have to tell him later.

He said, with a pretence of casualness, 'Well, I shall probably know him when I see him – it's tomorrow we're bidden to this welcome shindig, isn't it? God, how suburban!'

'It's a way of getting to know people. I think it's very nice of the Kendricks to take the trouble to introduce us – well, you,' Sarah said primly and rather pointedly. Though it had been Imogen Loxley who'd first telephoned to issue the invitation, who'd responded with alacrity to Sarah's suggestion to come over and join her for coffee, who'd afterwards donned a borrowed overall to cover her elegant casual clothes, picked up a paintbrush and spent an hour helping Sarah finish off the woodwork in the breakfast room. And a very nice small sitting-dining room it was now, thought Sarah – the walls a warm apricot, the paintwork a sharp white, Lisa's collection of porcelain plates on the walls, the smell of a summer evening drifting through the open window.

'I can recommend you an interior decorator,' Imogen had said, after being shown round the rest of the house and empathizing immediately with the enormity of the problem.

'One who doesn't want paying?' Sarah had laughed.

'Well, no, but she'd advise you on wallpapers and curtains,

if you bought them from her. I'll ask her along to meet you when you come over. She's Lois French, of Interiors, that shop at the corner of Butter Lane, just off the Cornmarket.'

'Oh, I've seen it! Much too grand for us.' But Sarah looked forward to meeting the woman. Dermot could use all the help and advice he could get.

'It doesn't matter to me, of course,' she told him now, as a preliminary to approaching the subject of her departure, 'but you'll still be here when I'm gone. You can't live in a community and not be part of it.'

'I don't see why not,' Dermot shrugged, but Sarah knew it was only a token objection. He was too gregarious not to want to meet his neighbours, especially now that Francis Kendrick's name had cropped up and sparked his interest. Dermot had a certain capacity for mischief, and she sensed he was ripe for it. She devoutly hoped he'd have the sense not to make waves at the party, or at any other time.

The antiquated telephone shrilled distantly from the hall. 'That'll be Simon.' She went to answer it with a certain amount of foreboding. She'd never been a match for Simon when he was feeling aggrieved, and if he started being really persuasive, she might well give in. She was feeling decidedly fed up with acting as Dermot's dogsbody, with the whole crackpot set-up here. If it wasn't for the children . . . well, if it wasn't for the children, she wouldn't be here at all.

By the time she got to it, the telephone had stopped, probably having been ringing for some time before they'd heard it and Simon having lost patience. She stood undecided, debating whether or not to ring him back, when there was a knock on the door, and when she opened it, there was the dark-browed Fitzallan on the step. He'd come downstairs from his attic eyrie to ask permission to have a bonfire in the garden, he informed her abruptly.

'A bonfire? There's a spot at the end of the garden that Dermot was using the other day, if you must – but I have to tell you I regard bonfires as extremely antisocial.'

He looked at her as he digested this, saying nothing for a

51

while. 'Perhaps I should find some other way of disposing of my rubbish.'

'Perhaps you should.'

They stood looking at each other. He finally spoke. 'Look. Please don't be uptight with me. I apologize for the other day. I'd had a right old morning, unexpected meeting called, when all hell was let loose. No excuse, none whatever, but please – let's be friends.'

He obviously couldn't exactly bring himself to smile, but equally obviously, in his own way, he meant to charm, and she was at least appeased, despite herself. She always found it faintly ridiculous to take umbrage, anyway, and he seemed to be wanting to make amends for his behaviour on her first day here. 'What is it you want to burn, Mr Fitzallan?'

'Fitz. It's James Fitzallan, but Fitz is what everyone calls me. Come and see for yourself how much there is before you allow me to commit it to the flames – and incidentally, you can take a look at that view – though I warn you, it's not all it's cracked up to be.'

She followed him upstairs and there was the famous view, from the famous window.

You *could* see the Rotunda, just – if you were pointed in the right direction and told what to look for. Otherwise, what you saw was a panoramic view of sky, and the tops of trees just below, and beyond them, between lights winking palely in the early evening, the seemingly endless, undulating landscape of houses, factories, blocks of high-rise flats and roads leading towards several blobs on the horizon, one of which he said was the Rotunda.

And behind her, on the walls of the room, a continuing cyclorama, in the paintings which covered them: the great sweep of skies and trees portrayed on the canvases hung, stacked and laid flat on the floor, all of them unframed.

'Do you do this for a living?'

'Good God, no! I'm not a professional, as you'll see only too well, if you look closely. I run a design consultancy. You could call this a hobby, if that's a word you'd use, though I wouldn't. Let's just say it's served its purpose.' She looked

52

quickly for that flash of raw pain which had struck her before, but his face was closed. 'Obsessive as to subject matter,' he went on, 'but it's the only thing I can do. I'd like to try a human figure, but I'm not sure . . . At any rate, I think I've painted myself out of this as a subject by now, hence the bonfire.'

She was shocked. 'You can't!'

His brilliant eyes lit with something which might possibly have been amusement as he followed her glance to the scores of canvases. 'As a painter, I'm a damned good designer. But maybe burning them is a trifle Draconian, what do you think? No –' He held up a warning hand. 'Don't answer that. I'd honestly rather not know.'

She wanted to laugh, having a suspicion that he'd never had any intention of putting all his work on the bonfire, it was simply a contorted way of arriving at an apology. 'It's no good asking me, anyway, I've no qualifications to judge. You should ask my – the man I work for,' she amended hastily. Bringing Simon into this was, she realized, the last thing she wanted to do, only she'd been thrown by James Fitzallan, his change of attitude. She'd written him off, but now, against all odds, she found she might be warming to him.

'What about you? What sort of work do you do?' he was asking. 'Sit down, if we can find you somewhere among all this, and I'll make some coffee while you tell me the story of your life.'

When she left half an hour later, she realized this was more or less what she'd done, while he'd skated the surface and she'd learned practically nothing about him.

6

Rodney Shepherd's mood couldn't be described as best pleased when he woke up the next morning to find the strange car still blocking his entry, when he was expecting customers and deliveries. He picked the telephone up and rang the police in a rage, ordering them to come and tow away this sodding BMW that was blocking his entry, or he wouldn't be responsible for the consequences.

The offending car was removed from behind his premises by the police with a speed which satisfied even Rodney.

The details having been input in to the National Computer, within minutes it was found to be registered to a Philip James Ensor, with an address in Solihull. The keys in the pocket of the man who had died at the Colley Street allotments were found to fit the car, and his prints corresponded with those all over the inside. A jacket was neatly folded on the back seat and his wallet was locked in the glove compartment. Jubilation all round at Milford Road Police Station was tempered by a telephone call Abigail made to his home which disclosed the presence of a wife who had thought he was still abroad on a business trip. Lord.

'I've made an appointment with Mrs Ensor over at Solihull,' she told Mayo. 'I'm taking Martin Kite with me, OK?'

She was impatient to be off. She'd convinced herself that she'd done all that was possible, and felt that the trail had gone cold, and now here was the break she'd needed, out of the blue.

'That's it, you stick with it, now that you've got a lead,'

Mayo advised crisply. 'Get over there as quickly as you can – the wife doesn't know yet?'

'Wish she did – but I didn't think it was the sort of thing to tell her over the telephone.' He nodded his understanding. Apart from breaking it gently, in a case like this, you had to take advantage of the situation to grasp anything that might give a possible clue as to why someone had taken Ensor's life.

'What kept us?' Abigail asked, inside half an hour later, as Kite eventually slowed down and began to thread his way competently through the built-up suburban areas on the out-skirts of Birmingham. She'd have preferred to do the driving herself, but Kite was a Class One police driver, and proud of it, and she decided it wasn't worth trampling on his mascu-line ego this time. She relegated herself to navigating from the map spread across her knees.

'No point in hanging around.' Kite's watchword. He should channel his energies into getting his inspector's exams, she thought. But Kite insisted he was happy where he was, and he was a damn good sergeant, very like Mayo, in that things moved when he was around. He ran his cases competently, without the need for flourishing trumpets.

It was a change, working with him, rather than the lugu-brious Sergeant Carmody, who usually doubled up with her when she needed partnering. He was at present on leave, no doubt bored to death on the Costa Brava with his wife and his mother-in-law, counting the days until he got back to work.

'You're too used to plodding along with old Ted,' Kite said, picking up her thoughts. 'When's he due back? Another week? God, it'd bore me stiff, sitting around the poolside with the ma-in-law for company.'

'Don't suppose Ted's too happy. He'd swap the Costa Brava any day for what we've got on. Hang on, we're nearly there.'

Another turning, and they'd reached their destination, a smart house on one of the new estates that were spreading out and stretching ever nearer towards Stratford-upon-Avon.

Judith Ensor was a woman in her late twenties, slim, small, with a gorgeous figure and a cloud of dark hair, a heart-shaped face, big grey eyes fringed with thick lashes, which she was inclined to flutter. She had a very slight, but attractive, lisp. She was ready for work, her clothes and make-up immaculate. Had Abigail been asked to hazard a guess as to what that work was, she'd have plumped unhesitatingly for beauty counsellor, hairdresser, fashion consultant or some allied occupation, but she would have been wrong. Mrs Ensor worked at a car-component factory as an industrial nurse. She might well constitute an industrial hazard herself, if she walked through the factory looking like that.

She sat very still when she was told the news. Under the pearly make-up it was impossible to see whether she had paled, but her eyes looked slightly unfocused and her lips were stiff when she spoke.

'I knew something would happen one day.'

'Would you care to elaborate on that, Mrs Ensor?'

'What?' She blinked several times in rapid succession. The big grey eyes were lustrous with what might have been tears. 'Oh, oh just – his car, you know – he drove it so *fast*.'

'I don't think you can have understood. It wasn't a car accident, I'm afraid.'

Shock took people differently. It was possible she hadn't taken it in when Abigail had told her how her husband had died. But Abigail didn't have the impression she'd been thinking of a car accident when she made that initial response. A quick recovery, though, if it had been a slip of the tongue. Judith Ensor began to interest her.

'Is there a relative or anyone you'd like us to contact, to be with you?' Abigail asked. 'Your children?'

'We have no children.' It was stated matter-of-factly, but with enough neutrality to show that it might seriously matter, and Abigail again shifted her perspective of the woman. Clumsy of me, she chided herself, you could never tell, and I should've noticed this isn't a family home. The room they were sitting in was as immaculate as its owner's person, furnished like a colour supplement, with all the material

56

possessions of a successful, childless couple. There were holiday souvenirs from abroad. A conservatory out of *House & Garden* added to the back. Mrs Ensor's own smart car was in the drive, this year's model. Yet there was something wrong, something empty about the set-up, and it wasn't only the lack of children.

'When did you last see your husband?' she asked. Judith Ensor sat back and crossed her pretty legs, shown off by the close-fitting short skirt she was wearing. Her expression hardened. Abigail, looking more closely, upwardly readjusted her assessment of her age by something like ten years.

'I saw him last a fortnight ago,' she said. 'He was supposed to be in Cologne, on business. I wasn't expecting him back until after the weekend.'

Philip Ensor, it turned out, had been the senior sales representative for a freight-forwarding firm based in Bletchley, a job which had necessitated him travelling all over the world on occasions, though his journeys were mainly restricted to Europe.

'It may have been business, then, that took him to Lavenstock last Saturday night?' Abigail asked, adding the name of the firm to her careful, methodical notes.

'Lavenstock?' It might have been on another planet and not simply a town in the next county. 'I don't know. What makes you think *I'd* have been told, anyway? As far as I was concerned, he was supposed to have been in *Cologne*, wasn't he?' The pretty hand with the immaculately lacquered nails was taut on the chair arm.

'Might he have been visiting someone there he knew?' Abigail suggested.

'Look, he didn't know anyone *here*! He wasn't the sort to socialize. We've lived here nearly a year and he scarcely knew the neighbours either side, he was away so much.' There was a bitterness in her voice she didn't trouble to hide now. 'That's why we moved here from Bletchley. With him away so much, at least here I'd be near Lew and Avis – that's my brother and his wife.'

Abigail's next question seemed by now unnecessary, but

the answer couldn't be taken for granted. 'Forgive me, but were relations between you and your husband friendly?'

She laughed shortly. 'Is it that obvious?'

'So it's possible he went to Lavenstock to see another woman?'

'No.'

'You're sure?' She'd sounded absolutely dead certain, but Abigail pressed on. 'All the indications were that he'd been involved in a fight, just before his death. If he's been seeing someone else, Mrs Ensor, it could have been with a jealous husband.'

'He didn't go there to see another woman,' she repeated flatly.

'That sounds pretty categoric.'

'So it should; I haven't been married to Phil for fourteen years without knowing him that well. And another thing – he'd never get involved in a fight. Never.' Her mouth twisted, marring the symmetry of the perfect oval face. 'Running away was more his style.'

If so, this time Ensor hadn't run far enough, poor devil. His wife may have been shaken, but her life didn't appear to have fallen to pieces on receiving the appalling news. She wondered what sort of life they'd led together, that Judith Ensor accepted the manner of his death so unquestioningly. But she'd said all she was going to say. Her lips were firmly pressed together, with the look of a woman who wouldn't be persuaded into saying what she'd determined not to.

'I'm afraid,' said Kite, 'there's the question of identification. We shall need someone to do it – you say your brother lives near. Would he be prepared to do the necessary?'

Her grey eyes turned a curiously assessing look on him, but she shook her head and spoke decisively. 'No. I don't want him bothered. I'm quite capable of doing it myself.'

The photographs displayed around the home were enough to leave no doubt that Philip Ensor was indeed the man last seen lying on the mortuary slab at his autopsy. But formal identification was a necessity in any sudden, unexplained death, when anyone had been unlawfully killed, one of the

more harrowing experiences which had to be gone through. Not, however, one which most wives willingly undertook.

'It might be an idea to have a word with your brother, all the same. He may know something about your husband's –'

'If Phil didn't confide in me, he certainly wouldn't in Lew! I might as well tell you they didn't exactly get on. But last Saturday, in case you're getting the wrong idea,' she added ironically, 'we – my brother and sister-in-law and myself – were at a family wedding over at Sutton Coldfield, and the celebrations went on until well after midnight. You'd be wasting your time.'

'Let's have his address, all the same,' Kite said.

She shrugged and gave it.

'When are we likely to find him in?'

'Most of the time. He's unemployed.'

Abigail considered briefly. 'Sergeant Kite will drive you over to Lavenstock and bring you back while I see your brother.' If Kite was surprised at this, he said nothing. 'In the meantime, would you mind if we took a look at your husband's belongings? It might give us some ideas where to start, help us to get a better picture.'

She readily gave permission. 'Go ahead, what there is. He wasn't a man for keeping things.'

Which proved to be absolutely true. Philip Ensor might have been a man living in a hotel, for all the personal possessions he'd left behind him. Some clothing, good but unexceptional. A few expensive but unused toiletries, the varying brands suggesting they might have been given to him as presents. An innocuous choice of books and CD discs, revealing nothing but a mediocre taste. The personal papers in the shared desk were only insurances, tax papers, documents relating to the house. He'd had a mortgage he could well afford, contributed to a pension fund that would leave his wife in comfortable circumstances – though not suspiciously so. His bills were paid. He'd evidently lived a life so blinding in its ordinariness that it was in fact quite extraordinary.

* * *

59

Lew Walker hadn't done anything like as well for himself in life as had his sister.

Not only was he unemployed, he lived in an undistinguished terraced house in a narrow, shabby street leading off the main Birmingham road, about as far a cry from Yorkfield Avenue as you were likely to get. He'd missed out on his share of the family good looks, too, though what he had would undoubtedly have been improved by a shave and a haircut, and less of a scowl. Sullen and uncommunicative, he reeked of cigarette smoke and left the television horse-racing blaring in the spotlessly unimaginative living room, while waiting for Abigail to state her business. In the background his wife hovered, a tired-looking, colourless woman, with bulging, thyroid eyes, dowdy and depressed. Abigail would have felt the same, married to Walker.

'Do you mind?' She had no compunction in going to the set and turning down the sound. The man stared at her, but said nothing. The woman's eyes flickered.

It took Abigail about two minutes to realize Judith Ensor had been right. She was wasting her time here. The shocking news she had to pass on seemed to have no more impact than if the victim had been some unknown politician who'd been assassinated at the other side of the world, rather than their brother-in-law. No expressions of sorrow or surprise escaped their lips. Not even a dear me.

She pressed on, feeling frustrated. The decision to spend time here she could ill afford, while Kite ferried Mrs Ensor to and from Lavenstock, had been prompted by a hunch that Judith Ensor didn't want her brother to talk to the police. She'd evidently boobed, and was now going to have to hang around at the pub where she'd arranged to meet Kite. Neither of the Walkers had anything relevant to contribute to the sum of her knowledge about Philip Ensor, much less the mystery of his death. Mrs Walker opened her mouth to speak only once, and looked at her husband for permission before she did. Abigail had posed all the questions she could think of, and was about to leave, when the woman surprised her

60

by speaking directly to her, and for the first time meeting and holding her eyes.

'You'll have to excuse me, I have to go to work. Down the road at the Shangri-la café on the corner. They don't like us to be late.' She left the room, a moment later the front door banged, and after a few more unproductive words with her husband, Abigail, leaving him to light yet another cigarette, followed suit.

The Shangri-la lived up to its name only in that it was clean, bright and reasonably comfortable.

'You've something you wanted to tell me, Mrs Walker?' Abigail asked of the woman behind the counter, as steaming water spat into the pot of tea she'd ordered.

She nodded. 'Table over there, in the corner – I'll join you in a minute.'

Abigail poured herself a cup of the strong brew, helped herself to a ginger biscuit from the cellophane-wrapped pack of two she'd bought. Avis Walker dispensed microwaved faggots and mushy peas to an elderly couple at a table by the window before coming across to lower herself on to the chair opposite, carrying a cup of tea for herself.

'Can't spare long, they'll all be coming in wanting lunches and sandwiches any time now.' She nodded in the direction of a builders' yard on the other side of the road. She was wearing a red plastic apron that matched the table coverings and its reflective glow added a little colour and animation to her pale face. Released from the presence of her husband, it seemed she was prepared to talk. 'You want to know about Phil, then? Well, I can't tell you much, but never mind what *he* says, there'd been something wrong between him and my precious sister-in-law, some big row or other recently. I don't know what about.' *He* evidently referred to her husband.

'Not a female, according to Mrs Ensor.'

She considered this, measuring sugar from a dispenser into her tea. 'No, I'll give Phil his due, I don't think he went after women, though who'd blame him? That Jude!'

61

'I thought you were friends? Didn't they move here to be near you?'

'To be near us? That's what she told you?' The humour of the remark struck her, and the sudden smile made her tired, drawn face nearly pretty. 'That's a laugh! First time I'd seen her for months, that wedding last week. Only went there to show off her new car and her fancy clothes.'

'So why do you think they did come to live here?'

'I've wondered about that. It was very sudden. He was still working at Bletchley, there seemed no reason.' She sipped her tea, then said suddenly, 'I'm sorry what's happened to him, he was a nice chap, you know, Phil. Not somebody you'd ever get close to, mind, you never knew what he was thinking. Deep, you know, and quiet. But very generous. He's lent Lew a fair old whack one way and another, and not got it back, either – and was Lew ever grateful? He was not! That's often the case, isn't it? Folks don't like to feel beholden – you noticed?'

'I know what you mean.' When you had no choice but to accept favours and had to remain under an obligation, gratitude could turn itself inside out. 'What did your husband do, when he was in work?'

Avis Walker shrugged. 'You name it, he's tried it. But nothing's worked out for him. He's got past bothering now.' She finished her tea and pushed her chair back as the elderly couple left and a group of displaced-looking teenagers wandered in. 'Sorry, but that's all I can tell you; I'll have to go now.'

'I'm very grateful to you. Could I wait here until I'm due to meet my sergeant? He shouldn't be more than ten minutes or so, now.'

'Stay as long as you like. You stay where you are and I'll get you another pot of tea when you've finished that – on the house.'

PART II

The party for the new neighbours is in progress at Simla, and Francis Kendrick, having downed a glass of wine and made what he considers is quite enough small talk, is about to make his excuses and leave them to it, when he glances outside and sees one of the children, Lucy, or the one they call Allie – he can't remember which is which, only that she's the shy one – standing alone under the big conifer on the lawn.

Maybe it's the height of the tree – they've just been discussing it in the drawing room and someone has estimated it to be nearly a hundred and fifty feet tall, which sounds about right, supposing it to have been planted at the time the house was built, a century and a half ago – maybe it's this height, juxtaposed with that of the small solemn child, three foot six at most, which holds his attention. He likes the way she's listened to the conversation and then gone out to see the tree for herself. She stands dwarfed by its immensity, overawed by its size.

He puts down his empty glass, steps over the low windowsill into the heat of the summer-evening garden and, unaware of Hope's eyes following him, walks across the grass towards the little girl.

She is Allie – properly Alice – he discovers, not Lucy. She wears a cotton frock, bare legs and sandals, and her hair is side-parted and held back with a blue hairslide in the shape of a butterfly. She has a small chip on one of her front teeth. He can't think who she reminds him of. They talk about the size and age of the conifer, and he tells her that it is correctly a Sequoiadendron giganteum, *known variously as the sequoia, the Wellingtonia, the Big Tree or the Mammoth Tree, that it belongs to one of the tallest and oldest family of trees in the world, and that its potential height is over ninety metres.*

He watches her listening to him, big eyed and serious, absorbing the information, which he imparts to her in the same way he would to an adult. He'd be hard put to it to know how to speak to her

otherwise, in what might be considered a more appropriate way, but in any case, he's never been one to underestimate what children can comprehend.

Allie thinks about it, scuffing the toe of her shoe in the deep, sun-warmed layer of brown needles beneath the tree, raising dust, and fingers a piece of the thick, fibrous, spongy bark which he tells her the tree regularly sheds. She reaches up to one of the sprigs of unripe green cones on the gracefully swooping branches, some of which touch the ground. She breathes in the resiny smell, it's like Dettol.

Belatedly, he says, 'What are you doing out here, all on your own?'

'I'd finished my lemonade and I wanted to see the tree. My friend Angel and me don't like grown-up parties.'

'Don't you? Then we should be friends, Allie. I don't like them, either,' says Francis, and the smile few are privileged to see lights his face. He knows now who she reminds him of. She is an Arthur Rackham child, thin and spindly, a child in an illustration, with windblown clothes and hair, who dances under witchlike trees with spiky, insubstantial fairies and elves. Or Titty in Swallows and Amazons, *still on occasions his preferred bedtime reading. He smiles again. 'Have you ever heard of a pianola?'*

'No.' She considers gravely. 'Is it some kind of piano?'

'That's right, a mechanical piano. I have one, a similar sort of thing at any rate, called a Polyphon, that plays a tune with the same name as yours. Would you like to hear it?'

'Yes, please.' She turns, says something over her shoulder, and reports back, 'Angel says she'd like to hear it, too.'

After a moment of attentive regard, Francis answers, seriously, 'Come along then, both of you.'

The sun has passed behind the sequoia and the shadows in the garden are lengthening, columns of midges dance around in what is left of the sunlight, making it thick and soupy, as the tall man and the little girl walk back to the house.

7

'What?' Hope turned from the window to answer something Dermot Voss had said to her. The word was sharp enough to come to Sarah's ears over the murmured conversation. She watched the pair of them as her own conversation with Meg Saunders, the wife of the self-satisfied man who owned a thriving local timber yard, wound down. Mrs Saunders was clearly disappointed to find Sarah was only incidental to the scene and would soon be gone, and had lost interest on hearing that Dermot didn't have a wife whom she could cajole on to the various committees she chaired. Someone else spoke to her and she turned to answer with alacrity, blocking Sarah's view of her brother-in-law.

Dermot was feeling hard done by, his worst fears about this gathering fulfilled, and not only because of the quality of the wine, which was indifferent. The information relayed to him through Sarah, via Doreen Bailey, about the occupants of the gloomy old house (even gloomier and quite as old as Edwina Lodge, he'd discovered when they arrived) had not filled him with enthusiasm, while meeting them had put even more of a damper on his easily dampened spirits . . . this middle-aged brother and sister, tall, thin and be-sandalled, unnervingly alike. Distantly polite, not the sort one warmed to . . .

He repeated his question to Hope. 'I was asking you what kind of books your brother writes?' He found her difficult and abrupt, though rather better than the brother, quite certainly the Cambridge professor whom he'd briefly met, years ago, but who showed no recollection of ever having met

Dermot. There was no reason why he should remember, of course. As far as Francis Kendrick was concerned, Dermot had merely been the young man behind the camera in a stiff, awkward interview with one of the outside-broadcast team, and, if he were wise, he'd have put the incident which had occasioned the interview firmly behind him. He'd spoken briefly when they were introduced, then retreated into an abstracted silence before disappearing into the garden.

'His books are mostly concerned with Byzantine art,' Hope Kendrick said in answer to his question at last, dragging her wandering attention back to Dermot and then becoming animated as she cited the number of books her brother had written, the critical acclaim he'd received . . .

Dermot listened with half an ear, but brightened as the other sister, Imogen, re-entered the room, ushering in more guests and seeing them settled in a hostessy kind of way. This was more the type of woman he could appreciate. She had talked amusingly, when he first arrived, about living in Brussels, a city he knew fairly well. He knew from gossip relayed through Doreen Bailey, via Sarah, why she no longer lived there, though she didn't mention this to him. He'd realized immediately that she was still committed to this almost-ex husband of hers, but the situation offered possibilities, all the same . . .

She now signalled across the room to Hope, who excused herself to Dermot and went to greet some newcomers, while he let himself drift in her wake towards Imogen.

Gil Mayo ate another handful of salted peanuts and wondered what the heck he was doing here. Parties of any kind were anathema to him, and as an overworked policeman his spare time wasn't so plentiful that he could afford to waste it in what he considered to be meaningless chit-chat with people he didn't know and would probably never see again. But he'd agreed to come, to take time out from the madhouse the station seemed to have become this week, a situation that had made his successful seminar no more than a beautiful

memory. He'd played his part tonight with good grace and circulated obediently around the crowded room, making himself pleasant. He'd now wedged himself into a corner, hoping to remain unnoticed until Alex gave him the sign they could depart – a forlorn hope for one of his size and personality: he was a big man, with a presence as solid as the Rock of Gibraltar – not easy to miss. But, alone for the moment, his policeman's eyes were everywhere, noting, filing, remembering, instinctively sensing the undercurrents, the feeling in the room of something not quite right.

His eyes lit on Dermot Voss and Imogen Loxley, whom Voss was entertaining with audible accounts of how he'd picked out Lavenstock with a pin, come across Mrs Burgoyne and become intrigued with the idea of himself as an entrepreneurial landlord. Intriguing chap, Voss, on several counts. Through his job, widely travelled in many of the most dangerous spots in the world. Quick-witted, with an Irish fluency with words which enabled him to recount his travels so as to make them seem both fascinating and amusing, when often they must have been neither, involving him as they did in the worst situations mankind could create for itself. As if he enjoyed living on the edge, or it hadn't quite got through to him. Mayo would have liked to continue their conversation, if only to find out whether he was right in his assessments. He mustn't, however, monopolize the guest of honour. Most of the women in the room were dying for the chance to talk to him. Voss was the sort who would be attractive to women, there was a sort of daredevil look about him that they seemed to go for . . .

'What are you doing here?' said a voice. 'Wouldn't have thought this was your scene.'

'Nor yours, Henry.' Mayo was relieved to find a kindred spirit at his side – Ison, the local police surgeon, looking as ill at ease as he felt himself to be in this gathering, far cry that it was from the less salubrious places and circumstances where they usually met.

'Viv brought me,' Ison replied, rather as if he were an umbrella picked up as an afterthought in case of rain, and

69

Mayo remembered that Vivien Ison taught geography at the Princess Mary where Hope Kendrick also taught, and that they were near neighbours of the Kendricks into the bargain, their home being just a little further down the hill, in a cul-de-sac off Albert Road. Ison was a short, brisk man, with a bristly moustache and bright eyes, reminiscent of some small, furry, bustling animal who, over the years, had become more than just a colleague with whom Mayo worked. Work, plus a mutual respect and liking, was what had initially formed a bond between them, but it was a shared passion for music which had fostered the friendship.

'Me, too,' Mayo said gloomily. 'I mean, Alex brought me along with her. She's standing in for Lois, who couldn't come tonight.'

'That situation working out all right?' Ison asked carefully.

'I think so.' Mayo's reply was equally cautious, given more in hope than in certainty. His glance travelled across the room towards Alex, at the moment talking with evident interest to the woman he'd been introduced to as Sarah Wilmot. He caught her reflection in the big, dim old looking glass over the mantelpiece, softened by the evening light, and was momentarily reassured. Too often, lately, he'd felt something overbright about her, like a splintered reflection of her sister, Lois, and it was bothering him.

She'd recently astonished all who knew her by throwing in her hand, leaving her successful and promising career as a police sergeant, and begun working with Lois in her smart interior-decorating business. She'd so far resisted any attempts to involve her in a partnership, for which Lois undoubtedly, if mistakenly, blamed Mayo. Hardly new. Lois French blamed most of Alex's misfortunes on Mayo, including the major one of living with him.

But Lois was wrong about him trying to influence Alex in any way. In fact, he had quite a load of guilt on his shoulders about her decision to quit the Force, though he'd never actively encouraged her in that. Stood objectively aside, and let her make up her own mind. And her own mistakes. *Had* it been a mistake? He was damn sure dabbling in interior

70

decorating wasn't going to prove stimulating or challenging enough for her in the long run.

The sun had passed behind the sequoia and dusk was gathering in the big dark room, the light absorbed by its heavy furniture, drawing its sombre colours into itself. It was a relief when Imogen began to move gracefully around, flicking on lamps that focused a kindlier radiance into the centre of the room, lighting faces, gleaming on glasses, on the women's clothes and their bare arms, leaving the shadows to the corners.

Alex was wearing a full patterned skirt that caught the light in its folds, and a kingfisher-blue silk shirt which emphasized the dark blue of her eyes. Her dark hair was a little longer than she'd worn it when in uniform. She wore his ring, a Victorian sapphire and diamond cluster – but still on her right hand. He swallowed a sigh.

He came to earth again to hear Ison harking back to the last time he'd been called out on police work. As usual, the doc couldn't resist the opportunity to talk shop. He was asking about Abigail's case. 'Any developments on your body by the allotments? I hear the theory that he staggered along and fell down in a drunken stupor is ruled out. Must confess, that was my first impression.'

'Not according to T-L. No alcohol present, for one thing.'

'Then who are we to doubt?' Ison grinned, but Mayo knew his amusement didn't reflect his high regard of his colleague's opinions. Sobering, he added, 'Poor devil. Chance in a million, drowning like that, in such shallow water.'

'Not if you've been hit on the head first.'

Ison was immediately interested, wanting to know the full details of the autopsy. Fortunately, or perhaps intentionally, no one else came near. Everyone in the room must know by now that Mayo was a policeman, and people trod warily when encountering the law, whether they had cause or not.

'Any ideas who he is?' Ison asked.

Mayo told him what they knew about Philip Ensor. 'We've pulled out all the stops and I must confess we're nowhere nearer knowing what he was doing here. Nothing in his line

71

of business in Lavenstock, though Abigail's tried several long shots. And nobody's come forward who'd seen him, despite that photo we issued to the media – not good, but the best we could do in the circumstances. Fortunately we now have a better one.'

Because of the ethics of showing a photograph of a dead face – nonproductive, too, given the state of Ensor's face when he'd been found – it had been a reconstruction involving facial enhancement by an artist. The result hadn't been bad, but the recent photograph of her husband which Judith Ensor had handed over and was shortly to be used revealed all the reconstruction's inadequacies. It was hoped this one might better bring forth recollections on someone's part.

'Early days yet, isn't it?'

'Long enough – nearly a week. We haven't given up yet, though.'

The case wasn't anywhere near being closed. Never would be, though the inquiry was growing sluggish and Philip Ensor was nearly as much of an enigma as he had been at first. Abigail was worrying like a terrier at the idea that Judith Ensor knew more about the circumstances than she was saying, but was getting nowhere with it.

The elder Voss child, Lucy, her job of handing round canapés over, and the attention she'd basked in at first now fading, was starting to whinge a little, fidgeting beside her aunt, bored in this grown-up gathering. He couldn't see Allie, who'd taken herself out into the garden. Francis Kendrick hadn't returned, either. Mayo decided perhaps he, too, might take a stroll around the garden.

He took another cautious sip of the diabolical wine and a glance at his watch, and thought of the pleasant, relaxed evening he and Alex could be having together at home.

The covert glance hadn't been lost on Ison, nor the fact that other people were beginning to leave. 'Tell you what, why don't you and Alex join us for supper?'

'Good idea. Where shall we go? Somewhere where there's no need to book?'

'Oh, join us at home's what I meant.'

'We'd enjoy that – thanks. But would Viv welcome guests at such short notice?' Mayo had no wish to be the cause of marital dissension.

'Rubbish! I believe it's only cold meat and salad. Anyway, Viv will cope. She'll be delighted.'

Mayo had no doubt about Vivien Ison's ability to cope. She was an energetic, practical woman with short grey hair, who took most things in her stride, including her husband's demanding, and sometimes macabre, job. Ison added, as further incentive, 'I have that new John Eliot Gardiner recording I know you're dying to hear.'

That clinched it. 'Well, if you're sure.'

'Sure I'm sure. Let's make tracks, then.'

The Isons departed to walk the short distance home, leaving Mayo and Alex to follow in their car. They made their round of farewells and were thanking Imogen and her sister at the door when, from somewhere in the back of the house, came a faint and gentle sound, the slow, sweetly measured musical-box notes of 'Alice Where Art Thou?'

'Oh, do listen!' Alex exclaimed, enchanted.

'That's Francis's Victorian Polyphon,' Imogen smiled. 'You put an old penny in it and it plays the tune you choose. Allie's very favoured to be allowed a demonstration.'

For a moment, they stood in the shadowed hall, lit only by gloomy stained-glass windows, the dark staircase with its tall carved newel posts winding upwards into infinity. What was it that held them all still? Those poignant echoes of the old house's past . . . musical soirees, drawing-room ballads, young ladies in ringlets and crinolines? Or some moment of precognizance? Mayo shook himself and moved to the door.

But in the weeks that followed, he was to remember time and again that haunting tune, the overpowering smell of roses from the garden, and the look on Hope Kendrick's face.

'Nice kids,' remarked Vic Baverstock over Monday-morning breakfast at Edwina Lodge. From the window of their downstairs flat, he watched Lucy and Allie trotting between their father's car and the house, importantly helping him to stow

photographic paraphernalia into the boot of his car, plus a grip for what looked like an overnight stay away from home, encouraged by Dermot, who knew the value of volunteer labour and wanted to get off as soon as possible.

'They're noisy,' replied Tina, without any reference to truth.

She'd been born with an argumentative and contrary nature, and disagreed with her husband on principle, contradicting him almost every time he opened his mouth to speak. He constantly reminded himself that, being thin and colourless, and of no great significance as far as looks went, this was her way of getting attention. If so, it wasn't a very successful ploy. People still did their best to avoid her. And Vic himself continued to air opinionated views, even on subjects he didn't much care about, simply to keep his end up, so that their conversation resembled an acrimonious game of pat-ball.

'All kids are noisy,' he said, although it had been only the elder child, when he'd met them in the garden the previous day, who'd seemed uninhibited and full of high spirits. The younger one had played with the ends of her hair, seeming too shy to open her mouth. They jigged about on the front doorstep now, waving as their father finally drove off, shouting goodbyes in their shrill childish voices before going indoors.

'Not all children make their presence felt so obviously, by any means, if they're well brought up,' Tina continued her complaint, punctuating it with a sniff.

Vic gave up the unequal struggle and poked without enthusiasm at his bowl of yoghurt and muesli, thinking it resembled sweepings from a stable floor, while his mouth watered for bacon, sausage, eggs, the works. Vegetarian food was all right in its way, but it needed imagination to give it a kick, you had to be committed enough to food to make such a regime palatable, and Tina was basically not interested in eating, regarding it as a necessary evil, nibbling minute quantities while barely giving herself time to sit down and consume them. Now there was a thing, he reflected, the

74

manager of a wholefood shop who wasn't interested in food! No wonder the customers didn't actually roll in – or quickly made some excuse to leave if they found themselves there by mistake. If you'd been born in Lavenstock and grown up with a centuries' old tradition of consuming the products of pork butchers' shops in the form of pigs' trotters and tripe, black pudding, pork pies, faggots and peas, you didn't take kindly to being lectured on the virtues of a healthy diet by someone who was patently no advert for her own products. Being skinny and intense wasn't admired around here. They thought her advice a bit of a cheek. Vic considered it a pretence.

Like this pretence that she found children a nuisance, when she pursued motherhood as determinedly as she pursued every other craze in her life – he couldn't think of it as anything else but a craze: Tina as a parent hardly conjured up visions of dewy-eyed madonnas or fruitful earth mothers. He switched off the subject, which he preferred to ignore – not the idea of having a family, for he was extremely fond of children, but the processes entailed in getting one. All these charts and temperature-taking and other things which he'd rather not think about, too damned clinical, by half. Not to mention sex at the approved time, whether one felt like it or not. Off-putting, to say the least. Especially since Tina didn't inspire him to feel much like it at all these days.

'That wretched paper girl's left her bike inside the gate again!' she declared suddenly, assuming her on-the-warpath expression as she spied Patti Ryman's bicycle in the bushes, and Patti talking to Henry Pitt.

'If she didn't hide it, it'd get nicked. You can't expect her to push it around while she's delivering that load of papers.'

'She shouldn't be delivering papers at all.'

Vic was inclined to agree – the bag for them was very near as big as the girl herself – but he couldn't be bothered to argue. He was going to have indigestion all day as it was from that bloody muesli.

'You don't need to go yet – and you haven't finished your

75

breakfast,' she accused him, as he pushed his chair back from the table. 'It's only quarter to eight.'

'Not really hungry,' he lied, thinking of the hot sausage sandwich he'd have time to pick up if he left now. 'And I want to be in early this morning. There's old Pitt – I can offer him a lift.'

'He likes to walk to work.'

'Well, he's only got to refuse, then,' Vic retorted, making his escape before he said more than he ought. He had his own reasons for keeping Tina sweet at the moment, apart from the fact that he was sorry for her over the way Mrs Burgoyne had let her down over her promise to let them have first refusal to buy Edwina Lodge.

He was just in time to catch Henry Pitt, from the upstairs flat, a plump, white-haired old man who was looking flustered, mumbling something Vic didn't catch, touching Patti's sleeve then edging away from her, his face growing even more pink as he spotted Vic.

'Well, thanks, Mr Pitt,' Patti said, giving Vic a bright smile as she hurried off to complete the rest of her deliveries. 'Don't forget to be there. It's really important.'

'Assignations?' Vic asked Henry jokingly, his gaze appreciatively following Patti's neat little back view. Even the hideous school uniform couldn't hide that Patti Ryman was growing up, fast. Her legs, when she'd worn those miniskirts during the holidays, were worth more than a second look.

Henry flushed even more deeply as he answered Vic's flippant remark. 'Oh, it's something and nothing.'

He didn't refuse Vic's offer of a lift, although it would mean abandoning his walk to work. He would arrive far too early at the town library, where he stamped books and put them back on the shelves contentedly all day long, where he made his way every day with his doddery-looking walk that must surely be deceptive, since he had no car and rarely took the bus, and sent for a taxi only on odd occasions. Couldn't be as old as he appeared, not yet retired and on the pension, Vic reflected, though he wasn't looking as benevolently smiling today as he normally did.

'How's things, then?' Vic asked when they'd joined the traffic flow and were bowling down the hill.

'Oh, coping you know, coping.' Henry paused. 'Well, to tell the truth, not happy with the way things are going at the library, Vic, not happy at all.' He had a gentle, cultivated voice, he wore knitted waistcoats and, in winter, a fur hat with ear-flaps. He'd lived with his brother, Charles, until Charles died and their house had become too much for Henry to cope with alone. Harmless old boy, a big soft Nellie, really, but basically OK.

'Oh, you mean the cuts and that.'

'Yes, that's just what I do mean.' Henry was silent for a while, then burst forth, growing more and more agitated as he elaborated on his theme. They were being forced to close down another branch library, due to spending limits set by central government ... 'Closing down *libraries*, imagine! We're becoming a nation of Philistines!' he cried. 'Not to mention the shortsightedness of it! How can we grumble about children doing nothing but sit in front of the telly, if we don't encourage them to read?' He went on in this vein for some time. 'It's hardly surprising they're growing up illiterate, can scarcely even write their own names!'

'I suppose not,' answered Vic, who rarely read anything other than *Exchange and Mart* and hadn't given the subject much consideration one way or another, although, working as a clerk in the council treasurer's department, he could hardly be unaware of the swingeing cuts in local government spending. He was rather taken aback at the gentle Henry's vehemence.

'Well, that's how it seems to me,' said Henry with an apologetic smile. 'I'm sorry, I can be a bit of a bore on the subject. It shouldn't matter to me, I'll be retiring shortly, but it does, I'm afraid, it still does.'

'Think nothing of it,' replied Vic, who'd been listening with half an ear anyway, thinking that if he got a move on, he'd still be in time to nip round the corner to the sandwich bar where the lovely Mandy would slip three sausages in his bap, rather than the stipulated two, at no extra charge. It

wasn't only the sausages that made his mouth water again. 'What are you going to do with yourself, then, when you retire? Got all your plans made?' he asked Henry heartily.

Henry looked bleak. 'I'm not sure. My brother and I – we used to spend our holidays in Greece, the country fascinated him, and we'd intended to go there more often when I retired – but I don't somehow feel inclined to go alone. To tell you the truth, I can't imagine what I shall find to do without my work,' he added, in a forlorn burst of honesty. 'I've worked in the library for forty-eight years.'

Forty-eight years! Jesus. Vic tried to think up something useful to say, but could only dredge up a cliché he was himself sick of hearing. 'Oh, I don't know. You wait. When I meet blokes that used to be in our office, they tell me they don't know how they found time to go to work. You've got plenty hobbies, I suppose?' Vic was a great believer in hobbies. His was singing in a male-voice choir. Very therapeutic, letting off steam by belting it out – and useful, too, if you needed an excuse.

'I like cooking. I read a lot.'

'You want to get yourself an allotment, keep you more fit than reading.'

'An allotment? Good heavens, I don't know the first thing about gardening!' Henry laughed gently. 'I am happy to say I have never *seen* a spade.'

Poor bugger, thought Vic, not realizing Henry was quoting, he's going a bit gaga already, even before they shove him out on to the scrapheap. Get worse if he wasn't watched. You could never tell with these old blokes when they got to that age, up to all sorts, they were. He thought with sudden unease of the empty sherry bottles he'd noticed recently in the shared dustbin, of lonely old men sitting on park benches, loitering outside school gates, of the two small girls at Edwina Lodge, and wondered what Henry could have been talking to little Patti Ryman about.

After those who went out to work had left, and the children been packed off to schools and playgroups, Ellington Close

78

took on its usual peaceful daytime languor. Mothers thankfully made themselves a quiet cup of coffee and looked for their horoscopes on the telly, the postman came and went, the three retired couples rose and had breakfast, and Stanley Loates put his mother's soiled bed linen into the washing machine.

Trevor Lawley, from number thirteen, went in search of his cat.

8

It had been a week of disasters, one of those weeks that occasionally descend like the wrath of God, even on well-conducted police stations such as Lavenstock Divisional Headquarters. Murphy's – or somebody's – Law, saying that if something can go wrong, it will, with Detective Superintendent Gil Mayo under pressure too, and – just another natural law of life – passing on the heat to the Poor Bloody Infantry below. A week best forgotten, but not yet over, culminating in this.

This was something the Super hated more than any other single crime, as his bleak face showed, and the reason he'd been one of the first on the scene. And not alone in that, Abigail Moon thought. Professionals, accustomed, but not yet, thank God, desensitized to the murder of a young person, a child – and this one not much more than a child, fifteen, sixteen at most. Life barely begun for her. Thought at first to be much younger, so small in stature was she, but underneath the dark-green school uniform the small round breasts, the smooth curves of her developing young body confirmed she was older. Yet the face of innocence looked up at them from the fallen carpet of leaves. Unblemished, but dead. Oh, certainly dead.

Patti Ryman, the paper girl.

Poor, poor child, poor creature, muttered Doc Ison, tight-lipped, he who had brought her into the world, and never thought to see her out of it. He knelt, shaken out of his usual professional detachment, beside Timpson-Ludgate as the pathologist delicately probed and examined: bluff and hearty,

renowned for his mordant humour, he too was silenced by the terrible waste of a young life.

'What could she ever have done to deserve that?' Ison asked.

Probably nothing, thought Mayo grimly, overhearing the muttered question. Nobody knew better than he that the times we live in mean that murder doesn't necessarily require provocation any more – or only one so slight as to be incomprehensible to any sane person, to anyone but the killer.

On the other hand . . .

There were many things on the other hand. Youth, however innocent it seemed, was rarely completely so these days. They knew more at eight years old than Mayo had known at twenty-eight – which wasn't to say he hadn't always wanted to know. He'd been born with an avid curiosity about the human race and what makes it tick, what causes it to go off the rails. It was what made him a good copper and occasionally a bad risk as a friend and companion. It was why he raged inwardly, in tune with Ison, against what could have brought little Patti Ryman to this violent end.

The playground drugs scene? A quarrel with a boyfriend, after experimenting with sex, becoming pregnant? Teenage prostitution, leading to murder? Unthinkable only a few years ago, any of them, but now all too possible.

But there was that other thing, the possibility of this being one out of a series of murders, which until now had been principally Hurstfield Division's problem, but now was in everyone's mind here: two other young girls over there had been raped and brutally battered to death within the last few months, another was missing. Younger than Patti, but two of them in school uniform, like her, and all of them with fair hair, like Patti's.

And yet . . .

Murder this undoubtedly was, though possibly not a sex crime. It seemed unlikely that she'd been raped or sexually assaulted, for although she'd been discovered lying on her back with her skirt rucked up around her thighs, she'd been fully clothed and there was no indication so far of any sexual

81

interference. Timpson-Ludgate had refused to be categoric about it until he'd had the chance to do a more detailed examination, but it wouldn't be what he expected to find. And, now that he'd gently turned her over, it could be seen that her mane of crimped fair hair was clotted with blood.

'There you are. Her skull's been smashed. With,' he added, looking more closely, 'what looks like a single blow to the back of her head. Savage, though, some weight behind it. And if you ask me what with, I can only say,' he went on, parting the hair carefully, 'it was probably something narrowish, flat, heavy, what say you, Henry? We'll get a better picture later, but take a look.'

Thus called upon, Ison squatted further down beside Timpson-Ludgate so that he, too, could examine the wound. Mayo didn't feel a minute inspection was called for on his part. He looked briefly, then at the rest of the body, the way her skirt had been dragged up, and at her black leather school shoes. He frowned.

There'd been no problem with identification. Everyone around her knew Patti. Knew her and liked her, a cheerful girl, delivering papers for pocket money before she went on to school. No problem with establishing the time of death, either: the doctors were saying she couldn't have been dead much more than an hour, which tied in with the time she normally arrived here on her round.

'PM nine a.m. tomorrow morning,' Timpson-Ludgate announced, peeling off his gloves. 'Best I can do.'

It was quicker than Mayo had expected.

As the doctors took their leave, the SOCOs moved in. Mayo took the opportunity – while the cameras flashed and captured the scene on video and Dexter applied his forensic skills to collecting the usual samples – to walk around and fix the scene in his mind: a roughly rectangular wooded area which sloped down behind the gardens of Edwina Lodge, Ellington Close, and the house called Simla, running down to the car park of an engineering factory on the lower road, from which it was separated by high chain-link fencing surmounted by barbed wire. The rest of the wood, except where

the residents had put up their own more decorative woven fencing panels, was fenced off with wire strung between concrete posts, fronted with scrawny quickthorn hedging. A narrow dirt path between the first house in the Close and the garden of Edwina Lodge – six-foot boarded fencing on the one side and a high brick wall on the other – led into this shared piece of private woodland, to which all the residents had legal access and where the older children played. Scruffy woodland of little more than an acre, the children probably thought it paradise. Ropes hung from trees, 'camps' had been dug, a stream, little more than a trickle, had been dammed with stones and diverted.

But now, apart from the shirt-sleeved police swarming all over the wood, and the sounds of their voices, the Close itself was silent as he guessed it rarely was – older children now in school, younger ones kept protectively indoors. Murder close to home had a sobering effect.

He completed his circuit of the wood and came back full circle. 'Somebody's going to miss this,' Dexter was saying. 'These don't come cheap. Hundred and fifty nicker at least, I'll bet, probably more.'

'Hundred and fifty, for a biro?' Kite echoed. 'Strewth!'

'It's a fountain pen. Last you a lifetime, this would.'

'If you don't lose it,' Kite said, looking at the slim, mottled brown-and-gold plunger-action pen with the gold fittings, engraved with a stylized gold flower, which Dexter was carefully putting into a polythene evidence bag. 'Or drop it at the scene of a crime.'

'There'll be prints, hopefully,' Dexter said, moving off.

'Who was it found her, Martin?'

'Chap at number thirteen,' answered the lanky sergeant, running his hand through his curly, fair hair. 'Name of Lawley, looking for his cat. He was going to take it to the vet today, for an operation on its ear, but he can't find it. Maybe the moggy's got wind of what's to happen to it and it's taken off, you know what cats are. Anyway, Lawley came in here calling for it and found the girl, recognized her immediately.'

His usually cheerful face was grim. 'Lucky it was him, and not any of the children.'

Every other policeman there, those who were parents and those who weren't, was undoubtedly thinking the same thing. 'Anyone taken his full statement?'

'On my way now.'

'Don't forget to ask him if he's lost a pen,' Abigail reminded him.

As she spoke, someone called out to Kite from the other side of the wood. The sergeant raised a hand in reply, but the dead girl was being placed in a body shell, and he remained quietly with the others while she was removed to the waiting ambulance, thence to be transported to refrigeration in the mortuary.

Her parents would have to be told.

'There's only one, her mother. Divorced,' Abigail said, 'and she was an only child.' She looked up from her clipboard, pushing her hair back. 'Life's rotten, sometimes.'

She didn't usually let things get to her, but this was different. This he could understand. In the rare moments when he was feeling low, when he'd been a parent coping on his own, his wife dead and his daughter Julie still a teenager, this was the sort of thing Mayo had always dreaded. But Julie had never remotely encountered any violence, she was alive and well and living abroad at the moment, he'd never personally had to confront such an appalling tragedy as was facing this unknown woman, Patti's mother, whose life would never be the same again.

And it was Abigail who was going to have to tell her.

Informing a parent that their child's life had just been snuffed out was the worst task any of them ever had to perform, but it was something they'd all had to do, and would no doubt have to do again. He thought about suggesting someone else do it, but he knew Abigail wouldn't appreciate it. She never asked for concessions.

He watched her for a moment, and was reassured. Cool, apparently unruffled, wearing a summer skirt and a light

cotton shirt this hot morning, her bronze hair drawn back into a thick plait. She'd cope.

'There's also an aunt,' she was saying, brisk with herself once more. 'She lives here in the Close, a Mrs Bailey, the mother's sister, and she wants to be the one to tell her . . . it seems they're very close. I'll give her time to break the news, get the worst over, before I go and see Mrs Ryman. By the way, she's asking to speak to you personally, before she goes to see her sister. She won't speak to anyone but the "top man". Claims she knows who did it.'

'She does?' He gave her a sharp glance. 'With good reasons? Or just suspicious?'

'I don't know. She wouldn't say anything more.'

'I'd better see her, then.'

Was this, after all, going to be one of those open-and-shut cases, where it was immediately apparent who the perpetrator was? Murder occurring out of the blue, for no reason, by some anonymous stranger, was a far rarer phenomenon than some of the more lurid press would have their readers believe. Trouble had more often been openly brewing before suddenly erupting, with disastrous repercussions. Friends, relatives, neighbours could, and often did, point the police in the right direction, leaving them few problems, save those of calming down the participants enough to make a coherent statement. If it was so in this instance, nobody would be better pleased than Mayo, but he doubted it. With nothing more than his gut feeling to go on, he somehow doubted it very much.

'We've talked to the neighbours, all sixteen houses in the Close, but no joy,' Abigail went on, tapping her clipboard, 'from those we've asked so far, that is – nobody saw or heard a thing. A lot of them had already left for work before she was found, mind, we'll have to see them later . . . and two families are on holiday. The rest are mainly mothers with young children, one or two retired couples. I'm just about to start on the two big houses, then we'll do the rest of Albert Road down as far as Patel's, the newsagent she worked for. It's going to be manpower-intensive again,' she added wryly.

Mayo's mind was already working on it, on the transfer of personnel from the Ensor case, which was now going to have to be put on to the back burner. With the department still working through the backlog of summer holidays, several people on annual leave, everything else would now have to go by the board. This investigation would take priority, he would personally see to it that it did. They'd give it all they'd got, work round the clock. Exhausted men and women, stretched resources, escalating overtime figures and budget allocations were the least of it.

'It might help if you left those two houses to me. I've met the owners – briefly, but at least it gives me a bit of an edge. I can make a start with them.' It was doubtful that they could have seen anything behind their shrubberies and high walls. But he knew instinctively that his personal involvement was needed here, that the occupants – the Kendricks at Simla, certainly – should be handled with care. They knew everybody that mattered, they still had poke. He couldn't afford any cock-ups where they were concerned. But there were other, less obvious reasons why he should concern himself with them, reasons he couldn't explain even to himself, but were amounting almost to a conviction ... shades of the party he'd attended, of something he'd missed, or subconsciously sensed out of kilter. Catches of that old tune, 'Alice Where Art Thou?', which had haunted him maddeningly ever since, began another replay in his mind.

'Right,' he went on, suddenly realizing that he'd been elsewhere while Abigail had been putting him in the picture, a bad habit of his that he knew irritated the hell out of other people, who thought he wasn't paying attention, especially since he rarely missed anything. The ability to think and operate on two levels was a facility he'd developed out of necessity. 'That seems to be it, then, so far?' he said, recapping correctly on what she'd been saying.

Patti, it appeared, had left her bicycle where she invariably parked it, just inside the gates of Edwina Lodge. After leaving the papers there and at Simla, she'd gone on to deliver in the Close. The canvas bag, with most of the newspapers and

magazines still in it, had been found at the entrance to the path leading into the wood. Traces of blood, still wet and sticky, indicated that she'd been attacked when she was half-way along it, and presumably by someone who must have come up behind her. But she'd actually been found here, a hundred yards further into the wood.

Why had she been going into the wood at all?

He stood back, hands in pockets, to get a better view. The Ellington Close houses were all set at angles to the wood, so that only the frosted-glass bathroom windows upstairs overlooked it. Number one had a bedroom window that obliquely looked over the path, but could be discounted, since the occupants were away. Only the upstairs windows at Edwina Lodge overlooked any part of the wood. Nothing could be seen of the path from Simla, the angle of vision was wrong.

Whoever had made the attack had still taken a very big risk of being seen. True, it was breakfast time, a busy hour of the day with everyone intent on their own concerns: preparing to leave for work, getting children ready for school, no time to be interested in what was happening outside. All the same, people must have been about all the time, walking past the end of the pathway, leaving in their cars.

They were making a fingertip search of the wood now, outside the taped area around the body and the delineated access path to where it had lain, looking for the murder weapon. Brambles and nettles grew in profusion at its edges, unidentified fungi grew in the undergrowth and on rotten tree stumps, nasty to the touch. There were still damp, muddy areas, even after weeks of dry weather, and evidence that dogs were irresponsibly let out to exercise here. Garden rubbish – and other things which had no business to be dumped there – had been thrown over the fences of those gardens backing on to the wood. 'The best of British,' he muttered under his breath as he left, on his way to see Mrs Bailey. It was a long time since that sort of thing had fallen to his lot, thank God.

'Sir!' It was young WDC Platt, hurrying to intercept him.

Her pretty face was pale, her curls damp with the heat.

'What is it, Jenny?'

'We've found the missing cat, sir. It's dead.'

She was looking upset, the way people did over animals, and shocked, evidently thinking, what a place to dump a dead cat, where children played! A hitherto safe area, where they wouldn't now be allowed to play for some time, even when the police were finished with the locus, Mayo guessed. Parents and children alike would, understandably, be wary of this little wood for some time to come.

'Perhaps you should come and see, sir,' Jenny suggested. He saw there was something more by her face.

Abigail accompanied him as he walked over to where Kite and a group of uniformed men were gathered around a deep tangle of undergrowth, and as she peered down at what was there, he heard her indrawn breath, and understood why when he also looked.

Not just any old cat. A big, sleek tortoiseshell, a handsome animal, plump and healthy-looking, despite its reputed ear trouble. It wasn't going to need the vet now. It appeared to have been stabbed, not once, but many times. It had had its throat cut. He gently touched the animal. The fur was still warm, the body not yet locked in rigor. He turned away, sickened.

'Poor beast. See we get blood samples.'

'Sir?'

'We'll need to establish which is the cat's blood out there, and which came from the girl.'

Jenny looked even more upset, but she pulled herself together quickly. She was turning out to be one of his best officers, proving to be hard-working and methodical, though she sometimes had to have things spelled out for her. She would probably do all right for herself in the Force, in a steady, unspectacular way.

'We'll have to have another think now about where Patti was killed, won't we?' Abigail, naturally sharper and more intuitive, was saying. 'If the traces of blood further back along

the path weren't hers, she might have been attacked right by where she was found.'

'Could account for why nobody saw or heard anything of the attack, too. And for the absence of any drag marks on the heels of her shoes or along the path into the wood,' Mayo said, 'or the unlikely possibility that her killer picked her up and carried her further into here. I suppose he could have dragged her by her feet, but if he did, there'd have been marks on her, on her clothing. And anyone who did this,' he said, jerking his head towards the body of the cat, 'he'll have blood on him, maybe scratches, unless he wore gloves. I'd guess by the size of it, this puss was a bit of a tiger.'

There was another shout. One of the uniformed constables had found what was almost certainly the weapon.

It was a flat, heavy length of iron, flaking with rust, about eighteen inches long by two inches wide, the sort used to brace the concrete posts between which the wires at the bottom of the gardens in the Close were stretched. Its narrow edge suggested the profile of the weapon used to inflict the wound on the back of Patti's head. Typically, the builders who'd put the fencing up in the first place had simply dumped the surplus material among the nettles and docks in the wood, rather than go to the trouble of carting it away. The killer had made no attempt to hide the piece of iron, perhaps thinking it would be lost among the dozens of similar pieces left lying around, that the blood would be indistinguishable from the rust marks on it, perhaps not thinking at all, only wanting to be rid of it. Only it wasn't, like the rest, half obscured in the encroaching bindweed and nettles, but had landed on a broken piece of the concrete fencing post, staining it with wet blood. Even then, it had needed someone as sharp-eyed as the youngest constable there to notice the stain.

'Nice one, Kevin,' commented Kite to the young PC, who flushed and tried to look nonchalant.

Dexter, summoned to look at it, pulled down his mouth. 'Don't expect we'll get any prints from that rough surface, even if he didn't wear gloves, but we'll collect some blood

and so on from it, all right. And there'll be some of this muck and rust in the wound.' He indicated the flaking surface of the rust-scabbed and soil-encrusted iron bar as he bagged it in a polythene evidence bag and labelled it.

'Do your best, Dave.'

Mayo was at last able to leave them to it and went, with Abigail, to seek out Mrs Bailey at number sixteen, while Kite went three doors down to take a statement from the man who'd found Patti's body.

9

The tortoiseshell cat's name was Nero, and the Lawleys had obviously been devoted to it. The news of how it had been killed devastated Trevor Lawley. 'God, that's sick!'

'Yeah. Makes you wonder, doesn't it?' Kite agreed.

'I mean, you hear about folk doing these sort of things to animals but you never think . . . hell, how am I going to tell the wife? Much less the kids!'

His Black Country accent came out strongly. He was a smallish man, thin and nervy, dressed in a dark-blue-and-red checked workshirt and jeans, and in his distress over his cat he seemed almost to have forgotten why he was being interviewed.

'Just my rotten luck, ain't it?' he moaned, when Kite managed to bring him back to finding Patti Ryman's body. 'I tell you straight, I rue the day we ever come here. It was only a council flat we had but we'd have been better stopping there. One thing after another it's been since the day we moved in. First the wife loses her job, then I'm made redundant, we haven't a snowball in hell's chance of paying the mortgage and no hope of selling the bloody house, neither. We don't need this! If anything'll put the kibosh on selling it, this will!'

With all these troubles, it was perhaps understandable that Lawley was morbidly self-obsessed with his ill fortune, and Kite schooled himself not to remind him too tersely that life wouldn't be fun for Patti Ryman any more, either, or her mother. 'Mr Lawley, just tell me what happened this morning,' he said shortly, making a mental note to ask whether

the Lawleys had quarrelled with anyone who might have taken their revenge through the cat, though Lawley was quite likely to be as paranoiac about that as everything else, to see himself surrounded by enemies. They were doing another quick round of the Close, anyway, after discovery of the cat, and in a close-knit community such as this, with everyone aware of everyone else's business, any quarrels between neighbours would soon come to light.

Kite's tone, if not the words, had got through to Lawley, making him pause in the airing of his grievances, gnawing his lip. 'Sorry. Just got to the stage where I can't take much more, know what I mean? It's a shame about the little wench.'

'How well did you know her?'

It wasn't a question to keep him calm. 'What do you mean, how well did I know her? Here, you're not thinking I had anything to do with it? Bloody hell, I only knew her through her bringing the papers!'

Trevor Lawley had been the one to find her, he might also have been the last one to see her alive. Why Patti Ryman had died was as yet a mystery, and there was no reason to believe Lawley had anything to do with it but there was every reason why he should, like anyone else, be subjected to questioning, and Kite told him so. He doubted whether Lawley even heard him.

'Look, she was a nice enough kid as far as I could tell, and I'm sorry this had to happen to her. Why, she used to stop and have a word with Nero of a morning,' he said, as if the cat had been a human being and their niceness to him was the criterion by which Lawley judged every other human being. 'He'd taken to sitting on top of the fence post by the path, and she'd stop for a minute or two and he'd let her stroke him under his chin, where he liked it – he wouldn't have let anybody do that, I can tell you! He was sixteen,' he said, back with his preoccupations. 'That's a good age for a cat, but he could've lived for years. He shouldn't have died like that! Just let me get hold of the bastard what did it! What sort of sicko could do that to a poor, defenceless animal?'

Kite had had enough of this. He said sharply, 'Patti Ryman was sixteen, too. Shall we keep to the point, Mr Lawley?'

Like a finicky housewife, the other man bent to straighten the fringe on the hearth rug, perhaps aware he'd gone over the top in his lament for his cat, more likely just out of a habit of obedience. The house was soulless and unimaginative, so immaculately clean and tidy, without a book or a magazine or a child's toy in sight, that it was hard to imagine any family life existing in it, much less any pet being allowed to form part of the household. Perhaps it only looked like this because it had to stand in permanent readiness for inspection by any possible client who might suddenly appear on the horizon. More likely Mrs Lawley was one of those obsessive housewives who have a personal vendetta against anything likely to harbour dust and germs.

Either way, Kite began to feel sorry for him. He thought of his own untidy, sometimes chaotic household, centred around two noisy, pre-teenage boys, and his cheerful, always on the go, slightly zany wife, Sheila, and was suddenly, thankfully, happy.

'So, to recap. You went looking for your cat and entered the wood at half past eight, when you saw the body of a young girl you recognized as Patti Ryman?'

'Well, I didn't know her last name. I only knew her as Patti.'

'Did you touch her?'

''Course I didn't touch her! I rushed home and dialled 999, for God's sake, for the ambulance.' He stopped. 'I think I knew she had to be dead, though, the way she was lying there – her clothes, know what I mean . . . Was she raped?'

When Kite didn't answer, he added, with unexpected sharpness, 'If you're looking for perverts, mate, you want to look at that bloke at number seven, not me. Can't keep his eyes off of the kids!'

At the door, Kite remembered he hadn't asked about the pen.

'A what?' Lawley said, when he'd described it. 'A bloody

93

pen, that price?' He jerked his thumb towards the For Sale sign. 'You have to be joking!'

At least, thought Kite as he left, he'd succeeded in bringing some amusement into Lawley's day.

The bay window at number seven gave Stanley Loates an oblique view of the police activity in the Close. Despite the uncomfortable racing of his heart, he watched their comings and goings compulsively, his jaws masticating one lump of treacle toffee after another from the paper bag in his pocket, telling himself repeatedly that he'd nothing to fear. He'd already been questioned twice – once about the girl, and then that young woman detective constable with the curly hair had come back about the cat. He'd told her that he'd seen nothing of Patti the paper girl that morning. She'd seen how surprised he was about the cat, and he was sure she'd believed him on both counts. She'd been very polite, thanked him and told him not to bother getting up out of his chair to see her to the door, sir, as though he was an old man.

Stanley wasn't old – nearly fifty, but that was young these days – a fattish, flabby man whose shirt and ill-fitting, baggy-bottomed trousers never met neatly, an unprepossessing man with sweaty palms and thinning, fairish hair. He lived with his mother, who was old and senile and ought by rights to be in a home, where she could be looked after properly, anyone said so. But to all such advice Stanley turned a deaf ear. She was his mother, he'd never let her be put away, he told them. He was a good son.

Maybe a few gullible souls were fooled by this, but not anyone who knew the two of them.

The truth was that the council-owned homes were full, with long waiting lists, and though Hilda Loates had enough funds in the bank to pay the costs of a private one, Stanley had no intention of wasting what was left of his inheritance. She'd sold his father's run-down business (thus depriving Stanley of the only job he'd ever had) and the old house in Grover Street, for what little they would fetch, having taken it into her head to buy this house as an investment, telling

him with a cackle he could always sell it at a fat profit when she was gone. That was five years ago. She hadn't gone yet and you couldn't give these houses away now.

All this, however, was only partly why he didn't trouble himself about finding another job, but stayed at home and cared for her. The truth was, Stanley didn't dare to suggest such a thing as a home to his mother, for he was still terrified of her, as he had been all his life. His brain told him it was quite impossible that she, a weak old woman, could take him, a grown man, by the shoulders and shove him into the dark cupboard under the stairs as she used to when he was a child, but his mind didn't believe it. She was capable of anything. She'd be able to rise from the dead, he was sure. She'd always had a vicious tongue, and though what she said nowadays, after her stroke, was mostly rubbish, she was aware of everything that went on, and she could talk intelligibly if she wanted to. The reason she didn't, very often, was that she knew her gobbledegook speech made life more difficult for him. So he gritted his teeth and carried on. He was prepared to do whatever he had to do for her. Whatever. He knew she couldn't last that much longer and after that – bingo! Life would begin, at last, for Stanley Derrington Loates.

She'd driven his father to an early grave. Alfred Loates, who built up a successful shoe-retailing business in the days when personal service to customers meant something, had been a small, spry, cheerful man, but even his unfailing optimism had eventually been defeated by her. He'd lost heart and his business had gone down the pan. But she wasn't going to defeat Stanley.

And he wouldn't be scared by the police, either.

He decided to have a doughnut and a cup of drinking chocolate to soothe his nerves before he went out and finished tying up his beans.

'Mrs Bailey's house is the first on the right, number sixteen, the one with the wishing well in the garden,' Abigail said.

And the frilly nets, and the ding-dong door chimes, and

the blaze of petunias and French marigolds lining the path, Mayo found as they walked up to the front door.

'This is Detective Superintendent Mayo, Mrs Bailey,' Abigail said as the door opened on the first ring. 'He's the senior officer in charge of the case.'

'Thank you for coming.'

Her eyes were red and swollen, her voice congested with weeping, but she was in command of herself. 'I was just off to work when I heard,' she began, indicating the pink tracksuit trousers and T-shirt that were presumably her working garb, evidently comfortable, if all too revealing of ample curves. 'It's my morning for Simla, but they'll have to do without me today. My sister's going to need me more than they do.'

The tiny hall was uncomfortably crowded with Mayo's large form, and Abigail, plus Mrs Bailey. 'What am I thinking of, keeping you standing here! It won't take any longer if we go and sit down somewhere,' she said suddenly, opening the door into a spotless front room that smelled of lavender furniture polish.

Waving them to a large, puffy, be-flowered settee with extra cushions embroidered in pansies, she sat down opposite. 'We've never had children of our own, me and Bob, and she was like my own daughter, our Patti.' Tears welled again and it was moments before she could speak, after employing an already sodden wad of tissues she pulled from her pocket. 'I'm sorry, but it's just – I blame myself, I blame myself. I told her, see, that there was nothing to worry about. If all he does is look, I told her – '

'Mrs Bailey, who are we talking about?'

She stared at Abigail. 'That Stanley Loates, of course, at number seven! Dirty old devil! Getting his kicks watching her bend down over the letter-boxes to push the papers in. She asked me what should she do and I said leave it, I'll give him the side of my tongue when I get the chance. And now look what he's done. I should've told you lot right away, when she first complained.'

'I doubt we could've done anything, except warn him off,'

Abigail said sympathetically. 'We can't stop anyone looking out of his own window.'

'Well, he wouldn't have gone on to rape and murder her if he knew you had your eye on him, would he?'

Mayo said, 'I'm afraid it's not quite so simple. For one thing, we don't know yet if she was raped, and it seems unlikely.'

But sexual motivation in some form or another couldn't be discounted, not when the victim was an attractive fifteen-year-old schoolgirl so small she might easily have been mistaken for a child, especially in her school uniform. Perhaps the name of Stanley Loates would appear when the computer came up with the names of all known child molesters, though it wasn't one known to Mayo. At any rate, along with all the others he'd be requestioned, minutely and at length, in a painstaking reworking, resifting and correlating of the data already collected in attempts to throw light on the deaths of the two little girls in Hurstfield.

'It seems more likely Patti died from a very violent blow to the head, Mrs Bailey,' Abigail said.

'What, him, violent? Hitting her? Stanley Loates?' Mrs Bailey's astonishment was enough to stem her tears. 'He'd be hard put to it to hit the top off a soft-boiled egg! Still, it just shows! You never know with that sort, do you?'

Ways in which the two deaths, the girl's and the cat's, could be – must be – connected, were running through Abigail's mind, all of them nasty. Yet however bizarre the possibility, it had to be assumed that the two killings, so closely related in time and place, were related in other ways, too.

She'd joined two of the other officers – Kite and Jenny Platt – for a quick sandwich in the snack bar a few doors away from Patel's paper shop. It was pretty basic, but when you were on a job like this, niceties didn't take priority. And since they were the only customers, inevitably, ideas began to be batted around.

'She heard what she assumed was someone torturing the

cat, went to investigate – and he hit her on the head –?' Kite suggested.

Abigail shrugged, gulping down coffee from a thick white beaker and finishing a hot sausage roll that filled a corner but didn't satisfy. 'I can't think of any other reason why she'd have gone in there. She couldn't have had much time to spare, with school starting at half past eight. But she was fond of this cat, you say, Martin?'

'According to Lawley. If she did hear the noise, she couldn't have known it was Nero, of course, but it seems he used to wait for her every morning . . . well, that's what Lawley said. And apparently Nero was everybody's favourite.' He paused. 'Though not for some sadistic bastard, he wasn't.'

'No ill-feeling between the Lawleys and anybody else in the Close – nobody likely to kill their cat to get at them?'

'It would seem not, and I'd have problems believing anyone killed it simply to lure Patti into the wood.'

'But she *was* there, Martin, they died at about the same time; she may have seen who was harming the cat.'

'And the bastard killed her for that?'

It was an unlikely scenario, Abigail had to admit. 'And in any case, if he was behind her, as he must've been for her to have got that wound on her head, he would surely assume she hadn't seen him anyway.'

'Unless she saw him and turned to run away. Scared he was going to turn on her, maybe?'

It was, at that moment, fruitless speculation. Of more immediate moment was the question of the allegations against Stanley Loates, as she pointed out. How much credence could be given to them, apart from the fact that they came from two independent sources? How much of it was simply malicious gossip and suspicion? Loates was known as a loner, an oddball, a man who kept himself to himself and apparently didn't mix with his neighbours, who didn't fit into the same pattern as those other families in the Close . . . and people were always suspicious, ready to point the finger at what they didn't understand.

'Well,' Jenny Platt put in, unexpectedly, 'all I can say is that if I had a life like his, I'd stare out of the windows a lot, too. You should see that mother of his! Can't be much else for him to do except look after her and that'd be enough to get anybody down.'

Except for the coffee machine burping behind the counter, there was a silence after this outburst. Jenny's young face was flushed, earnestly trying to put another point of view.

'Is she bedridden?' Abigail asked.

'No, she just sits in a chair by the fire – full on, even today – and makes life miserable for him. It's difficult to understand what she says but she can convey a lot with her eyes. He never goes out unless one of her old cronies comes to sit with her, would you believe, but there's no love lost between them. Mind you, he's pretty loathsome himself, but just because he's always looking out of the window doesn't mean he had anything to do with Patti . . .'

'Don't forget the kids he watches, Jenny.'

'Yeah.' Jenny looked down at the grey coffee in her beaker.

'I know we can't jump to conclusions, but you don't suggest we ignore the possibility?'

''Course not. That wasn't what I meant. I'm only trying to be fair.'

Abigail was quite aware that, despite her defence of Stanley Loates – or at least, of his rights – the last thing Jenny wanted was to go back to number seven and talk to him again. She'd no need to say how much he made her flesh creep, that she hated the foetid smell of the house, the overpoweringly heated sitting room where that ancient old woman sat silently in the chair by the fire, but Stanley Loates had to be questioned, and the sooner the better. And Jenny's – or anybody's – feelings, however, weren't paramount in this, something Jenny knew, and accepted.

It was unfortunate for DC Farrar, tall, blond and good-looking, with his propensity for saying the wrong thing at the wrong time, that he should have entered the café in time to overhear the last exchanges, and to have summed up the situation with his quick intuition.

'Just lie back and think of England, Jen,' he advised, smirking as he came back from the counter with his coffee and a pie.

Abigail gave him one of her looks. 'There won't be any need for that, Keith,' she said, making her mind up. 'Sergeant Kite will be interviewing Stanley Loates, and you'll be going with him. I want Jenny with me when I go down to see Patti's mother.'

'Right, ma'am,' said Kite, catching her eye and turning a look on Farrar that wiped the smile from his face.

10

Mayo drove himself back up to Albert Road, after a snatched
lunch and a couple of hours at his desk, during which he
returned numerous phone calls and spent a brisk half hour
with his part-time secretary, Delia, disposing of all but the
most pressing of his commitments for the next couple of days
and dealing with the reports that had landed on his desk. He
noted in passing that Abigail had left him word that another
prestigious car had gone missing, this time a top-of-the-range
Rover, and that the file on Philip Ensor had grown no thicker.

He drove out of Milford Road and was caught, as usual,
by the badly phased traffic lights at the corner of Victoria
Road, swearing as he waited for them to change. Like every
other frustrated motorist in Lavenstock, he didn't understand
why the devil Traffic couldn't get it sorted, why you only
went forward two or three cars before the lights went again
to red, why there had to be these long periods when no
traffic lane at all moved, as if frozen at the whim of some
higher authority.

But it was this hiatus which afforded him the glimpse of
Alex in the Italian restaurant on the corner. She was sitting
at a table a little way from the window and facing him,
though she was too immersed in conversation with the man
sitting opposite her to look up and see him. Her companion
had his back to the window and Mayo had no chance, before
the lights changed again, to assess who it might be. He
frowned a little. A client? She hadn't said she was lunching
with anyone – but then, of course, there was no reason why
she should have.

She'd been smiling, leaning forward in a friendly, even intimate, way. There'd been wine on the table.

His first call was to Simla, the house he'd previously visited in vastly different circumstances – the welcome party for Dermot Voss and his family – but he was unlucky in that only Imogen Loxley was at home. She'd told him when he'd telephoned to arrange his call that her sister Hope, as he'd expected, would still be at the Princess Mary School where she taught and wouldn't be home until around half past five. He intended to see her when he made a visit to Patti's school the following day, but he was disappointed now to find that her brother Francis was in London, lunching with his publisher, combining the day with doing some research at one of the museums – Imogen couldn't recall which – and had arranged an overnight stay in the hotel he always used on such occasions.

He was informed of all this in a prettily furnished room which overlooked the garden, a large room giving an overall impression of lightness – an astonishingly attractive room to find in that dark house, whose heavy, fusty, last-century ambience he'd found so depressing on his last visit. Here, there was a thick blue carpet, with a Chinese hearth rug in creamy pastels and deep, chintz-covered armchairs. Taupe-grey velvet curtains stirred in the breeze from the open window. Flowers were massed in bowls, and the walls painted in a shade that glowed like lighted alabaster, iced with a delicate white cornice and frieze. Imogen Loxley looked equally elegant, and expensive, decorated with the sort of gold jewellery he thought should be described as 'understated', wearing a slip of a dress, cream coloured, short and sleeveless, nothing to it – though one thing he'd learned was that the cost of women's clothes couldn't be judged by how much there was of them.

Come to think of it, Alex was spending a lot on clothes lately. He'd accidentally come across one of her bills and had to be resuscitated by a large malt. Not like Alex, to be extravagant . . .

102

Imogen had offered him tea but he'd declined, and they sat opposite each other on twin sofas set at right angles to a pretty marble fireplace that was crowded with silver photo frames, where she gave him the information he needed. Hope Kendrick, it seemed, had left that morning to drive to school at about twenty to eight, earlier than she normally set out, having allowed time to run her brother to the station to catch his train; he would take a taxi when he returned home the following day.

'And you, Mrs Loxley?'

It had been Christian names when they'd been introduced at the party, but somehow the circumstances didn't seem to warrant their use now. She'd addressed him formally when he arrived and he'd responded likewise, feeling it was better to keep this on an official footing.

'Oh, I like to start my day in a leisurely fashion. I made my breakfast and brought it in here while I watched the breakfast news until after the headlines came on at eight. I didn't realize anything was amiss until I noticed all the cars arriving.'

'But you didn't see them from here.' Simla was a house with a long frontage, narrow from back to front, with most of the principal rooms facing the garden at the rear. From this window could be seen that giant tree they'd all been talking about at the party, and the rose beds which stretched across the garden in front of the windows. Though extensive, sloping down to the wood at the bottom, with overgrown banks of laurel and rhododendron separating it from the back gardens of Ellington Close, it wasn't a garden to write home about, apart from the roses, which were magnificent, their heady and pervasive scent mingling with that of the roses in the room. 'You can't see the road from this room.'

'No, I was in my bedroom at the front by then. I sat by the window, looking out for the postman, but he was late, he didn't get here until after nine.'

It was a long time to sit watching for the postman. But as she spoke, he caught the hint of pain in her voice, perhaps over an expected letter that hadn't come, the almost

103

inaudible indrawn breath, a small, abrupt dismissive movement to herself. The hairs actually stood up on her slim, bare brown arms, as if a goose had walked over her grave. He was reminded that Alex had told him she was separated – from Tom Loxley, wasn't it? That Euro MP who'd made his mark over European Agricultural Policy ... Hadn't he had something pungent to say recently on the subject of British cheeses (as one smart-aleck journalist had it) and the European diktat as to how they should be manufactured?

'She'd delivered our paper as usual, you know, poor child.'

'You saw her bring it?'

'No, she must've left it before I went back to my bedroom. She used to deliver first to next door – Edwina Lodge – and leave her bicycle there before she came on here.'

'You'll have a good view of the entrance to the Close from your bedroom, then?'

Ellington Close was approached by a narrow road between the two older houses, walled either side, after which it broadened out into a rough crescent shape.

'Yes, there's a side window, as well as one at the front, but I saw no one, other than the people who lived round about, setting off for work in their cars. I'd no idea what was happening until Doreen Bailey rang to say she wouldn't be in today and told me why. I'm so sorry I can't help you. Believe me, I would if I could – I've a daughter about the same age, away at school.'

Following the direction of her involuntary glance at the collection of photos on the mantel, he saw a girl with a thin, clever face, smiling up at the man next to her, who had his arm around her shoulder. 'Is this her?' he asked, studying it with interest. 'I can see the resemblance.'

'Yes, that's Melissa. Mel, we call her.' Her smile was that of any proud mother, but it also seemed to him slightly strained. Understandable, if her marriage was breaking up, and there was a daughter to consider ... She said nothing about the man in the photograph, whom Mayo had recognized from TV appearances as Tom Loxley.

There seemed nothing more to pursue here at the moment,

until Francis Kendrick returned. He left with a general impression that despite her outwardly cool poise, she had been distinctly on edge throughout the interview, and had been relieved when it was over.

Sarah Wilmot hadn't been in when he telephoned but it was possible she'd returned meanwhile. It was unlikely, he thought as he crossed the road, that she'd be of much help, in view of the short time the Voss family had been in residence, and he'd have to see her brother-in-law later, but both had to be routinely questioned, and it would fit in with his busy schedule if he could see her now.

Edwina Lodge was one of those red-brick Gothic edifices whose ornate and irregular design seemed to have no relevance to its function. Having received no answer to his first ring, he circumnavigated the house but found no one at the back either. He guessed that it had been converted vertically, with the three flats in one half, but he gave up trying to work out what the interior layout might be. The back of the house overlooked the wood; it would be difficult to see very far into it through any of its lower windows because of the garden's slope, though it didn't seem impossible for anyone to have made an escape from the wood via the garden and then the front entrance. The same, of course, would apply to the garden at Simla.

Both front gardens had very little depth, probably due to the widening of Albert Road at some time, and were filled by dusty spotted laurels. Here, a heavy, ornate arch attached to the side of the house marked the entrance to a broad driveway leading to something that looked like a fairly derelict coach house at the end. The drive was paved with blue bricks and a high wall ran alongside, behind which ran the road into Ellington Close. This was the wall, presumably, against which Patti had been wont to prop her cycle.

He was standing back and trying to decipher the entwined initials below the date, 1859, on the stone cartouche in the centre of the arch when someone came up behind him.

'Were you wanting anything?' asked a suspicious female voice.

He turned to see a thin, sharp-featured young woman, laden with carrier bags, with hair that appeared to have been cut with a knife and fork, wearing a grey T-shirt stretched across her nonexistent bosom, and baggy flowered shorts.

On hearing who he was, Tina Baverstock, for so she announced herself, with a gleam in her eye and the eagerness of the inveterate gossip, promptly invited him in for a cup of tea. Such people being as gifts from the gods to policemen hard pressed for information, Mayo accepted. He was lucky she was here, she informed him, Monday being the day when her wholefood shop closed. 'A lot of people don't like it – they expect everybody to keep open all hours nowadays, but I have my customers who know when I'm open and when I'm not. Anybody wants anything, they'll take the trouble to come at the right time.'

Or go somewhere else, he thought, amused, as he followed her in.

The entrance to her ground-floor flat was via a side door, where a back staircase, originally built to keep the sight of servants from offending the eyes of visitors, ascended to the upper storeys. The inside of the house confirmed his assumption that the house would be a rabbit warren. Its division into flats seemed to have happened more by an unforeseen accident than through any planning on the part of an architect. The Baverstock living room, at any rate, was an uneasy compromise, wrought from what must once have been a gracious reception room, now ruined by having had a partition thrown across it to make the kitchen, cutting the deep cornice in half and regrettably bisecting a large window.

Tina Baverstock emerged from this kitchen area with tea, predictably a herbal infusion. Well, he'd drunk worse in the interests of getting at the truth. In any case, he suspected she might take offence if he didn't drain it to the dregs. She began talking at once while she was pouring the tea, greedy for excitement, the way some people always were, even in the face of tragedy; perhaps, he thought, striving for charity,

through the need for drama in their lives . . . there couldn't, after all, be much of that, working in a healthfood shop.

'She shouldn't have been delivering papers, that Patti, it isn't safe, they shouldn't allow girls to do it –' was the first thing she found to say of the murdered girl.

'She used to leave her cycle here, I understand,' he interrupted without too much compunction, abandoning charitable thoughts, but all that did was to start her off on another tack.

'Yes, but not with *my* approval. It fell over once and scratched our new car. She was cheeky when I reprimanded her about leaving it there – but what could I do when the landlord supported her?'

It was clear that her opinion of Dermot Voss was not high, either. Rankling amongst other things was his refusal to promise them a new bathroom installation, and his disturbing them by leaving home at ungodly hours in the morning. 'Half past seven this morning – and by the look of what he was stowing in the boot, he won't be home tonight, either. Not much of a father to those children.' She sniffed, unattractively.

'Presumably that's part of his job.'

She must surely know Voss's circumstances, he thought, but she seemed to have taken against the poor devil, without a good word to say for him.

'But he was back within half an hour, in a right old state about something or other,' she said with satisfaction. 'Then another car came and picked him up about an hour later. I should think his own had broken down, it doesn't seem to be very well maintained. My husband says the engine sounds as rough as – well, rough.'

She'd evidently expected things to take a turn for the better when the house ownership had changed hands and was disappointed that they hadn't, and she'd turned her spite on to Dermot Voss. Her neighbours fared no better when she moved on to them: Henry Pitt, who worked in the library and who let horrid cooking odours float down the stairs,

with never a thought of opening a window. And James Fitz-allan, who rented the attic as a sort of *studio* –

'He's an artist?'

Her look suggested there were artists and artists. He suspected she'd never actually seen his work or been into this studio and that it ate into her soul. The gossip continued, spilled out, venomous, unlovely.

'I saw her talking to him, you know, this morning.'

'To Mr Fitzallan?'

'No, no, Henry Pitt.'

'What time was this?'

'Quarter to eight. They seemed to be having what I can only say was a very *animated* conversation! Not the first time I'd seen them talking, either. Of course, I'm not one to gossip, but he scuttles away quicksticks every time any other woman approaches him and it's funny he happened to be on his way out so often, just at the time she was here to deliver the papers, when the library doesn't open until half past nine! Well, I mean, a young girl and an old man like that – *unhealthy*, I call it.'

'Are you saying, Mrs Baverstock,' Mayo asked coldly, 'that Mr Pitt could have had something to do with Patti Ryman being murdered?' He was aware by now of disliking her extremely.

She flushed bright red at his tone and bridled. 'How could he have? He got straight into Vic's car – my husband's – and went into town with him. Naturally, I didn't mean to imply –'

Why, he'd wondered while she was complaining, if she equally disliked her neighbours and living here so much, didn't she move, surely she and her husband earned enough between them for something better? Her last words as he left were enlightening on this point. 'Of course, things would've been different if that woman had kept to her promises – Mrs Burgoyne. She always promised she'd give us first refusal to buy this place when she left, that's the only reason we've stayed here, but she conveniently forgot that when she had a better offer.'

'Thank you for your time,' he said, and with relief went to where he'd left his car, further up Albert Road.

For a moment, there, he'd contemplated asking her if he might look through her bedroom window, which must overlook the back garden, but had immediately decided that the unlikely chance of there being a possibility of seeing into the wood from there wasn't worth it. He wished he hadn't been such a coward, but he'd a strong feeling there was every possibility of her being the type of woman who'd immediately think the suggestion an invitation to rape.

11

It was the young, uniformed constable, Kevin Marsden, he who had distinguished himself by finding the murder weapon and was now keeping an eye on the entrance to the wood, who first noticed the commotion.

He set off at a run towards the end of the Close, from where shouts and scuffles travelled on the still, early-afternoon air, putting out a call on his radio as he did so. Kite and Farrar were, as it happened, just rounding the corner on their way back to the crime scene and within seconds, close behind Marsden, they all arrived at the spot where two people were struggling on the pathway outside number seven, Ellington Close.

Mrs Loates had finally flipped. She had somehow tottered out of the house before Stanley could stop her, and in the struggle to get her back inside, had fallen to the ground, where she now lay, mumbling and muttering and offering passive resistance. Her flowered quilted dressing gown had fallen apart to reveal a dingy flannel nightdress that had ridden up over her mottled, varicosed legs. The legs terminated in zipped felt bootee slippers. Her hair, stiff and iron grey, hung in two rat's-tail plaits down her back.

Stanley was trying to yank her to her feet, desperately begging her to come back inside the house. 'Come indoors, do, you'll do yourself a mischief!' When that failed, he tried another tack. 'Everybody's looking at you, Mother, you're making a spectacle of yourself.'

Groups of neighbours stood around, embarrassed, unwilling or unable to intervene. A mother with a baby in her

arms clutched her toddler's hand. An elderly couple stood together by their gate, stunned by this further chaos and disorder which had descended on their hitherto quiet and respectable Close. Trevor Lawley came out and hovered on the sidelines for a moment or two, then went back indoors.

Stanley's normally doughy face was red. Hilda Loates had once been a big, strong woman and his belly quivered with the effort of trying to lift her. She looked at him balefully and let her weight sag slackly against him. The three policemen arrived.

Thankfully, Stanley left them to it. He relinquished his hold on his mother and stood back, breathing heavily as they manoeuvred her bodily into the house and put her in her chair.

The spectators muttered together in shocked tones and presently went back into their own houses.

Inside the house, Stanley said, 'Should we give her some brandy?'

'Don't let him near me,' the old woman said suddenly, muffled but quite clear. 'He's after me – he wants to kill me!'

'Now then, Mrs Loates,' Kite said, and to Marsden, 'Get an ambulance,' not liking the bad colour of the old woman's face.

'Right,' Marsden said, thankful to have something to do that didn't involve watching the old woman. Domestics of any kind he hated, one involving a batty old woman without her teeth in he could do without any day.

The others stood around, keeping a wary eye on her. She seemed to have shot her bolt with her accusation at Stanley, however, and sat slumped into the chair where she'd been placed, her mouth opening and shutting like a fish. Kite sent Farrar to find a blanket and he came back with an old-fashioned pink sateen eiderdown which they wrapped around her. Her eyes wandered and her colour came and went alarmingly. She sat speechlessly now, huddled into the eiderdown, chumbling her lips, seemingly unaware of the crowded room.

'What brought this on?' Kite asked her son.

111

'God knows.'

All at once the old woman began talking again. Kite was getting used to her and had no trouble in understanding her when she said, 'He did it, him, our Stanley! He did it, I saw him.'

'Take no notice of her,' Stanley said scornfully. 'She's daft as a brush. She doesn't know what she's saying.'

It was possible to feel sorry for him. His eyes swivelled round in his head like a hare's, the sweat stood thickly on his pale skin.

A malicious spark glinted in his mother's old, black eyes. 'Threw it over the fence, he did.'

Stanley gave a groan.

'Threw what, Mrs Loates?' Kite asked, and guessed: 'The cat?'

'Ar. Been peeing all over his lettuces, that's why. Used to fancy a nice salad, I did, but not now.'

Marsden gave a snort and was quelled by a look from Kite. But once started, there was no stopping Hilda Loates, though she wasn't making sense any more. Her face was plum-coloured. Farrar had made tea for everybody but she knocked the mug out of Stanley's hand when he attempted to get her to drink. 'Where's that ambulance, for God's sake?' Kite muttered.

'It's here.'

'Now, what's all this, Mrs Loates?' the paramedic was beginning, when she made a sort of bubbling sound. She went rigid and the dark colour drained from her face. In a flash, she was wrapped in a blanket, lifted on to a stretcher and borne away in the ambulance.

'You can come with her,' they said to Stanley but he refused, though he promised to assemble what she'd need and take it to her later, and when the ambulance had disappeared, sat down heavily on the sofa. He looked drained and exhausted, and sagged against the back cushions with evident relief. His eyes, however, were surprisingly bright and alive. At one point he put a hand over his mouth and Farrar thought, *The bugger's laughing!*

112

'I've said, I know nothing about all this,' he grumbled in answer to Kite, who chose to lead in with a question about the cat when it came to question time, but he knew he was cornered, with little alternative now but to tell the truth. He showed no remorse for what he'd done. The animal, it appeared, had been annoying him for years. It seemed to regard anywhere it chose to roam as its own territory and nothing Stanley could do deterred it. 'Scratching in the seed-beds and piddling all over the veg!' His indignation mounted. 'If I had a dog, I'd be had up if I let it roam all over other folks' gardens, but cats – they can let 'em go where they bloody well like and nobody can do anything about it!'

'Doesn't mean to say you can go around killing 'em,' Kite stated, staring out into the small garden, dominated by tidy rows of vegetables and a small greenhouse, with espaliered plums against the side fence and a couple of ballerina apple trees dead centre.

'I tried everything else – cat-pepper, string, you name it, made not a blind bit of difference.' A painted tin cat with glass eyes, meant to intimidate genuine members of the species, leaned impotently against the fence, bearing witness to Stanley's wasted efforts. 'It used to sharpen its damned claws on my apple trees!'

'All the same.'

'Didn't mean to kill it, though,' he said suddenly. 'I was cutting string to tie the beans up, see, and there it was, bold as brass, behind me. It shot off when I shooed it away but it caught its claw in the netting. I lunged out at it and nicked it with the knife. After that – well, it was yowling fit to bust – I had to put it out of its misery.'

Kite, sickened, recalled the number of slashes in the cat's body and didn't believe a word. 'And then you threw it over the fence.'

'As far as I could.'

There was no reason to doubt this, at least. A good heave and the cat, thrown over the hedge from here, could conceivably have landed where it had been found.

'I'd like to talk to you about Patti Ryman, Mr Loates,' he said.

Stanley's eyes swivelled. His eyes lost some of their brightness. 'I've already said, I don't know anything about her. I didn't even know what she was called till today. She was only the paper girl.'

Beads of sweat stood on his pallid forehead. Unappealing at the best of times, now, stressed by what had happened with his mother and under pressure about Patti, he was probably showing up at his worst. Kite by now had an inkling of what Jenny Platt had been getting at but he wasn't going to let up out of a misplaced sympathy, simply because Stanley was inadequate, pathetic, because he'd been screwed up by his mother. The man was a toad.

'You like children, Mr Loates?'

Stanley blinked. 'Like them? I suppose so, they're all right.'

'You give them sweets, watch them when they're out playing.'

'What of it? I wouldn't do them any harm. I like them, yes, and what's wrong with that? Don't you like kids?'

Nothing wrong with liking them. Maybe something wrong with a society that had to suspect everyone who was kind to children of having an ulterior motive. But.

'Patti –' Kite said.

'I liked her as well,' Stanley interrupted defiantly. 'She was a bonny little thing, she used to wave to me at one time, I don't know why she stopped. I wouldn't have harmed a hair of her head.'

There was a certain ring of truth about this, but Kite had heard protests of this nature too many times to have much faith in them. He gazed out of the window, at the garden into which Stanley had put most of his time, energies and talents. The chain-link fencing at the bottom was completely obscured by the quickthorn planted in front of it, which he kept well clipped and which had consequently by now thickened into a well-nigh impenetrable barrier. There was no way that this man, flabby and out of condition, could have got over that and into the wood, and back, not without

114

some assistance, such as a ladder which he might have pulled over after him – had he been more athletic – still less reason for him wanting to do so.

And if he'd gone into the wood by the conventional route, Stanley Loates, slow, lumbering, ungainly, would have been hard to miss, making the return journey between the front of his house and the path.

'What'll happen to me?' he asked. 'About the cat?'

'A report will be made to the Crown Prosecution Service. What happens then is up to them, and Mr Lawley, whether he wishes to bring charges or not. And if he doesn't,' Kite added, piling it on, 'you'll be lucky if the NSPCC doesn't.'

Whichever way things went, he couldn't see life being very happy for Stanley Loates in Ellington Close.

Abigail Moon leaned forward, peering through the windscreen for a possible parking space amongst all the vehicles parked nose to tail either side of the streets, while Jenny Platt drove slowly.

'How the heck do the people who live round here manage?'

'Anybody's guess.'

They were at the bottom of Albert Road, near to the house where Patti Ryman had lived. A run-down area of terraced houses, small factories, corner shops, a deserted Methodist chapel and a huge, hangar-like building painted in shouting primary colours that was a DIY store proclaiming itself open 8 a.m. to 8 p.m., with an enormous, near-empty car park. Jenny was muttering about leaving theirs in the car park and be hanged to it when a battered Cortina was driven conveniently away from the kerbside.

The area on the whole was not, in any sense of the word, attractive, and Mailer Street, when they walked round the corner and came to it, stood out like a beacon in comparison, being on the edge of what had been selected by the council as an experimental improvement area, extending from here to the Leasowes. The street itself was short, comprising decent little terraced houses built of dark brick, sloping down

to the fish-and-chip shop on the corner of the main road. Now restored to its original appearance when it was first built at the turn of the century, it had a rather self-conscious charm. Encouraged by what the council had done, the residents had made their own contribution by way of window boxes and tubs. The steps of every house were swept clean, the windows polished, as if vying with each other for points on the respectability scale. Bollards, painted a handsome dark blue and gold, had been set into the cobbles, top and bottom, to prevent vehicle access, presumably in the interests of safety as well as nostalgia: the road at the bottom provided a never-ceasing flow of traffic, much of it heavy, on its way to the motorway, less than a mile off.

By the door of Linda Ryman's house, petunias and helichrysum spilled luxuriantly from a trough, and the brass knocker was highly polished.

Doreen Bailey was still with her sister. The two of them were in the living room at the front of the house – there was probably only a kitchen behind – drinking the last of what, in Abigail's experience of these sort of situations, was likely to have been an endless succession of cups of tea. Unlike her older sister, Linda Ryman showed no signs of tears, but her eyes were huge and overbright in a face drained of all colour. She gazed unseeingly into the dead coals of a living-flame gas fire, her feet neatly together on the hearth rug, her hands clasped tightly on her lap.

'Go easy on her when you see her,' Mrs Bailey had warned. 'She's had some hard knocks.'

Yet however difficult life had been for her, it hadn't left its physical stamp. At the moment, her face was set into a mask of grief, yet it remained unlined, pretty, incredibly youthful-looking. The age gap between the two women was so large she might have been Doreen Bailey's daughter rather than her sister. They bore a faint, family resemblance to each other, but otherwise they were quite unlike. Where Doreen was a large and comfortably upholstered mother figure, Linda was a small, slim, blue-eyed blonde, as her daughter had been.

116

But Abigail guessed, despite the air of helplessness, that she was a fighter, one who hadn't let life get her down. She'd done wonders with the house on a limited budget. The sitting room was attractive in a do-it-yourself stripped pine, dried flowers, Laura Ashley way. Built-in shelves in the corner were painted matt green and displayed a collection of pretty white china ornaments. Some old chairs were neatly slip-covered in a blue and green patterned fabric. A school photograph on the mantelpiece showed a younger Patti, her fair hair long and silky, unpermed.

'Come on, m'duck, drink your tea,' Doreen said gently, lifting the cup and saucer from the coffee table and putting it into her hands. Linda drank as obediently as a child, evidently still in that state of shock where Abigail doubted any possibility of getting anything useful from her.

'What will happen now?' she asked dully. 'What about the funeral?'

Abigail explained that there would be an inquest, probably on Thursday, which would be adjourned for further police inquiries to be made, after which the coroner would release Patti's body, and the funeral could take place. 'The inquest will be resumed as soon as we've found out who killed Patti, and why,' she added gently. There was no need to mention to her the necessity for identifying the body, since this appalling task Mrs Bailey had already offered to relieve her of. And, mercifully, her mind seemed to have blanked off the horrors of a postmortem.

After telling her what she needed to know, Abigail stood up and Jenny followed suit. 'We'll leave you now, Mrs Ryman. I have to ask you some questions, but they'll wait until you feel able to answer them.'

'Now's as good as any time,' Linda said unexpectedly. 'I'm not going to feel any better tomorrow. And it helps to talk.'

Abigail hesitated. 'If you're sure . . .' She glanced at Mrs Bailey inquiringly.

'She'll be all right, won't you, m'duck?'

Linda nodded.

117

'Well then –' They reseated themselves. Jenny took out her notebook.

There were the usual routine questions, designed to establish the normal course of Patti's days and to find out whether anything unusual had happened during them which could give a lead on her murder. But her life appeared to have followed its usual innocent pattern of school, homework, sports practice, with all her spare time spent with her friend, Gemma Townsend. They were bosom friends and did everything together.

'Nothing in the least unusual happened? Nothing she seemed worried about?'

'She was a bit preoccupied last week – her new school project was bothering her a bit, I think. She was doing well at school, she always worked hard – but it was the start of a new term, different teachers. If there was anything else, she'd have told me. We've always been like that with one another. I've never kept anything from her and she wouldn't keep anything from me.'

Parents often said that, and the truth was hard to bear. 'What about boyfriends?'

That roused Linda enough to earn Abigail a sudden, sharp look. 'Are you asking was she pregnant? Well, I can tell you she wasn't, not yesterday, anyway. And she didn't have any one particular boyfriend. I made her swear she'd tell me if there was anybody, I didn't want her making the same mistake as me, did I? I was only sixteen when she was born, you know, and that's a rotten start for anybody.'

'You're divorced now, I believe?'

Doreen Bailey intervened tartly: 'He pushed off when Patti was eighteen months old.'

Linda shrugged. 'Things were never right between us from the start. He was only a couple of years older than me and he wasn't ready for marriage any more than I was.'

'It must've been hard for you, left on your own.'

'I wasn't sorry. We've managed. I'd always kept my job on at Nancy's – the hairdresser up the road, worked there ever since I left school – and I've had a good family behind

me.' She attempted a smile at Doreen, and Doreen put her arm round her shoulders and squeezed.

'Come on, Lindy, bear up, you've done wonderful, so far.'

'Does her father keep in touch with Patti?'

'He's dead,' Doreen Bailey informed them, pursing her lips. 'Killed just after he left them, in a motorbike accident, and good riddance.'

'Doreen.'

'All right, I'll say no more.'

'I should never've let her take that paper round!' Patti's mother said suddenly. 'I tried not to be overprotective – you need freedom when you're young, but it was a mistake – I wouldn't have let her keep it on when the dark mornings came but I thought, this time of year . . . and it's a nice neighbourhood. She begged me, see, wanted to feel she was pulling her weight. Girls that age want clothes and things like their friends, and she knew I couldn't afford them.'

'It's unlikely the paper round had anything to do with it,' Abigail said gently, and as the difficult, unshed tears began at last to threaten, she thought it might be tactful to leave the sisters alone for a while. 'Is it all right if we take a look at her room, Mrs Ryman?'

'Linda, please. It's just at the top of the stairs.'

No more than a boxroom, really, with the dressing table doing duty as a desk, a T-shirt draped over the mirror to avoid distraction. Bookshelves showing a fairly wide reading for her age, with copies of *King Lear* and *A View from the Bridge*, plus A level text notes, on the bedside table. The top dressing-table drawer held a brush, comb and electric hair-curler, the others nothing but underclothes, T-shirts, tops and sweaters. In the single wardrobe were a couple of summer school-uniform cotton dresses, some school shirts, two very short skirts, jeans and a leather jacket. Sandals and a pair of the ugly, clumpy shoes girls favoured at the moment stood on the floor. The walls were covered with the usual pop-idol posters, pictures of animals and two RSPCA posters. There was also an RSPCA collecting box. It was the

room of any teenage girl, with nothing in it to give any sort of clue as to why she'd been murdered.

When they returned to the living room, Linda's tears had dried. 'We've been talking over what you said about there being anything different, well, it's probably nothing –'

'Anything at all, it doesn't matter how unimportant it seems.'

'It's just that she came home in a taxi last Saturday from Gemma's.'

'Taxi?'

'I made it a rule she had to be in by ten unless it was something special, and she always kept to it, she knew how I worried.'

'But it wasn't usual for her to take a taxi?'

'Heavens, no! Gemma's mother always brought her back if it was late, but she's a doctor, and she was called out during the evening. She knew she was likely to be away for some time, so she told the girls to ring for a taxi when Patti was ready to go home, and gave her a ten-pound note to pay for it. She rang up a minute or two after ten – Dr Townsend, I mean – to see if she'd got home all right. She's a single parent, too, so she knows the problems. Patti came in the door just as I was putting the phone down and wanted to know who'd been ringing and – well, it ended up with a bit of an argument.'

'Why was that?'

'It didn't amount to much, but she went on a bit about being checked up on, and having to be sent home in a taxi, and taking money from Gemma's mother like that – why couldn't she come home on the bus, she was old enough, you know the sort of thing.'

'It's not what happens on the bus, it's when you get off – I hope you told her that,' her sister said.

''Course I did, but girls of that age, you can't tell them anything. Though I think it might just have got home to her. She went a bit quiet after that, and then said she was sorry for giving me all that hassle. It wasn't long before she went up to bed.'

12

By the time Mayo had finished talking to Tina Baverstock, he felt in need of something long and cool to wash away the taste of her nasty herbal tea. And not only the tea. The Drum and Monkey was just around the corner. What was ten minutes to a thirsty man?

It was a pleasant pub with a forecourt and tables, and a shady corner, fortunately empty. He carried his half of ginger-beer shandy to the table under a sycamore, threw his jacket on to the bench beside him, took a long, cool swallow and sat back, reviewing his thoughts.

Going straight from one house to the other had given him no opportunity so far to assess the interview with Imogen Loxley, but uppermost in his mind was the notion that if she'd been truthful about sitting at her window like the Lady of Shalott, looking out for the postman – and there was no reason at this stage to think she'd any conceivable reason to lie, or conceal the truth – it seemed clear that Patti's murder had occurred after she'd delivered the paper to Simla and before Imogen arrived upstairs at, say, five past eight, no more than a fifteen-minute time span. Unless the assailant had either been lurking in the wood before she was attacked, or entered it via one of the gardens which adjoined it – and presumably escaped the same way. But how could he have known Patti would go into the wood?

He didn't in any case see how anyone planning a murder would have contemplated one such as this, with all the attendant risks. There could have been no guarantee that the perpetrator would have got away without being seen or

heard. When questioned about their movements, few people could be exact about what they'd been doing at a precise time during the day, but breakfast-time was different. The human race is on the whole more habit-orientated than it cares to admit. Morning routines are established by office, school and factory starting times, and in his experience, people usually knew exactly where they were, or should have been, when the day was beginning – and which people they normally encountered. A stranger hanging around was almost certain to have been noticed. On the other hand, a moment only would have sufficed to slip along that path and disappear from sight, and the same would apply when he emerged from the wood, not much later.

But it was fruitless at this stage in a murder inquiry to start looking for any sort of pattern. Until more facts were collected, names of witnesses had been obtained, others eliminated from the inquiry, until a suspect emerged and the motive became clear. Speculating before that, there was always the danger of jumping to wrong conclusions . . .

A kamikaze wasp, intent on suicide, zoomed in on his beer mug. He moved his glass further into the shade, covering it with his hand. The wasp decided to concentrate on his ear. He flipped irritably at it and watched it land on the table, legs in the air. Gotcha! Where were we? Wrong conclusions . . . ah, yes.

It's a well-known fact that nobody can ever concentrate wholly on one subject for any length of time. According to the shrinks, at any rate. The more you try, the more the mind wanders . . .

All right, then. Who had he been, the man with Alex? Jealousy was an immature emotion, not to be considered in well-adjusted senior police officers. Anyway, it wasn't part of his make-up. He was curious, that was all. Far be it from him to be suspicious of every man Alex had dealings with. She'd worked for years in a man's world, and not without exciting admiration, and it had never been a problem for him. And it was months – well, a long time, anyway, since he'd thought of Liam, the Irishman. The bad-news man, the

playboy of the western world, the hound who'd spoiled so many of the best years of Alex's life, kept her dangling with promises he'd no intention of ever fulfilling, playing up his so-called need of her, until at last, seven years on and no further forward, she'd come to her senses, seen things as they really were: the wife in the background, still the semi-invalid she'd always been, and Liam, no nearer asking for a divorce than he'd ever intended.

It was several years now since she'd gathered her courage, moved away and given him the push.

He'd gone, gone forever, hadn't he? Hadn't he?

Of course he had. But Alex had never blamed him entirely, always made excuses, always saw the other side of the equation. Could it explain that brittle, nervous excitement about her recently that he couldn't understand and didn't want to ask about, not even tentatively or obliquely? And she'd been smiling and lifting her glass to the man opposite her in the restaurant . . .

What the hell.

He took a long, reflective pull of his shandy.

And became aware of increasing activity outside the church on the opposite side of the road, of the number of cars parking there. He watched more arrive, driven mostly by women, but with one or two men among their number. As they walked up the path to the church door, and he decided from their casual clothes and their demeanour that it was unlikely to be either a wedding or a funeral they were attending, a red Renault drew up. Sarah Wilmot got out, locked the door and also made for the church.

Mayo finished his drink, strolled across the road and followed the rest of them up the yew-bordered path through the old churchyard, shaded by ancient oaks, renowned in spring for its great sheets of daffodils, its tombstones now laid flat and the graves grassed over for easy maintenance, their occupants far too long dead to care.

Sarah was sitting motionless in one of the back pews, while the people he'd seen entering moved purposefully about the church. A regular hive of activity, it was. Someone was prac-

tising on the organ. 'Jesu, joy of man's desiring'. Trite, but gentle and oddly appropriate, and played well. There was to be an organ recital next month – he'd spotted a notice stuck up in the porch as he came through. He made a mental note that it might be worth attending.

Sliding into the pew beside Sarah, he was struck by her unexpected sombreness. She looked as wholesome and healthy as when he'd met her at the party, her face, as well as her smooth bare limbs, tanned pale gold, and her short, toffee-coloured hair streaked with the sun. She smelled of bluebells and fern. She glanced up when she saw him and smiled, and immediately the impression of some dark shadow hanging over her was gone.

'Did you want to see me? I thought someone from the police would be coming round, but to tell the truth I'd forgotten you were a policeman. I suppose you have to ask me questions.'

He hesitated. 'I don't want to disturb you if – '

'That's all right, I just came in for a few minutes' quiet. It isn't often churches are open on weekdays, these days. Go ahead – unless you'd rather we went across to the house?'

He shook his head. 'This'll do. I haven't much to ask you ... you don't know the neighbourhood yet, won't know which comings and goings are normal, which are out of the ordinary, who's a stranger and who isn't. For the moment, we're just checking on when people left home this morning.'

Routine comment. True, of course, but also, even at this stage, a matter of being alert to catch nuances, things let slip, of patiently picking up discrepancies or seemingly irrelevant pieces which might eventually fit together.

'Oh, that's easy,' Sarah said. 'Dermot left at half past sevenish, or maybe a bit later. I suppose by the time he'd walked back home it must have been after eight. I wasn't there, I'd left with the children for school at five past eight.'

'Walked back?'

'Didn't you know? He had his car pinched this morning.'

'I wouldn't necessarily be told about it. Not my department.'

'Oh. No, of course, it wouldn't be. He parked it outside Patel's while he went in to get some cigarettes. There was quite a queue and when he came out it was gone. He had to come back home to report the theft and make arrangements for another car and so forth. He's not due home tonight and of course, his overnight bag was taken as well – plus his personal camera. His company's lent him another car but it's really messed up the day for everyone. He was livid.'

Tina Baverstock, though she'd been wrong in her assumptions about the car breaking down, would testify to this fury. She'd heard the door bang. Mayo mentally slotted these times in with the others. Picaddilly Circus in the rush hour wasn't in it, all of them milling around at the same time, and still no one seeing hide nor hair of the murderer.

The church was High, with lace on the altar cloths, candles and a sanctuary lamp burning, a faint smell of incense mingling with the flowers. A young priest in a black cassock moved quietly among the groups. A faint murmur of conversation made a background susurration.

'What are all these people doing?' he asked, curiosity finally overcoming him as a woman with a large tote bag and a camera slung over her shoulder passed them and took up a determined stance in front of a marble monument on the wall, produced a notebook and started making notes. 'Who are they?'

'Oh, church recorders,' she answered, smiling at his mystified expression. Here, she explained, to make a detailed inventory, to record minutely every part of the church and its furnishings, whether it be silver, woodwork, memorials, books, or anything else . . . 'In case of damage, or loss – or theft, which I don't suppose I need to remind you about. My mother's in a similar group, that's how I know about it.'

St Gregory's was a fourteenth-century church which had been enlarged and overrestored by the Victorians. Pevsner hadn't found much to remark on in Lavenstock, other than the public-school buildings, the Tudor almshouses and various ancient inns and dwellings in the mediaeval streets

leading from the Cornmarket down to the river. St Gregory's, if Mayo remembered correctly, had received scant mention, apart from the fine organ and some stained-glass windows by Kempe. What a pity. As with the town, there were more subtle attractions than the patently obvious.

'Did you see Patti at all this morning?'

Her face clouded. 'Not this morning, no. I didn't see any-one; I left Dermot to it, got the children into the car and drove off.'

The music changed. More Bach. 'Lovely,' she said.

'Do you like music?'

'Oh yes – but that's not why I'm here.' She gave him a quick, sideways glance. 'I – I actually slipped in to say a quick prayer for her, for Patti, and her mother, but – I'm not sure part of it wasn't for myself. My own sister, dying so recently . . . it brings it back. How little we *know* anyone, really.'

Now why had she added that last remark? What did she mean by it? Her head was bent and the wing of butterscotch hair partly obscured her face. She looked up with an unread-able expression and gave a little embarrassed half-laugh.

'When are you expecting to return home?' he asked.

'I don't know, but I can't stay here much longer. I've a job – and a flat I must get back to – but there's millions of things to do here, yet –' She looked at her watch. 'Today, I've to find a *chimney-sweep*, would you believe, before Dermot can have gas fires fitted . . . buy new curtains . . . pick the children up.' She laughed. 'I'll be glad to get back to work! No reason why I shouldn't, now. I've actually found a housekeeper. Mrs Bailey's agreed to come in when I've gone, to see to the cleaning and cooking and look after the children when Dermot's not there. She's very good with them and they adore her. She's delighted with the idea, it means she can give up her job at the supermarket. But now this has happened she may not want to start for a while . . . Patti meant an awful lot to her.'

'Mrs Bailey doesn't seem to be the type to let it knock her off her peg for long.'

'I expect you're right. Imogen Loxley did offer to see to

the children pro tem, she and her brother and sister seem to have taken a shine to them, Francis is trying to teach them to play Mah Jong but – I don't know . . .'

Francis, he thought, jolted. Francis Kendrick? That dry, intellectual stick. Well, well. Then he remembered the Victorian music box and the tall man holding the hand of the little girl as they crossed the lawn.

'Tell me about the other people at Edwina Lodge. I've already met Mrs Baverstock.'

She met his glance and grimaced. 'Her husband, Vic, he's OK. He's nice to the children, makes them laugh. I've scarcely spoken to Mr Pitt. He seems a sweet old soul but I suspect he's shy of women. He ducks his head and scoots whenever we meet.'

'What about the mysterious man who has the attic floor – Mr Fitzallan?'

'Fitz? Oh, there's nothing mysterious about him,' she said casually. 'He's a spare-time artist and he rents the attics as a studio, that's all. He runs a successful design consultancy in real life.'

'Fitzallan Associates?'

'Yes, I think that's the name – d'you know it?'

'I've heard of it.'

A faint smile played round her lips. 'He's painting a portrait of Allie. Oh Lord, that reminds me!' She looked again at her watch. 'If there's nothing more – I have to go and find a pet shop before the children come home. Disaster struck this morning. Goodness knows how it happened, but after they'd gone to school I found their hamster lying dead in its cage. I'll have to get another, otherwise they'll be heartbroken. Will they know the difference, d'you think?'

'Wouldn't bank on it,' Mayo answered, remembering a similar experience in Julie's childhood. However, he told her where the nearest pet shop was, gave her a few minutes and then followed her out into the bright sunlight, pausing to make a note of the organ recital. The organist was not to be the woman he'd just heard playing, but Francis Kendrick. A

127

man of many parts, Kendrick. And high time he made contact with him.

As he walked back between the yews he thought of the other name that had been mentioned – James Fitzallan. He remembered the case, and nearly all the details. The wife who'd died in suspicious circumstances. And that other woman, and her child.

Abigail Moon came into his office as soon as he got back to the station, with a report on the Stanley Loates incident. 'He's a creep,' she said forthrightly. 'Anyone who could do that to a dumb animal could do anything.'

'And that, of course, makes it certain he killed Patti, as well as the cat.'

'Oh Lord, of course not! But – I don't know – he could have, I suppose – not intending to kill, but a mindless reaction because she saw what he'd done –? All right, I know – I'm letting my prejudices show.' She ran a hand through her hair. 'More to the point, there's someone come in with some information. He's in with Martin Kite at the moment – his name's Pitt, Henry Pitt.'

'I feel I ought to tell you,' Henry Pitt had begun, nervously looking around the interview room as though expecting to see jack-booted inquisitors behind him and thumbscrews on the wall, rather than a tattered copy of PACE and Martin Kite sitting opposite. He coughed, blinked like a nervous rabbit, smoothed back his hair. His hands, Kite noticed, were smooth and white, the backs covered with freckles and pale gold hairs.

'Yes, Mr Pitt? What is it you have to tell us? I take it it's about Patti Ryman?'

'Patti, oh dear, yes. Someone at the library heard about it on the local radio.' For a moment Henry looked as though he were about to burst into tears. His soft lower lip trembled, tears did actually come to his eyes, but he took out a large handkerchief, blew loudly into it and then said, 'I'm sorry, it was such a shock . . .'

128

He'd taken time off from his work at the library, come in of his own accord and asked to see the detective superintendent in charge of the case, at what cost to himself Kite could only guess. In Mayo's absence, he'd been offered Sergeant Kite as a substitute, plus a sympathetic presence in the shape of WPC Platt, and a cup of tea, which he hadn't touched. None of it seemed to have had any effect. 'It's all so difficult –'

'Well, let's begin with the last time you saw Patti,' Kite said, patiently.

'Yes. Yes, of course. It was this morning, when she was delivering my paper. We often used to have a little chat. I was very fond of her.' His lips began to tremble again but as he met Kite's gaze, kindly but sharp, his hesitant manner suddenly left him. He may have given the initial impression of being a doddery old fool, but he was an intelligent man, must be well aware of how this conversation might be interpreted, and Kite had no doubt it had taken some courage to square up to what he had to say.

'Take your time, Mr Pitt.'

'Thank you.' He breathed deeply, and then began to speak slowly, anxious to get things in the right order. 'I first met her when I was taking a collecting box round the Close for the RSPCA. She was at her aunt's house – Mrs Bailey, you know – and she started chatting. I could see she was as passionate about cruelty to animals as I am, and she wanted to know if she could become a collector as well, but of course she wasn't old enough. I gave her a collecting box for her own use, and she used to put a small amount in every week, and something out of her birthday and Christmas money, that sort of thing. Well, that's how it began – I came to look forward to seeing her smiling face every morning. Occasionally we had a few minutes' conversation, but usually it was just to pass the time of day and so on, nothing more, you understand.'

'Yes, I understand.' Kite had heard similar protestations hundreds of times. This time, there was more than a ring of truth in what the old buffer had been saying so far. Kite, who wasn't easily fooled by anyone, thought him almost

painfully honest and well-intentioned. 'And this morning?'

Pitt licked his lips. 'This morning was different . . . she said she had a problem. That was how she put it, a problem, and could she talk it over with me. I asked her why me – was it something to do with her schoolwork? You see, sometimes I'd help her to find books she needed for her school projects and so on, but she said no, it wasn't that, it was only that she couldn't think of anyone else who'd understand. That made me think it was something the RSPCA should know about, and I told her she should report it, but apparently what was bothering her was something quite different. "I think it's what you'd call a moral dilemma, Mr Pitt," she said. "Like when you think you know something bad about a person, but you're not quite sure."'

'Was it anything that had a bearing on what's happened to her?'

'I don't know. She said she'd no time to talk about it then. I suggested she came to the library after school and I'd take my tea-break in the library cafeteria with her, and we'd discuss it then. But of course . . . when I heard the news . . . dear God, what are we coming to?'

'All this happened before she went to deliver her papers in the Close?' Kite asked, shuffling papers to give Henry time to get over his distress.

'Oh yes, she always came to Edwina Lodge first – and then Simla – before she went on there.'

'If it wasn't anything to do with the RSPCA that was bothering her, why do you think she came to you, in particular?'

'I really can't think,' Henry said humbly.

13

Police cars were still parked at the entrance to the Close when Sarah arrived back at Edwina Lodge after picking the girls up from school, but luckily the children either didn't notice them or saw nothing untoward in them being there. It wasn't going to be possible to keep them in ignorance of the terrible events which had happened in the wood for long, however. News of that sort couldn't be kept secret. They'd met and talked to Patti, been promised a go on her grown-up bicycle. But how did you tell young children something like that without frightening them half to death? Especially now, just when they were beginning to come to terms with the loss of their mother.

Later that evening, when they were in bed, Sarah sat back, nursing a whisky, richly deserved, she felt, after a day of enforced domesticity – how did mothers stand it, day in, day out? – coupled with the terrible news about Patti Ryman, and ending with a protracted scene with Lucy over the hamster.

'This isn't Goldie!' Lucy had declared, immediately she opened the cage to give the animal its food. 'It's somebody else! What's happened to her?'

'What makes you think it's not her?' Sarah had prevaricated, furiously cutting Marmite sandwiches, pouring juice, knowing she was being cowardly.

'I just do! It's not Goldie! What have you done with her?'

Sarah knelt down by the cage and tried to tell both children as gently as she could what had happened, wondering if she could use the hamster's demise to introduce the subject of Patti, but to her horror both children had burst into noisy

sobs and whatever she said couldn't pacify them, especially Lucy, who could create a scene better than anyone when the occasion demanded it.

It was at this point, when she was kneeling on the floor with her arms around both children (at least around Lucy – Allie was pulling away, as usual, stiffening whenever she was touched) that blessed intervention came in the person of Imogen, there to deliver a parcel for the children, from Hope. The tears gradually subsided. When opened, the parcel was found to contain a pair of dolls, one for each child. Hope, it appeared, had been embarrassed about giving the presents herself, as well might she be, considering the one intended for Allie, Sarah thought, considerably taken aback by it.

'I know, I know!' Imogen said, holding up a hand, forestalling comment. 'I did try to dissuade her, but you know what Hope's like. They've no sentimental value for her – she was never one for dolls.'

It was obvious to Sarah that she *didn't* know what Hope was like. She was stunned by her generosity, but at the same time, appalled. Mainly at the total unsuitability of Allie's present, which was not a plaything but an expensive antique in near-mint condition, a genuine, simpering Victorian doll with a rosebud mouth, wearing plum-coloured, lace-trimmed silk, and kid boots. But the sight of Allie's enraptured face, besotted with love at first sight, like a mother with her first-born baby, effectively scotched any possibility that somehow, tactfully, the doll could be returned.

The one designated for Lucy wasn't nearly such a thoroughbred, but that didn't matter. Lucy hardly ever played with dolls. She thanked Imogen politely for the jointed wooden Dutch doll, dressed in national costume, and was playing with it for the moment, introducing the now apparently accepted hamster to it, with the hamster receiving most of the attention. It wouldn't be long before she put the doll on one side in favour of her new computer game.

Allie was sitting on the floor with her doll cradled tightly in her arms, covering it with wet, messy kisses, boding ill for the pristine, the pink and white face. 'Now come along,

Angel,' she announced, prim as a Victorian nursemaid, 'I'll read you a story I've written and draw you a picture, but then you'll have to go straight to bed.'

Sarah exchanged looks with Imogen. *Angel*? Maybe Hope, even if unwittingly, had done more than she realized.

Now, Angel having been tucked up in bed beside Allie, and Lucy's doll, as yet nameless, lying on the floor in the corner of the bedroom with its limbs at all angles, Sarah abandoned the whisky, which she didn't really care for and, disappointingly, always looked better than it tasted, and escaped from Dermot, if you could be said to escape from someone who barely seemed to know you were there. He was ostensibly immersed in a fat file concerned with the legal intricacies of being a land-lord, but he didn't look as though his heart was in it. Something of greater moment was absorbing his thoughts.

Out in the garden, the new swing hung loose on its ropes from the old pear-tree branch. Sarah perched on it, absently propelling it back and forth, one toe barely touching the ground. In the dusk, the Welsh poppies which had seeded themselves between the cracks of the old blue bricks of the path glowed like small harvest moons, orange and gold. The deep honey scent of dame's violet hung on the air. On the other side of the great beech hedge was the wood, silent now, where the sound of men's voices had rung for most of the day.

Although Sarah hadn't known Patti, had barely spoken to her, the poor girl's murder seemed to add another dimension to the shock of her own discovery of the previous day.

She'd been putting off thinking about *that* for too long – ever since yesterday, in fact, when she'd knelt on the floor of her bedroom with the old tin trunk beside her, but no amount of procrastination was going to make it go away.

The trunk had held the last of Lisa's personal possessions to be disposed of. The rest – the pretty shoes and slender suits she'd been so looking forward to wearing again after the baby was born – Dermot had donated to charity shops immediately after the funeral. It wasn't until yesterday that he'd asked Sarah if she'd mind going through the trunk. He

133

simply couldn't face it himself, he said, and she'd steeled herself to do the task straight away, in order to get it over with, though suspecting it might awaken memories grown neither less painful nor less vivid.

Lisa, surprisingly for one so much of the moment, had kept more memorabilia from her childhood and adolescence than Sarah had. Perhaps she'd just never got around to throwing them out. Sarah began to sift through the oddly assorted layers – toothily smiling Donny Osmond posters, the ivory-backed prayer book her godmother had given her when she was confirmed, a pair of ballet shoes, a riding crop and hat, old school photographs – one of them with Sarah, taken when they were gap-toothed six- and seven-year-olds. She shook out an acid-yellow minidress Lisa had begged and schemed and cried for – just why, wasn't now clear, and put it on the 'discard' pile, before turning to Lisa's jewellery box.

'I've kept her engagement ring myself,' Dermot had said, 'and if there's anything you think the girls might like when they're older, put them on one side. Anything else, you're welcome to have for yourself, or to get rid of, just as you think best. There's one or two things of value, but you know she mostly preferred costume jewellery, though none of *that* was cheap, as I remember!' he added, with a wry lift of the eyebrow.

Sarah didn't imagine there would be much to her own taste. Lisa had, surprisingly, loved the sort of dramatic costume jewellery that made an impact, as if feeling her personality lacked some definition. Whereas, small and sparkling, full of life, she hadn't needed jewellery at all.

Sarah set aside a couple of gold chains for herself, then a heavily laden silver charm bracelet that she was sure would delight Lucy, and for Allie the single strand of cultured pearls, identical to the one Sarah herself possessed, chosen as eighteenth birthday gifts by their father. She gathered up the rest and put them back carefully in the velvet-lined trays to return them to the box. The girls might like them when they were older. It was a large box, covered in ivory leather and lined with red velvet, whose loose, padded bottom had col-

lected a little fluff and dust. Lifting it to give it a brush, she saw a manila envelope underneath. Inside was a photograph. Taken somewhere foreign-looking, hot. Italy? Greece? A blinding light, deep shadows, a café table under a tree. A man with a thin face, smiling into the sun.

On the back was written: *Darling Lisa, as requested. Until I can be there again in person. Ever and always, my dearest, yours.* It was unsigned, but dated New Year's Day of the previous year.

The face smiling from the photograph wasn't Dermot's.

Sarah found it hard to accept that Lisa, open and honest as the day, could have risked everything – her marriage, her children's happiness – by carrying on a secretive, underhand affair. That it was an affair, Sarah had no doubt. There'd been no dubiety about the message. Unmistakable. Darling Lisa. A few lines on the back of a photograph, and Lisa's memory was diminished, tarnished. Lisa, the last person to have done such a thing. Well, she hadn't been canonized, no one had ever said she was better or worse than the next woman. But – Lisa!

Perhaps she'd really been in love with him, this 'yours'. Sarah paused. Would *I* do *that* for Simon? Better not think about that.

Ever and always, yours. Darling Lisa. Who was he, and did it matter now, anyway? Yet Sarah had a sudden sense that it did, a feeling of impending disaster. The hairs on her skin stood on end. Nonsense.

She slid off the swing and walked to the grainy, splintery wooden seat set under the wall which supported a great swathe of honeysuckle, facing the view over Lavenstock. In the dusk, lights twinkled palely below; in the distance, the hills, blue in the daylight were now dark against a sky the colour of a 'Peace' rose. Night insects danced, moths fluttered dustily in the grass.

Behind the puzzle of why Lisa, of all people, had had this secret, was a plunge of unexplained fear.

A footfall on the path. Fitzallan, looming tall beside her. A hand on her shoulder, his deep voice: 'Something wrong? You're shivering like a leaf.'

'Oh! Oh, Fitz, it's you.' She came back from a long way, feeling that she had to make an immense effort. 'It's nothing, a ghost walking over my grave.'

'I'm sorry. I'm intruding.' But he didn't go away. Instead, he pulled his Aran sweater from his shoulders and draped it around hers, and sat on the seat beside her, where a warmth that had nothing to do with the sweater presently enveloped her. She'd hoped he would come and join her. Since showing her his paintings in the attic, it was becoming almost a nightly ritual to sit here on the seat before he went home to his house, fifteen miles away. They never talked much. He had a great capacity for silence, this man. Quite often, she'd wondered about that house of his, his lonely life since his wife had died.

'Want to tell me what's wrong?' he asked.

That face, the one in the photograph. Undistinguished, a stranger's face, yet half recognized. No one she'd ever met, she was sure of that, there was no voice that went with the face. A man glimpsed in the street, across a shop counter? A restaurant? Some politician or other in the paper? Not recently, or she'd have remembered – surely . . . ?

Fitz would know what to do if she told him. He was that sort of man – partly due, she felt, to having gone through his own personal hell while his wife had been alive, about which she now knew a little – but mostly because that's how he'd been born. Knowing what to do, and unswerving, once he set his mind to it.

'I *can't*,' she said, hoping this didn't sound as feeble as she felt it did, but she was unused to bottling things up. 'I would, believe me, but I just can't.'

'Well, if you start to feel differently – I'm here.'

He smiled at her, his brilliant eyes lighting up. He wouldn't press her, she knew, but yes, if anything could have made her feel better at this moment, it was to know that Fitz was there.

'The police came to see me today,' he said suddenly.

'They're talking to everyone.'

She waited but he didn't say anything more.

She had a feeling that he was trying to bring himself to

136

tell her something, but she knew him well enough by now to know that he'd only do it in his own time.

Down at the police station in Lavenstock, those who could were going home. It had been a long, long day.

Abigail Moon drove home to her cottage under the hill, thought about a glass of wine, thought about having to open a bottle when she only wanted a glass and decided against it. Thought about ringing Ben, then looked at the clock and decided against that, too. Made herself a tunafish sandwich, went to bed, thoroughly restless, knowing she wouldn't sleep, and went out like a light immediately her head touched the pillow.

Detective Constable Keith Farrar slipped his key into the lock of his front door, let himself in quietly, wiped his feet on the mat and without putting on the light – so as not to disturb Sandra – tiptoed into the spotless, state-of-the-art kitchen, where a corner of the table was set out for one. A meal of unimaginable dreariness awaited him in the fridge. Cutting into the cold lamb and beetroot, he saw the letter on the table, propped against the glass dome that covered a plate of bread spread with healthily polyunsaturated margarine. His heart sank. Another hospital consultation for Sandra. Almost certainly another disappointment. He felt deeply sorry for her, but even sorrier for himself, wistfully imagining a life with a wife who had a baby to occupy her, rather than needing to fill in her time by keeping the house as sterile as an intensive care unit, and nagging him about promotion.

Martin Kite arrived at his warm, untidy home, as different from the house where he'd interviewed Trevor Lawley that morning as chalk from cheese, just as his wife was going to bed. She saw how tired he was but he surprised her by putting his arms fiercely around her and holding her head against his shoulder, and even more by not uttering a single complaint about Daniel and Davy not yet being in bed and having the television on loud enough to keep half Lavenstock awake.

*   *   *

137

Gil Mayo was in that state of wakefulness which even a steady walk home through the dark, sleeping streets of his manor had failed to lull. He was happy on two counts when he walked through the door of his upstairs flat: to find Alex not yet in bed and that he'd missed her sister Lois by about ten minutes.

'Shut up, Bert!' he said by way of greeting to the parrot, who was resenting the close attention being paid to Alex and was responding in his inimitable way. When he could make himself heard, Mayo asked carefully after Lois and Alex responded just as carefully. Relations between himself and the spiky Lois, he sometimes felt, were rather like that of his cat and his parrot. Correction. His *landlady's* villainous-looking grey cat, and his daughter Julie's parrot, wished on him when she'd decided to leave for foreign parts. Pesky old Moses, who also answered to the name of Go Away, sometimes now managed to insinuate himself into the flat because Alex couldn't bring herself to boot him out, and with the bars of the parrot cage between them, the two nonhumans regarded each other warily, like Tweetie-pie and Sylvester, like himself and Lois.

He poured himself a dram of The Macallan while Alex went to prepare him something to eat, sank on to his favourite sofa and put his feet up on the new upholstery, letting a warm feeling of home envelop him. Clean, tidy, stylishly decorated, smelling faintly of polish. He'd once questioned the wisdom of living with someone who was so congenitally tidy-minded as Alex, even fearing it might break up a beautiful relationship, but in fact he'd come to see certain advantages. He now made no objections to having his books alphabetically arranged, or his CDs neatly shelved, and even responded positively to having his socks paired and tucked together, rather than having to search for a mate.

He sipped his Scotch and began to rehearse variations of the same question: 'So who was that you were having lunch with?' – 'Who was that man I saw you with in the Italian restaurant?' – 'Why didn't you tell me you were meeting a man for lunch?' Worse and worse.

A loud clattering was issuing from the kitchen, the volume

of which was unfortunately not guaranteed to be commensurate with the quality of what was produced. Farrar's wife, Sandra, wasn't the only one who wasn't interested in cooking, though Alex was learning, having begun to get a grasp of the situation when she'd cottoned on to the number of times Mayo mentioned his mother's treacle sponge, or one of Julie's more exotic dishes. Plain, unimaginative food, mostly salad, was the order of the day when it was her turn to cook. Perhaps Julie would come home one day and teach her properly.

'I forgot – letter from Australia on the mantelpiece,' she said, popping her head round the kitchen door, tuning into that telepathy between them which was still a source of wonder to him.

Slitting the envelope open, he skimmed it quickly for what he always hoped to read – but his daughter wasn't coming home, not yet, nor likely to be, he saw as he came to the last paragraph. Since giving up her place at catering college, eschewing meat and opting for a life in faraway places, she'd found an exciting life in Australia and was now planning to start up a restaurant with a friend.

He went to tell Alex what the letter had said. 'Vegetarian restaurant in Sydney – wonder what the Ozzies'll make of that?' he grinned, hovering hungrily in the kitchen door. 'Good smell.'

She waved a fork at him. 'Go away. You know I can't do anything properly when anyone's standing over me. I'm not your Julie and this needs concentration. I'm doing you a steak, with a pepper sauce I got from a recipe in the paper. Don't mind if I don't join you? I'm not hungry.'

Whisky glass in hand, he leaned against the doorjamb, seeing himself reflected in the dark window, relaxed in his shirt sleeves, the whiteness of the fabric making his dark face look all the darker, the slatey eyes under the thick brows watching her steadily, his dark hair crisped with grey. He said the last thing he meant or ought to have said, albeit with a smile: 'You won't, not after eating with Lois and stuffing yourself with pasta at lunch-time.'

She barely missed a beat. Smiling in return, she said, 'How did you guess I had lunch at Gino's?'

'I saw you when I was stopped at the traffic lights.'

There was a short silence, accompanied by a horrid smell of burning. 'The sauce! Hell's teeth!'

Alex grabbed the pan and rushed it to the sink, where she turned the tap on and spent some time getting rid of the ruined sauce before turning round and leaning with her back against the sink unit. 'So much for that. Plain grilled steak, I'm afraid.'

'You'd better turn it over, then, otherwise that's going to be charcoal as well.' He liked his steak rare.

He realized, when he was finally sitting down to what he considered to be a near-cremated steak, that his ill-judged remarks were going to be passed off, as though nothing had been said, but when she'd brought cheese for him, a small slice of hazelnut chocolate cake to satisfy her own sweet tooth and late-night, decaffeinated coffee for both, she sat down opposite and said seriously, 'Something quite exciting's appeared on the horizon, Gil. I do want to talk to you about it sometime, I'd appreciate your advice, but it's not the right time now, not while you've got your plate full with this case.'

Had she really been going to tell him, or had he forced it into the open with his snide remarks, for which he was truly sorry? And had the rug pulled from under his feet? Wasn't that just like a woman – whet your appetite and then refuse to satisfy –

'Sure you won't have a piece of this cake? It's from Dowley's.'

'No, thanks, and I thought you weren't hungry.'

'It's longer than I thought since supper-time. And that pasta I was stuffing myself with at lunch was an omelette.'

'Don't forget the wine.'

'You saw a lot in a few seconds at the traffic lights. What can I do to convince you that –'

'Try me and see,' he said, pulling her to her feet.

PART III

Hope Kendrick is sitting in her empty classroom, waiting to be summoned to talk to the police in the headmistress's study. The weight of Patti Ryman's death feels heavy on her shoulders. It brings back painfully, in a roundabout way, memories she's striven for years to forget.

She'd dreamt of him last night, as she regularly does, as she has for more than twenty-five years, though his face is becoming less clear with every year that passes. Sometimes, she can't remember his face at all, and that really frightens her.

Well, he'd been tall, had to be, of course. Taller than she is, but even so, not the same height as Francis. A big, blond man with light, Scandinavian blue eyes, broad shouldered and athletic-looking. Not the usual picture of an academic, but Sven had never been what was expected. A brilliant mathematician, he was first her tutor at Cambridge, then her lover. Her face twists. She's aware that everyone considers her a dried-up old prune, who has never known love, much less sex . . . even Francis, perhaps especially Francis, never suspected, though neither of them, Sven or herself, had ever deliberately sought to keep it a secret.

She'd introduced him to Francis with caution. Her brother received him with his usual suspicious reserve, but as it became apparent that Sven was going to be part of the continuing scenery, when it was obvious that he was intellectually at least Francis's equal, his wariness gradually gave way to respect, liking, and finally, acceptance. She had, ironically, been delighted.

After that, it was Francis with them everywhere they went: she, Francis and Sven, their friend. Cycling out for tea at one of the villages, picnicking in the river meadows, the Cambridge college gardens, punting on the Cam, tennis, music at King's . . . a summer of roses and wine. And love, unsuspected by head-in-the-clouds Francis, as she'd never hoped or expected to find it. Sven, making her come alive, filling her with passion. Sven, watching her, smiling

when their eyes met, Sven watching her watching Francis . . .

And then, the summer was over and the days were lengthening. Something was wrong. Sven growing very cool towards Francis. Then Francis catching flu, really bad flu, so that she had to cancel the week with Sven in Prague, where he'd been invited to lecture. After which Sven had bowed out, saying, 'I can't compete, and I won't play second fiddle.'

She'd managed to reply, though she was choking, scarcely able to breathe. 'He couldn't help catching flu.'

'No, but there was no need for you to stay behind with him. He wasn't that bad.'

This time she couldn't answer.

'I don't know why I'm surprised. It's only what I should have expected. He always comes first, doesn't he? Doesn't he?' His gaze had held hers. 'He always has and always will.'

Scalded, she'd refused to think about the subtext there. It was over without argument, without the opportunity to speak in her own defence, though she would have offered none. And she'd been too proud to tell him she was pregnant. No one had ever known that, not even Francis. Well, by then, Francis had had troubles enough of his own.

She sits now in the quiet room, seeing what she has become, a gaunt, desiccated, angular spinster, nearing fifty. Motionless, the sun focusing on her clasped, ringless hands like a burning glass, allowing herself for once to think of the child – the children – wonderful bright children, like Patti Ryman and the little Voss girls – that she might have had, not resolutely shutting them out of her life and thoughts as she normally does.

The head comes in to say the police are ready to see her. A woman fifteen years younger than Hope, smartly dressed, made-up, a woman whose style the girls secretly admire, in contrast to Hope, whom they pity. She has children of her own, a husband who is a captain of industry. She runs her school, her home and her family with equal efficiency. She is successful, dazzling. What a terrible thing this is, Miss Kendrick, we mustn't let it get out of hand, though. Keep the girls busy, life must go on.

Hope gets to her feet, her shoulders sagging. She feels drained, but she must talk sensibly to the police. She follows the head to her study. Life must go on.

14

Patti had been a model pupil, according to her headmistress, conscientious and hard-working, homework always handed in on time, consistently high marks in class and in exams, popular with staff and pupils.

Her form tutor, Miss Kendrick, neither as young nor enthusiastic (and nowhere near as ambitious of her school's position in the league tables) as the head, gave a modified version of this when she was left alone with the two police officers in the latter's room. 'Patti hadn't been with me for long – I'd had her as form pupil only from the beginning of this year, but I taught her maths for the last two. She was conscientious, though she did not, in my opinion, have a first-class brain . . . I wouldn't have encouraged her to have too high expectations, it would have been unrealistic. She *might* have gone far – but only by overstretching herself.'

There was implied criticism of the headmistress here, and when Hope Kendrick spoke of high expectations, she was probably meaning Oxford or Cambridge, but Mayo looked at her with more interest, seeing in her an authority he hadn't expected, and finding himself in agreement with what she'd said. He'd never seen the point of pushing children beyond their limits, either, a counterproductive act if ever there was one.

'Well, we're not here to assess her academic prowess,' he said. 'We just want to get a general impression of what she was like, to find out if anything might have been worrying her, if anything happened lately that could possibly have led to her death.'

'Teachers, I assure you, are the last to be told if anything's worrying children! I can only say that she didn't appear to be worried. I always found her a cooperative girl, lively in class, not half asleep as some of them are from staying up too late watching television – not even from getting up early to deliver those papers. I saw her collecting them from Patel's yesterday as we passed.' She softened the implicit disapproval by adding in a low voice, 'Poor child,' yet flushed as she did so, almost as if embarrassed to show compassion.

'What time would that be?'

Quickly recovering herself, she gave the time as twenty to eight, or thereabouts, which agreed with the time her sister Imogen had given. She was absent-mindedly fiddling with the cap of a biro she'd picked up from the orderly array set out in a tray on the large clutter-free desk, and staring at Mayo in a slightly puzzled way; when she saw he'd noticed, she looked away, confused. 'I left earlier than usual, though I had a couple of free periods first thing. I was driving my brother to Birmingham New Street to catch the eight fifteen to London.'

My brother. Three syllables, with a wealth of undertone. He remembered the way Hope's eyes had followed Francis, on the evening of the party, as he stepped over the window-sill from the crowded, chatter-filled room into the silence of the rose-scented garden. That damned tune began re-echoing through his head again, 'Alice Where Art Thou?', the measured notes tinkling like drops of water, sweet, melancholy, maddening.

'I'm afraid I haven't been much help,' she apologized, still fiddling with the pen. The plastic clip finally snapped off. 'I was ... fond of Patti – she was a sensible girl, if a little immature for her age in some ways – though in my opinion that's no bad thing. They're grown up before they've left the cradle, these days.'

He'd heard she was a bit of a martinet, and could well believe it, suspecting that she was respected, if not liked. She was more at home here, mistress of her own environment, than she had been in the party scene, when she'd been tense

and uneasy, out of place. But she wasn't comfortable, being questioned. Something odd and unaccountable about both her and her brother remained lodged as a question in his mind.

'As to what Patti did, or what she was like out of school,' she said finally, 'I don't know, you'll have to see her friends for that.'

A bubbly personality, Patti, ready to have a go at anything, according to her friends when spoken to, some of them in tears, all of them subdued, overawed by having the make-believe horror of the telly made real, brought so abruptly into their own young lives.

Anything? Well, anything for a laugh, nothing heavy.

Not, according to her special friend, when Abigail and Mayo drove off to talk to her at her home, anything *forbidden*. Patti liked fun, but knew where to draw the line, said Gemma Townsend severely, a tall and self-possessed girl, neat and conservative with long, smoothly combed, silky dark hair. A direct contrast to Patti, little and fair, liking fun clothes and fun hairstyles. Patti certainly wasn't into drugs. Boyfriends? Gemma shrugged. Nobody special, though a lot of boys fancied her. She and Patti had decided they weren't going to get themselves seriously involved. They wanted to get good A levels, and the two didn't mix. Neither was all that interested in boys, anyway.

'I see,' Abigail said, noncommittally, wondering if the two girls had gravitated towards each other subconsciously, each seeing the other as a foil. Where Patti had apparently seemed young for her years, Gemma appeared much older than hers, very controlled, though her dark eyes still revealed a bewildered and youthful misery when she spoke Patti's name.

'More coffee, anyone?' asked Gemma's grandmother, graciously.

'Thank you, no, Mrs Sinclair.'

The grandmother, a slightly flustered, faded woman with faraway eyes who lived with her daughter and granddaughter, seemed to be regarding this visit of the police as some

sort of social occasion, the rules of which they were transgressing by asking questions not quite in the best of taste. Gemma was actually being seen at home because she was allegedly suffering from a heavy cold, though there were precious few signs of it, apart from the fact that she was extremely pale. A diplomatic cold, perhaps, because she couldn't face school and all the fuss and melodrama and emotional hoo-ha among the other girls over what had happened to Patti. Abigail felt some sympathy with that.

'Think about the last few days, Gemma. Did Patti mention anything that had upset her, anything unusual?'

Gemma looked down at her feet, neatly shod in well-polished tan leather, smoothed her carefully pressed skirt over her nyloned knees. Her clothes looked as though they'd been bought by her mother at Marks and Spencer. On her slender middle finger, oddly, gleamed a cheap little brass ring, decorated with a skull and crossbones. 'She was going to ask to be given a different paper round. She didn't like the one she had.'

'She'd had it for some time, hadn't she?'

'Yes, but it was a pain having to lug that great heavy bag halfway up the hill from the paper shop. And she said some creepy old man in one of the houses was watching her all the time. It was a rush to get to school on time, as well.'

'OK,' Abigail said. 'Let's talk about last Saturday night, Gemma, Saturday the second.'

A wariness in Gemma's eyes. 'What about it?'

'Patti was here, with you, wasn't she?'

'Oh dear, poor little Patti! She so enjoyed the lemon pudding I made for supper!' Mrs Sinclair interjected, dabbing at her eyes, as if the news had just struck home.

There was an awkward pause, during which nobody seemed to know what to say. Mrs Sinclair smiled vaguely and picked up her knitting. Abigail began again.

'Yes, well, you – er – had supper, then she left in a taxi,' she stated again. 'What time would that be?'

Gemma glanced sideways at her grandmother. 'About quarter to ten, I think. I'm not sure.'

'Mrs Sinclair?'

'Oh, don't ask me!' the grandmother answered vaguely. 'I went to bed early with a migraine.'

Mayo wondered who was supposed to be keeping an eye on whom, when Gemma's mother wasn't here. 'Which firm did you ring, Gemma?' he asked.

She was smoothing her skirt again. 'I don't remember, not really. I think we got it from the Yellow Pages.'

'If we looked at the Yellow Pages now, would it jog your memory?'

'It might.'

But the book couldn't be found. 'I expect my mother has it in the surgery, and she always locks the door before she goes out.'

It was a group practice, two other doctors besides Amanda Townsend, housed in the one half of a pair of large Edwardian semis, with the Townsends living in the other half. The receptionist had gone home, and neither of the other two doctors were in.

'We always used Woodruff's when my husband was alive,' Mrs Sinclair remarked inconsequentially as they left. 'A very reliable firm. We never had any trouble with *them*.'

'Very cool, our Gemma,' remarked Abigail, as they left the doctor's house.

'Telling lies, what's more. Can you see her not remembering the name of the taxi firm? Well, we'll find out, it'll take us a bit longer, that's all; there aren't that many taxi firms in Lavenstock. Though my guess is, for some reason Patti *didn't* go home in a taxi. But I can't see any way of making Gemma tell us why.'

'There'll be a boyfriend in it, somewhere,' Abigail said, not believing Gemma, either. 'If Grandma hadn't been there, she might've told us.'

'If Grandma hadn't been there we couldn't have interviewed her, at her age, could we? Not without breaking all the rules in the book.'

*   *   *

149

A man known to Mayo, Chief Inspector Uttley of the Hurst-field Division, a colleague of long-standing, was in charge of the investigation there into the murders of the two little girls, and the disappearance of the third, all of which had fallen within his jurisdiction.

They'd made arrangements to see him and went in Mayo's car, which he allowed Abigail to drive. Mindful of the honour, she reciprocated by not talking, leaving him to enjoy the music he preferred when driving but which, truth to tell, sometimes got on her nerves. Hers not to reason why. Twenty miles, and a good deal of Shostakovich's Ninth later, they arrived at Hurstfield Police Station, where Uttley was waiting for them with coffee and sandwiches.

'A right bugger, all this,' he greeted them, shaking his head, waving a hand like a ham in the direction of the several fat files in readiness on his desk. Fred Uttley was an old sparring partner of Mayo's, a big, solid man whose belly strained the waistband of his trousers, a tough copper of the old school. But, handing the bulging folders over, knowing what they contained, his usually genial face took on a greyness. 'Help yourself to what you want from them, but I warn you, it won't be much.'

They leafed through the material while they drank the coffee, but what they read choked the bread in their mouths, and in the end the sandwiches were left uneaten and curling up at the edges.

It was seven months, in January, since the first child, Nicola Marchant, aged eleven, had been found, raped and brutally battered, lying in the snow. She'd been out toboganning one Saturday afternoon with her friends, on a hill not a hundred yards from her home, and had left them at three-thirty, as instructed, before the winter afternoon began to get dark. She had never reached home. Her body, with her long blonde hair cut off at the roots, had later been found tossed into the ditch by the roadside, her sledge thrown on top of her. Snow had fallen intermittently all that day, until well into the evening, obliterating any tracks or traces the killer might have left.

Rachel Williams, thirteen the day before she disappeared in April, was on her way home from school when she was killed. She'd waved goodbye to her friends on the school bus, turned down the country road on which she lived and was never seen alive again. She hadn't been found for six weeks, when council workers using a mechanical hedge-flail had come across her, dumped like discarded rubbish in the ditch below, six miles from her home, and, like Nicola, her fair hair had been hacked off. She too had been raped and repeatedly bludgeoned with a heavy instrument.

'A hammer,' Uttley said. 'Same bloody hammer in both cases, or identical ones. The bastard probably saved it to use again.'

The MO had been similar in all respects. DNA tests confirmed it was the same man responsible in both cases. There had as yet been no trace of the third missing child, Tracey Betteridge. A few weeks ago, she'd gone to visit her grandmother who lived just around the corner from her own suburban road, and hadn't been seen since. Her disappearance might, or might not, be connected to the other two.

A lifetime of police work had rendered Uttley not insensitive, but not easily upset, either, yet these events had shaken him to the core. He had grandchildren of his own and obscurely and needlessly blamed himself for not yet having got to grips with the situation. 'I shan't sleep at nights, and that's a fact, until we've put the scumbag that's responsible where he can't do any more harm. Preferably pinned to the floor by his balls.'

But his turned-down mouth suggested his hopes weren't high, snatched at random as the children appeared to have been, with nothing at all to give a clue as to their abductor, not a shred of evidence, anywhere. Appeals, reconstructions on *Crimewatch*, miles of foot slogging, knocking on doors, hundreds of hours of tireless questioning, thousands of witnesses, yards of computer print-outs, nothing had come of it.

If Patti's death had indeed been linked to these other murders, it was a depressing prognosis for the apprehension of her killer.

Uttley was bitter. 'The only way we're going to catch him is if little Tracey turns up and he's made some mistake.' His eyes boded no good for whoever was found to be responsible. 'Or if it turns out he's made one with your Patti.'

'But they've nothing to do with Patti, have they?' Abigail remarked in an unusually dispirited voice on the way home. During the last couple of hours, she seemed to have lost some of her resilience. 'If we're looking for a pattern, we're not going to find it there.'

Mayo, chin sunk into his collar, thinking over the last depressing session, didn't think so either. Serial killers were creatures of habit, apt to keep to more or less the same modus operandi, and Patti's murder was unlike the ones they'd been reading about, in almost every respect. The full autopsy report on her body had confirmed Timpson-Ludgate's original opinion that she hadn't been raped, for one thing, and for another, it had been a single blow which had killed her – wielded with enough savagery and strength to shatter her skull, to be sure, but she hadn't been senselessly and repeatedly battered, as the other two girls had been. It wasn't a hammer belonging to the assailant which had been used, either, but the first weapon that had come conveniently to hand. Nor had she been abducted and taken somewhere else to be killed. All the victims had in common, in fact, was their fair hair – hardly conclusive proof of any connection. And Patti's hair hadn't been cut off.

He sat back with his eyes closed, the radio switched off, his thoughts grim. Like Uttley, he promised himself no rest until they'd found the killer. The burden was heavy, but it was his responsibility. The third day after the murder, and the bastard still free. Yet he knew that the search could go on for months, years even. If you didn't find them fast, often you didn't find them at all.

As the tree-crowned Kennet Edge flashed by on their left, and they entered the outskirts of Lavenstock, children were coming home from school, humping the oversize bags they all seemed to find necessary to carry their school kit around

152

in. There'd been nothing in Patti's school bag to excite attention – her school books, plus gym kit, towel, a hairbrush, deodorant and a small leather purse containing less than a pound. The newsagent she'd worked for, Surinder Patel, had been worried that she hadn't returned to leave the empty delivery bag and to pick up her school bag and hat, which she always left with him before cycling off to school for half past eight. He blamed himself for not raising the alarm earlier, but his corner shop, as well as being a newsagent's, was also a sub-post office and general grocery store, and that was his busiest time of day, when people were coming in for papers and cigarettes, and bread and groceries were being delivered. Long before he'd had the chance to do something about it, Patti was dead.

Just why had Gemma been pulling the wool over their eyes? Farrar had been detailed to canvass all the local taxi firms, and, knowing Farrar, it would be done thoroughly, but Mayo was damn sure none of them would have received any call on Saturday evening for a taxi to take a young schoolgirl home. Narrowing his eyes, he visualized the town map which occupied most of one wall in his office.

'Turn off and drive round the ring road,' he said suddenly to Abigail as the Kubla Khan glass domes of the new shopping centre at the top of the town came into view.

She obeyed without so much as raising an eyebrow. They followed the road as it skirted the main thoroughfares and swung round into Colley Street. At the stop by the Punch Bowl they had to wait until a number 12 bus pulled out, which lumbered in front of them all the way to Milford Road, where Mayo instructed Abigail to abandon the ring road and drive into the police-station car park.

Back in his office, he traced the same bus route on the map with the arm of his spectacles. It went along the ring road, then made a detour into the town centre. Past the Saracen's Head and across to join Albert Road and thus into Colley Street. Past the police station, and eventually round to the end of Mailer Street, where Patti lived.

'But – have a look at this – from the bus stop in Colley Street –'

'The quickest way to Mailer Street is the path across the back of the allotments.' It hadn't taken Abigail long to pick up his reasoning. Her eyes took on a gleam of realization. 'And you think –?'

'It's a possible hypothesis,' Mayo said slowly.

'More than that, surely? It was the same Saturday night Ensor was killed there, wasn't it? So it's not out of the way to think that she might have seen something!' The idea had re-energized her. 'I think I should go and see Gemma again. And this time get the truth out of her. I'll go carefully,' she promised, pre-empting any warning he might see fit to give. 'After what happened to Patti, no wonder she didn't want to talk, poor kid.'

Abigail would have preferred to speak to Gemma on her own, but since Gemma was in the eyes of the law still a juvenile, it was necessary to go by the book and have an appropriate person present. In this case, Gemma's mother, not the grandmother. The evasions didn't trip quite so easily from Gemma's tongue in her presence.

Amanda Townsend was several inches shorter than her daughter, a pretty, dark, energetic-looking woman in her mid-forties, but one whose every gesture indicated that she wasn't one to stand any nonsense. She sat next to Gemma on the sofa, looking expectantly at Abigail, wearing a beige cotton skirt and a plain white shirt, no make-up. Too busy, perhaps too self-fulfilled in her career to feel the need to bother about her appearance. Maybe it was the grandmother who'd chosen Gemma's clothes.

'I just want to go over what you said again, Gemma,' Abigail began. 'About the taxi on Saturday night. We haven't been able to trace a taxi firm that came here to pick anyone up.'

Gemma, this time dressed in jeans, albeit carefully pressed ones, and worn with a neat print blouse, gave a choked sort of gasp and then burst into tears.

154

Her mother let an arm rest across her daughter's shoulders for a few seconds, gave a squeeze, then announced briskly, 'That's enough of that, Gemma. Dry your eyes and tell Inspector Moon what she wants to know. She's not going to bite.'

It seemed as though that might be the least of what Gemma feared. In a rush, scrubbing at her eyes at the same time with a tissue, she gulped, 'She didn't take a taxi home.'

'Well!' Her mother eyed her speculatively. 'How is it you were able to give me the correct change, three pounds fifty?'

'We just guessed that's what it might have come to, about six fifty. Patti put that, apart from her bus fare, into the RSPCA box, so it wasn't really dishonest. It wasn't her fault about the taxi, anyway – it was me! She only did it because I asked her to, Mum!'

'Did she, indeed?' The tone was not encouraging, but Gemma knew now there was no going back.

There was, as Abigail had known there would be all along, a boyfriend in the picture. Not Patti's, however, but Gemma's. 'What boyfriend's this?' Dr Townsend interrupted sharply.

'His name's Nige.' Gemma's chin went up, a small act of defiance, but she skated on hurriedly with the rest of the story, twisting the little brass ring with the skull and cross-bones on it around on her finger. Gemma had known, she said, that if she went down to the amusement arcade by the market he'd be there, it was where he spent his evenings –

'Hm,' was her mother's only comment.

Hearing the tone of it, and as familiar as Gemma's mother evidently was with the arcade and the sort who hung around there, Abigail saw immediately why this Nige hadn't been introduced into the Townsend family. She wondered briefly where Gemma's father was. Divorced, as Patti's had been? One could see that drawing the two girls together. Orphans of the marital storm, perhaps.

They'd all had a coffee together, Gemma was saying, when Patti had caught the bus and – Abigail listened impassively – Nige had brought Gemma home on the back of his motor-

bike. Her grandmother was still in bed and hadn't known a thing. Not even that Gemma had been out.

In view of all this, looking at Amanda Townsend's determinedly noncommittal face, Abigail had it in her heart to feel sorry for Gemma. Threats of wasting police time, which had been in her mind when she arrived, she pushed away as unnecessary.

'I'm sorry, Mum,' Gemma apologized tearfully, swallowing hard, and turning to Abigail. 'I suppose I should've told you before, but I – There's something else.'

'More?' repeated her mother ominously.

'Patti got off the bus at Colley Street and took a short cut across the allotments. She could've stayed on and ridden round to the end of Mailer Street but it would've taken ages and she was already a bit late.'

Bingo! Even the fact that the idea had been Mayo's, and not hers, couldn't lessen Abigail's small surge of triumph. 'And?'

'She was halfway along the path at the back of the allotments when she saw two people struggling. One of them seemed to knock the other flat to the ground. She wondered if she ought to have gone to fetch help or something, but it would have made her even later, and, well – you don't interfere in anything like that if you've any sense, do you?'

'That's right, Gemma, you don't.'

Abigail visualized the allotment site, the small green huts amid the neat rows of vegetables, here and there a vivid patch of flowers for cutting, beans climbing up their supports. The colour would have been leached out by the moonlight, but the same moonlight and residual light from the sodium streetlamps in Colley Street would have cast enough light for Patti to see clearly as she took the path towards the Leasowes, giving her a good view of the central road, the place where Ensor had been found, and possibly even a good view of their faces.

'But then,' Gemma said, licking her lips, 'there was that piece on Radio Lavenstock about that man who'd been found

dead there. And she began to be worried that she ought to tell someone.'

'She didn't know who they were? Didn't describe them, or anything?'

'No – but I think she might've known, really, after she'd thought about it. She kept saying she didn't know what to do. I think she was just too scared to say.'

15

Speculation ran like a buzz of adrenaline through the incident room where the team waited for the Superintendent. The ending of another frustrating day. Largely unproductive routine: legwork, telephoning, questioning, with sources beginning to run dry, a feeling that the inquiry was reaching stalemate. And now, with tidings of this new development filtering through, it was kiss goodbye to any thoughts of taking it easy. They revved up with cigarettes and coffee, in the circumstances not a man or a woman there begrudging the extra effort that would be needed.

Kite alone was bouncing around as if it were first thing in the morning. Keeping up with his high energy levels was other people's problem. He began opening more windows before Mayo had the chance to do it himself. It hardly made a dent in the atmosphere, since Inspector George Atkins had his pipe well away. He came back to the front desk and reread the information Gemma had given them, propping himself against a desk, arms folded, crossed legs stretched across the gangway. 'Silly kids. If they'd simply come straight out with it –'

'It's obvious why they didn't.' Abigail pressed the last drawing pin into the visual-aid board and laid down the black marker pen. 'Patti thought at first that it was nothing more than a fight she'd seen. According to Gemma, it was only after she heard on the news on Sunday night that a man had been found dead down there on Sunday morning that she began to worry. She dithered about coming forward because she knew both she and Gemma would be in dead

shtuck over her not taking a taxi home, not to mention compounding it by short-cutting through the allotments, that time of night.'

'What devious lives adolescents lead!'

'And the ones you'd least expect to. Gemma Townsend, of all people, and this Nige.'

'Nigel Worsfield, a name not unknown to us down here.'

'OK, I know, bunking off school, petty shoplifting when he was younger – but fair's fair, he's had a job down at Everett's garage since he left school and not been in trouble since. Hardly someone her mother's likely to approve of, though.'

'Excuse me, Sarge.' A WPC, looking pointedly busy, with a file under her arm and balancing two styrofoam cups of coffee, was endeavouring to get past.

Kite amiably angled his long legs to one side. 'Any mates Patti might have been pairing off with?' he asked.

'Apparently not. Patti had been covering up for Gemma – you know, saying she was with her when Gemma was really with Nige and so on, but she doesn't seem to have had any particular boyfriend of her own. Don't think we shall get anywhere pursuing that line – the odds are that she saw Philip Ensor being murdered – and that makes it an entirely different ball game.'

Mayo evidently thought so as well. When he showed his face in the incident room, the buzz of talk died down in the expectation of what was to come, the cigarettes of the circumspect were put out as officers grouped themselves in front of him to hear what he had to say.

'Firstly, thanks for staying on. You should all have made yourselves familiar with the new developments by now, but just to make sure everything's crystal clear . . .'

He drew their attention to the diagrams Abigail had drawn on the board: the names of Philip Ensor and Patti Ryman, side by side, with details of the assaults on each circled and radiating from them. Lines from each circle were now joined together at the bottom.

'None of you need me to spell out what this means. We

now have a possible motive for Patti's murder – I say possible, we must keep an open mind, but at least it gives us something to work on, in both cases. It's beginning to look something like this: she takes a short cut home, via the path that runs along the back of the allotments, and sees this struggle going on between the two men. They're milling around on the road which runs through the centre of the allotments, but they're not so far away that she couldn't have recognized their faces – or the face of one of them, at least. There was a full moon that night and in any case, she must have passed fairly close. One of the men dies. Leaving aside the question of whether it was accidental or not, the other man panics, fearing this girl will tell what she saw.'

And that, Mayo was convinced, was why she'd died. He made a positive effort to sound unemotional about it, to control his own anger that Patti's life should have been forfeit – not to satisfy the urges of a random child killer, something quite outside the boundaries of comprehensible human behaviour – but worse, in a way, simply because the poor unfortunate child had stumbled upon an act of mindless violence against another person. And had been deemed expendable because of it.

'Understood so far?'

The queries which followed were mostly routine, until Farrar asked keenly, 'If it was the same perpetrator in both cases, why did he wait so long to kill her – more than a week later?'

'Good question. Patti at first told Gemma Townsend she didn't know who the two men were, but it seems she might have had second thoughts about that. Presumably the killer didn't realize who she was, either. Not then. I believe it must have come to him later that she was the girl who'd passed them when they were fighting. And had reason to think she'd realized this, too.'

'Wouldn't that rule out anybody who lives on her paper round? They'd have recognized her on the spot, wouldn't they?'

'That may be so, Keith, but I still want every resident in

the vicinity retargeting. I recognize how tedious this going over old ground is becoming, and I'm sorry. But we need to find out if there were any links at all, however tenuous they might seem, between any of them and Philip Ensor, and – it goes without saying – especially where they were on the Saturday night that Ensor died. And I particularly want to know what the hell he was doing in Lavenstock that night, OK? Try the hotels again, bed and breakfasts, see if someone's memory can be jogged. It's just possible he was staying under an assumed name.'

Though if he'd been staying overnight, why had his car been left out of sight behind Rodney Shepherd's premises, rather than in a hotel car park? Mayo frowned, studying his methodical notes for a moment. Ensor was where it all began, he was convinced, everything else was the after game. Find out what he'd been doing here and . . .

'As to why he chose the time and place he did to kill Patti, when he could so easily have been seen . . .' Mayo paused. 'It was a risk I don't think he did choose – in that particular sense.' This, he reminded them, was no psychopath they were looking for, but someone out to protect himself from the consequences of the original killing. Whatever the outcome, the intention had simply been to shut Patti up. It looked as if Ensor's murder fell into the same category, an impulse, or possibly accidental killing after a fight. 'We seem to have come up with a profile of a spur-of-the-moment killer, someone who lands out unthinkingly when he's upset, but sharp enough to seize the opportunity when it offers – remember, in neither case did he go equipped, simply picked up what was lying around for a weapon.'

'What about the cat, sir?' It was Farrar, once again.

'I think we have to look on the cat as only incidental – important only in so far as it was the cause of Patti going into the wood. We know that Loates killed poor old Nero, but he's not, for my money, a credible suspect in Patti's murder – and it's even less likely that he could fight and overcome a man like Ensor, so much younger and fitter – just supposing he had cause. Unless whoever killed her was

161

conveniently lurking inside the wood at the same time, which doesn't make much sense, we might line it up something like this: Patti hears the cries of the cat – not on his usual perch – and goes to investigate. The murderer – probably watching out for her – seizes his opportunity and follows her into the wood. He speaks to her, still not entirely sure whether she's recognized him as one of the men she saw fighting, but what they say to each other convinces him that she does. She turns away, perhaps having told him that she must tell the police – and he picks up the iron bar and kills her.'

There was a silence.

'You want to say something else, Keith?'

'Could've been someone who had legitimate business around the Close, like the postman or the milkman, somebody not likely to be regarded as a stranger.'

Mayo followed a rule that at these briefings no one was to feel they couldn't put forward a theory or a suggestion – but why was it always Farrar? It was a perfectly legitimate observation he'd put forward, but Farrar got up his nose, in the way he got up most people's noses. Maybe because he was always so damn right, but – There was always a but where Farrar was concerned. Mayo had had a hint from Kite that the DC was having domestic troubles. Not exactly unusual in the police service, as Mayo knew to his cost. Before Lynne had died, things had not gone smoothly in his own household, so he was even more inclined to make excuses for Keith Farrar, who was in any case a damned good police officer, and would have gone further, had it not been for his attitudes.

'Oh, come on, Keith! Milkmen and postmen have already been accounted for, as you should know,' Abigail reminded him sharply. 'Too busy doing *The Times* crossword, were we?'

Somebody sniggered and Farrar looked at the inspector sourly, smarting at the quip about the crossword, which everyone who hadn't been at the South Pole lately must know he could do in under half an hour, but aware that he'd uncharacteristically slipped up. The first woman Chief

Constable in Britain had recently been appointed. Moon was obviously hopeful of being on her way to becoming the second. And he was still a bloody DC, he couldn't think why. Life was a bugger, sometimes.

'Worth repeating, ma'am,' he couldn't resist adding, but Abigail swallowed her irritation and didn't reply.

Mayo kept his eye on Farrar for several seconds. An exchange of good-humoured insults was as common currency in the CID room as anywhere else, but Abigail had been unwontedly sharp, and it showed how on edge they all were. He wondered if the public ever realized how much murder, in particular this sort of murder, affected the men and women inquiring into it.

He was ready to wind the meeting up. He himself had two people still to see – Dermot Voss, who was proving elusive, and Francis Kendrick. He thought it might be a good idea to take Abigail with him when he went to see the latter.

'Right, that's about it. We work all out on this. Any extra hours, let Inspector Atkins know. OK, George?'

Atkins nodded, already relighting his pipe in the expectation of Mayo's departure, drawing his lists towards him.

Back in his office, he found a print-out on his desk concerning the motor thefts Abigail was investigating, plus the details he'd asked for about Dermot Voss's stolen car. He studied it for a while, swinging his glasses back and forth while he thought about it. The beginning of any murder investigation was always a time of frenzied activity – gathering statements, collating alibis. Mayo was quite happy to leave all that sort of thing to be worked out by the computers, after all the relevant names and times had been fed in – as far as he was concerned computers had definitely made a policeman's lot a happier one. They hadn't yet entirely replaced the human element, thank God, but meanwhile, a computer print-out beat pencilled lists on the backs of envelopes, any day. Now that both cases had opened up – or rather, come together – he looked at his list of possibles with a new eye. Excluding

163

those residents in and around Ellington Close, eliminated for one reason and another, he was left with:

'X'. The unknown factor, the mystery man who might exist but who hadn't yet appeared on the scene, whom nobody had ever seen.

Stanley Loates. Mayo couldn't for the life of him see Loates wielding a heavy iron bar on the girl, still less as being involved in a fight with Ensor – apart from the fact that Patti knew him well enough, and would have recognized his flabby form immediately. The same thing applied to Henry Pitt, who'd said he'd stayed at home all night listening to a concert of Viennese music on the radio and had in any case left home on the morning of the crime with Vic Baverstock, while Patti was still alive. Vic also appeared to have a watertight alibi for the Ensor murder, having been out practising with his male-voice choir.

Trevor Lawley had sworn Patti was already dead when he found her. It would be worth checking on him to see if there were any links between him and Ensor. It was believable – just – that he could have hit Patti hard enough to kill her, if he thought she'd done that to his precious cat, at least according to Kite, but Mayo was fed up with theories about that damned cat. Better to work on something with more substance, like his own conviction that Patti's murder had a direct connection with what she'd seen when she was walking home that night.

Which left Francis Kendrick, whom he still had to interview today, time permitting, and Dermot Voss, both of whom should prove interesting. He thought about that for some time, then, after several minutes, he added Hope Kendrick to his list, whom he could believe capable of doing anything to protect her brother. A little mischievously he listed Tina Baverstock, whom he could believe capable of doing anything.

After a moment, thoughtfully, he added Imogen Loxley.

They were talking about mildew, black spot and other esoteric subjects. They'd been going on in this vein for some

time. It seemed that Kendrick had a sure-fire way of getting rid of aphids. Abigail passed on her father's hint for using soft soap as a spray. Mayo looked at his watch. He signalled with his eyes to Abigail that the preliminaries were over, and prepared for confrontation.

He'd assumed from the first that the interview with Kendrick would *be* a confrontation: Professor Kendrick, Cambridge intellectual, versus Gil Mayo, ignorant copper, which was why he'd taken Abigail along with him. Ignorant copper he might seem to someone like Kendrick, but he was also a professional one, and apt to get shirty when people forgot. Abigail being there would have a restraining influence on him. He was willing to be proved wrong, but this was the impression Kendrick had given him when they first met. Kendrick had hardly given him the time of day at the party.

They'd found him dead-heading his roses in the cool of the evening. The shadow of the sequoia fell long over the lawn, there was a spectacular sunset over the distant hills. Mayo had decided to play the part expected of him and to keep initially in the background, letting Abigail do the talking. She was the expert here, after all. She'd struck the right note from the beginning, murmuring something about the roses being a credit to him, which had the effect of loosening Kendrick up a bit and bringing a smile to his face.

'Oh, I didn't plant them. They were here when we came. I don't know the first thing about gardening in general, but the roses were so magnificent, it seemed a pity not to learn how to look after them properly.'

He would, Mayo thought. He'd approach the subject with as much rigour as if it were another academic exercise, master it once and for all and that would be it. Mayo, to whom all gardening was a mystery, could admire that. Perhaps if he himself didn't live in the upstairs flat of a house whose elderly owners lived on the ground floor and kept the garden looking neat and pleasant, if unremarkable, he might be encouraged to broaden his knowledge. Rather like Abigail Moon had done with the garden of her cottage, only it had grabbed her in the way Mayo doubted it would ever grab

him. The furthest he got in that line was mowing the lawn, whenever he had the time, for the Vickers. Give him a clock that needed setting to rights, any day ... not like weeds and grass, which never stopped growing, even after you'd attended to them.

Abigail, catching his glance, smoothly brought the discussion to a close and said immediately, 'You know that we're here to investigate the death of Patti Ryman, Mr Kendrick. Did you know her?'

'The paper girl? No, I never set eyes on her, to my knowledge. My study's here at the back of the house and I'm normally working there when the papers are delivered.'

'I'm told you go jogging in the early morning?'

'I walk,' he corrected shortly. 'And sometimes in the evening, too, for that matter. I try to do six or seven miles, most days.'

Mayo, also a dedicated walker, to whom half a dozen miles was little more than a limbering up, didn't comment, but Abigail asked, 'Any particular routes?'

'Sometimes as far as Scotley Beeches, or Kennet Edge, quite often just to the other side of Lavenstock and back.'

'Did you go out on Monday morning?'

'No, as a matter of fact, I didn't. I had papers to sort out before my trip to London and was rather pushed for time.'

Mayo spoke up for the first time. 'You drove up to Birmingham New Street to catch the London train, rather than go from Coventry. Why was this?'

The big, raw-boned hand tightened on the secateurs. Kendrick leaned forward to snip off a dead head, precisely before the next bud, dropping it into the wheelbarrow before he answered. 'It may have escaped your notice, Superintendent, but Lavenstock is more or less equidistant from both points.'

'But the train starts at least twenty minutes earlier from New Street. What made you decide to go from there, since you hadn't much time to spare?'

Kendrick treated him to the sort of glance reserved for backward students. 'Oh come, that time in the morning? With all the traffic on our famous one-way system? Any

time you might have in hand you're likely to lose it – whereas you can use the bypass the other way. Whichever station you choose there's nothing to it in terms of time. You save nothing but your temper. But in any case,' he added blandly, 'I had a manuscript to deliver to my typist on the way there.'

Manuscript my backside, thought Mayo, becoming more bloody-minded northern the more patronizing Kendrick became. And the traffic wasn't that bad. Unless Kendrick had, in fact, gone from Coventry and used the spare time otherwise. It could be checked. 'The address of your typist, please?'

Kendrick gave it with an amused smile.

'And how did you pay for your ticket? Cash, credit card?'

'In cash.' Kendrick's look managed to convey the impression that credit cards were only for the lower orders, or the feckless who lived beyond their means, and how he paid for his ticket was no business of anyone else, anyway.

'All right.' Mayo changed tack. 'Back to these walks of yours. You didn't go for one last Saturday evening – Saturday week, that is, did you?'

'Are you telling me, or asking me? I don't remember so far back.'

'That was the evening you had your party here.'

'So it was. You were one of our guests, I believe.' Mayo tried not to imagine that the word 'guest' was stressed. 'No, as a matter of fact, I didn't get my walk in that evening.' He smiled suddenly and Abigail, at least, saw that there might, in different circumstances, be a more appealing side to him. 'I play the organ at St Gregory's on alternate Sundays and I usually practise for an hour or so on Saturday evening. I saw no reason why the party should make any difference. I went across after everyone had gone home.'

'That would be – what? Eightish? I myself left just before that . . . while you were demonstrating your Victorian music box to young Allie.'

'It's called a Polyphon,' Francis said, after a pause. 'The children and their father and aunt went home shortly after eight.'

167

'So you'd be home after your organ practice at what time?'

Another fractional hesitation. 'I suppose it may have been around nine thirty. I don't believe I noticed the time.'

'One of your sisters would no doubt confirm this.'

'No doubt they could. Unfortunately, Hope is at a PTA meeting, and Imogen is also out. But I should regard it as an unpardonable liberty if they were asked to. What reason do you have for checking up on me? That night or any other?'

'Oh, we're only eliminating you from certain inquiries, on another murder, sir.' Mayo gave the time-honoured assurance with only the merest glint of irony in his eye. Did the man visibly relax? 'We just wanted to be sure you'd nothing to tell us. Seems you haven't, so we'll leave you to your roses. Unless,' he added, 'the name of Philip Ensor means anything to you?'

'Ensor? No. I don't know anyone of that name. Who is he?'

'You may have read about him in the papers. He was the man who was found murdered last Saturday night, sir, on the Colley Street allotments.'

But Francis Kendrick shook his head.

Mayo felt by no means as cheerful, nor even as insensitively brusque, as he'd sounded on leaving Francis Kendrick. On the contrary, he was, quite suddenly and inexplicably, overwhelmed by the feelings of sadness and loneliness he'd sensed in the man. It wasn't something he'd expected to feel. But that last glimpse of his face, lost and tormented, stayed with him.

Ten days since Ensor's killing, and the days were growing cooler, a different quality could be discerned in the light. Evening was coming on appreciably quicker. The sun was going down over Kennet Edge, in a sky streaked with turquoise and rose-gold. The scent of Kendrick's roses seemed to cling to them as they bowled down the hill once more towards Milford Road.

168

'Well, do you think he *has* nothing more to tell us?' Abigail asked, turning his own words back to him.

'Remains to be seen.' Mayo did his best to shake off the feelings that Kendrick had stirred up. 'Somebody might remember him buying a ticket at Coventry – stands out in a crowd, that height, doesn't he? But I think he's probably telling the truth.'

'What about the Saturday night, and Ensor?'

'Fisticuffs doesn't seem exactly his thing. Words are more his weapon.' He relapsed into an abstracted silence, until they reached the station.

Once there, they found all the accumulated work of the day awaiting them.

'With all there is to do yet, it looks like being a late session again tonight, Abigail – sorry.'

'No problem. Nobody makes plans when we've something like this on if they've any sense.'

He rang Alex, warning her not to expect him home until late. 'Tell you what, I'll give you a ring when I'm ready, and if you haven't already eaten, you can come down and meet me and we'll grab something quick in the town, save the bother of fixing something when I get in.'

'Good idea. Ask Abigail to join us. How about a quick Chinese? We can be in and out in twenty minutes.'

Well, he'd suggested it.

By the time they'd worked their way through the bean-curd soup and the king prawns and the fried won ton, Mayo couldn't face even a bowl of lychees, never mind the hot banana fritters in syrup which the two women were ordering with every anticipation of enjoyment. Chinese food always had the same effect on him: by this stage in the meal he was replete, full to saturation point, but knowing with certainty that an hour later he'd be feeling hollow, craving a thick ham sandwich with plenty of mustard. What was more, there was the vexed question of what to drink with that sort of food: perish the thought of a decent wine – and the diuretic effects of jasmine tea, late at night, was a problem he could do

without. He settled, as usual, for a lager. He always grumbled about coming to the overpriced Jade Lotus, supposedly renowned for its Peking cuisine, but in the end gave in because he knew Alex liked it. The decor was restful, it was discreetly lit and the chairs were comfortable, at any rate.

Plus, it was a chance to step aside for an hour from the sort of case that took over every waking thought – and sometimes sleep, as well. One which he'd had no intention of talking about over this meal, though, not even to Alex, who could usually be relied on to lend a sympathetic and understanding ear, often making valuable suggestions of her own, having been in on the sharp end and knowing what it was like. But tonight, he was a little disgruntled, his intention when suggesting supper out having been to direct the conversation into other, quite different channels. He'd be discreet about it, but steer them back to the point where she'd sidestepped the other day. He needed to lay a few ghosts. And then she'd included Abigail. But Abigail, now having demolished the last of the sizzling bananas, was making noises about an early start in the morning, preparing to leave. Maybe there was still time to approach the subject uppermost in his mind.

It was not to be.

Someone stopped near their table. He looked up to see Dermot Voss, smiling, stretching out a hand, making surprised noises about fancy seeing them here and why didn't they come across and join them for coffee or whatever. Pointing to a table just around the corner, with a mirror opposite his seat, through which he'd presumably seen them, though they hadn't seen him. Damn. Damn it to hell. He liked the volatile Voss and his amusing conversation, but he was in no mood to be entertained. However . . . Swallowing hard, he decided it might after all be opportune.

Alex, in her calm way, was beginning to make excuses, but Mayo smoothly intervened, Abigail said no more about going home, and in no time they were all sitting round the same table, he and Alex, Abigail, Dermot and Imogen Loxley.

Imogen Loxley. Well, now, there was a turn-up for the book. Mayo watched them and wondered what Sarah

170

thought about being left at home with Dermot's offspring while Dermot was out wining and dining an attractive woman – if she knew about it, that was. It occurred to him that young woman wasn't exactly getting a wonderful deal out of all this.

The other four were drinking jasmine tea and Mayo was understanding why they'd chosen it in preference to the coffee he'd ordered. On the same principle, presumably, that you didn't order fish and chips outside the British Isles if you were wise. The coffee was undrinkable.

He put the cup down and caught Imogen's stare before she looked quickly away. If she was supposed to be enjoying herself, she wasn't giving that impression. She joined in the conversation, in a social way, but she wasn't really there. She fidgeted with her spoon. Her white silk blouse was scarcely paler than she was. Dermot, on the other hand, was rattling away like an express train. He was explaining his new job, and how it had necessitated him leaving Milton Keynes, how he'd had the amazing luck to find a profitable investment like Edwina Lodge ... enthusing rather too much, Mayo suspected, over something which had seemed like a good idea at the time but was already turning out to be rather a boring commitment.

'Not a very auspicious start to life here in Lavenstock,' he was saying. 'Food poisoning on the first night, my car nicked – what next? Nothing like this ever happened in MK!'

'Yes, I remember you said before that you'd had food poisoning.'

'Did I? Well, it's not something I'm likely to forget. From some shellfish I ate for dinner, I suspect. Had to rush out of the restaurant.'

'The food's usually pretty dependable at the Saracen's. Did you complain to the management?'

'No. There was no point. Once I'd got rid of whatever it was, I felt all right.'

'Well, as far as your car goes, the problem may have solved itself,' Abigail told him.

'You've found it?'

'We caught someone stealing a car today, and he's asked for others to be taken into consideration, yours among them. You should have it back shortly.'

Dermot's face was a study. 'Well, what do you know.'

Imogen said drily, 'Even Milton Keynes couldn't beat that.'

Later, Mayo was to wonder why the connection hadn't occurred to him earlier, but it was only in the dawn reaches of a sleepless night, the hour between wolf and dog, when everything seems suddenly clear and simple, that a sudden flash of the obvious came to him, illuminated his mind for a single moment and then drifted foggily away as sleep came at last.

A busy day crowded in on him, and it wasn't until later events had brought things to a head that the idea came back to him.

16

In another part of the town, while Mayo was consuming his Chinese won ton, Vic Baverstock was struggling with his conscience, aided by a pint of bitter in the Black Bull.

The Black Bull wasn't his first choice – in Vic's opinion, a low-class dump if ever there was one – but if he'd gone to the Saracen's, Mandy would've been there, at her part-time job behind the bar, and he wasn't exactly flavour of the month with Mandy just now.

He stared gloomily into his beer, trying to shut out the sounds of the jukebox. He wasn't the sort who lied to the police on principle and it bothered him that he'd had to, out of necessity. It had been his rotten bad luck for that bloke to have got himself killed when Vic had been parked on the bit of spare ground in the allotments. Just when he was getting well away with Mandy. Not that he'd known then that the bloke had snuffed it, he hadn't stayed long enough to see. When he'd realized that a serious struggle was going on, he'd got the hell out of it before the police arrived, though he knew Mandy would blame him for choosing a spot like that in the first place, so near the town centre, and he'd been right, she had. To say that she was pissed off was an understatement.

He knew he ought to go to the police and admit he'd lied when he said he'd been out practising with the choir that Saturday night. They'd find out, of course, if they bothered to check, but so far they hadn't seemed to think it necessary. He wasn't in their line of suspects, he'd convinced them that he hadn't known the dead bloke from Adam, and he'd a

173

bomb-proof alibi for the time Patti had been killed. But the other one – the one who'd done it – well, Vic knew who he was, all right. He'd seen him clearly, though Mandy hadn't, being in no position to be able to, at the time.

But, Mandy apart, Vic had his reasons for keeping stumm about knowing. Tina, chiefly. All the same, he hadn't reckoned with that terrible thing that had happened to poor little Patti having had anything to do with what he'd seen.

Upset, he looked down at the evening paper again, folded small on the table, so that the last paragraph about her murder was uppermost. He'd sweated blood – though he wasn't the only one to be questioned – wondering what interest the police had in *his* whereabouts that Saturday night, why they'd wanted to know if he'd known this bloke Ensor. Now, the paper said they were working on a theory that Patti being killed like that might have some connection with the dead man found in the Colley Street allotments ten days ago . . . Vic took a long swallow of his beer. Gawd.

The thought of an anonymous letter or telephone call crossed his mind, but not seriously. That wasn't his style. Then he remembered DC Deeley, Pete Deeley, used to live across the road when they were kids. Good sort, Pete, a word in his ear and maybe he'd be able to make sure that Vic's name was kept out of it – that was what they said, didn't they? Any information will be treated in the strictest confidence. What they meant was, if you'd been out having it off with the neighbour's wife, they wouldn't let on.

Near enough.

He needed to sleep on it, though.

By eight o'clock the next morning, there was a coffee pot with two china cups and saucers on Mayo's desk, not thick white canteen pottery or nasty plastic cups from the machine. The coffee was real, too. A rich aroma of freshly ground Arabica rose between them as Abigail poured two cups and pushed one across the desk towards Mayo, ready for when he'd finished telephoning. The shot of caffeine felt good, jolted her system into full wakefulness. All the same, she

swore she'd lay off it for the rest of the day. She'd drunk too many cups yesterday and her mind had been jumping around all night like a Scud missile.

She was tapping her teeth with a pencil, looking thoughtful, when he finally put the receiver down. 'Right, where were we? Dermot Voss and his car, wasn't it?'

'Yes, but I've been thinking about those Belgian francs in Ensor's pocket.'

'He travelled to Belgium in the course of his business. There only a few weeks ago, wasn't he?'

'That's right, and Imogen Loxley was living in Brussels until very recently.' She stopped, looking down at her notes. 'She's married to Tom Loxley, the Euro MP . . . The marriage is on the rocks, by all accounts.'

'Like a lot more,' he commented drily, but his glance was interested. 'Any ideas why, in this particular case?'

She shook her head. 'Not for certain. But Loxley's been acquitting himself very well in Brussels, making quite a name for himself over the Common Market Agricultural Policy, working hard. Perhaps too hard, leaving her too much to her own devices.'

'Par for the course, in that sort of job. Women like Imogen Loxley, they cope, better than their husbands sometimes. What did you think of her and Voss, dining together last night?'

'Interesting. I gathered we came as something of a reprieve, rather than an interruption. The tension was thick enough to cut with a knife when we joined them.'

He nodded. 'My impression, too. And Alex's. So, what are you thinking?'

She frowned. 'I don't know what Voss can have to do with this, if anything. It's a long shot, but it's possible, I suppose, that Imogen could have met Philip Ensor in Brussels and had an affair with him, which broke up her marriage. Supposing she blamed Ensor for it and finished with him, came back to Lavenstock, but Ensor was still pestering her. She arranged to meet him, Patti saw them struggling – remember, she appears to have been unsure at first about the attacker,

and this could have been because she wasn't sure if it was a man or a woman, say if she was a tall woman like Imogen Loxley and was wearing trousers. She'd ample opportunity to watch for Patti and follow her into the wood . . . T-L didn't rule out the possibility that a woman could have wielded the murder weapon, if she'd had the bottle for it. And there's the pen, too. A woman's sort of pen – '

'Has it been traced yet?'

'To the manufacturers, yes. But they can't give us the specific retail outlet – Deeley's sifting through all the people they supplied that type of pen to. The makers say the engraving was done after it was bought.'

'Mm.' He brought his gaze back from the Town Hall clock, checked it by his own watch. Two minutes slow. 'She's a bit of a dark horse altogether, Imogen Loxley,' he murmured absently, draining his coffee.

'But you're not sure you can see her as a double murderess.' She sighed. 'Well, neither can I, not really.'

'We should see her again,' he temporized. 'But let's get down to this business of Dermot Voss, first. He says he left his car outside Patel's while he went in for his cigarettes, about seven forty, came out five minutes later and it was gone. That young toerag – what's his name? Oh yes, Mitchison – says he didn't nick it until ten to eight – if he's telling the truth for once in his life.'

'He's no reason not to. He nicked it on the way to work, because his own wouldn't start and he was late, would you believe?'

'I believe it. So what was Voss doing between say, twenty to eight and ten past, when he came back home? Plenty of time for him to have followed Patti into the Close and killed her.' He frowned. 'Voss hadn't moved into Edwina Lodge when Patti saw the fight at the allotments, so she wouldn't have known who he was, then. But she could have recognized him when she did meet him – and very likely put two and two together.'

He poured himself more coffee and needlessly stirred the black, sugarless liquid. Abigail declined one for herself and

waited for him to carry on. He'd had the faraway look of a man with something at the back of his mind ever since they'd begun to talk.

Mayo felt as though he was suddenly on to something.

That mention of meeting Voss in the Chinese restaurant had reminded him of how Voss had been enthusing about the advantages of the modern house, specially designed for energy-saving, that he'd left behind in Milton Keynes, and in the way these things do, his own pre-dawn flash of insight had come back to him. His subconscious, though possibly not entirely unrelated to the stimulation of a couple of stiff, late-night drams, had been working for him while he slept, gone on working and was now coming up with some interesting conclusions of its own.

Milton Keynes. A place Mayo knew nothing about, a new town, a railway-station sign flashing past the window on the journey to and from London: Milton Keynes, Bletchley . . . He said slowly, thinking as he spoke, 'There had to be a reason for Ensor being in Lavenstock that night, for meeting the man who killed him. Milton Keynes isn't a million miles away from Bletchley, where Ensor worked. If he and Voss had known each other before . . .'

That encompassed a whole load of suppositions, and he knew it. But hell, wasn't that where it started from, a 'what if' that led on to the truth? Thousands of people lived in each place. The odds on them knowing each other were so long as to be hardly worth considering, without any other connection. Yet he had an irrational certainty that he'd somehow – God help him, he didn't know how – stumbled on to something . . .

He reached out for Ensor's file. 'We know he worked in Bletchley, but where did he live before he moved to Solihull? Let me have another look on what we've got on him, while you find out his previous address.'

Abigail picked up the phone and made the request for an outside line, while Mayo began to read. A glowing report on Ensor had been received from his employers. His business life had evidently been as exemplary as his private one. C L

177

Freightlines had been more devastated to hear of his death than any of his relatives had, including his wife. He'd started in the firm as a trainee salesman at the Bletchley head-quarters and had moved up the managerial ladder until he was chief salesperson, or whatever, next stop sales director. Moving house to Solihull had surprised his employers but, although it was less convenient from his point of view, it hadn't made any difference as far as his work was concerned. Solihull was within commuting distance – if you didn't object to getting up that much earlier in the morning – and he was out of the office a good deal, working elsewhere, often abroad, anyway.

The MD to whom Abigail had previously spoken had said, regarding his move to Solihull, 'Gave it out that his wife was missing her family – as if we're in Outer Mongolia here! Still, no telling with women, after all. He did have to leave her on her own a good deal, must admit – all part of the job, though.' He admitted that he'd only met Mrs Ensor a few times, at social functions connected with the firm, but she'd obviously made a hit. He remembered her very well. 'Did him credit, damn good-looking woman,' he said admiringly.

He was elderly, white-haired. The sort to take it for granted that a man would have the sense to choose a wife who looked the part.

'Thanks very much.' Abigail finished her call and put the receiver back. 'Ensor *did* live in Milton Keynes.'

They looked at each other. 'So they both moved, Ensor and Voss. Why did Dermot Voss come here? I can see why he couldn't have carried on with his other job – it would've meant wishing his children on to relatives – not that he seems averse to that! – or sending them to boarding school, I suppose. If that's the reason he gave it up, then I'll hand it to him. But why buy that damned great house – he's surely got enough problems without that? I daresay it would work for somebody like that Mrs Whatsername who used to run it – somebody there on the spot, doing nothing else, but –'

'He says it's a paying proposition. Pays his mortgage and a bit over. Maybe he's strapped for cash.'

'That wouldn't surprise me.'

Abigail said slowly, 'Avis Walker, Ensor's sister-in-law, said something, when we were talking about Ensor lending her husband money, which has stuck in my mind. Folks don't like to be beholden, she said. Assuming Ensor and Voss did know one another, and say Voss had been in difficulties and Ensor had bailed him out –'

'And Ensor was dunning him to pay it back? They met, had this argument, things got out of hand, and Ensor ended up dead?'

'I was going to say maybe being obligated to Ensor had stuck in Voss's craw to the point where he'd grown to hate him – but yes, it's more likely to be as you suggested.'

'Anyway, at this point we're not concerned with why. Motivation's a slippery notion at the best of times. Find out who and we'll know why. But the night Ensor was killed,' Mayo said, warming to his theme, 'Voss was staying at the Saracen's. Twice he's gone out of his way to mention that alleged food poisoning he got there – which could have been an excuse to leave Sarah because he had an appointment with Ensor he didn't want her to know about, for whatever reason. Colley Street is only round the corner from the Saracen's. Based on the assumption, of course, that Voss and Ensor did know each other. Whatever, Ensor is the key to all this. We have to find out more about him. When someone's life is so damned tidy, I worry about it. It's not natural. Abigail, I want you to get over to Solihull again. Have another talk with Judith Ensor. Put pressure on her, if needs be, bring her over here if necessary.'

'I'm not sure how she'd respond to pressure – she struck me as being very stubborn, the type just to dig her heels in more. But the softly-softly approach didn't get me anywhere last time, so it has to be worth a try.'

'Get her to talk, somehow.'

'OK, I'll take care of it. I'm due in court in an hour, and I'll be there most of the day, but I'll get over as soon as I can.'

*　　　*　　　*

Imogen had risen early, after a restless night. She buttered toast, poured herself another cup of tea, then let it go cold as she reread yet another accusing letter from Melissa.

It hadn't really been necessary to read it in the first place. It was the same as all the others – Mel, from her sixteen-year-old vantage point, offering criticism and telling her mother what she must do. They knew it all, today's children, potted psychology from television soaps. But not from experience. All very well for Mel to tell her she was being selfish, she *must* go back to Daddy, whatever was wrong wasn't wrong enough to split the family up. Imogen hadn't told her exactly what the rift was about, nor, presumably, had Tom – only that the marriage wasn't working. Which must have seemed patently untrue to Mel. She'd been home the weekend before Imogen had so precipitately left, and everything had been quite normal. Mel would have noticed if it hadn't been, she was sharp and very intuitive, possessive even, where her parents were concerned. Except that she seemed to have got it into her head somehow that she, Imogen, was following up some women's lib prescription, doing her own thing, making a menopausal bid for freedom. Yet Imogen shrank from telling her the truth . . . to a child of Mel's generation, it would surely seem a trivial reason for breaking up a marriage . . . most of the parents of her friends at that expensive school were in and out of bizarre relationships like jack rabbits. Perhaps Mel had seen the effect on their children . . .

She stared down at her toast, which appeared to have got itself cut into minute squares, scarcely big enough to feed a mouse. She scraped the lot into the bin. She wasn't hungry, anyway. Her appetite had disappeared halfway through that Chinese meal last night, when Dermot's heavy hints left no room for doubt as to how he was expecting the evening to end.

She couldn't blame him. She'd been expecting the same thing, which was why she'd accepted his invitation. Defiantly. Sauce for the goose, she'd thought. I can't go on living my life like this. I'm not like Hope. And Dermot Voss was a very attractive man. Free, what was more.

And then, for some inexplicable reason, she'd chickened out. She'd had no need to say anything, he'd sensed her change of mood immediately, and correctly guessed the reason for it. He hadn't bothered to hide how he felt; while keeping up a semblance of conversation for form's sake, he'd been incandescent with anger underneath. The waiters had impassively removed her half-eaten food, managing to convey intense Oriental disapproval without blinking an eyelid and then, as if to humiliate her further, Dermot had gone to ask Gil Mayo and the two women he was with to join them, without so much as asking her whether she would mind or not.

Not that she did. It was a relief at first, until the conversation had slid, inevitably, around to Patti Ryman's murder. Mayo, however, had skilfully avoided making comment on that. Professional etiquette or something, she supposed, but those watchful, slate-grey eyes were alert, she knew he'd missed nothing of what was said.

She suspected that he'd known right from the beginning, when he'd first come to interview her, that she was keeping something back, and she knew, if he questioned her again, she wouldn't be as successful this time in avoiding him. They could do you for obstructing the police in their duty, that much she knew. Did that include lying by omission?

She was dodging the issue. Anyone with any sort of social conscience would have told them before now. It wasn't loyalty, or that she couldn't imagine something that had happened all those years ago not having any bearing now – all too easily she could imagine that. Human nature didn't change, human failings remained constant. You could keep the lid on a can of worms for half a lifetime but sooner or later it would burst open and the fat would be in the fire. God, her metaphors were as confused as her thoughts.

The truth was, she was frightened, thrown badly off balance by a fear she thought she'd conquered years ago . . . She'd wanted so desperately to believe that the past was over and done with, but that little girl, Patti, had made it impossible.

The awful loneliness that had rolled over her yesterday morning – fear as well, rearing its head from her childhood – grabbed her again. Feelings of hurt and injury, memories of being left out of their shared secrets. But more than that, much more. She'd been so frightened of them, of Francis especially, but of Hope as well. They'd been thoughtlessly cruel to her, terrifying her with their peculiar games and their closeness and their half-understood innuendoes, in that hateful old house, Heath Mount. She had thought, when it was pulled down, that its power would have been destroyed forever, but the past, like some frightful miasma, hung over this house and its occupants, too. Something terrible was happening here.

She was alone in the house. Hope was at school and Francis nowhere to be found – probably on one of his long walks, or shut up in his study with his icons and his books, and his holy pictures. Where she could not – dared not – disturb him.

She couldn't cope with this by herself. Her life hadn't equipped her to deal with this sort of situation, but there was no one else she could confide in, she'd lost touch with most of her old friends when she went away to live. She wanted, needed, Tom. But would Tom, after everything that had happened, want her?

17

Lucy had been invited to tea with her new friend Jodie, and Jodie's mother had telephoned to say she would meet both children out of school, arranging to have Lucy at home by half past six.

Sarah could see that it would be no bad thing just now that Lucy should have the chance to do something on her own. She was being difficult, and it all had to do with the people at Simla, with Imogen and, to a certain extent, Francis. It was on Allie, for some reason, that their favour had especially fallen. Anyone else might have been in danger of becoming spoiled through all the attention being paid to her, but Allie, being Allie, accepted it without appearing to notice. Poor Lucy, who was used to being the one in the limelight and couldn't be blamed for not understanding what was going on, had her nose sadly out of joint.

Hope, despite the gift of the dolls, remained detached from all this, which Sarah had decided must be due to diffidence, in view of how she'd sent the children's presents over via Imogen, rather than giving them herself. 'I think she's basically a very shy person,' she'd told Fitz.

His reaction had been disconcerting. 'Don't let the children get too close to the Kendricks, Sarah. They're an odd bunch.' He wouldn't say anything more and she wondered what he meant. But Fitz had grown up in this area and had known the Kendricks all his life, he'd gone to school with Francis, they'd both been day boys at Lavenstock College. She sometimes forgot what a tight community this was, compared to

a big, anonymous city like London, how well known so many people were to each other.

She drove up to the school at home-time, parked in the long line of cars belonging to waiting mothers, and settled down until Allie should put in an appearance. The children came out, Lucy and her friend Jodie (hair *definitely* highlighted, ye Gods!) piled into Jodie's mother's car after she (*her* hair improbably auburn) had had a brief word with Sarah, and were driven away. Other children followed, until Sarah's car was the only one left. Lisa had often laughed about how she and an impatient Lucy had sat thus outside their former school, times without number, waiting for Allie to emerge. She was invariably one of the last, if not *the* last, trailing out, clutching her slipping possessions, dreamily unaware how long she'd taken.

Sarah sat staring through the windscreen at the pleasant grouping of the red-brick school buildings and, as seemed to happen every spare moment now, her own problems swam into focus.

She'd spoken to Simon last night. He was becoming increasingly irritated at her refusal to say when she was coming back. Fending him off had been just another cowardly excuse for not coming to grips with what she really ought to say to him – that this space between them had given her time to think, that she was now sure that her own future couldn't include him, not in any way meaningful to him. But, apart from the fact that she didn't want to ask herself why this decision was connected with Fitz, telling Simon the truth took more courage than she'd been able to summon up last night, after she'd at last remembered where she'd last seen the face in the photograph.

The knowledge lay like a heavy, indigestible lump in her stomach. She couldn't yet bring herself to do what she knew she must, eventually. She'd once despised others in the same situation, not seeing it as a viable choice. She understood better now. Yet there was no decision, not really. It was not a matter of if, but when. And not really even that – it must be now.

The last, lingering child had departed, and still no sign of Allie. She should have been out ten minutes ago. Sarah got out of the car and went to jolly her along.

Three minutes after that, she was on the telephone to the police.

Dermot was furious with the school. 'What the hell do they mean, they let her go with that woman? They're supposed to be responsible for the children in their charge, for God's sake!'

'*That woman*', DC Jenny Platt reminded him gently, was Hope Kendrick, a well-known and respected member of the community, another teacher, and although not of their school, known to most of the staff at Greymont JMI as well. Known also to live next door to Allie, her affection for Allie obviously returned. All the same, Sarah could see that she agreed with Dermot. The school was in serious dereliction of duty, they should have checked, there was simply no excuse for letting her go off with anyone, no matter how plausible the reason for taking Allie out of school. Allie's class teacher, now appalled at what she'd done, had been far too ready to accept that Hope had been asked by the child's father to pick Allie up for him that morning – a forgotten appointment, she'd said, with the orthodontist who was building up that chipped front tooth. Reasonable enough to be accepted by a busy teacher.

It was now nearly eight o'clock, and the house fully lit up, with a heavy police presence everywhere, doorbells ringing, people coming and going. In view, presumably, of what had happened to Patti Ryman, they were taking no chances, they'd sent this policewoman round to stay in the house, and they'd put out a search for Hope's car. But this must be a different matter to Patti's murder, entirely. Yet it seemed equally impossible to associate Hope with taking Allie away like that.

'She won't get far. We'll pick her up. It isn't as though we don't know who's taken her,' they'd said. Which made it all the worse in Sarah's eyes. It was such an irrational thing to

have done, and when reason went out of the window . . .
She tried not to think what might be going on in Allie's
mind, by now. Rigid-faced and making cups of tea for all as
if her life depended on it, she couldn't make any sense of
any of it.

With all her heart, she wished Fitz here. She'd telephoned
him at his office, at the first available opportunity. 'What?'
He'd listened without interruption until she'd blurted out
the story, but when he answered seemed not anxious to
prolong the conversation. 'Sarah, this is terrible. Don't worry,
I'm sure she'll be all right. I'm sorry, but I can't come over
straight away, I've made other plans for this evening. I'll try
and get over later.'

It wasn't what she'd hoped for. She'd never spoken to him
on the telephone before and hadn't realized how clipped and
abrupt his voice would sound, more so than usual. Perhaps
she'd rung at an inconvenient moment, but all the same,
she'd expected concern and warm sympathy and felt depress-
ingly let down.

They were all sitting in the cheerless drawing room with
its incongruous furniture – why there, of all places, Sarah
couldn't imagine, except that it was next to the hall and only
a few strides from where the telephone was, and there was
more room for all the people who were coming and going.
Every time it rang, they all sat up, as if pulled up by wires
attached to their shoulders, only to sag like puppets when
one of the police answered it and there was no news.

Dermot sat with his head in his hands. Suddenly he looked
up. 'What the hell are you all hanging around here for, doing
nothing, when you should be out finding Allie?'

The policewoman, who said they should call her Jenny,
had a clean-scrubbed appearance and well-polished shoes.
She was young, but not afraid of showing her disapproval.
All she said, however, was, 'There's still time for Miss Kendrick to bring her back. She may just have taken some misplaced notion into her head to take Allie out for the day.'
She didn't look convinced. No one else did, either.

Doreen Bailey came downstairs at last from seeing Lucy

calmed down and tucked up in bed. She'd insisted on staying with her, apparently thinking that someone was going to steal into the house and spirit her away, too. 'Asleep, poor lamb,' she said.

The doorbell rang. The lanky sergeant, Kite, looked round the door and summoned WDC Platt with a jerk of his head. A murmur of voices came from the hall and then Jenny Platt returned, shaking her head at their hopeful faces.

'Anyone fancy a cup of coffee?' Doreen asked.

'To hell with coffee, we're all awash with it,' Dermot said, jumping up and beginning to pace the room. 'Sorry, Mrs B. In God's name, how much longer?'

Sarah, clutching Angel to her like a talisman, as if the doll could somehow summon Allie back, saw defeat traced on his features, defeat and something dark and deep in him that Sarah had never recognized before. Some realization of his inadequacy as a parent? At seeing the whole bright enterprise collapsing? A need for Lisa at this time – who could tell?

Abigail hadn't been able to leave for Solihull until the late afternoon, but a telephone call had established that by the time she got there, Judith Ensor would be home from work.

She was dressed in pale blue this time, in a matching dress and jacket that only needed a picture hat to make it suitable for a wedding. Her enamelled make-up was flawless as ever, colour-coordinated pink-frosted lips and nails, like strawberry sorbet, hair like dark candyfloss.

'Dermot and Lisa Voss?' At first it seemed as though she wasn't going to admit to having known them, but after a time it appeared to dawn on her that denial was pointless and she gave a grudging admission. 'We used to know them, once.'

'Used to?'

'They lived near us. Then we moved down here and we lost touch.'

'You mean you didn't see each other again? You didn't visit, or write?'

'No.'

'Not even a Christmas card?'

'No.'

'Had you quarrelled?'

She lifted one immaculate shoulder. 'These things happen.'

'Well. Did your husband ever lend Dermot Voss any money?'

'He may have done. He didn't tell me if he did.'

She crossed her legs and smoothed her skirt. Her expression was unyielding. It was going to be like drawing teeth. 'Mrs Ensor, don't you *want* to know who killed your husband?' Abigail asked gently.

For a moment, it seemed that might have got to her. Her colour came and went. Tears appeared at the corner of her eyes. Then she remembered her mascara. 'Would you like a glass of sherry?' she asked suddenly. 'I would.'

Why not, if it would get her to talk? After the first sip of the sweet, brown liquid Abigail left the little crystal glass to one side, waiting while Judith drank hers.

'How did you meet the Voss family? Were they near neighbours?' she prompted after a while, hoping the drink might have given Judith a bit of Dutch courage. Either it had, or she'd decided to give a little more. She began to speak, softly and quickly.

'Near enough. Philip met Dermot at some airport or other when their flight was held up for hours and hours. They got talking and found we lived in the same place, and that was how it started. We played bridge together. I used to babysit for them when Dermot was home. A faint smile momentarily softened the hard little face in its frame of cloudy dark hair. 'I liked the children. They were great.'

She sat elegantly on the settee, glass in hand, staring out of the window. 'This other murder you mentioned, this young girl,' she said suddenly. 'What's Dermot's involvement in that?'

'I can't say that, yet,' Abigail replied cautiously.

She didn't say anything for a while, then seemed to come to a decision. 'After you'd gone, the other day, I found some-

188

thing that might interest you. Excuse me while I get it, will you?'

When she came back, she silently handed over a packet of letters, enclosed with an elastic band. They were addressed to Philip Ensor, at his business address, handwritten in a stylish hand, with swooping loops and Greek Es. The ink was brown, the paper was thick, creamy-yellow, with a curlicued stylized flower in brown at the top right-hand corner.

Abigail skimmed through them. They were love letters, not of the most steamy kind, but love letters, all the same, and all from Lisa Voss. The writing paper interested her.

'Very distinctive, this paper,' she said, putting the last letter back into the envelope.

'Dermot got it for her. He used to buy her lovely things all the time – a new supply of these every birthday, and once a special pen to go with it.'

'A fountain pen – with this same flower engraved on it?'

'It's not a flower – it was her monogram. She drew her initials like that!' Well, yes, Abigail saw that with the curved downstrokes of the V joining together at the bottom, and the L curling extravagantly around it, it did look exactly like a flower. 'He had the pen specially engraved to match. She didn't know when she was well off – a lot of women would've given their eye-teeth for a husband like that.'

Including Judith Ensor? She'd evidently liked Voss, which wasn't surprising. Good-looking, good-humoured, a good line in blarney. A way of talking to women that made them feel special . . . whereas her husband had been, to her at least, a very different proposition.

'She was like that, Lisa – always had to be different – her clothes, her house . . .' She glanced round in a dissatisfied way at the pristine, conventional room which had everything that money could buy. 'It was all right, if you didn't look beneath the surface – I mean, she wasn't too fussed about housework, for all she'd spend hours doing up old furniture and things.'

Her lips pursed together as if she'd been sucking a lemon.

189

The female half of the Voss partnership, at least, had cut no ice with her.

Abigail snapped the elastic band round the letters Judith had conveniently 'found', while Judith drank her sherry and poured herself another, and stared at the carpet while tears gathered in her eyes. 'You see how it was,' she said. This time she didn't bother about her mascara.

'May I take these with me? I'll give you a receipt.'

'I don't want them back, I never want to see them again. You can keep them.' Her voice tinkled like icicles.

Abigail understood what she meant. In Judith's position she wouldn't have wanted them back, either. They explicitly charted the progress of Lisa Voss's affair with Philip Ensor, the secret meetings when Dermot had been away and Ensor supposedly on business elsewhere, the growing angst about not being able to be together permanently. Then the tone of the letters changed. Despite the care they'd taken to keep their affair secret, Dermot had somehow found out, and was taking it badly, refusing even to discuss a divorce, becoming abusive . . . it was in the last letter that Ensor was told that Lisa was pregnant.

'How did Dermot find out about Lisa and your husband, Mrs Ensor?'

She shrugged. 'How should I know that?' She avoided Abigail's eye.

Jealousy was an ugly word. An ugly emotion. Maybe it was an assumption on Abigail's part, though she didn't feel it was unjustified, that Judith Ensor was not childless from choice. How cruel then, to find out that her husband's mistress, with two children of her own already, was pregnant with her own husband's child. She said gently, 'Was it before or after Lisa Voss died that you moved here? Whose suggestion was it, yours or your husband's?'

'It was before, but does it matter? We both wanted to leave the place behind.'

That was understandable, on Judith's part, at least. Who would want to live within spitting distance of reminders of her husband's infidelities? But it also implied that she'd

190

known what was going on, and that it was probably the cause of the split between the families.

Standing up, ready to leave, Abigail asked Judith Ensor, 'Why didn't you tell us this before?'

She sat in her baby-blue suit on her flowered settee, a sparkly little brooch in the form of an arch-backed cat with green eyes on her neat lapel, her beautiful grey eyes wide and unblinking. 'I always liked Dermot, he was good fun, and if he had killed Philip – well, it was only what Philip deserved, wasn't it?'

Down at Milford Road Police Station, Fitzallan was being shown into the nearest room, which happened to be one of the interview rooms. He'd appeared at the front desk with a curt request to see the senior officer on the Patti Ryman case, stating that he had something important to say. When the request came, Mayo shrugged on his jacket, adjusted his tie, drank the dregs of yet another coffee, and went downstairs. Summoning a PC to join them, he introduced himself, saying, 'I believe you've already answered the questions my officers put to you – is there something you've remembered?'

He spoke more impatiently than he knew. The whole station was alive with activity and tension, events were piling up, occupying his thoughts and his time – notably this latest worrying development, the disappearance of the little girl, Allie. He couldn't see how, yet, but if it was a coincidence, unconnected with the other happenings they were working on, then he was a Dutchman. He was in no mood to put up with time-wasting grumbles from the public, wherever they came from.

An abrupt man with deep-set eyes, not given to smiling easily at any time, now Fitzallan positively glowered. Tall and broad-shouldered, in a casually expensive suit, he dominated the cheerlessly functional surroundings, throwing himself on to the hard chair offered without seeming to notice its comfort or otherwise. Then he startled Mayo by asking abruptly, 'First of all, do I need to go into my personal background? Are you familiar with what happened to my

191

wife some years ago?' He added tersely, 'The officers who've already questioned me seemed to know all about it.'

'It's part of their job to know. I remember the case, too.'

'Yes. Well. I only mentioned it because I think it has some bearing on what I've come about.' He took a moment to organize his thoughts, and Mayo, beginning to be intrigued by the man and his purpose in coming here, didn't push him.

Fitz looked down at his hands, breathing deeply. He was fully aware that he wasn't one of the world's best communicators, and this was something he'd never yet been able to talk about freely, not to anyone: those reasons why it had been necessary for him to have the attic flat at Edwina Lodge as a bolt hole, where he could paint, and leave behind for a measure of time the woman who had been his wife, his responsibility, his burden but ultimately, as he'd continually reassured himself, his enduring love.

Elspeth, cool and beautiful when he'd married her, neurotic and unstable within a few years, bringing the structure of their lives crashing down. Her illness, a disturbing and little understood dysfunction with an unpronounceable name, had made her impossible to live with, impossible to abandon. It had resulted in a steady erosion of their marriage, problems with drink, drugs, suicide attempts. There were those who'd urged him to have her 'put in care' but, hellish though life had become, it would have shamed him not to cherish her as he had in the days before her illness, at least to try and love her and care for her as much as when she'd been well, and whole. All the same, when eventually she did manage to take her own life in that monstrous way, he blamed himself for not listening to the advice.

That day, she'd pumped into herself a cocktail of drugs and drink, taken her car out and driven it at speed along a busy road, with the inevitable conclusion: an appalling pile-up, with the people in the other car, an eight-year-old boy and the driver, his mother, being killed instantly.

'Mr Fitzallan?'

He blinked rapidly, then opened his briefcase and passed

a sheet of grey drawing paper across the desk. 'I think you should look at this.' It was a child's drawing. There was a silence as Mayo studied it.

'Who drew this?'

'Allie, Voss's little girl. I'm doing a portrait of her, trying to, and she likes drawing, so I usually give her pencils and paper and let her draw while she sits for me. Can't expect a little girl to sit unoccupied for any length of time.'

It was a drawing in thick crayon, not remarkable for its talent. It was crude and childish, but it made the hairs on the back of Mayo's neck stand on end. The sheet of paper was large, and the simple outline filled it. A staircase in profile, with a man at the top, standing with arms out-stretched. At the foot of the stairs lay a woman, flat out, arms and legs stretched out like a fly. Against the grey back-ground, the crayoned lines were slashed on to the paper, heavy and thick, the chosen colours angry deep red and black. The circle that represented the man's face had been furiously scribbled over in black.

'Why did you bring this here? You said you thought it had some relevance?'

'You're familiar with art therapy? The theory that you get disturbed people to paint or draw, in the hopes that they'll bring out their anger, or fear, or whatever's hidden inside and troubling them. Something like that, anyway – a simplis-tic way of putting it, no doubt, but I'm no expert. My wife had years of therapy, it was one of the things they tried . . . But it wasn't deliberate on my part when I gave Allie a paper and pencil, it was only for her to amuse herself while I painted her.' He paused, eyeing them from under his brows. 'I suppose you knew that Voss's wife died from a fall down the stairs?'

'She fell downstairs?' Mayo had known only that Lisa Voss had died during pregnancy, there'd been no reason to assume her death hadn't been caused by some condition arising from that. 'What are you suggesting?'

'I'm not suggesting anything. Only that Allie's apparently had a history of sleepwalking and nightmares since her

mother died – and you must agree, it's a pretty morbid subject for a child to choose. And now that she's disappeared . . .' He left the rest of the sentence unsaid.

After a moment or two, Mayo said, 'Right, Mr Fitzallan. Thank you for bringing this to our attention. Leave it with me, if you would.'

Fitz stood up. He hadn't expected it to be any better received. He wasn't sure whether he ought to have spoken at all, whether he'd made a fool of himself or not, uneasily aware that this policeman might well think the picture nothing more than a childish scrawl, and himself some sort of crackpot amateur psychiatrist. He hesitated, then decided to say nothing more, took his leave and strode out.

When Fitzallan had gone, Mayo took the drawing back to his office and then stood in front of the window, staring out. The sky was a soft, heavy pearl-grey, one of those still, windless, moody evenings of late summer. It would be dark in an hour. A pigeon sat on the sill of one of the Town Hall windows opposite, listening to the grinding of gears at the traffic lights, the hiss of air brakes, looking too bored to move. The top of a red double-decker bus cruised past . . .

Rather than money, perhaps the source of the quarrel between Voss and Ensor had been Lisa Voss.

He turned his back on the window and went to look at the childish, disturbing drawing where it lay on his desk, depicting – what? Something Allie had actually witnessed? Was that scribbled-out face Ensor's, or was the whole thing something imaginary, an invented scene to explain to herself the deeply disturbing shock of her mother's death? Was it even possible that the child had seen it happening in reality? And told her father? Or had she done other similar drawings, which he'd seen, and drawn his own conclusions? If Voss had had reason to believe it possible that Ensor had pushed his wife downstairs, it was more than a motive for him to have killed the other man.

Yet why should Philip Ensor, if he *was* guilty of murdering Lisa Voss, have come to Lavenstock to meet her husband?

It would surely have been more logical for him to have kept out of the way. Why should he have killed Lisa, anyway – unless they'd quarrelled – if they'd been having an affair? He picked up the phone. 'Somebody get me details of the inquest on a woman called Lisa Voss,' he requested, giving the necessary details. 'Get them to fax it through. I'll be in my office for a while yet.'

When it came, he read it through carefully. The inquest recorded a verdict of accidental death. She had apparently tripped over the loose belt of her dressing gown and fallen to the bottom of a flight of polished, open-tread stairs. Her neck had been broken. She'd been alone in the house, except for the children, who hadn't wakened. She'd been discovered the next morning by the cleaning lady when she let herself in. Dermot Voss had been expected home the following day, and had in fact arrived about four o'clock, to find his wife dead.

'Check out Voss's flight from Belgrade,' Mayo said to Farrar, slapping the details on to Farrar's desk in the CID room. 'See what time he actually arrived. I'm on my way up to Edwina Lodge. When Inspector Moon comes in, ask her to meet me there.'

The doorbell rang yet again. Voices sounded in the hall, then the Superintendent came into the drawing room. 'Nothing new, yet, I'm afraid,' he said gently. 'There's a call out for Miss Kendrick's car, as you know, but it hasn't been seen yet.' His face was grim and set. 'We still don't seem to be able to contact anyone else at Simla.'

'*What*?' Dermot looked up, his eyes wild. 'What did you say?'

'We're finding difficulty getting hold of Mr Kendrick. He doesn't seem to be at home, nor does Mrs Loxley.'

'Imogen?' Sarah suddenly remembered that she and Imogen had tickets for an open lecture on William Morris in the Ferraby Hall, part of Lavenstock College. She looked for the hundredth time at the clock on the mantel. The lecture would be over, they'd be well into the cheese and wine

which was to follow by now. She hadn't given anything else a thought since hearing about Allie, but she couldn't understand why Imogen hadn't let her know if there'd been a change of plan. The disappearance of everyone from whom she might have expected moral support suddenly took on a frightening aspect.

'*No one there at all*? Are you sure?' For a moment Dermot looked nonplussed, then his eyes narrowed. Sarah saw that his mind was working in that peculiarly fast and connective way it sometimes did. Then he said, coldly and deliberately, 'There's something you should know about Francis Kendrick.'

'*Francis* Kendrick?' Mayo's voice was sharp as a whip.

'There was an incident – when he was a young professor at Cambridge. He played the organ at one of the churches – there was a young choirboy . . . It was all hushed up, just a piece of gossip – I only came across it incidentally because we happened to be making a documentary about his college at the time. Several people thought the boy was being mischievous, because Kendrick had reprimanded him over something, but . . .' He shrugged his shoulders.

Mayo was staring at him in speechless disbelief which echoed Sarah's own. When he found words, he said, incredulously, 'A young girl's been murdered – you have two of your own, one's disappeared – and you kept all this to yourself?'

'This was *Francis* Kendrick, not his sister. Choirboys and little girls – hardly the same, are they?' But Dermot avoided his eyes.

Sarah stood up abruptly and left the room.

'Anyway, I reckoned you'd have found out,' Dermot was saying, cockily – 'that's your business, isn't it?'

'We've no reason to go into a man's past unless he's a suspect.'

'Well, you've plenty bloody reason to suspect him now – what are you going to do about it?'

'My men are effecting entry to the premises now.' It was the way people expected the police to speak. He often found it useful when he was stalling.

Sarah came back, holding a manila envelope. 'Can I have a word with you, in private, please?' she said to Mayo. 'Come into the small sitting room.'

When they emerged, the telephone was once more ringing in the hall. The shrill, insistent note of the old-fashioned instrument, unlike the present-day warble, made everyone jump. Jenny went to answer it. Everyone grew silent, listening to what she said. 'What? *What*? Yes, I'll tell him. I expect he'll be over immediately.'

18

Mayo sprinted across the few intervening yards between Edwina Lodge and Simla, though he didn't know why he was running. It was far too late for that.

His thoughts were spinning, and in the space of those few seconds all the reasoning which had caused him to send Abigail off to Solihull again was overturned. He'd been so sure he'd had the right answer. But could he have been wrong – had he been dangerously guilty of manipulating the facts to fit a theory? Maybe Patti's murderer *had* been someone with a penchant for young bodies, little girls – or little boys, come to that – after all.

The dismal hall, its upper reaches dark with shadows that swooped down from the ceiling, was lit with one central light that barely made inroads into the gloom. It was enough, however, for Mayo to see everything that needed to be seen: a longer shadow depending from one of the newel posts, a Modigliani figure, grotesquely elongated, its own shadow dancing alongside as it gently swung, a heavy, carved-oak upright chair kicked away and lying on its back.

Ison had been sent for and since he was at home when the summons came, he covered the short distance within minutes and was there almost as soon as Mayo. The body was cut down, and after a brief examination Ison was able to estimate that Francis Kendrick had been dead for only a few hours.

'It appears to be a straightforward suicide. No note, you say? Unusual. They usually do, poor sods, don't they, if it's only to leave the blame with someone else?'

That was true, though Mayo had often suspected that more notes were ever destroyed than came to the notice of the police. 'Hardly been time to look, yet,' he said.

Kendrick was dressed in his old, baggy cotton trousers and a short-sleeved cotton shirt, with a complete absence of that self-absorbed vanity of some suicides – those who tidied their houses, wore clean clothes before they finished it all, concerned to the end with leaving behind a good impression of themselves, not even a thought of cruelty to the living. Anyone who'd seen the number of suicides he had couldn't fail to be struck by how much humanity clung to its vision of itself.

'What's that in his pockets?'

A piece of paper protruded very slightly from the pocket of Kendrick's shirt. Extracting it in the prescribed manner, Mayo read aloud the four words written on it. *The book is finished.* 'And what,' he asked the doctor, 'is that supposed to mean?'

'Some cryptic reference to his life having come an end?' suggested Ison imaginatively.

Mayo blew out his lips. He could imagine some people putting it like that, but not Kendrick. Surely too uncharacteristically dramatic a gesture for such an apparently unemotional man as Francis Kendrick. More likely it meant just what it said, that the book he was working on was finished, it was ready to be dealt with. He, like everyone else, had ultimately had his little vanities. He could not leave the world behind without making sure that something of him would live on after he'd gone.

A uniformed constable came into the room. 'There's an unsealed letter here, sir – it was on the kitchen table.'

Reading between the lines of the hastily scrawled note from Imogen, addressed to Hope and Francis, explaining that she had suddenly returned to Brussels, it wasn't difficult to guess at the state of mind which had made her leave so precipitately. 'I shall be back in a few days, either to collect my belongings, or to return permanently. It will all depend on Tom,' she wrote sadly.

199

They were not a happy family, the Kendricks.

But there were no more notes, nothing from Hope to say why, or where, she had taken the child, and nothing more written by her brother Francis to indicate what had brought him to take this final step. Remembering the last time he'd seen him, the unexpected sympathy he'd aroused, Mayo felt he might hazard a guess. He hoped he was wrong, that the reason Francis Kendrick had taken his own life, in a way that Mayo always found particularly gruesome and horrible, was not because of the weight of his sins preying on his conscience. But either way, the conclusions were not particularly comfortable.

'Sir, they've found the little girl!'

'Found?' All Mayo's sense of dread was contained in the word as he turned to Jenny Platt, framed in the open doorway.

'She's all right, on her way home with Mr Fitzallan.'

'*Who* did you say?'

'Fitzallan, sir. D I Moon's just arrived, and she took a telephone call from him. He found Miss Kendrick and the little girl. At their country cottage in Shropshire. They're on their way back now.'

He knew the full story now, what had led up to Ensor's murder and why Patti's death had followed. He and Abigail had exchanged information and the whole sorry scene was clear. He could now act, but there was no hurry.

About eight o'clock, a car drew up outside Edwina Lodge. Fitzallan's Range Rover. Fitzallan, dark-browed, strode into the house with Allie in his arms, fast asleep, her head cradled against his shoulder. Her face was dirty, she had lost her hairslide but otherwise she seemed unharmed and opened her eyes for a moment, smiling sleepily when Sarah put Angel into her arms before following Fitz as he carried the child upstairs to her room.

Hope Kendrick was beyond questioning that night. Possibly overcome by the realization of what she'd done, she sat rigidly in the passenger seat of the Range Rover until she

was requested to come into the house. She had to be told about her brother's death and it was done as gently as possible but, dazed and emotionally exhausted, she hardly seemed to take it in.

'You'll not get anything out of her tonight,' Ison said. 'I'll give her a sedative and you can question her in the morning. Is there anyone who can be with her? I wouldn't advise her being left on her own.'

'We've already contacted Imogen Loxley in Brussels. She and her husband are coming over. I should think Mrs Bailey can be persuaded to stay with her until they get here.'

Fitzallan, meanwhile, was ready to explain his reasons for charging up to Shropshire, when a call to the local police there would have simplified matters. Did he have some personal stake in the fortunes of this family? Mayo wondered, and saw from the way he and Sarah Wilmot looked at each other there wasn't much room for doubt what that was. 'I had this idea,' he said. 'I knew the Kendricks had a cottage in Shropshire, not exactly where, though I'd a fair idea, so I decided to go and have a look. I suspected,' he said gloweringly, 'that you wouldn't take my idea seriously, any more than you did the drawing. In any case,' he confessed with a smile that was all the more disarming for being unexpected, 'I wasn't all that convinced myself. I went, without giving it too much thought.'

Mayo cut short further explanations. Fitzallan would have to be dealt with later, Hope Kendrick, too, but both could wait. Now that the child was safe, there were other matters to be attended to. He turned to Allie's father.

'Dermot Voss, we'd like you to come down to the station and help us with our inquiries into the murder of Patricia Mary Ryman.'

19

Mayo drove slowly back to the station. After the last few dry, sunless, still and cheerless days the weather had taken a turn. With the new moon, a wind had sprung up, bringing rain with it. It had become heavy by the time Mayo returned from Edwina Lodge, with clouds obscuring the moon. The station, with all its lights on, glowed like a lighted ship against the black surrounding hills as he made a dash for the door.

Abigail arrived just behind him. By the time they had finished setting out the line their questioning was to take, despite her resolve, she was drinking coffee, and making no excuses for herself.

'Those children,' she said softly. 'Didn't he give a thought to his children?'

'I don't for one minute imagine that Voss gives a thought to anybody but himself. There's nothing to him. He's one-dimensional. Come on, I think we've left him cooling his heels long enough.'

They went downstairs and Mayo stood in front of the table that separated them from Voss, leaning forward, his hands flat on the surface. He spoke to the man he'd once thought of as a pleasant acquaintance, with whom he'd shared social congress. 'OK, we're ready to start, and I want it straight. Don't give me any bull on this. You've already wasted enough of our time as it is.'

Dermot Voss lolled in the opposite chair, smoking, a faint amusement on his face, unperturbed by the presence of a detective superintendent, a detective inspector, a sergeant

and a constable. 'Do I have the impression you're about to interrogate me?' he asked, his smile deepening.

'I don't know why else you think we've brought you down here. And I don't much care *what* impression you have. What matters is that you answer my questions.'

'Dear me. Well, fire ahead.'

Mayo settled himself into the chair next to Abigail, taking his time, spreading his papers out on the table in front of him. Voss had totally dismissed the idea of being represented by a solicitor.

'Interview commences eleven thirty. Those present are Superintendent Mayo, DI Moon, DS Kite and WDC Platt.' He nodded to Jenny Platt, ready to take back-up notes, then turned back to Voss. 'First of all, I'd like you to explain to me what you were doing between seven thirty a.m. and five past eight on Monday, eleventh September.'

'I told you, I stopped at Patel's to get cigarettes. There was a queue, and God knows how long it took me to get served. When I came out again my car had gone. Disappeared. Vanished. Into thin air.'

'What were you doing between that time and arriving back at Edwina Lodge at five past eight?'

'Well, I cast around for a bit, looking for the car. It took me some time to grasp what had happened. At first, I thought I must have left it down that street, what's it called? – Allegar Street – and forgotten – you know, the one that turns off Albert Road just past Patel's. Sometimes, if there's no parking space outside the shop, I do leave it there.'

'Must've taken you all of two minutes to find out you hadn't.'

'Plus more time, wandering a bit further, wondering if someone had moved it for a joke. It *has* happened to me before, you know,' he added, as their faces said what they thought of this as an excuse. 'It must have been about ten to eight when I got back to the house.'

'Mrs Baverstock has stated that it was five past eight when you arrived back at Edwina Lodge.'

'And who's to prove her word against mine? That nosy bitch would say anything against me.'

'Your sister-in-law, Sarah Wilmot, didn't leave the house until after eight o'clock.'

'All right, so I arrived a bit later than I thought. I wasn't checking my watch every five minutes! Now, suppose you tell me something – this is all to do with that girl, Patti, being killed, right?' His good humour was slipping a bit. 'So give me one good reason why you think I should be concerned in that?'

'We'll come to that. First I'm going to put forward what we believe happened, then you can tell me where you think we're wrong. I think you called for cigarettes, yes, but I also think you intended to waylay Patti, which you did – you followed her into Ellington Close and then into the wood, and killed her there.'

'You lot – you really are something else!'

'I haven't finished yet. You must have had one hell of a shock when you came back and found your car missing. If it had still been there, you'd have been away and nobody the wiser. So you did the best you could – got out of sight as quick as possible, back to Edwina Lodge, where everyone would be out, as you thought. I don't suppose you knew Tina Baverstock was at home on Mondays.' He saw by the flicker of Voss's eyes that he'd hit the nail on the head.

'Well, naturally I came back – I had to sort myself out, report the car missing, get picked up and all that. And all right, I did see Patti. We met at the entrance to the Close, as a matter of fact, as I was going back to the house. She asked me if I could hear a noise. It sounded like an animal in pain, and it was coming from the direction of the wood. She ran in and I followed. I found her in tears, crouched beside a dead cat. It had been mutilated and she was terribly upset, she said she'd have to tell the owners. I offered to do it for her but she wouldn't have that. In the end, I had to leave her and go home. I was due on an important assignment that morning, and I had to report my car missing and arrange for another to pick me up.'

'This is a substantially different version of your first story.'

'Since she was alive and well when I left her, I didn't see the need to complicate matters.'

'It complicates things a good deal more when people take it on themselves to lie to us.' Dermot looked pained. 'And that was the last you saw of her?'

'It was.'

Like all good liars, he was keeping to the truth as much as he could, but there wasn't enough of it to support his story. 'What you haven't given me,' he complained, 'is one plausible reason why I should have killed that girl?'

'It might become clearer to you if we went a bit further back, then – to the Saturday night Ensor was killed.'

Dermot frowned, puzzled. 'Ah yes, the man on the allotments.'

'The man who was your very good friend, Philip Ensor,' Mayo reminded him sharply.

'Oh, *Philip* Ensor,' he said, as though there were other Ensors who had met with the same unfortunate end.

'Don't pussyfoot around, Mr Voss, we've already established how far your acquaintance with him went.'

'I knew him at one time, yes. Slightly.'

'Rather more than that, I believe.'

Abigail bent over the briefcase which stood on the floor to extract a bundle of what looked like letters. She put them on the table, without saying what they were. Creamy yellow paper, brown ink. Dermot rocked back in his chair and stared at the ceiling.

'You were in fact very good friends,' she said.

'At one time, maybe. Not of late.'

'Why was that? Did you quarrel?'

'They moved house, we lost touch, you know how it is, it's the women who keep these things going, and Lisa didn't bother.'

'But the friendship was mainly between you and Philip Ensor, wasn't it? You'd known each other for several years, I think.' Her hand went out absently and touched the creamy

yellow bundle. She slid out one of the letters and laid it flat, facing herself.

'Can I have another cigarette?' Voss asked, lowering the chair and leaning forward while it was lit for him.

'That's true,' he said eventually, 'to a point. I met Ensor when we were marooned in an airport – Athens, I think. We got talking and struck up a rapport. Then a few weeks later, by an amazing coincidence, we found ourselves in adjoining seats on another flight home from Germany. Discovered we lived not far from each other, liked golf. One thing led to another . . .' He shrugged.

'And you did, in fact, become close friends.'

'We used to see quite a bit of each other. Our wives weren't all that keen. But they went along with it. I think Judith was inclined to be jealous of Lisa – she couldn't have a child, and we had two.'

'And maybe she began to have further cause for jealousy. Especially when your wife became pregnant again.'

Dermot raised an eyebrow, apparently not seeing fit to reply to that, so Mayo went on.

'By that time, they'd moved from Milton Keynes – at Mrs Ensor's insistence, since she didn't like the association that was growing between her husband and your wife.'

'I don't know anything about that.'

'That's not exactly true, is it?' Mayo tapped the letters. 'It's all here – what was going on between them, your reactions when you found out.' He let that sink in for a while, then suddenly changed tack. 'The night Ensor was killed, you were staying at the Saracen's Head, here in Lavenstock. You gave it out you had food poisoning.'

'I did have food poisoning.'

'If you say so. But your sister-in-law ate the same food and wasn't affected. It was nothing but a ploy to slip out and meet Ensor, wasn't it? At a place you'd sussed out when you'd previously stayed at the Saracen's, when you were house-hunting.'

'That's a load of rubbish. And I repeat, I did not go out and meet Ensor.'

'I must tell you that we have a witness who saw you.'

'Probably when I slipped out for a breath of air for a few minutes, after I'd thrown up.'

'The witness recognized you and will swear he saw you and Ensor fighting.'

'You can't witness something that didn't happen,' Voss said, but with much less conviction.

'There were, in fact, two separate witnesses. Perhaps you were too occupied to remember the car that drove away – but you did remember Patti, when you met her later, as being the girl who'd walked through the allotments when you and Ensor were fighting, which is why you killed her.'

'No. I'd as little reason to kill her as I had to kill Ensor.'

Mayo began sifting through the papers on the table and soon found what he was looking for. 'Do you recognize this?' He held up the polythene-encased photograph of Ensor that Sarah had found, then turned it over so that Voss could read what was written on the back, explaining what he was doing for the benefit of the tape recording.

Voss stared at it. 'Where the hell did you get this?'

'It was found in the bottom of your wife's jewel box, by Sarah Wilmot.'

'Sarah?' He sounded as though he'd had a blow, right where it hurt.

'She found it a couple of days ago but she'd never met Philip Ensor and knew nothing about him. She only connected it yesterday with the E-fit picture we'd issued of him – which wasn't all that good a likeness, but as near as we could get. Show him the other exhibit, Inspector Moon, if you will.'

Abigail held up the drawing that Allie had done. The colour drained from his face. 'What are you trying to do to me? Who drew that?'

'It's one of your daughter's drawings – Allie.'

For once he was silenced.

'The night your wife died, you took an earlier flight from Belgrade and arrived home a day sooner than you were expected. We've checked with the airline, and we've found

a taxi that left you at your home at ten o'clock in the evening. The driver remembered you very well, on account of your photographic gear. I believe a quarrel blew up almost immediately between you and your wife about her association with Ensor, which ended with you pushing her down the stairs.'

'Your imagination's in overdrive, Mayo,' Voss said, stubbing out his cigarette. But his hand had begun to shake, and he avoided looking at anyone.

'But that's a substantially correct account of what happened, isn't it? You must have woken your daughter with the noise, and she saw it happen. She's pushed it to the back of her mind, as children – and not only children – do with traumatic events that are too terrible to deal with. But it's been there in her subconscious ever since, manifesting itself in sleepwalking, drawings like this . . .'

'Stop it!'

Voss put his folded arms on the table, laid his head on them and began to weep. 'I didn't kill Lisa. And I never meant to kill the others,' he mumbled indistinctly.

'Will you raise your head, Mr Voss, and say that clearly for the benefit of the tape?'

There was no response, except for the sound of his weeping. Eventually he raised his congested face and after being prompted again, repeated what he'd said.

'Why don't you tell us exactly what happened?'

'What'll happen to me if I do?' he asked abjectly.

Mayo looked at him as he swiped the tears away with his hands. 'That's not for me to say. I've already cautioned you, and I must warn you that we have enough evidence to support a charge against you of murdering Patti Ryman.'

'What evidence?'

'We found this pen at the scene of the crime. Do you identify it as one belonging to your wife, which you'd occasionally used since her death?'

'It looks like the one I bought for Lisa, yes.'

'We've also found traces of burnt, bloodstained clothing

208

in your garden incinerator, fibres of which match those found on Patti's school blazer, and – '

'I didn't push Lisa down the stairs! She tripped over that damned belt – she'd been warned often enough about leaving it unfastened. I did come home early, and yes, we did have a row – she'd been asking me for a divorce, she was pregnant, and I knew the child wasn't mine. The children were asleep, and she was already undressed, ready for bed. She said she wasn't going to argue any more and was going downstairs to make some tea. I followed her and grabbed at her at the top of the steps, but she twisted away from me and fell. I swear I didn't push her downstairs. If – if Allie saw it, it may have looked like that to her, but it was an accident. I tried to grab her but her dressing gown was satiny stuff and it slipped through my fingers . . . She was dead when I got to the bottom of the stairs. I didn't know what to do, so I just left, walked to the station and took a train to London, came back next day as if I'd just arrived. Nobody ever questioned me.'

There was a long silence.

'And on Monday the eleventh of September?'

'It's basically true what I told you. I stopped the car outside Patel's to get some cigarettes and saw Patti coming along with the papers. I'd recognized her a few days earlier, when that Baverstock bitch was bawling her out about leaving her bike outside the house. I went out to tell her it was my house and the paper girl could leave her bike where she damn well liked. God, I got a shock when I saw who the girl was! That hair, you know, impossible to mistake.' He was speaking fast, his words tumbling over each other, anxious to justify himself. 'I was pretty certain she'd recognized me, too, but I couldn't be sure. It happened as I told you on the Monday morning, I went with her into the wood, we saw the cat and all that, but then, as we were leaving, she suddenly burst out, "It was you, wasn't it, the other night by the allotments? You were fighting – I shall have to tell the police, but it'll be all right, Mr Voss. I looked back but he was standing up, so it couldn't have been you who killed him, could it?" She

209

was so innocent, so naive. But if she'd told you what she'd seen, it would've been all up with me. She walked away and – I hardly remember how or why – I picked a piece of iron up that was lying around and hit her with it. Then I went back to pick my car up and found it had gone.'

He'd walked away, just as he'd walked away from Ensor – and his own wife. He'd gone into the wood with Patti, and emerged a few minutes later, without a soul having witnessed his entry or exit from the wood.

'I'm sorry I did it, I never would have killed her if I'd thought about it,' he said, beginning to weep again.

'And you wouldn't have killed Philip Ensor either, if you'd thought about it?'

'That was different. We were fighting. I knocked him down once and he got up. I picked a stone up and hit him with it. I left him lying in a puddle – I thought it would cool him off. How was I to know he'd die?'

'Tell me exactly what you were fighting about – how he came to be in Lavenstock that night.'

'He'd been threatening me. I'd had a letter from his wife, Judith, telling me what was going on. I found it hard to believe – I'd always thought Philip a decent sort, we'd always got on well, but he was hardly the sort a woman would die for.' Seeming not to have noticed his unfortunate choice of words, he went on, 'We'd been going through a bad patch, Lisa and I . . . she wanted me to get another job where I could spend more time with her and the children, for one thing. But I never thought things were that bad. It was hard to stomach the idea of her and Philip. I wrote her some rather strong letters, telling her she must give him up.'

'You mean threatening letters, don't you?'

'What do you think? She'd been playing around while I was in the thick of it in Bosnia. I wasn't exactly happy about that. I told her she'd better come to her senses, or else. She wrote and told Ensor – those letters, I suppose,' he said, gesturing to the pile on the table, 'telling him that I'd threatened to kill her. The baby was his, you know. He was abroad when she died, but when he came back and heard about it,

he threatened to take the letters to the police, unless . . .' He couldn't finish the sentence but Mayo finished it for him.

'Unless you paid him back the money you owed him. Your wife mentioned the debt, several times, in her letters.'

'Yes, she would. She didn't like me not paying it back. I don't think he was bothered about it, he had a good job and never squandered his money – but I'd have paid it back if I could. Wouldn't you hate the idea of owing money to a man who'd been sleeping with your wife? When he began to pester me, I paid some of it back, but eventually I told him that was it. I'd no more to give him.'

'What was his reaction to that?'

'He said he had a proposition to put to me. He'd found out about my move to Lavenstock and demanded I met him that night, which I did.'

'Where?'

'Where? Oh, I didn't want him inside the hotel where Sarah might see us, so I arranged to meet him outside, in the car park. He was late.'

'He didn't park in the hotel car park.'

'No, it's not very big and there was a function on that night, and all the spaces round about were taken up, too. He said he'd had to shove his car up some back alley. He wasn't the sort to let things upset him, usually, but I think it had annoyed him that he couldn't find anywhere. At any rate, he became abusive with me over – over Lisa's death. I thought he meant to kill me, but I pushed him down and ran off – anywhere, I didn't know that road led to the allotments – but he followed me and – well, I've told you what happened then.'

There was silence when he'd finished.

'Thank you, Mr Voss. We'll take a break, and then go through all this once again. And I'd advise you to change your mind about getting a solicitor.'

211

EPILOGUE

Down a short, steep drive leading off the country lane, there is the house, a small, irregular brick-and-timber Elizabethan manor, tucked into a fold of the hill. Sarah sits curled in the window-seat, reading a letter.

The first time she saw Fitz's house was nearly three months ago, shortly after Dermot's arrest, on a warm October day. The front door and several windows had been wide open, and the sounds of a violin concerto floated across the garden.

'That's Mrs Mac's radio,' Fitz explained. 'She's tuned in to Classic FM all day.' But she'd evidently heard the car, and had come into the hall to greet them, a raw-boned, ginger-haired Scots woman with a soft, sibilant Highland accent. 'Och, I was not expecting you so soon! I'll be having your tea ready in half an hour,' she said. 'Maybe the wee girls would like to help me make some drop scones while you two make yourselves comfortable?' and bore the children away.

'She doesn't usually come over all stage-Scottish like that,' Fitz said. 'She's either embarrassed or wants you to get a good impression.'

'I'm impressed, all right,' Sarah said, following him as he led the way from the wide, stone-flagged hall into a pleasant room with a big stone fireplace where now a huge log fire burns. The room was slightly shabby, the slipcovers faded, some of the rugs on the wide polished boards threadbare, but the furniture was old and beautiful and everything bore witness to Mrs McLaren's meticulous Scottish housekeeping, right down to the squarely placed cushions and the single pot plant on a mat, dead centre of a shining, gate-legged oak table. 'It's a lovely, lovely house,' Sarah said.

Fitz's shoulders relaxed. 'I've been hoping you'd say that. I didn't know how you'd react. It was a small farm at one time, with quite

a bit of land round it when my parents bought it, but now there's only the house.'

'And the garden,' Sarah had said, looking out of the low-silled, latticed windows on to a stone-flagged terrace with a garden beyond, glowing with dahlias, asters and chrysanthemums, beech trees at the bottom just turning gold. 'That's beautiful.'

'I'll take you round later, though it's no thanks to me it looks the way it does. My father moved into a cottage in the village with no garden to speak of when I married, so he's very happy to look after this. It was my mother who laid it out and we just try to keep it as she did.' He gave a gusty sigh. 'Like the rest of the house, I'm afraid. Nobody's done anything to it for years. Elspeth and I were always going to do it up, but somehow we never did.' He could mention her name now, not yet easily, not entirely without pain, but without too much awkwardness. 'You can do what you want with it, when we're married.'

That was in October, and Sarah Wilmot is now Sarah Fitzallan. She looks up from her letter at the now familiar room. The changes she's made have been small – a few lamps and some of Fitz's skyscapes that she's persuaded him to let her hang, huge jars of leaves and berries, new loose covers, supplied by Lois French, but it's made all the difference . . . It has a heart, it's a home now, for her and Fitz, Lucy and Allie.

'A ready-made family, Fitz,' she'd reminded him, gently. 'It's a lot to be taking on.' A lifetime's commitment, maybe.

Dermot had been kept in custody, awaiting trial. Superintendent Mayo refused to speculate about what would happen when the trial came to court. He'd had nasty surprises from juries before. Dermot refused to plead guilty, and the police might fail to secure a murder conviction – but whatever happened, there were huge difficulties regarding the children's future, and though there was no question for Sarah about where their immediate future lay, she could see Fitz might not feel the same about it. 'If it's a problem –'

'That's a bonus, not a problem,' he'd interrupted firmly. Straight down the line, Fitz. He'd had it all worked out, he wasn't under any illusions that it was all going to be plain sailing, but he'd accepted what it would mean and it hadn't made any difference. Why had she thought it would? If anybody could cope, it was Fitz.

214

'I love both of them dearly,' he told her gruffly, 'but if they were the most horrible brats in Christendom, I'd still love them for your sake.'

'Fitz,' she'd said, laughing, close to tears, 'that's almost a romantic thing to say!'

'What I mean is – ' But what he'd meant to say had been interrupted by the arrival of tea.

'I made them, I made the drop scones all by myself!' Lucy said, presenting a plate of rather odd-sized and misshapen scones, liberally spread with butter.

'No, you didn't! Angel and me helped,' said Allie.

'I put the batter on the griddle from the spoon!'

'I turned them over!'

'That's why they're such a yukky shape!' countered Lucy, getting in the last word, as usual.

'Well, it doesn't matter who did what, they're delicious,' Sarah said, placatingly. 'You'd better show me how to make them before Mrs Mac goes back to Scotland.'

It's now two months since Mrs Mac departed to live with her sister in Arisaig, the garden is winter-bare, the children are looking for cones from the Scots pine, to take to school and gild for Christmas decorations. Allie stands under the tree, looking up, reminding Sarah unbearably of the day she'd stood under the sequoia, the day of the welcome party at Simla, and the notes of 'Alice Where Art Thou?' sounding through the house.

'Do you think the children would like to have the Polyphon?' Hope had asked, when she was clearing out the house. Then, painfully, seeing Sarah's face, 'No, better not.'

Allie had talked constantly at first about the wonderful day when she was unexpectedly taken out of school by Hope, when they had the long ride in the car and she was given all sorts of treats and Hope was so kind to her. Everyone was so interested in what she had to tell them, but after a while they stopped questioning her and by now it's only a memory. Any scars left are Hope's.

Haltingly, at intervals, Hope had forced herself to tell Sarah everything, about Francis, and Sven, and the child which had never been born, and the unsatisfied longings which had built up over the years. The events surrounding Patti's death had brought it all

back, and suddenly there had been a confusion in her head, a compulsion to take Allie away, to have her just to herself. The madness hadn't lasted long. If Fitz hadn't appeared that night, she would have brought Allie back the next day, she swore that.

Sarah believed her. The letter which she now rereads is from Hope. She has taken up a live-in teaching post at a school near Shrewsbury. It isn't far from her cottage on the Long Mynd, where she spends most weekends. Imogen is back in Brussels, Simla is empty, and up for sale. The Baverstocks have bought Edwina Lodge. 'Thank you for the invitation to spend Christmas with you,' Hope writes, 'but I've already arranged to spend the holiday in Madeira, with a colleague from school.'

The tragedy has brought the two women together in a tenuous friendship, one that Sarah has deliberately worked on. Both of them have lost someone they loved very much as a direct consequence of what happened. Sarah has lost Lisa, and Hope has lost her brother, and this has formed a bond between them. Predictably, Hope found it nearly impossible to express her feelings about this, but Sarah, sensing the necessity for Hope to untangle her emotions about Francis, and what had caused him to take his life, wouldn't give up.

The inquest on Francis recorded a verdict of suicide while the balance of his mind was disturbed. By what, it was not stated. But later, when the first shock had worn off and, encouraged by Sarah, Hope was able to talk about it, she admitted, 'I know that it was Patti being killed that tipped him over the edge, being questioned about it. He knew that Dermot had recognized him that day at the party and felt it was bound to begin again . . . the gossip, the persecution. That was what ruined his career, the first time. It was groundless, and cruel . . . I was his twin, as close to him as his own self, and I know. There was never any room for anyone, or anything else, between us. Believe me, I know what he was capable of, what he himself was, and wasn't. It nearly broke him, the first time. He'd eventually made something of his life, but he couldn't have stood up to it a second time.'

'You might like to know,' she writes now, 'that I sent Francis's book to his publishers, and I heard this week that they've accepted it for publication. They think it's the best thing he's ever done.'

Sarah smiles and uncurls herself from the window seat. She goes into the room at the back of the house that Fitz now uses as a studio. It's empty but for the paraphernalia of painting. The completed picture of Allie is on the easel. The drawing, to be more accurate, in pastels.

Allie is shown kneeling on the floor, drawing, caught as she looks up at the painter with a glancing smile, her expression one of perfect trust.

It's the best thing Fitz has ever done, too.